The Magical Adventures of Phoebe and Her Unicorn

Complete Your Phoebe and Her Unicorn Collection

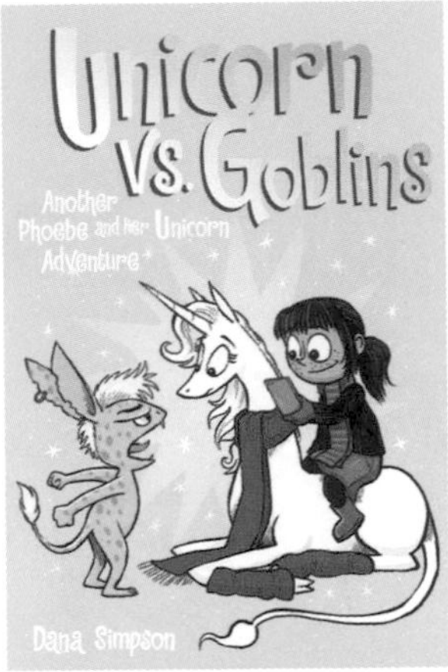
Unicorn vs. Goblins
Another Phoebe and Her Unicorn Adventure
Dana Simpson

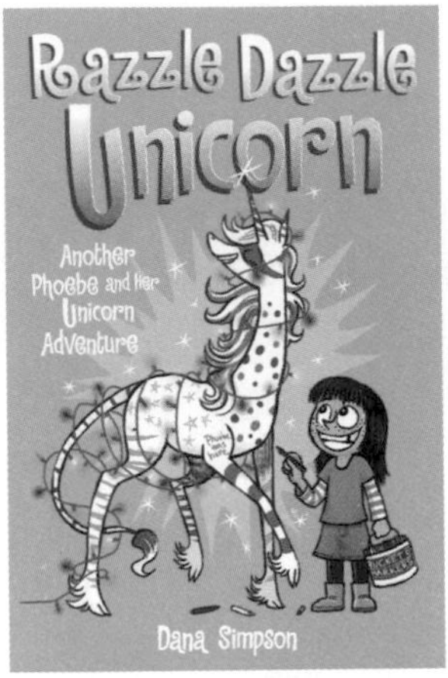
Razzle Dazzle Unicorn
Another Phoebe and Her Unicorn Adventure
Dana Simpson

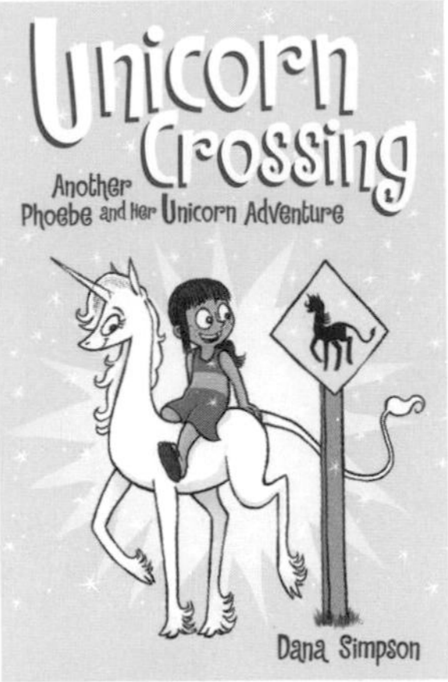
Unicorn Crossing
Another Phoebe and Her Unicorn Adventure
Dana Simpson

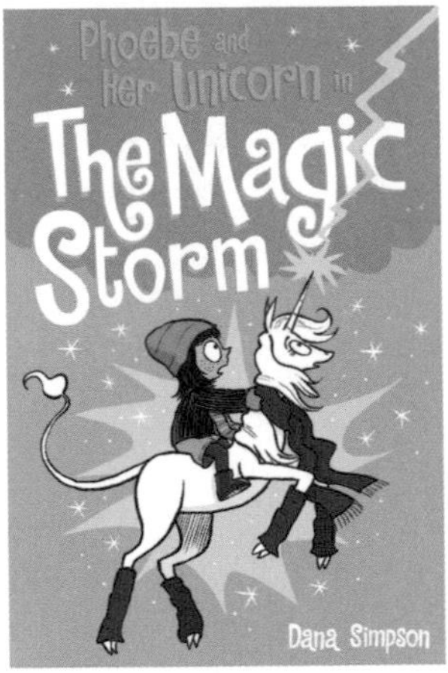
Phoebe and Her Unicorn in
The Magic Storm
Dana Simpson

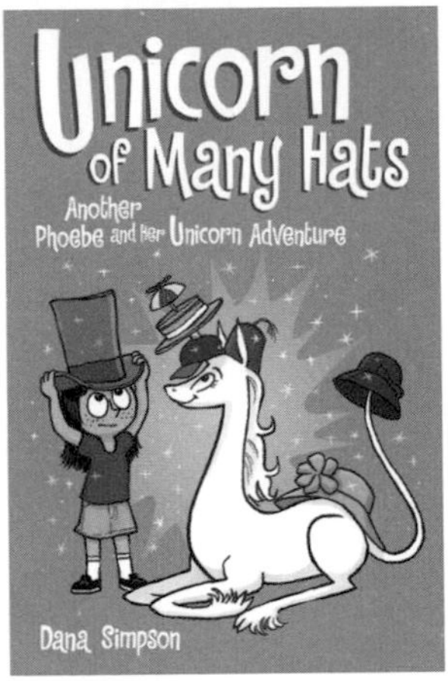
Unicorn of Many Hats
Another Phoebe and Her Unicorn Adventure
Dana Simpson

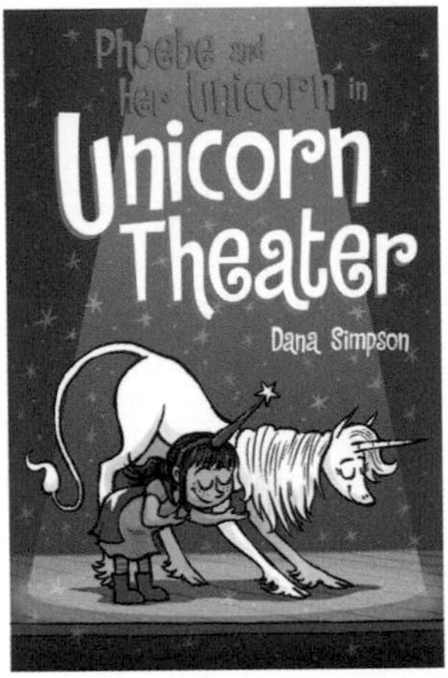
Phoebe and Her Unicorn in
Unicorn Theater
Dana Simpson

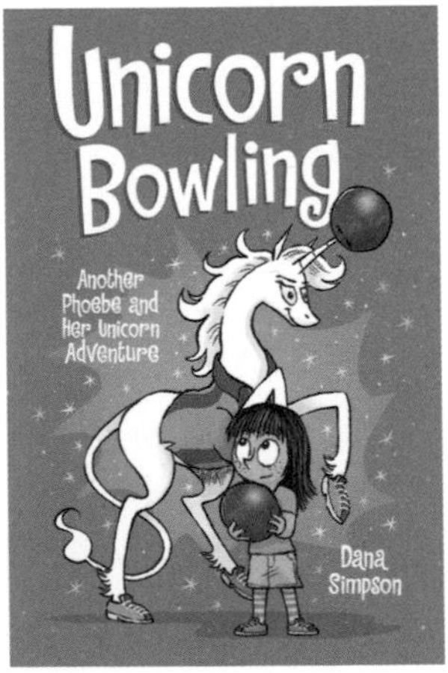
Unicorn Bowling
Another Phoebe and Her Unicorn Adventure
Dana Simpson

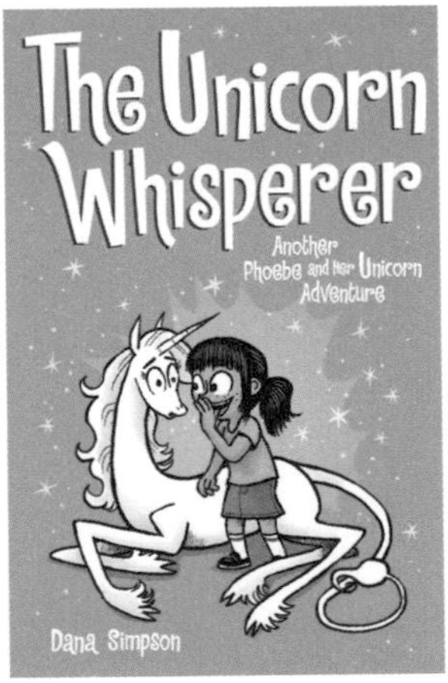
The Unicorn Whisperer
Another Phoebe and Her Unicorn Adventure
Dana Simpson

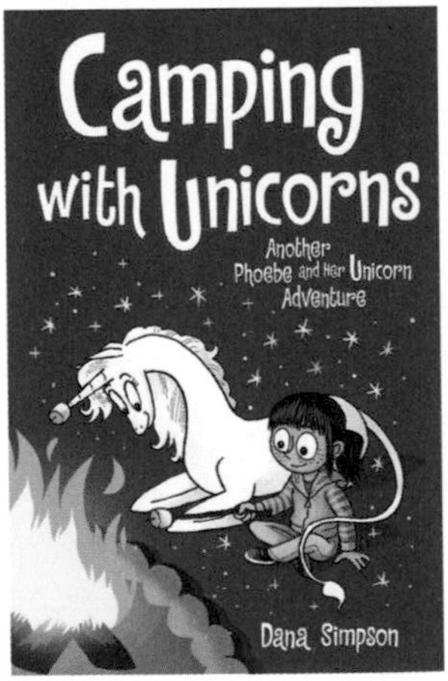
Camping with Unicorns
Another Phoebe and Her Unicorn Adventure
Dana Simpson

The Magical Adventures of Phoebe and Her Unicorn

Dana Simpson

Featuring comics from
Phoebe and Her Unicorn and *Unicorn on a Roll*

Andrews McMeel
PUBLISHING®

Phoebe and Her Unicorn

INTRODUCTION

i would dearly love to claim at least some connection to the origins of Marigold Heavenly Nostrils, the innocently arrogant unicorn who preens so charmingly through Dana Simpson's delightful comic strip bearing her name. And perhaps I can. Scholarly articles have been written, after all, about the fact that prior to my 1968 novel *The Last Unicorn* there were no female unicorns to be found in any of the world's varied mythologies. And in the early pages of that book I did write "Unicorns are immortal. It is their nature to live alone in one place: usually a forest where there is a pool clear enough for them to see themselves—for they are a little vain, knowing themselves to be the most beautiful creatures in all the world, and magic besides . . ."

A little vain . . . Marigold would be an appalling monster of ego, utterly self-concerned and completely unlikable, if it weren't for her sense of humor and her occasional surprising capacity for compassion—both crucial attributes when bound by a wish granted to a nine-year-old girl in need of a Best Friend to play invented superhero games with, to introduce to slumber parties and girl-talk gossip and to ride through the wind after being called nerd and Princess Stupidbutt one time too many. For Phoebe is a remarkably real little girl, as bright and imaginative as Bill Watterson's Calvin, as touchingly vulnerable as Charles Schulz's Charlie Brown. And if these strike you as big names to conjure with, I'll go further and state for the record that in my opinion *Phoebe and Her Unicorn* is nothing less than the best comic strip to come along since *Calvin and Hobbes*. Simpson is that good, and that original.

Part of the charm of *Phoebe and Her Unicorn* is the way in which Simpson plays her two characters' opposed world views—immortal and contemporary— against each other, along with their egos: for Phoebe's determination to be recognized as Awesome quite matches Marigold's impregnable superiority to the entire human species. Consequently, both delight in sticking the needle in where they can, and on this ground they are equals. There is real affection between them, but it grows by degrees. Simpson takes her time with this, always remaining in full control of her material, including artful cultural references and the gradual development of additional characters and themes.

The temptation is to quote at least every gag and panel, but that would be wrong. Enchantment doesn't retail well at secondhand; like Robert Frost's definition of poetry, it gets lost in translation. I'll simply suggest that you go read *Phoebe and Her Unicorn* in a serious hurry.

Like now!

— Peter S. Beagle
Oakland, California
September 2013

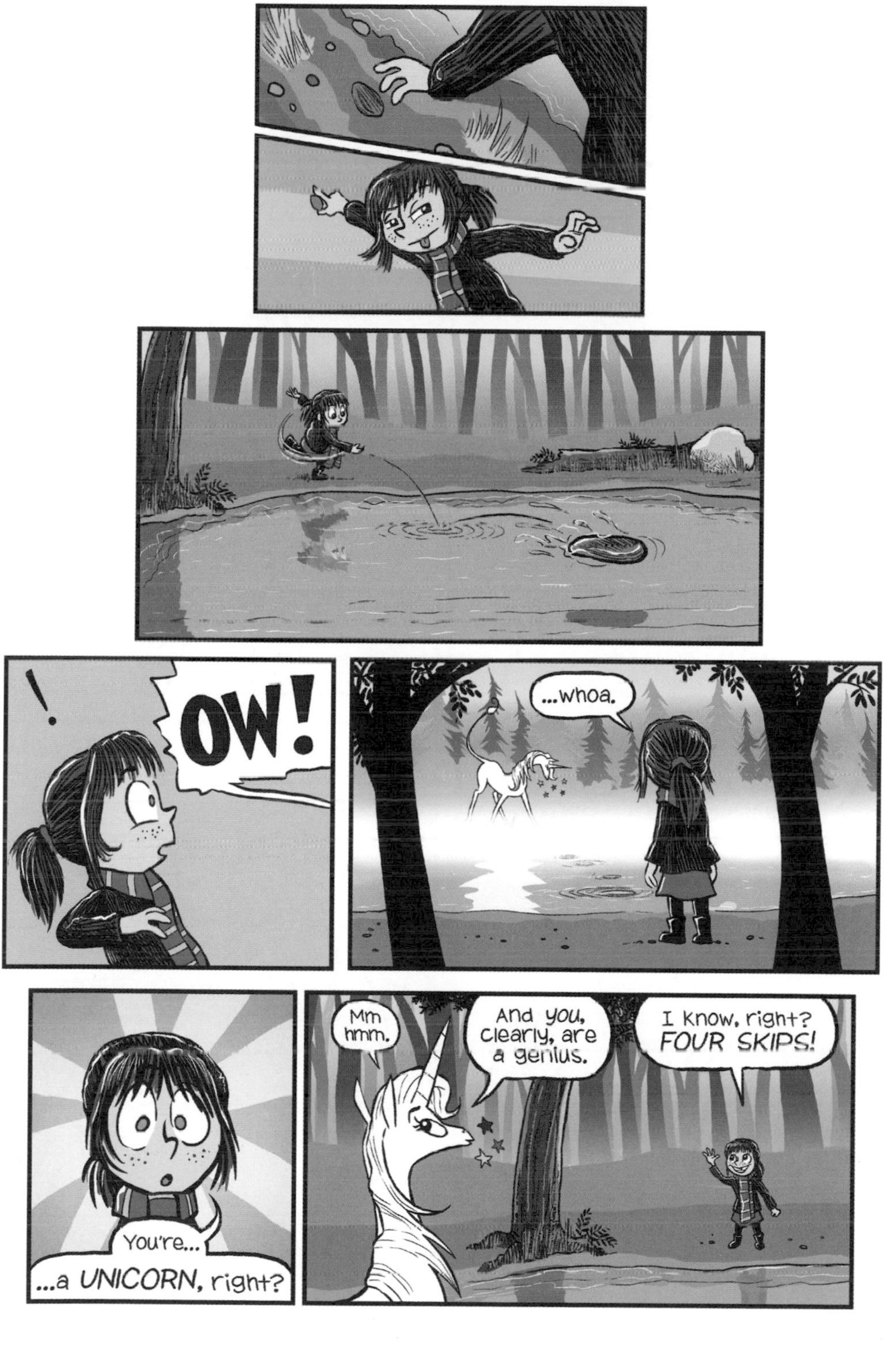
!
OW!
...whoa.
You're...
...a UNICORN, right?
Mm hmm.
And you, clearly, are a genius.
I know, right? FOUR SKIPS!

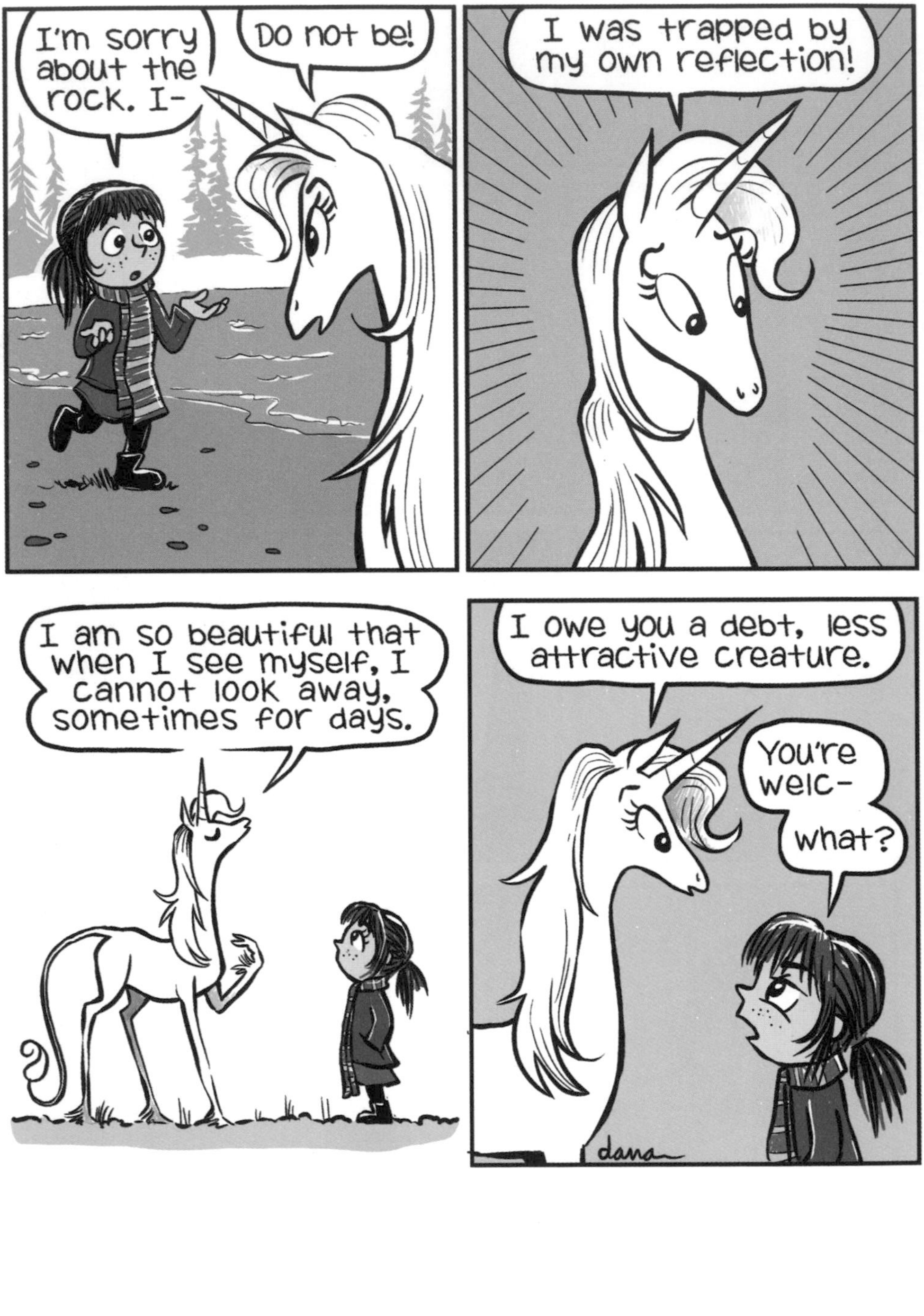
I'm sorry about the rock. I-
Do not be!
I was trapped by my own reflection!
I am so beautiful that when I see myself, I cannot look away, sometimes for days.
I owe you a debt, less attractive creature.
You're welc-
what?
dana

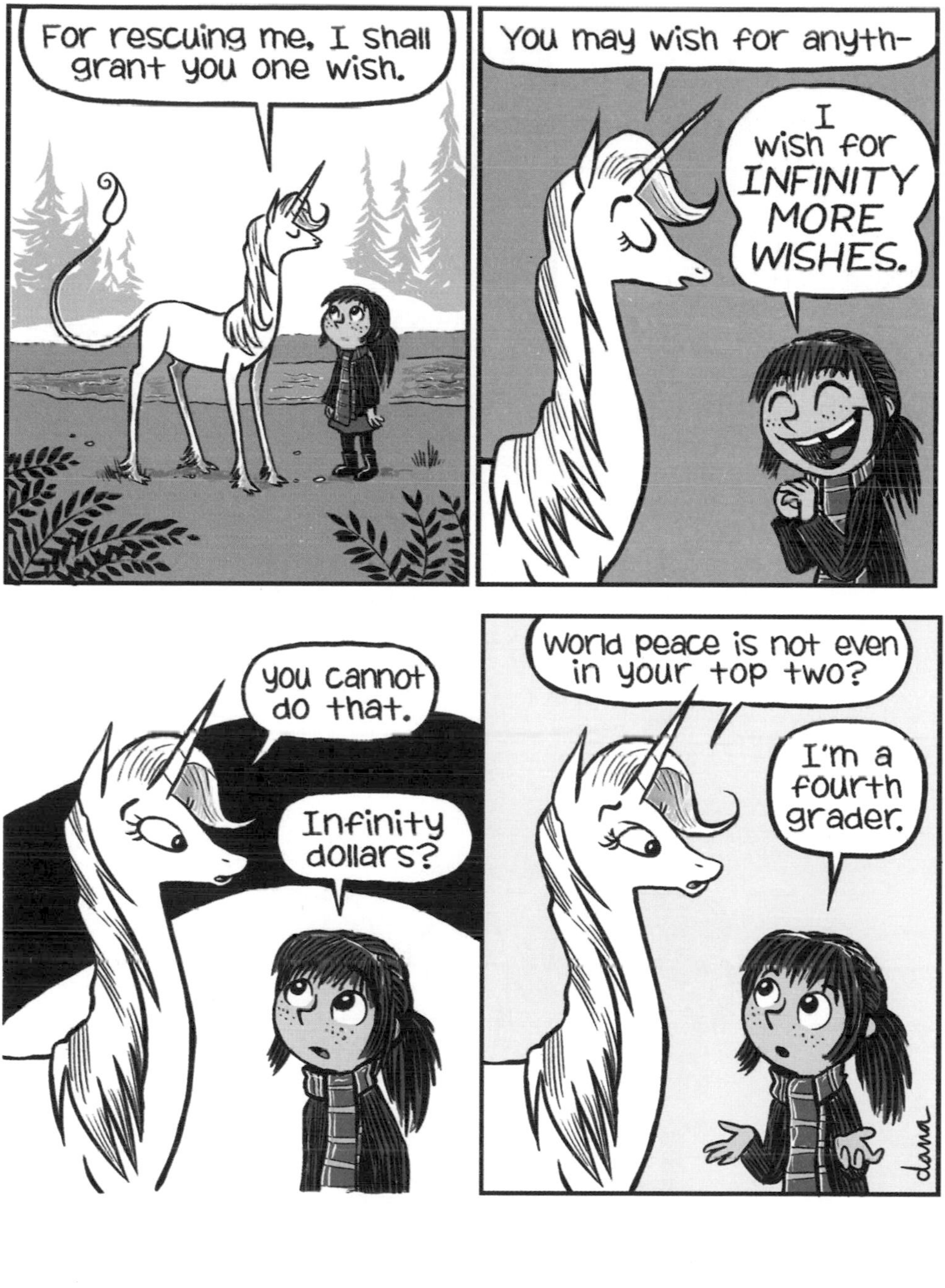
For rescuing me, I shall grant you one wish.
You may wish for anyth-
I wish for INFINITY MORE WISHES.
you cannot do that.
Infinity dollars?
World peace is not even in your top two?
I'm a fourth grader.
dana

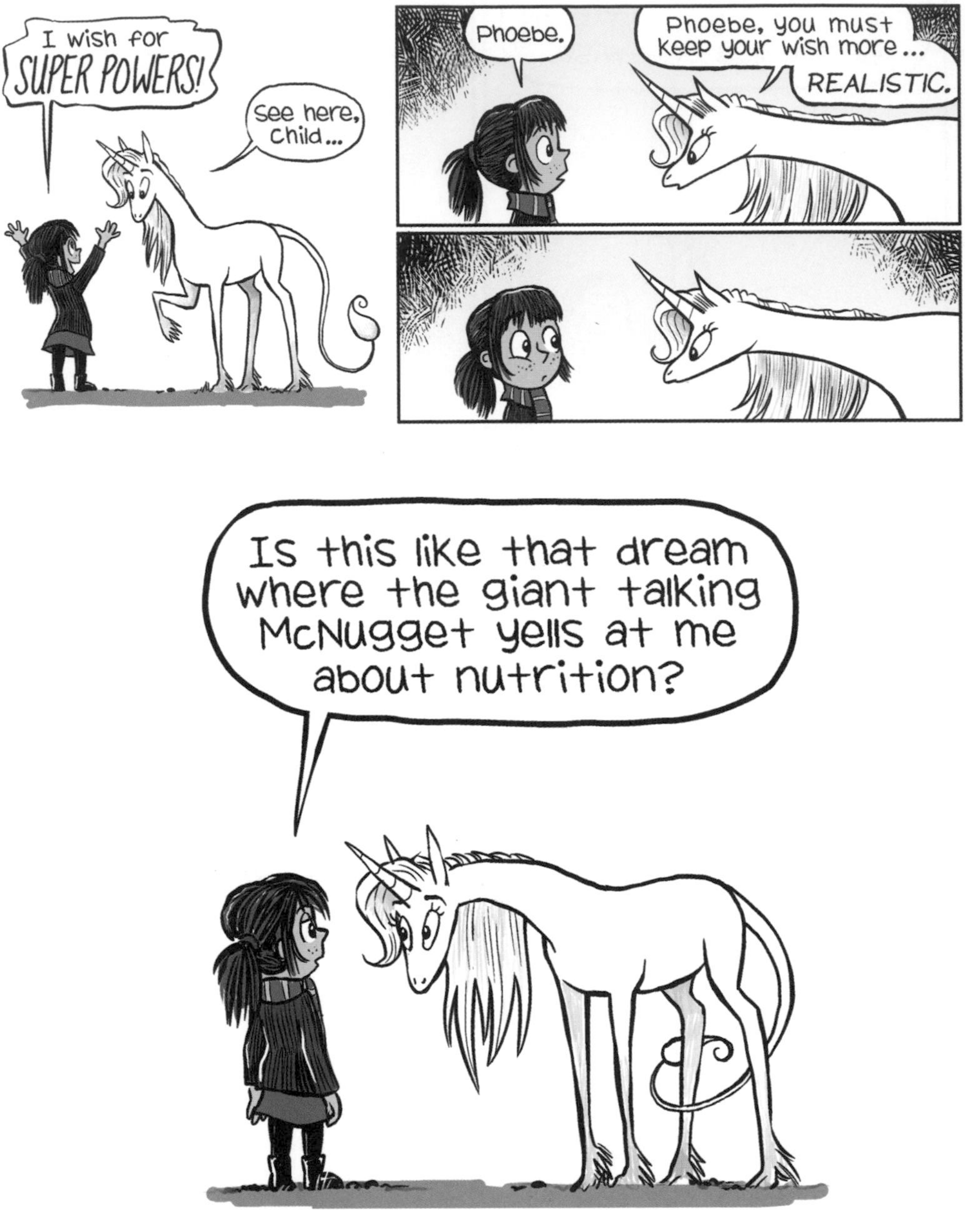

I wish for SUPER POWERS!
See here, child...
Phoebe.
Phoebe, you must keep your wish more... REALISTIC.
Is this like that dream where the giant talking McNugget yells at me about nutrition?

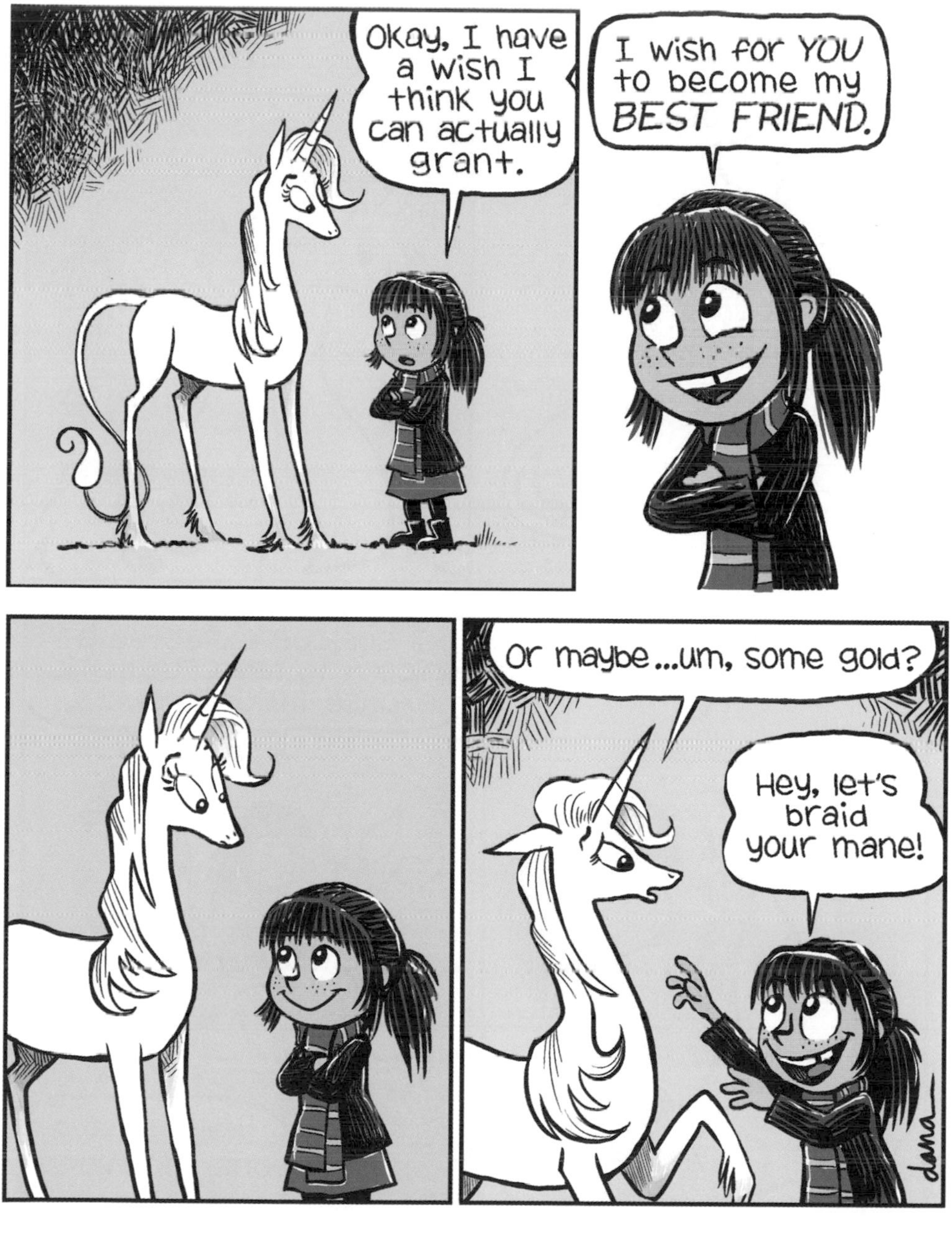
Okay, I have a wish I think you can actually grant.
I wish for YOU to become my BEST FRIEND.
Or maybe...um, some gold?
Hey, let's braid your mane!
dana

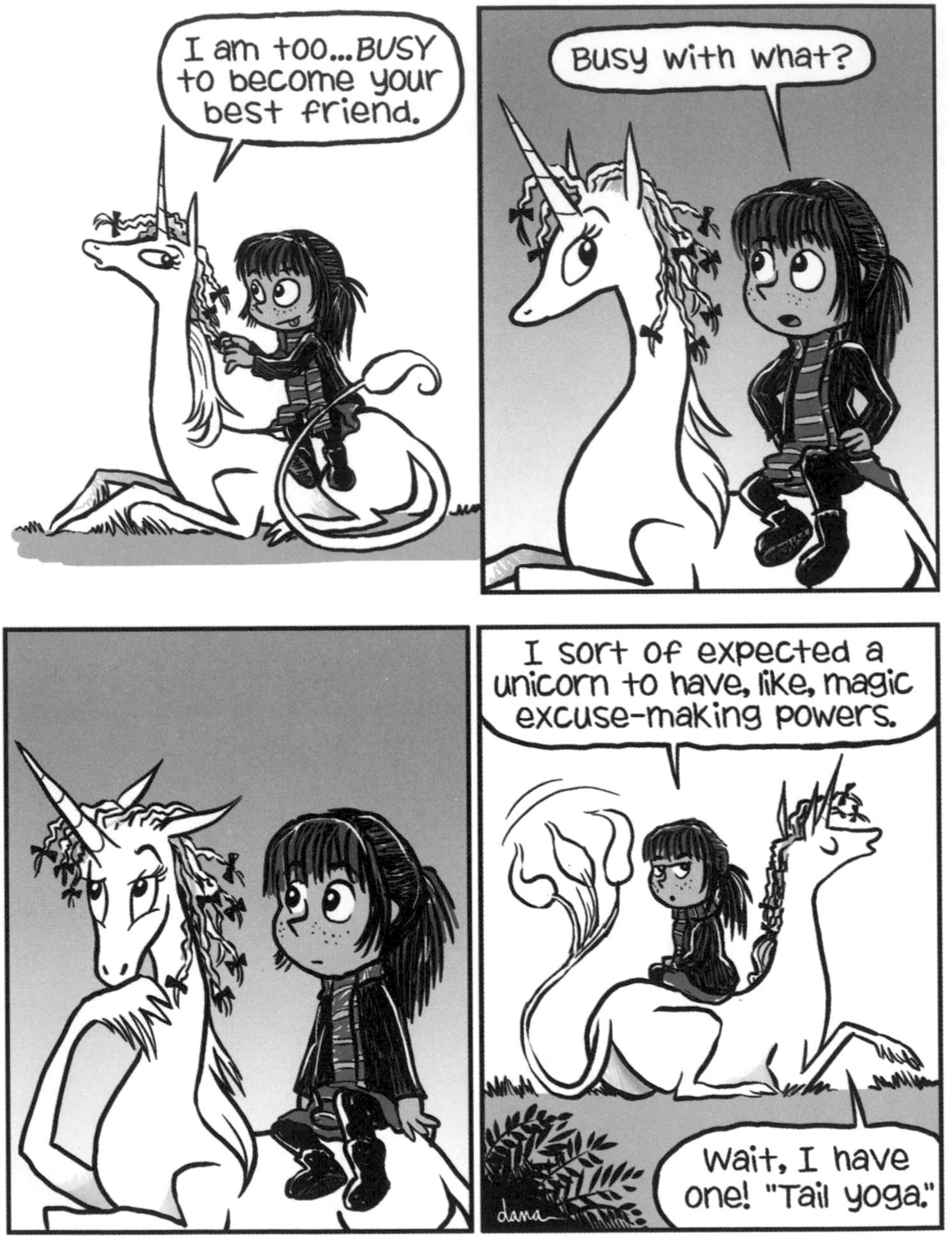
I am too...BUSY to become your best friend.
Busy with what?
I sort of expected a unicorn to have, like, magic excuse-making powers.
Wait, I have one! "Tail yoga."
dana

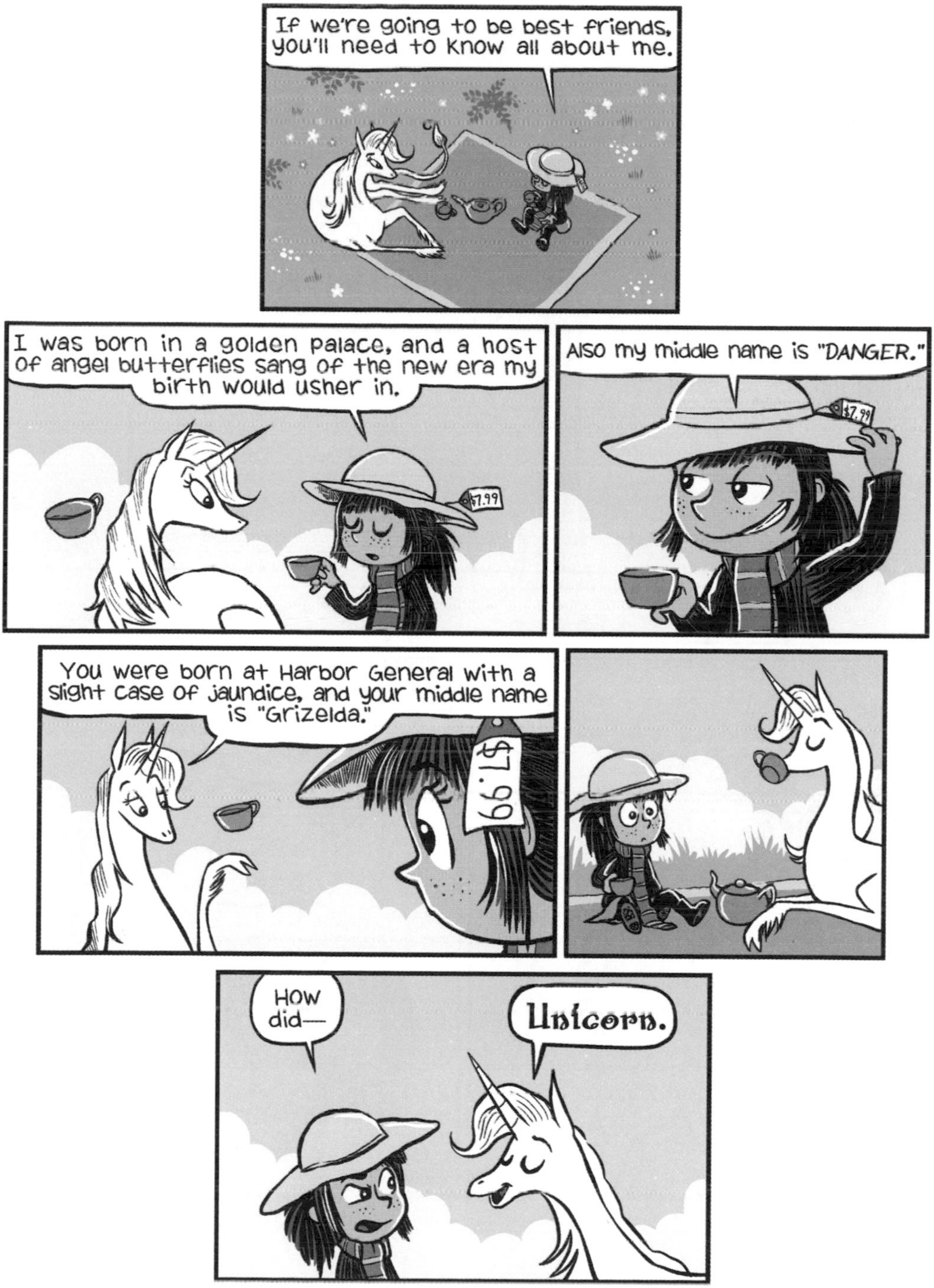
If we're going to be best friends, you'll need to know all about me.
I was born in a golden palace, and a host of angel butterflies sang of the new era my birth would usher in.
$7.99
Also my middle name is "DANGER."
$7.99
You were born at Harbor General with a slight case of jaundice, and your middle name is "Grizelda."
$7.99
How did—
Unicorn.

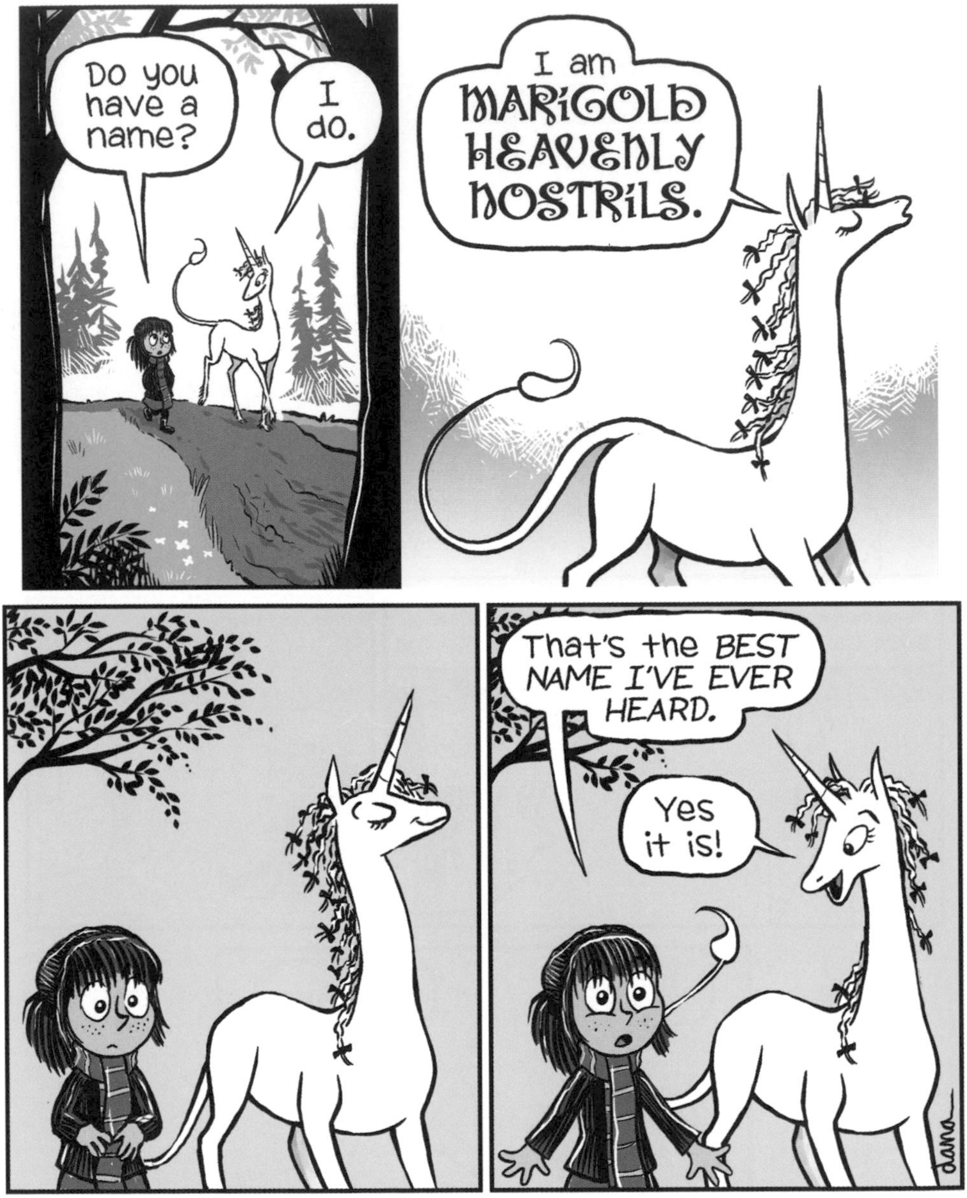
Do you have a name?
I do.
I am MARIGOLD HEAVENLY NOSTRILS.
That's the BEST NAME I'VE EVER HEARD.
Yes it is!
dana

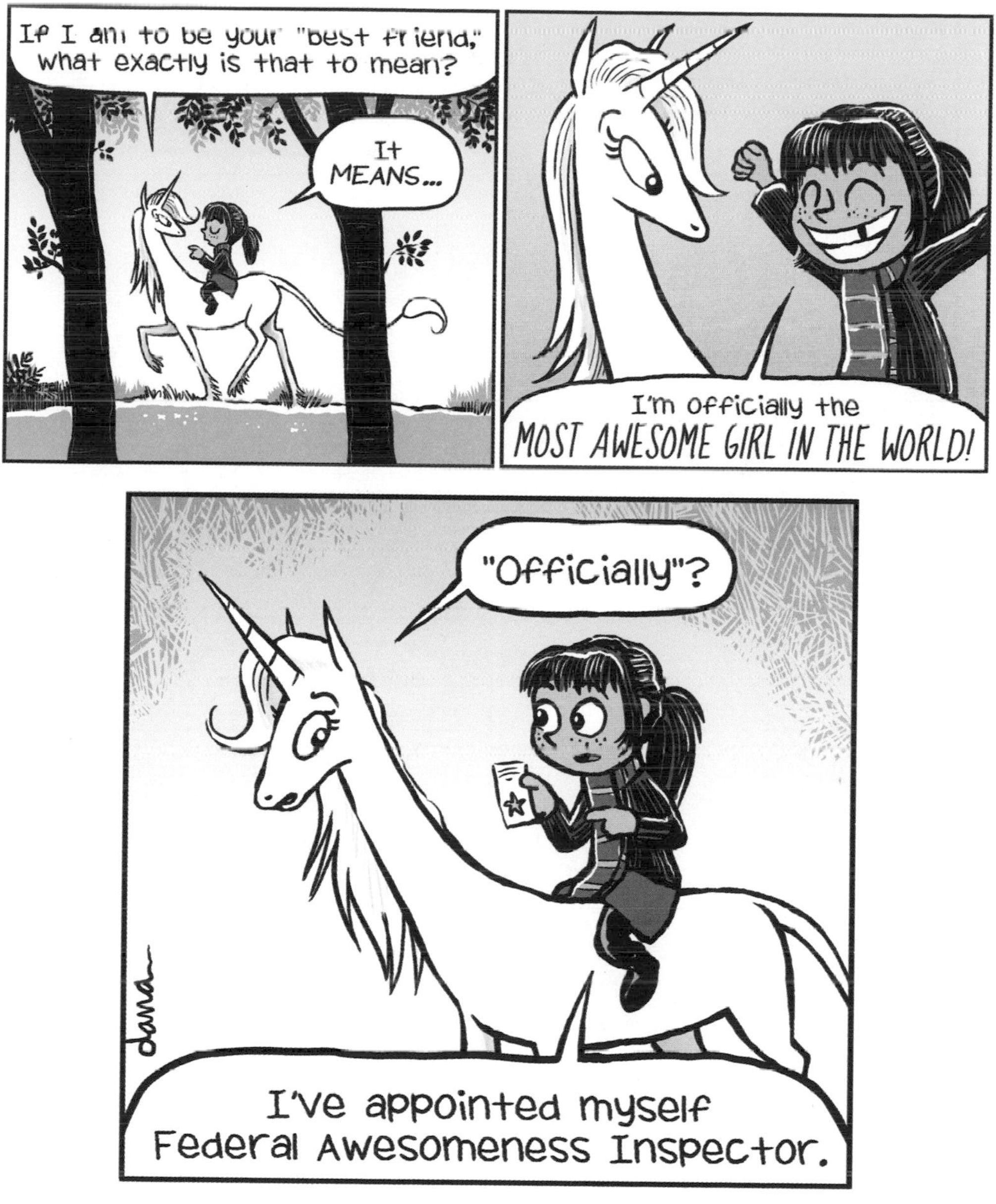
If I am to be your "best friend," what exactly is that to mean?
It MEANS...
I'm officially the MOST AWESOME GIRL IN THE WORLD!
"Officially"?
I've appointed myself Federal Awesomeness Inspector.
dana

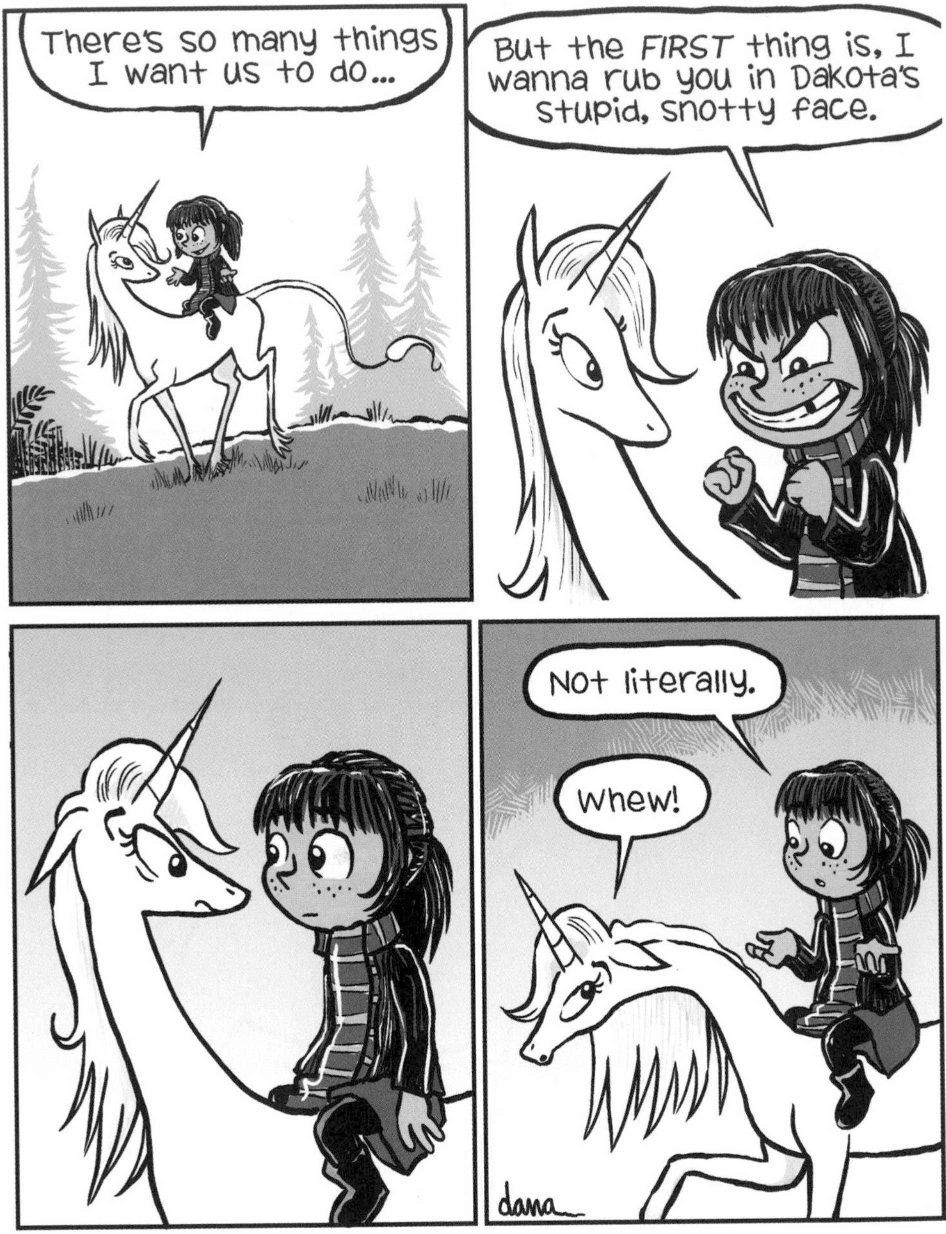
There's so many things I want us to do...
But the *FIRST* thing is, I wanna rub you in Dakota's stupid, snotty face.
Not literally.
Whew!
dana

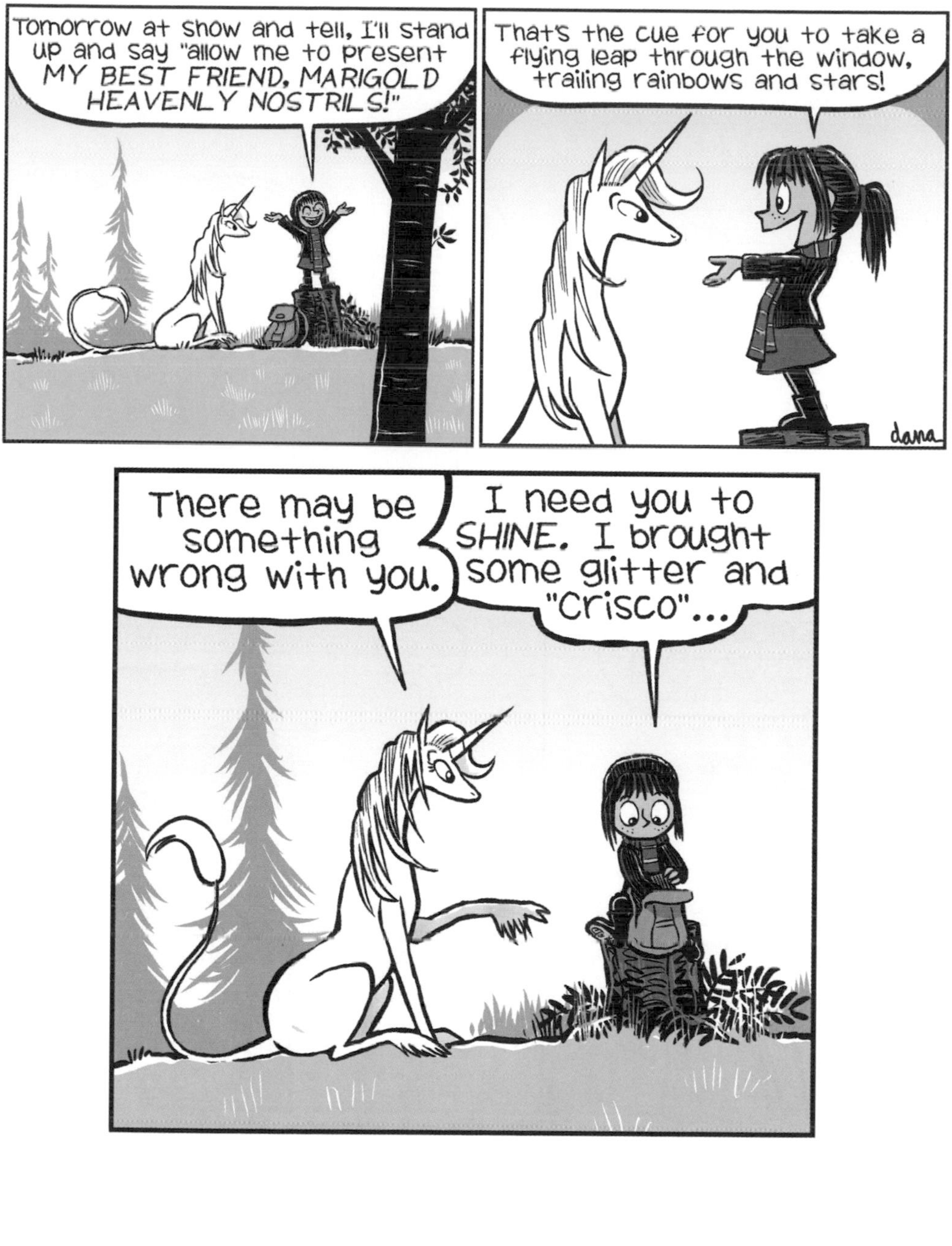
Tomorrow at show and tell, I'll stand up and say "allow me to present MY BEST FRIEND, MARIGOLD HEAVENLY NOSTRILS!"
That's the cue for you to take a flying leap through the window, trailing rainbows and stars!
dana
There may be something wrong with you.
I need you to SHINE. I brought some glitter and "Crisco"...

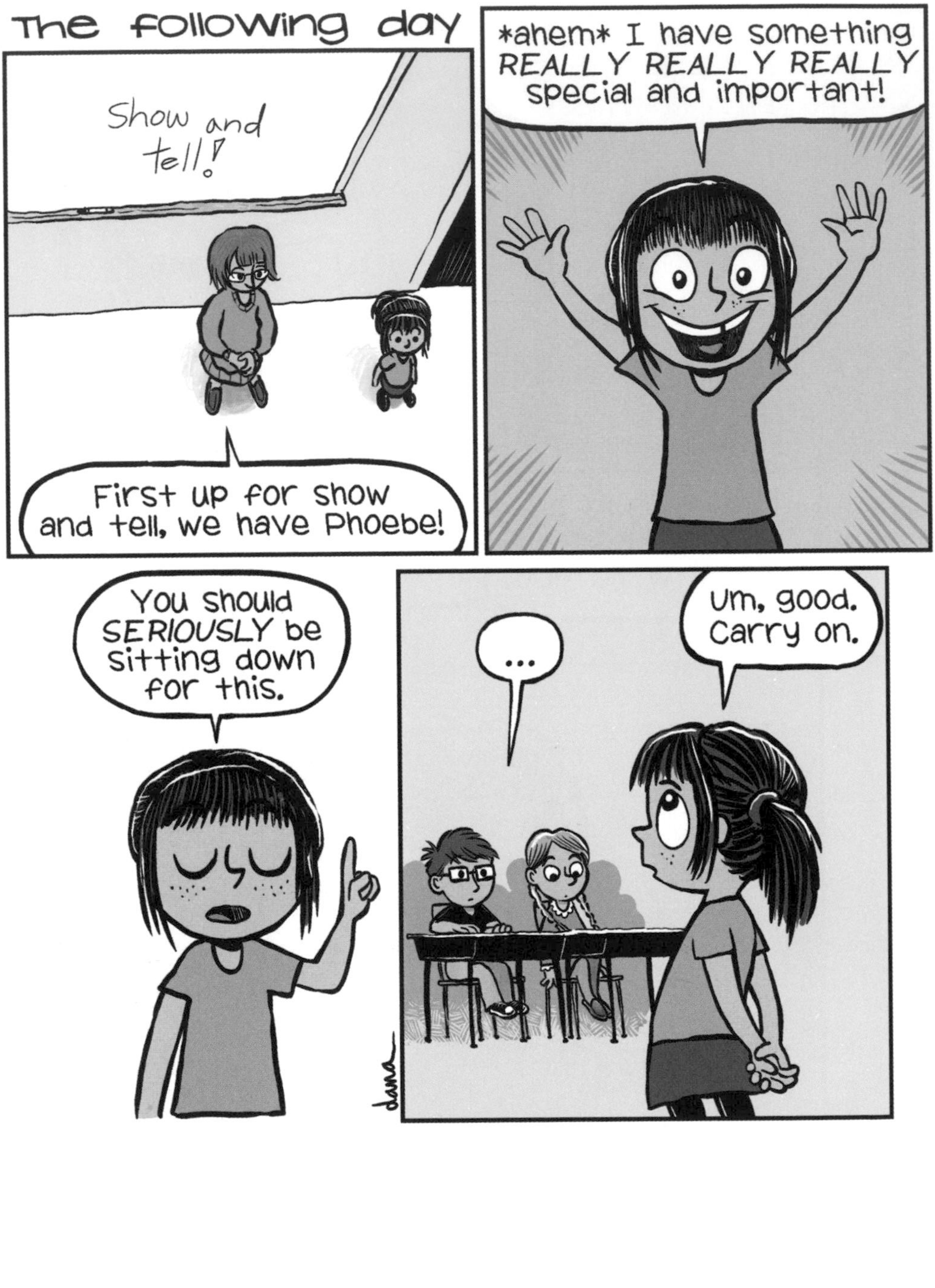
The following day
Show and tell!
First up for show and tell, we have Phoebe!
ahem I have something REALLY REALLY REALLY special and important!
You should SERIOUSLY be sitting down for this.
...
Um, good. Carry on.
dana

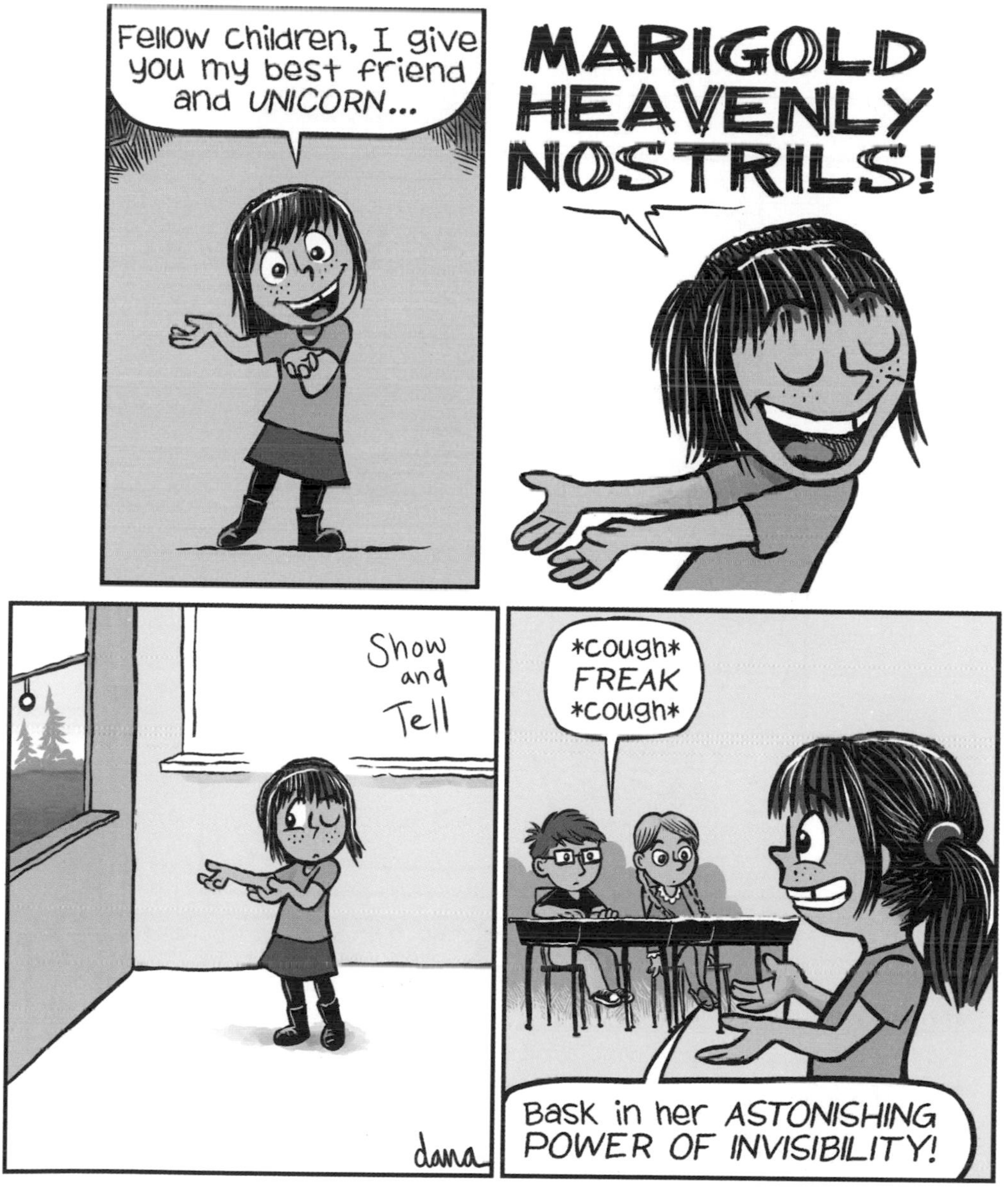
Fellow children, I give you my best friend and UNICORN...
MARIGOLD HEAVENLY NOSTRILS!
Show and Tell
dana
cough FREAK *cough*
Bask in her ASTONISHING POWER OF INVISIBILITY!

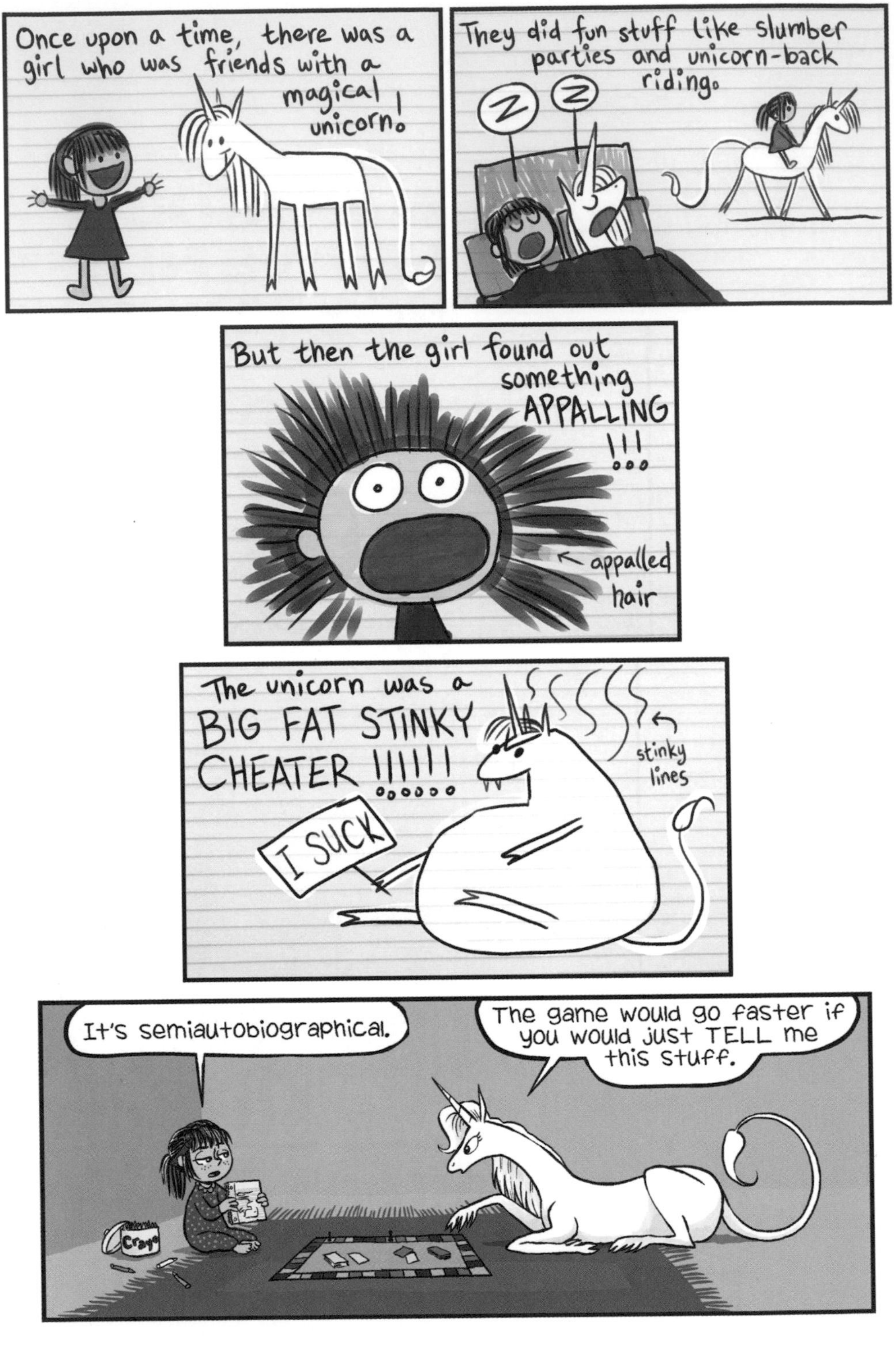
Once upon a time, there was a girl who was friends with a magical unicorn!
They did fun stuff like slumber parties and unicorn-back riding.
Z
Z
But then the girl found out something APPALLING!!!
appalled hair
The unicorn was a BIG FAT STINKY CHEATER!!!!!!
stinky lines
I SUCK
It's semiautobiographical.
The game would go faster if you would just TELL me this stuff.

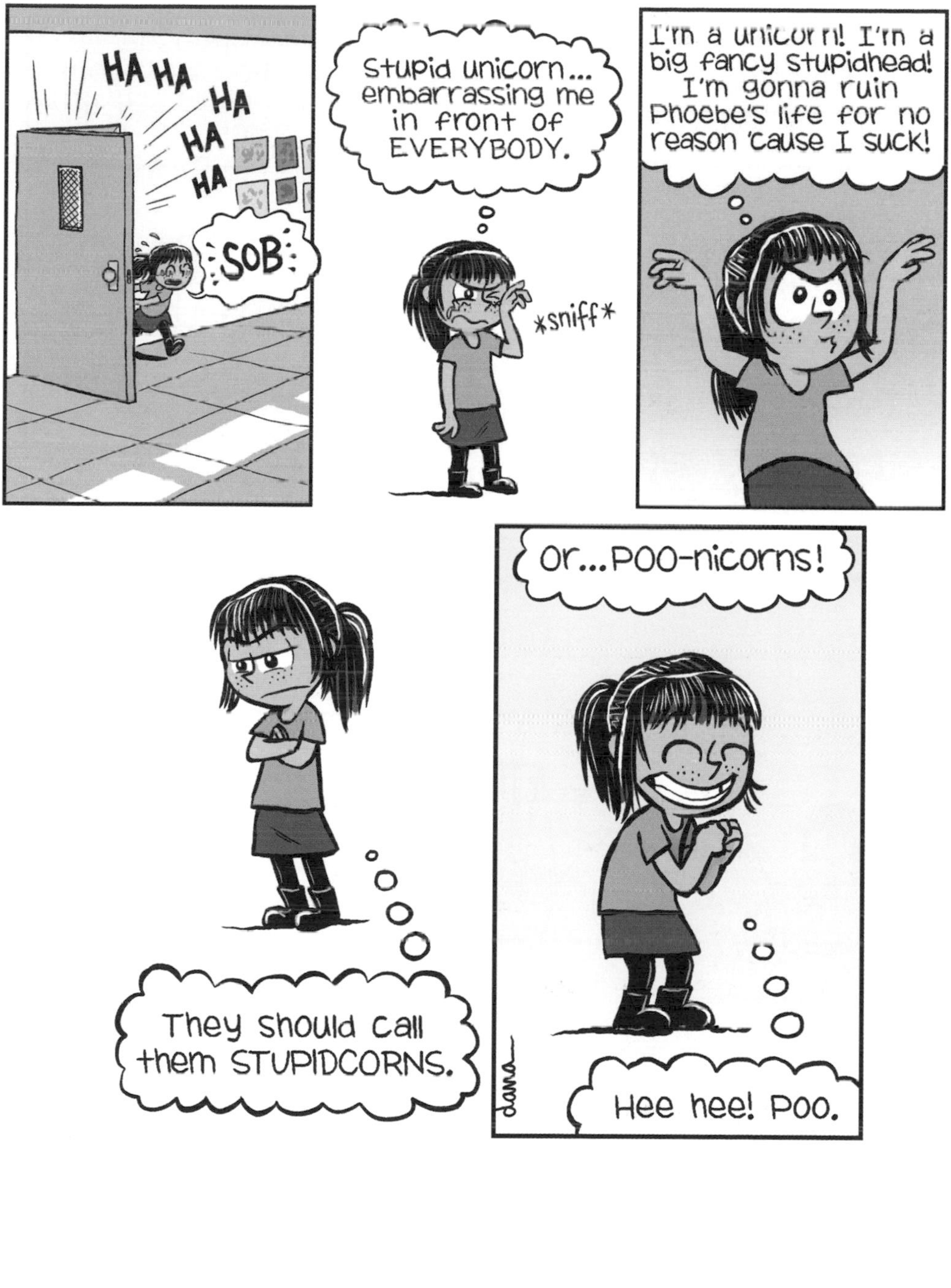
HA HA HA HA HA
SOB
Stupid unicorn... embarrassing me in front of EVERYBODY.
sniff
I'm a unicorn! I'm a big fancy stupidhead! I'm gonna ruin Phoebe's life for no reason 'cause I suck!
They should call them STUPIDCORNS.
Or...POO-nicorns!
Hee hee! Poo.
dana

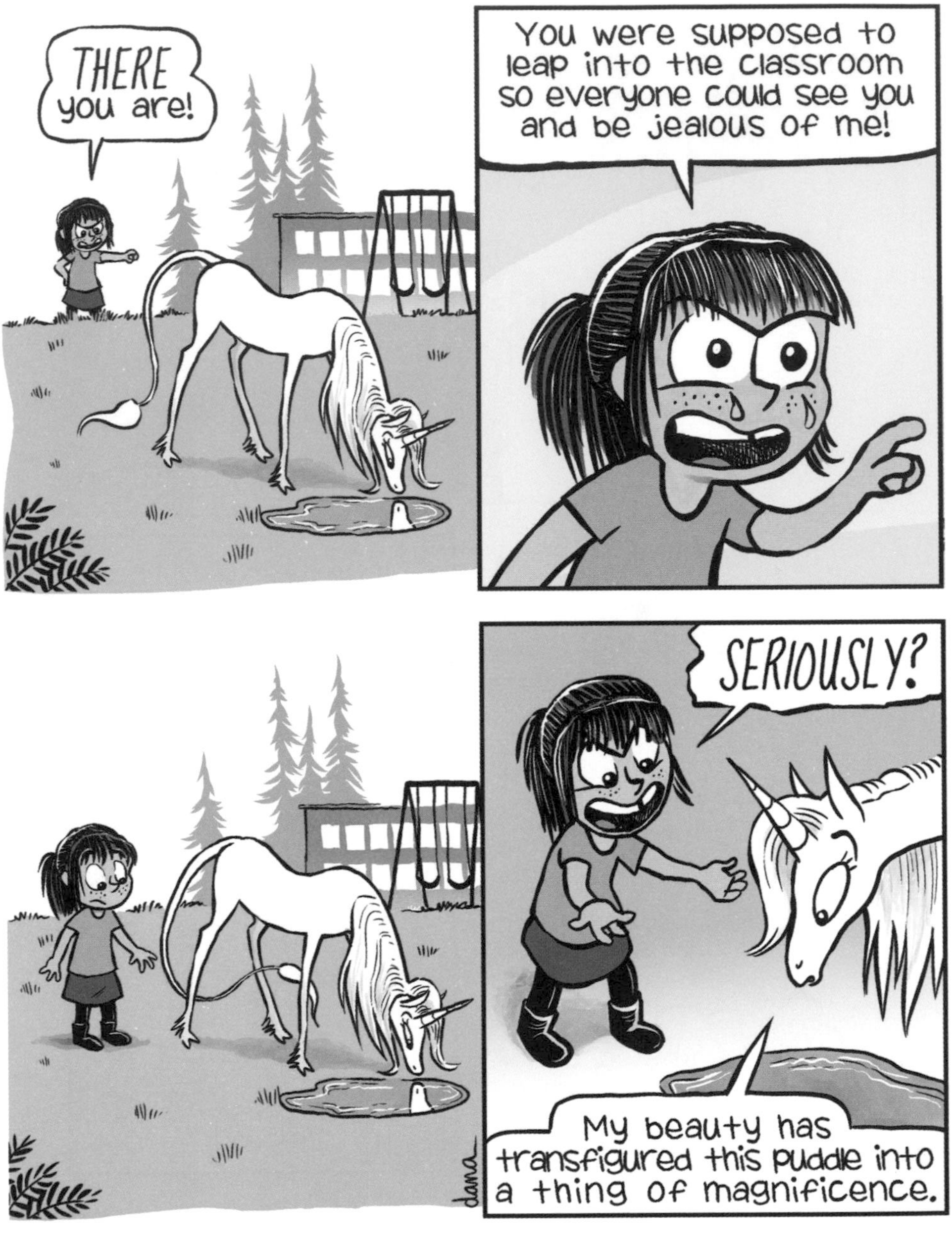
THERE you are!
You were supposed to leap into the classroom so everyone could see you and be jealous of me!
SERIOUSLY?
My beauty has transfigured this puddle into a thing of magnificence.
dana

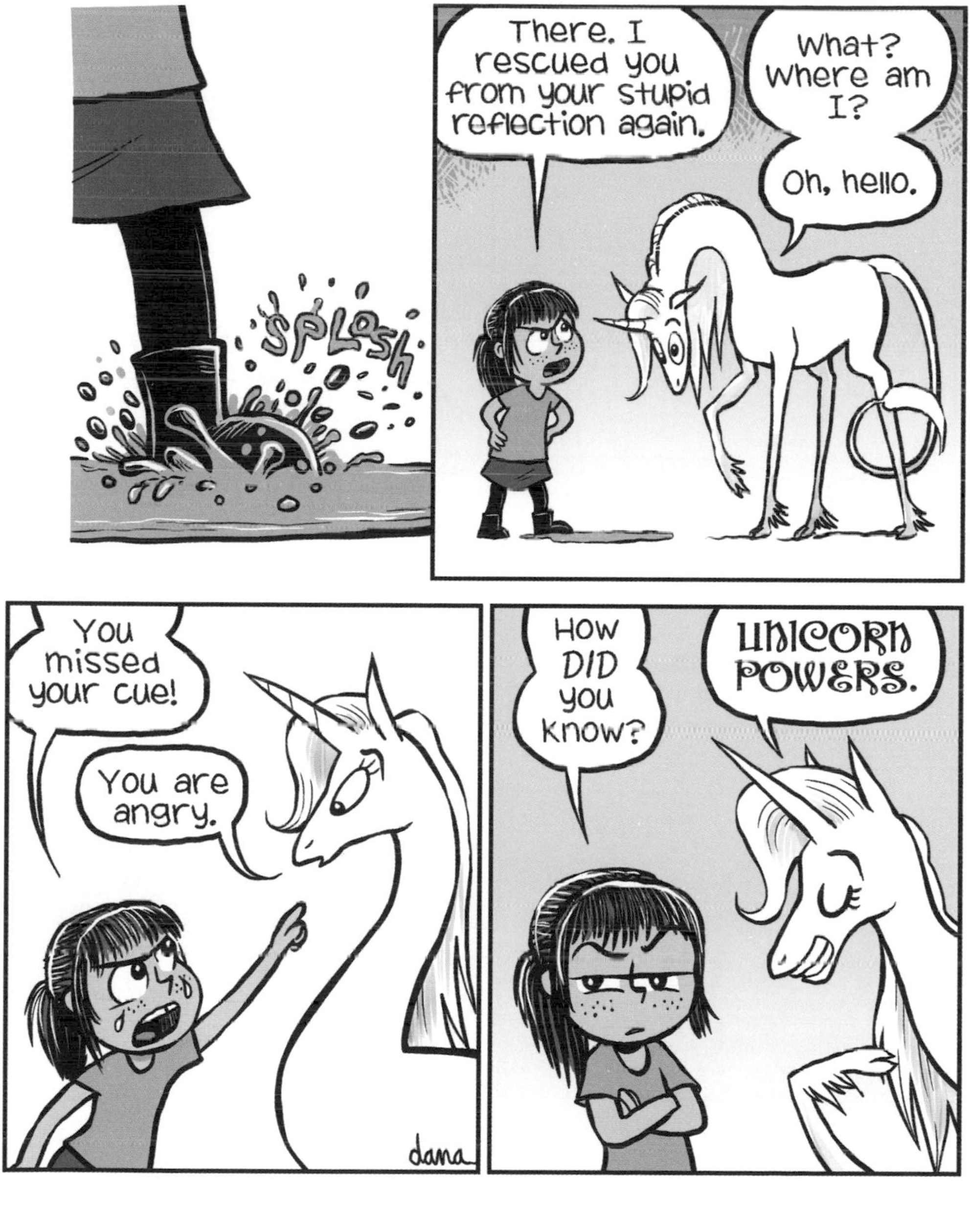
SPLOSH
There. I rescued you from your stupid reflection again.
What? Where am I?
Oh, hello.
You missed your cue!
You are angry.
dana
How DID you know?
UNICORN POWERS.

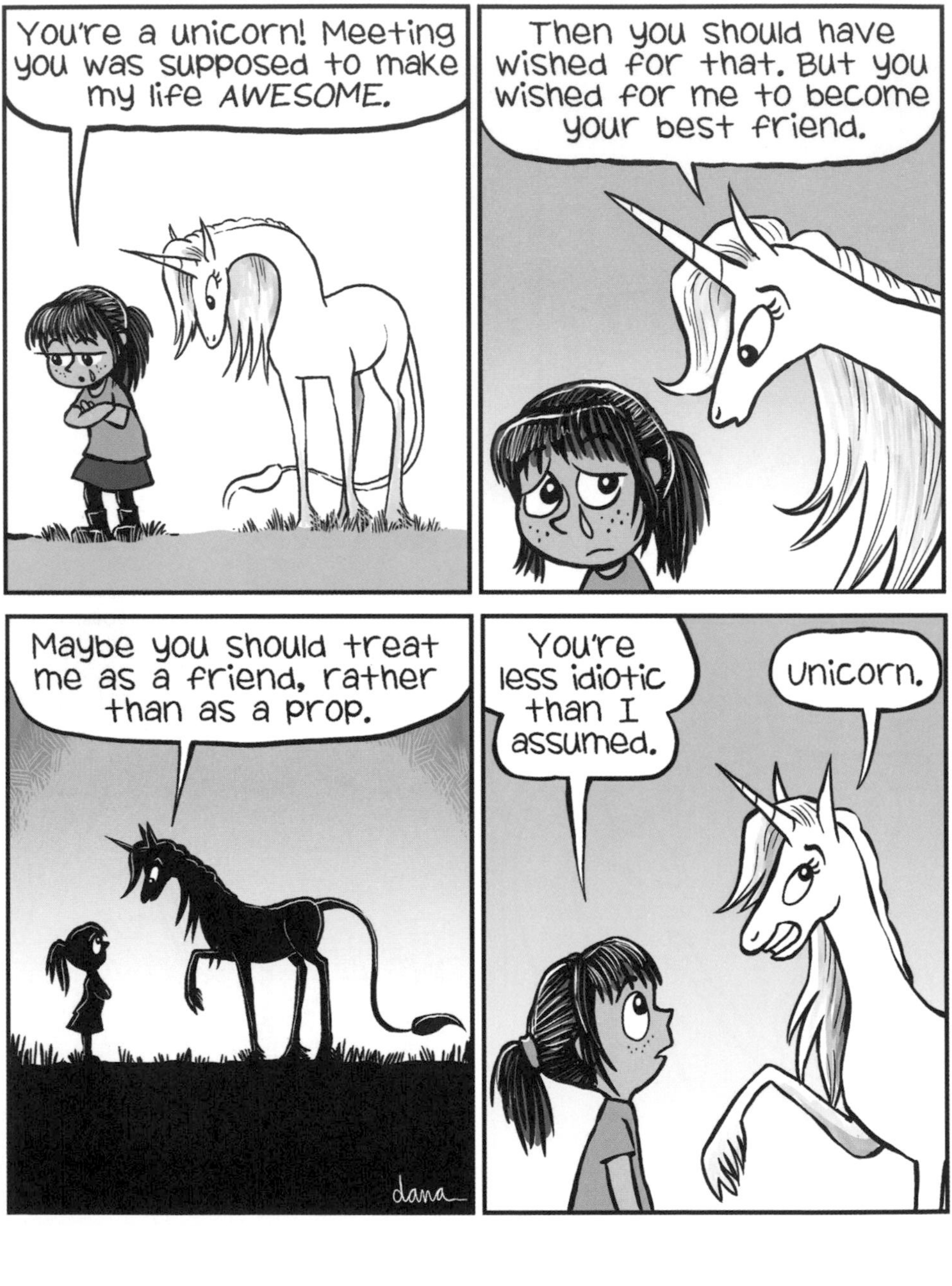

You're a unicorn! Meeting you was supposed to make my life AWESOME.
Then you should have wished for that. But you wished for me to become your best friend.
Maybe you should treat me as a friend, rather than as a prop.
dana
You're less idiotic than I assumed.
Unicorn.

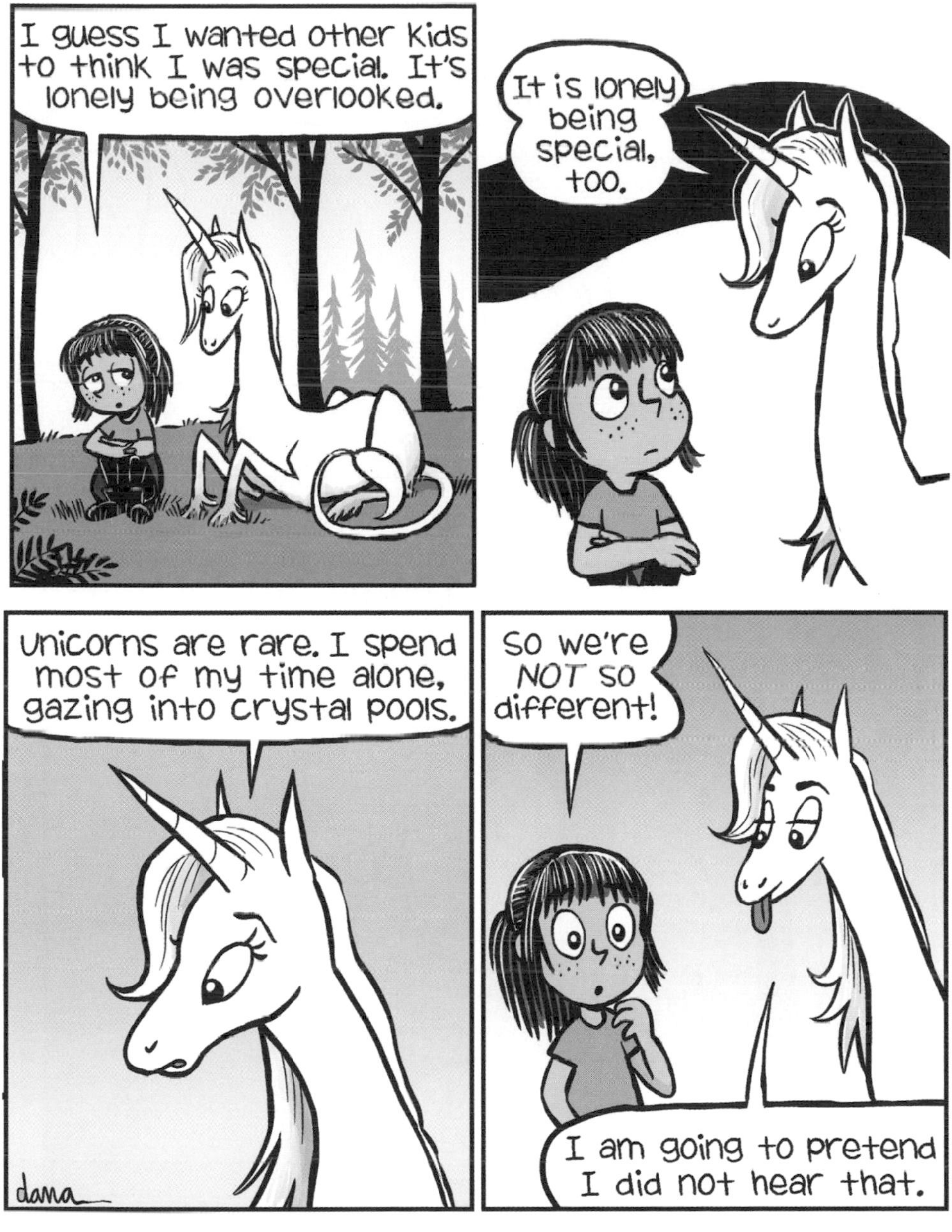
I guess I wanted other kids to think I was special. It's lonely being overlooked.
It is lonely being special, too.
Unicorns are rare. I spend most of my time alone, gazing into crystal pools.
So we're *NOT* so different!
I am going to pretend I did not hear that.
dana

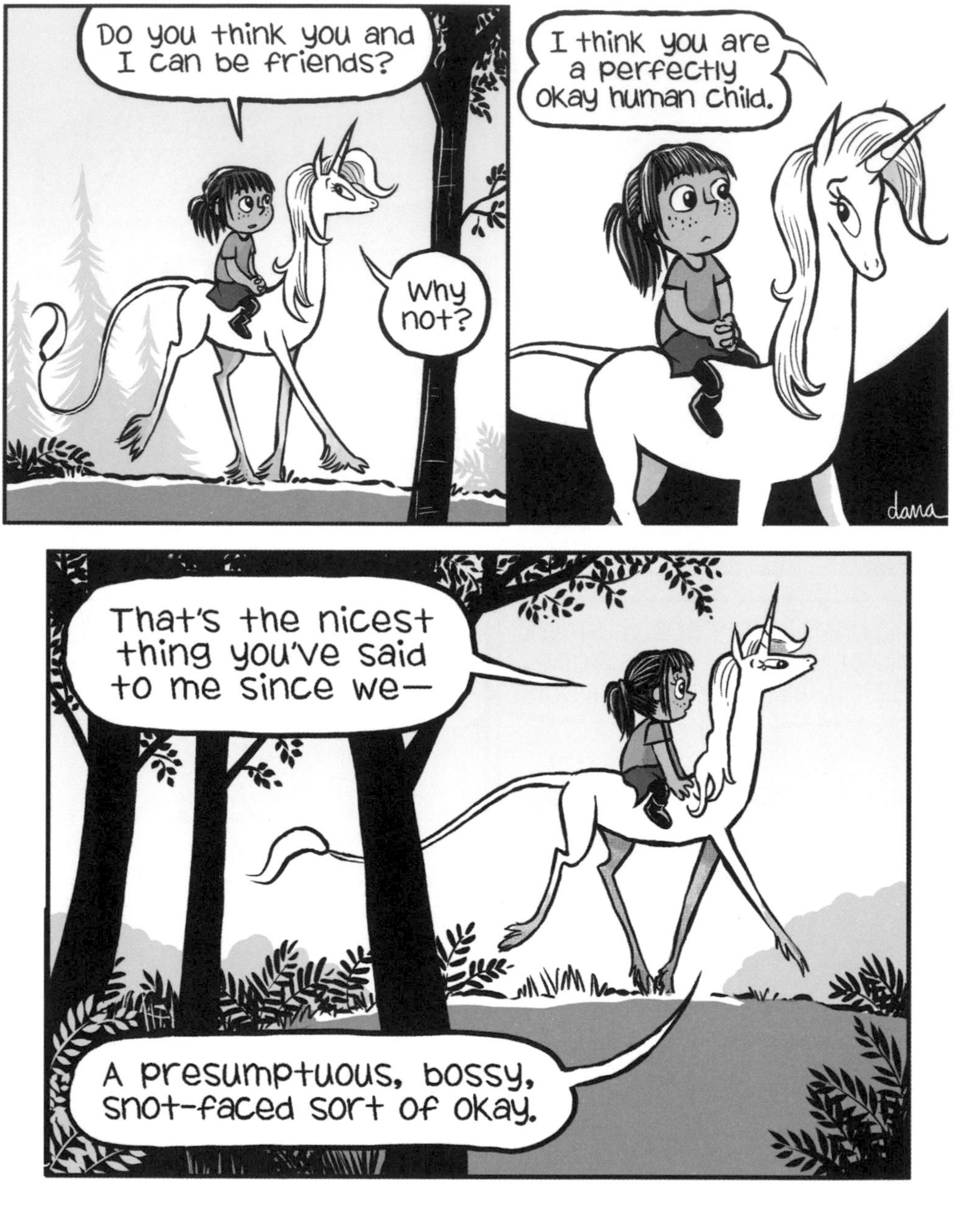
Do you think you and I can be friends?
Why not?
I think you are a perfectly okay human child.
dana
That's the nicest thing you've said to me since we—
A presumptuous, bossy, snot-faced sort of okay.

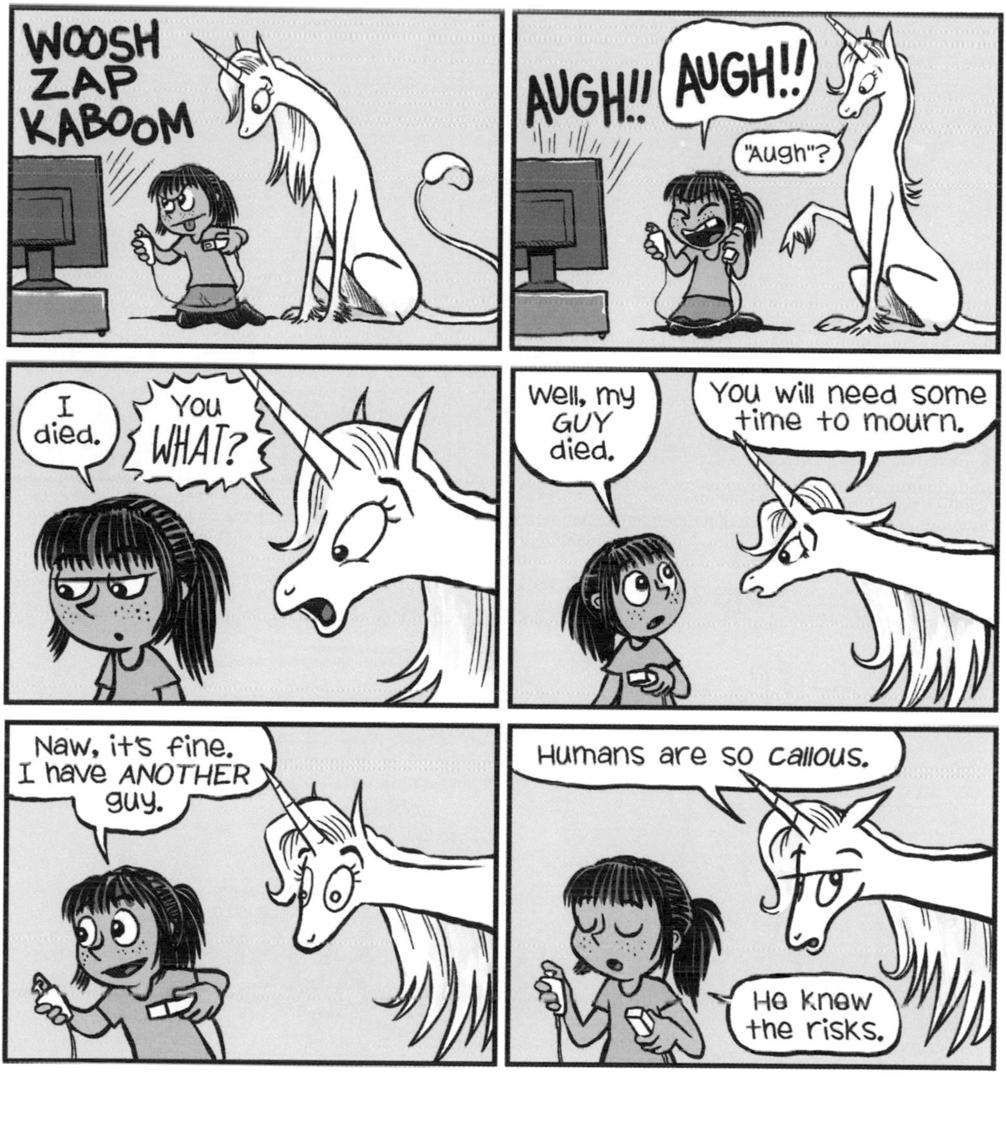
WOOSH
ZAP
KABOOM
AUGH!!
AUGH!!
"Augh"?
I died.
You WHAT?
Well, my GUY died.
You will need some time to mourn.
Naw, it's fine. I have ANOTHER guy.
Humans are so callous.
He know the risks.

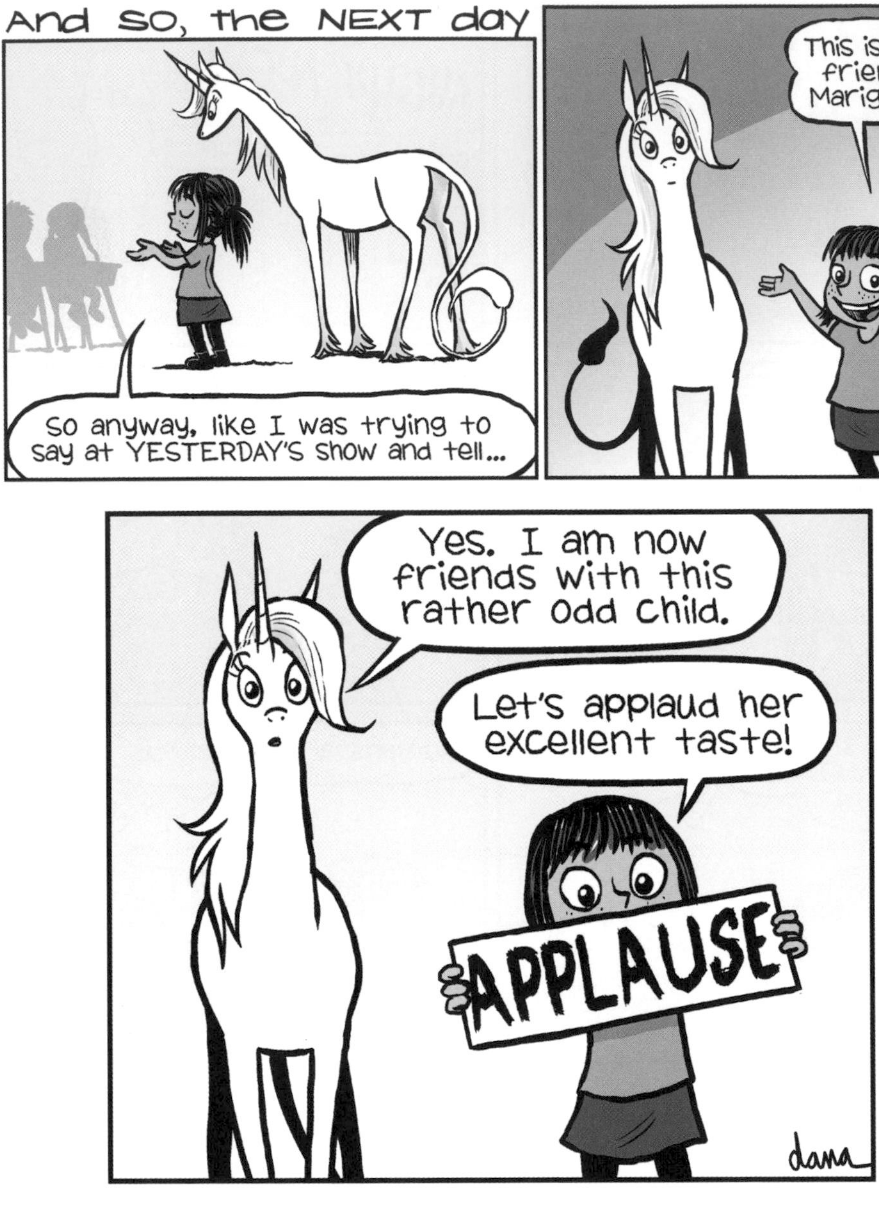
And so, the NEXT day
So anyway, like I was trying to say at YESTERDAY'S show and tell...
This is my friend Marigold.
Yes. I am now friends with this rather odd child.
Let's applaud her excellent taste!
APPLAUSE
dana

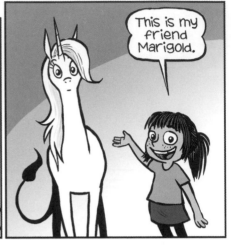

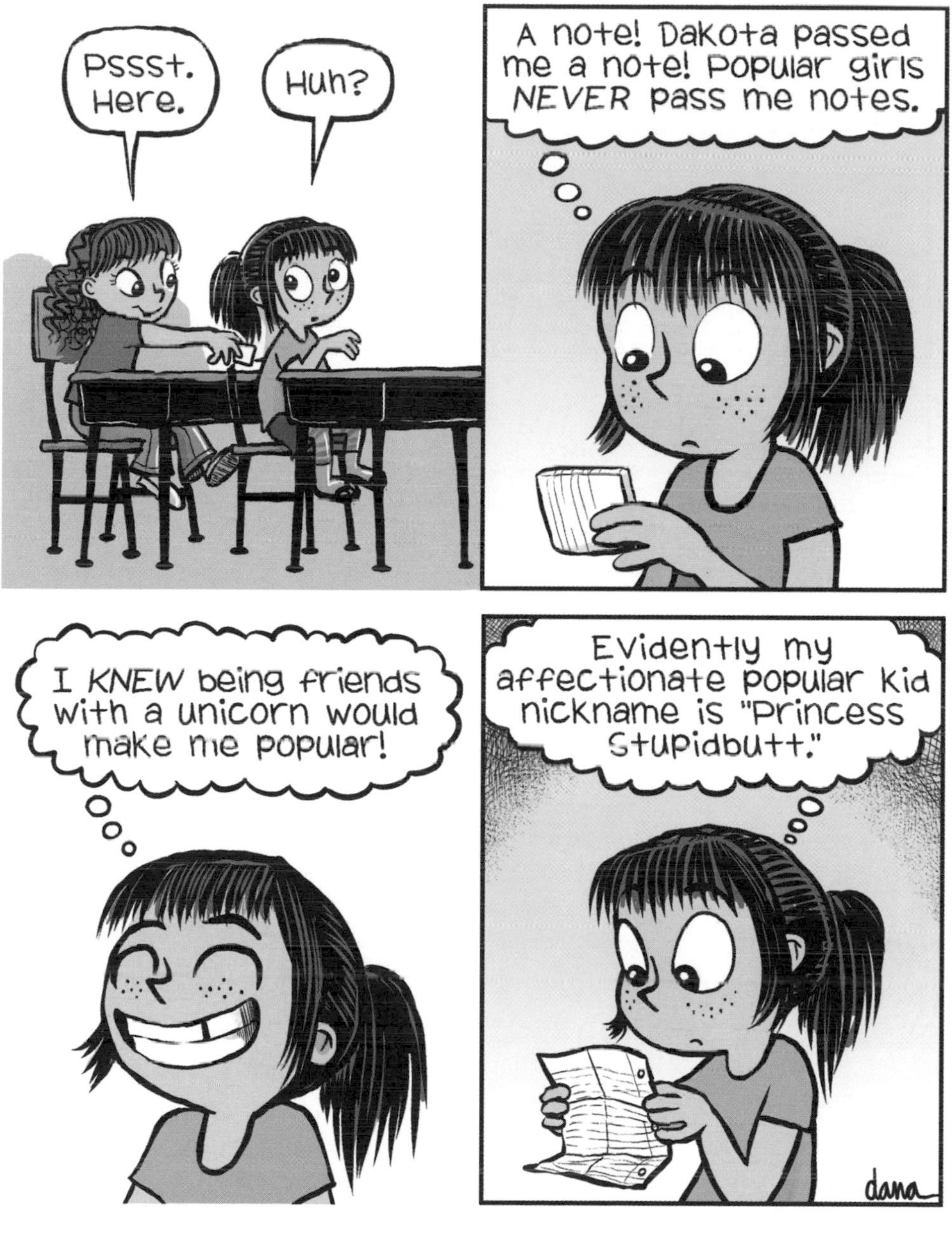
Pssst. Here.
Huh?
A note! Dakota passed me a note! Popular girls NEVER pass me notes.
I KNEW being friends with a unicorn would make me popular!
Evidently my affectionate popular kid nickname is "Princess Stupidbutt."
dana

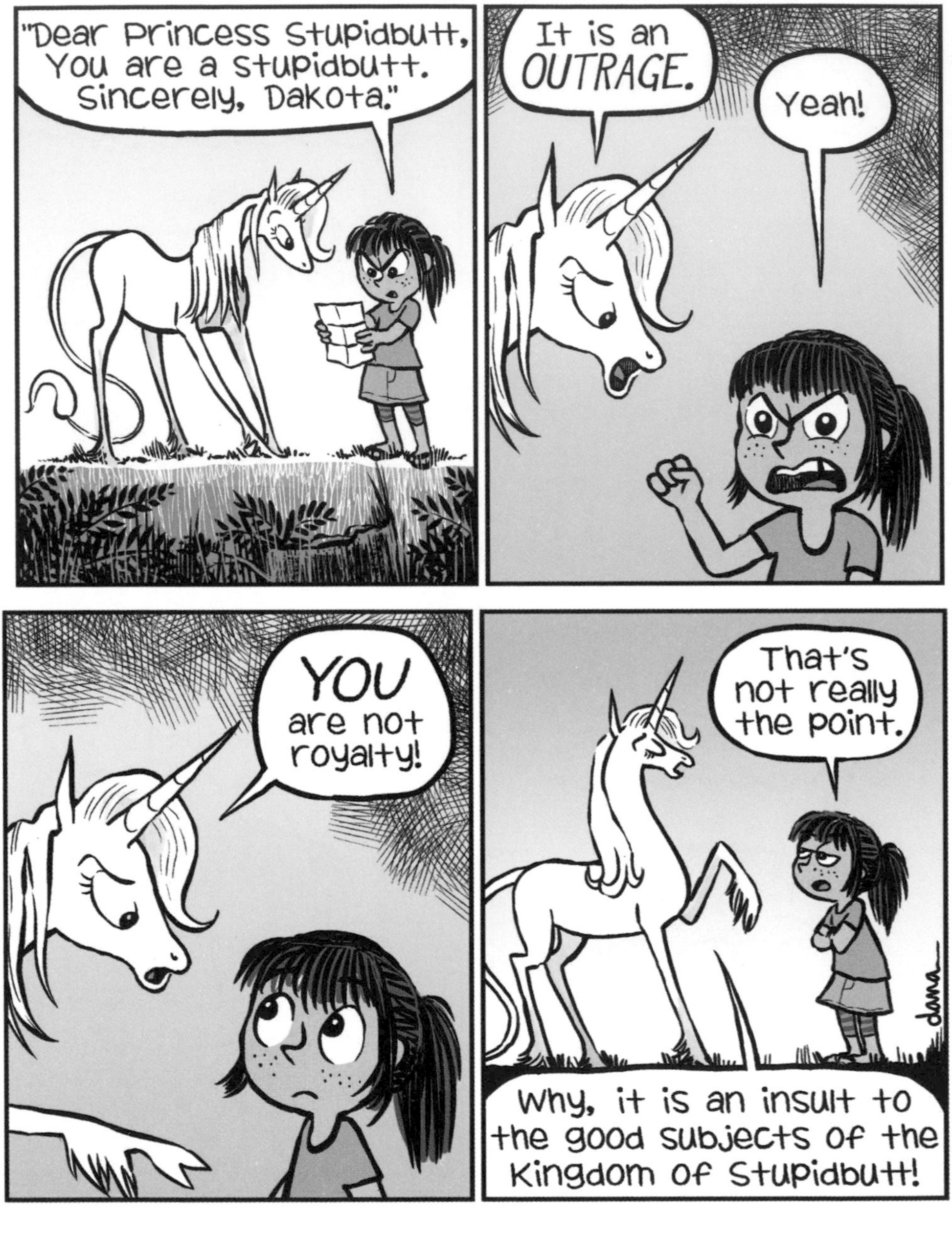
"Dear Princess Stupidbutt, You are a stupidbutt. Sincerely, Dakota."
It is an OUTRAGE.
Yeah!
YOU are not royalty!
That's not really the point.
Why, it is an insult to the good subjects of the Kingdom of Stupidbutt!
dana

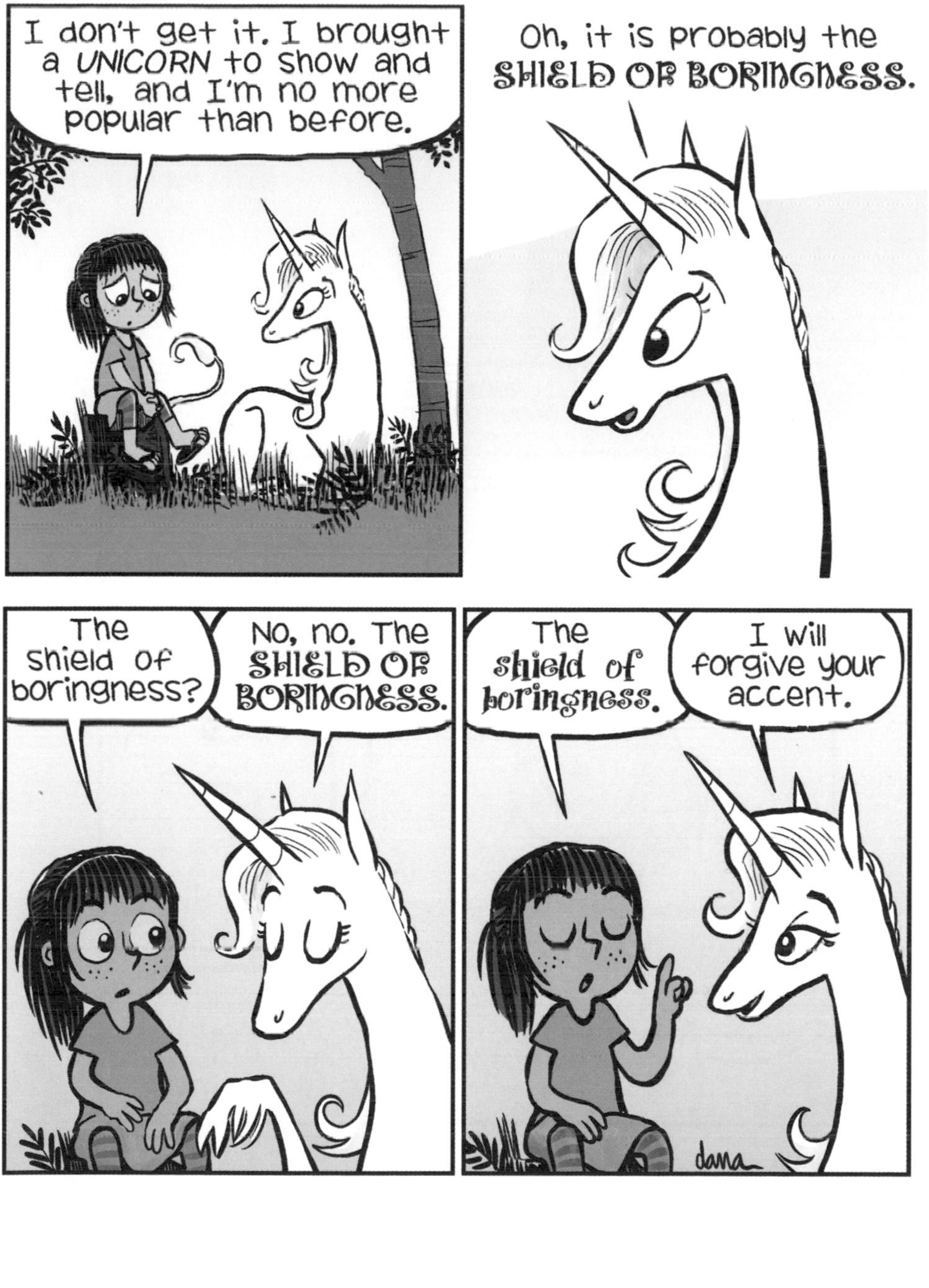
I don't get it. I brought a *UNICORN* to show and tell, and I'm no more popular than before.
Oh, it is probably the SHIELD OF BORINGNESS.
The shield of boringness?
No, no. The SHIELD OF BORINGNESS.
The shield of boringness.
I will forgive your accent.
dana

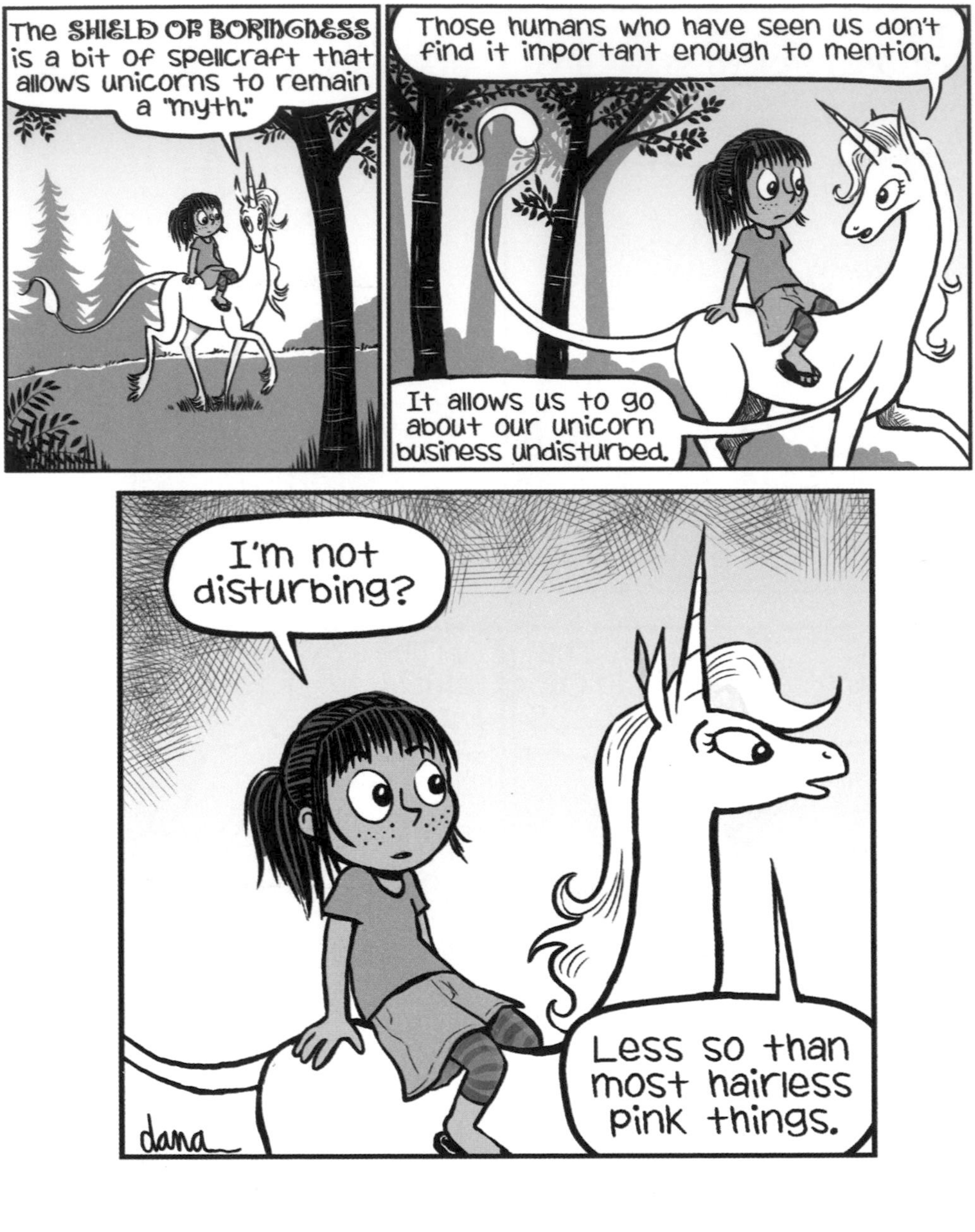
The SHIELD OF BORINGNESS is a bit of spellcraft that allows unicorns to remain a "myth."
Those humans who have seen us don't find it important enough to mention.
It allows us to go about our unicorn business undisturbed.
I'm not disturbing?
Less so than most hairless pink things.
dana

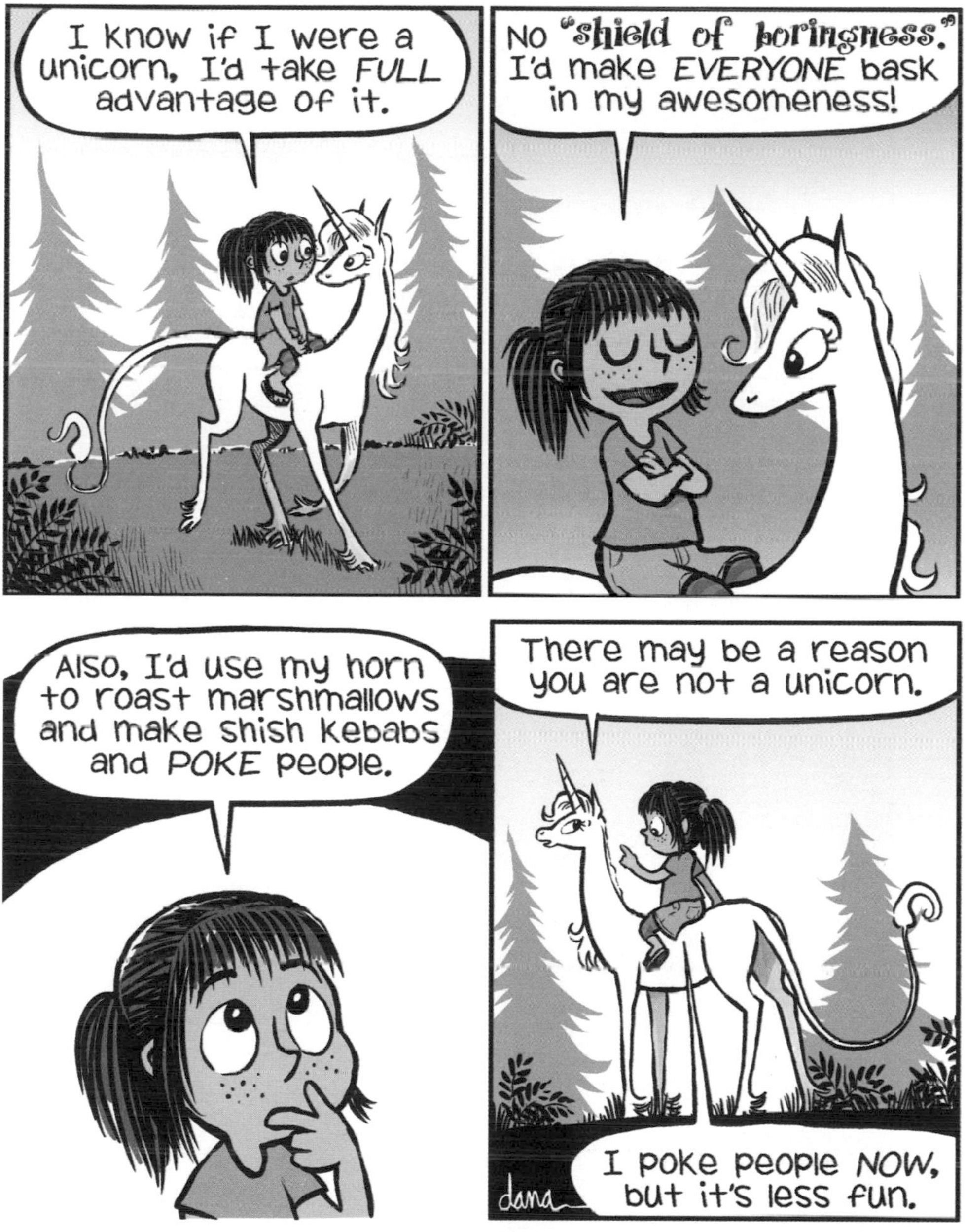
I know if I were a unicorn, I'd take FULL advantage of it.
No "shield of boringness." I'd make EVERYONE bask in my awesomeness!
Also, I'd use my horn to roast marshmallows and make shish kebabs and POKE people.
There may be a reason you are not a unicorn.
I poke people NOW, but it's less fun.
dana

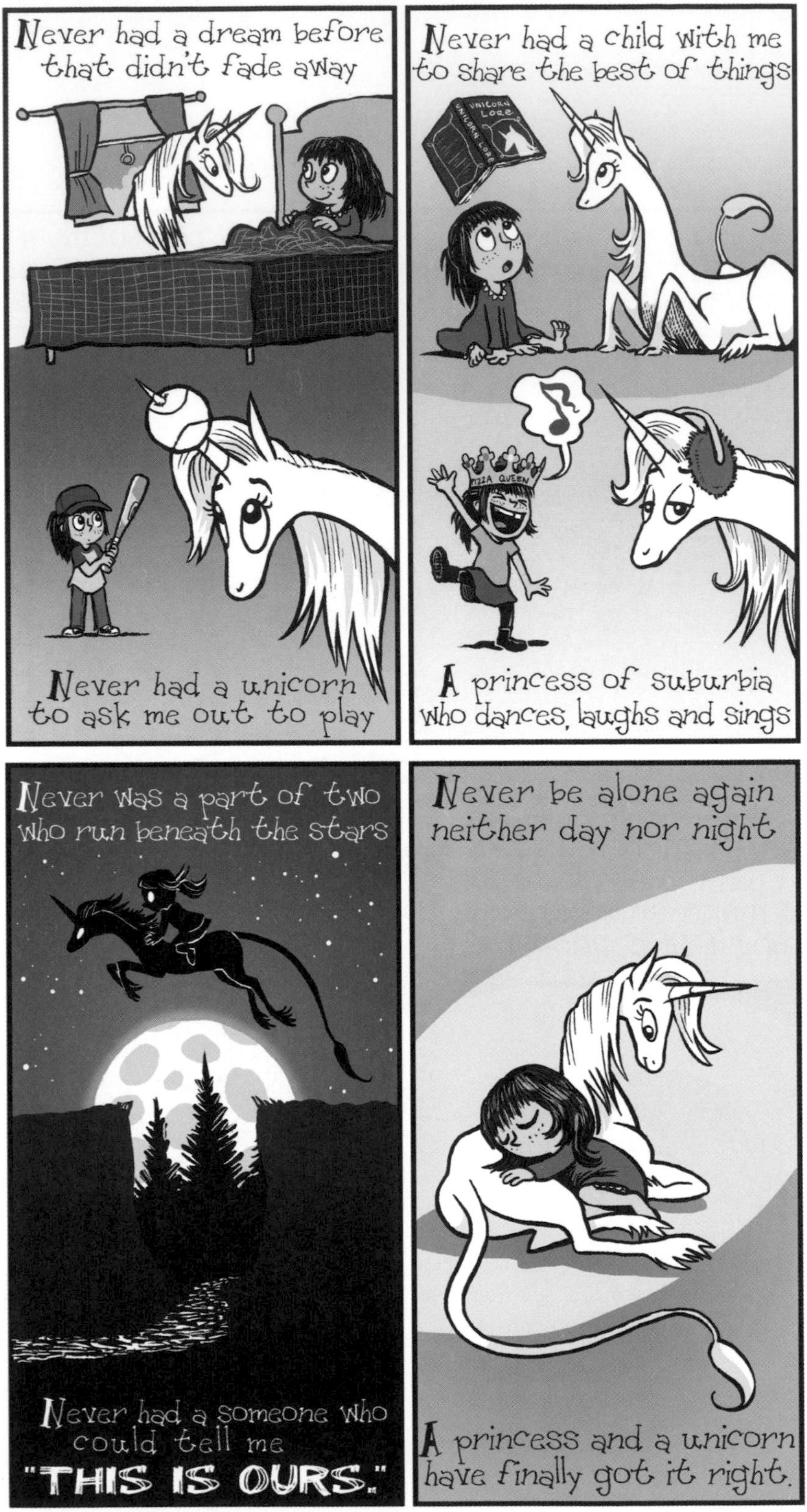
Never had a dream before that didn't fade away
Never had a unicorn to ask me out to play
Never had a child with me to share the best of things
UNICORN LORE
PIZZA QUEEN
A princess of suburbia who dances, laughs and sings
Never was a part of two who run beneath the stars
Never had a someone who could tell me "THIS IS OURS."
Never be alone again neither day nor night
A princess and a unicorn have finally got it right.

Last night I dreamed I had spaghetti for hair.
Together, we will make that dream come true.
I don't *WANT* it to come true.
Then it's good that you said something!
dana

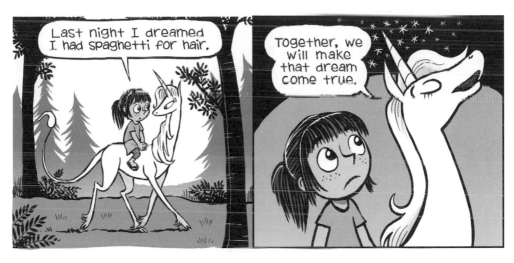

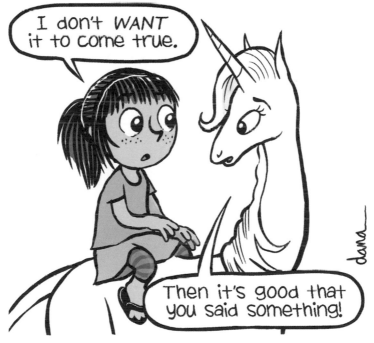

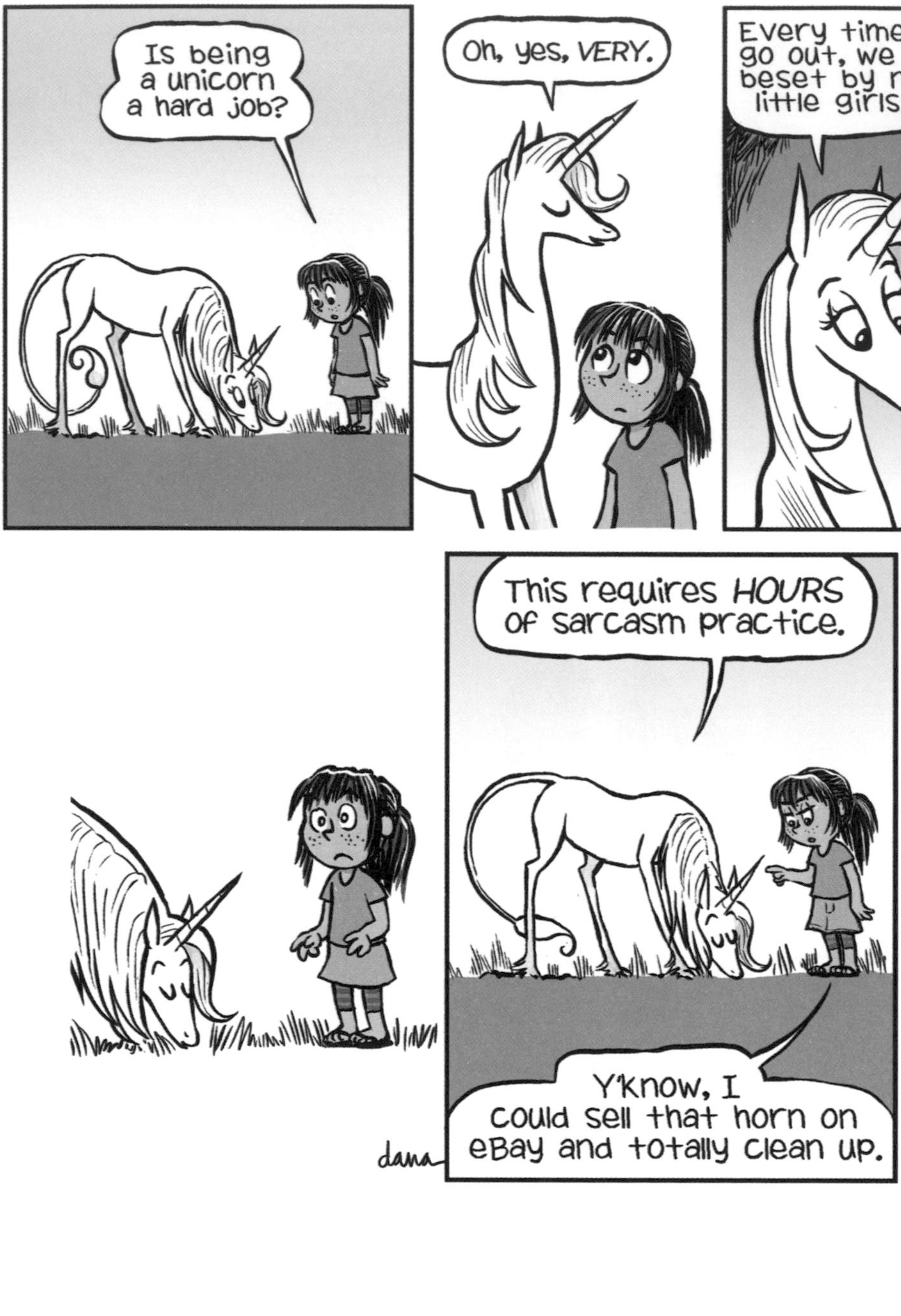
Is being a unicorn a hard job?
Oh, yes, VERY.
Every time we go out, we are beset by nosy little girls.
This requires HOURS of sarcasm practice.
Y'know, I could sell that horn on eBay and totally clean up.
dana

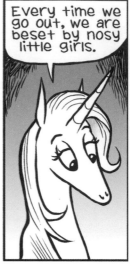

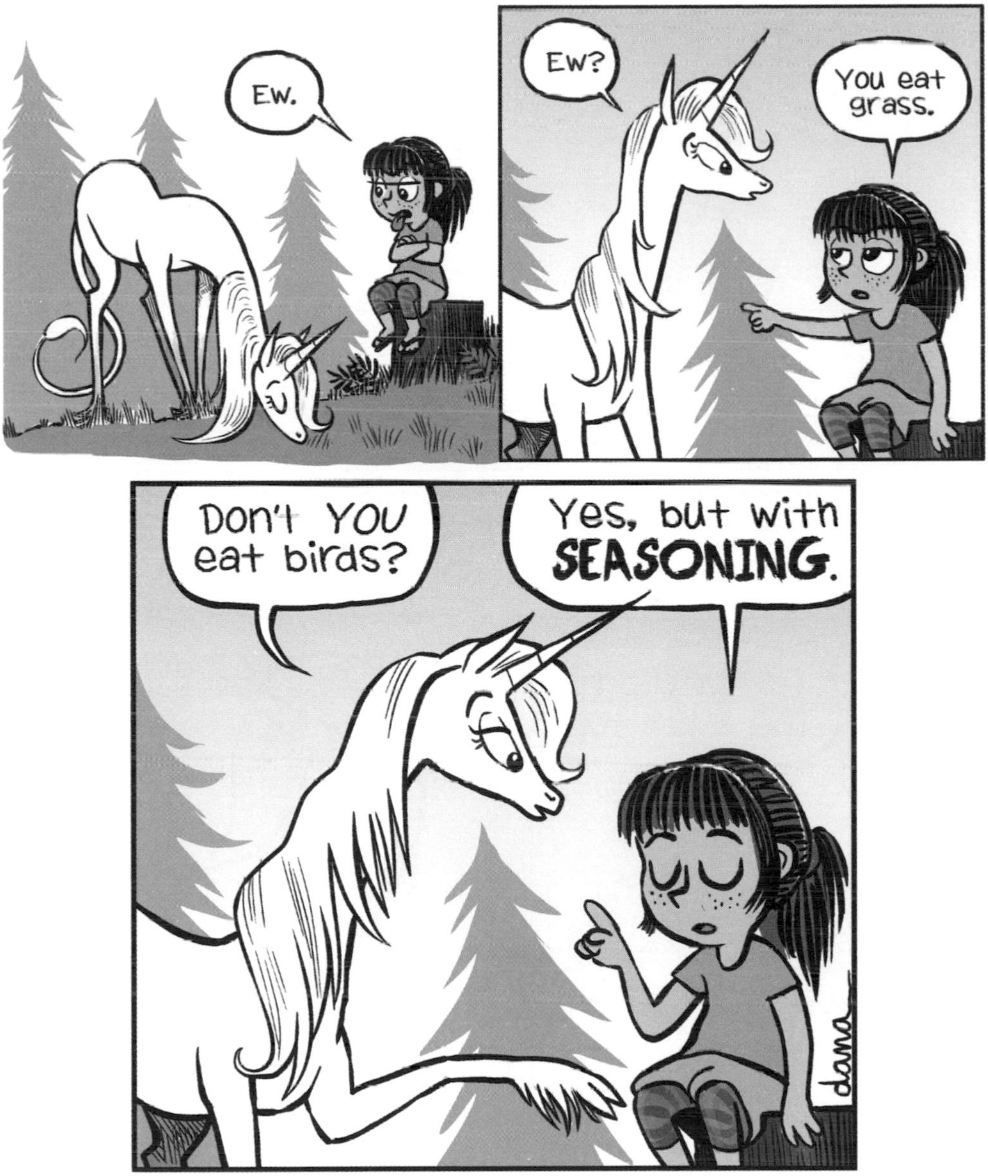
Ew.
Ew?
You eat grass.
Don't YOU eat birds?
Yes, but with SEASONING.
dana

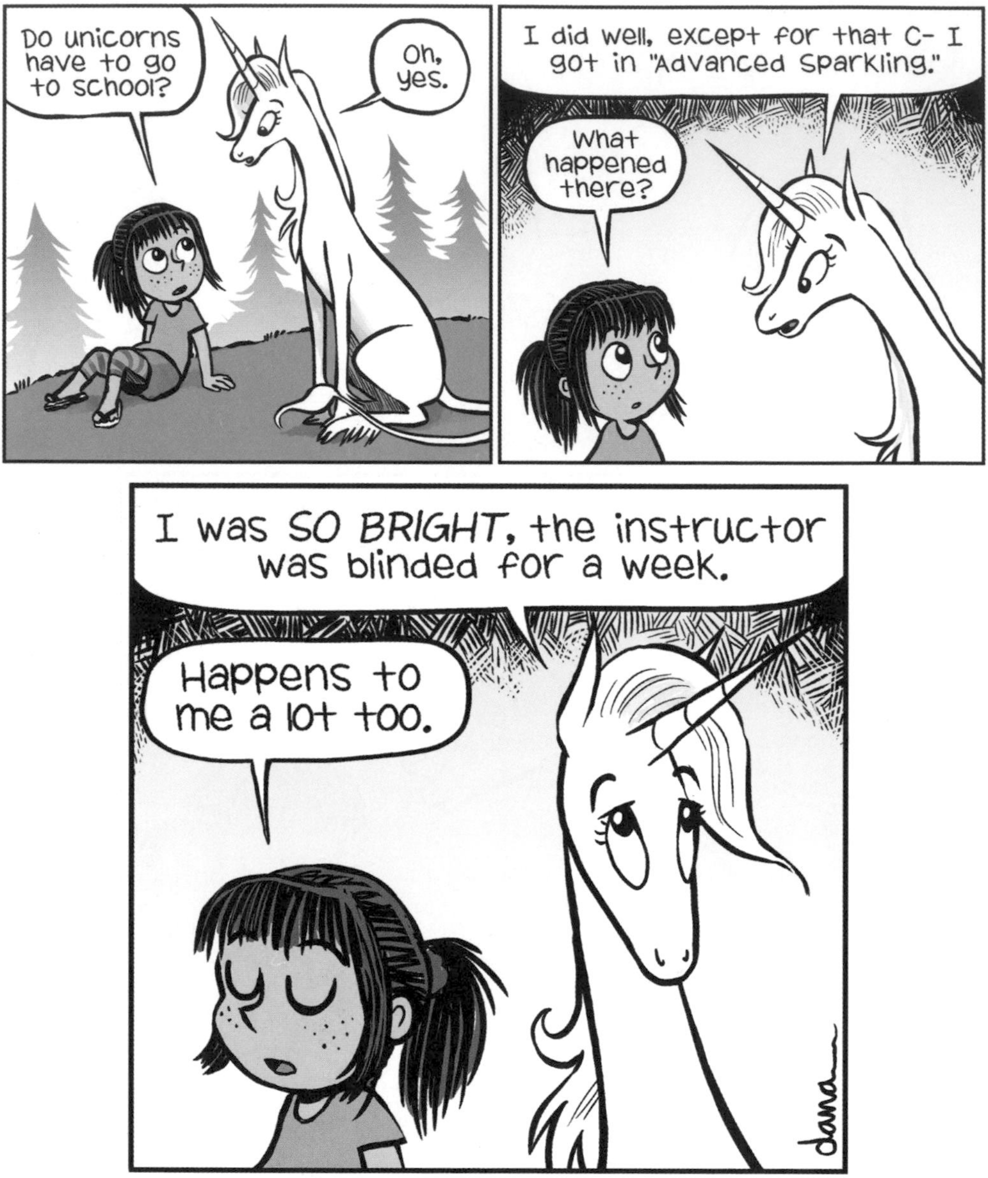
Do unicorns have to go to school?
Oh, yes.
I did well, except for that C- I got in "Advanced Sparkling."
What happened there?
I was SO BRIGHT, the instructor was blinded for a week.
Happens to me a lot too.
dana

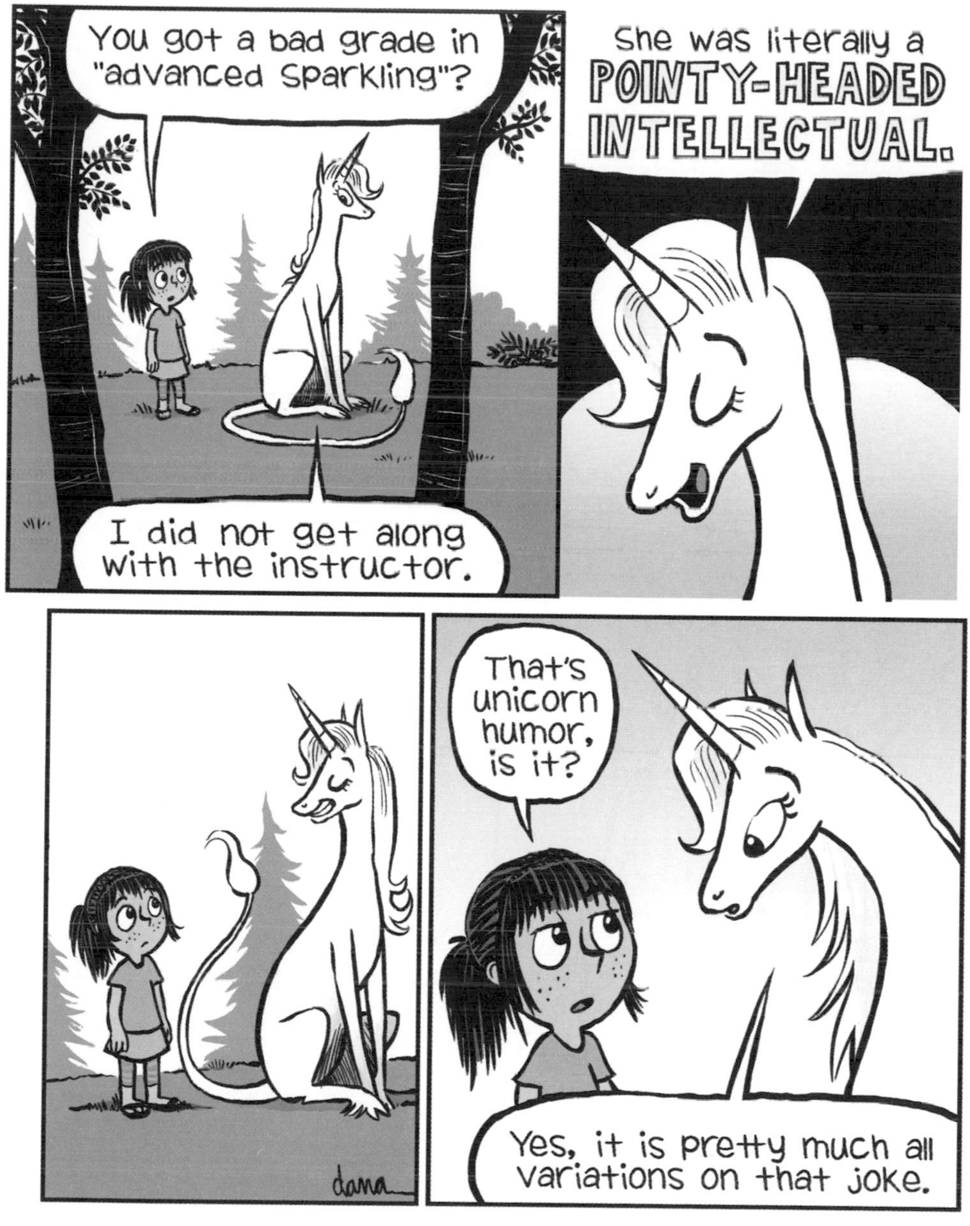
You got a bad grade in "advanced Sparkling"?
I did not get along with the instructor.
She was literally a POINTY-HEADED INTELLECTUAL.
That's unicorn humor, is it?
Yes, it is pretty much all variations on that joke.
dana

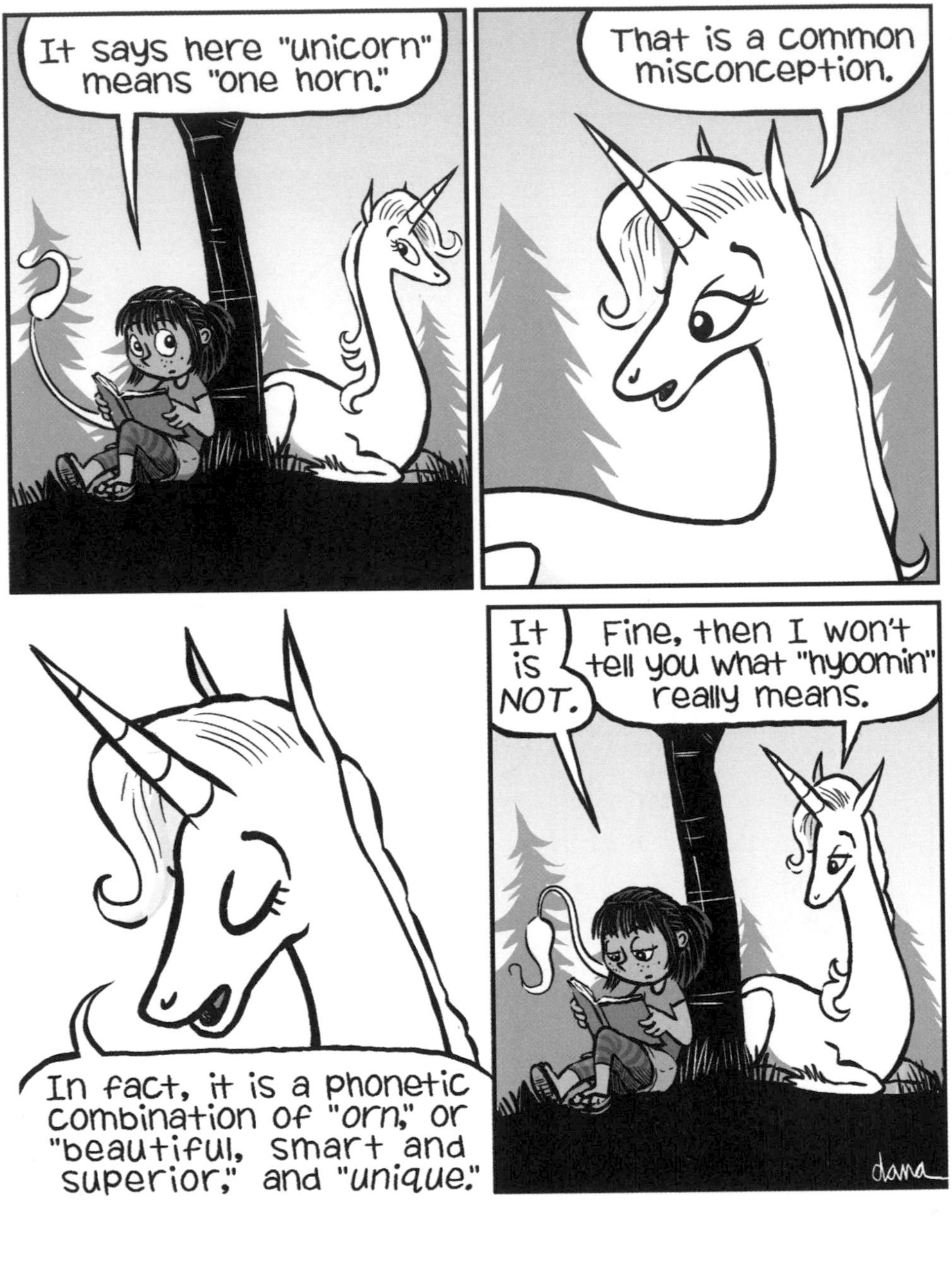

It says here "unicorn" means "one horn."
That is a common misconception.
In fact, it is a phonetic combination of "orn," or "beautiful, smart and superior," and "unique."
It is NOT.
Fine, then I won't tell you what "hyoomin" really means.
dana

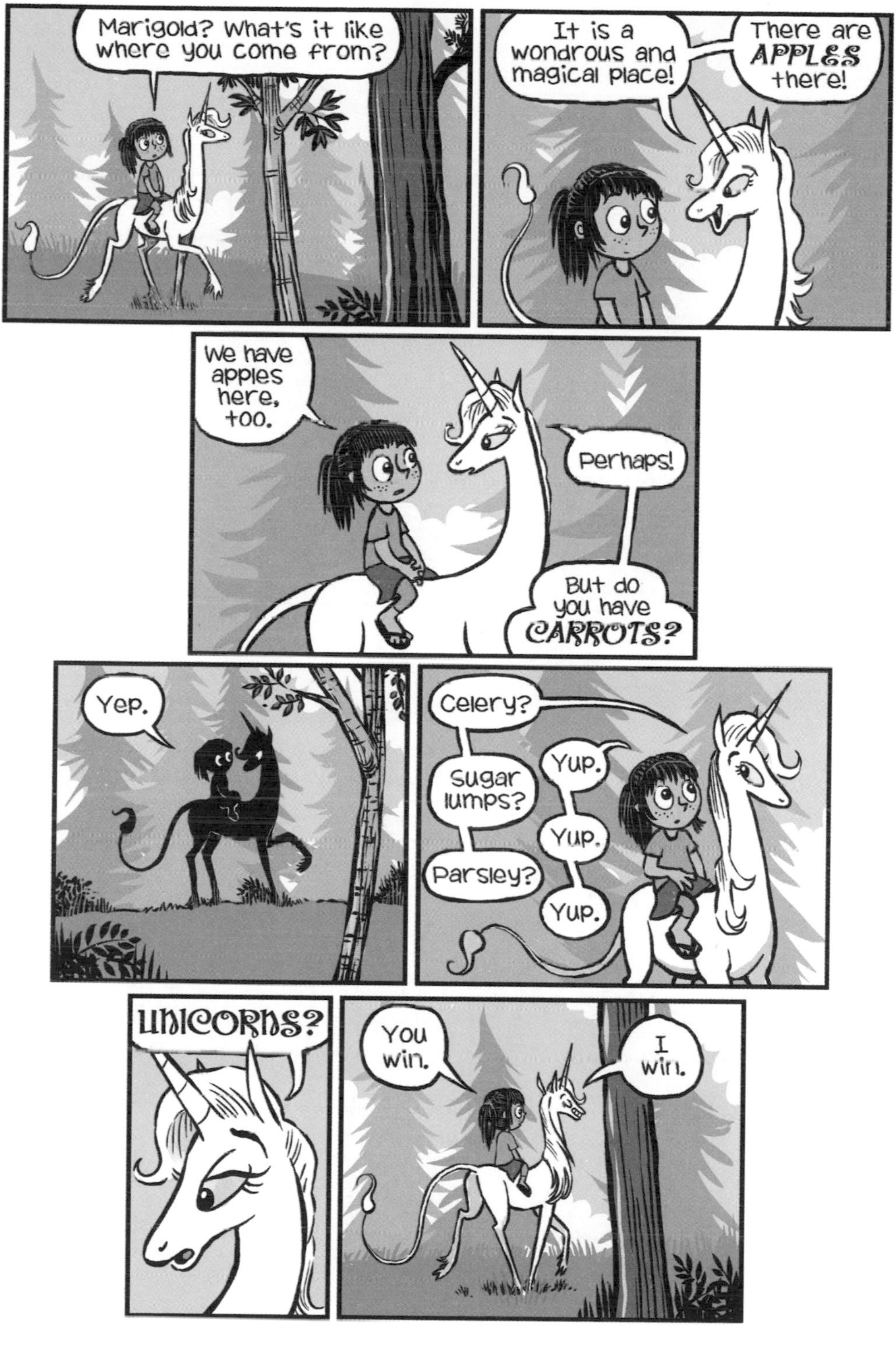
Marigold? What's it like where you come from?
It is a wondrous and magical place!
There are APPLES there!
We have apples here, too.
Perhaps!
But do you have CARROTS?
Yep.
Celery?
Sugar lumps?
Parsley?
Yup.
Yup.
Yup.
UNICORNS?
You win.
I win.

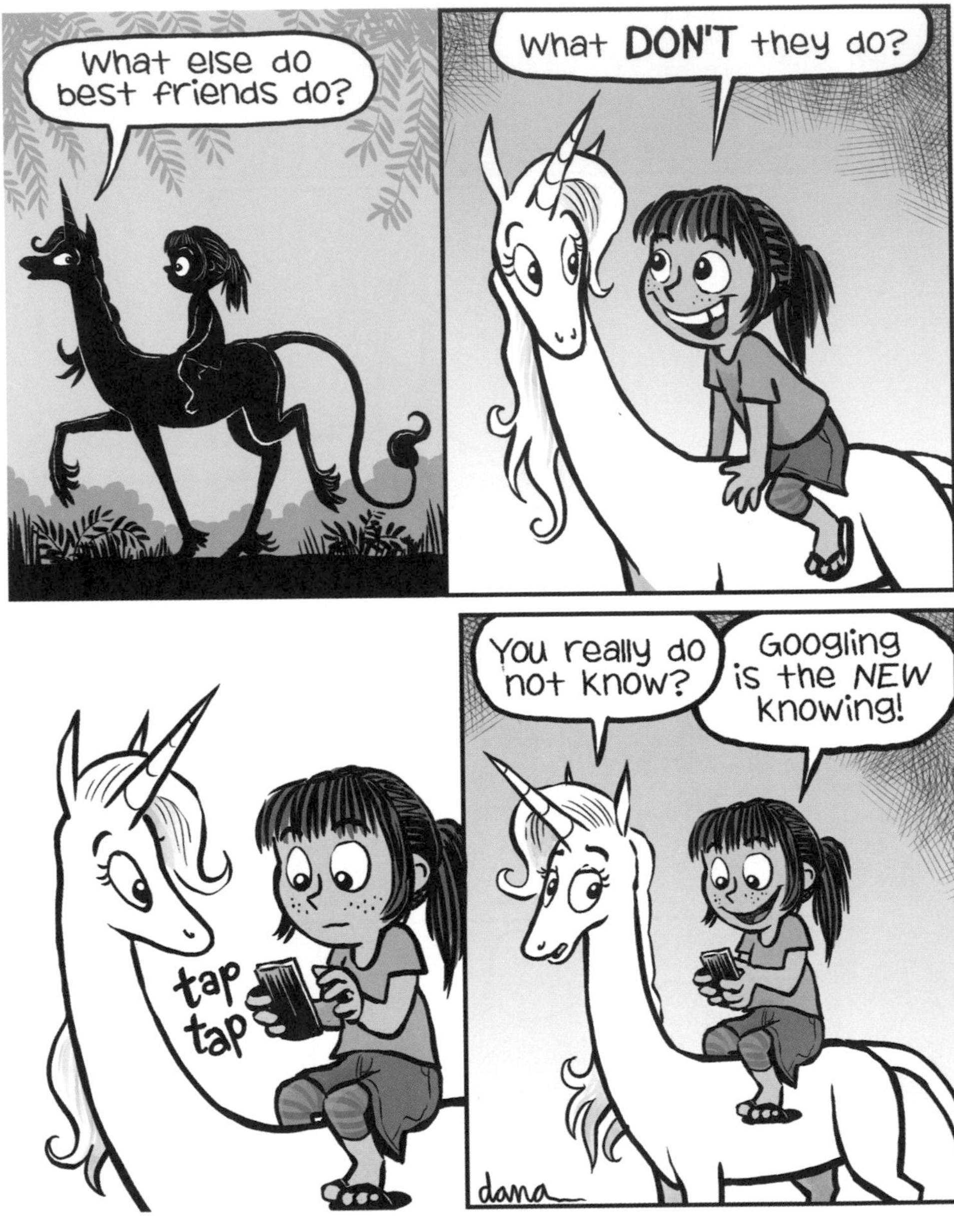
What else do best friends do?
What **DON'T** they do?
tap tap
You really do not know?
Googling is the *NEW* knowing!
dana

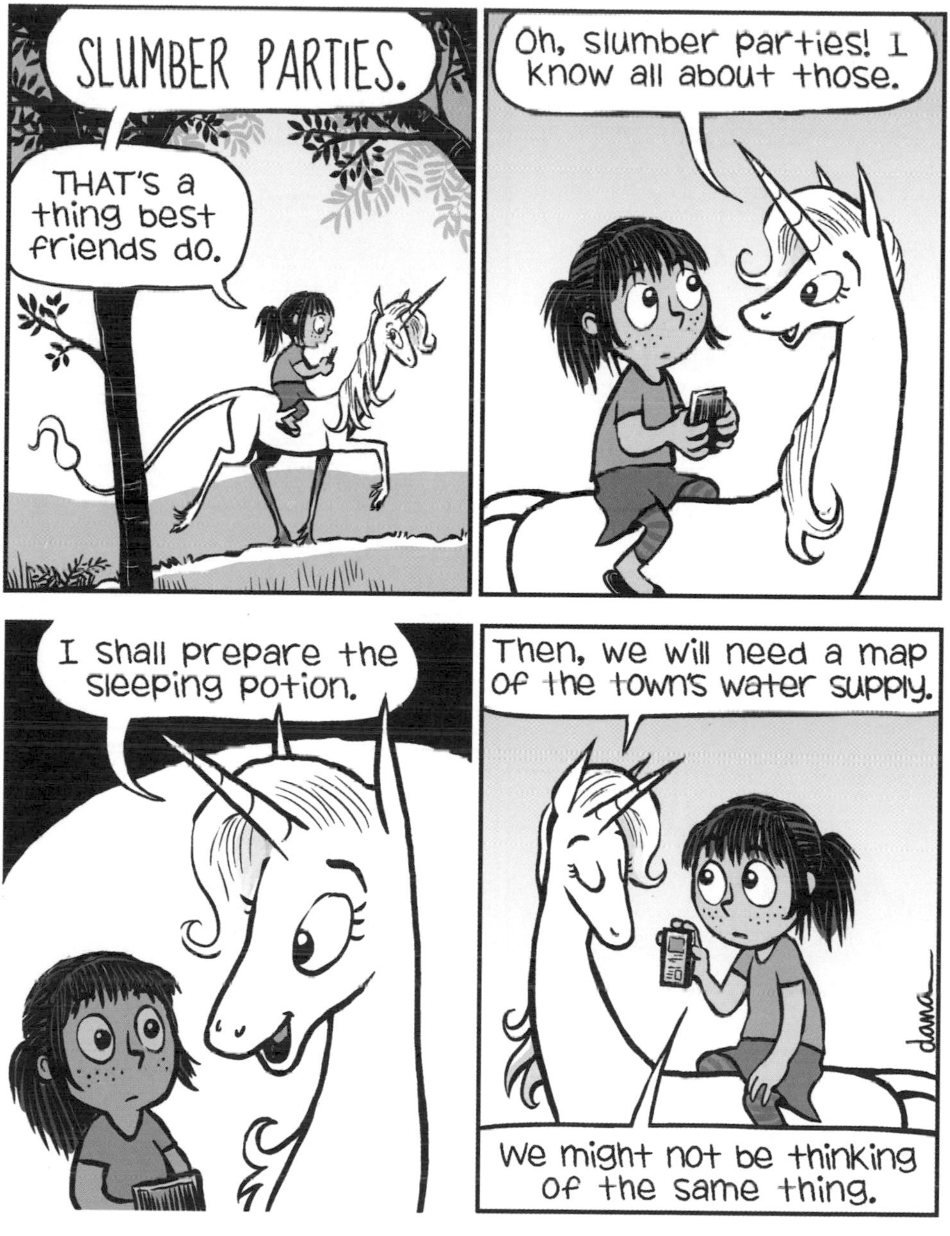
SLUMBER PARTIES.
THAT'S a thing best friends do.
Oh, slumber parties! I know all about those.
I shall prepare the sleeping potion.
Then, we will need a map of the town's water supply.
We might not be thinking of the same thing.
dana

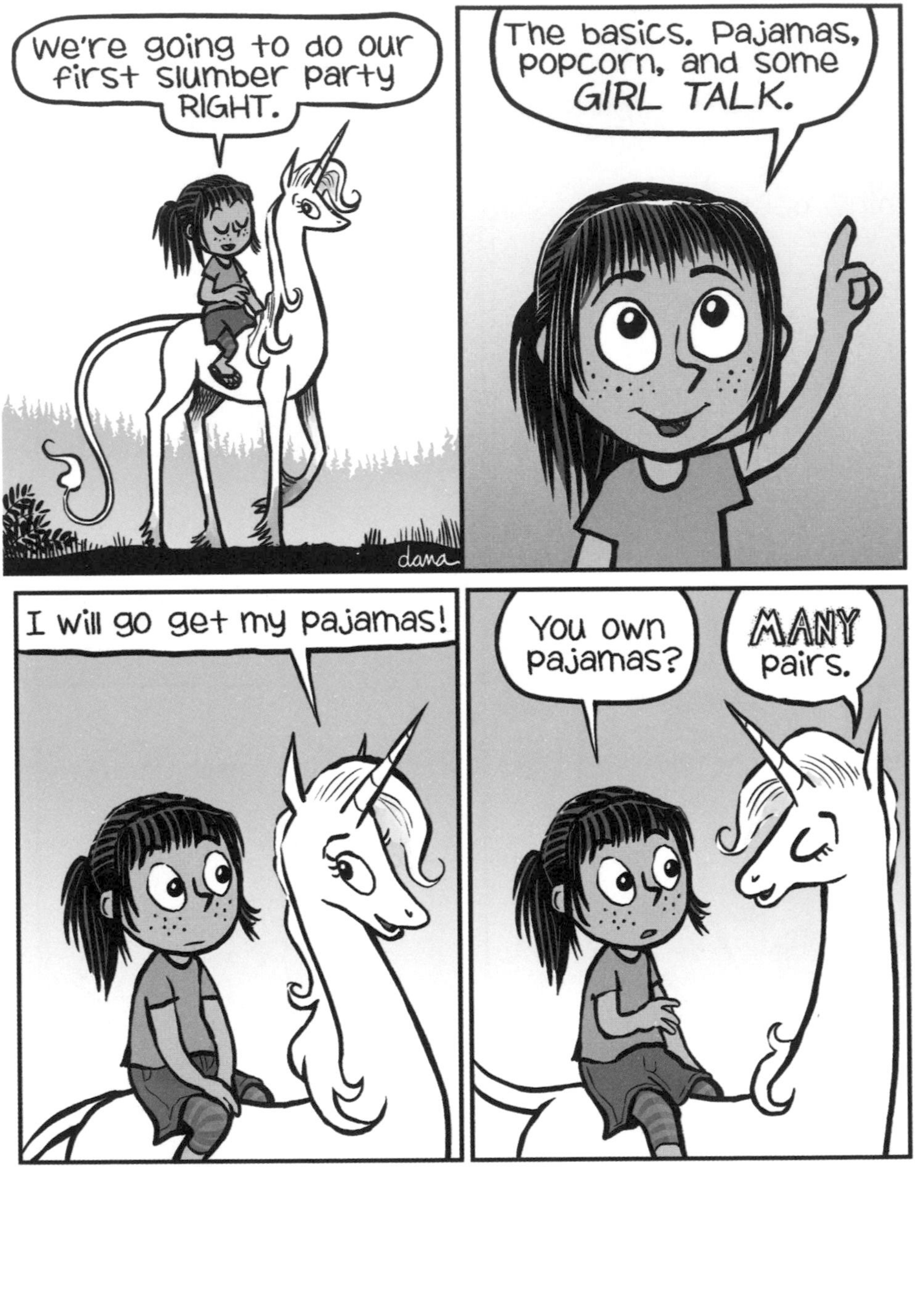
We're going to do our first slumber party RIGHT.
dana
The basics. Pajamas, popcorn, and some GIRL TALK.
I will go get my pajamas!
You own pajamas?
MANY pairs.

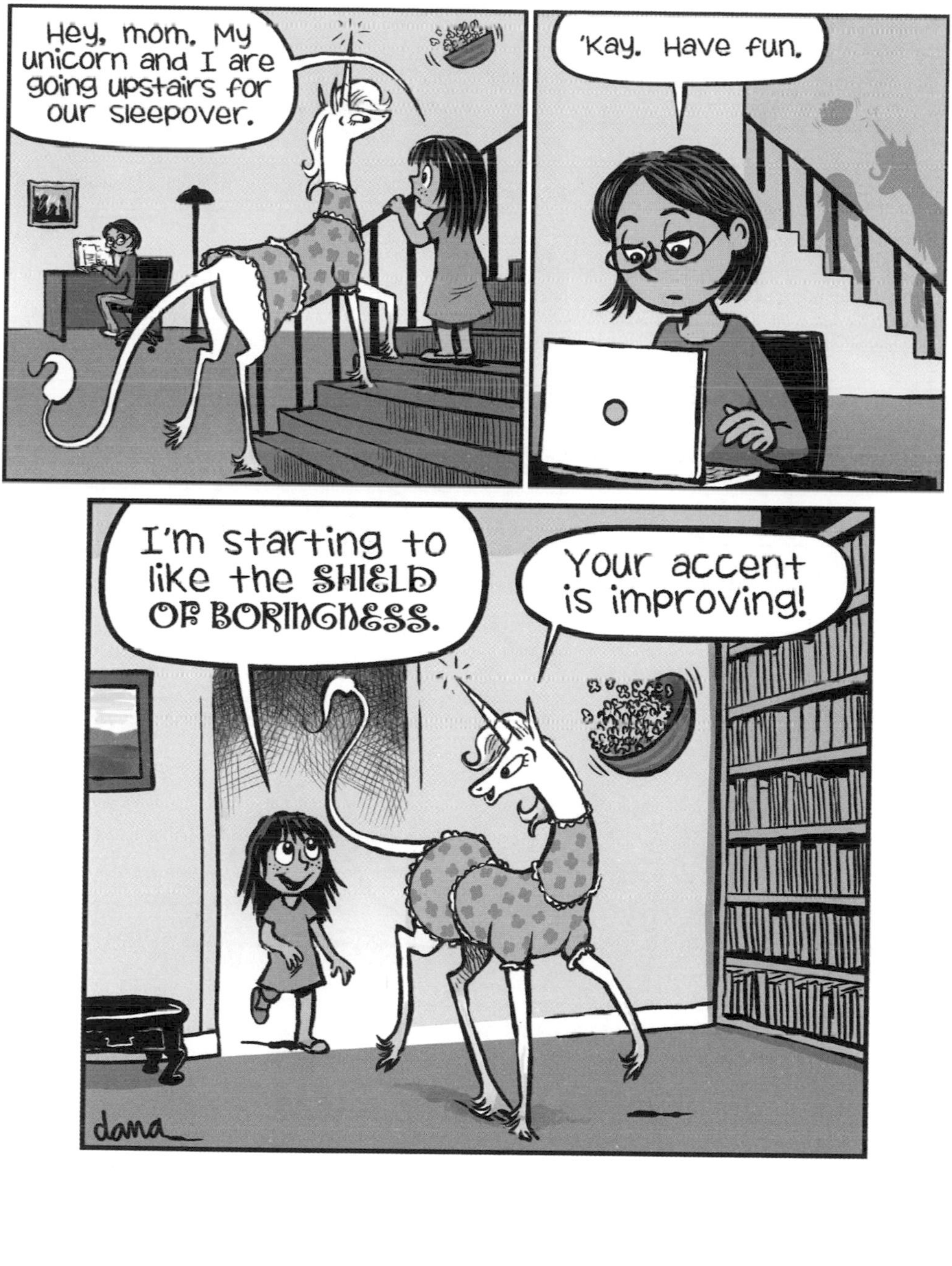
Hey, mom. My unicorn and I are going upstairs for our sleepover.
'Kay. Have fun.
I'm starting to like the SHIELD OF BORINGNESS.
Your accent is improving!
dana

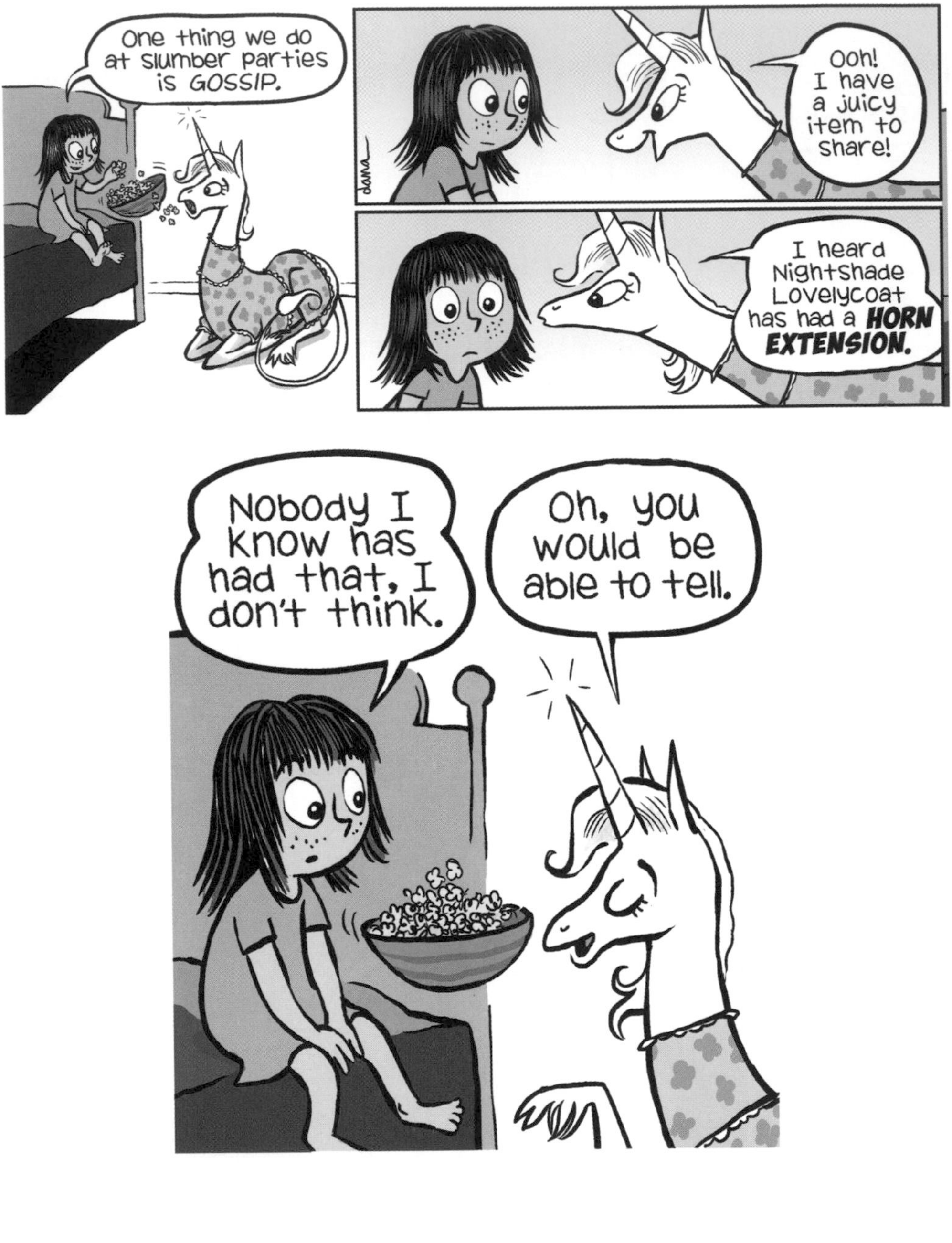
One thing we do at slumber parties is GOSSIP.
Ooh! I have a juicy item to share!
I heard Nightshade Lovelycoat has had a **HORN EXTENSION.**
Nobody I know has had that, I don't think.
Oh, you would be able to tell.

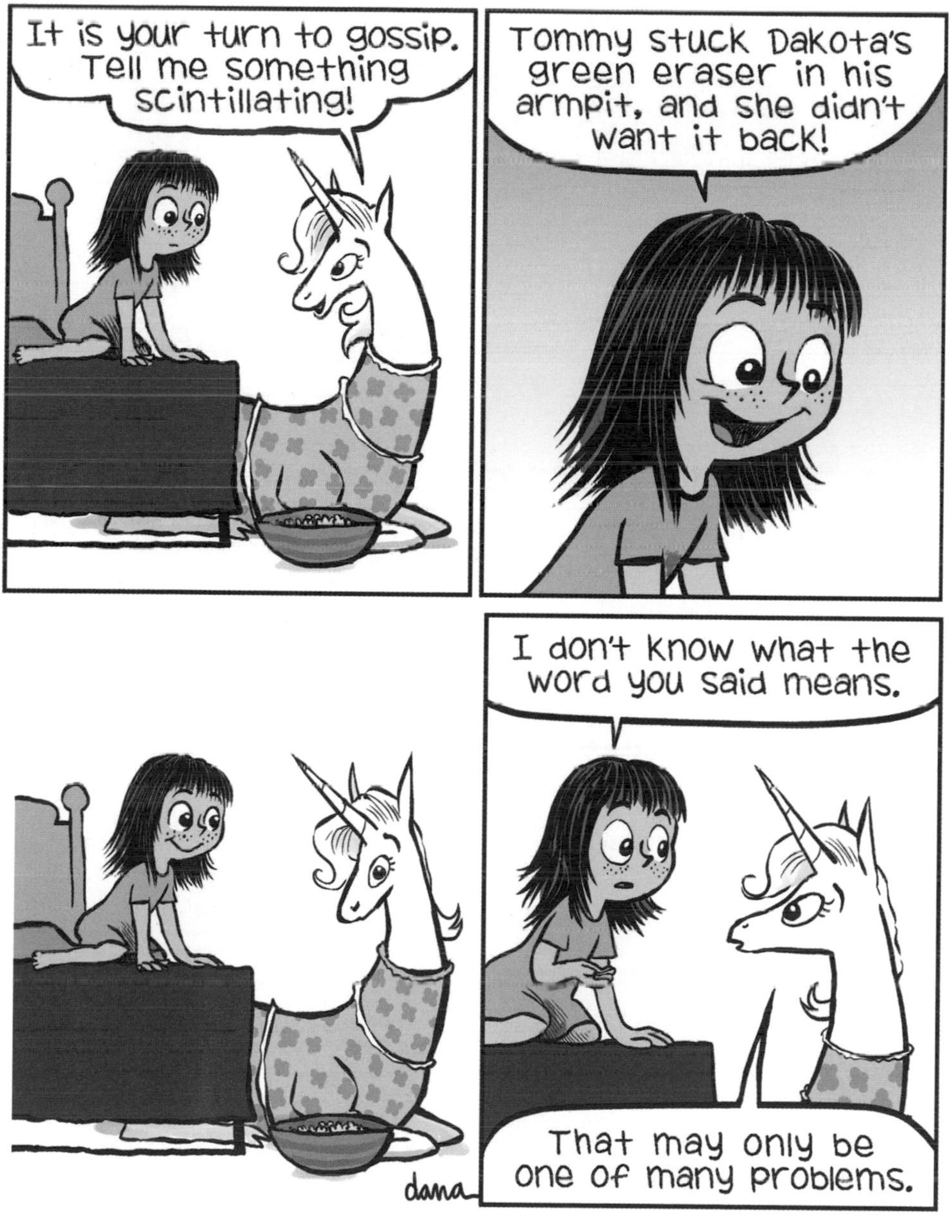

It is your turn to gossip. Tell me something scintillating!
Tommy stuck Dakota's green eraser in his armpit, and she didn't want it back!
I don't know what the word you said means.
That may only be one of many problems.
dana

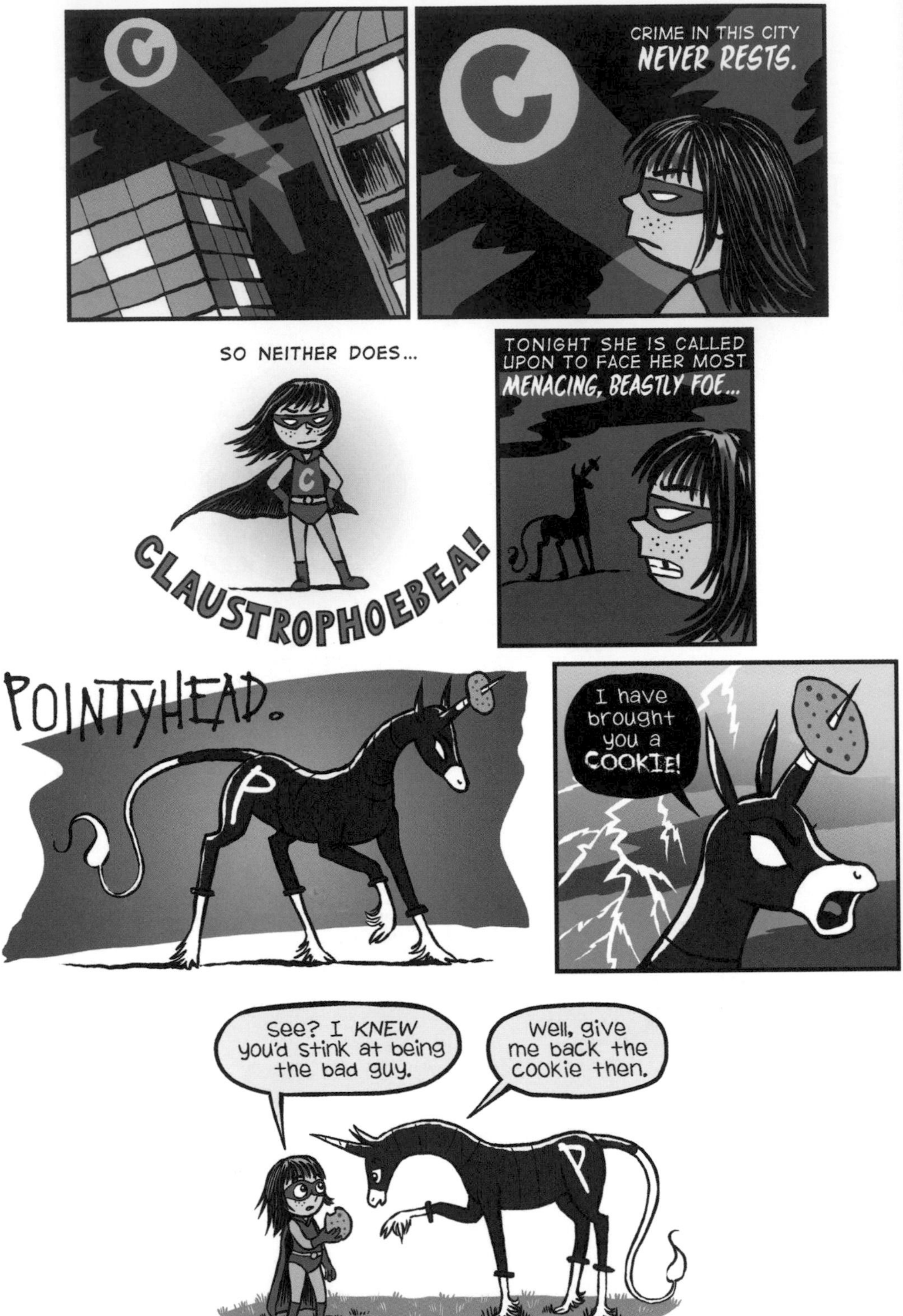
CRIME IN THIS CITY
NEVER RESTS.
SO NEITHER DOES...
CLAUSTROPHOEBEA!
TONIGHT SHE IS CALLED UPON TO FACE HER MOST
MENACING, BEASTLY FOE...
POINTYHEAD.
I have brought you a COOKIE!
See? I KNEW you'd stink at being the bad guy.
Well, give me back the cookie then.

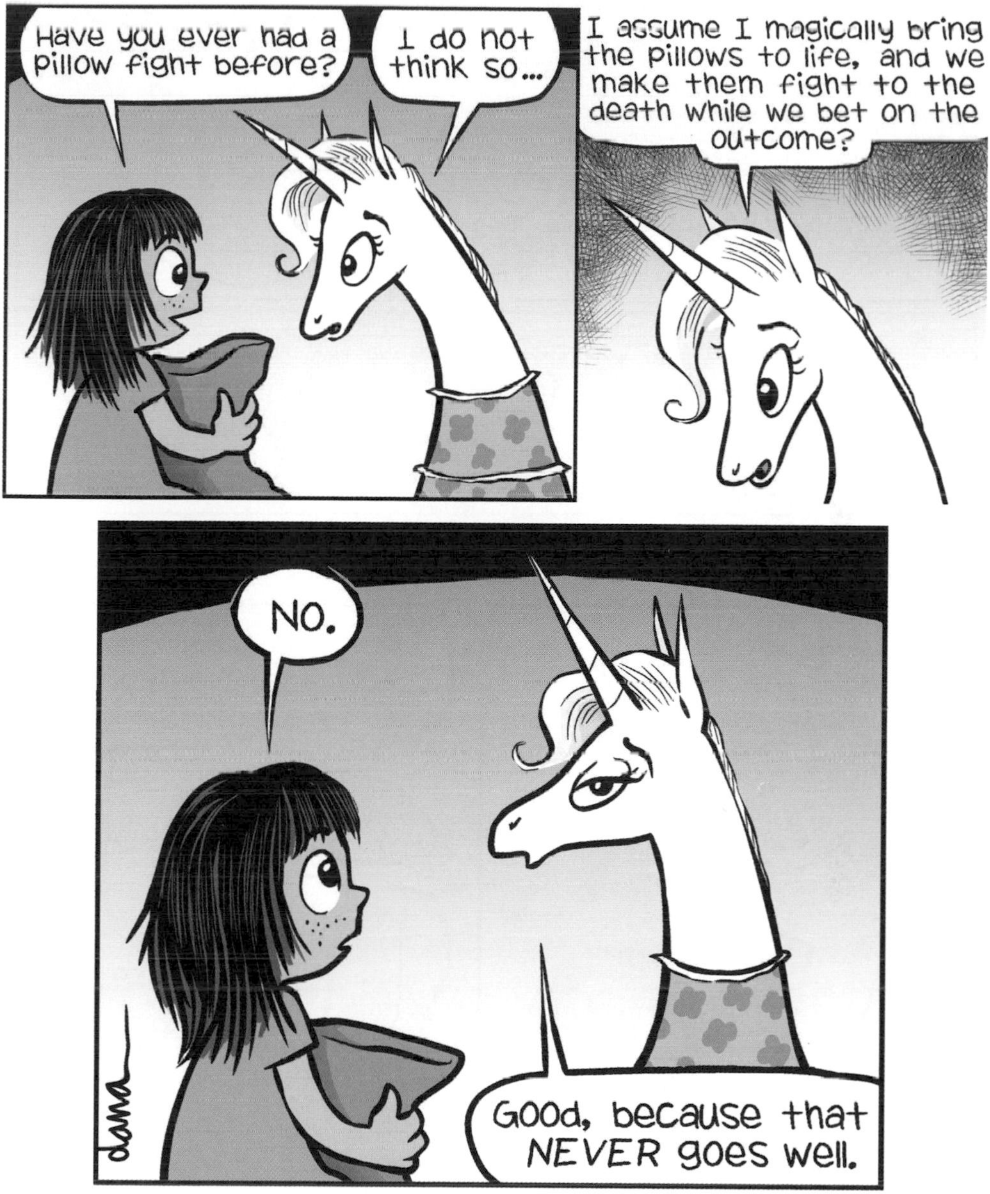
Have you ever had a pillow fight before?
I do not think so...
I assume I magically bring the pillows to life, and we make them fight to the death while we bet on the outcome?
NO.
Good, because that NEVER goes well.
dana

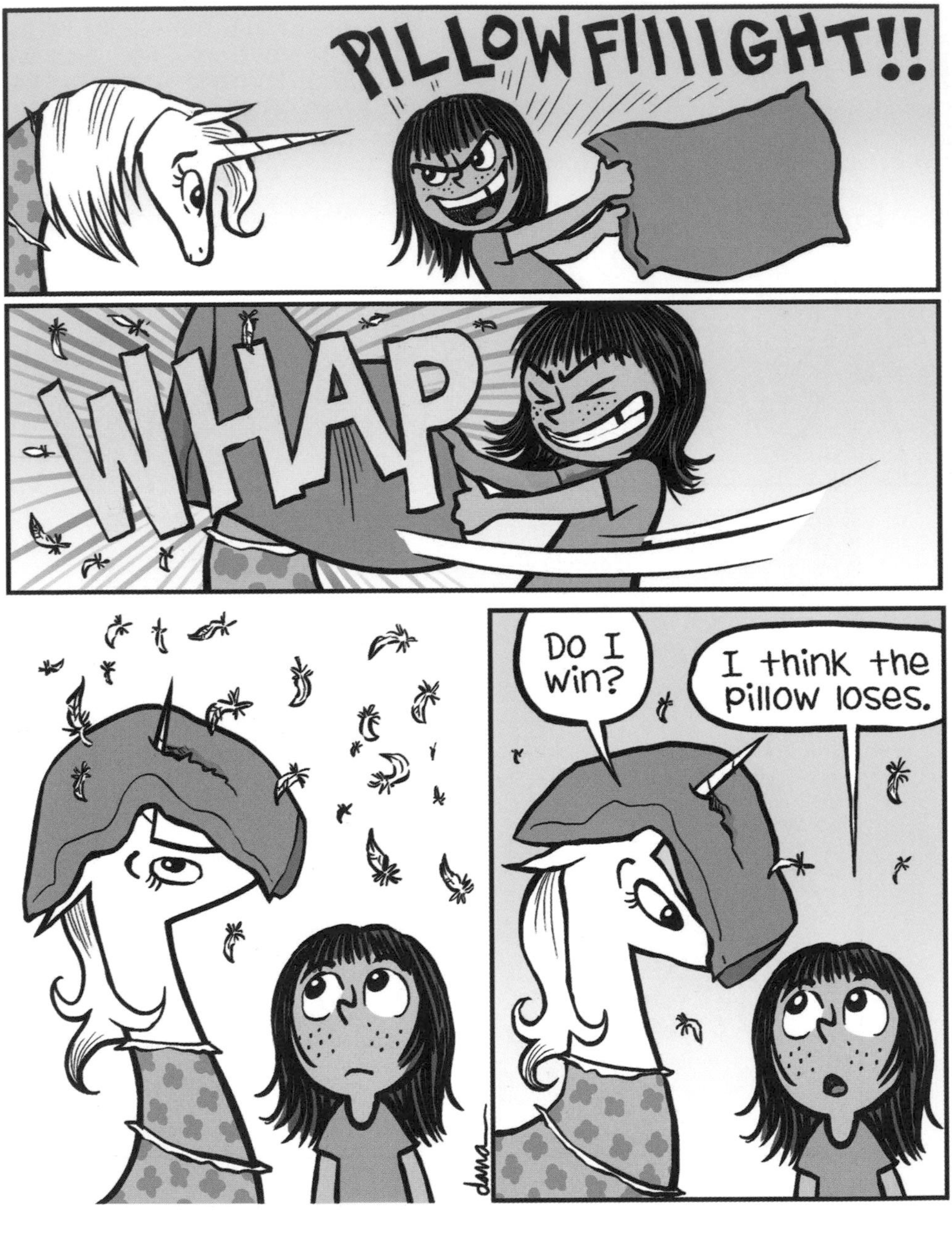
PILLOWFIIIIGHT!!
WHAP
Do I win?
I think the pillow loses.
dana

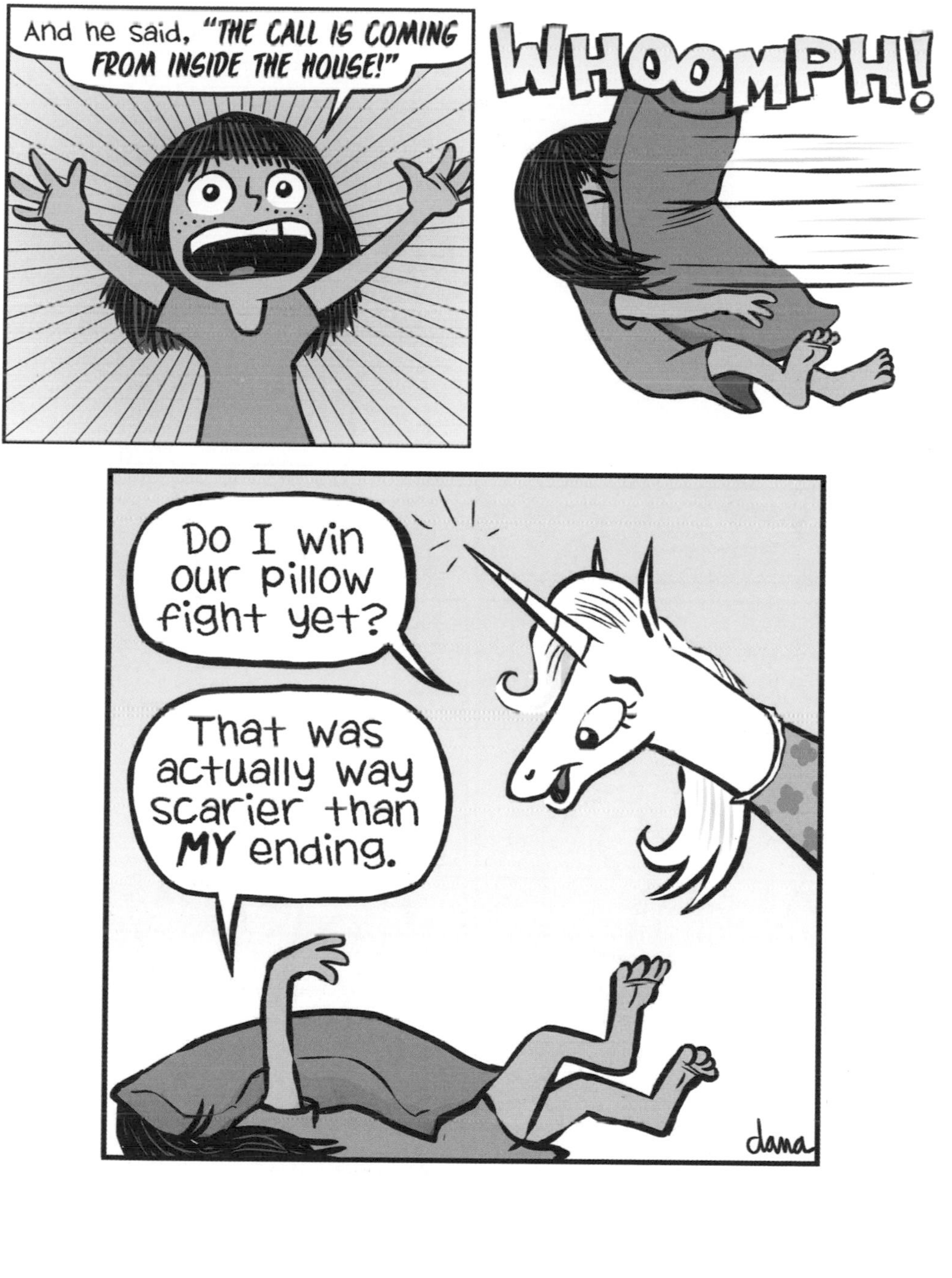

And he said, "THE CALL IS COMING FROM INSIDE THE HOUSE!"
WHOOMPH!
Do I win our pillow fight yet?
That was actually way scarier than MY ending.
dana

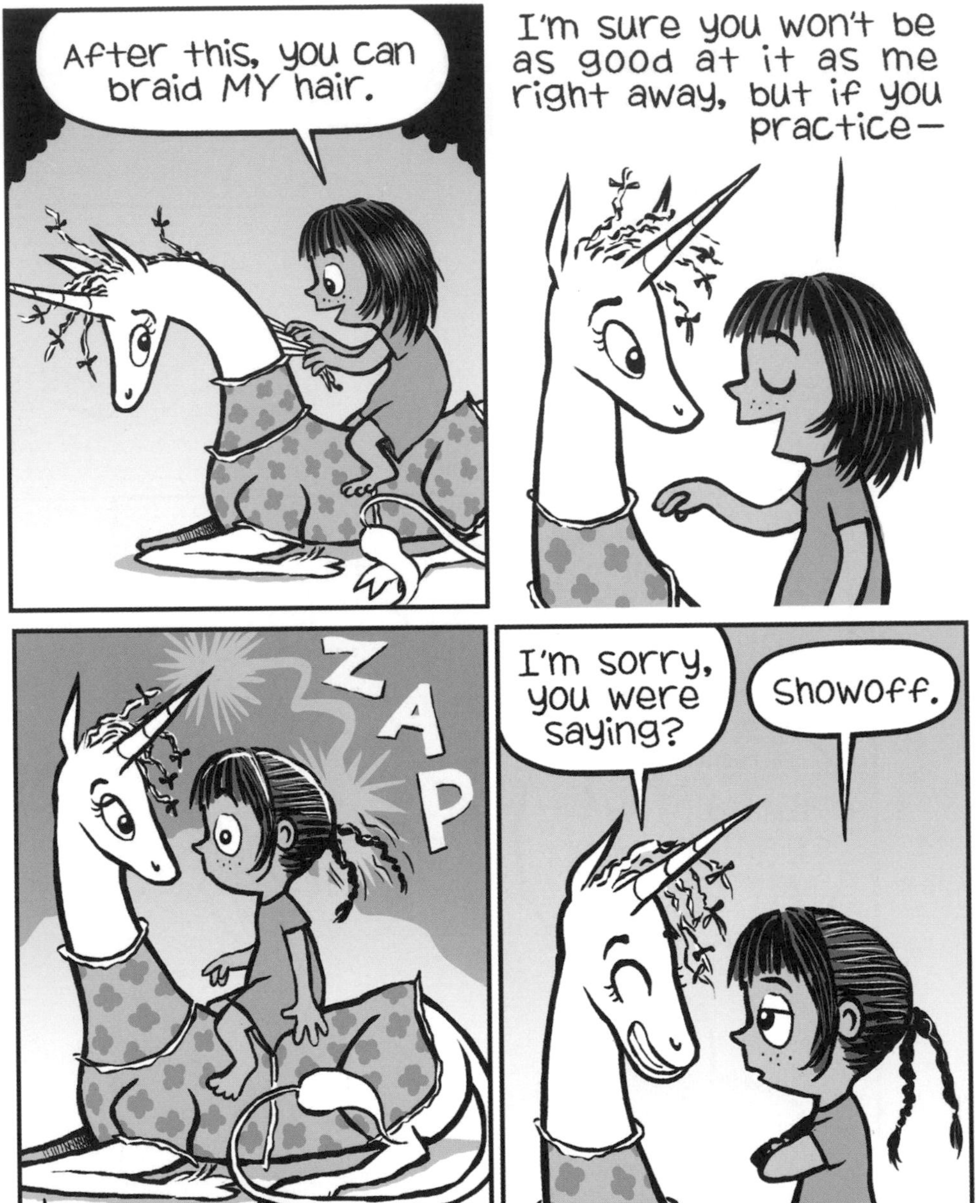
After this, you can braid MY hair.
I'm sure you won't be as good at it as me right away, but if you practice—
ZAP
I'm sorry, you were saying?
Showoff.
dana

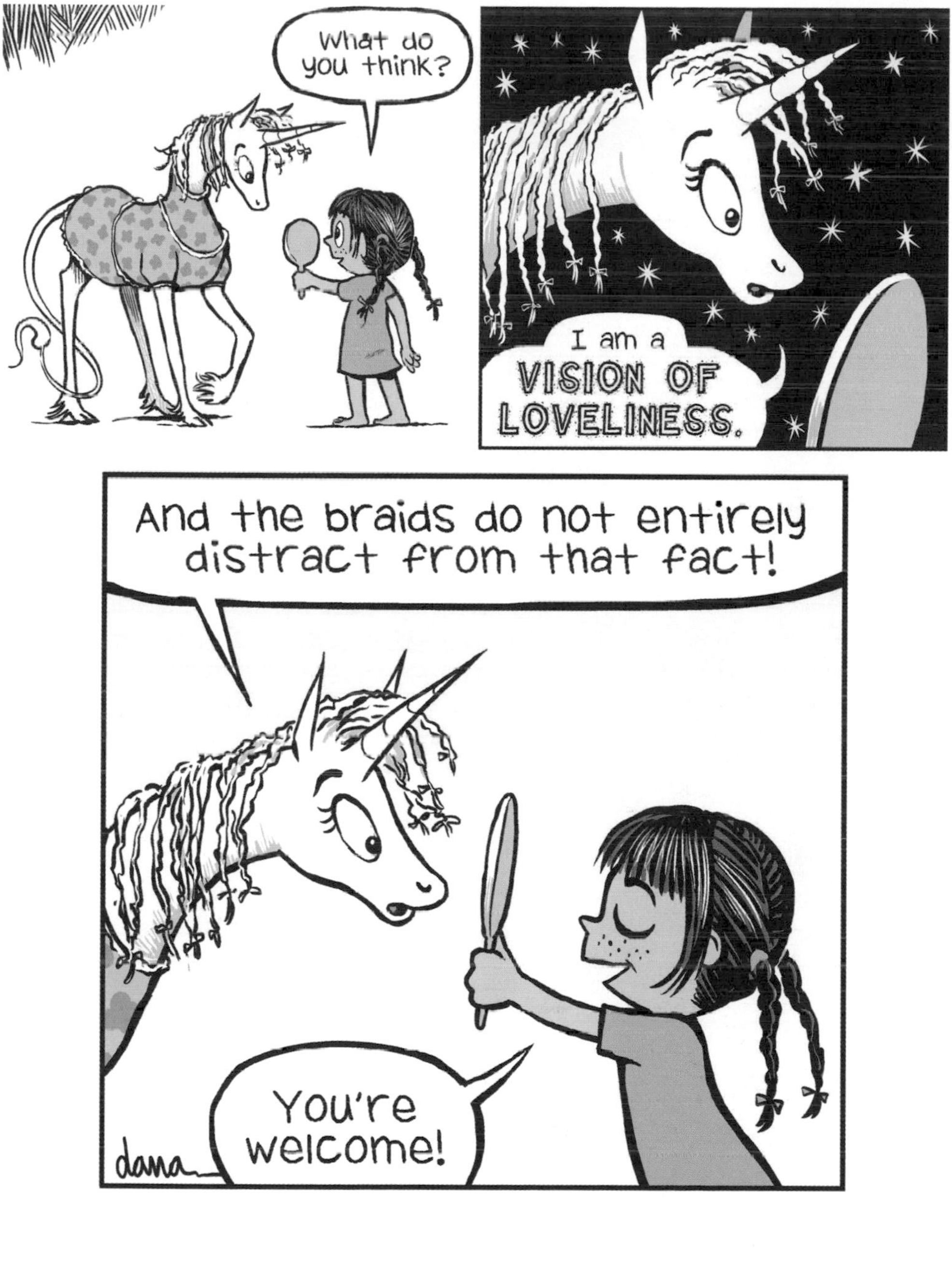
What do you think?
I am a VISION OF LOVELINESS.
And the braids do not entirely distract from that fact!
You're welcome!
dana

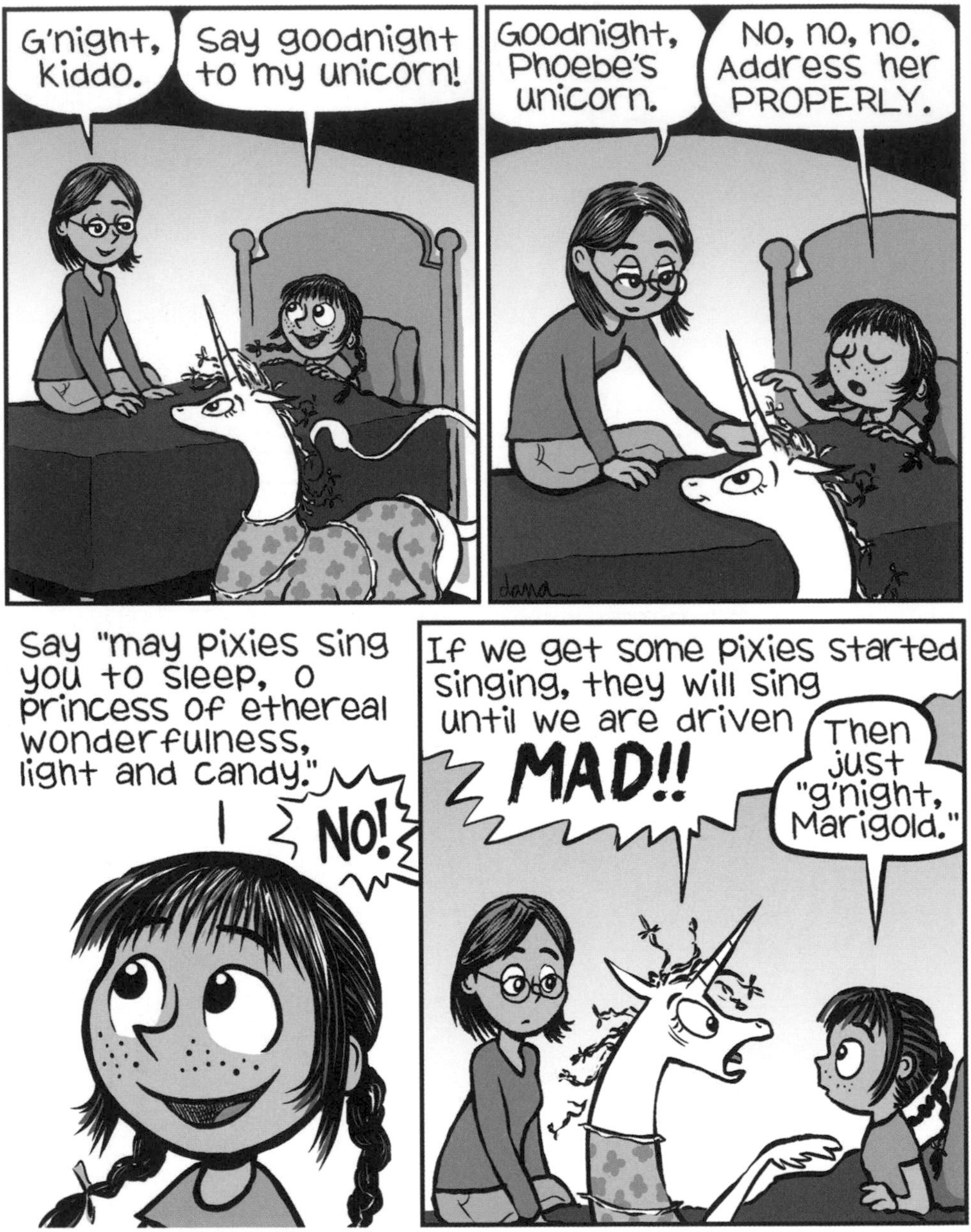
G'night, Kiddo.
Say goodnight to my unicorn!
Goodnight, Phoebe's unicorn.
No, no, no. Address her PROPERLY.
Say "may pixies sing you to sleep, O princess of ethereal wonderfulness, light and candy."
I
NO!
If we get some pixies started singing, they will sing until we are driven MAD!!
Then just "g'night, Marigold."

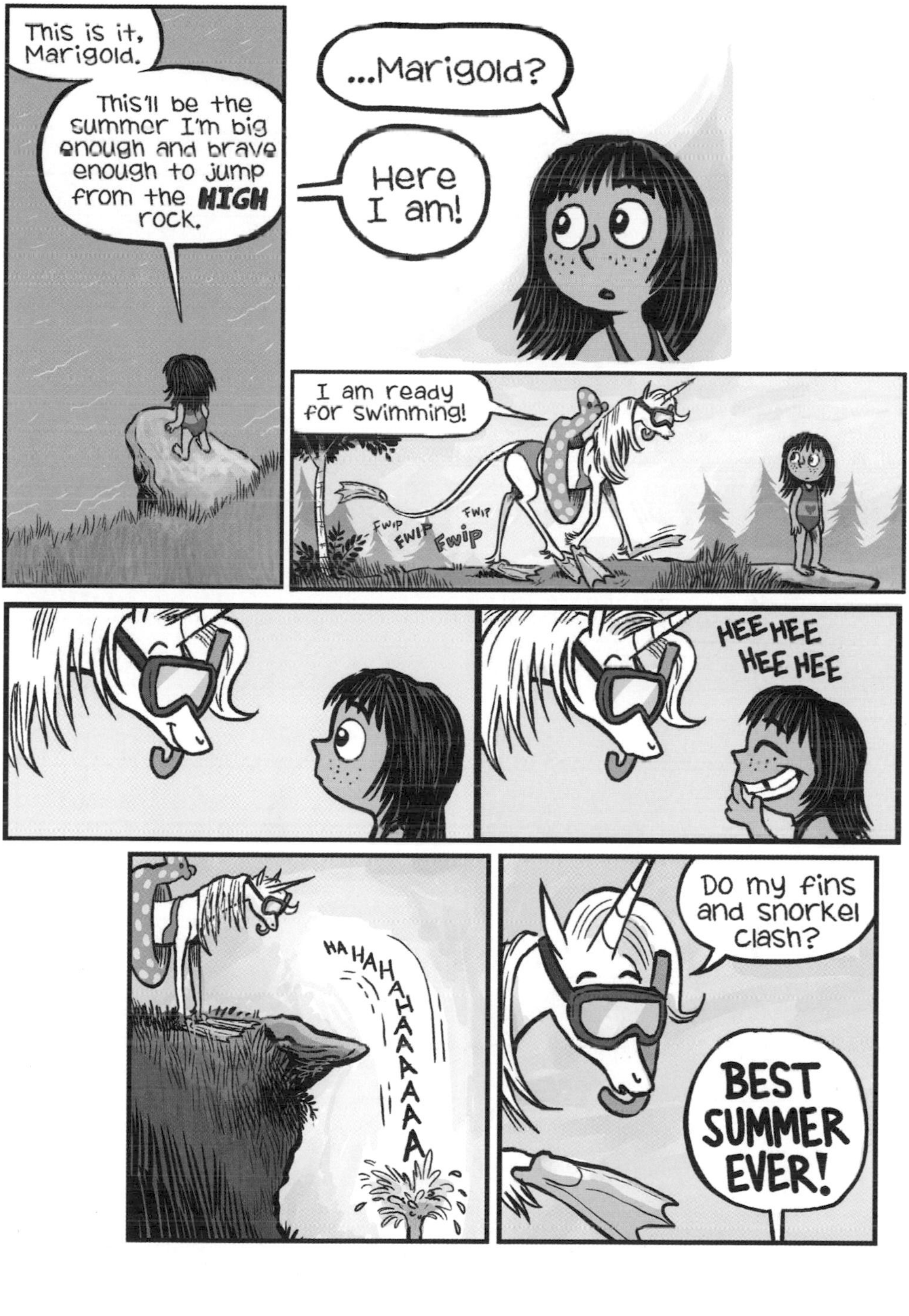
This is it, Marigold.
This'll be the summer I'm big enough and brave enough to jump from the HIGH rock.
...Marigold?
Here I am!
I am ready for swimming!
FWIP
FWIP
FWIP
FWIP
HEE HEE HEE HEE
HA HA HAHAAAAAAAA
Do my fins and snorkel clash?
BEST SUMMER EVER!

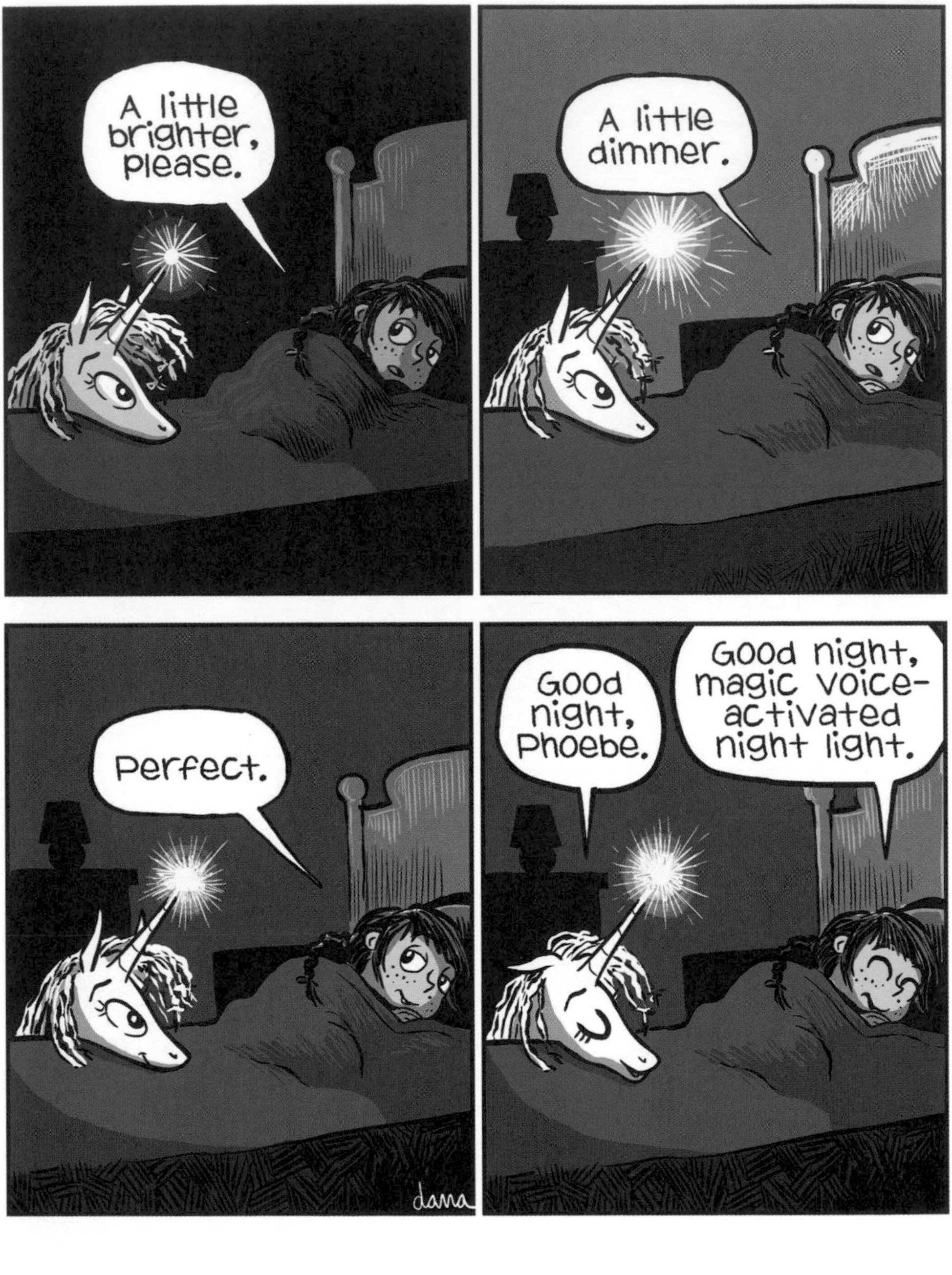
A little brighter, please.
A little dimmer.
Perfect.
Good night, Phoebe.
Good night, magic voice-activated night light.
dana

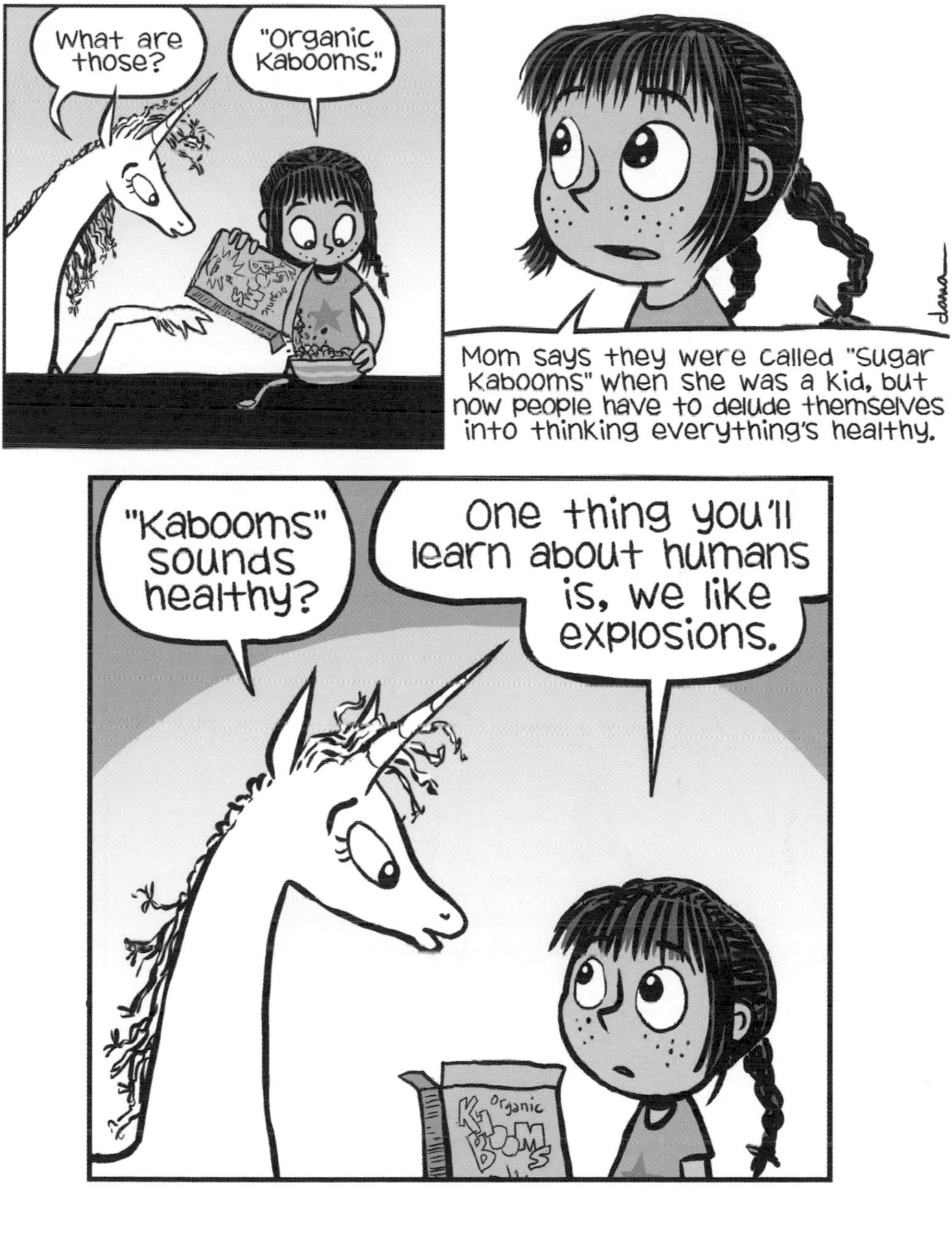
What are those?
"Organic Kabooms."
Organic
Mom says they were called "Sugar Kabooms" when she was a kid, but now people have to delude themselves into thinking everything's healthy.
dana
"Kabooms" sounds healthy?
One thing you'll learn about humans is, we like explosions.
Organic KABOOMS

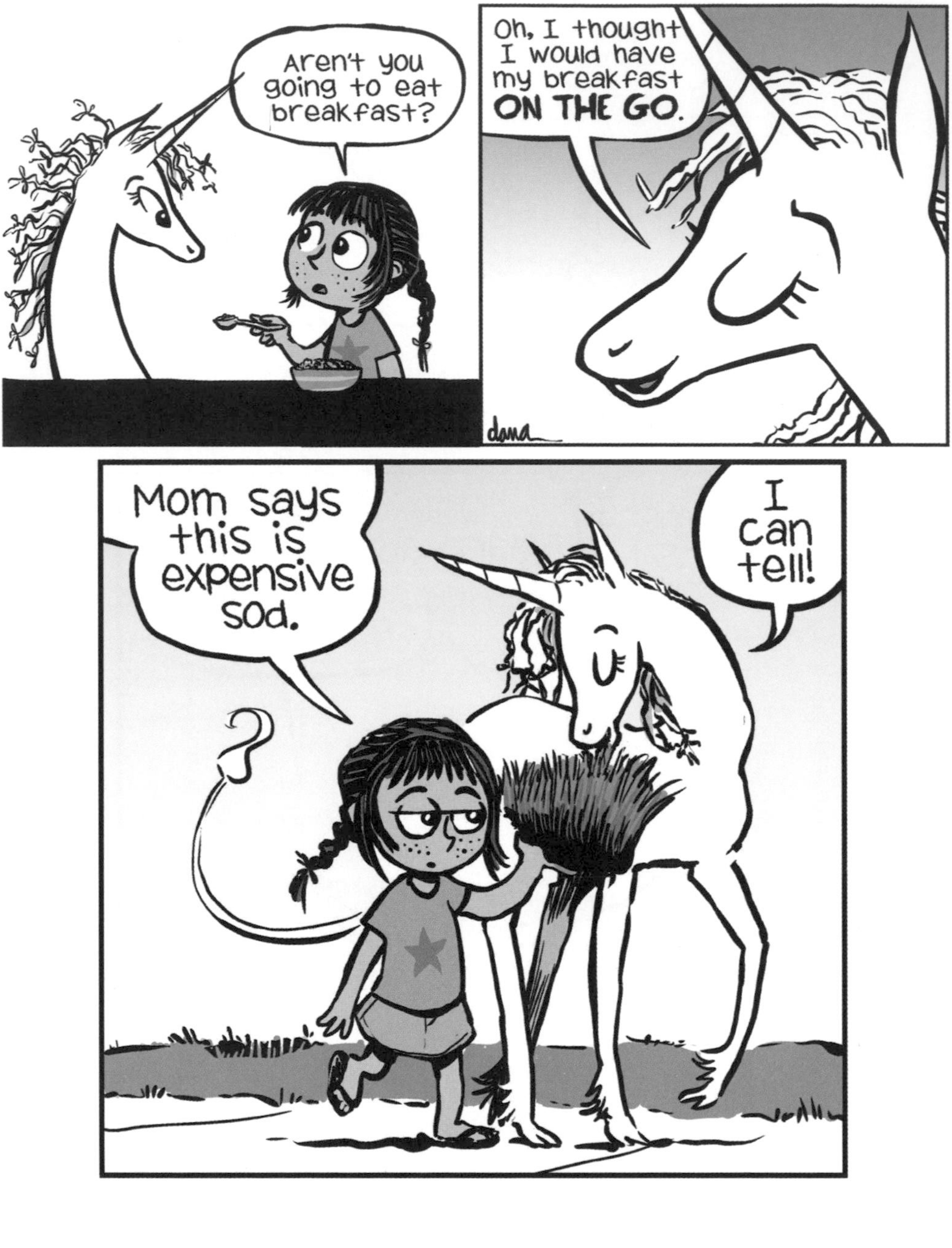
Aren't you going to eat breakfast?
Oh, I thought I would have my breakfast **ON THE GO**.
dana
Mom says this is expensive sod.
I can tell!

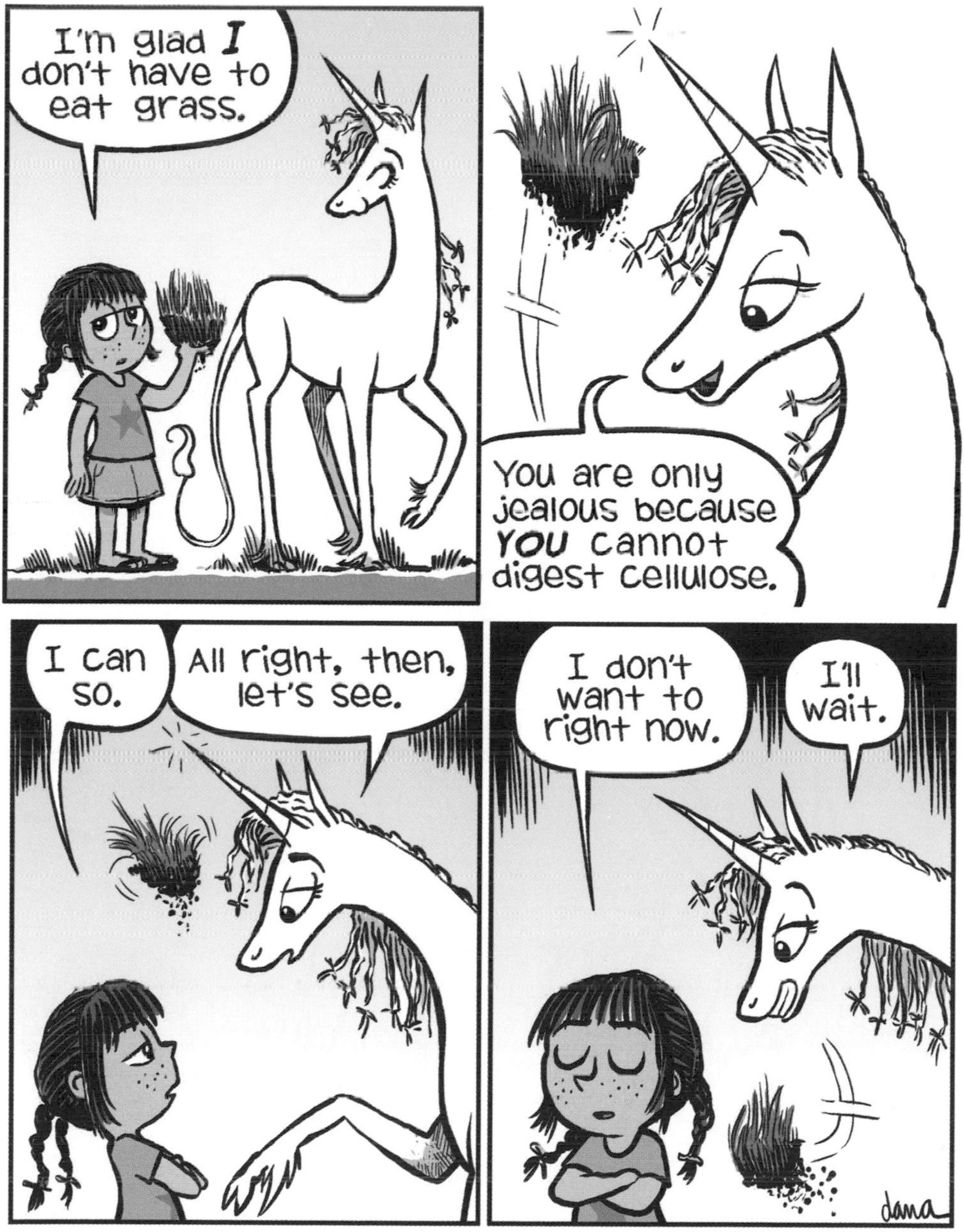
I'm glad I don't have to eat grass.
You are only jealous because YOU cannot digest cellulose.
I can so.
All right, then, let's see.
I don't want to right now.
I'll wait.
dana

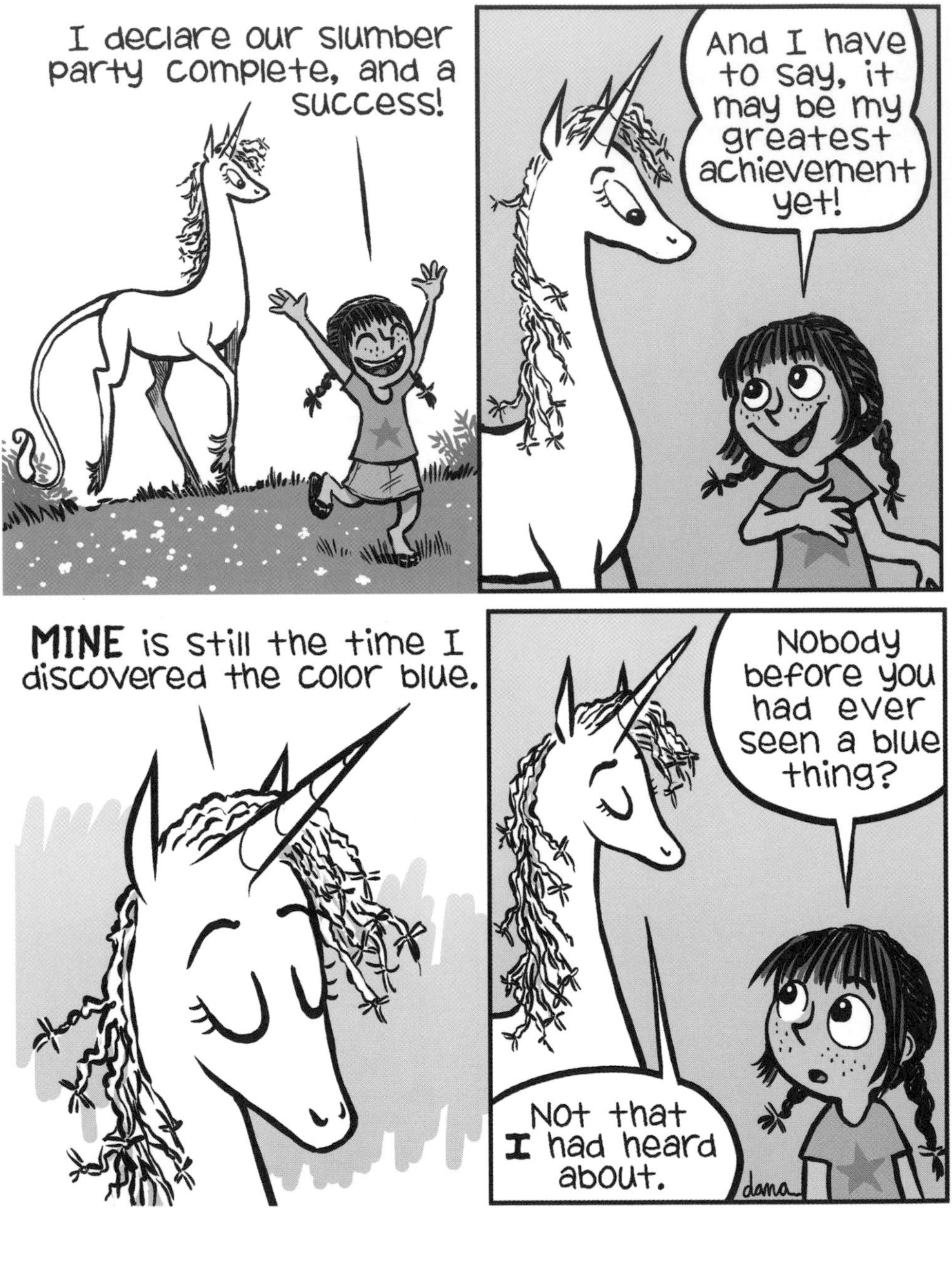
I declare our slumber party complete, and a success!
And I have to say, it may be my greatest achievement yet!
MINE is still the time I discovered the color blue.
Nobody before you had ever seen a blue thing?
Not that I had heard about.
dana

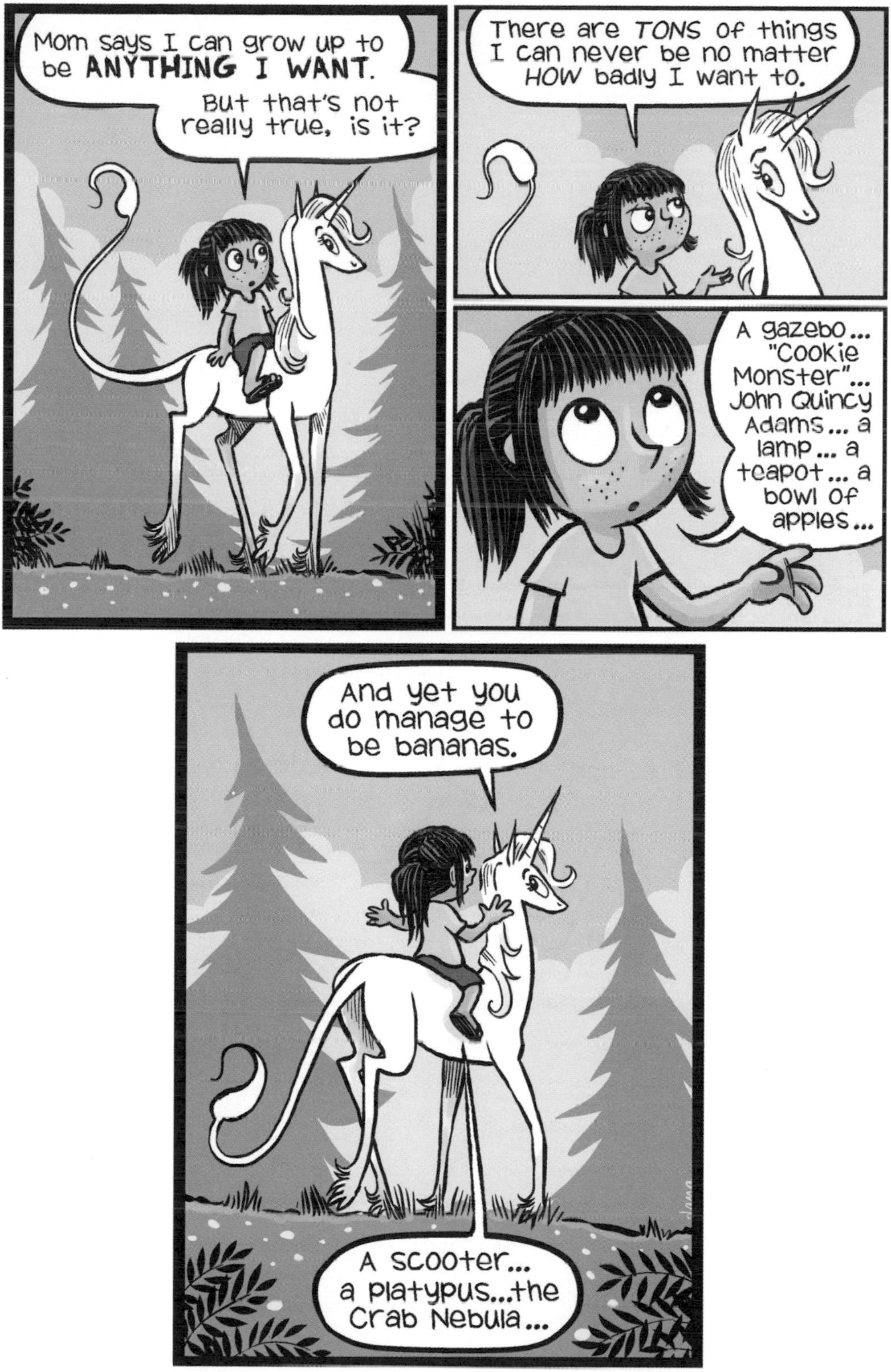
Mom says I can grow up to be **ANYTHING I WANT**.
But that's not really true, is it?
There are *TONS* of things I can never be no matter *HOW* badly I want to.
A gazebo... "Cookie Monster"... John Quincy Adams... a lamp... a teapot... a bowl of apples...
And yet you do manage to be bananas.
A scooter... a platypus...the Crab Nebula...

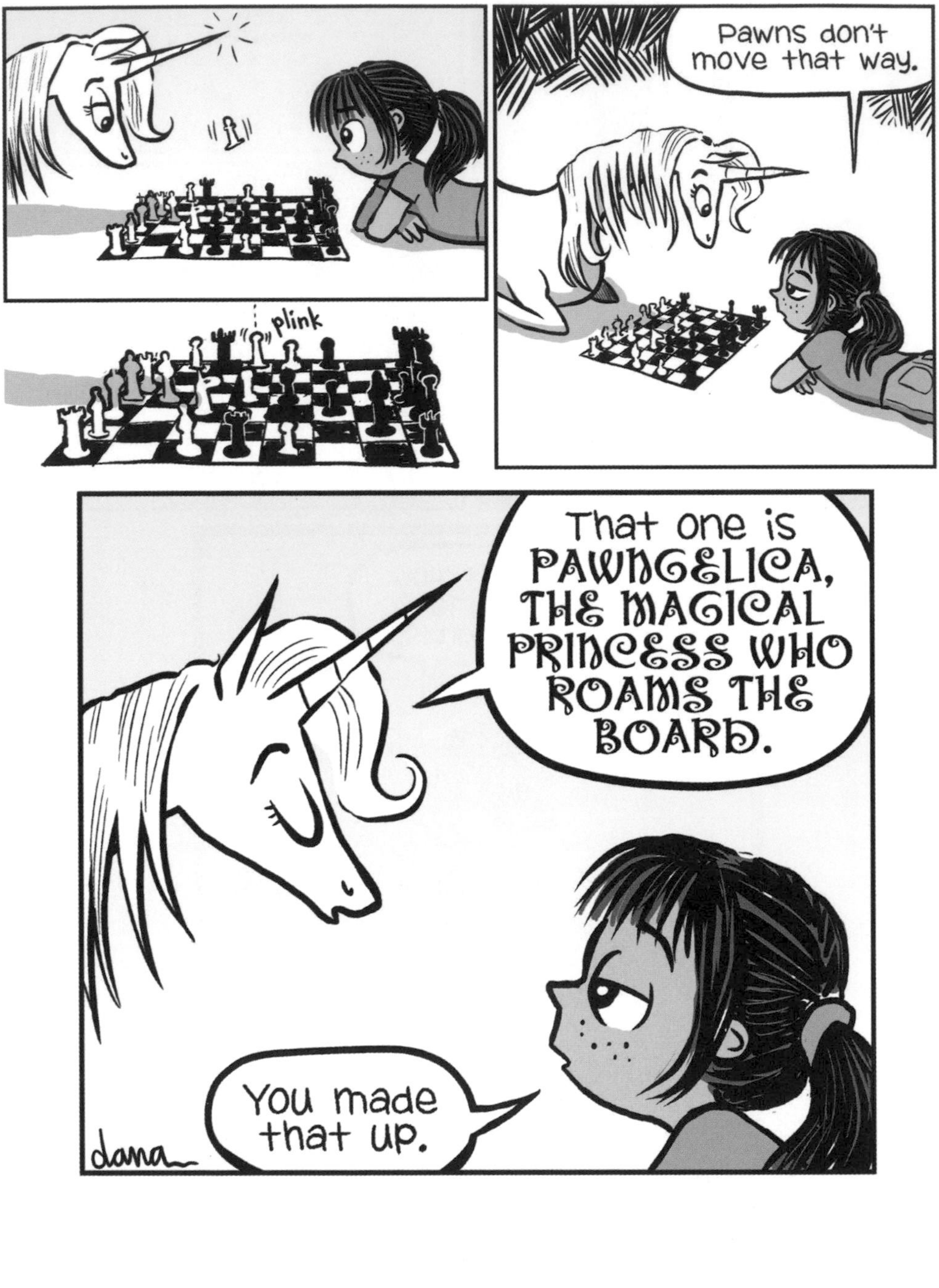
plink
Pawns don't move that way.
That one is PAWNGELICA, THE MAGICAL PRINCESS WHO ROAMS THE BOARD.
You made that up.
dana

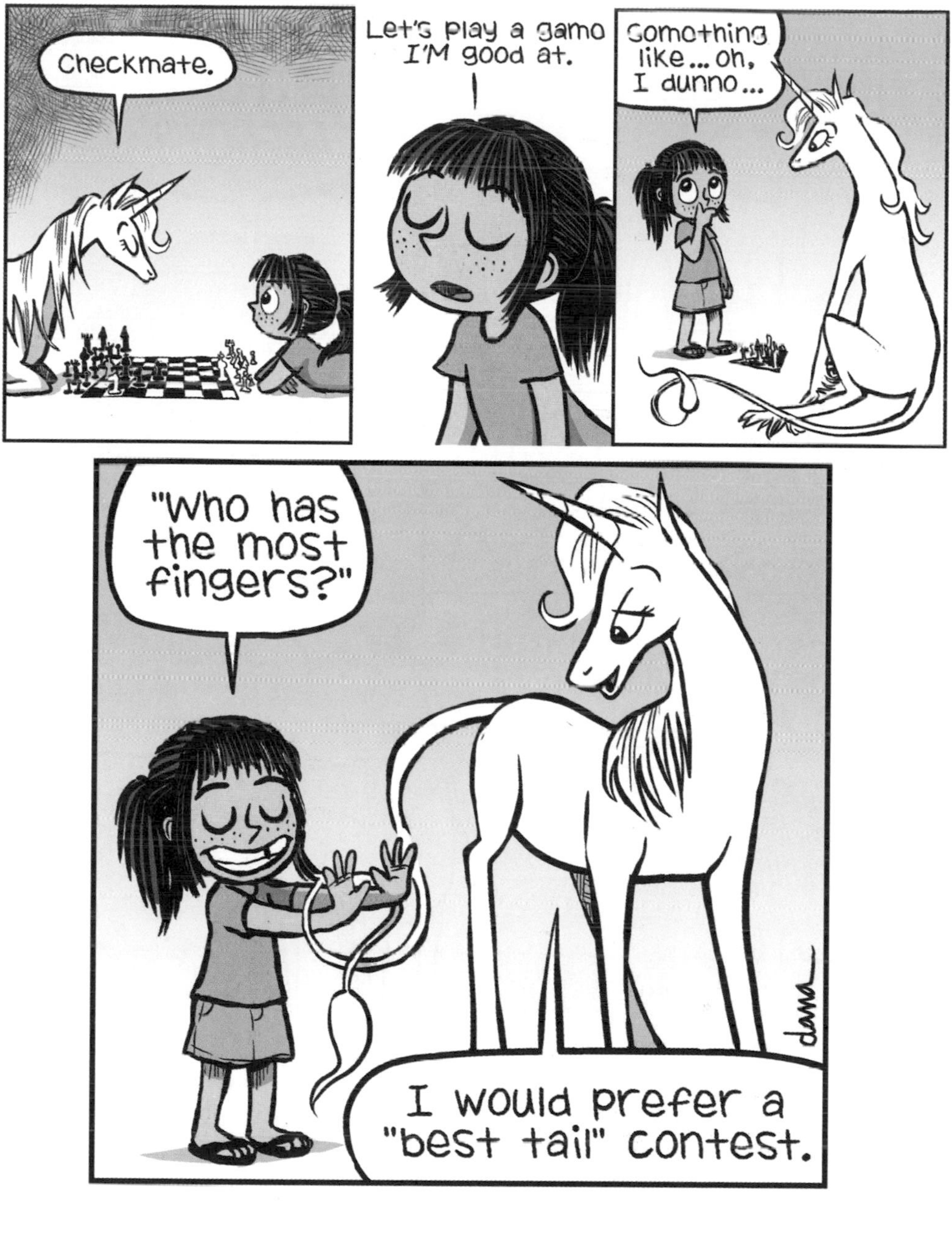
Checkmate.
Let's play a game I'M good at.
Something like... oh, I dunno...
"Who has the most fingers?"
I would prefer a "best tail" contest.
dana

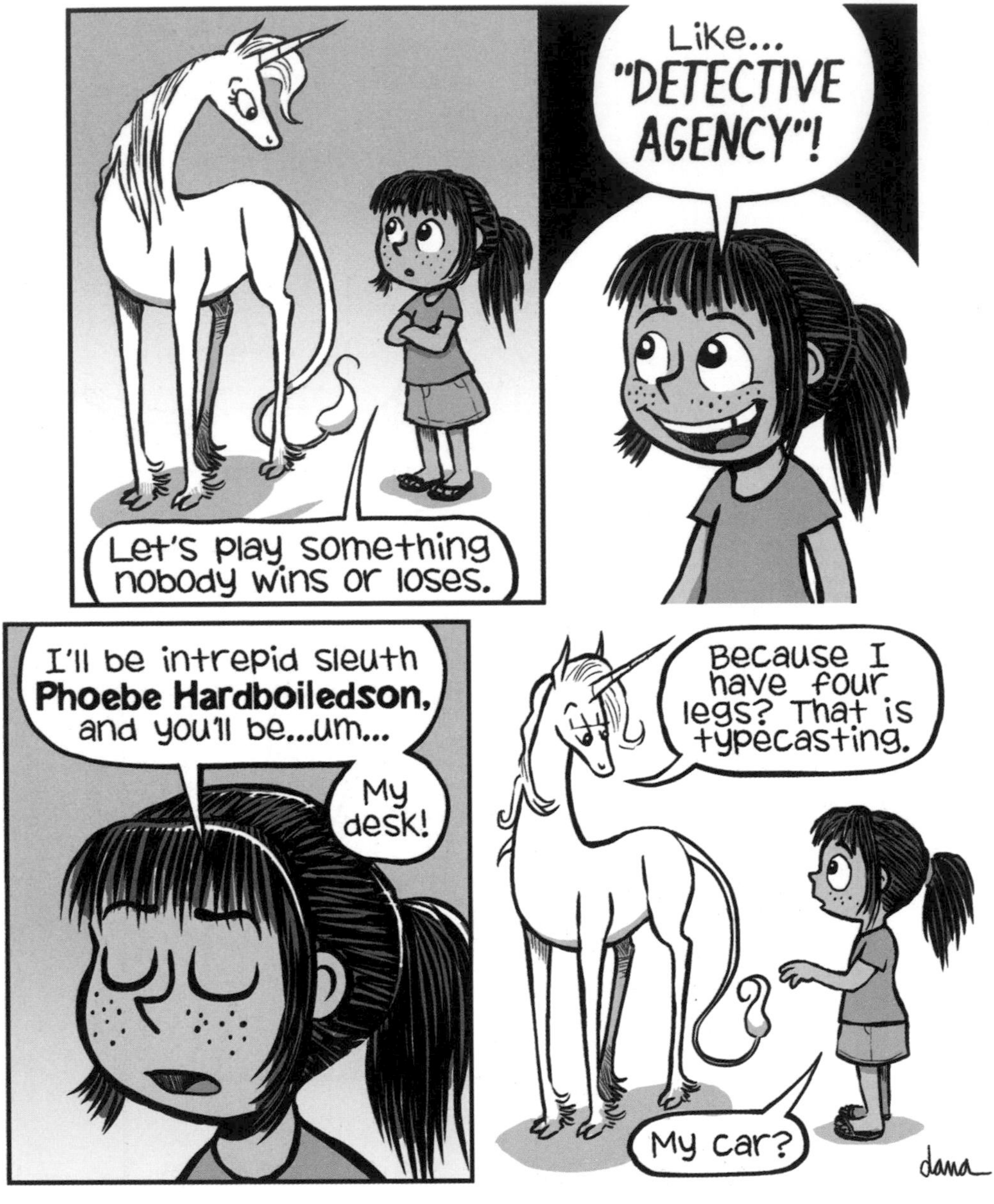
Let's play something nobody wins or loses.
Like... "DETECTIVE AGENCY"!
I'll be intrepid sleuth Phoebe Hardboiledson, and you'll be...um...
My desk!
Because I have four legs? That is typecasting.
My car?
dana

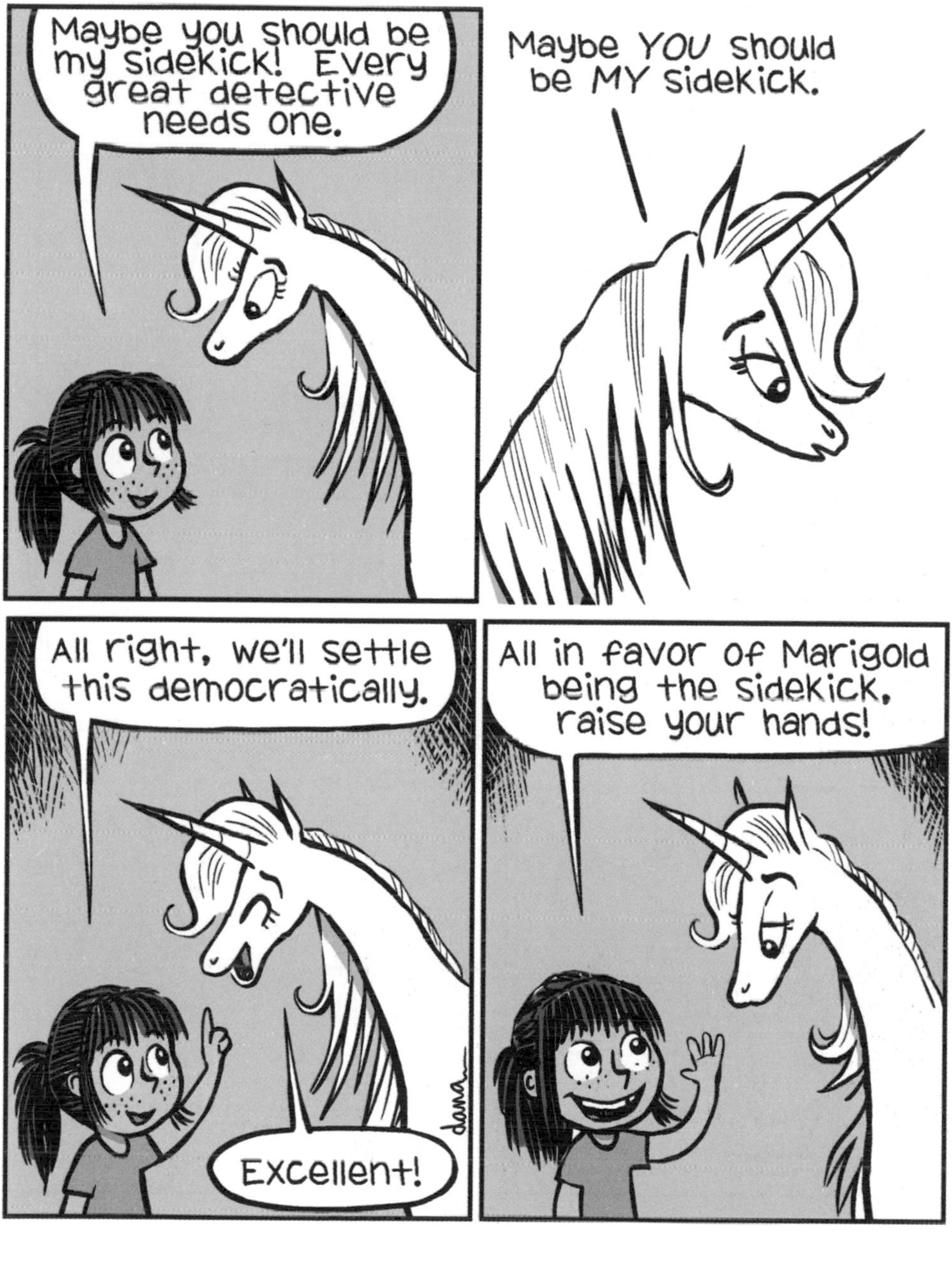
Maybe you should be my sidekick! Every great detective needs one.
Maybe YOU should be MY sidekick.
All right, we'll settle this democratically.
Excellent!
All in favor of Marigold being the sidekick, raise your hands!
dana

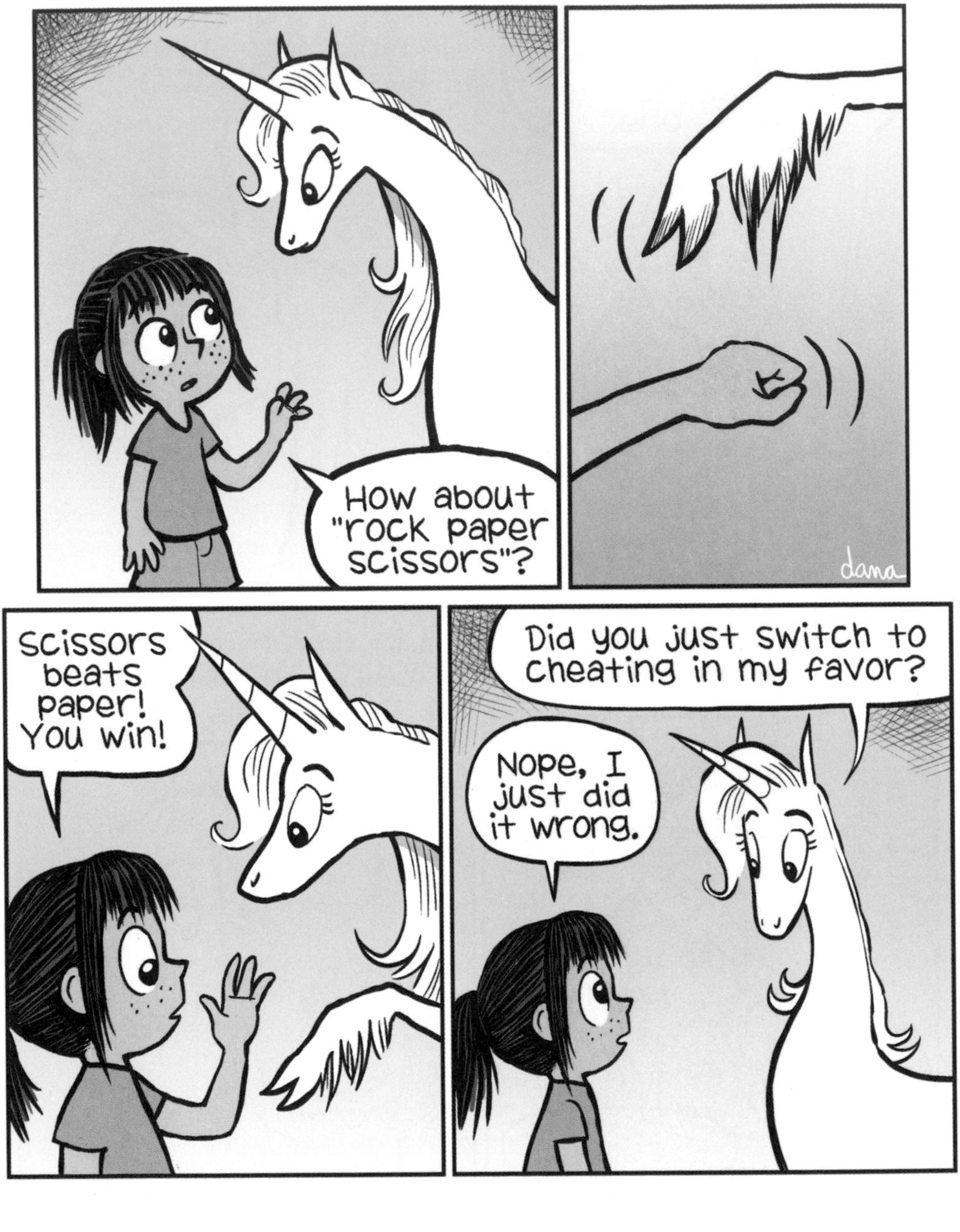
How about "rock paper scissors"?
dana
Scissors beats paper! You win!
Did you just switch to cheating in my favor?
Nope, I just did it wrong.

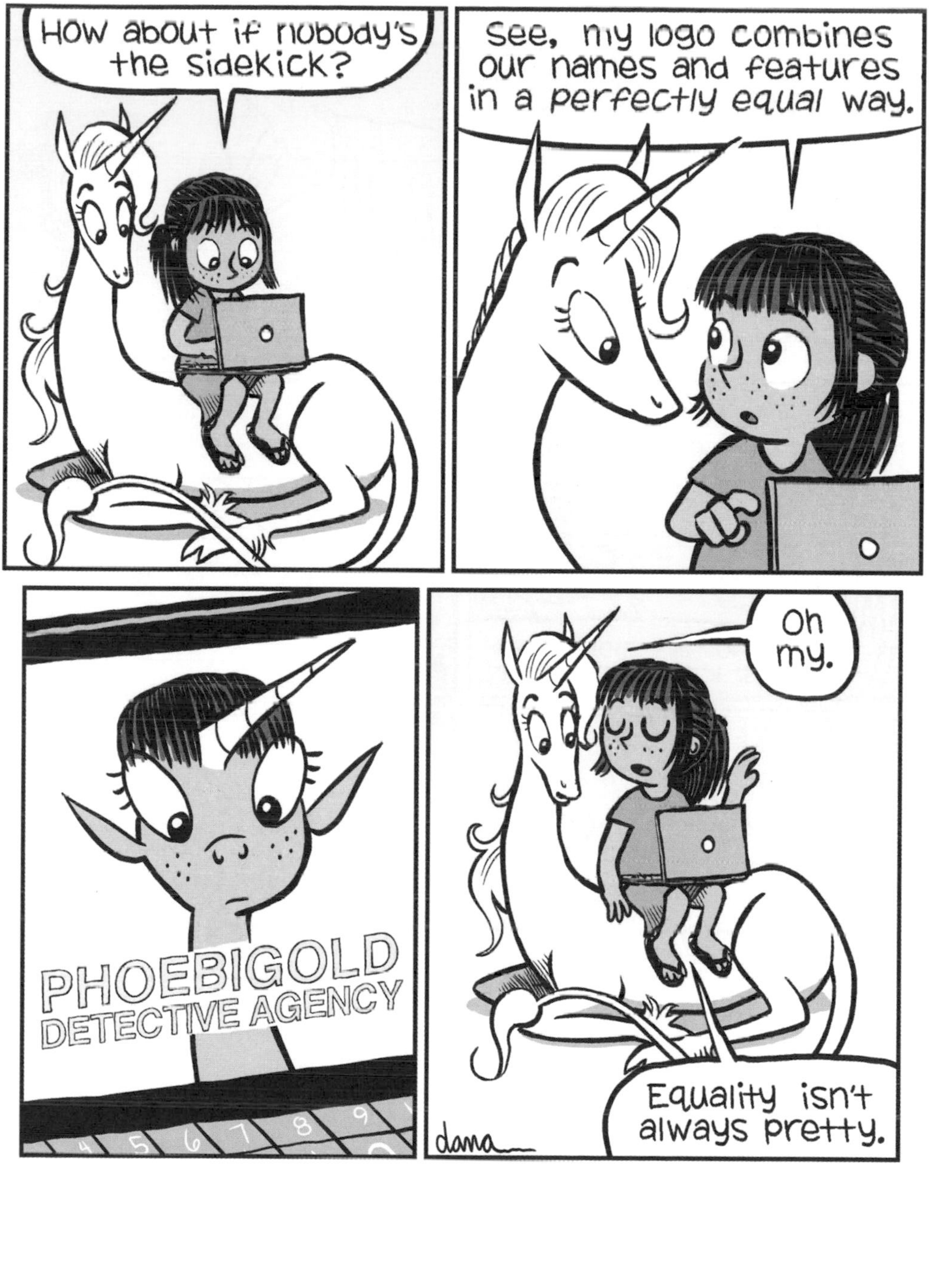
How about if nobody's the sidekick?
See, my logo combines our names and features in a perfectly equal way.
PHOEBIGOLD
DETECTIVE AGENCY
Oh my.
Equality isn't always pretty.
dana

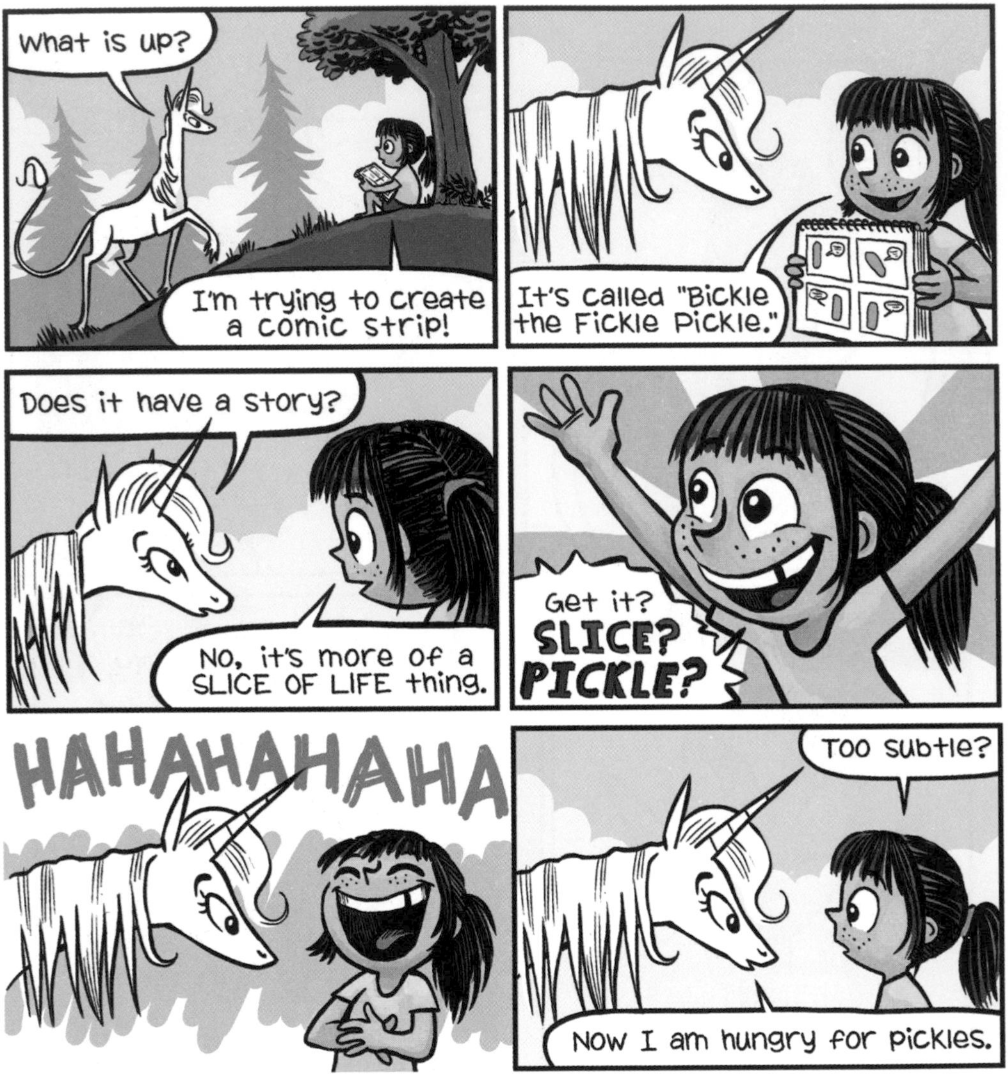
What is up?
I'm trying to create a comic strip!
It's called "Bickle the Fickle Pickle."
Does it have a story?
No, it's more of a SLICE OF LIFE thing.
Get it? SLICE? PICKLE?
HAHAHAHAHA
Too subtle?
Now I am hungry for pickles.

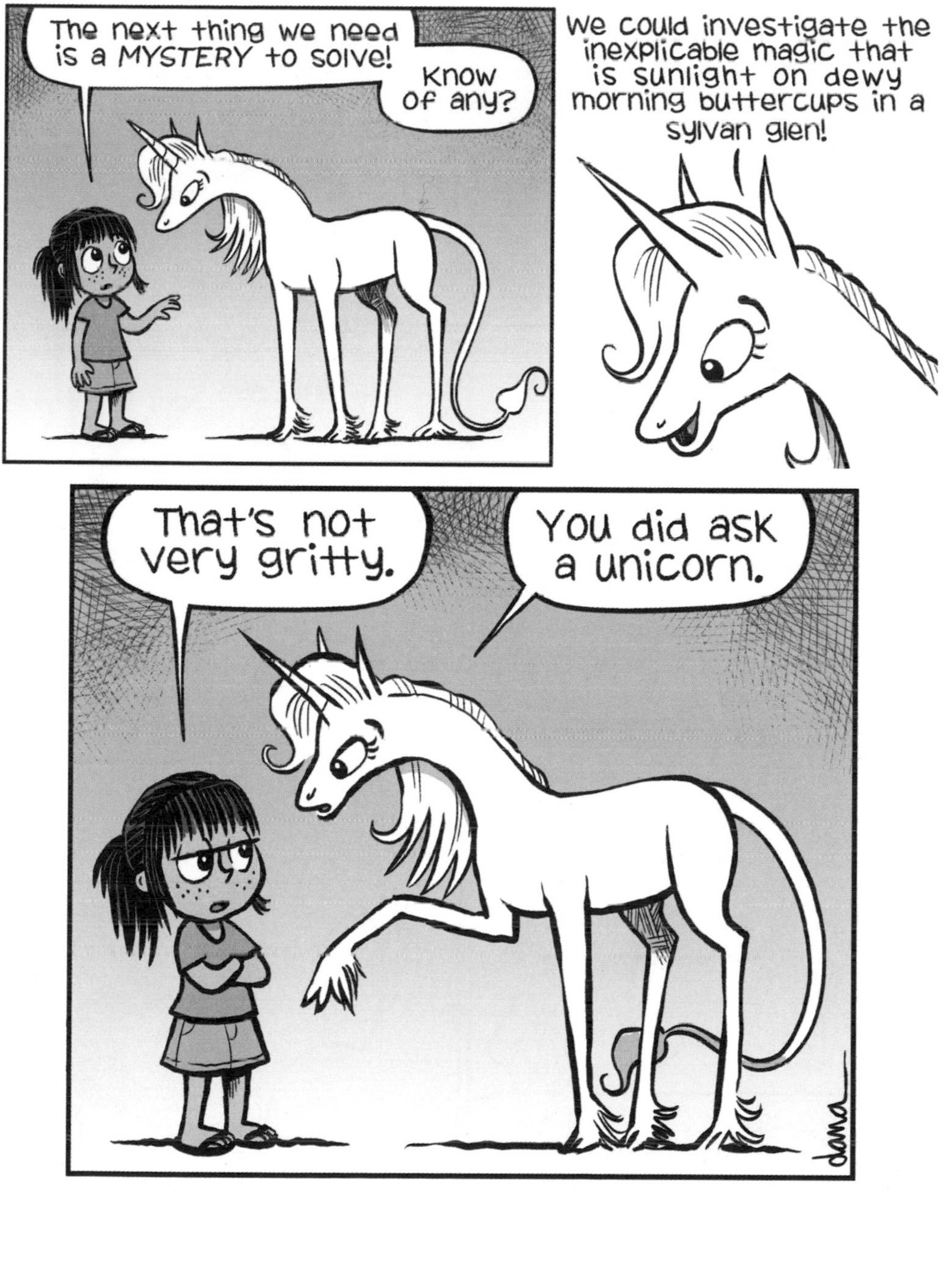
The next thing we need is a MYSTERY to solve!
Know of any?
We could investigate the inexplicable magic that is sunlight on dewy morning buttercups in a sylvan glen!
That's not very gritty.
You did ask a unicorn.
dana

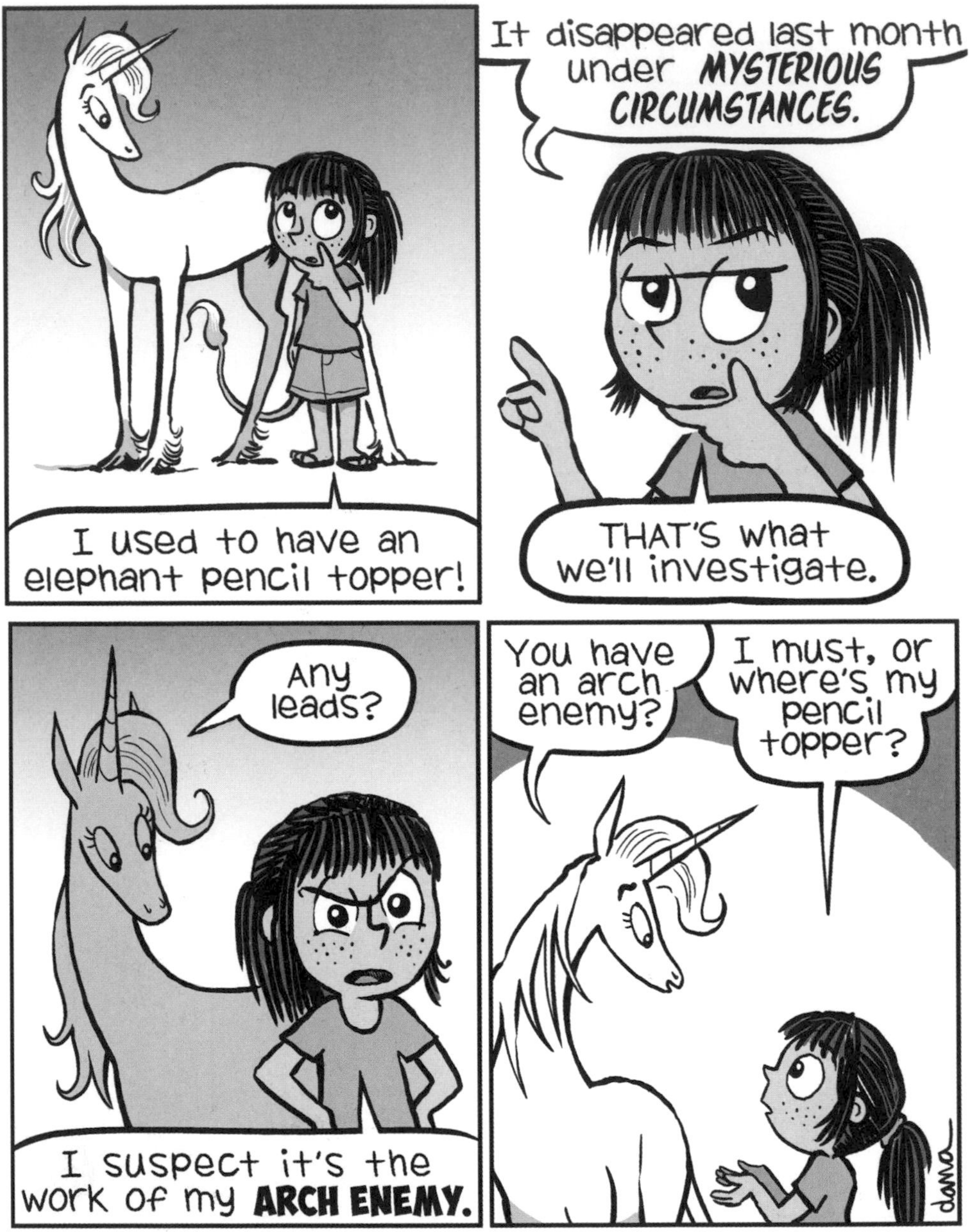

I used to have an elephant pencil topper!
It disappeared last month under MYSTERIOUS CIRCUMSTANCES.
THAT'S what we'll investigate.
Any leads?
I suspect it's the work of my ARCH ENEMY.
You have an arch enemy?
I must, or where's my pencil topper?
dana

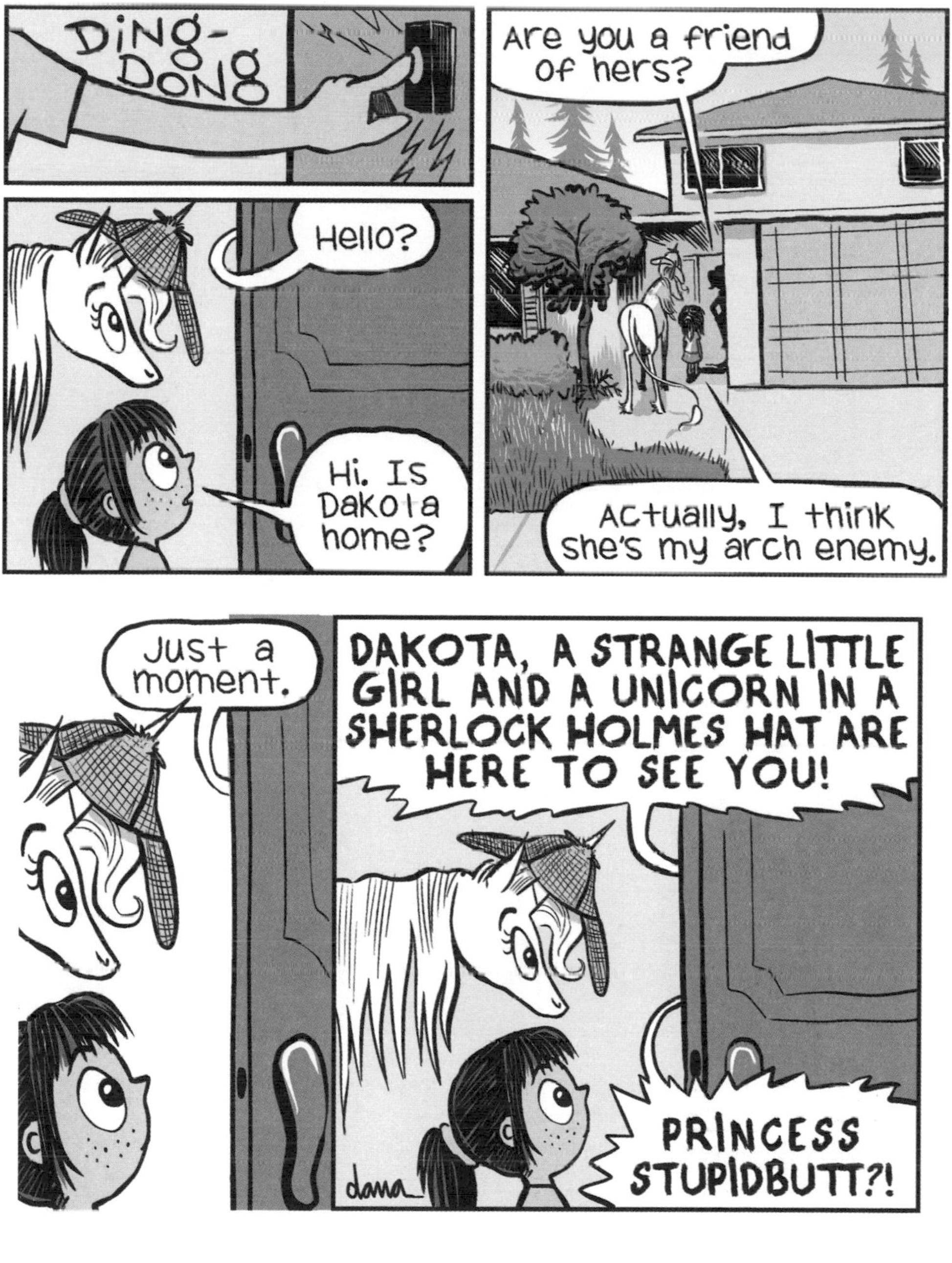
DING-DONG
Are you a friend of hers?
Hello?
Hi. Is Dakota home?
Actually, I think she's my arch enemy.
Just a moment.
DAKOTA, A STRANGE LITTLE GIRL AND A UNICORN IN A SHERLOCK HOLMES HAT ARE HERE TO SEE YOU!
PRINCESS STUPIDBUTT?!
dana

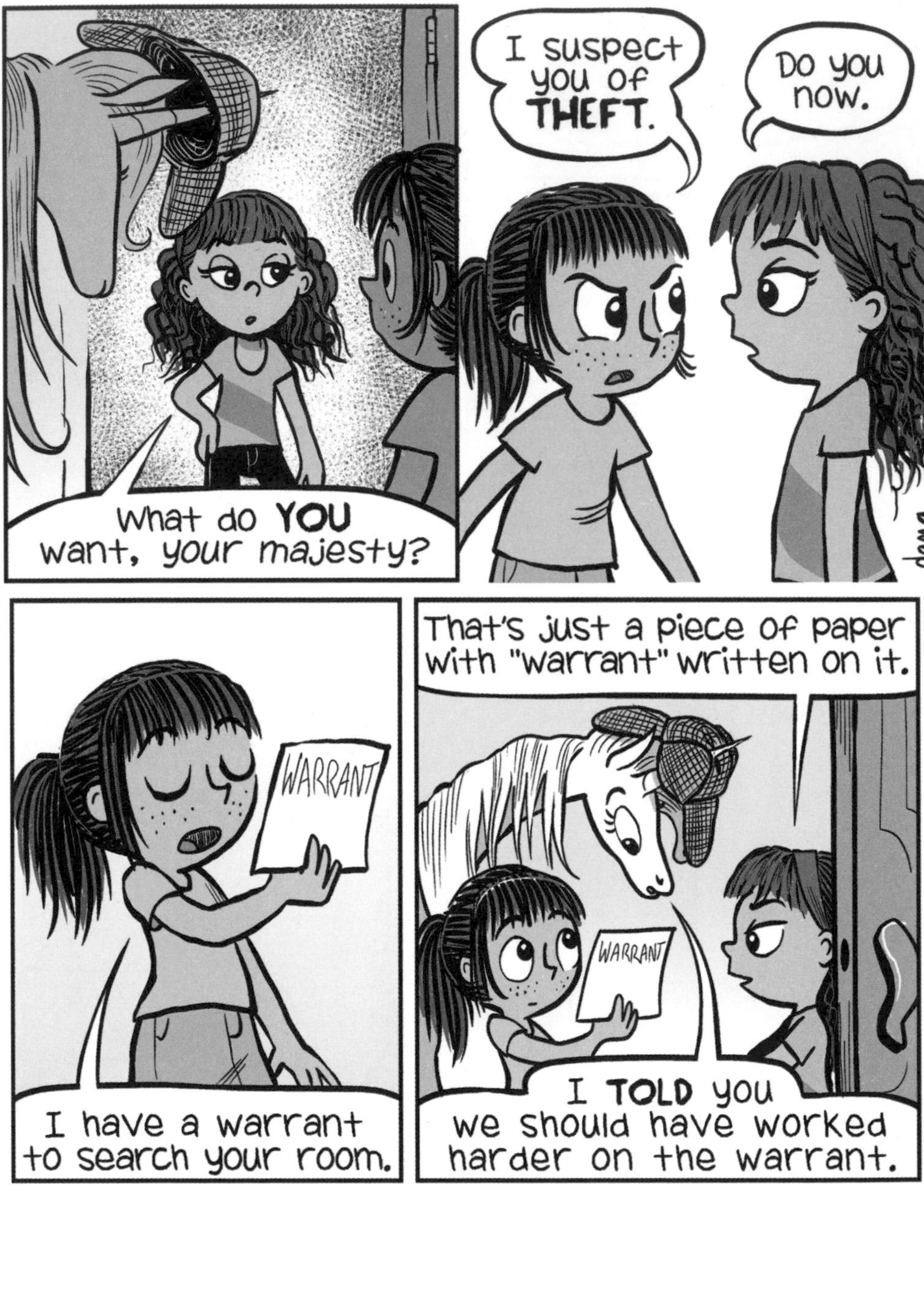
What do YOU want, your majesty?
I suspect you of THEFT.
Do you now.
dana
I have a warrant to search your room.
WARRANT
That's just a piece of paper with "warrant" written on it.
WARRANT
I TOLD you we should have worked harder on the warrant.

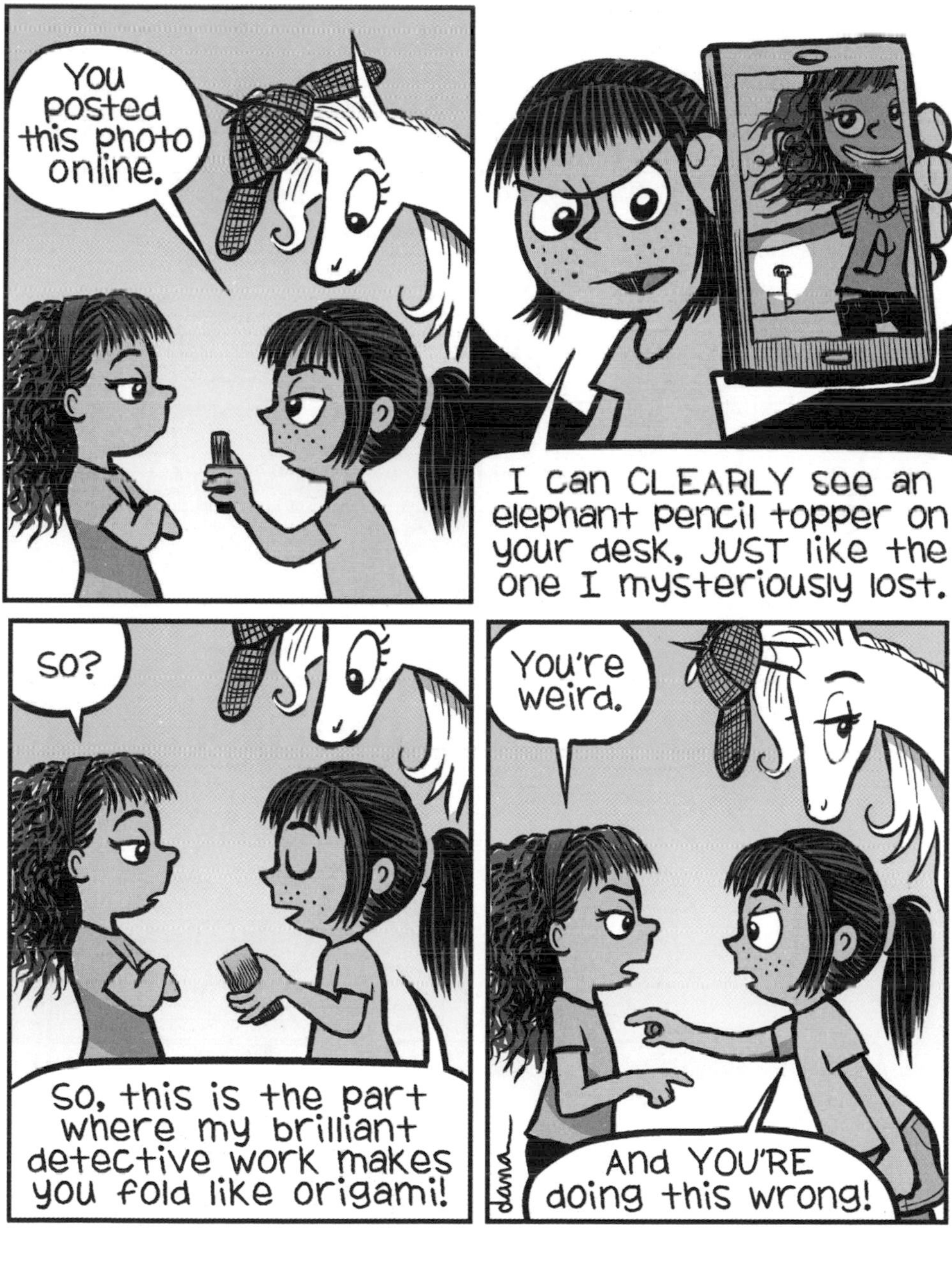
You posted this photo online.
I can CLEARLY see an elephant pencil topper on your desk, JUST like the one I mysteriously lost.
So?
So, this is the part where my brilliant detective work makes you fold like origami!
You're weird.
And YOU'RE doing this wrong!
dana

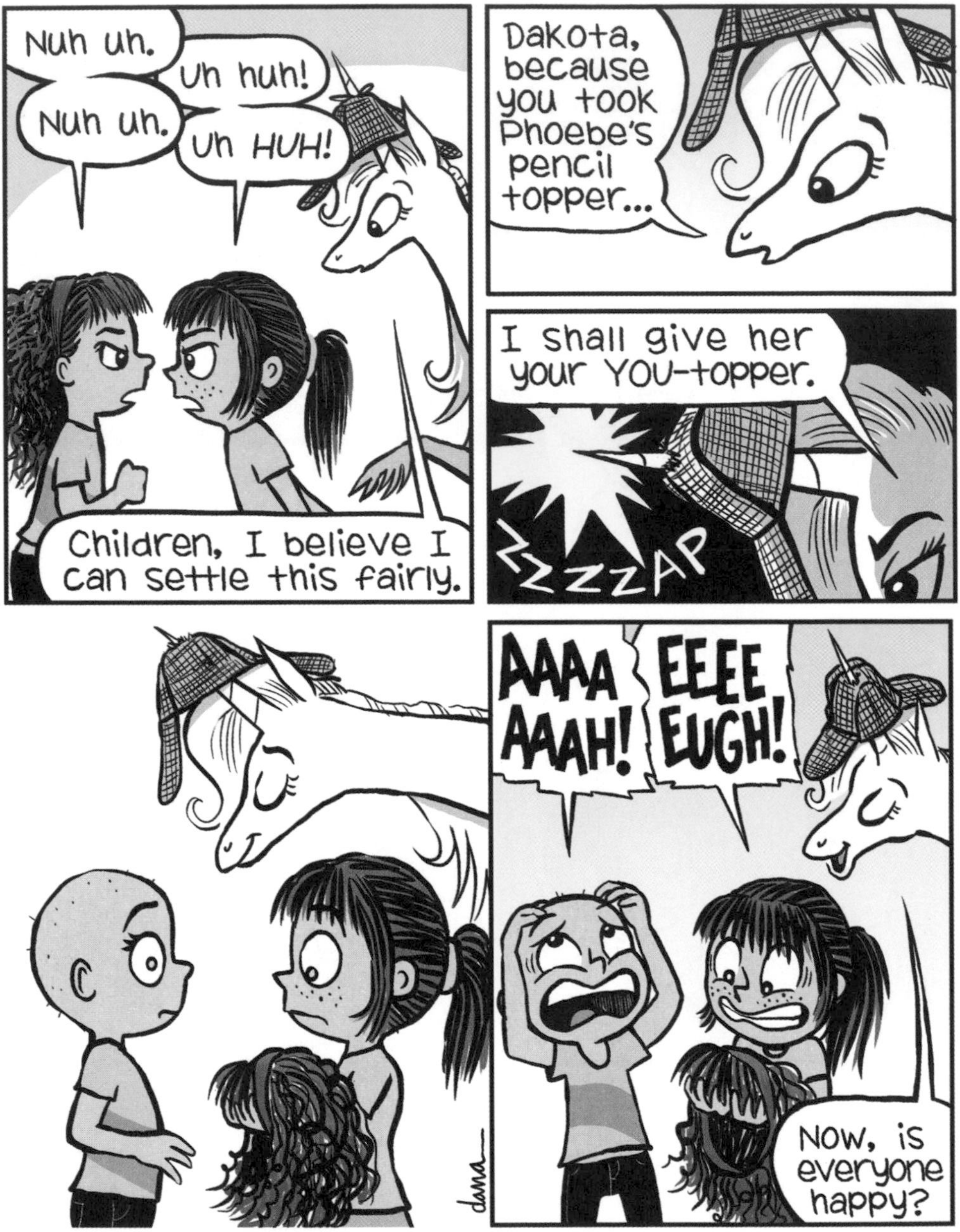
Nuh uh.
Uh huh!
Nuh uh.
Uh HUH!
Children, I believe I can settle this fairly.
Dakota, because you took Phoebe's pencil topper...
I shall give her your YOU-topper.
ZZZZZAP
AAAA AAAH!
EEEE EUGH!
Now, is everyone happy?
dana

AAAAAAAAAAAAAA!

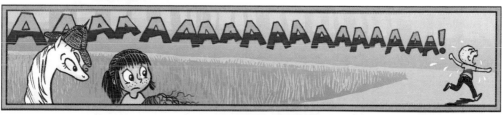

AAAAAAAAAAAAAAAAAAAAAAAA!

She is upset!

You **ZAPPED HER HAIR OFF.**

That is a big deal?

YES!

You humans are *MOSTLY* bald anyhow. I did not know you cared so much for what little hair you have.

I...can actually kinda see your logic, but...

What is a tiny bit of extra pink in a sea of fleshy human disgustingness?

Remember what I said about knowing when to stop talking?

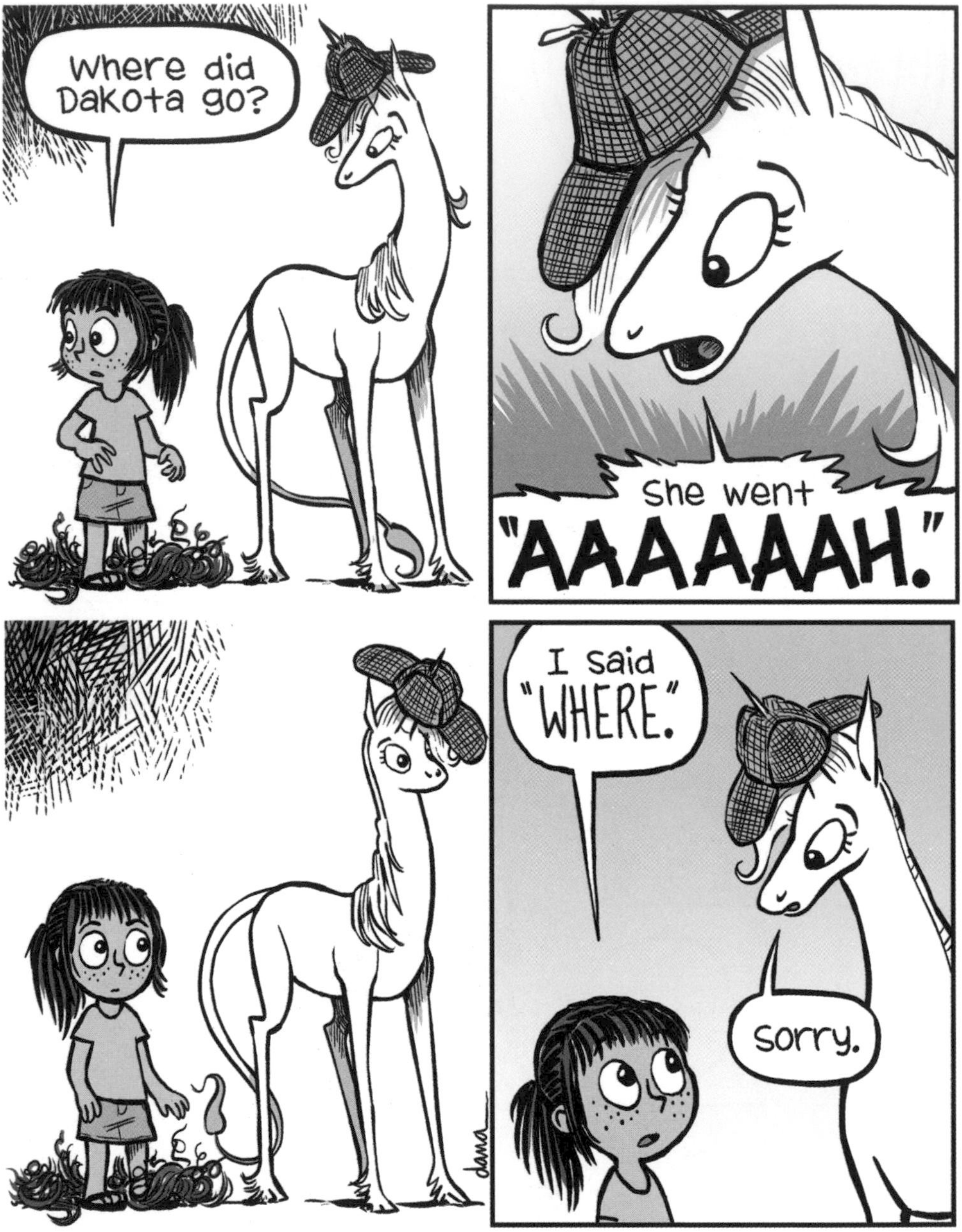
Where did Dakota go?
She went "AAAAAAH."
I said "WHERE."
Sorry.
dana

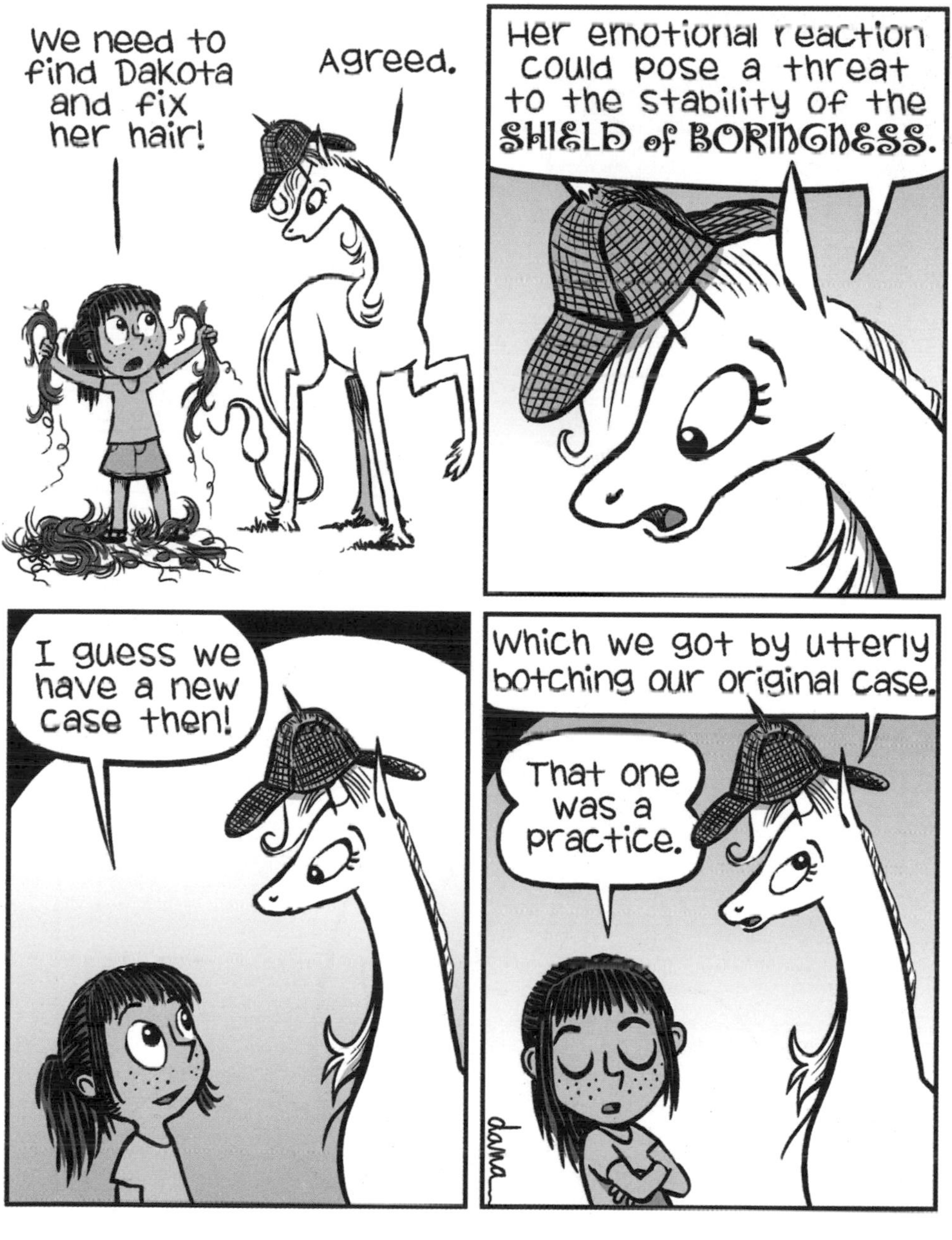
We need to find Dakota and fix her hair!
Agreed.
Her emotional reaction could pose a threat to the stability of the SHIELD of BORINGNESS.
I guess we have a new case then!
Which we got by utterly botching our original case.
That one was a practice.
dana

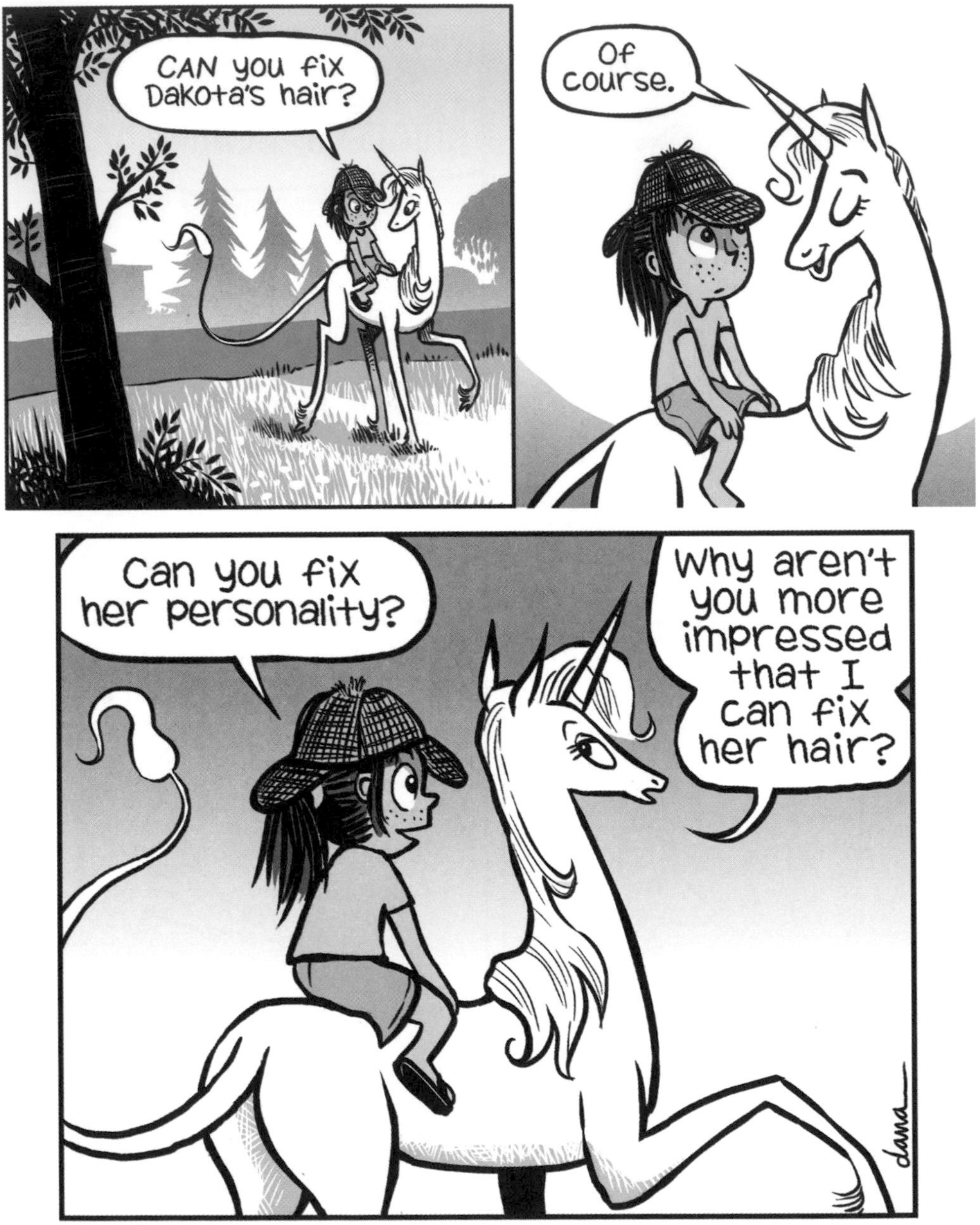
CAN you fix
Dakota's hair?
Of
course.
Can you fix
her personality?
Why aren't
you more
impressed
that I
can fix
her hair?
dana

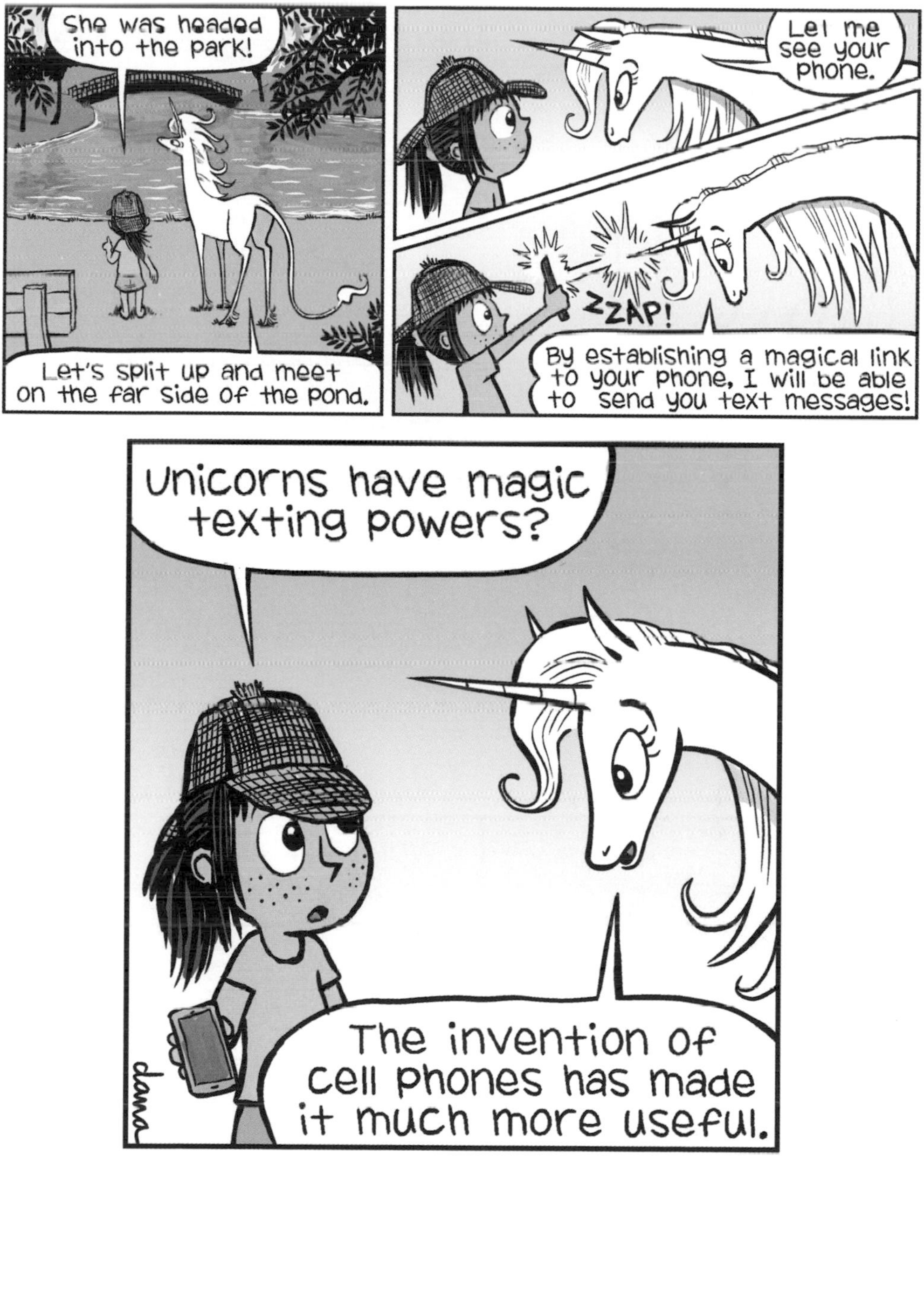
She was headed into the park!
Let's split up and meet on the far side of the pond.
Let me see your phone.
ZZAP!
By establishing a magical link to your phone, I will be able to send you text messages!
Unicorns have magic texting powers?
The invention of cell phones has made it much more useful.
dana

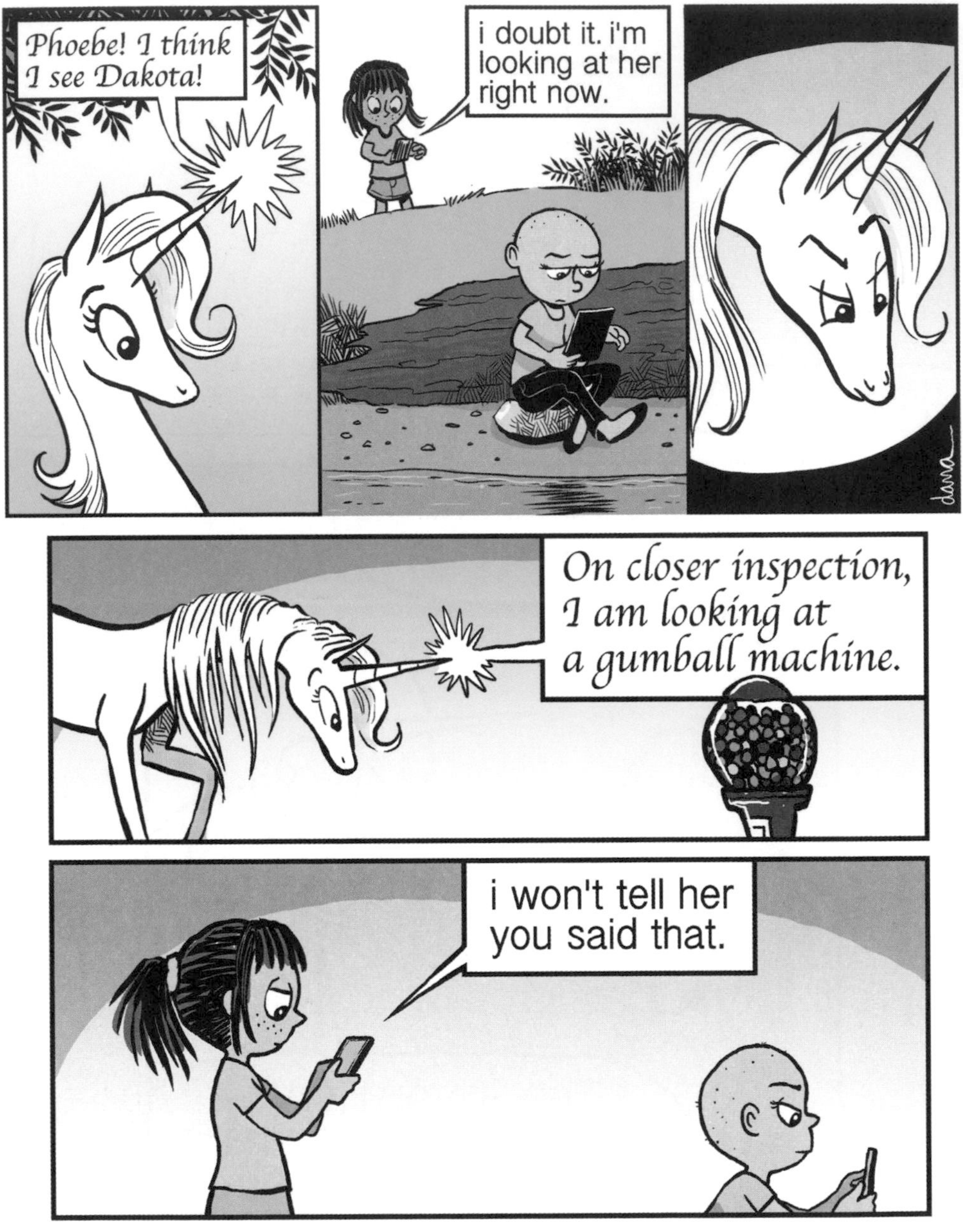
Phoebe! I think I see Dakota!
i doubt it. i'm looking at her right now.
On closer inspection, I am looking at a gumball machine.
i won't tell her you said that.

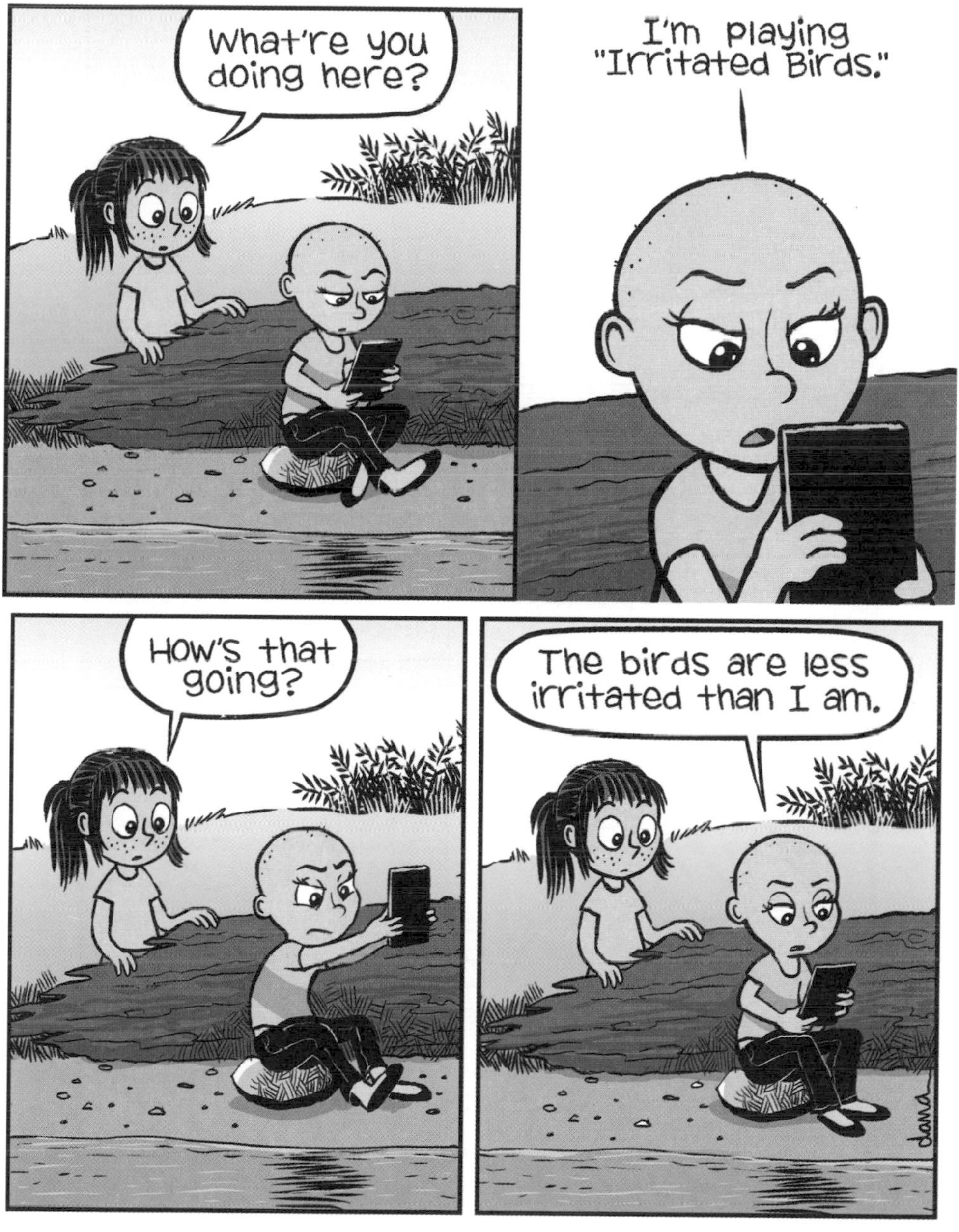
What're you doing here?
I'm playing "Irritated Birds."
How's that going?
The birds are less irritated than I am.
dana

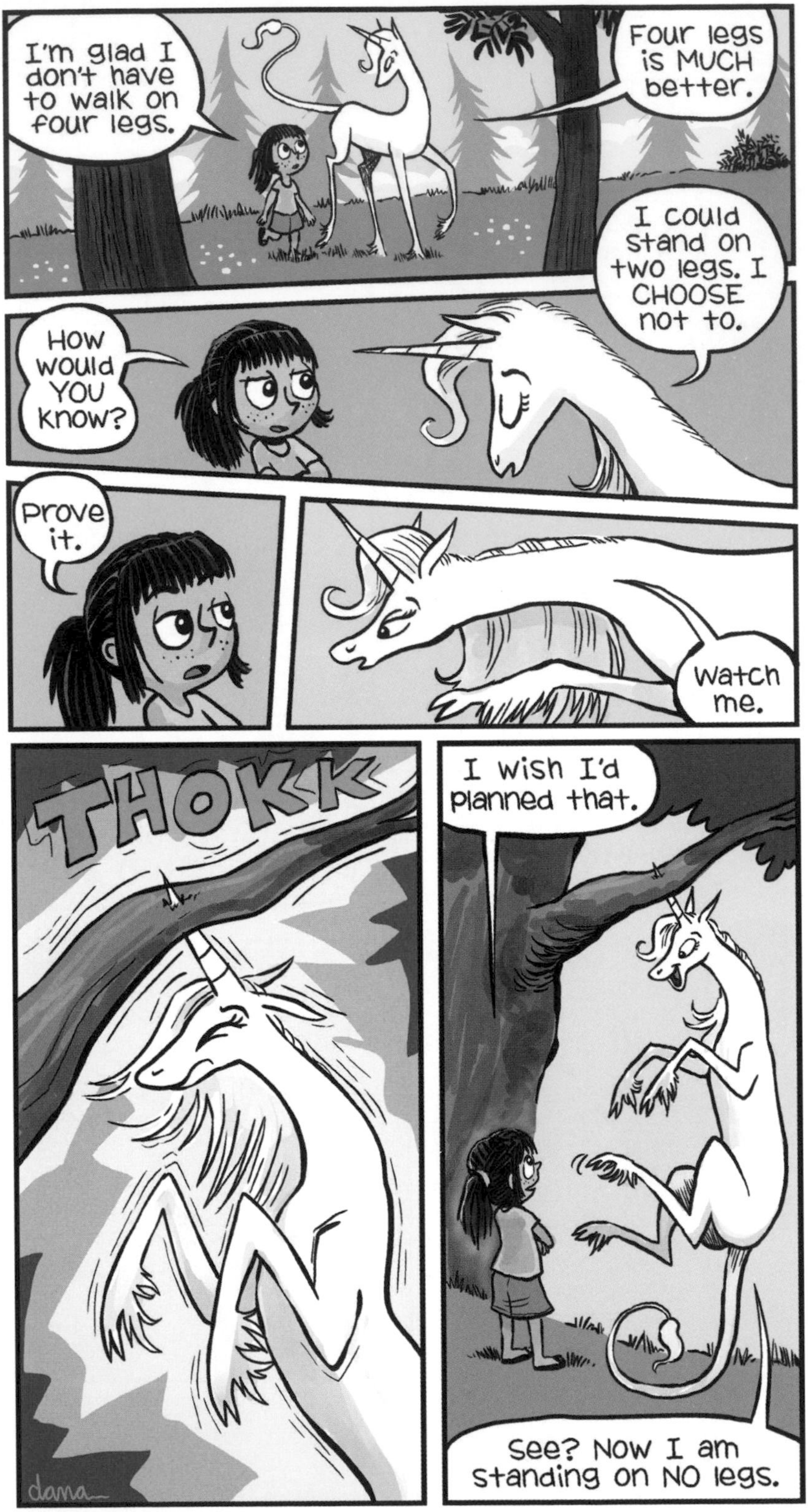
I'm glad I don't have to walk on four legs.
Four legs is MUCH better.
I could stand on two legs. I CHOOSE not to.
How would YOU know?
Prove it.
Watch me.
THOKK
I wish I'd planned that.
See? Now I am standing on NO legs.
dana

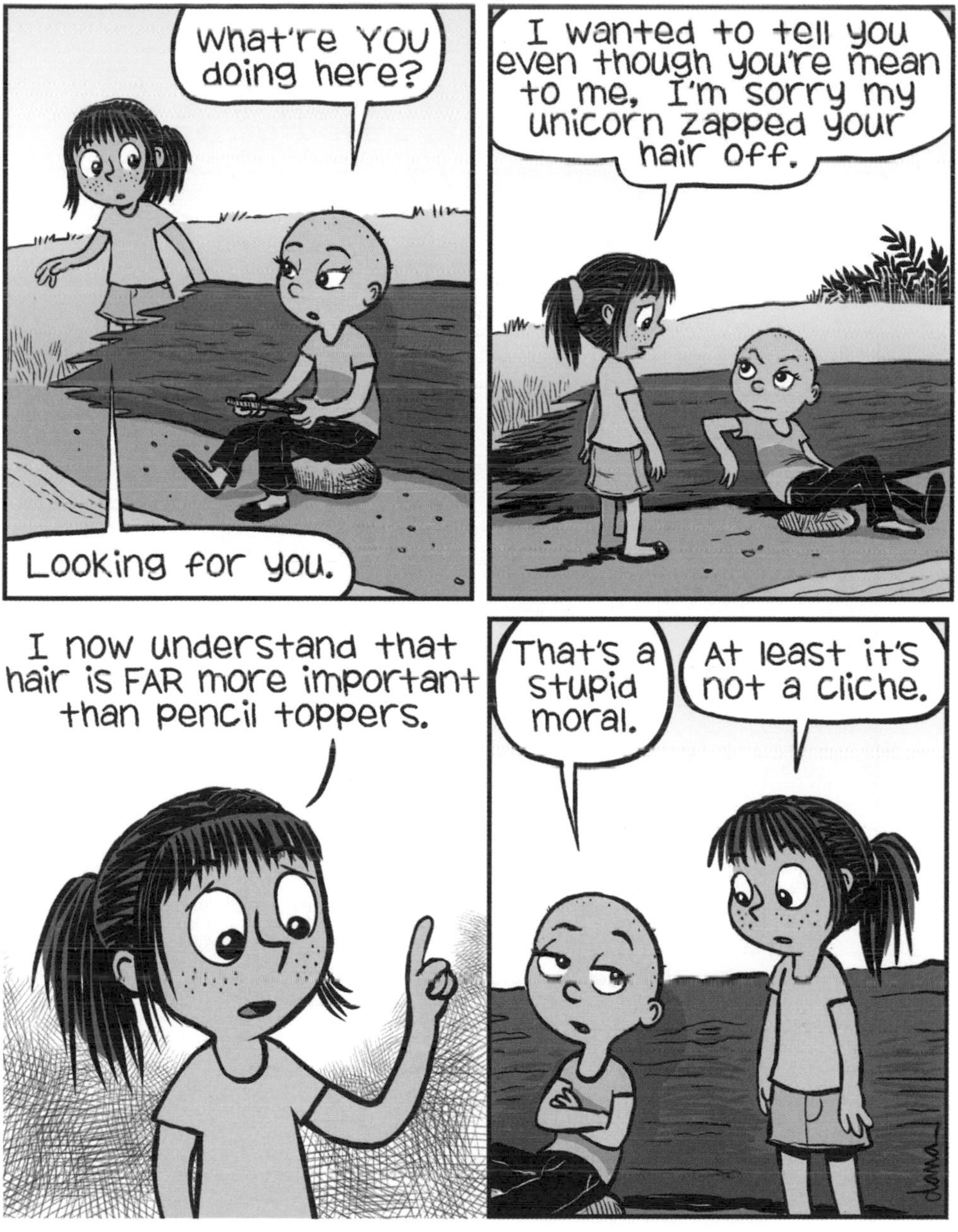
What're YOU doing here?
Looking for you.
I wanted to tell you even though you're mean to me, I'm sorry my unicorn zapped your hair off.
I now understand that hair is FAR more important than pencil toppers.
That's a stupid moral.
At least it's not a cliche.

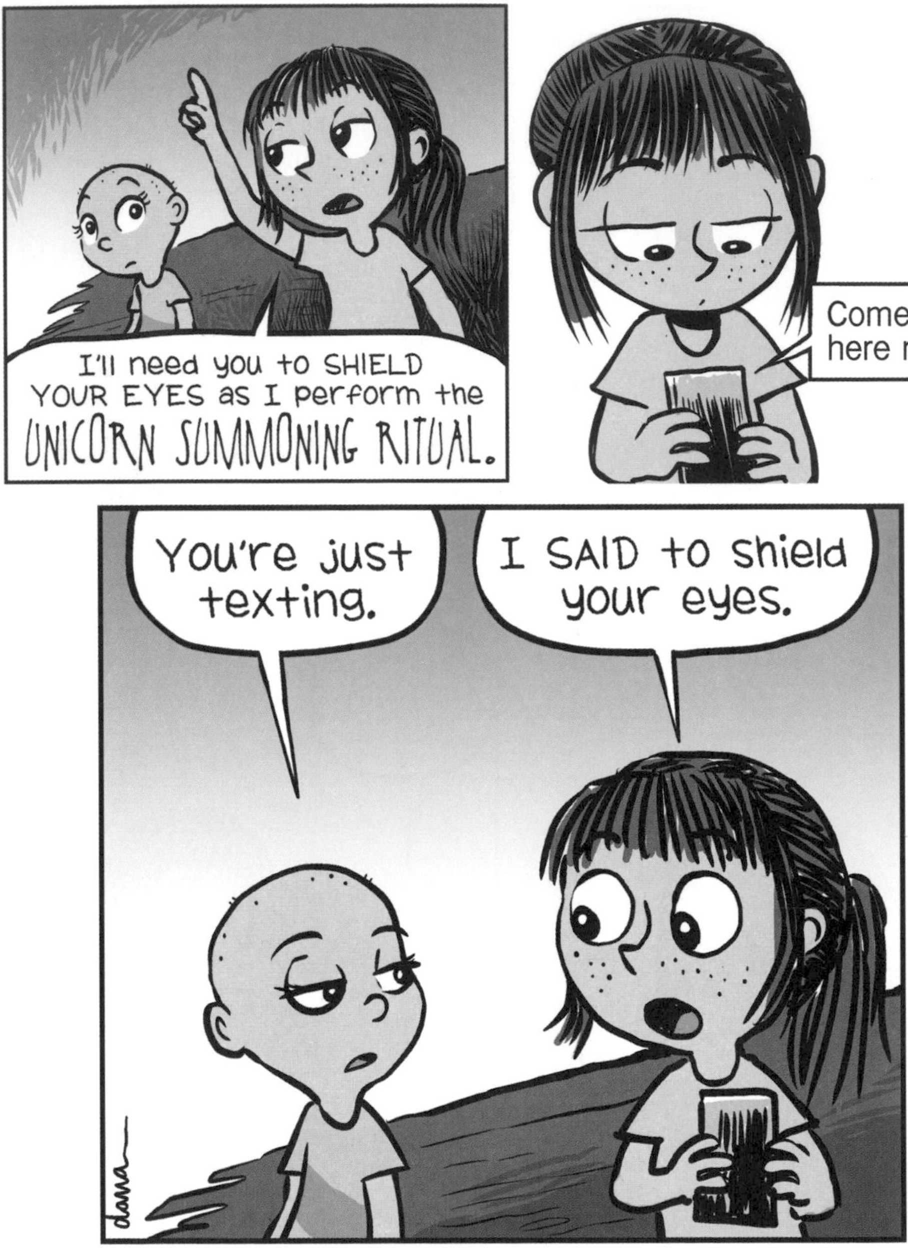
I'll need you to SHIELD YOUR EYES as I perform the UNICORN SUMMONING RITUAL.
Come over here now
You're just texting.
I SAID to shield your eyes.
dana

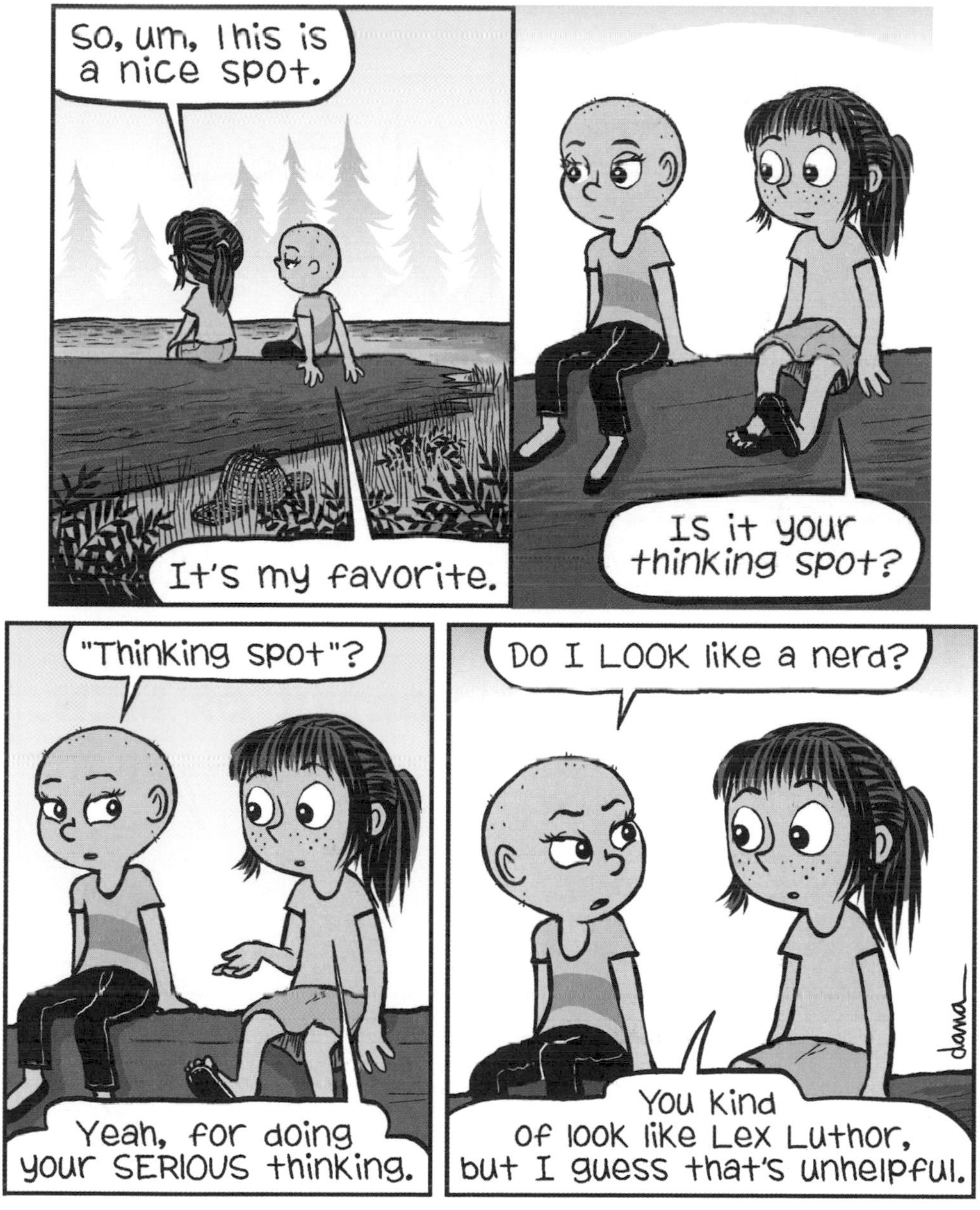
So, um, this is a nice spot.
It's my favorite.
Is it your thinking spot?
"Thinking spot"?
Yeah, for doing your SERIOUS thinking.
Do I LOOK like a nerd?
You kind of look like Lex Luthor, but I guess that's unhelpful.
dana

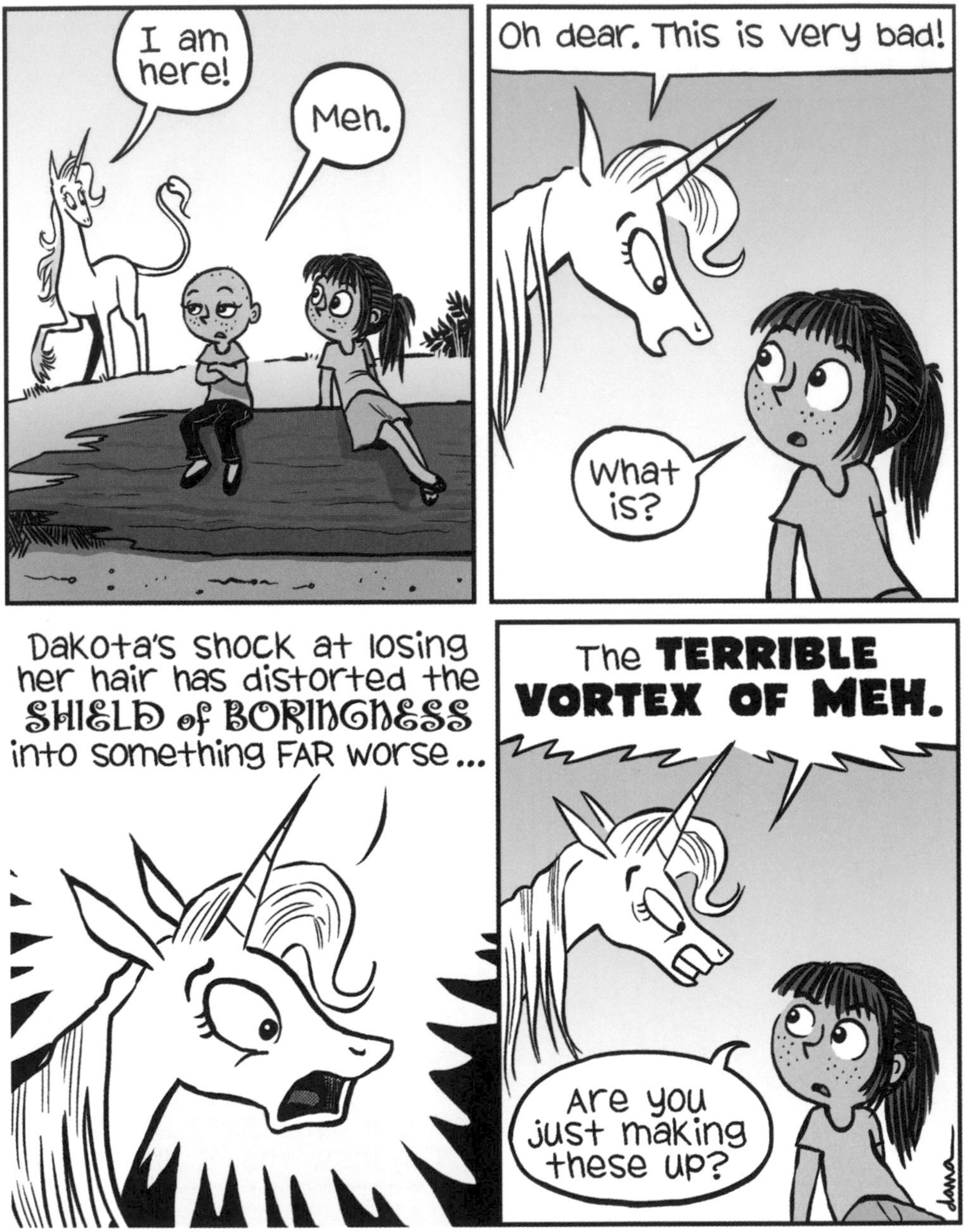
I am here!
Meh.
Oh dear. This is very bad!
What is?
Dakota's shock at losing her hair has distorted the SHIELD of BORINGNESS into something FAR worse...
The TERRIBLE VORTEX OF MEH.
Are you just making these up?
dana

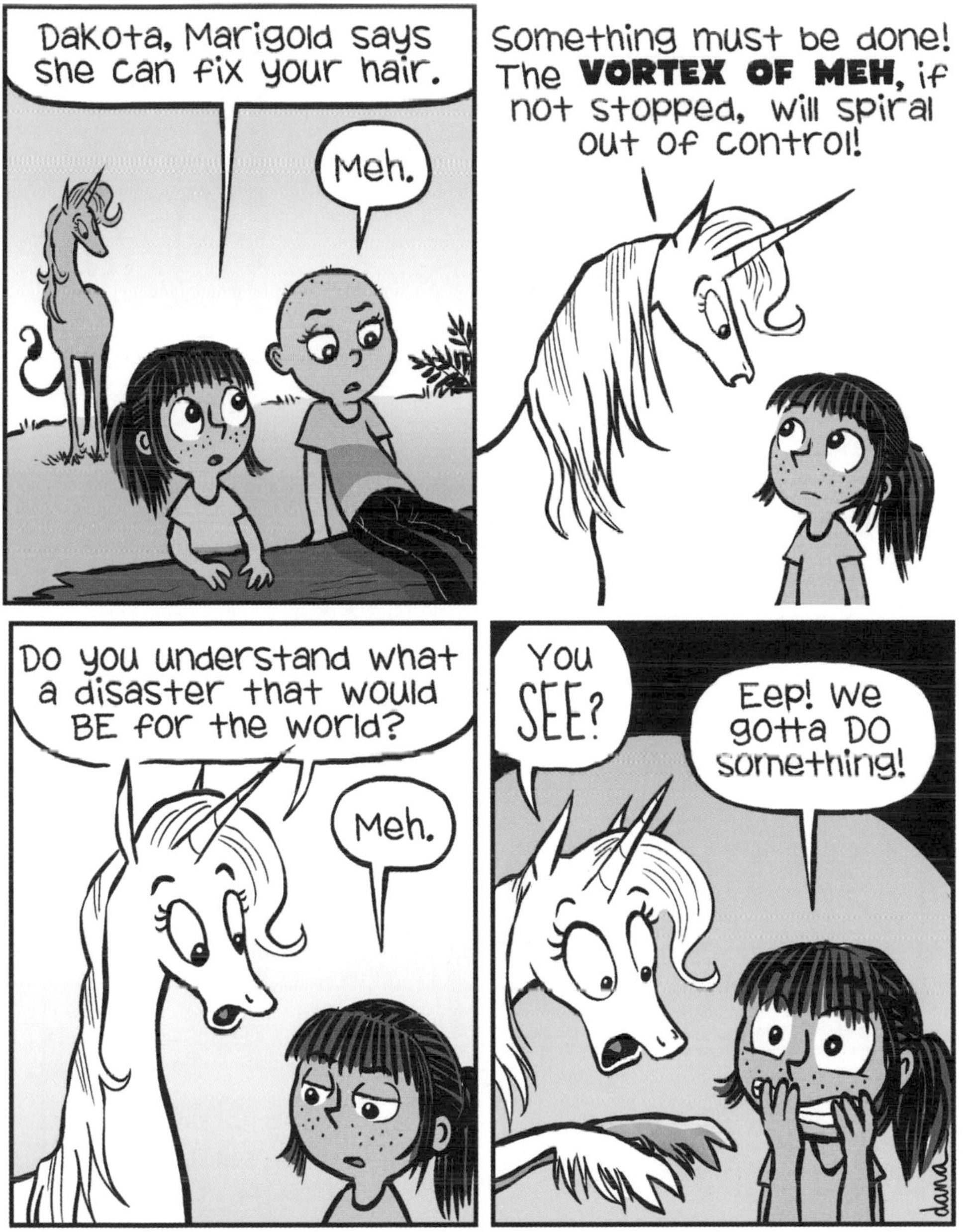
Dakota, Marigold says she can fix your hair.
Meh.
Something must be done! The **VORTEX OF MEH**, if not stopped, will spiral out of control!
Do you understand what a disaster that would BE for the world?
Meh.
You SEE?
Eep! We gotta DO something!
dana

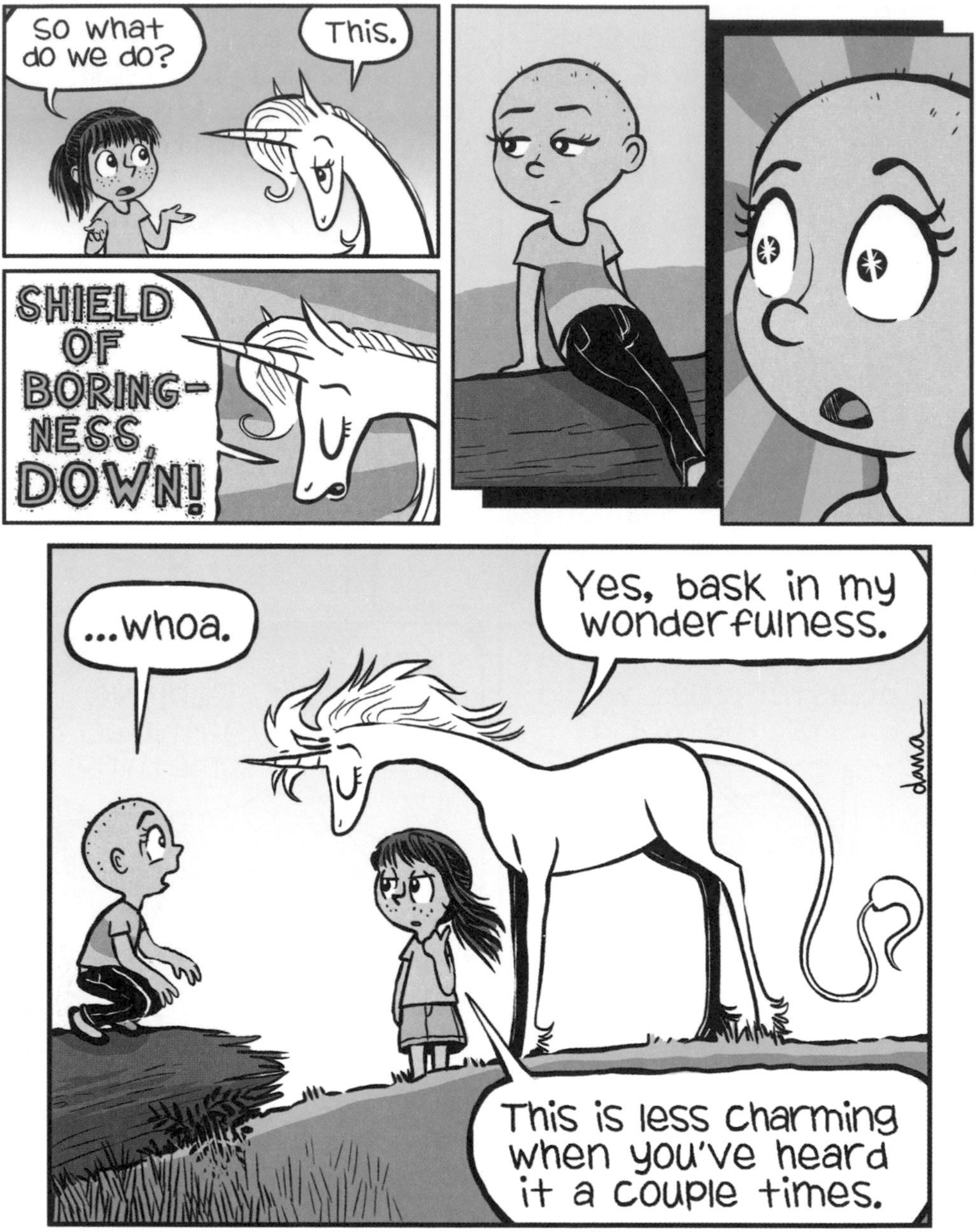

So what do we do?
This.
SHIELD OF BORING-NESS, DOWN!
...whoa.
Yes, bask in my wonderfulness.
This is less charming when you've heard it a couple times.
dana

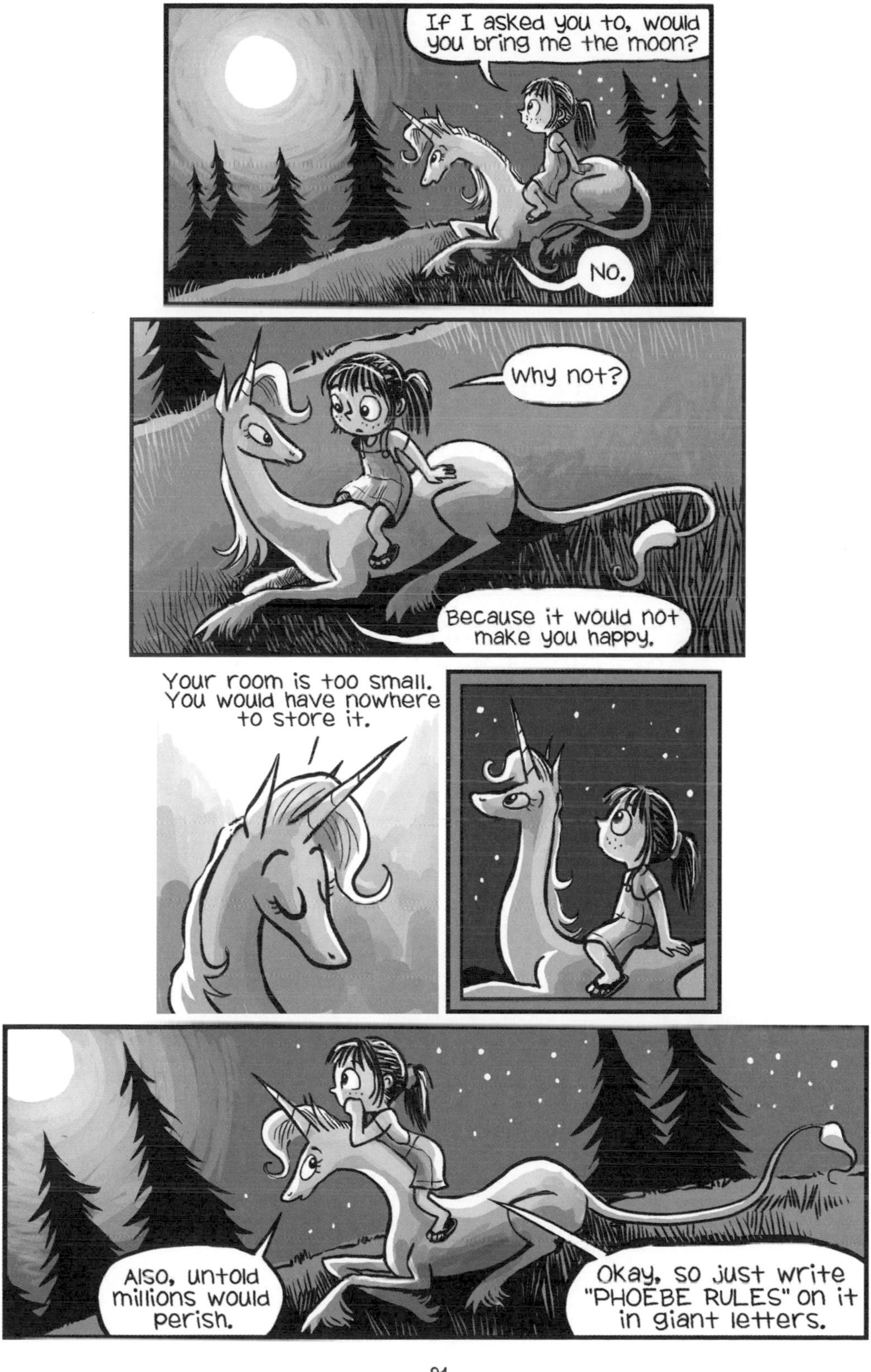
If I asked you to, would you bring me the moon?
No.
Why not?
Because it would not make you happy.
Your room is too small. You would have nowhere to store it.
Also, untold millions would perish.
Okay, so just write "PHOEBE RULES" on it in giant letters.

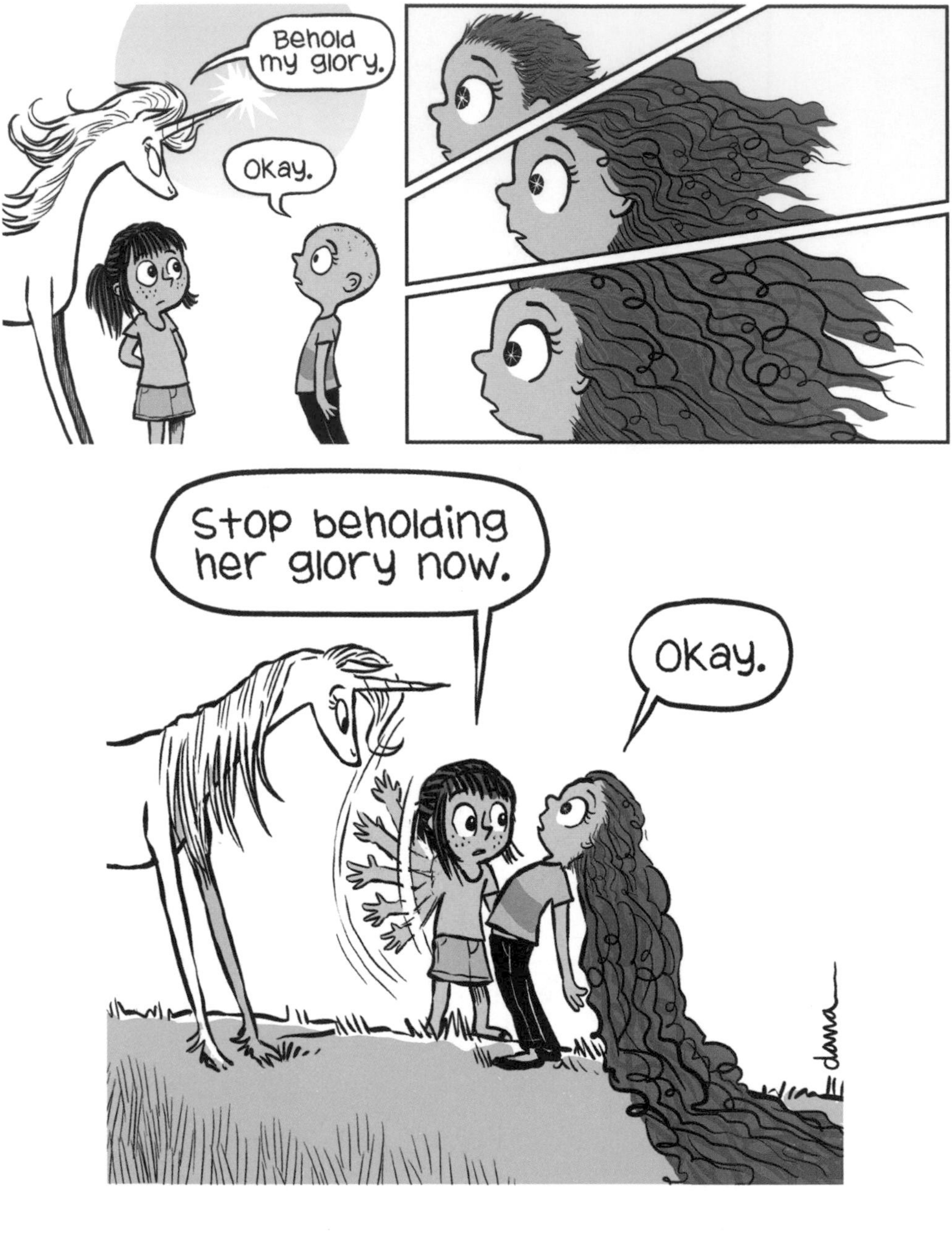
Behold my glory.
Okay.
Stop beholding her glory now.
Okay.
dana

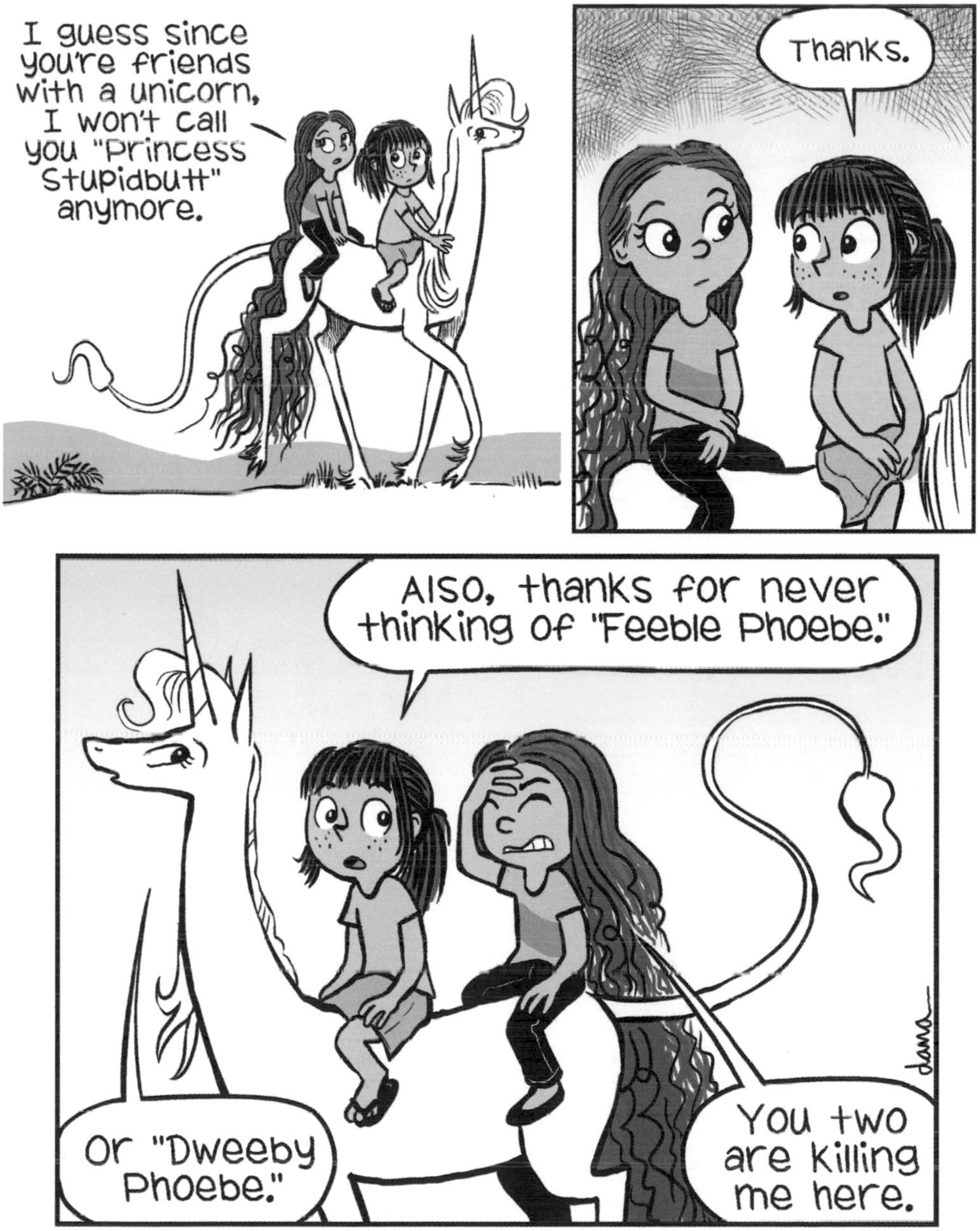
I guess since you're friends with a unicorn, I won't call you "Princess Stupidbutt" anymore.
Thanks.
Also, thanks for never thinking of "Feeble Phoebe."
Or "Dweeby Phoebe."
You two are killing me here.
dana

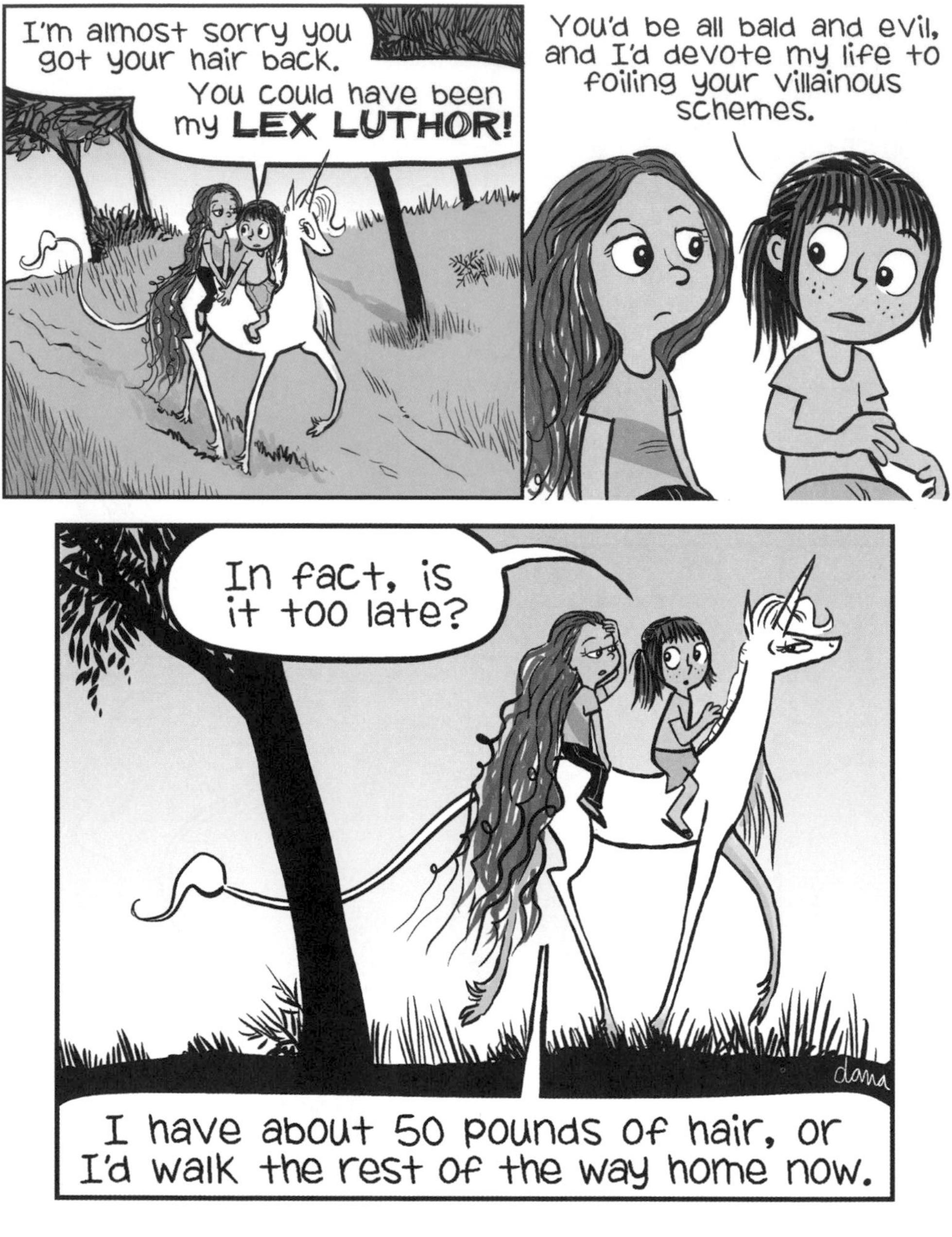
I'm almost sorry you got your hair back.
You could have been my LEX LUTHOR!
You'd be all bald and evil, and I'd devote my life to foiling your villainous schemes.
In fact, is it too late?
I have about 50 pounds of hair, or I'd walk the rest of the way home now.
dana

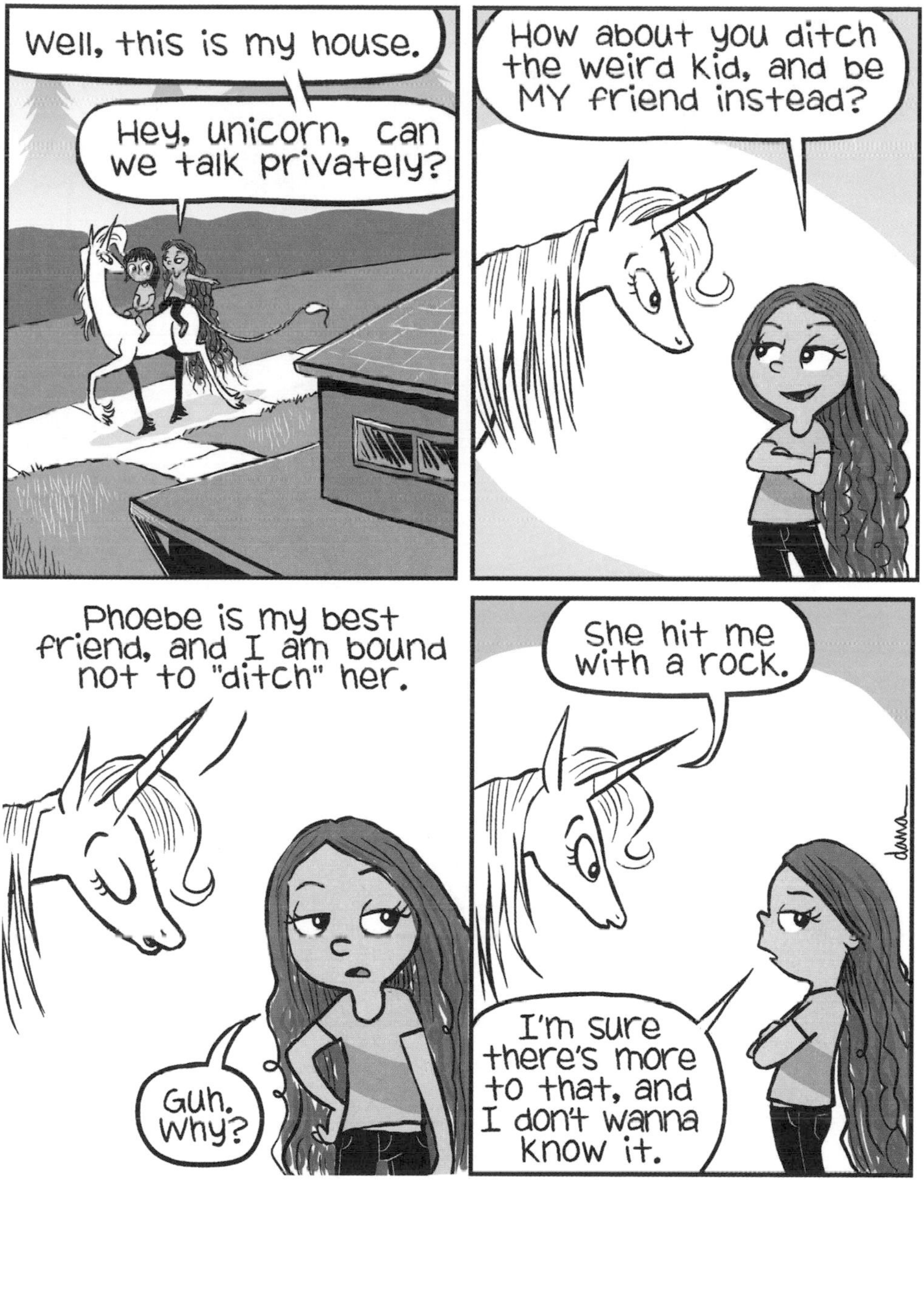
Well, this is my house.
Hey, unicorn, can we talk privately?
How about you ditch the weird kid, and be MY friend instead?
Phoebe is my best friend, and I am bound not to "ditch" her.
Guh. Why?
She hit me with a rock.
I'm sure there's more to that, and I don't wanna know it.
dana

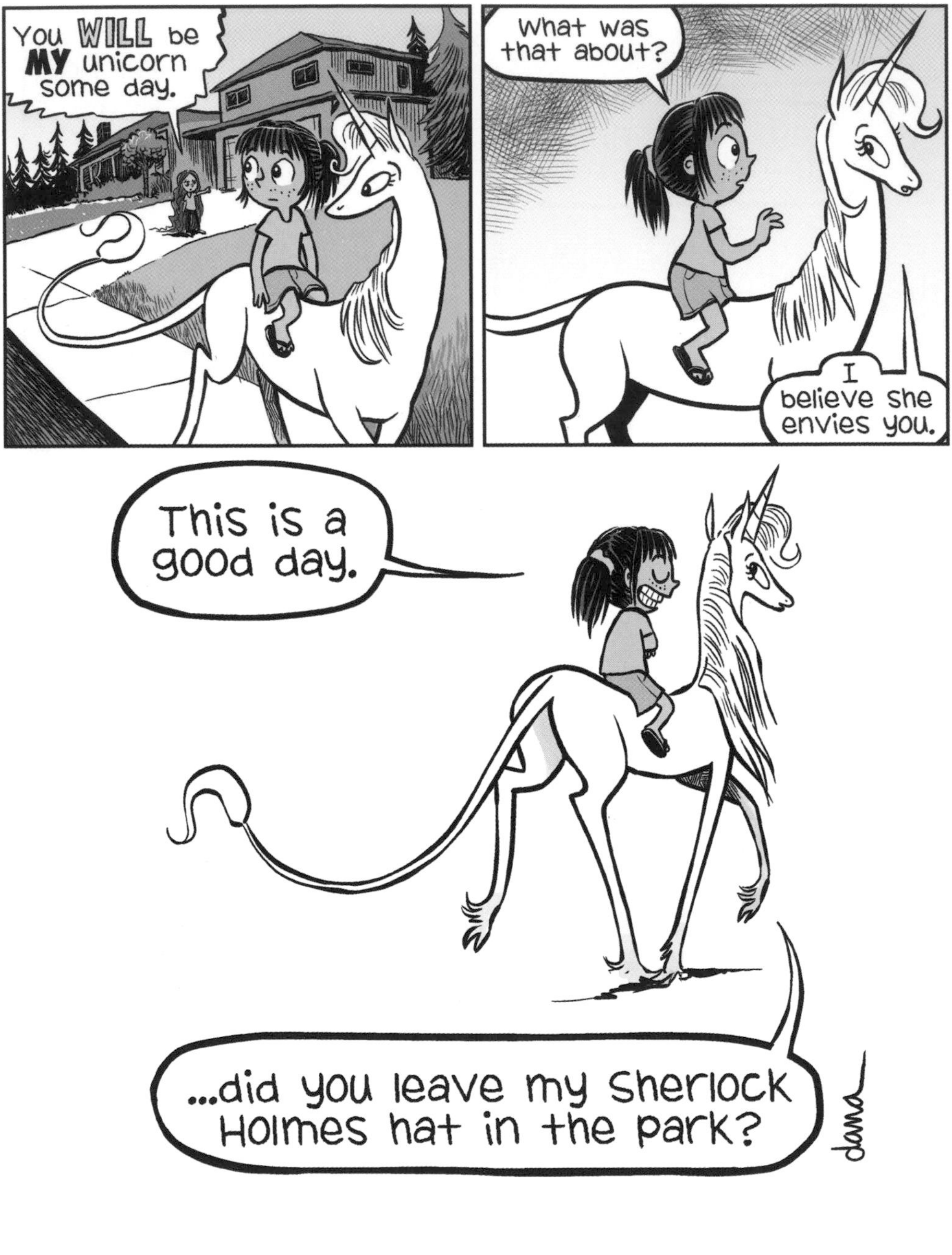
You WILL be MY unicorn some day.
What was that about?
I believe she envies you.
This is a good day.
...did you leave my Sherlock Holmes hat in the park?
dana

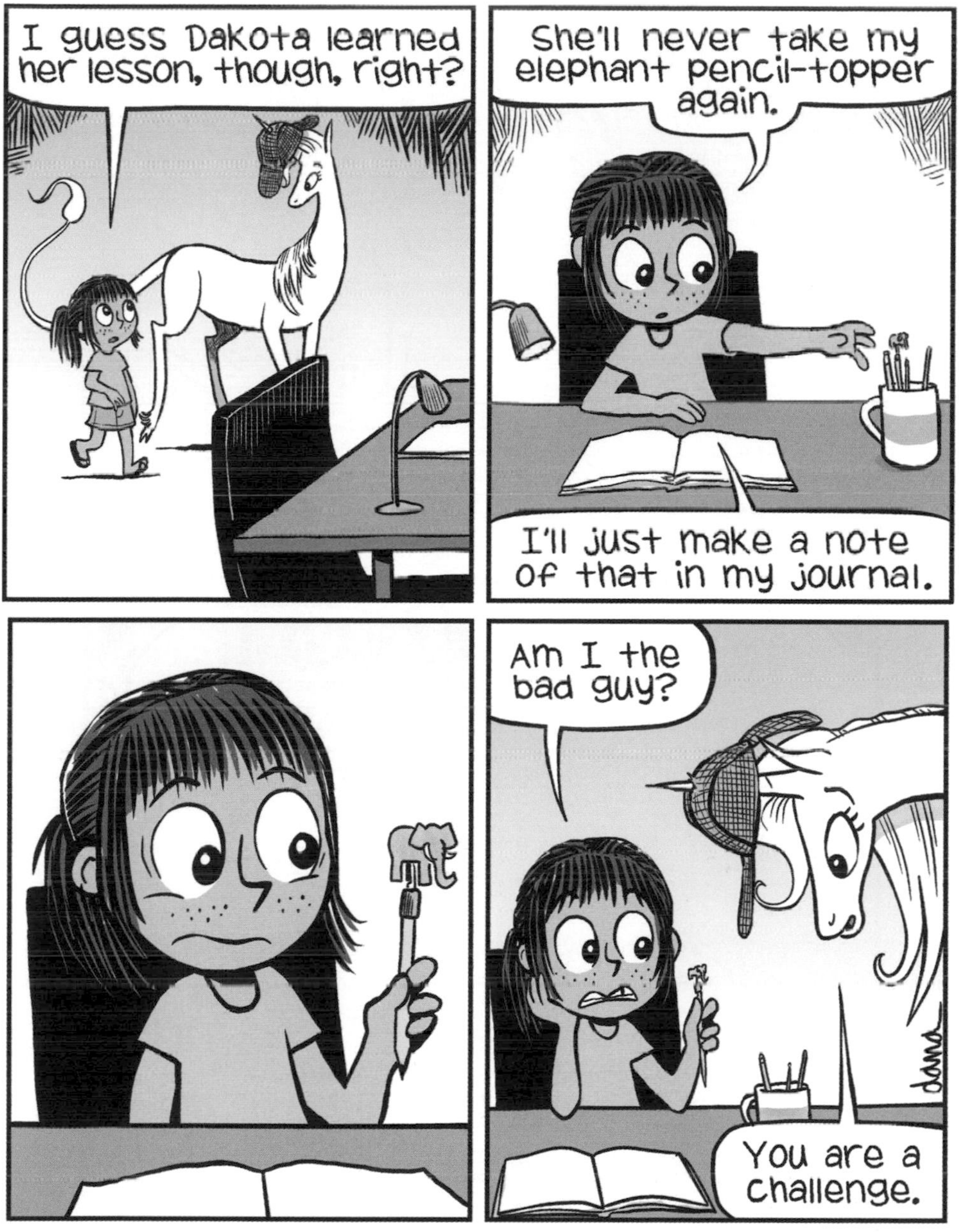
I guess Dakota learned her lesson, though, right?
She'll never take my elephant pencil-topper again.
I'll just make a note of that in my journal.
Am I the bad guy?
You are a challenge.
dana

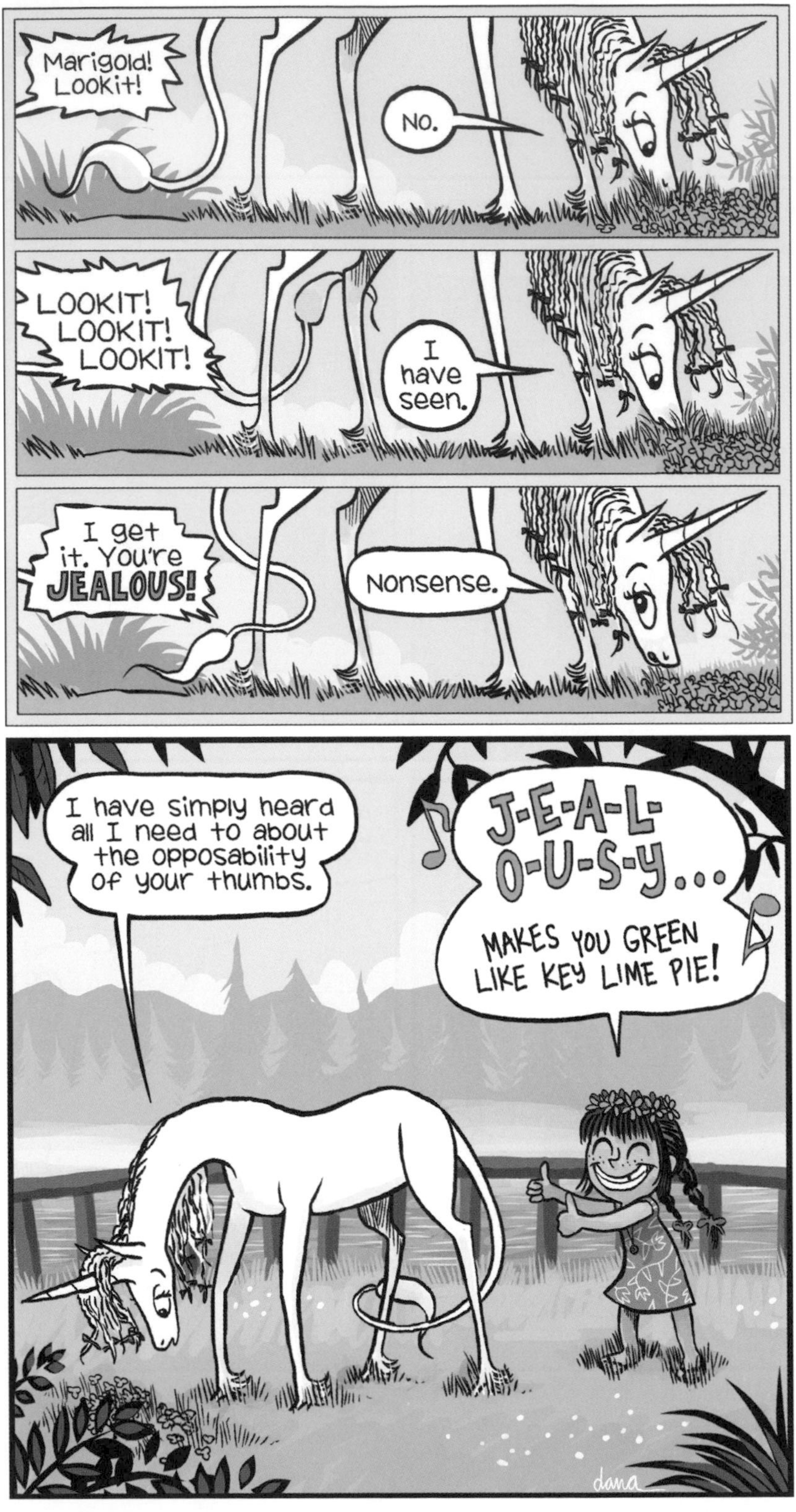
Marigold! LookIt!
No.
LOOKIT! LOOKIT! LOOKIT!
I have seen.
I get it. You're JEALOUS!
Nonsense.
I have simply heard all I need to about the opposability of your thumbs.
J-E-A-L-O-U-S-Y...
MAKES YOU GREEN LIKE KEY LIME PIE!
dana

I guess I failed at being a detective.

There is no shame in failing, sometimes.

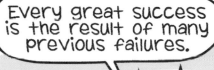

Every great success is the result of many previous failures.

Let me tell you about the first time I failed at not being perfect.

You had me, and then you lost me.

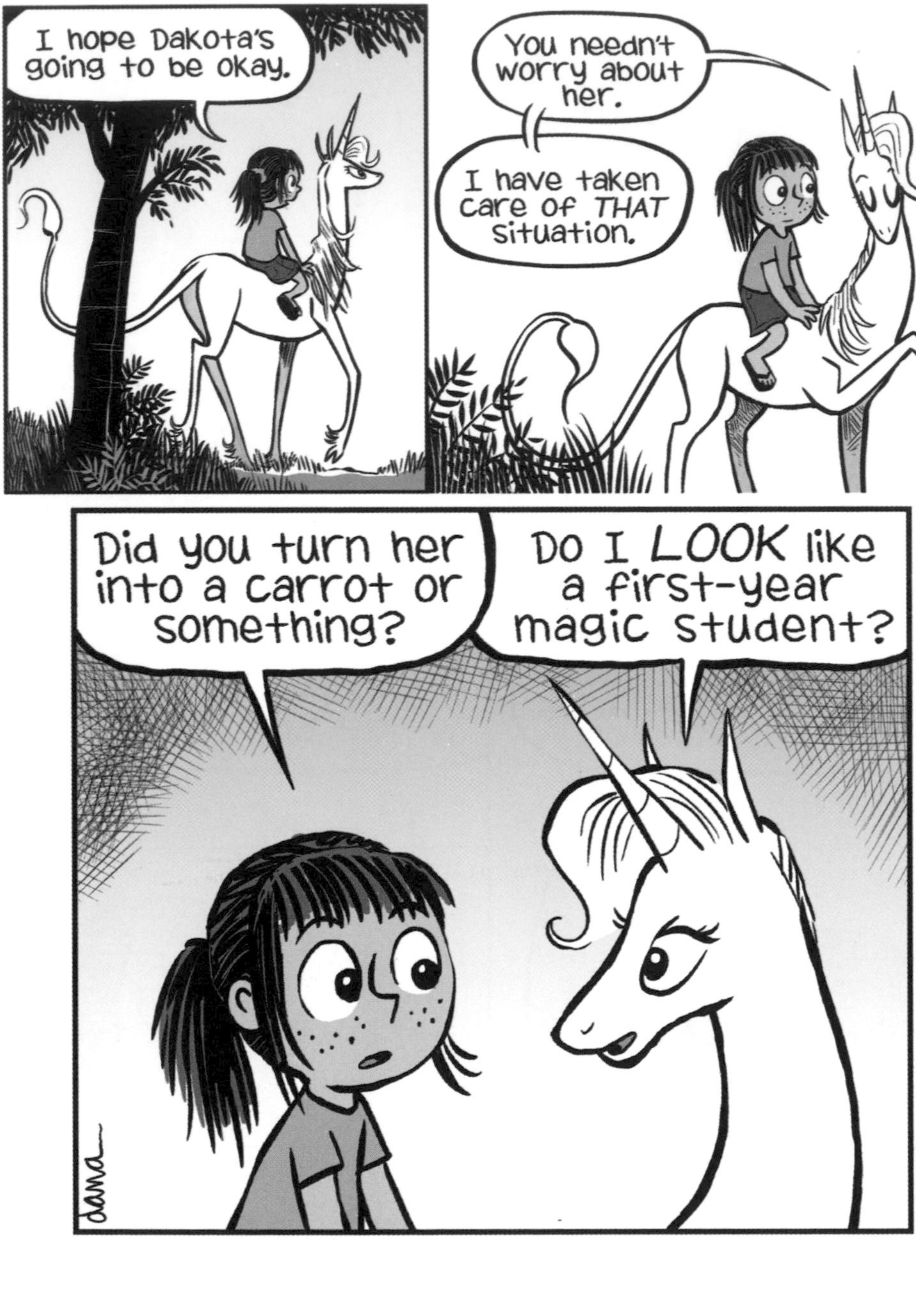
I hope Dakota's going to be okay.
You needn't worry about her.
I have taken care of *THAT* situation.
Did you turn her into a carrot or something?
Do I *LOOK* like a first-year magic student?
dana

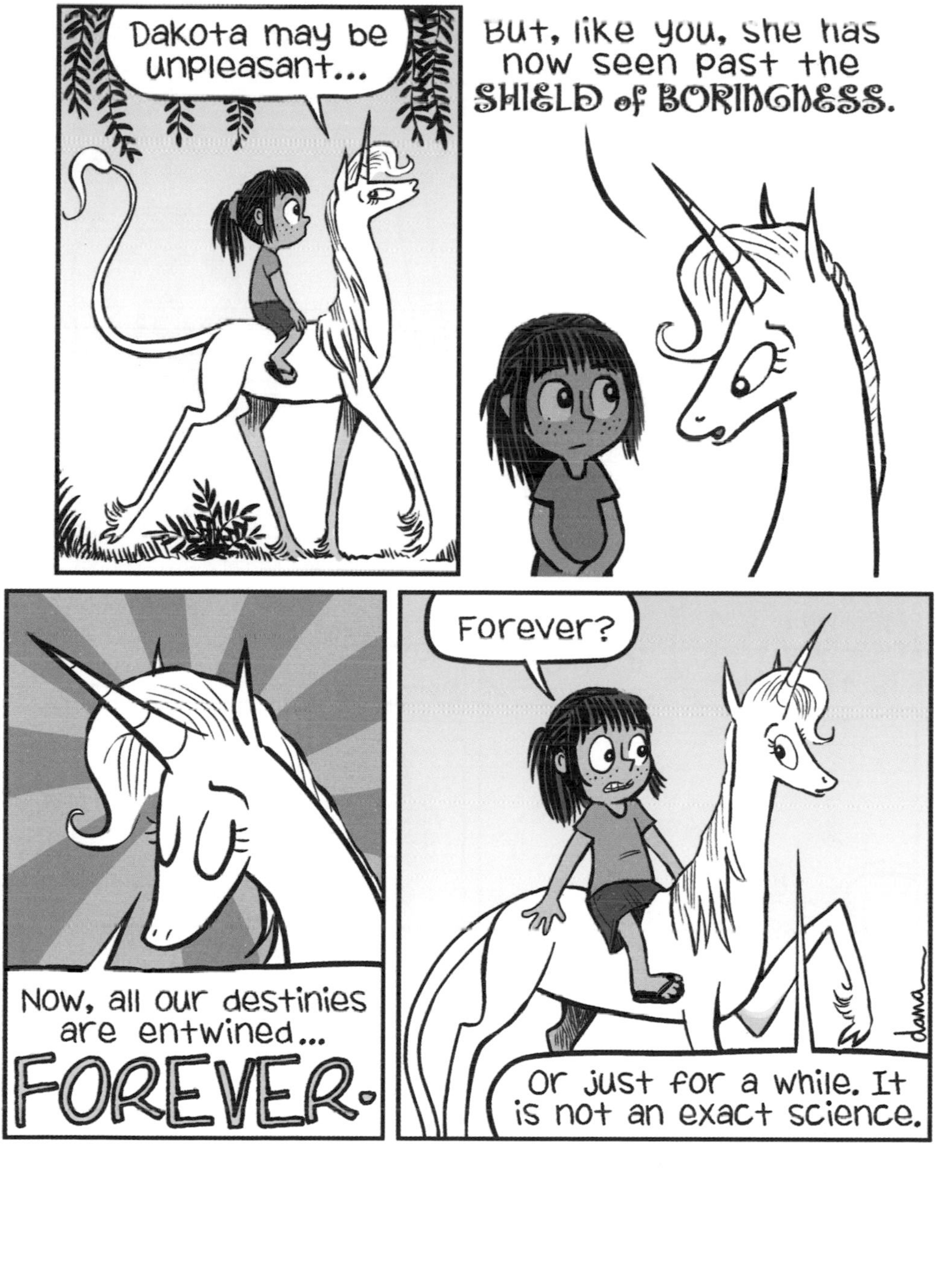
Dakota may be unpleasant...
But, like you, she has now seen past the SHIELD of BORINGNESS.
Now, all our destinies are entwined... FOREVER.
Forever?
Or just for a while. It is not an exact science.
dana

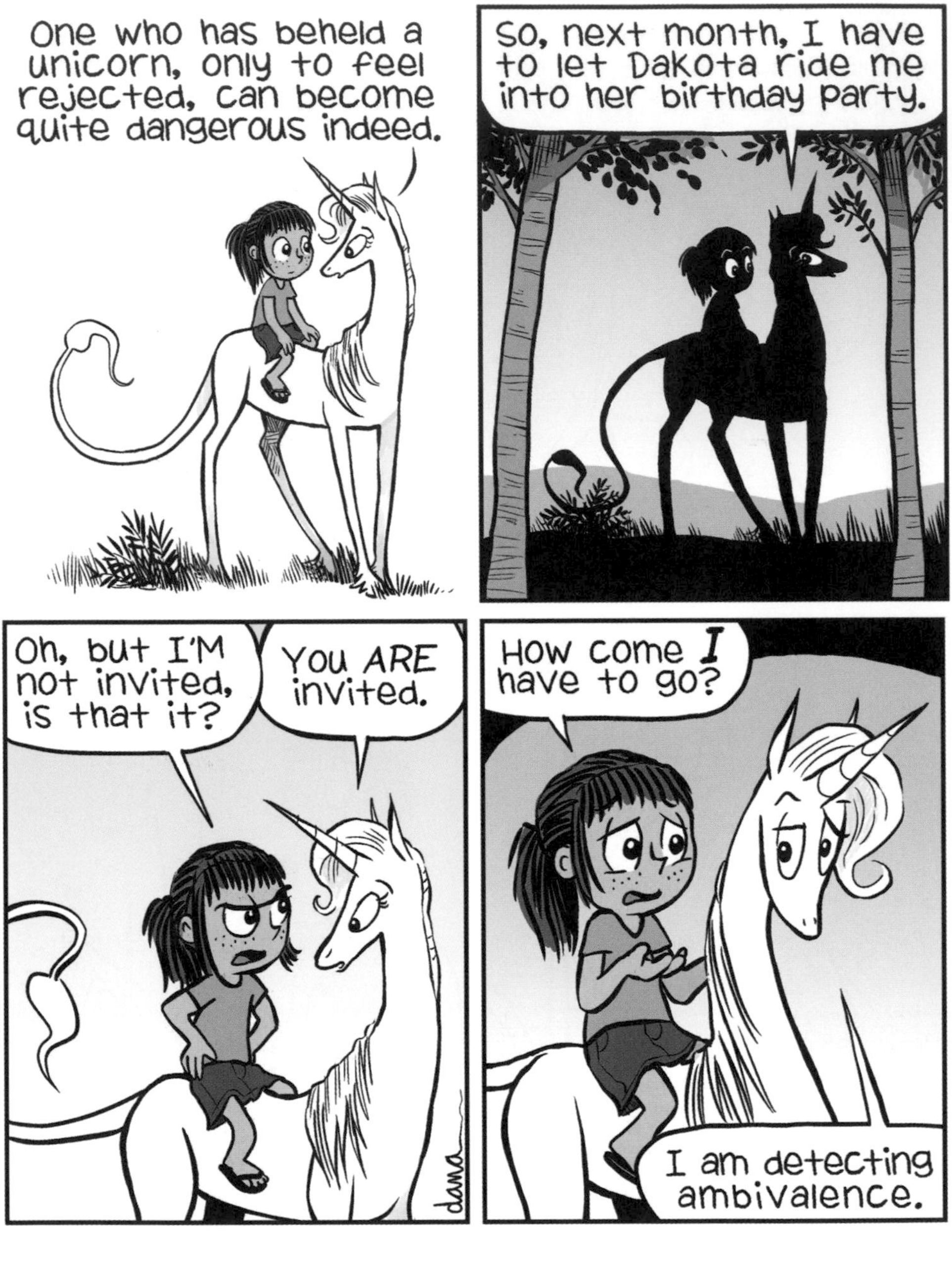
One who has beheld a unicorn, only to feel rejected, can become quite dangerous indeed.
So, next month, I have to let Dakota ride me into her birthday party.
Oh, but I'M not invited, is that it?
You ARE invited.
How come I have to go?
I am detecting ambivalence.

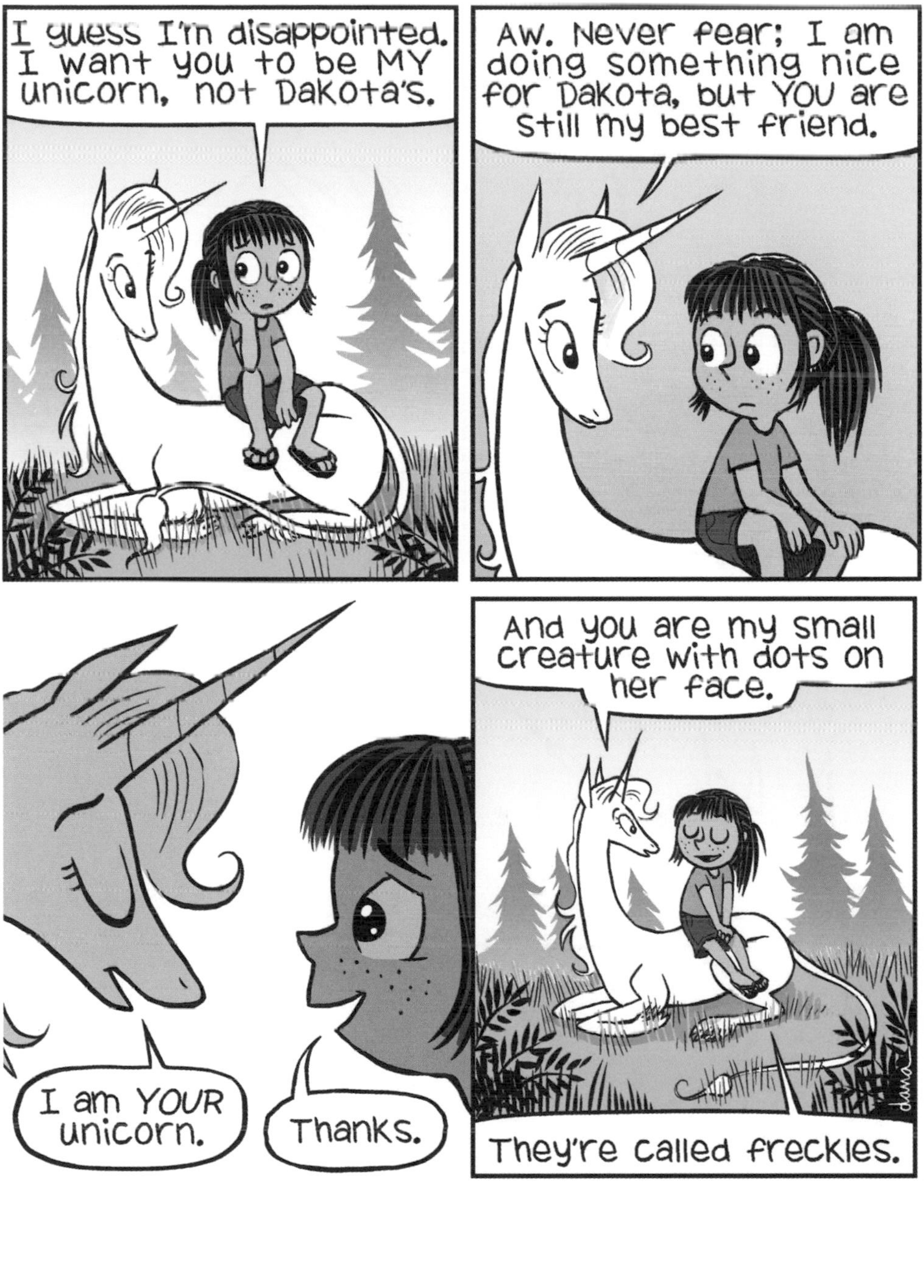
I guess I'm disappointed. I want you to be MY unicorn, not Dakota's.
Aw. Never fear; I am doing something nice for Dakota, but YOU are still my best friend.
I am YOUR unicorn.
Thanks.
And you are my small creature with dots on her face.
They're called freckles.

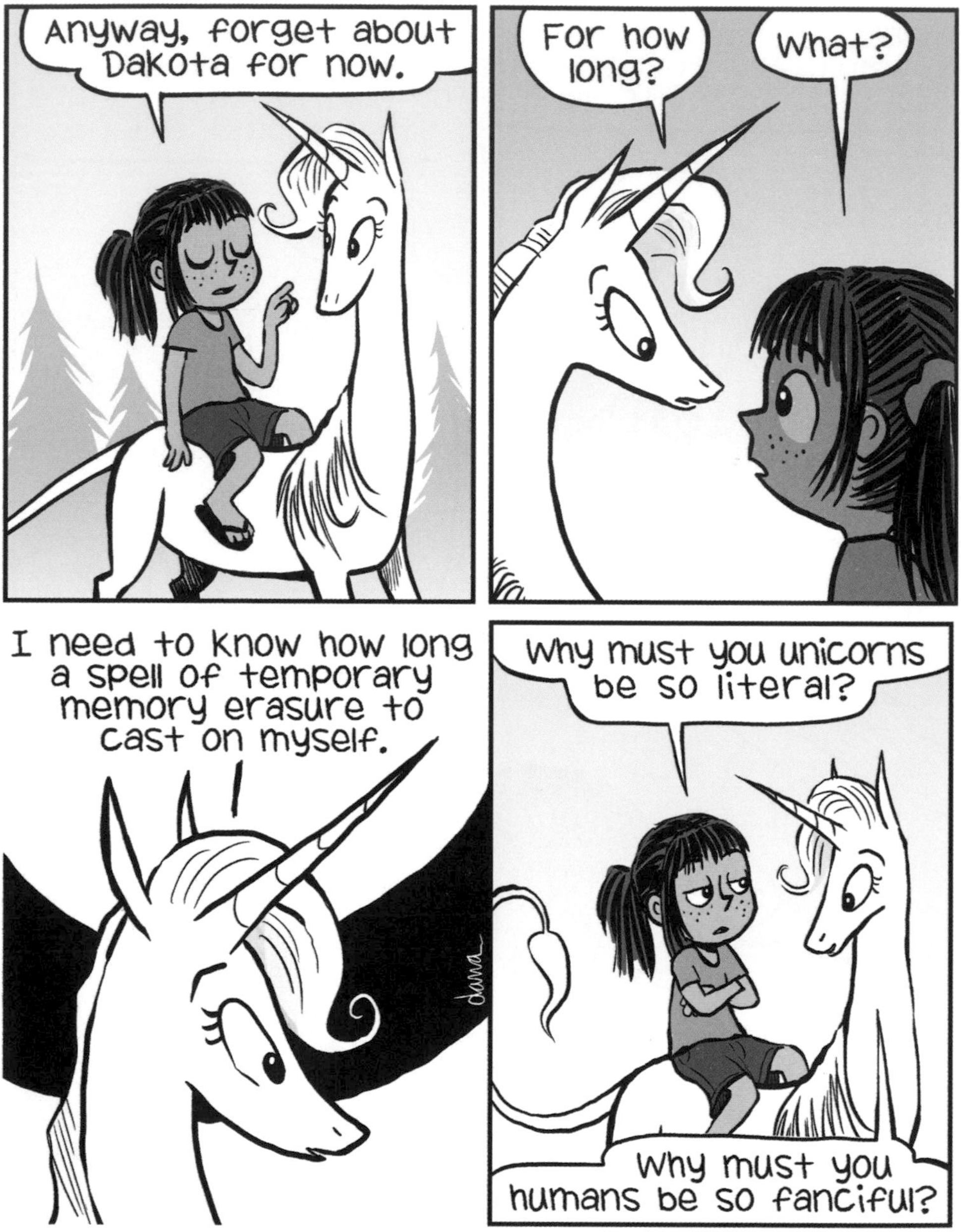
Anyway, forget about Dakota for now.
For how long?
What?
I need to know how long a spell of temporary memory erasure to cast on myself.
dana
Why must you unicorns be so literal?
Why must you humans be so fanciful?

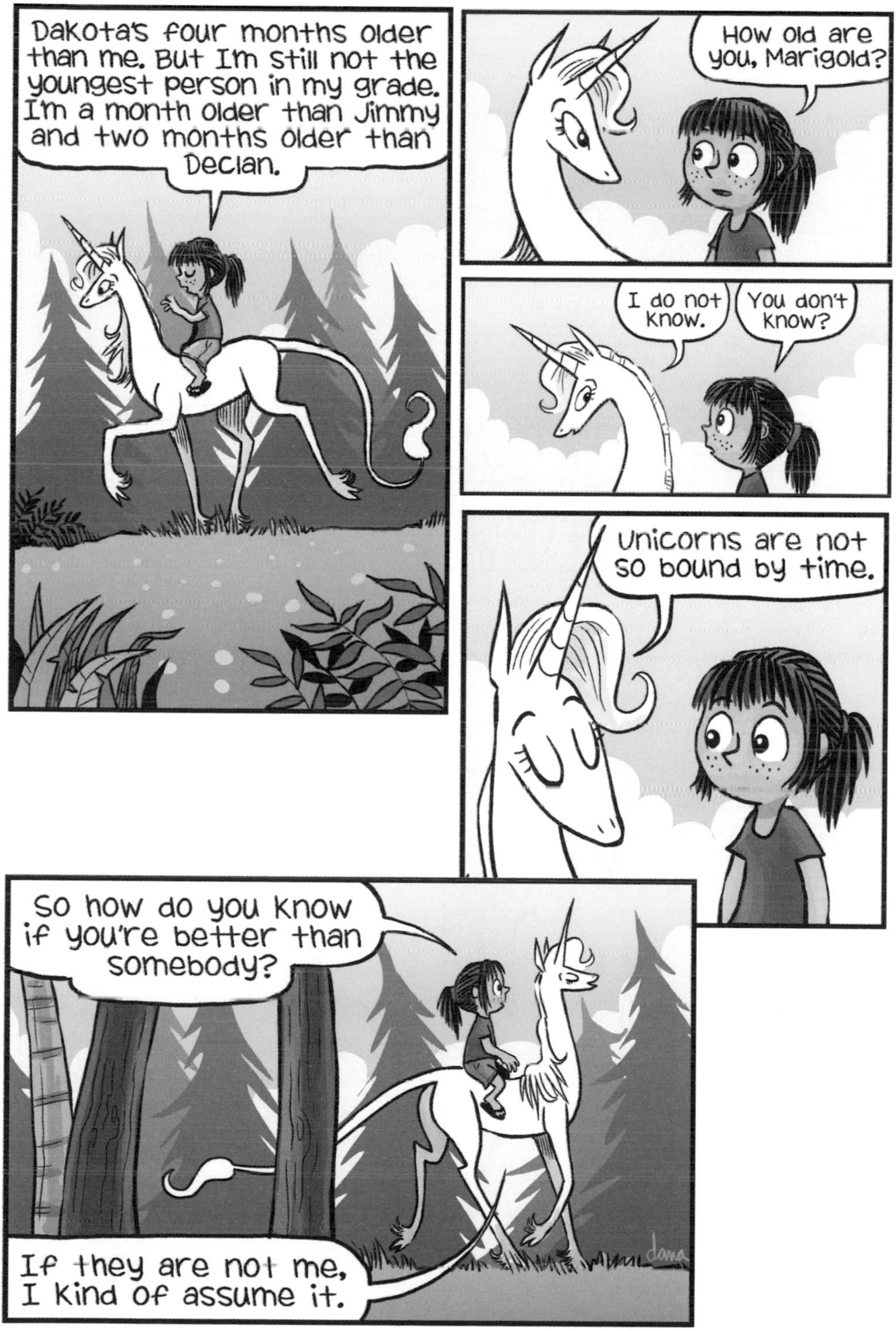
Dakota's four months older than me. But I'm still not the youngest person in my grade. I'm a month older than Jimmy and two months older than Declan.
How old are you, Marigold?
I do not know.
You don't know?
Unicorns are not so bound by time.
So how do you know if you're better than somebody?
If they are not me, I kind of assume it.

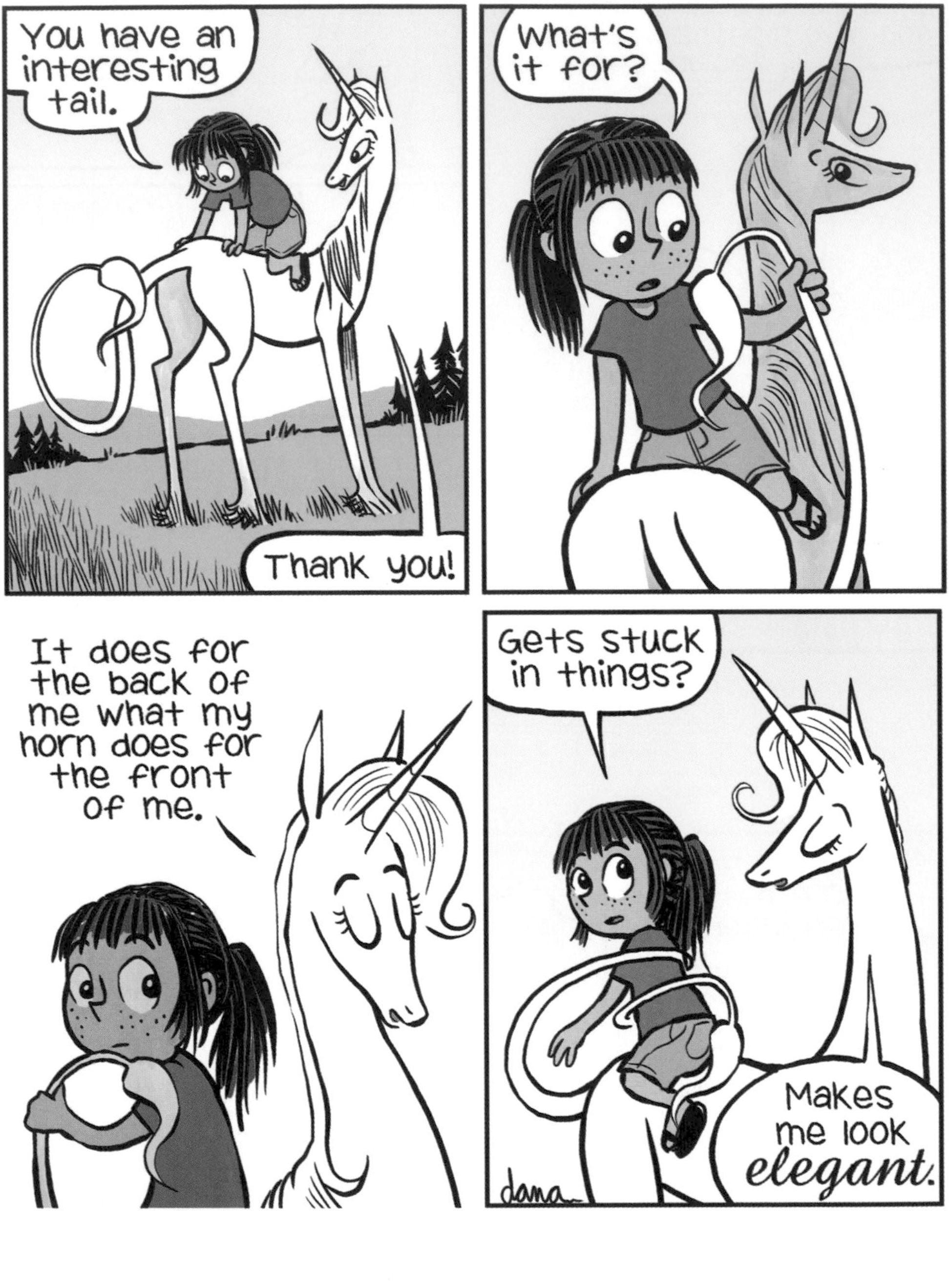
You have an interesting tail.
Thank you!
What's it for?
It does for the back of me what my horn does for the front of me.
Gets stuck in things?
Makes me look *elegant*.
dana

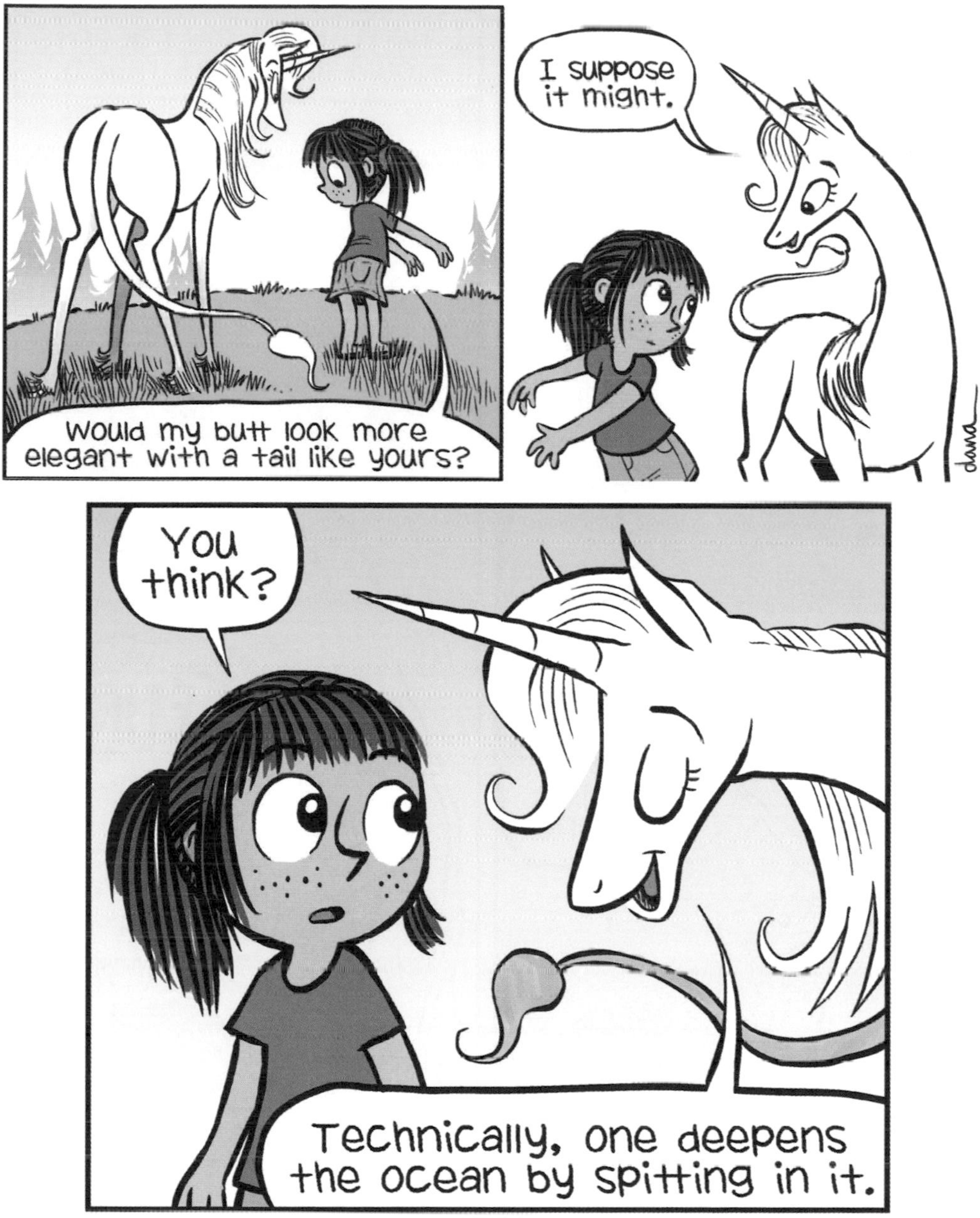
Would my butt look more elegant with a tail like yours?
I suppose it might.
dana
You think?
Technically, one deepens the ocean by spitting in it.

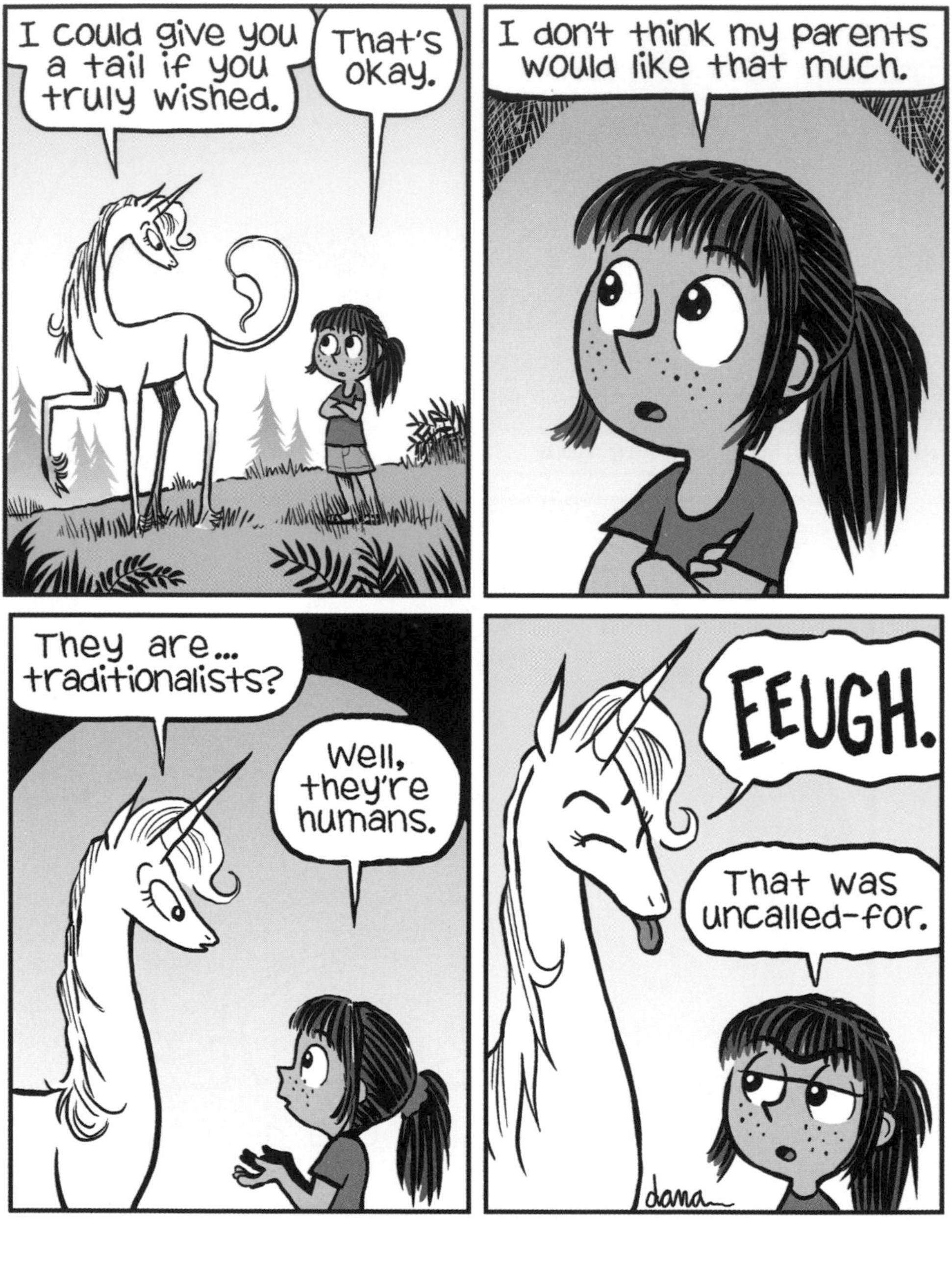
I could give you a tail if you truly wished.
That's okay.
I don't think my parents would like that much.
They are... traditionalists?
Well, they're humans.
EEUGH.
That was uncalled-for.
dana

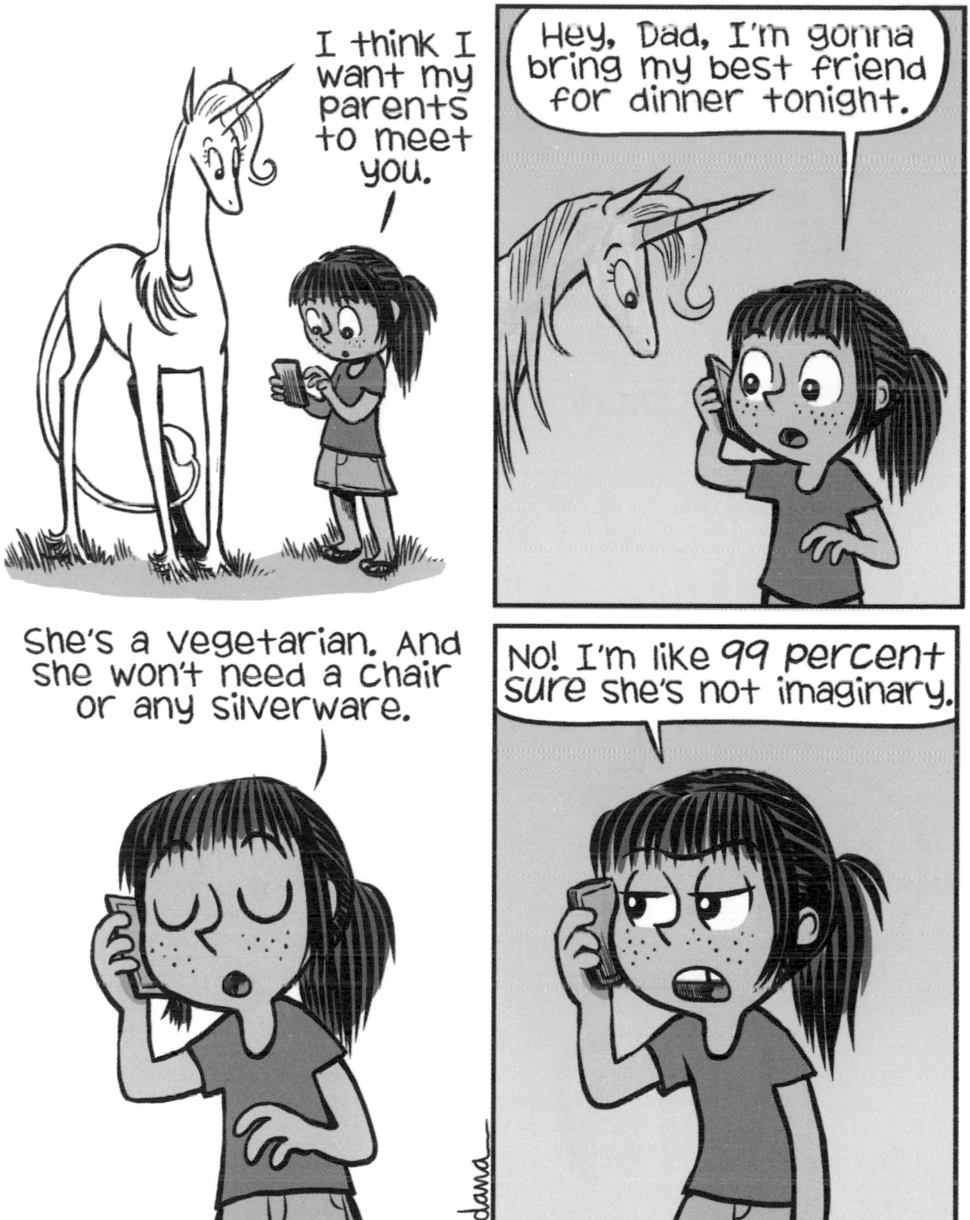
I think I want my parents to meet you.
Hey, Dad, I'm gonna bring my best friend for dinner tonight.
She's a vegetarian. And she won't need a chair or any silverware.
No! I'm like 99 percent sure she's not imaginary.
dana

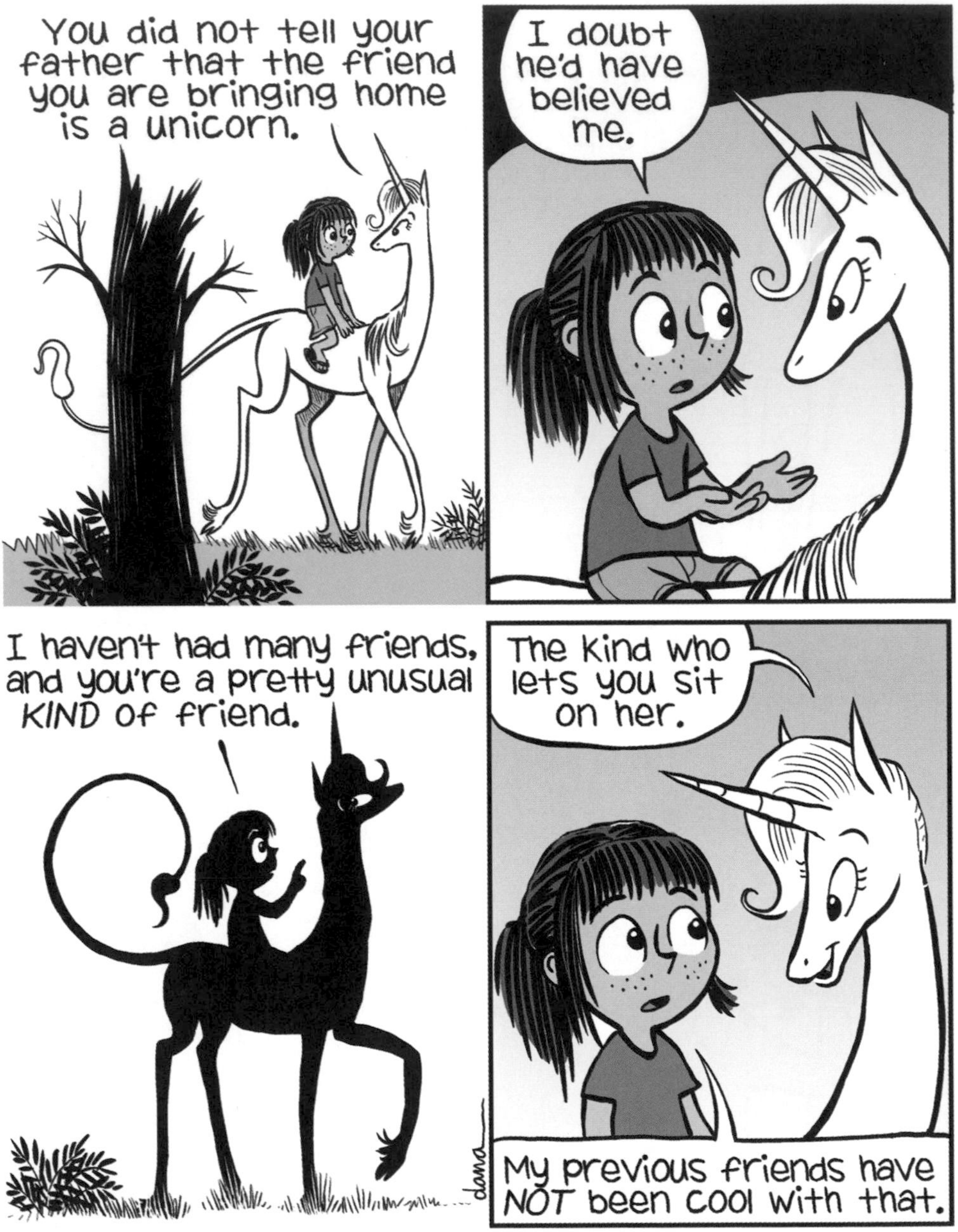
You did not tell your father that the friend you are bringing home is a unicorn.
I doubt he'd have believed me.
I haven't had many friends, and you're a pretty unusual KIND of friend.
The kind who lets you sit on her.
My previous friends have NOT been cool with that.
dana

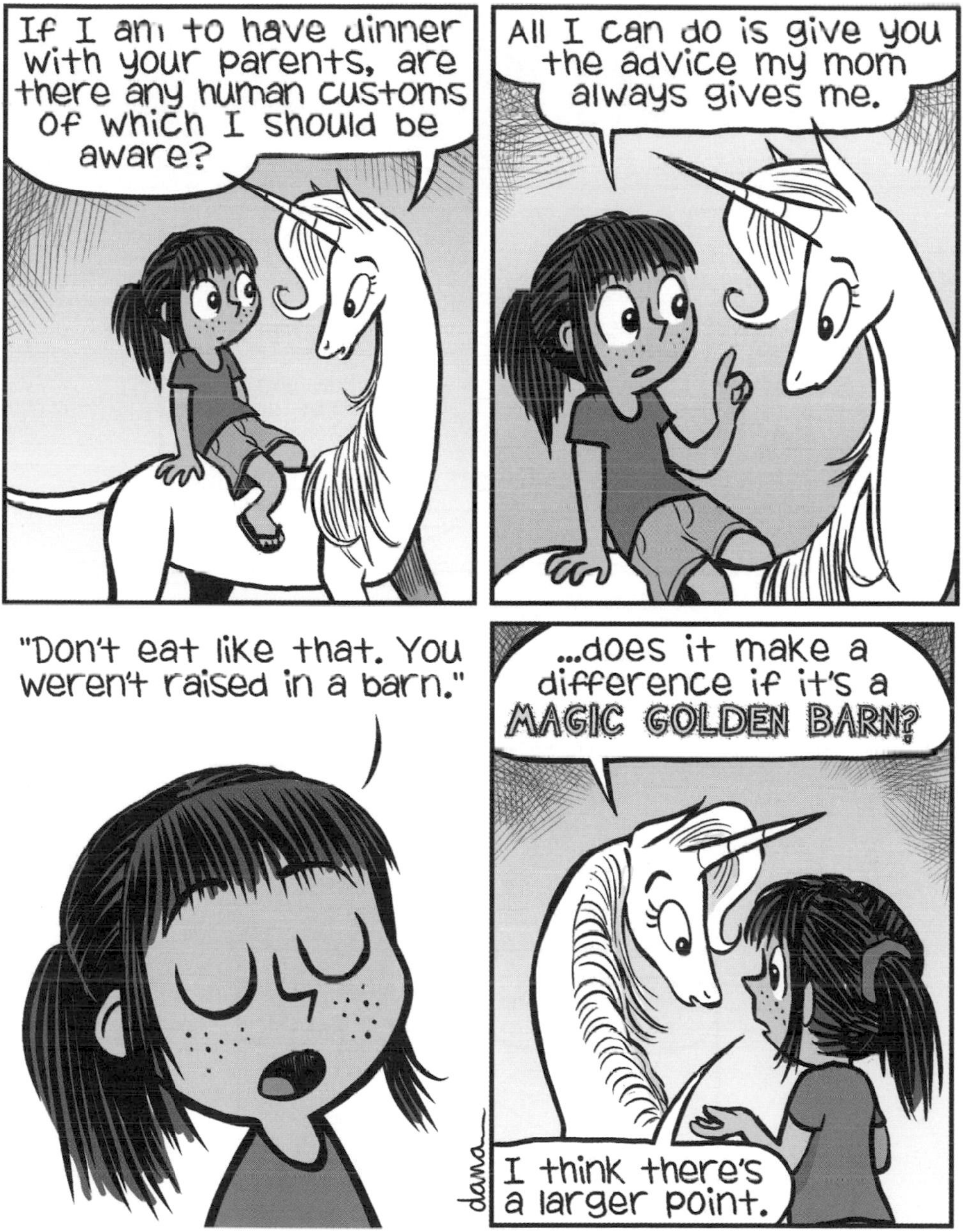
If I am to have dinner with your parents, are there any human customs of which I should be aware?
All I can do is give you the advice my mom always gives me.
"Don't eat like that. You weren't raised in a barn."
...does it make a difference if it's a MAGIC GOLDEN BARN?
I think there's a larger point.
dana

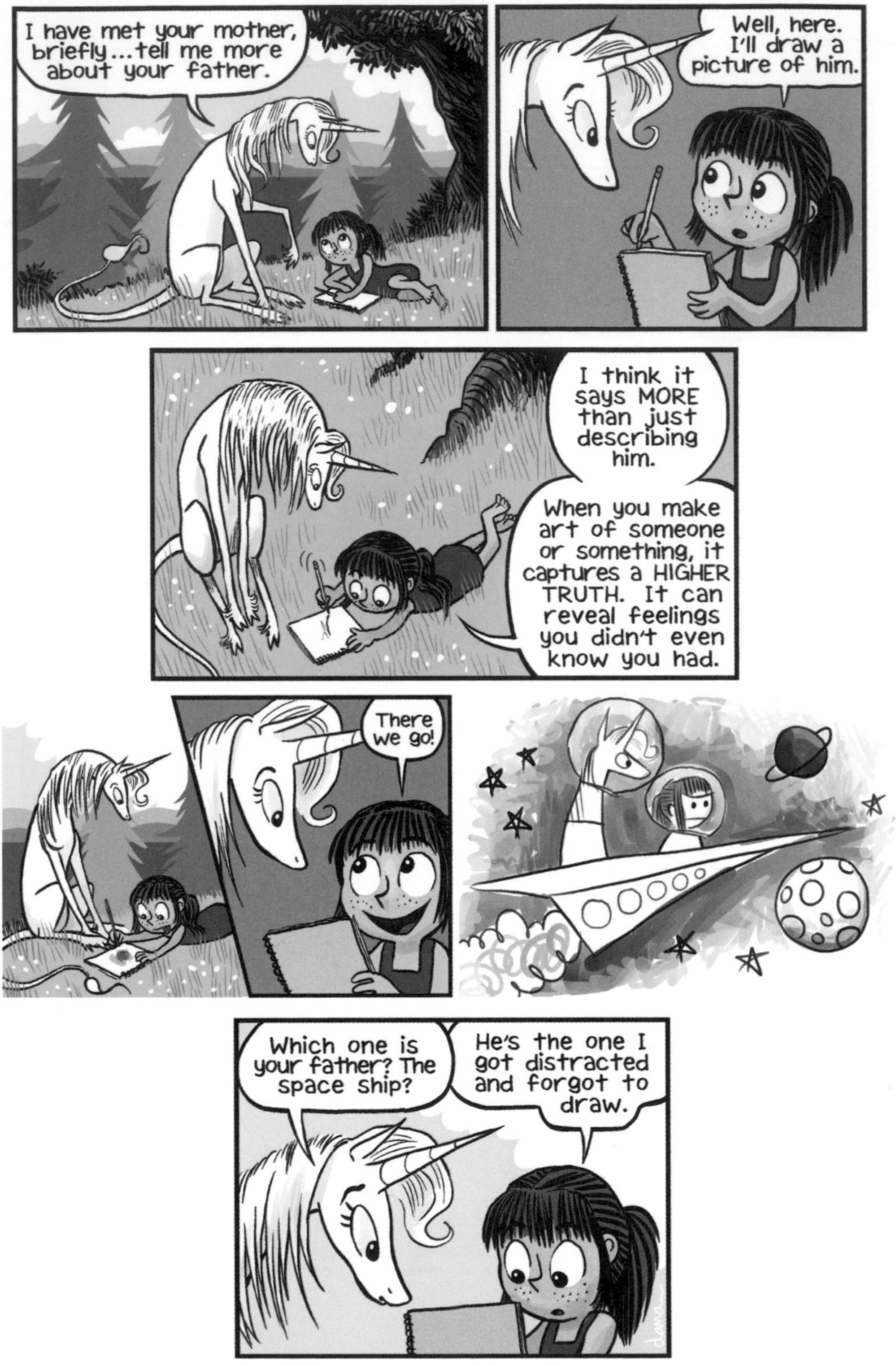
I have met your mother, briefly... tell me more about your father.
Well, here. I'll draw a picture of him.
I think it says MORE than just describing him.
When you make art of someone or something, it captures a HIGHER TRUTH. It can reveal feelings you didn't even know you had.
There we go!
Which one is your father? The space ship?
He's the one I got distracted and forgot to draw.

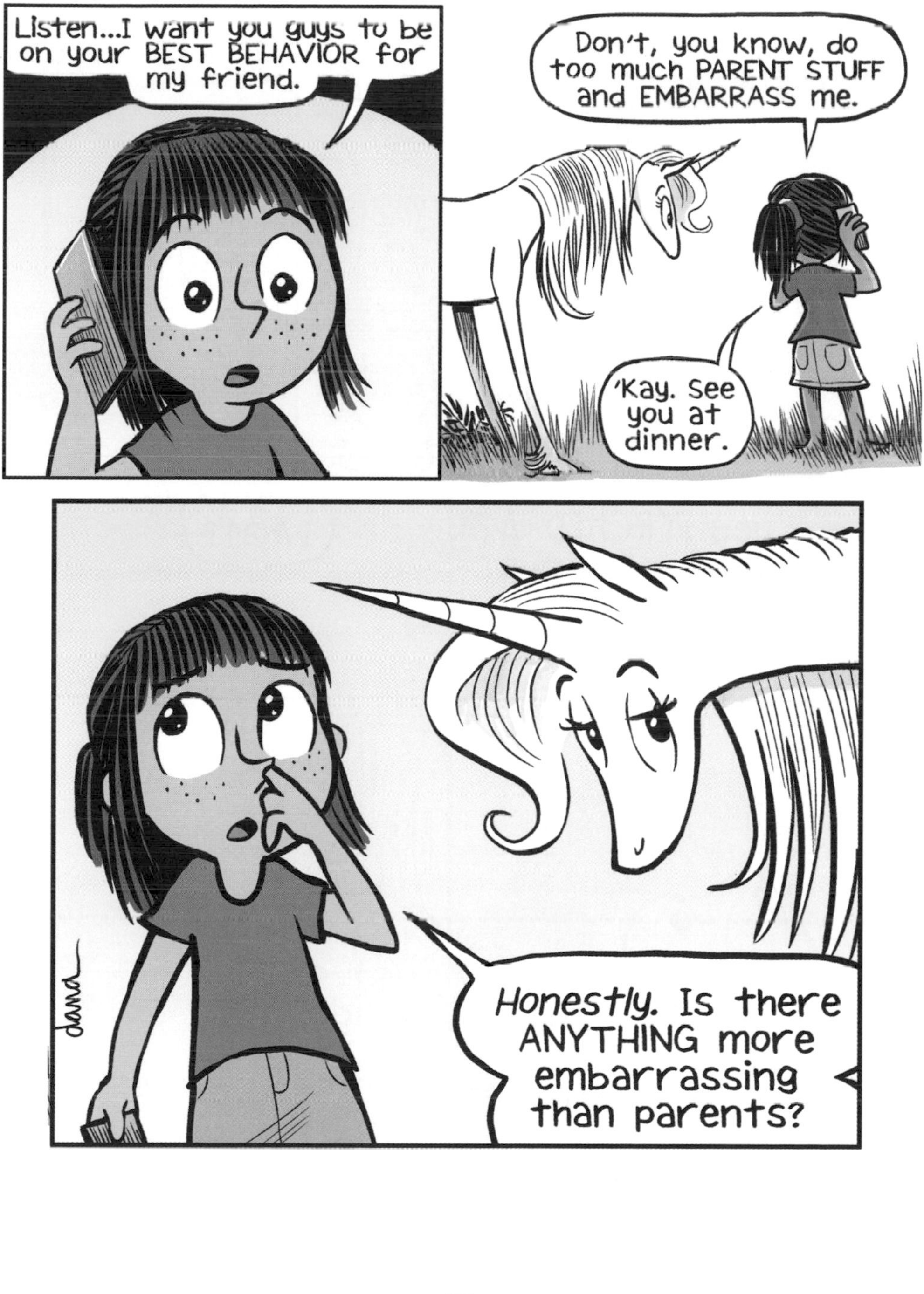
Listen...I want you guys to be on your BEST BEHAVIOR for my friend.
Don't, you know, do too much PARENT STUFF and EMBARRASS me.
'Kay. See you at dinner.
Honestly. Is there ANYTHING more embarrassing than parents?

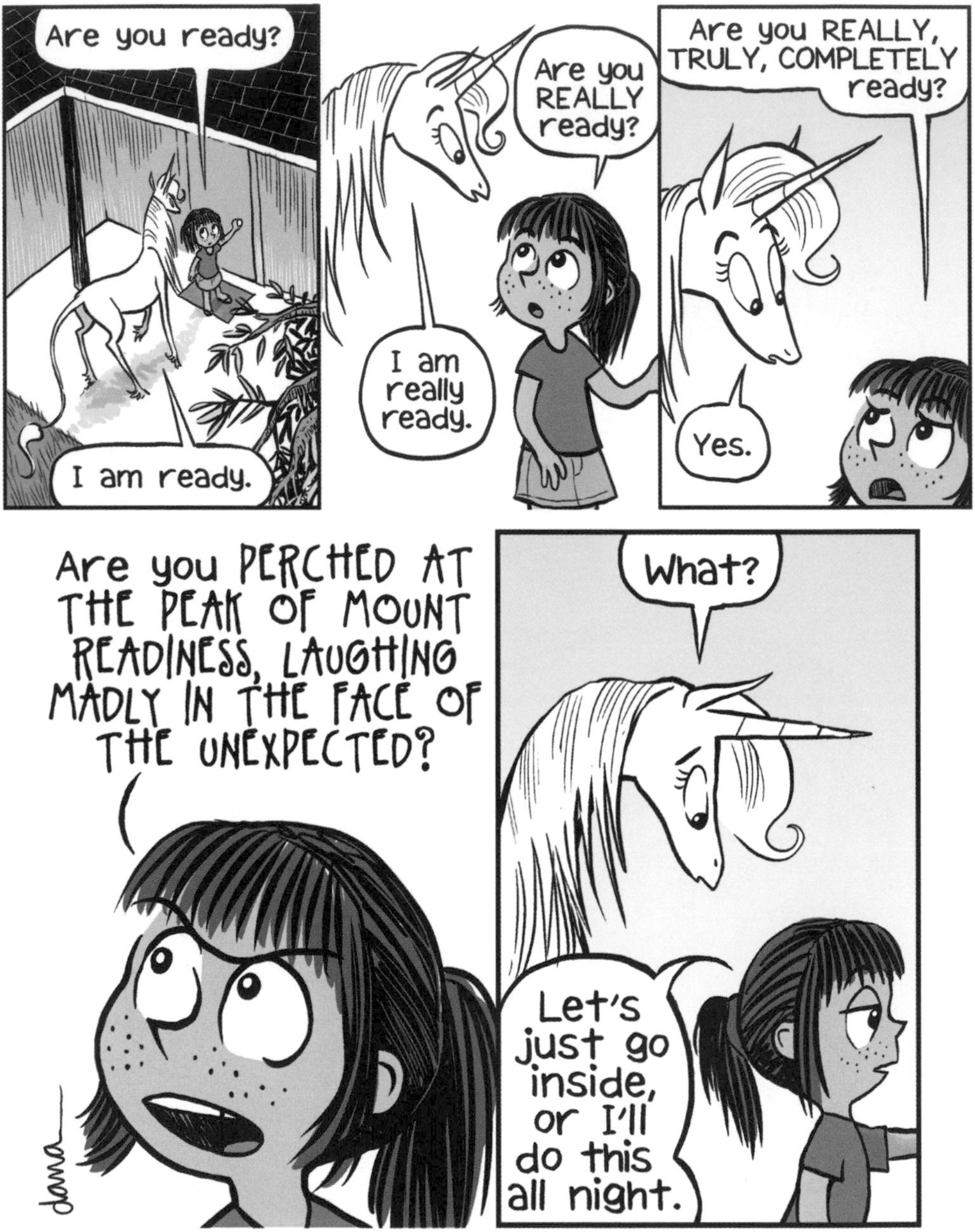
Are you ready?
I am ready.
Are you REALLY ready?
I am really ready.
Are you REALLY, TRULY, COMPLETELY ready?
Yes.
Are you PERCHED AT THE PEAK OF MOUNT READINESS, LAUGHING MADLY IN THE FACE OF THE UNEXPECTED?
What?
Let's just go inside, or I'll do this all night.
dana

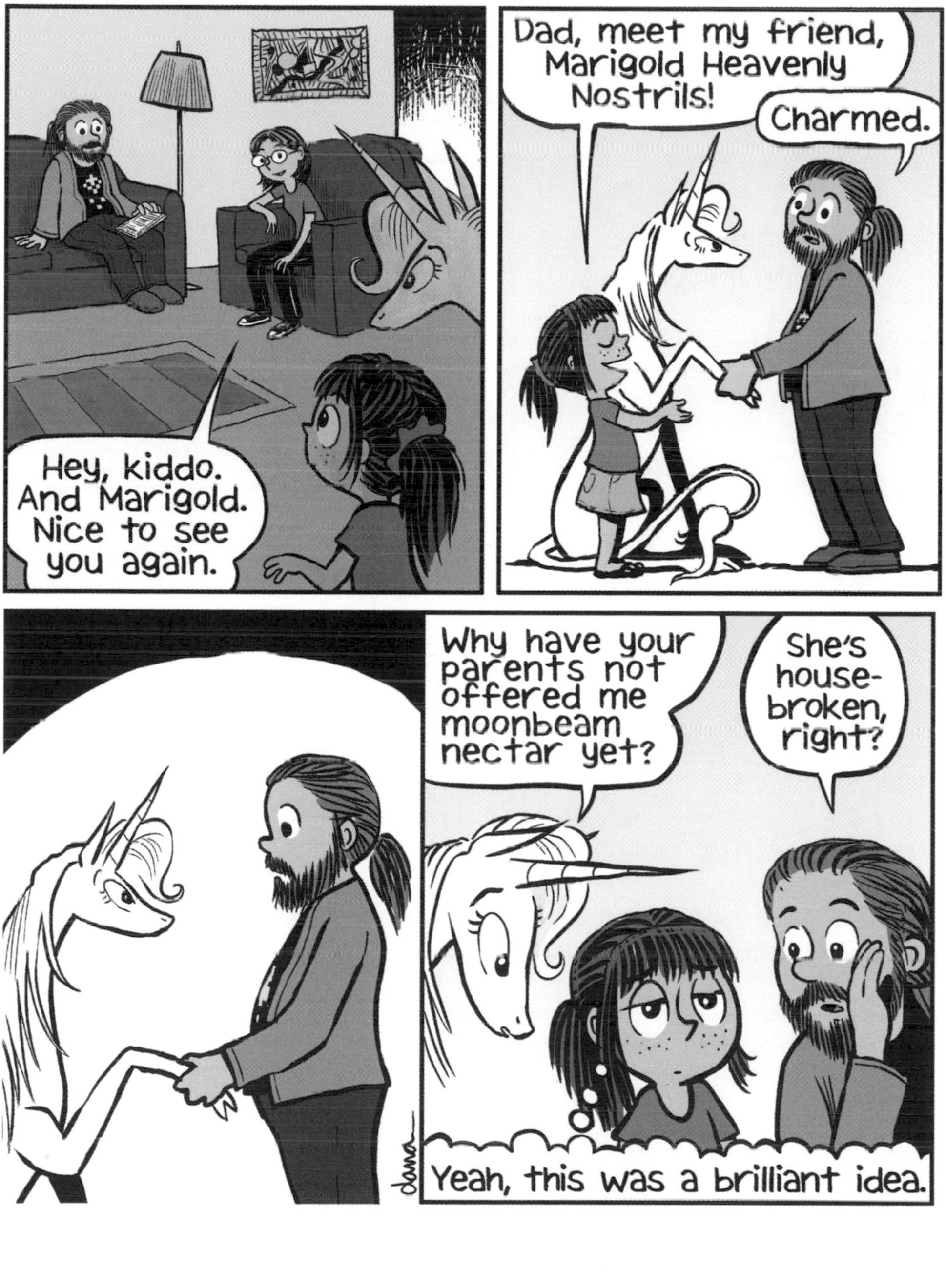
Hey, kiddo. And Marigold. Nice to see you again.
Dad, meet my friend, Marigold Heavenly Nostrils!
Charmed.
Why have your parents not offered me moonbeam nectar yet?
She's house-broken, right?
Yeah, this was a brilliant idea.
dana

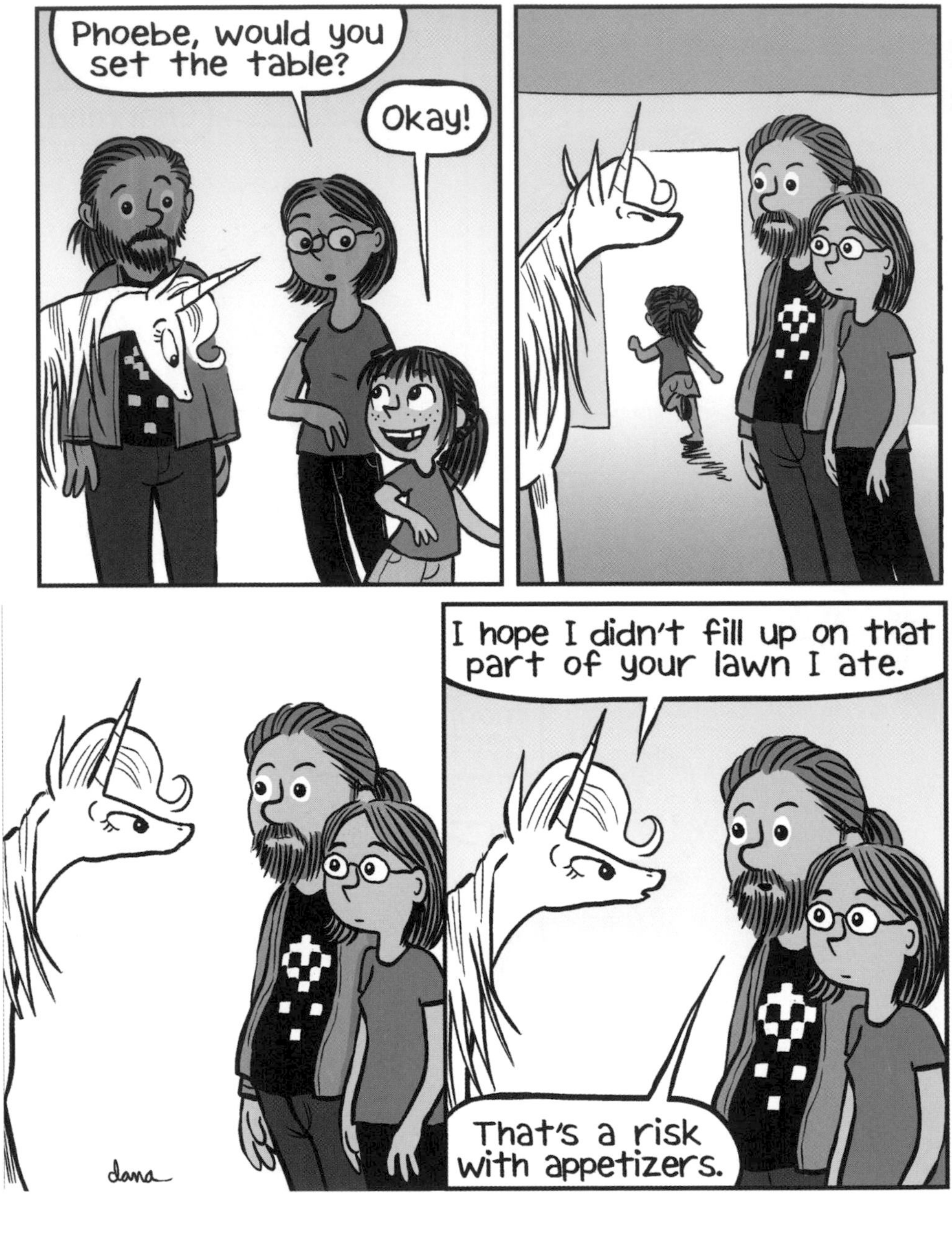
Phoebe, would you set the table?
Okay!
I hope I didn't fill up on that part of your lawn I ate.
That's a risk with appetizers.
dana

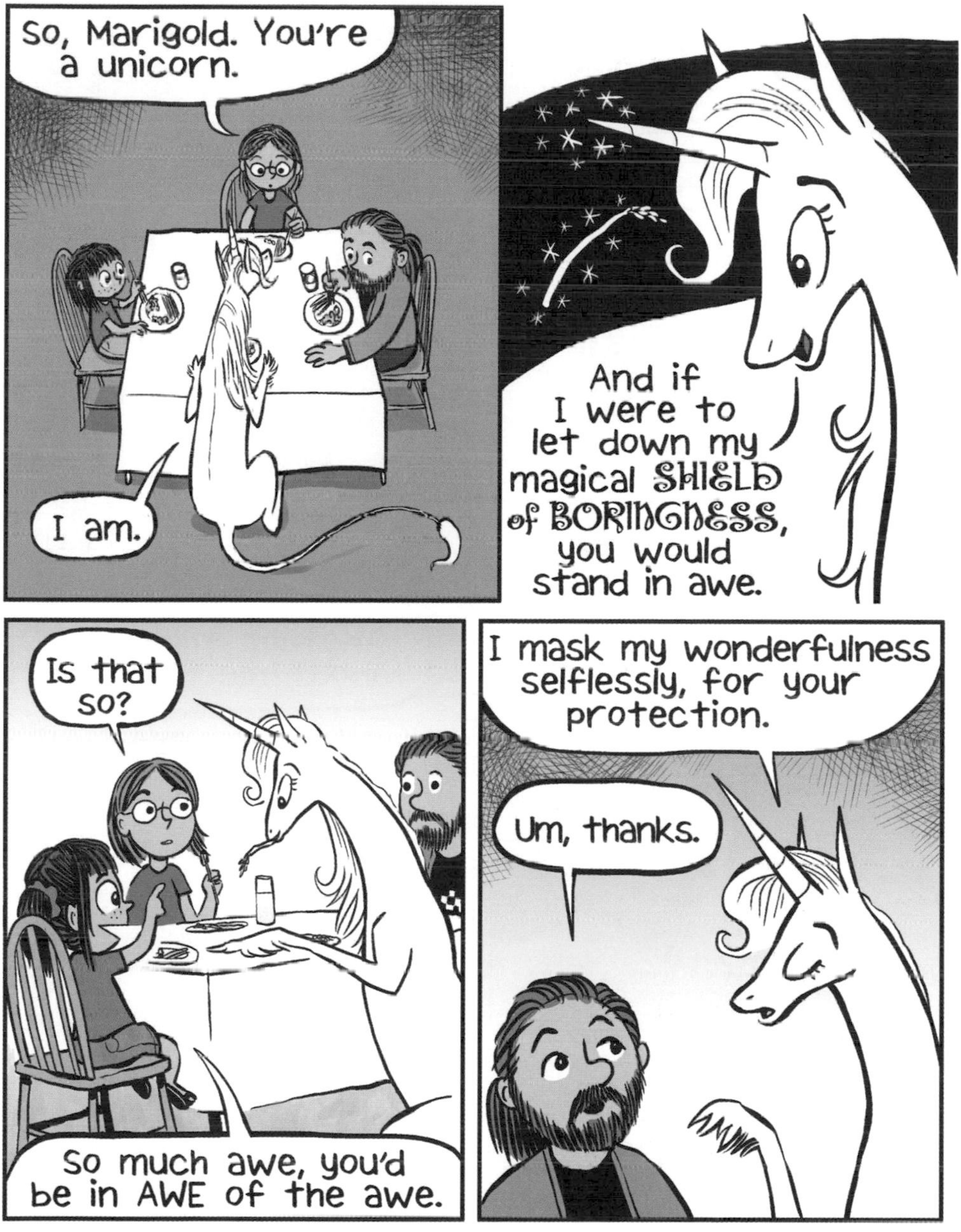
So, Marigold. You're a unicorn.
I am.
And if I were to let down my magical SHIELD of BORINGNESS, you would stand in awe.
Is that so?
So much awe, you'd be in AWE of the awe.
I mask my wonderfulness selflessly, for your protection.
Um, thanks.

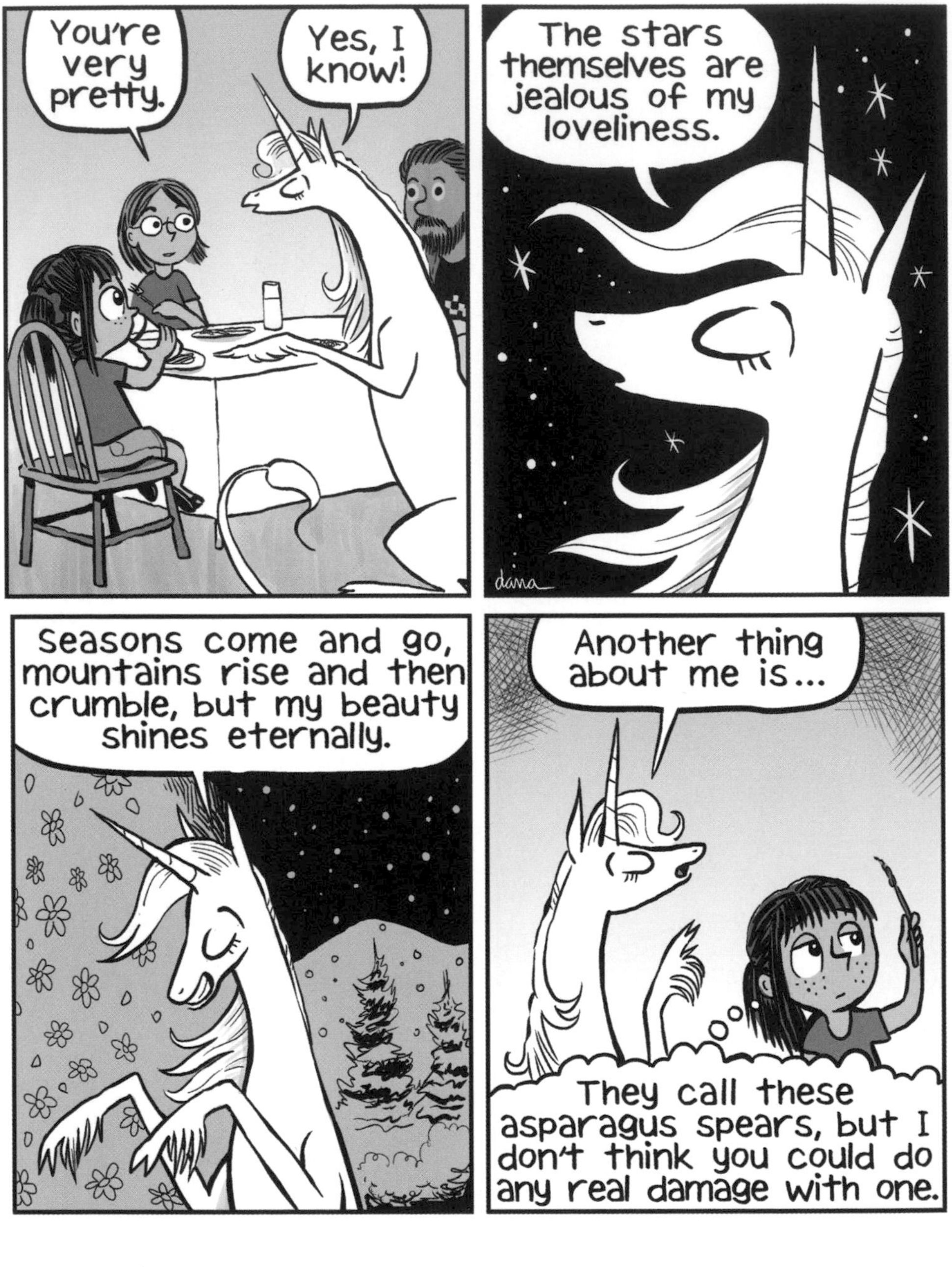
You're very pretty.
Yes, I know!
The stars themselves are jealous of my loveliness.
dana
Seasons come and go, mountains rise and then crumble, but my beauty shines eternally.
Another thing about me is...
They call these asparagus spears, but I don't think you could do any real damage with one.

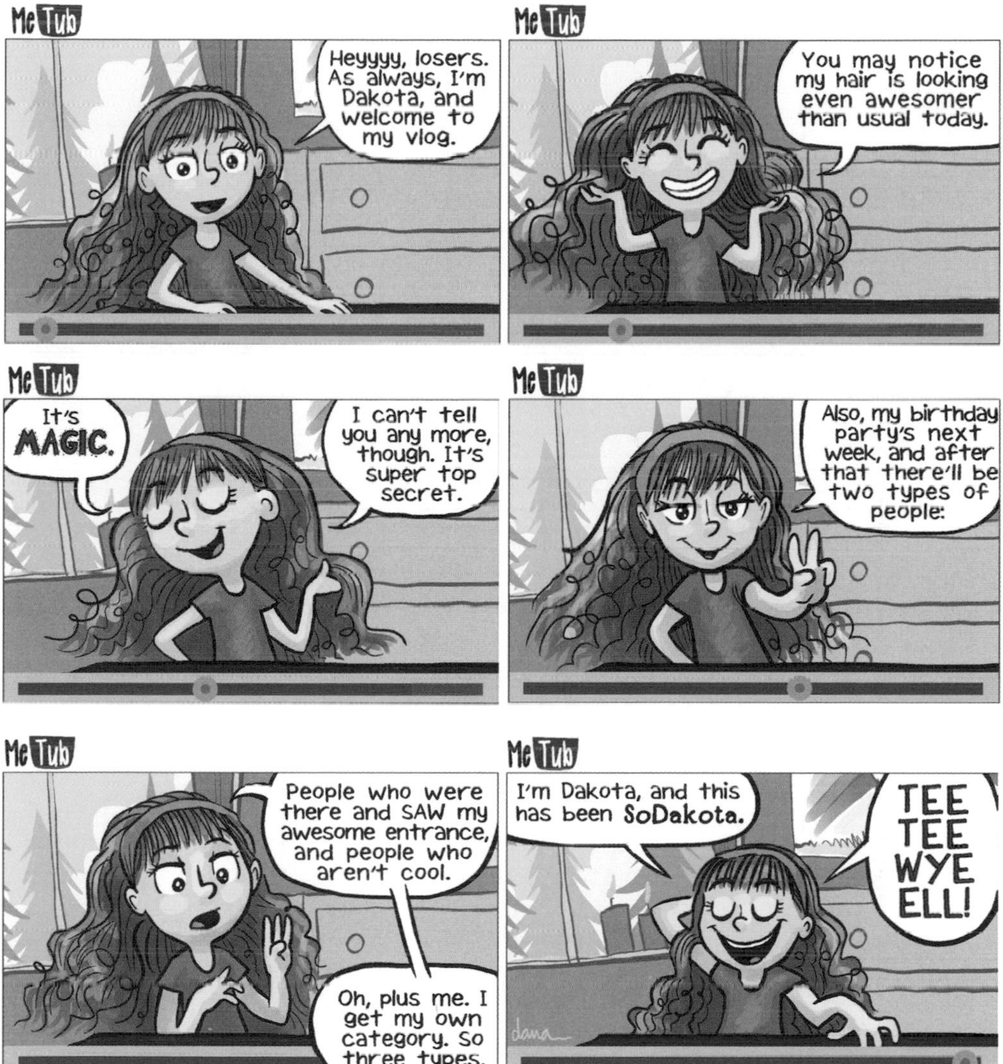
MeTub
Heyyyy, losers. As always, I'm Dakota, and welcome to my vlog.
MeTub
You may notice my hair is looking even awesomer than usual today.
MeTub
It's MAGIC.
I can't tell you any more, though. It's super top secret.
MeTub
Also, my birthday party's next week, and after that there'll be two types of people:
MeTub
People who were there and SAW my awesome entrance, and people who aren't cool.
Oh, plus me. I get my own category. So three types.
MeTub
I'm Dakota, and this has been SoDakota.
TEE TEE WYE ELL!
dana

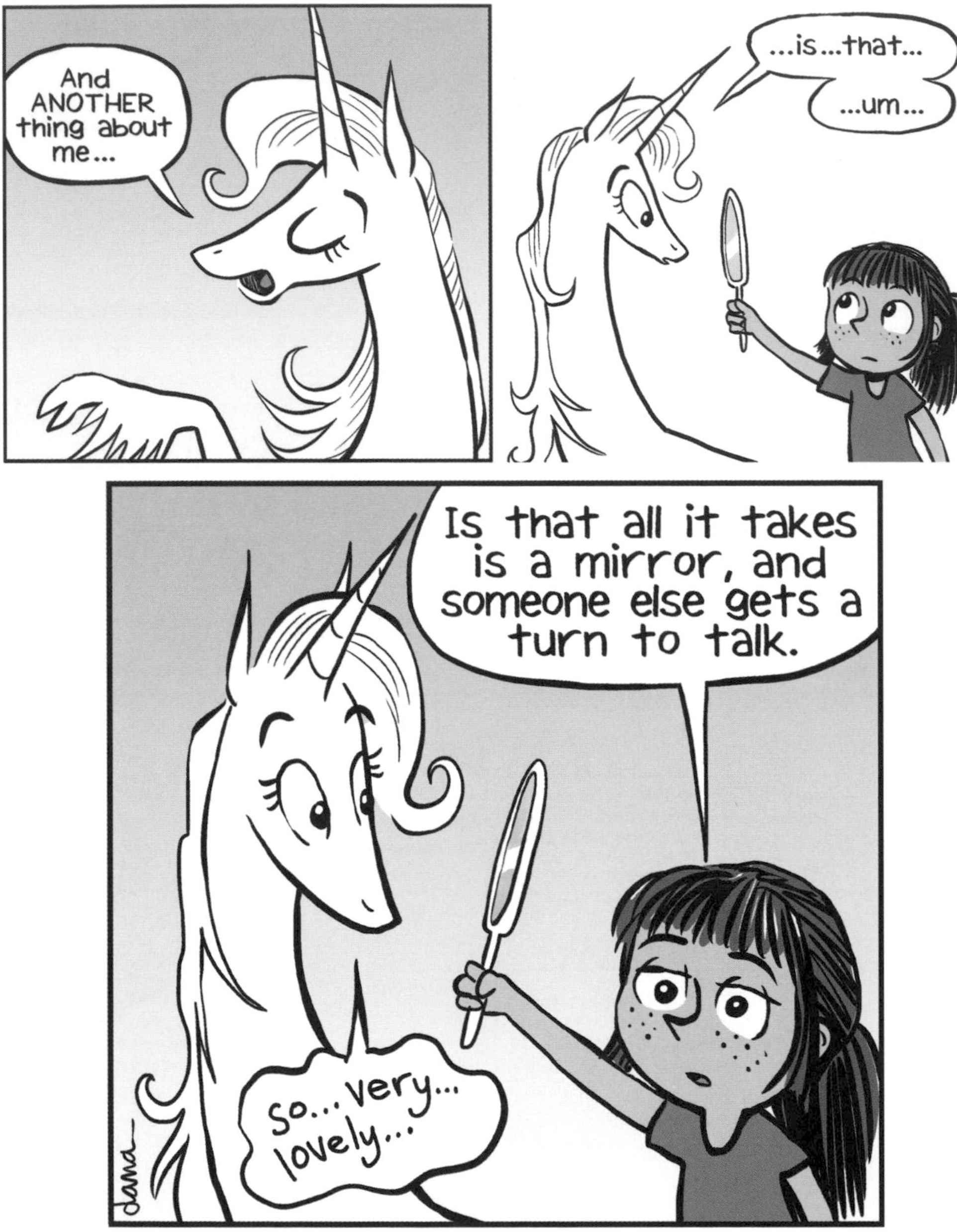
And ANOTHER thing about me...
...is...that...
...um...
Is that all it takes is a mirror, and someone else gets a turn to talk.
so...very... lovely...
dana

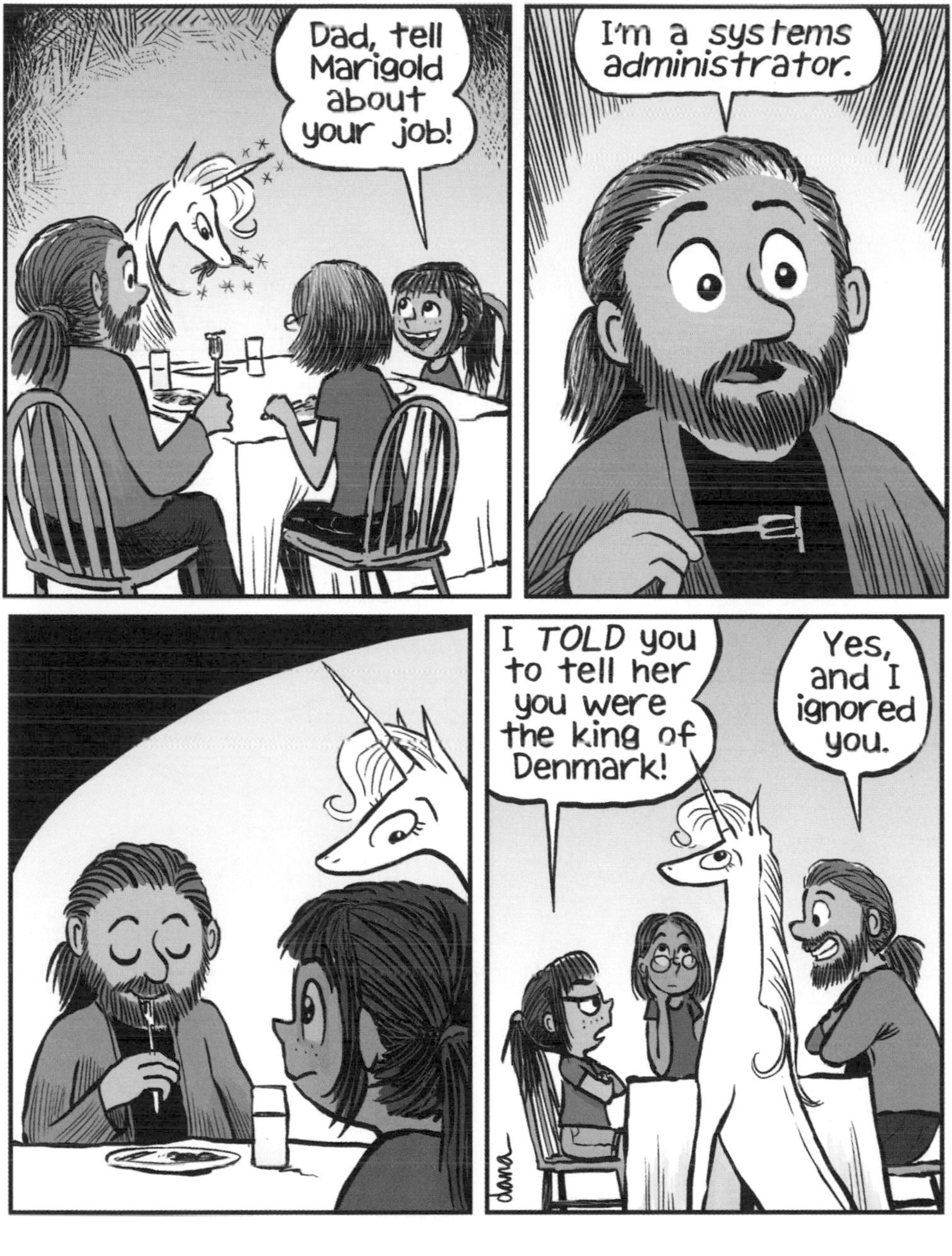
Dad, tell Marigold about your job!
I'm a *systems* administrator.
I *TOLD* you to tell her you were the king of Denmark!
Yes, and I ignored you.
dana

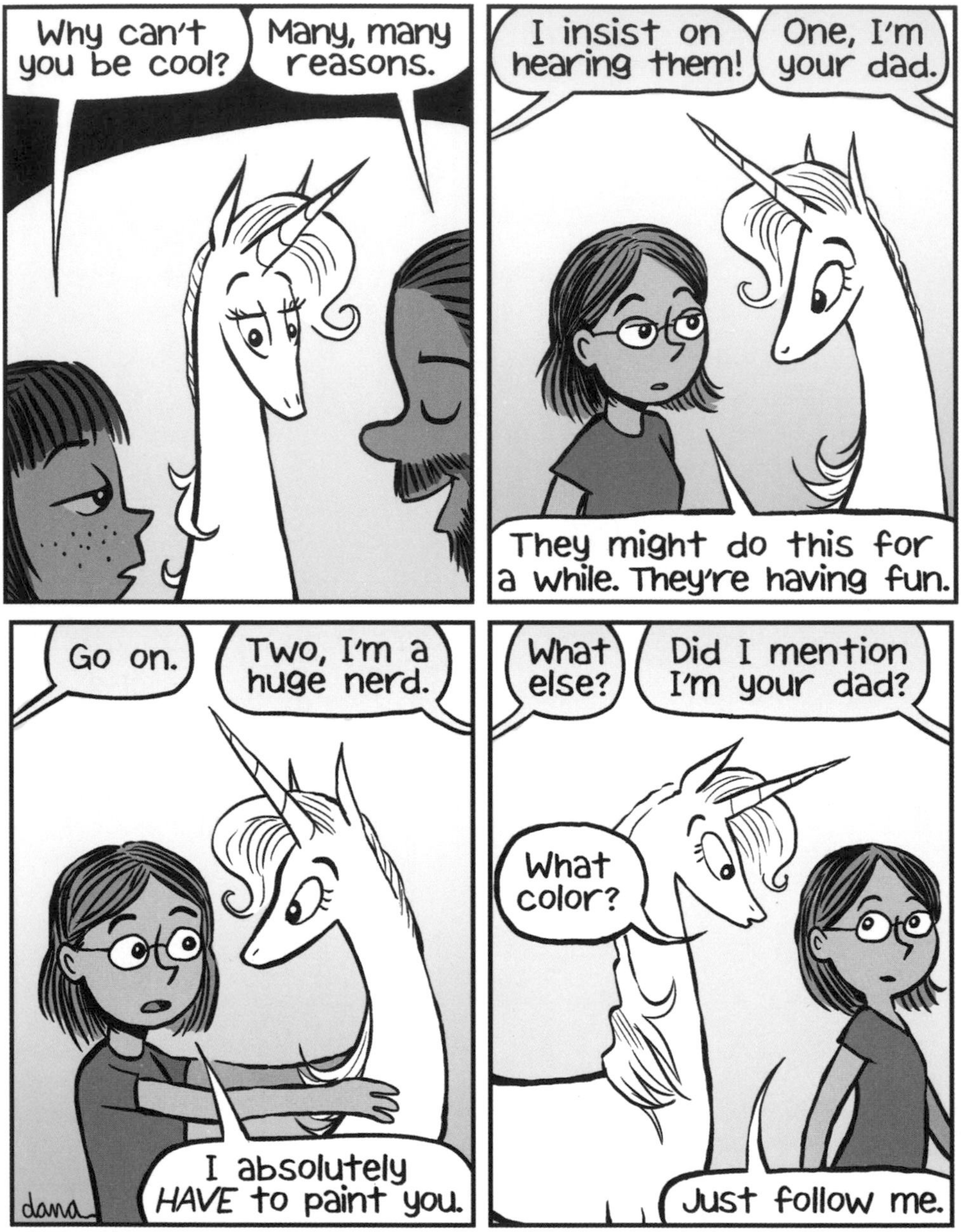
Why can't you be cool?
Many, many reasons.
I insist on hearing them!
One, I'm your dad.
They might do this for a while. They're having fun.
Go on.
Two, I'm a huge nerd.
I absolutely *HAVE* to paint you.
dana
What else?
Did I mention I'm your dad?
What color?
Just follow me.

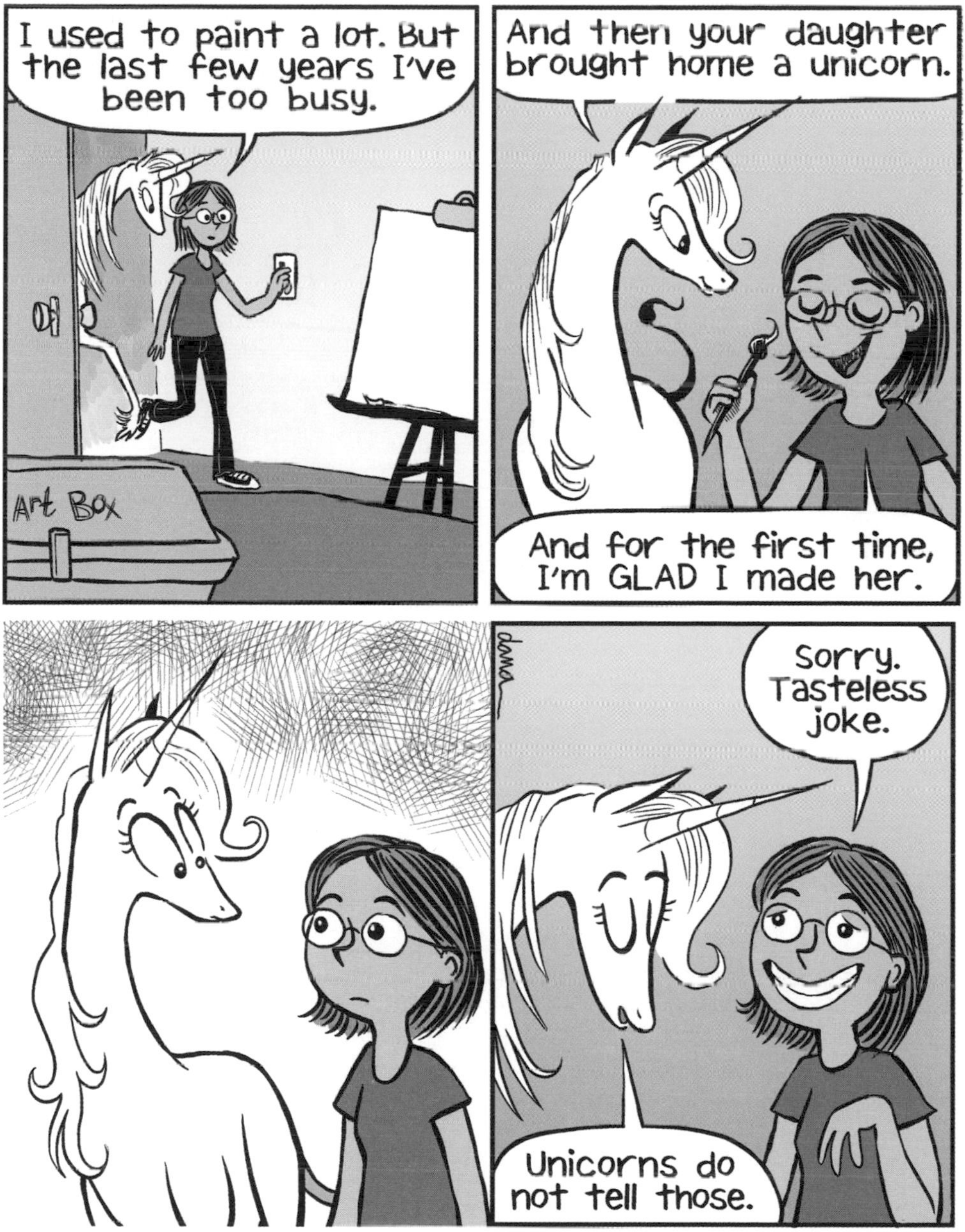
I used to paint a lot. But the last few years I've been too busy.
Art Box
And then your daughter brought home a unicorn.
And for the first time, I'm GLAD I made her.
dana
Sorry. Tasteless joke.
Unicorns do not tell those.

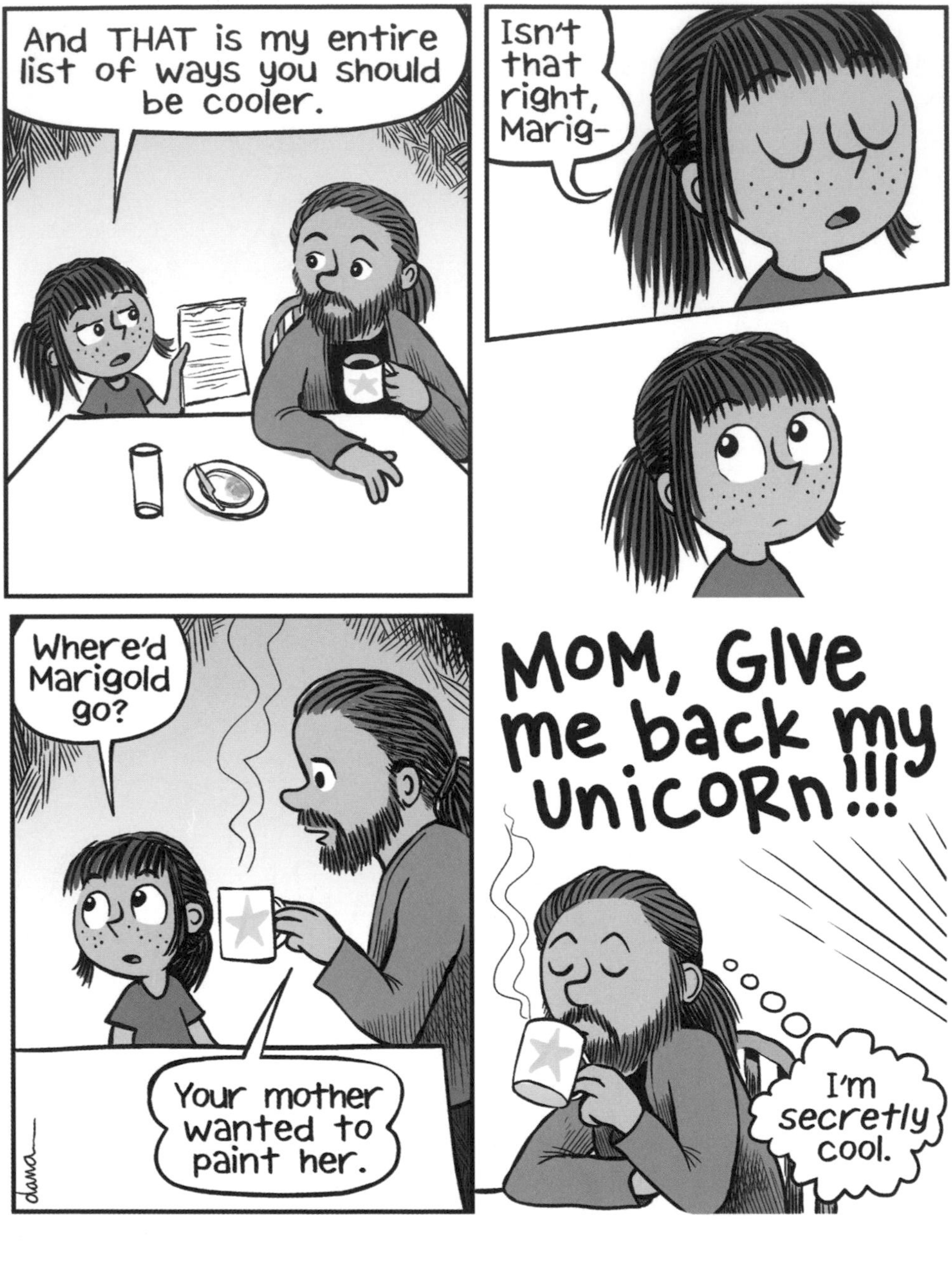
And THAT is my entire list of ways you should be cooler.
Isn't that right, Marig-
Where'd Marigold go?
Your mother wanted to paint her.
MOM, GIVE me back my UNICORN!!!
I'm *secretly* cool.
dana

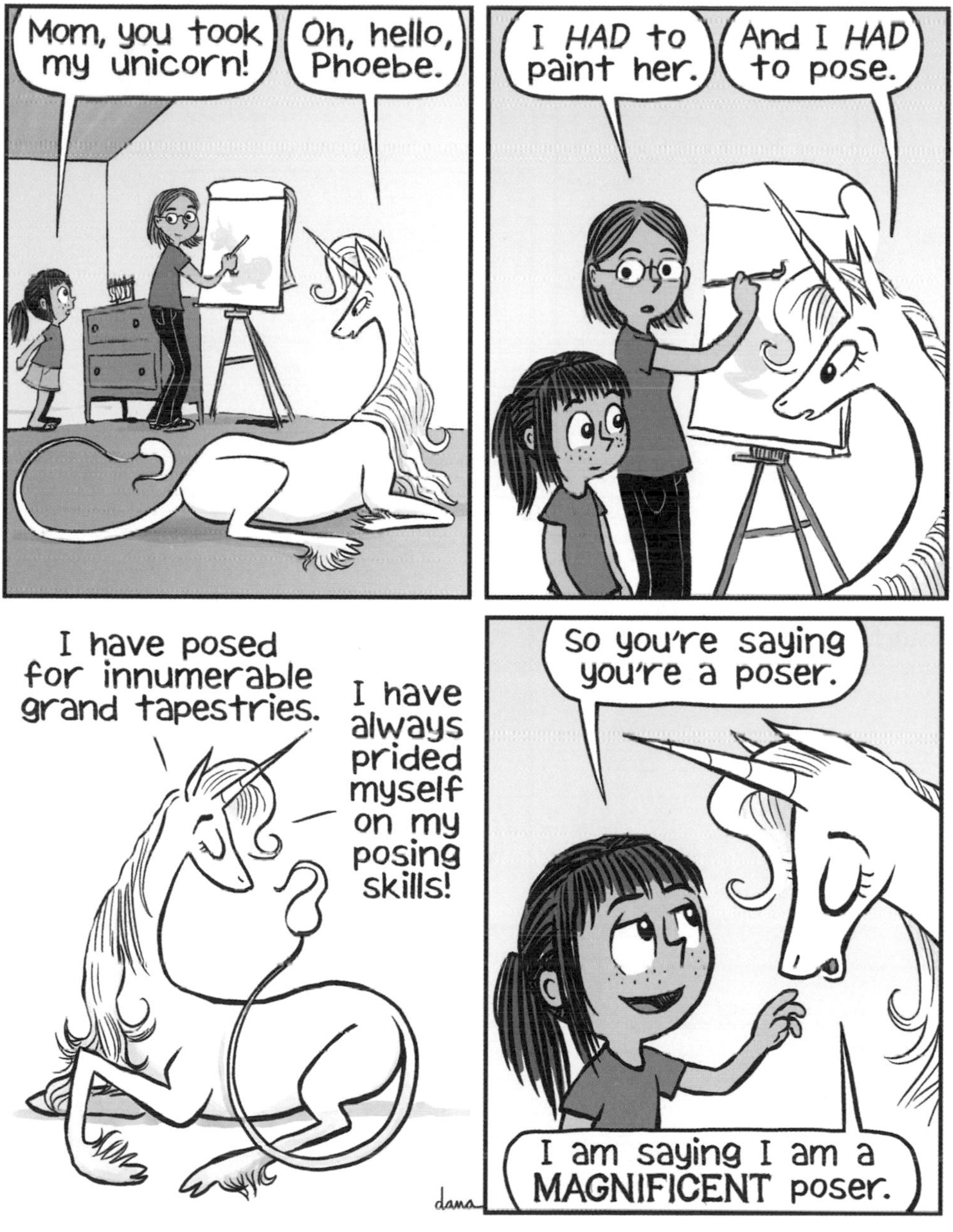
Mom, you took my unicorn!
Oh, hello, Phoebe.
I *HAD* to paint her.
And I *HAD* to pose.
I have posed for innumerable grand tapestries.
I have always prided myself on my posing skills!
So you're saying you're a poser.
I am saying I am a **MAGNIFICENT** poser.
dana

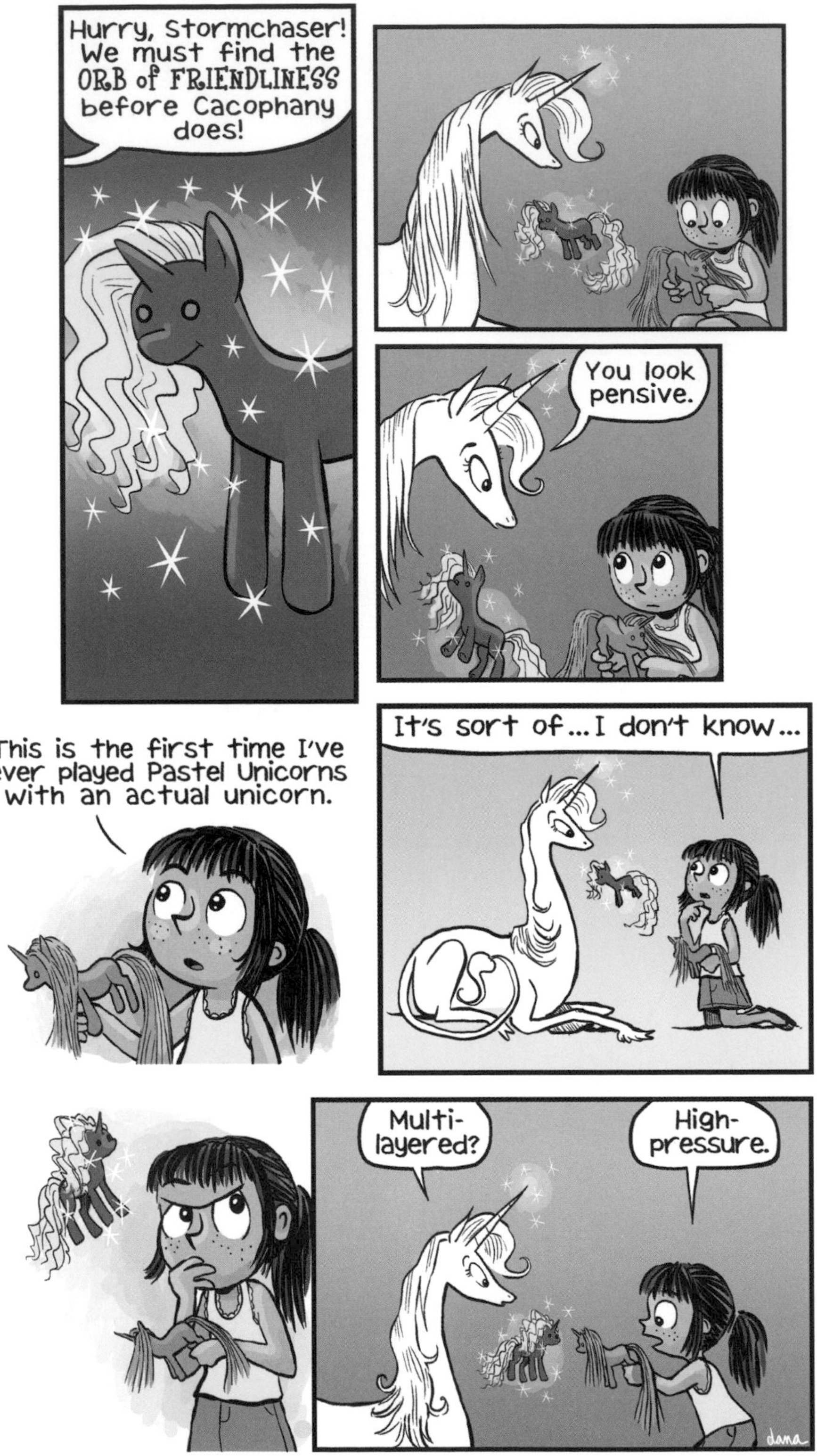
Hurry, Stormchaser! We must find the ORB of FRIENDLINESS before Cacophany does!
You look pensive.
This is the first time I've ever played Pastel Unicorns with an actual unicorn.
It's sort of... I don't know...
Multi-layered?
High-pressure.
dana

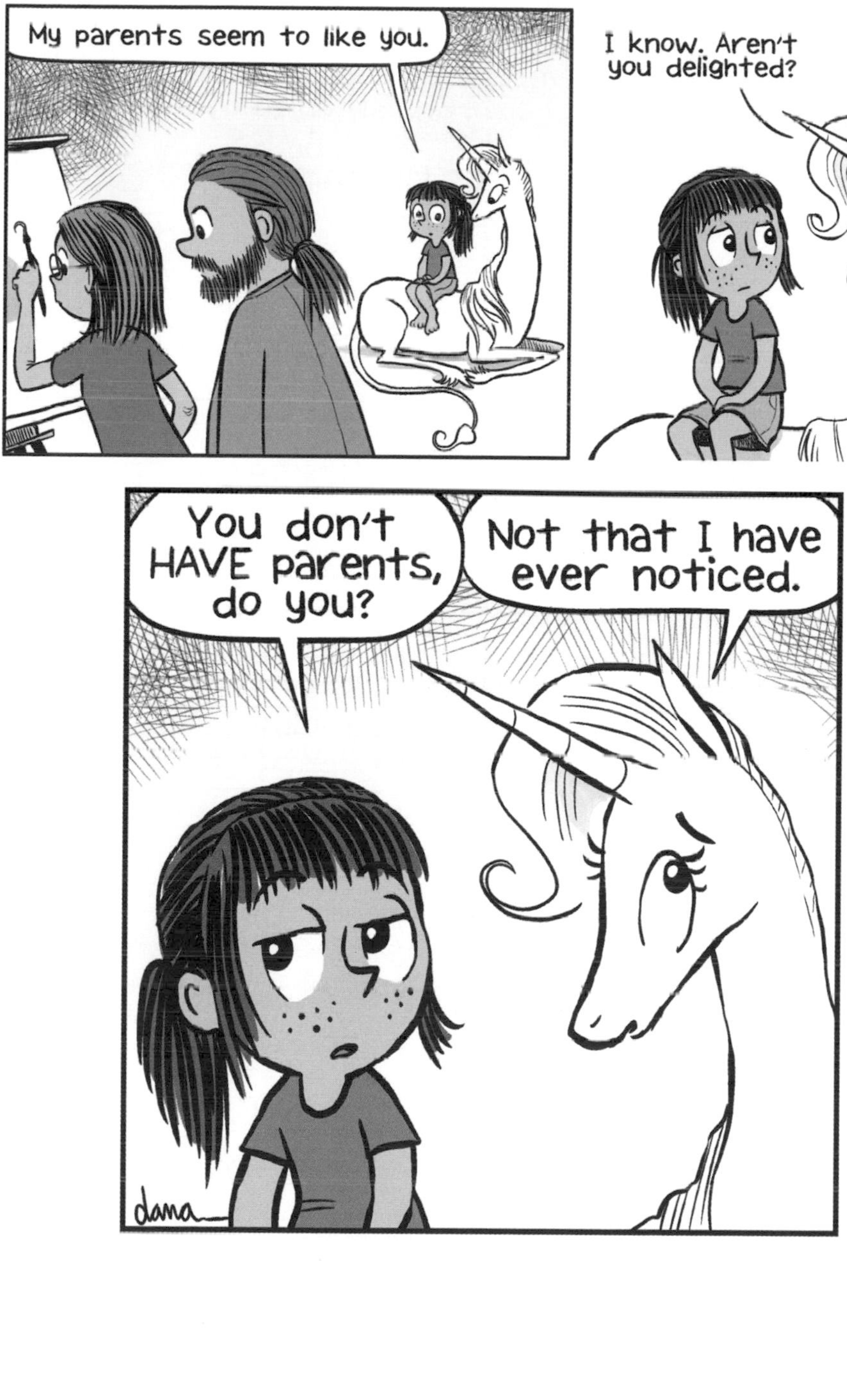
My parents seem to like you.
I know. Aren't you delighted?
You don't HAVE parents, do you?
Not that I have ever noticed.
dana

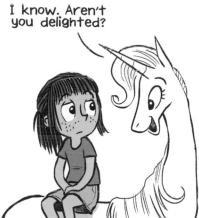

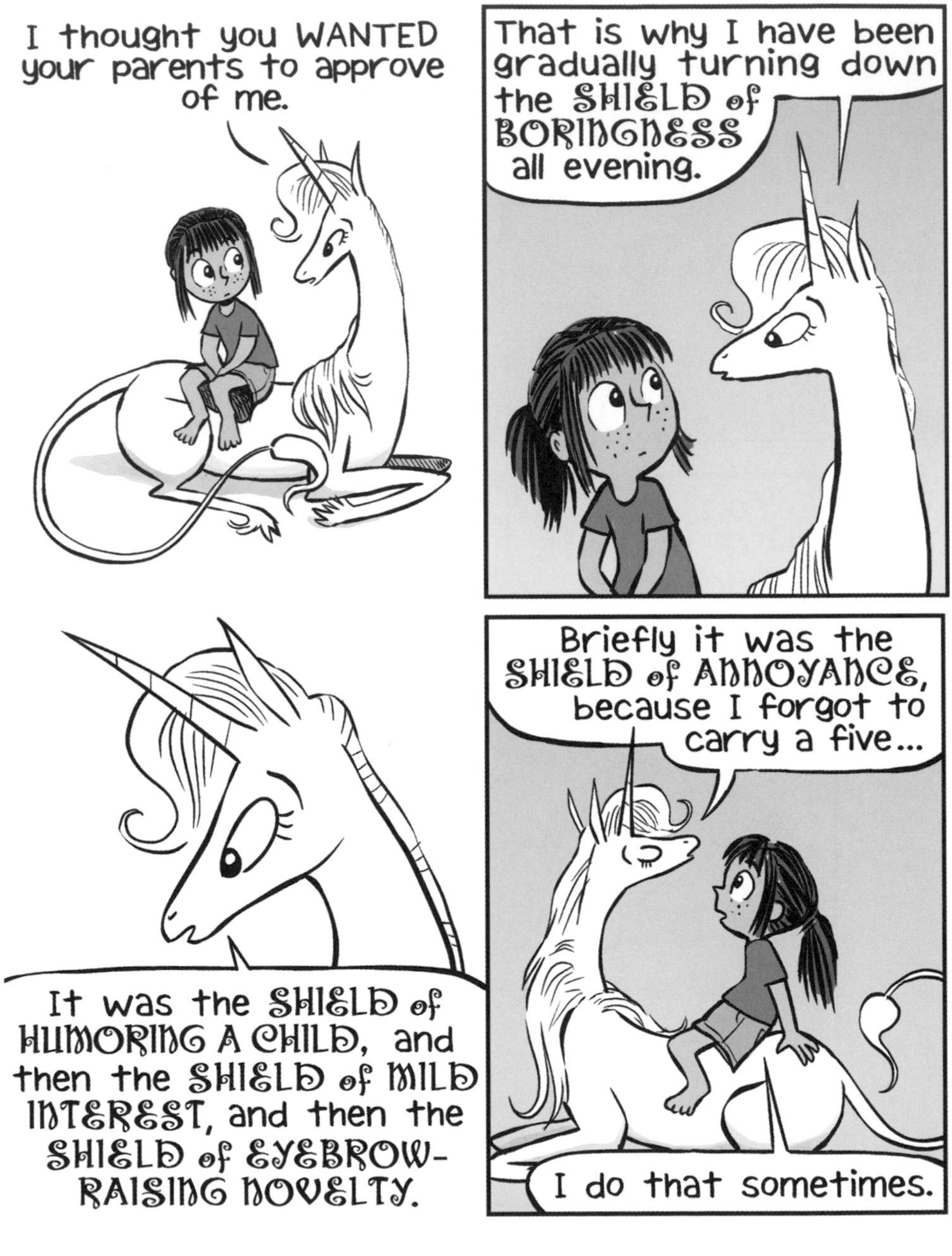
I thought you WANTED your parents to approve of me.
That is why I have been gradually turning down the SHIELD of BORINGNESS all evening.
It was the SHIELD of HUMORING A CHILD, and then the SHIELD of MILD INTEREST, and then the SHIELD of EYEBROW-RAISING NOVELTY.
Briefly it was the SHIELD of ANNOYANCE, because I forgot to carry a five...
I do that sometimes.

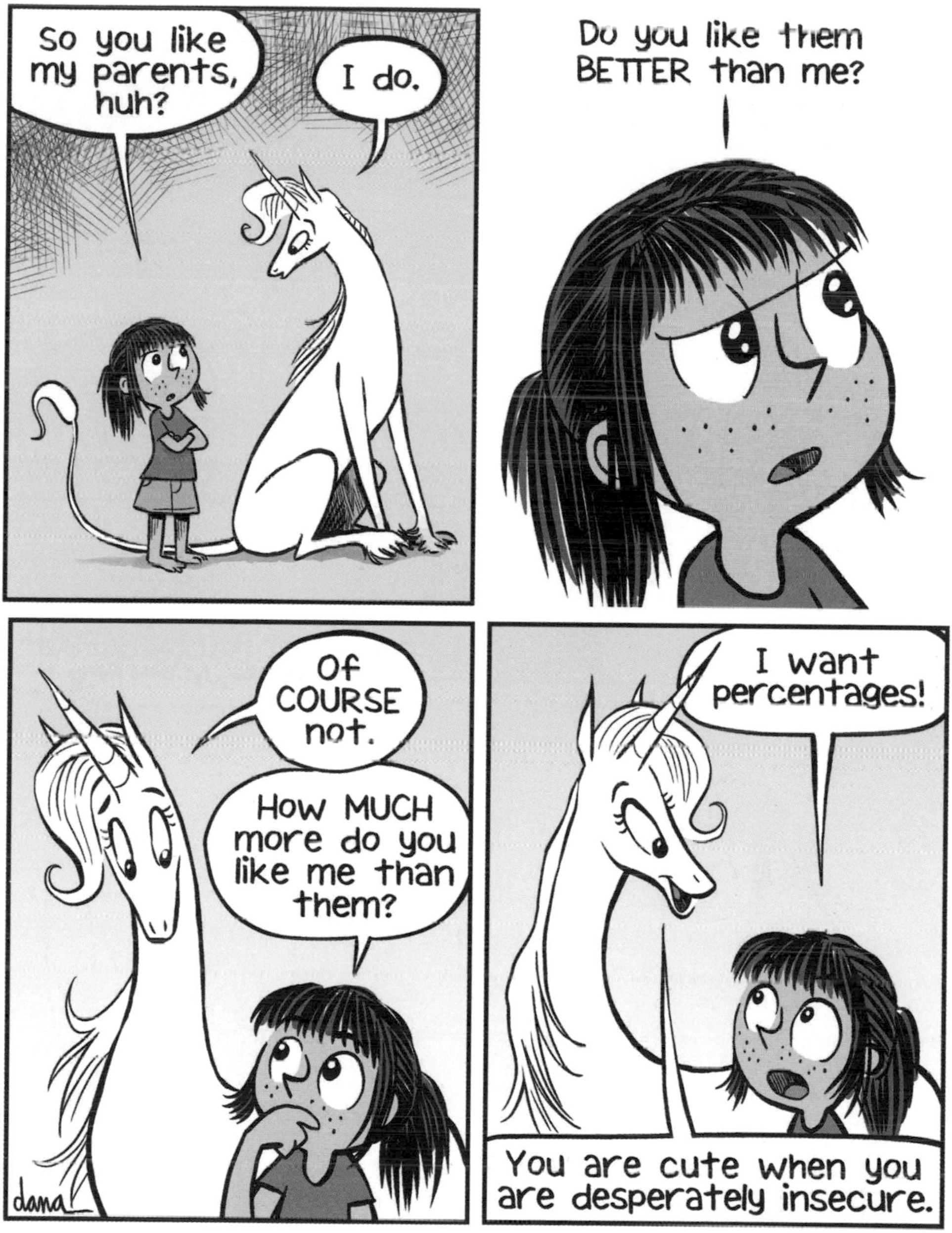
So you like my parents, huh?
I do.
Do you like them BETTER than me?
Of COURSE not.
How MUCH more do you like me than them?
dana
I want percentages!
You are cute when you are desperately insecure.

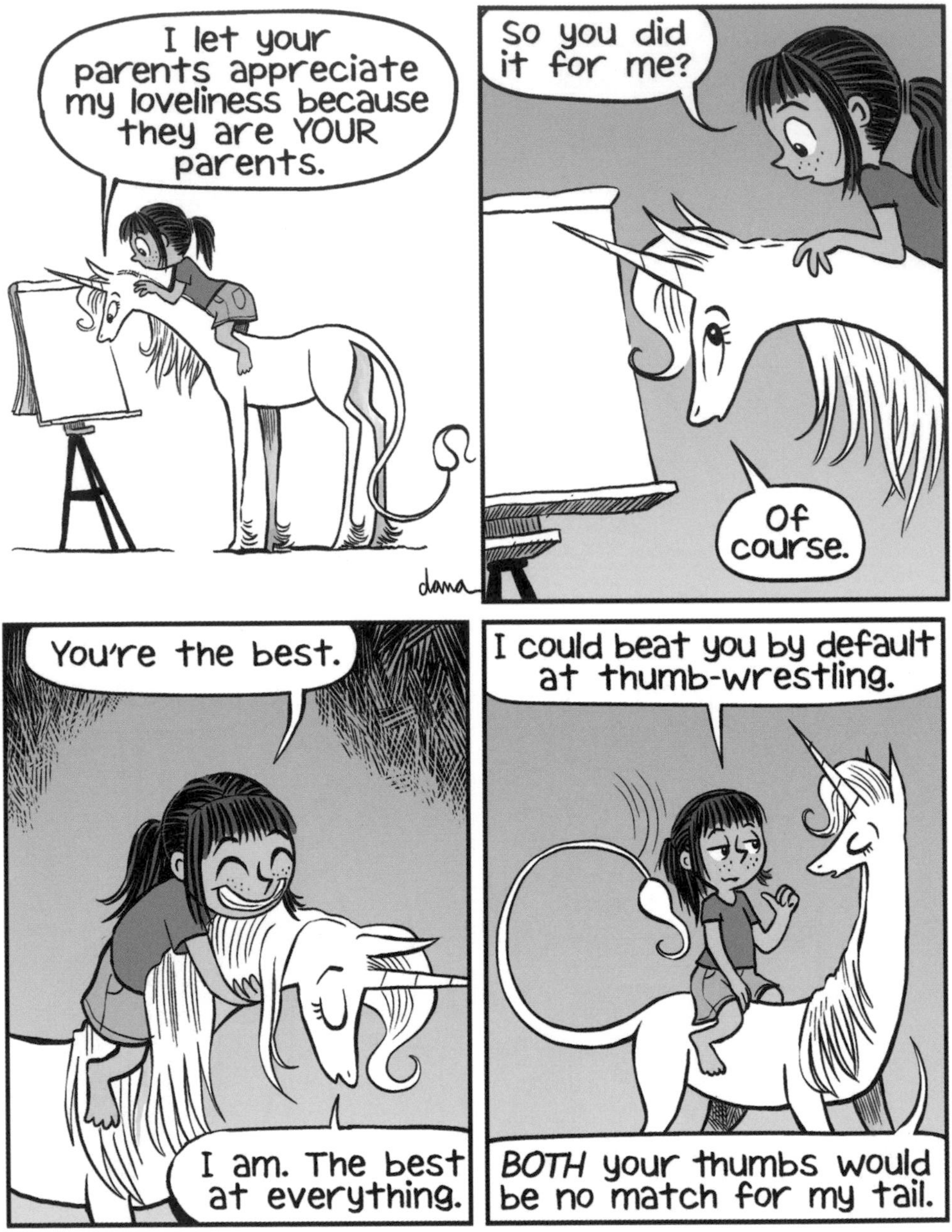
I let your parents appreciate my loveliness because they are YOUR parents.
dana
So you did it for me?
Of course.
You're the best.
I am. The best at everything.
I could beat you by default at thumb-wrestling.
BOTH your thumbs would be no match for my tail.

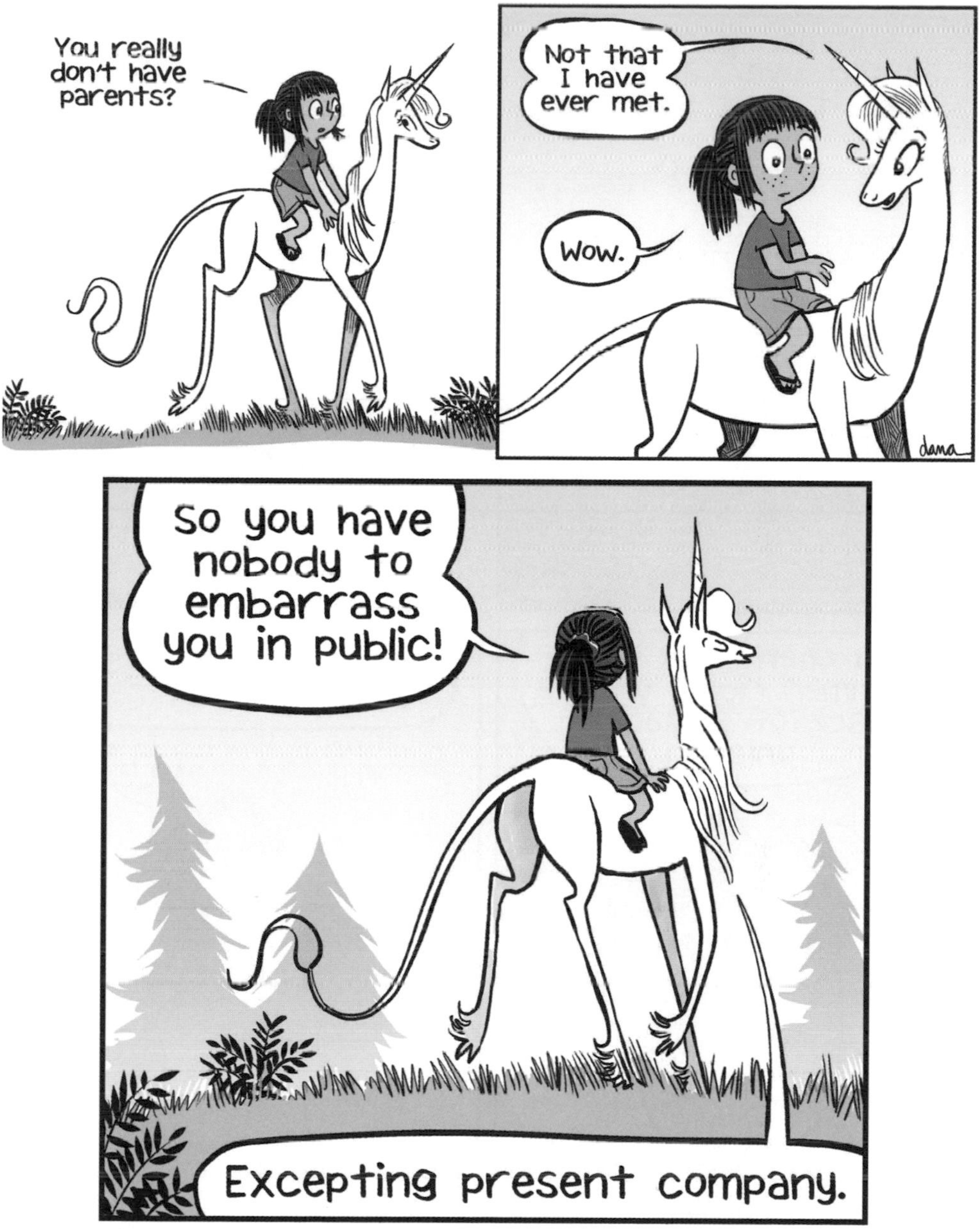
You really don't have parents?
Not that I have ever met.
Wow.
So you have nobody to embarrass you in public!
Excepting present company.
dana

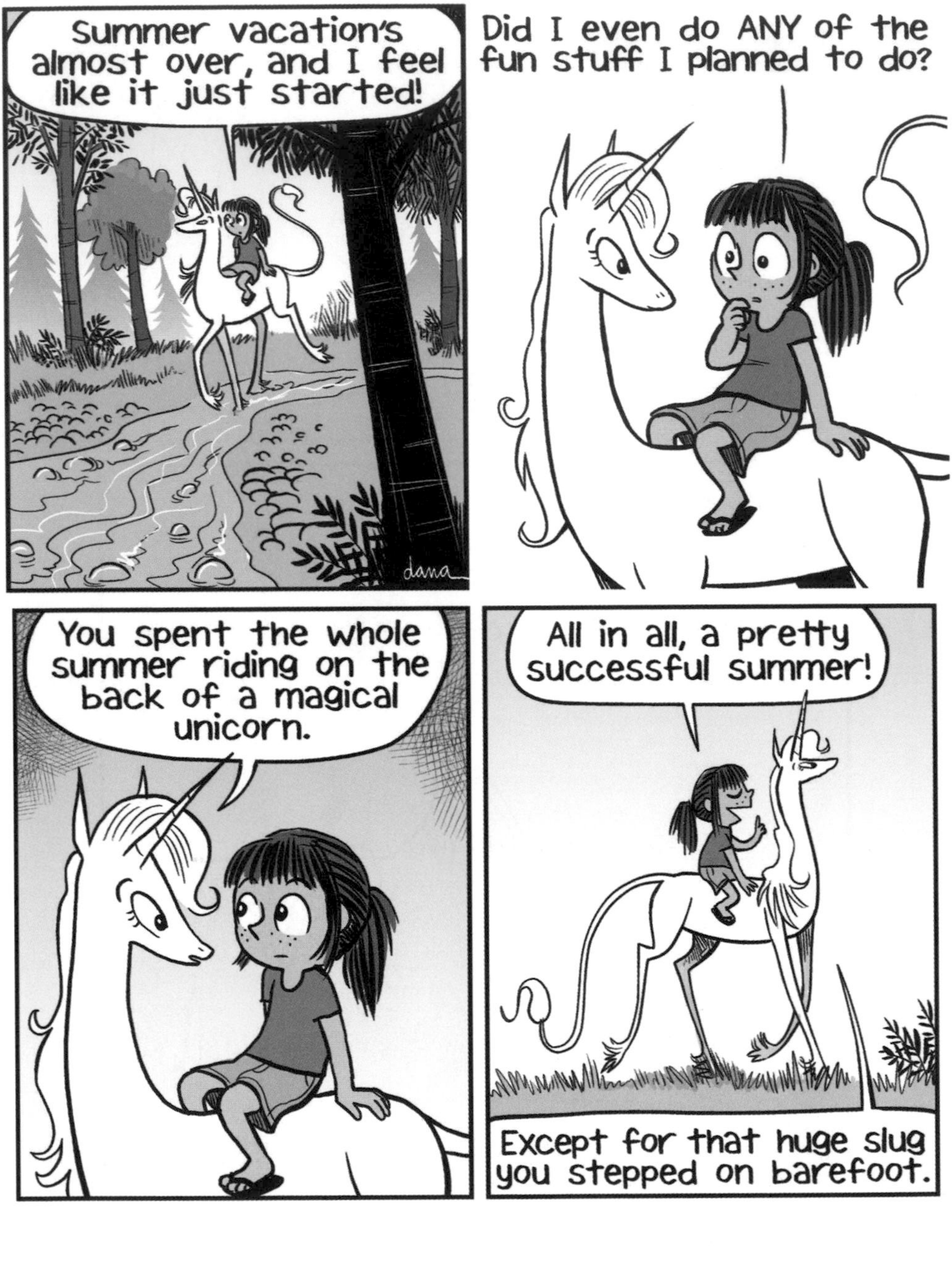

Summer vacation's almost over, and I feel like it just started!
Did I even do ANY of the fun stuff I planned to do?
You spent the whole summer riding on the back of a magical unicorn.
All in all, a pretty successful summer!
Except for that huge slug you stepped on barefoot.
dana

Dad, what was life like before the internet?
I knew this day would come.
That one day, you would ask about the BEFORE TIMES.
It was a dark and brutal age, when typewriters roamed the land and IGNORANCE and BOREDOM reigned.
It was VERY DIFFICULT to waste time watching videos of cats.
I'm going outside now.
Outside! I remember outside.
maow

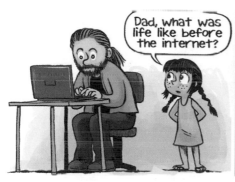

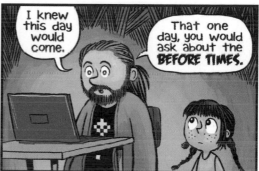

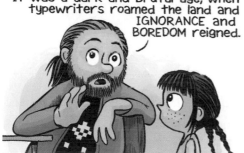

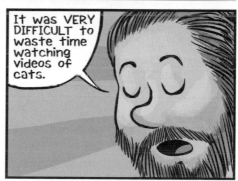

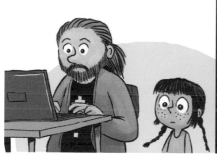

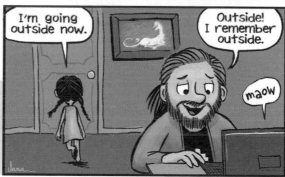

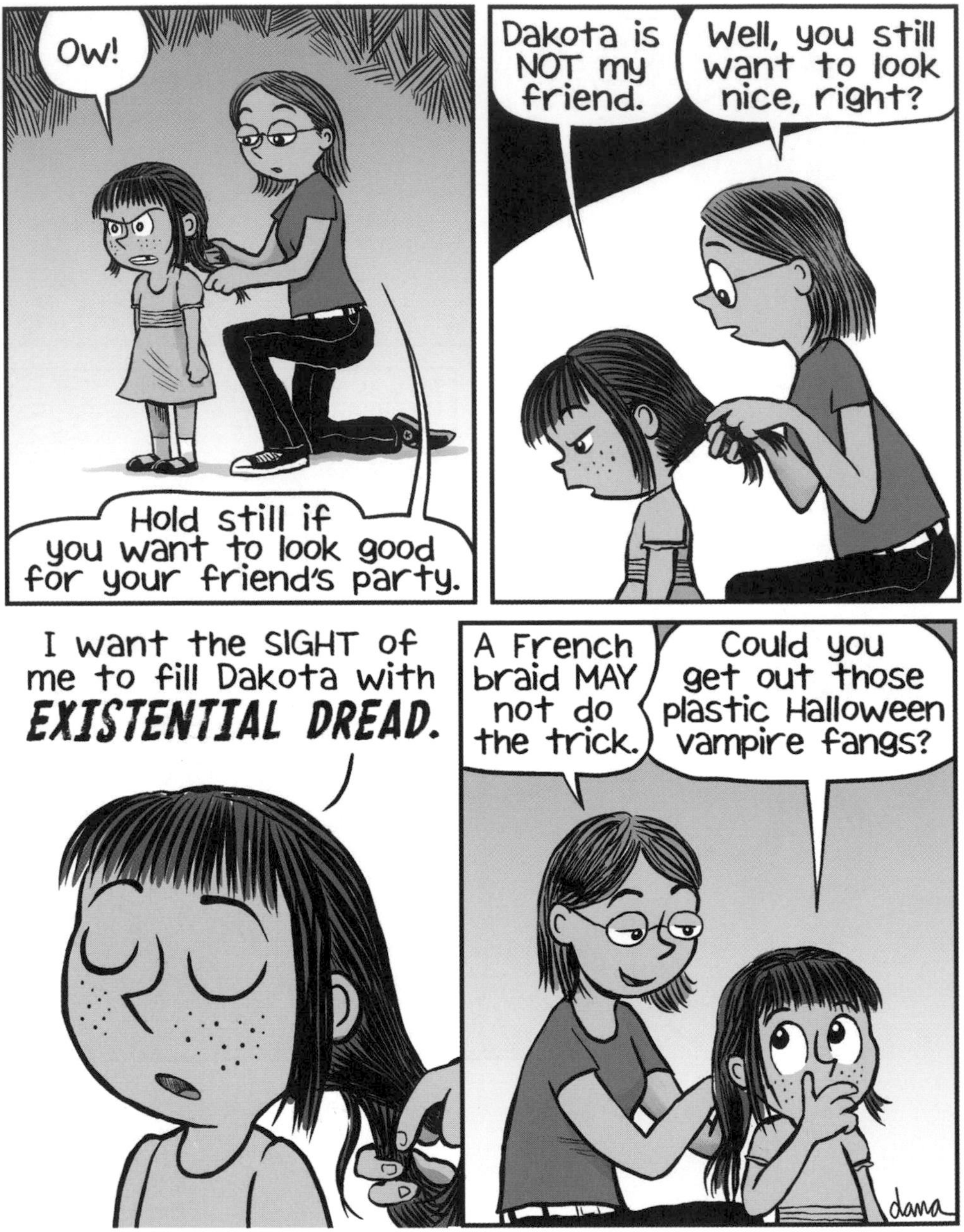
Ow!
Hold still if you want to look good for your friend's party.
Dakota is NOT my friend.
Well, you still want to look nice, right?
I want the SIGHT of me to fill Dakota with EXISTENTIAL DREAD.
A French braid MAY not do the trick.
Could you get out those plastic Halloween vampire fangs?
dana

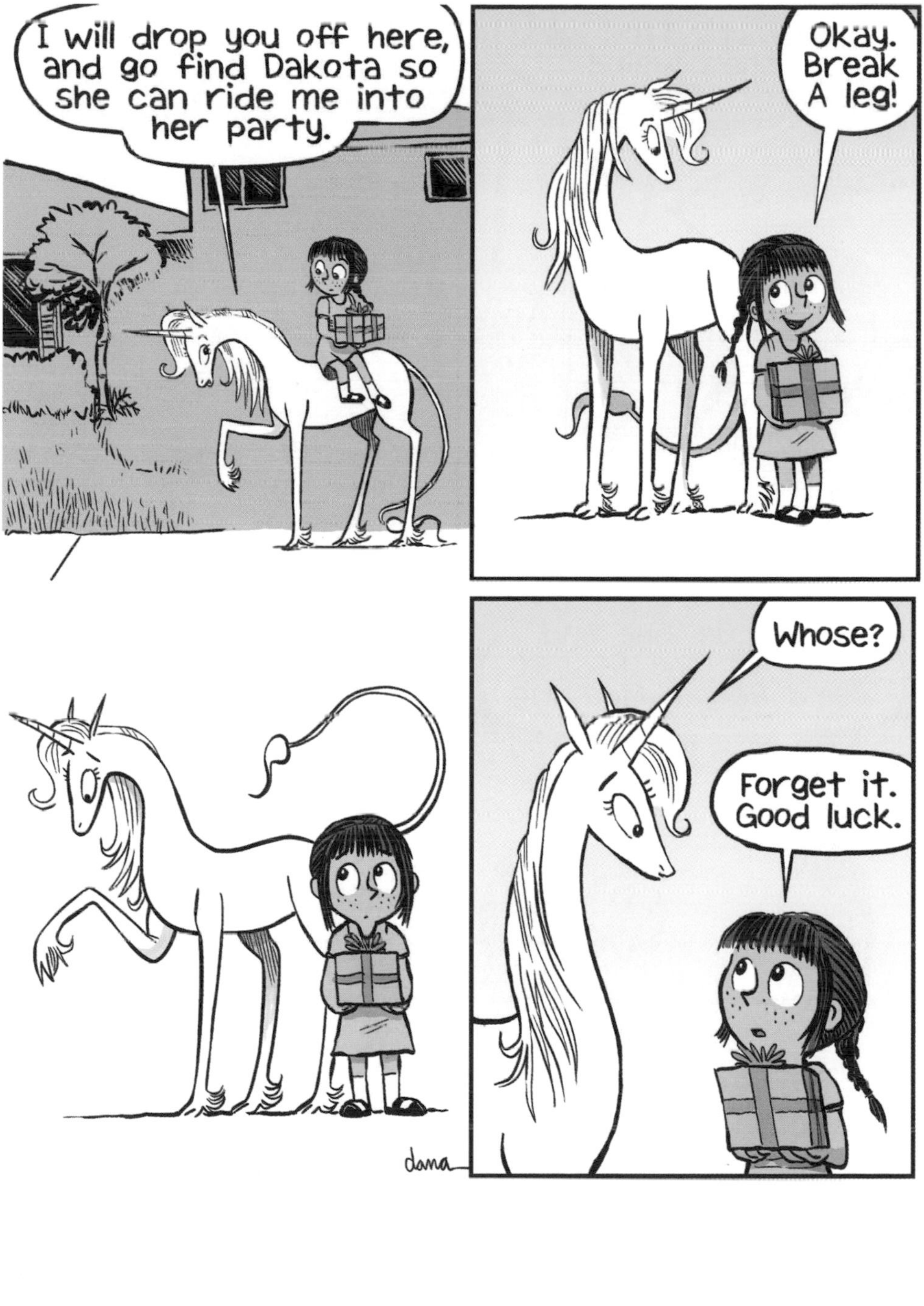
I will drop you off here, and go find Dakota so she can ride me into her party.
Okay. Break A leg!
Whose?
Forget it. Good luck.
dana

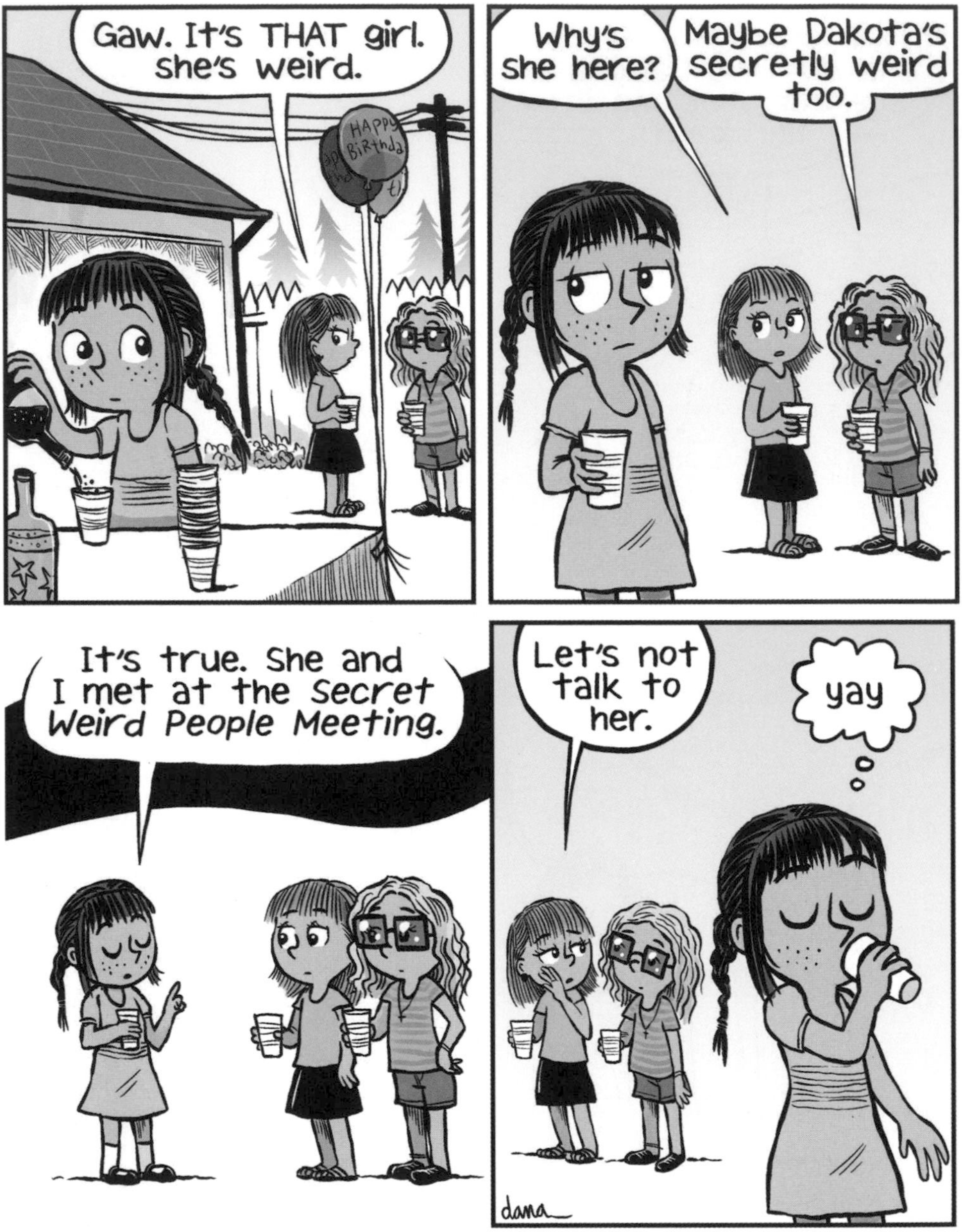
Gaw. It's THAT girl. she's weird.
Why's she here?
Maybe Dakota's secretly weird too.
It's true. She and I met at the Secret Weird People Meeting.
Let's not talk to her.
yay
dana

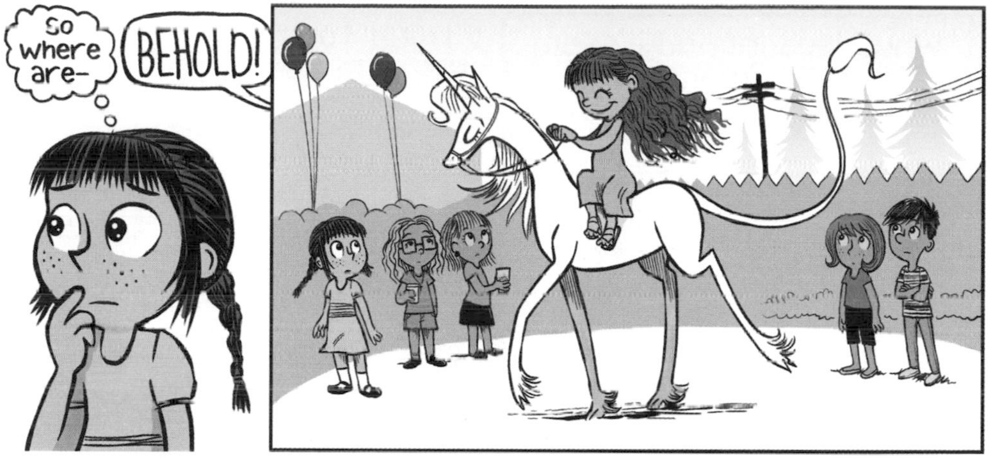
So where are-
BEHOLD!

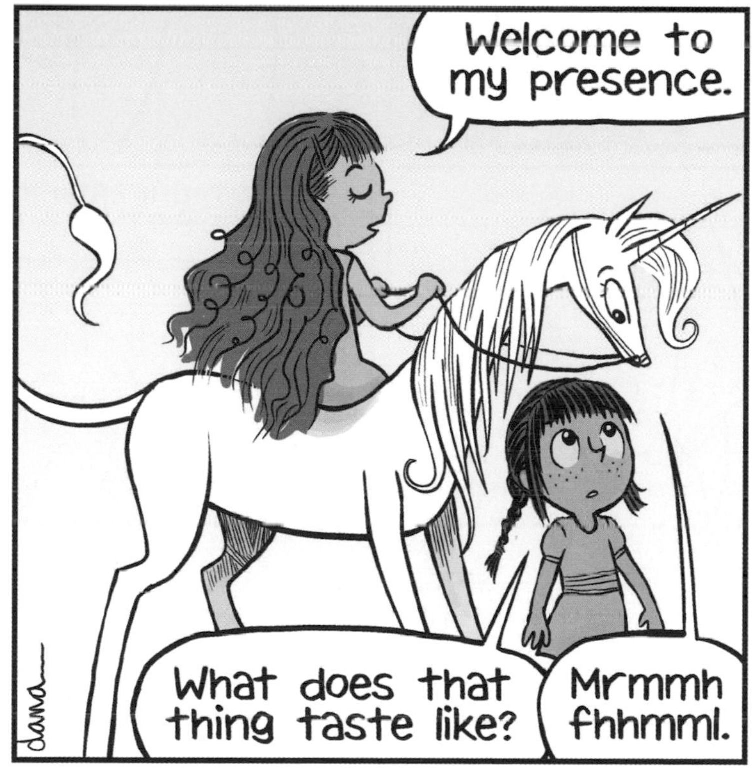
Welcome to my presence.
What does that thing taste like?
Mrmmh fhhmml.

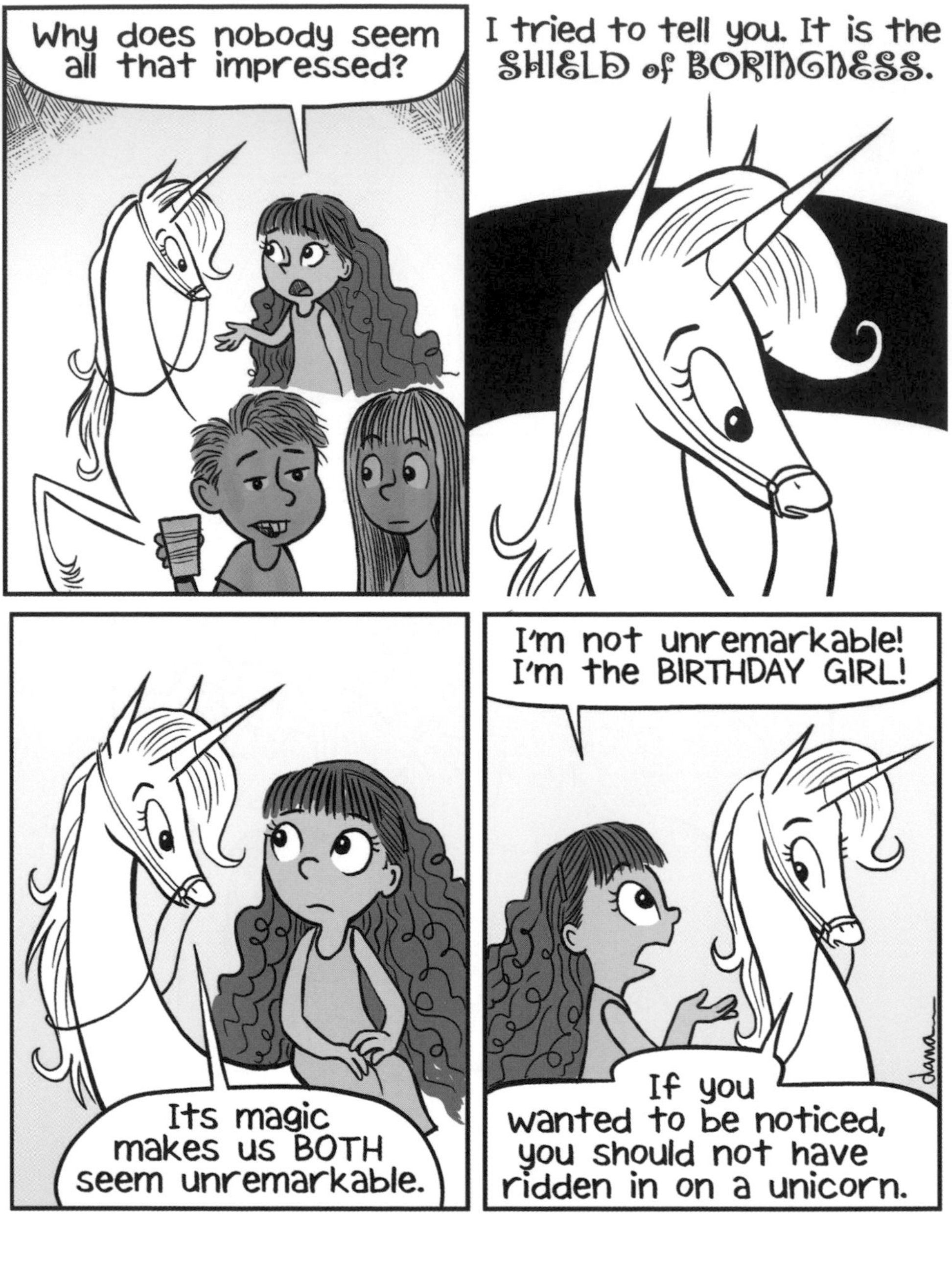
Why does nobody seem all that impressed?
I tried to tell you. It is the SHIELD of BORINGNESS.
Its magic makes us BOTH seem unremarkable.
I'm not unremarkable! I'm the BIRTHDAY GIRL!
If you wanted to be noticed, you should not have ridden in on a unicorn.
dana

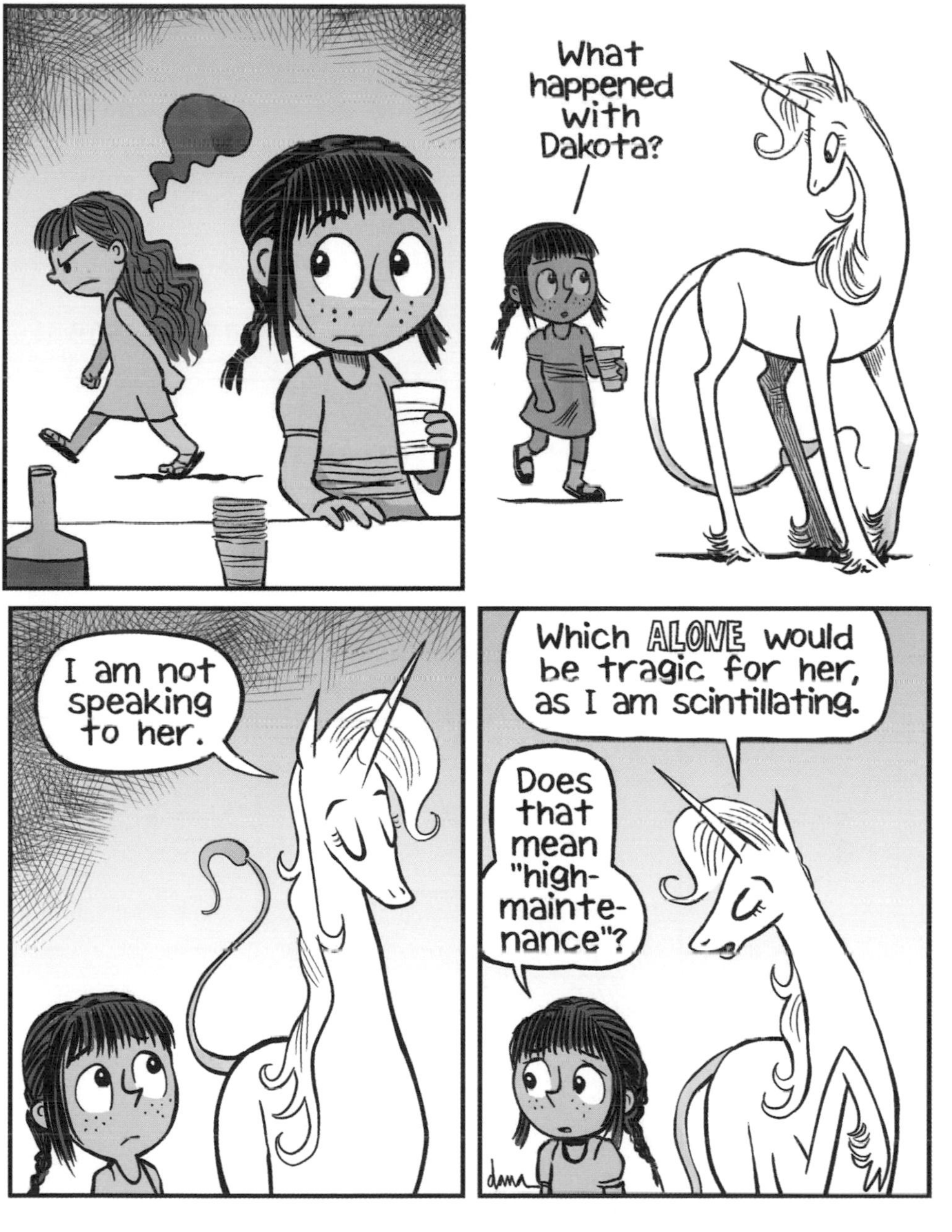
What happened with Dakota?
I am not speaking to her.
Which ALONE would be tragic for her, as I am scintillating.
Does that mean "high-maintenance"?

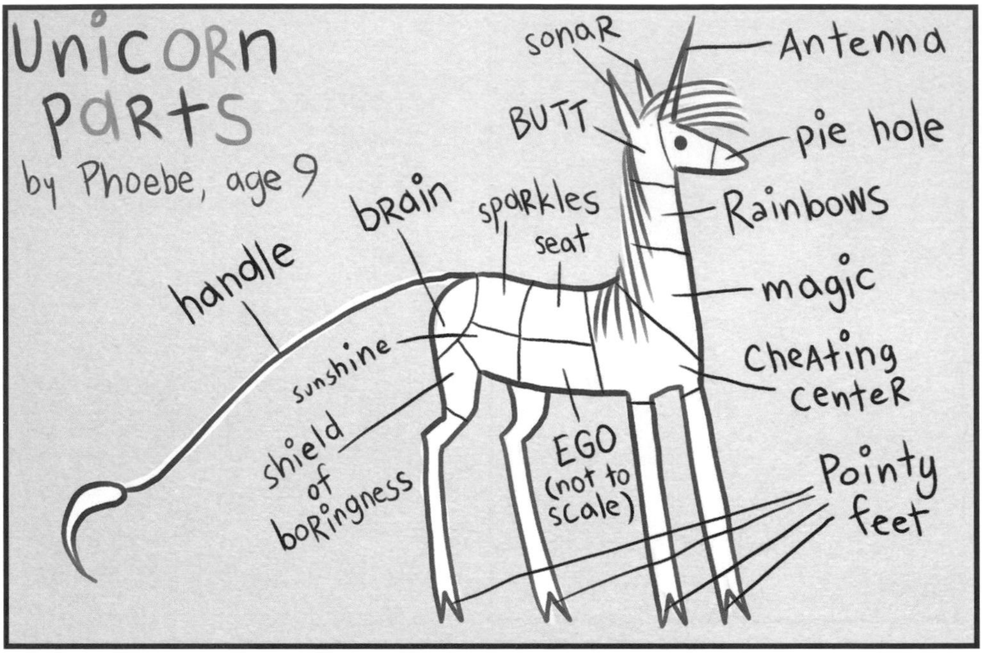
Unicorn parts
by Phoebe, age 9
sonaR
Antenna
BUTT
pie hole
brain
sparkles
seat
Rainbows
handle
magic
sunshine
Cheating center
shield of boringness
EGO (not to scale)
Pointy feet

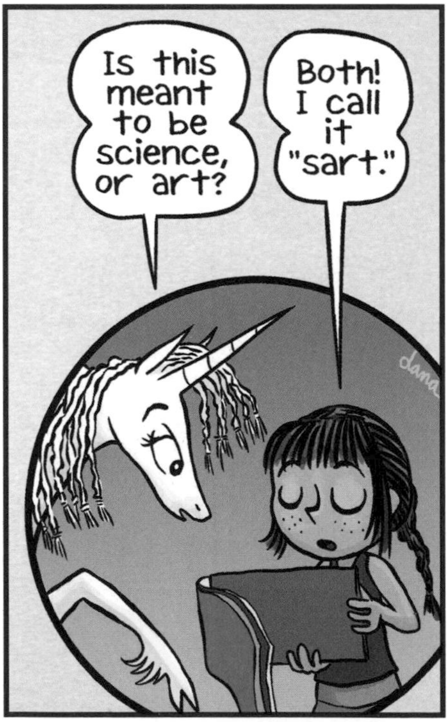
Is this meant to be science, or art?
Both! I call it "sart."

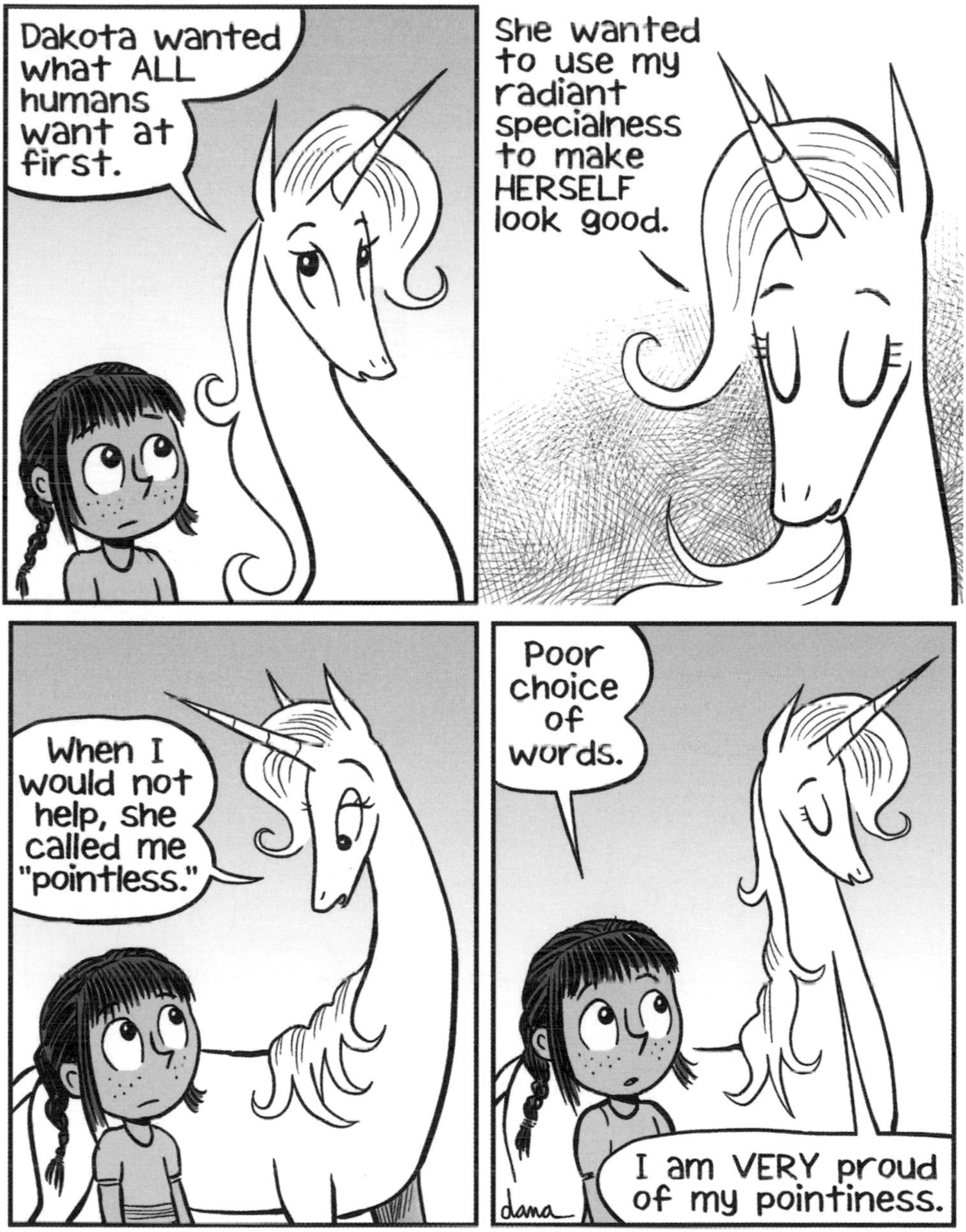
Dakota wanted what ALL humans want at first.
She wanted to use my radiant specialness to make HERSELF look good.
When I would not help, she called me "pointless."
Poor choice of words.
I am VERY proud of my pointiness.
dana

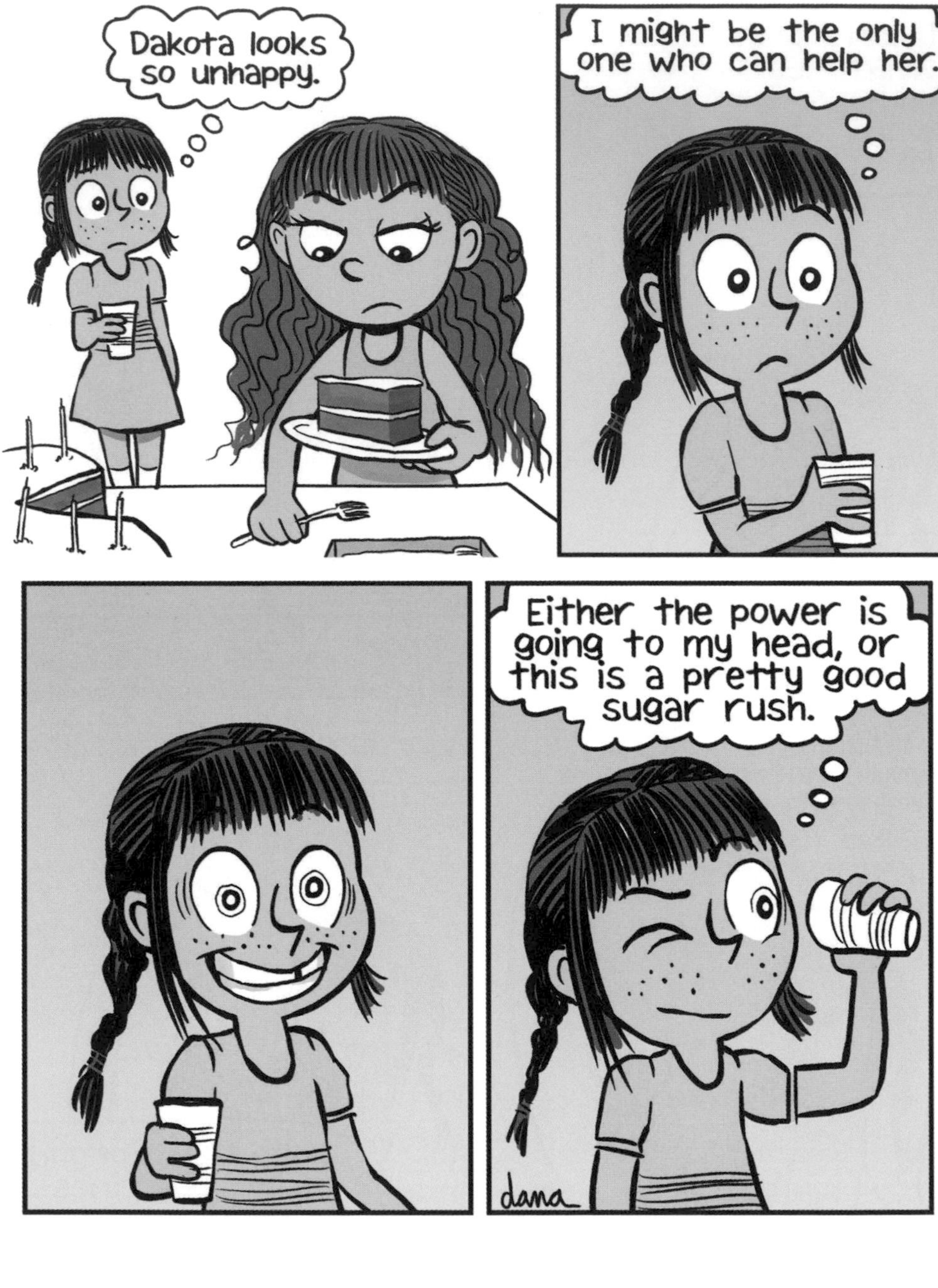
Dakota looks so unhappy.
I might be the only one who can help her.
Either the power is going to my head, or this is a pretty good sugar rush.
dana

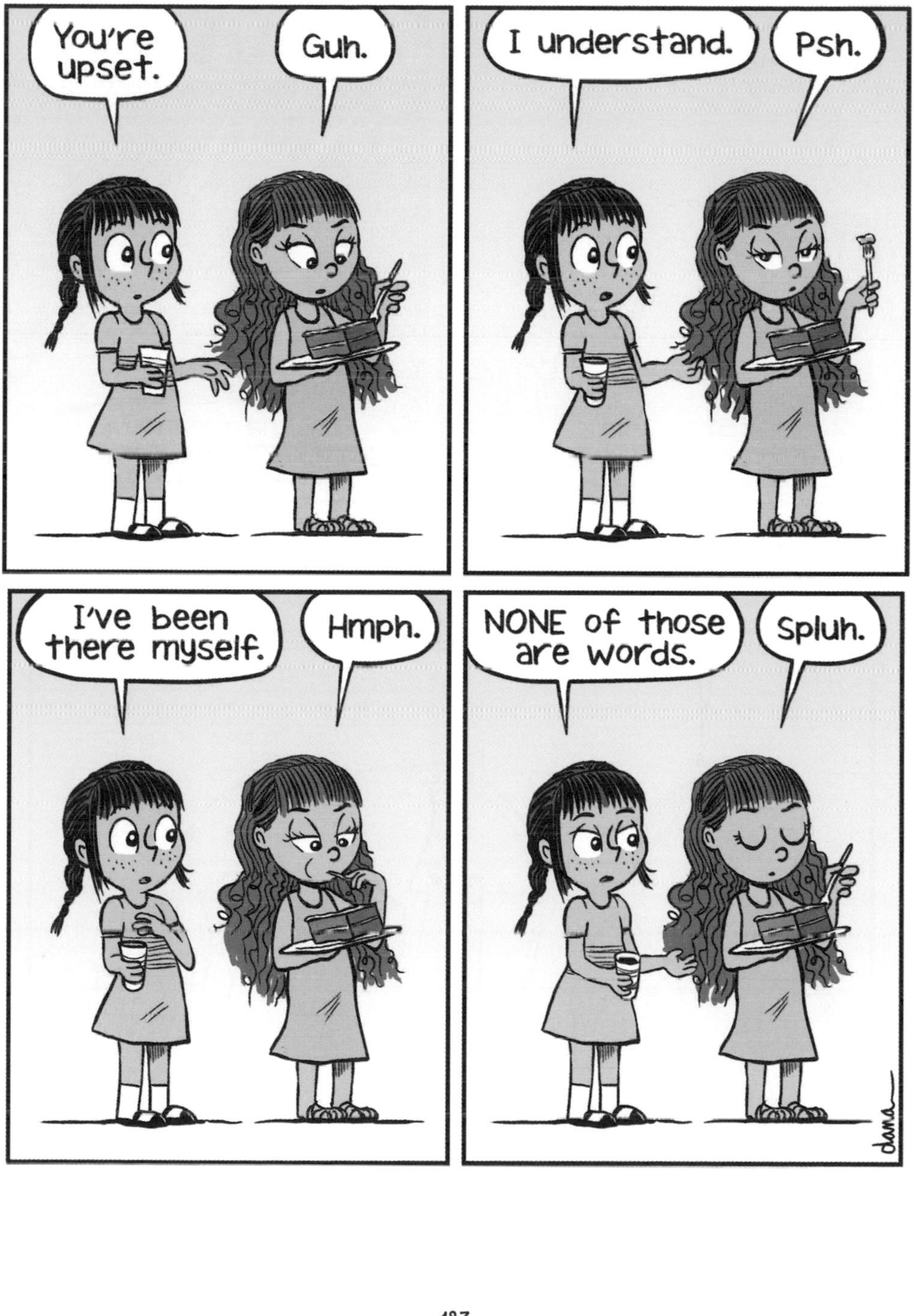
You're upset.
Guh.
I understand.
Psh.
I've been there myself.
Hmph.
NONE of those are words.
Spluh.
dana

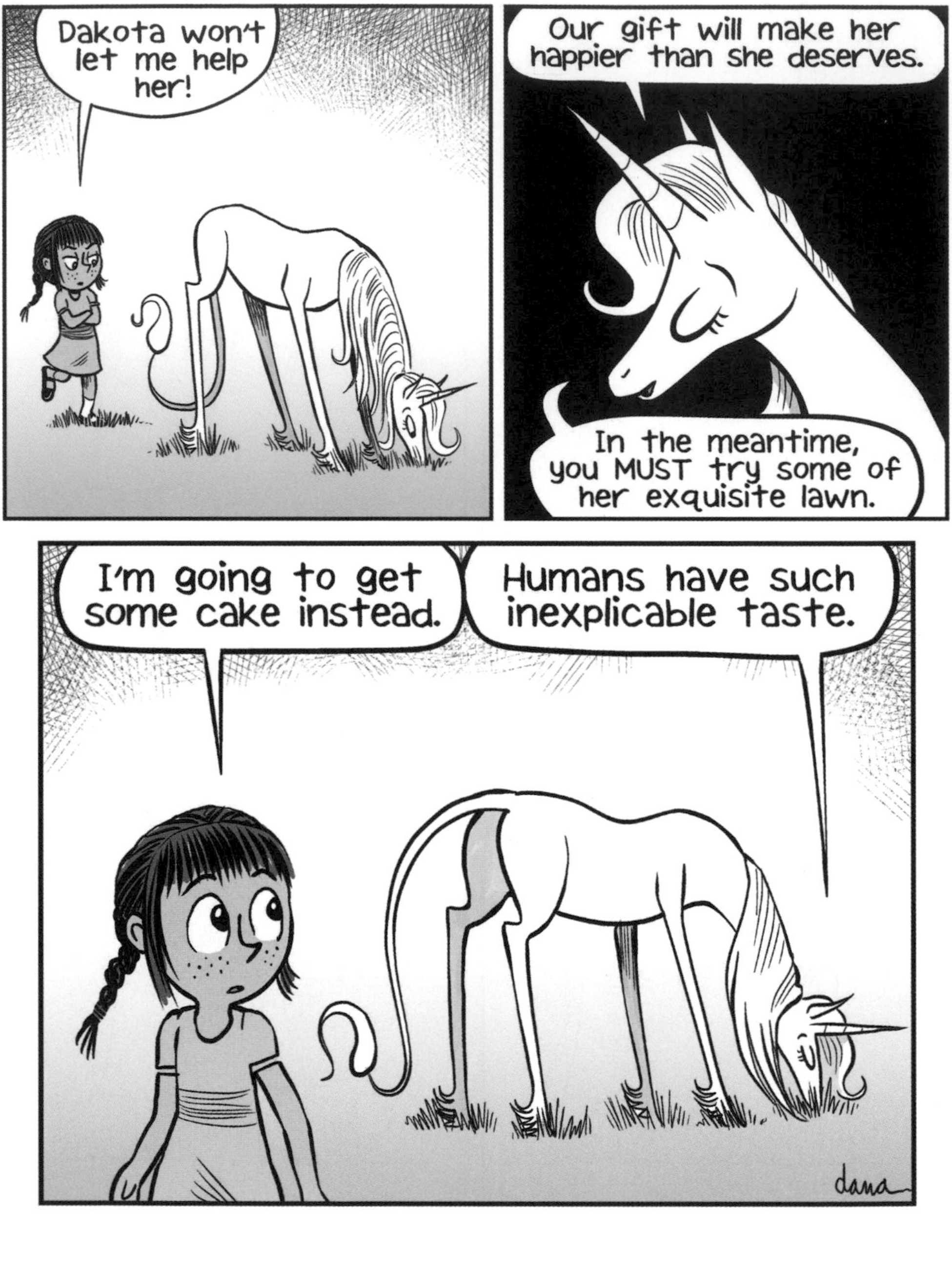
Dakota won't let me help her!
Our gift will make her happier than she deserves.
In the meantime, you MUST try some of her exquisite lawn.
I'm going to get some cake instead.
Humans have such inexplicable taste.
dana

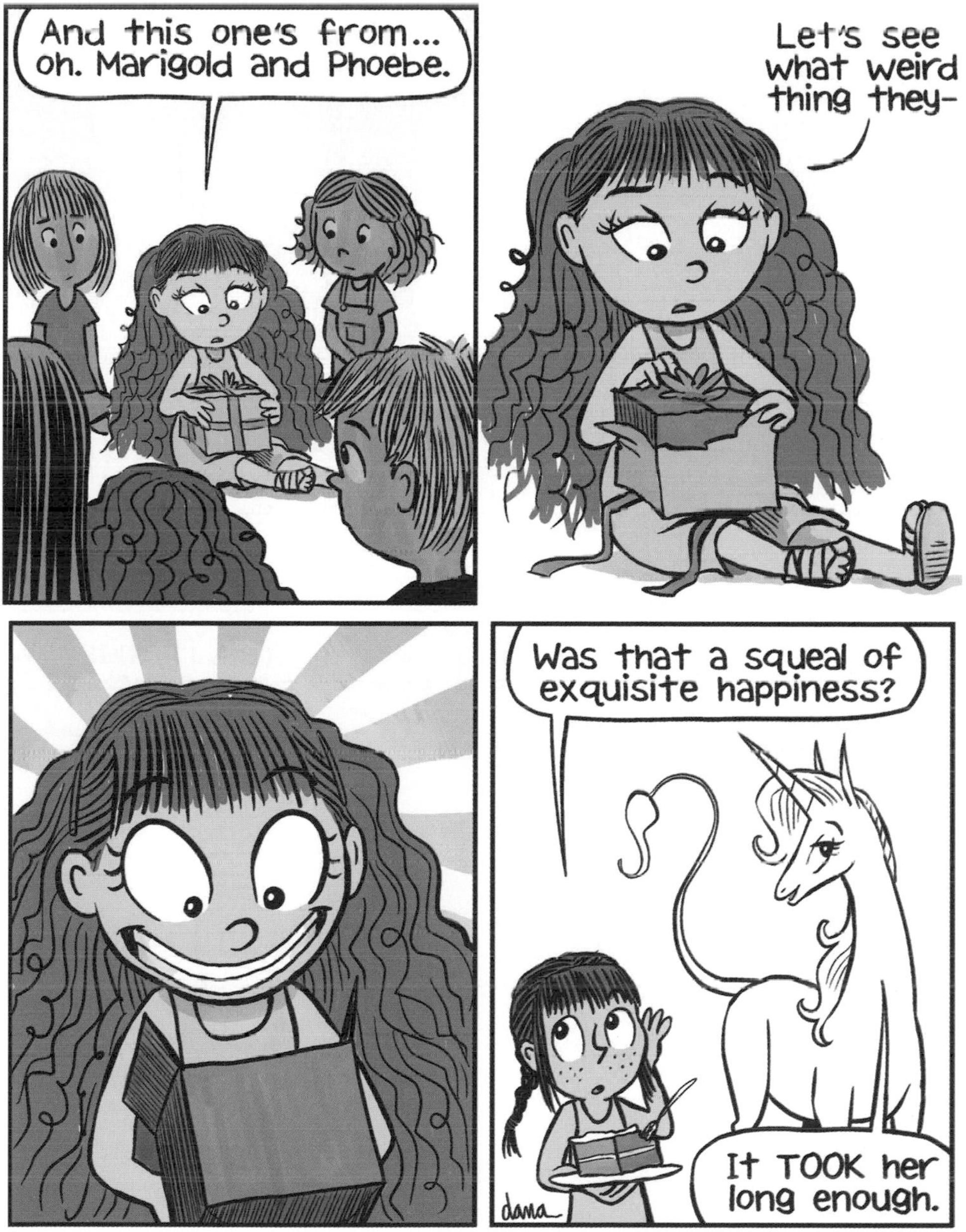
And this one's from... oh. Marigold and Phoebe.
Let's see what weird thing they-
Was that a squeal of exquisite happiness?
It TOOK her long enough.
dana

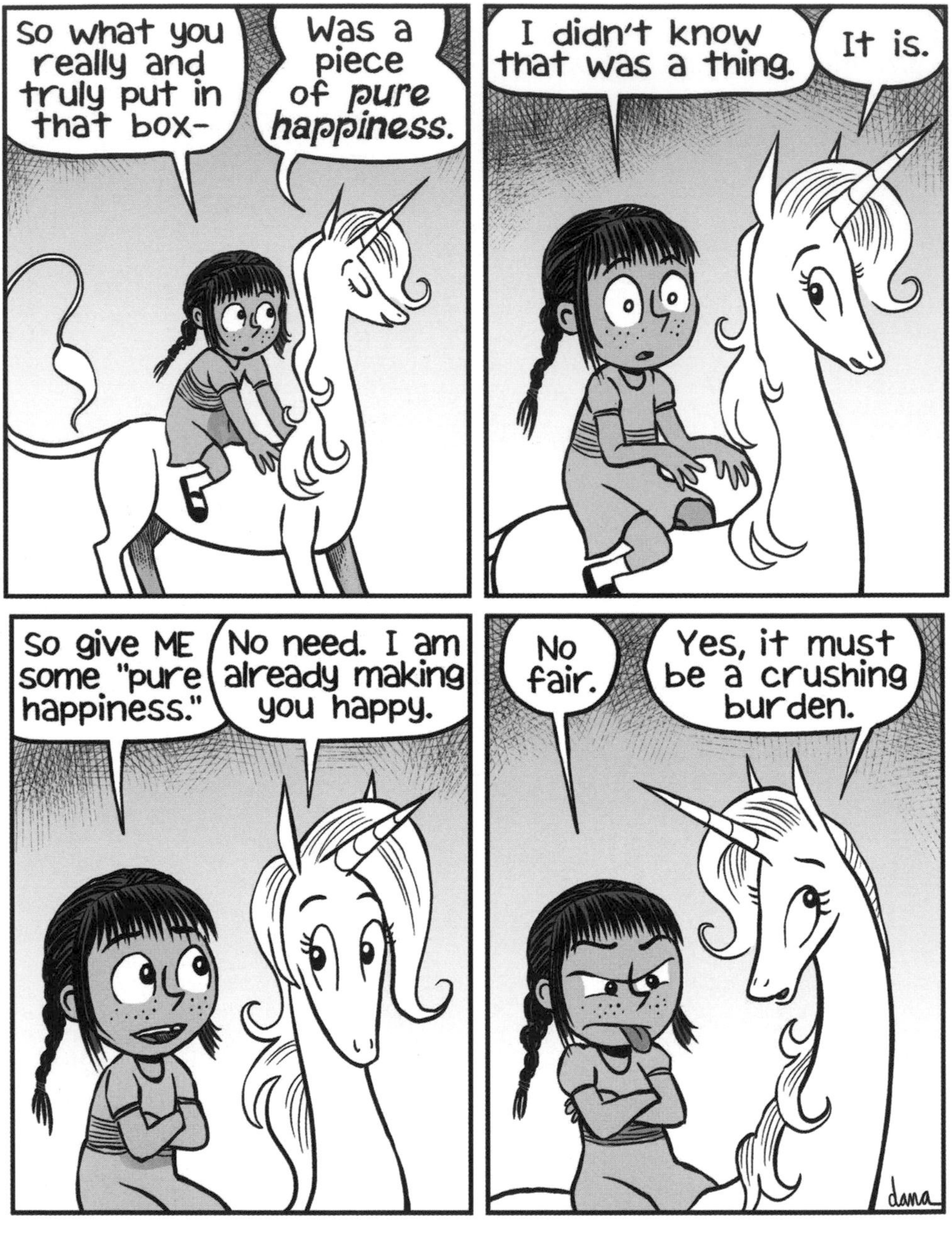
So what you really and truly put in that box-
Was a piece of *pure happiness.*
I didn't know that was a thing.
It is.
So give ME some "pure happiness."
No need. I am already making you happy.
No fair.
Yes, it must be a crushing burden.
dana

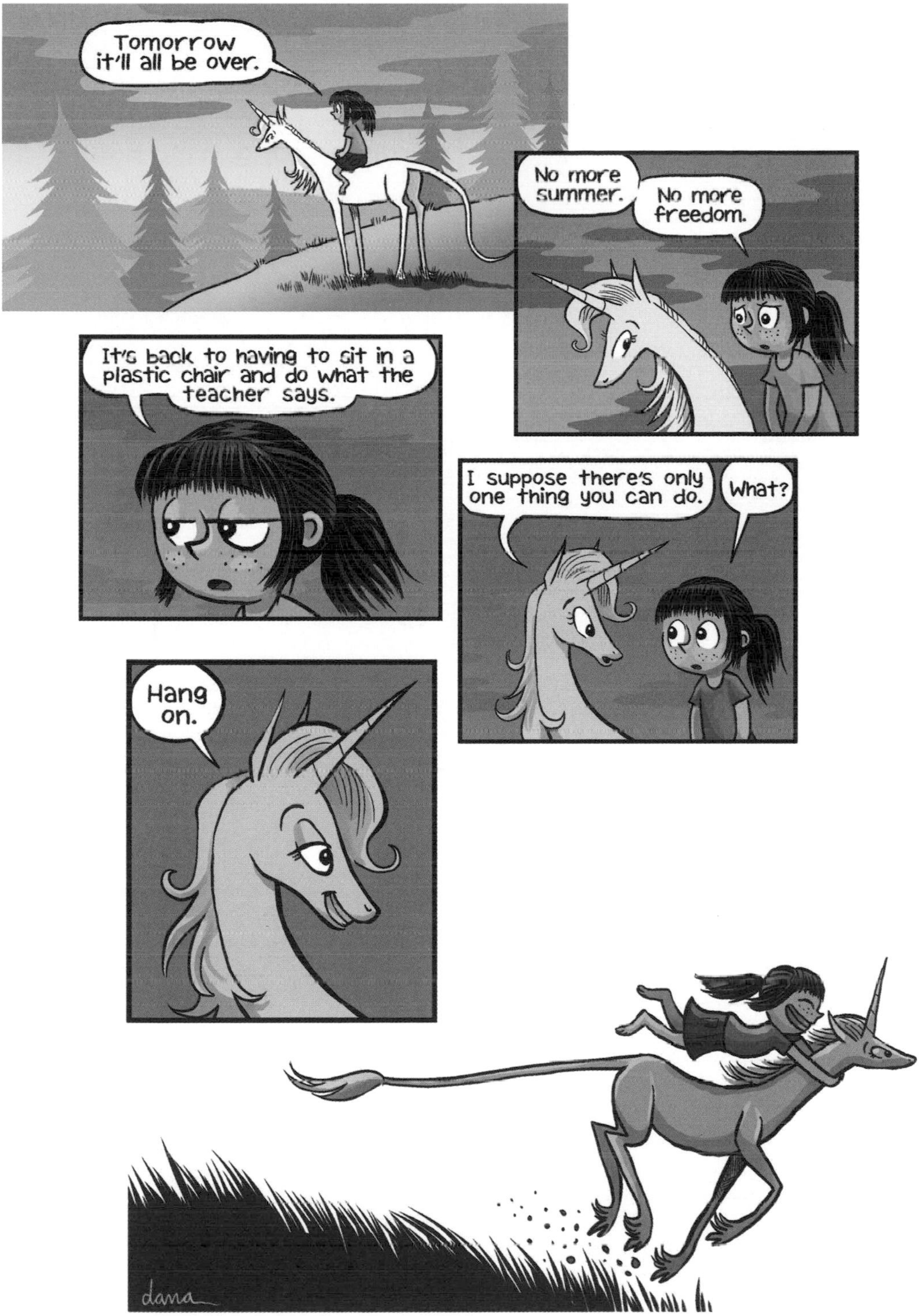

Tomorrow it'll all be over.
No more summer.
No more freedom.
It's back to having to sit in a plastic chair and do what the teacher says.
I suppose there's only one thing you can do.
What?
Hang on.
dana

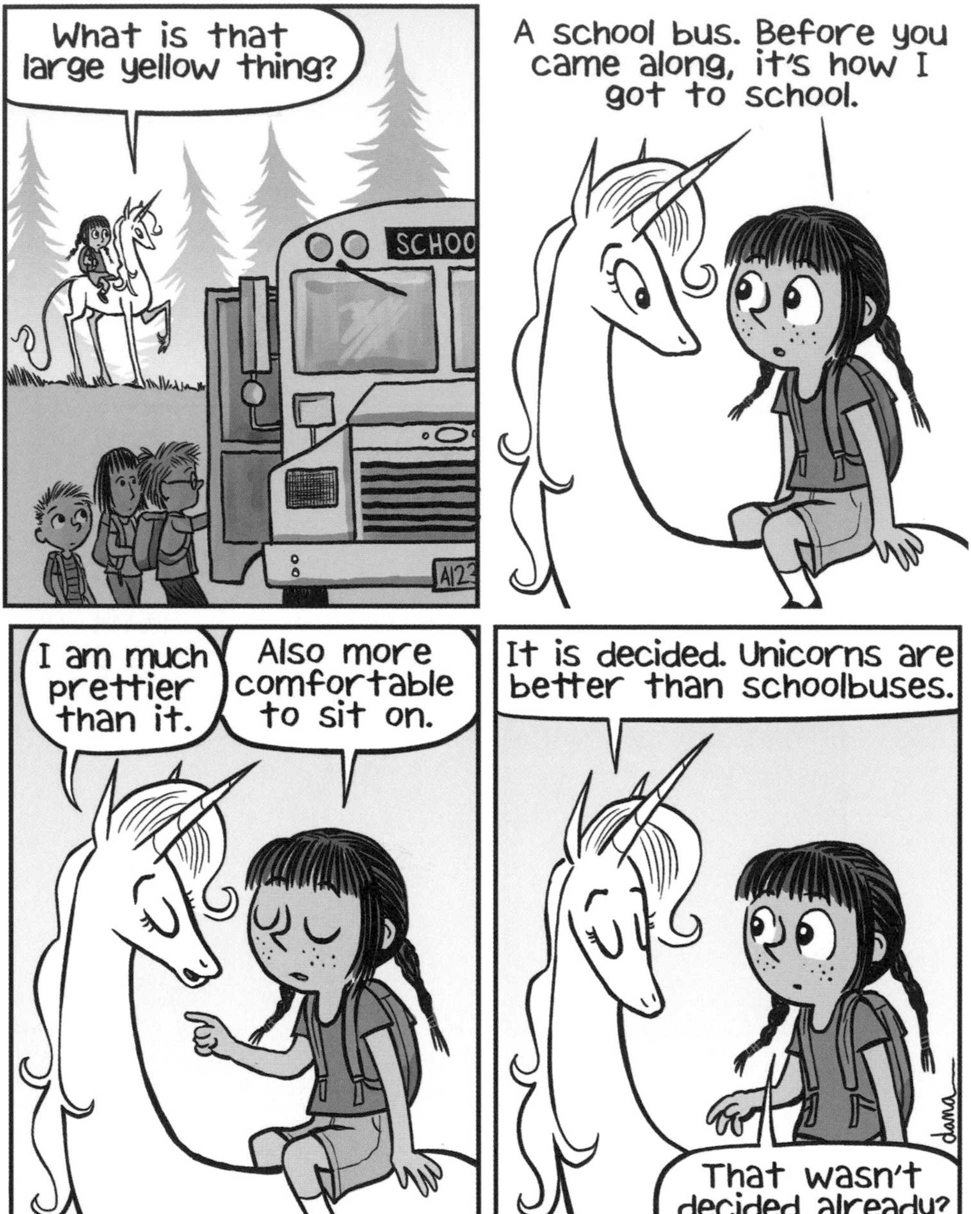
What is that large yellow thing?
SCHOO
A123
A school bus. Before you came along, it's how I got to school.
I am much prettier than it.
Also more comfortable to sit on.
It is decided. Unicorns are better than schoolbuses.
That wasn't decided already?
dana

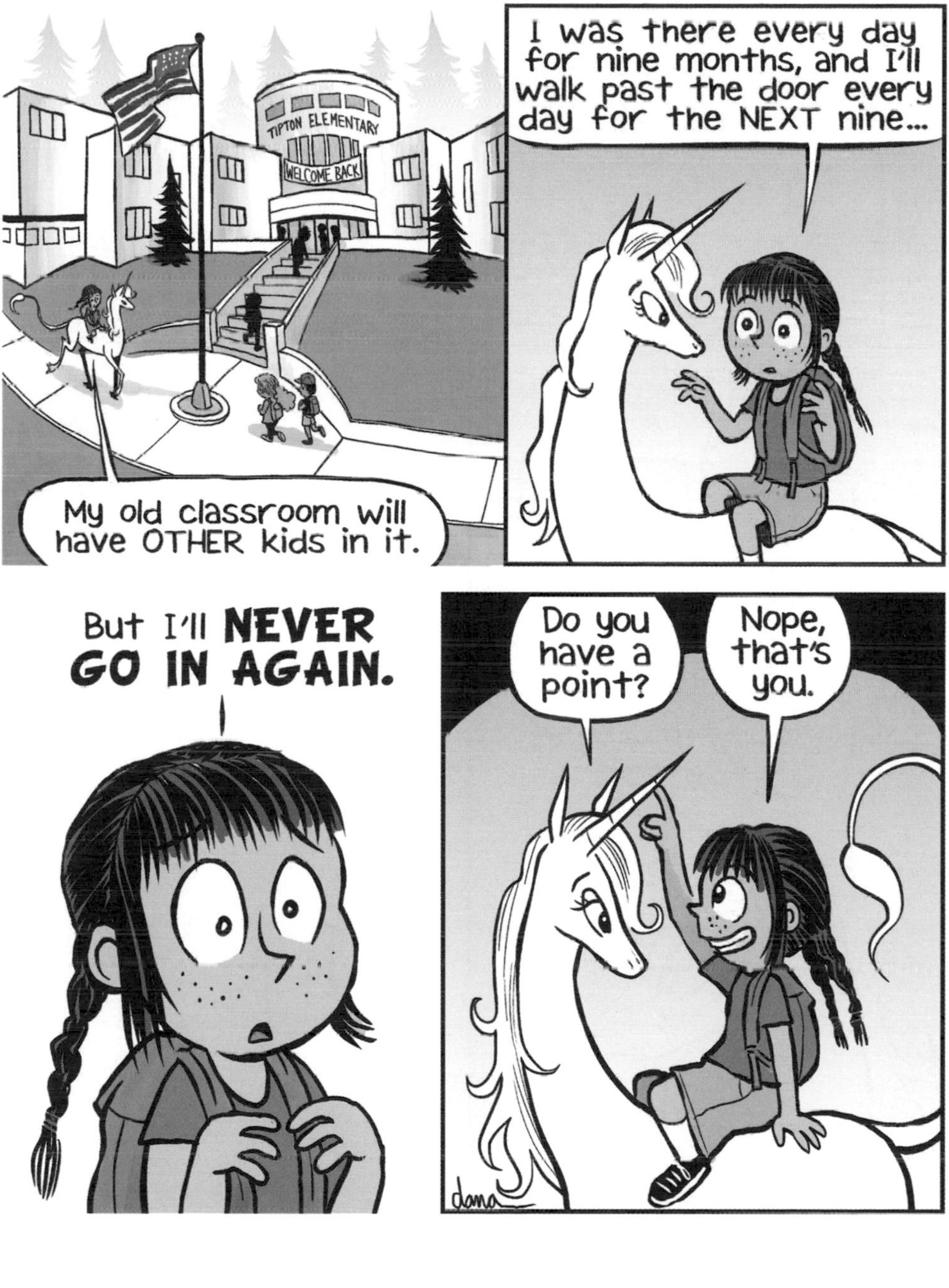
TIPTON ELEMENTARY
WELCOME BACK
My old classroom will have OTHER kids in it.
I was there every day for nine months, and I'll walk past the door every day for the NEXT nine...
But I'll **NEVER GO IN AGAIN.**
Do you have a point?
Nope, that's you.
dana

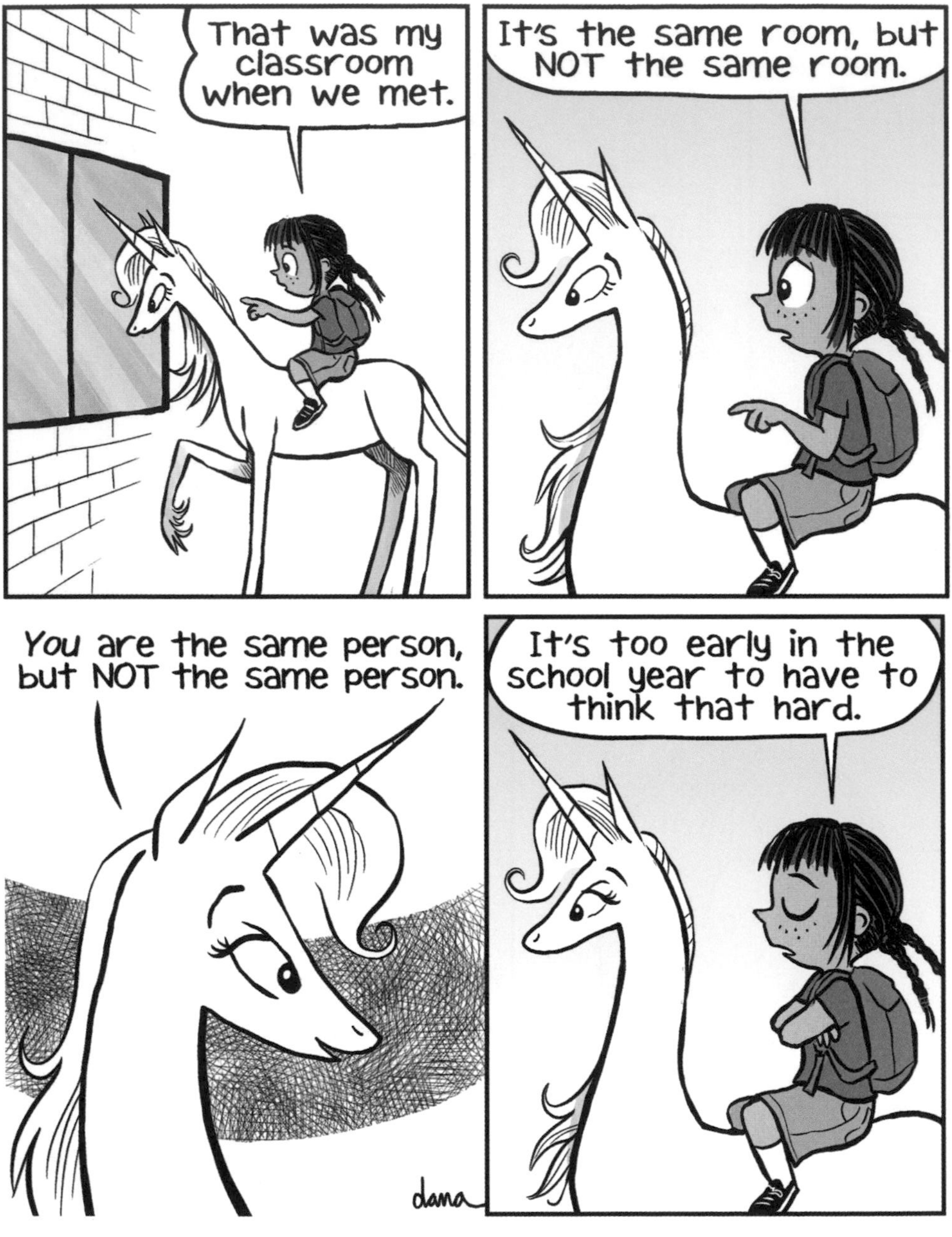
That was my classroom when we met.
It's the same room, but NOT the same room.
You are the same person, but NOT the same person.
It's too early in the school year to have to think that hard.
dana

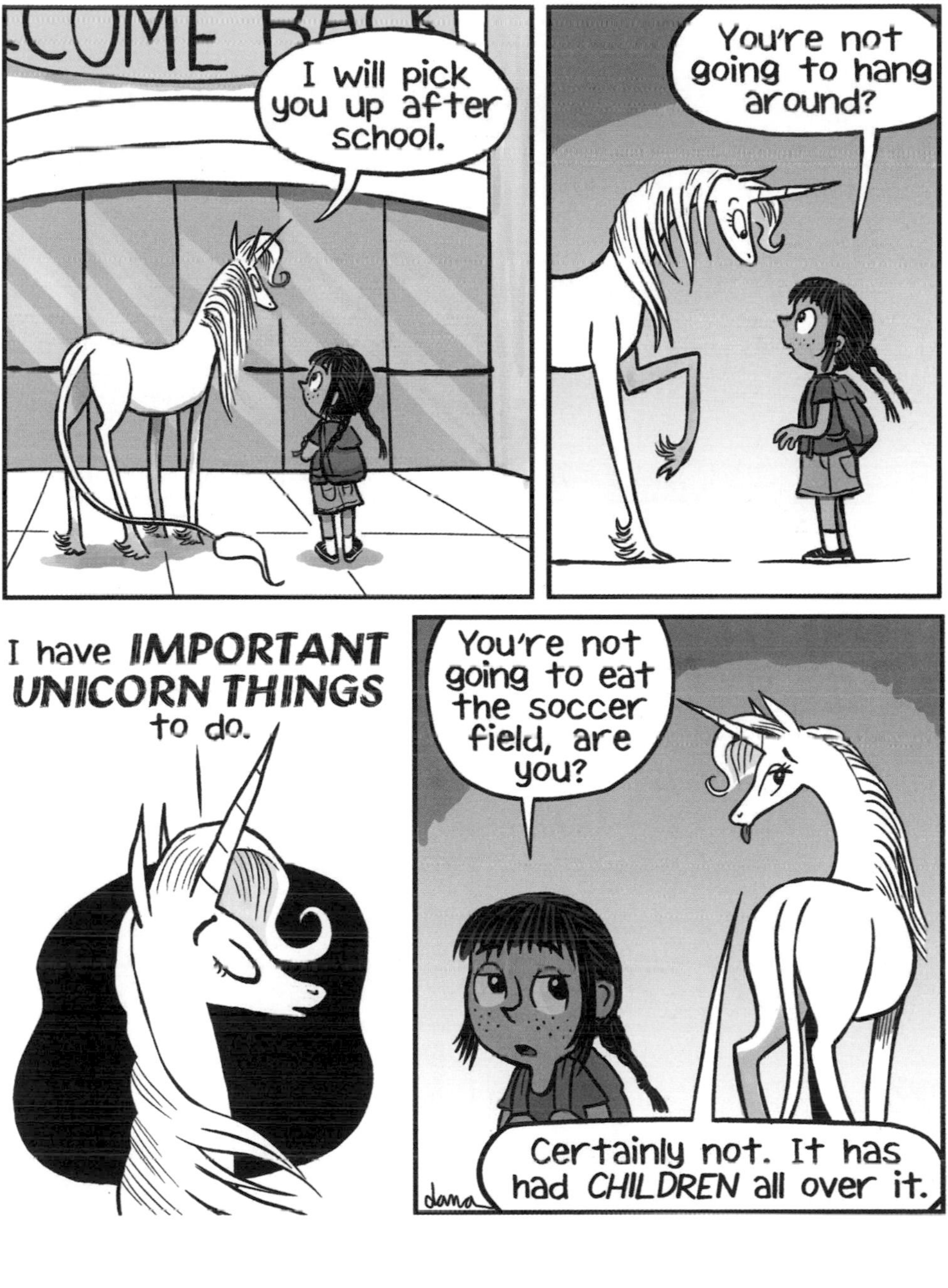

I will pick you up after school.
You're not going to hang around?
I have IMPORTANT UNICORN THINGS to do.
You're not going to eat the soccer field, are you?
Certainly not. It has had CHILDREN all over it.
dana

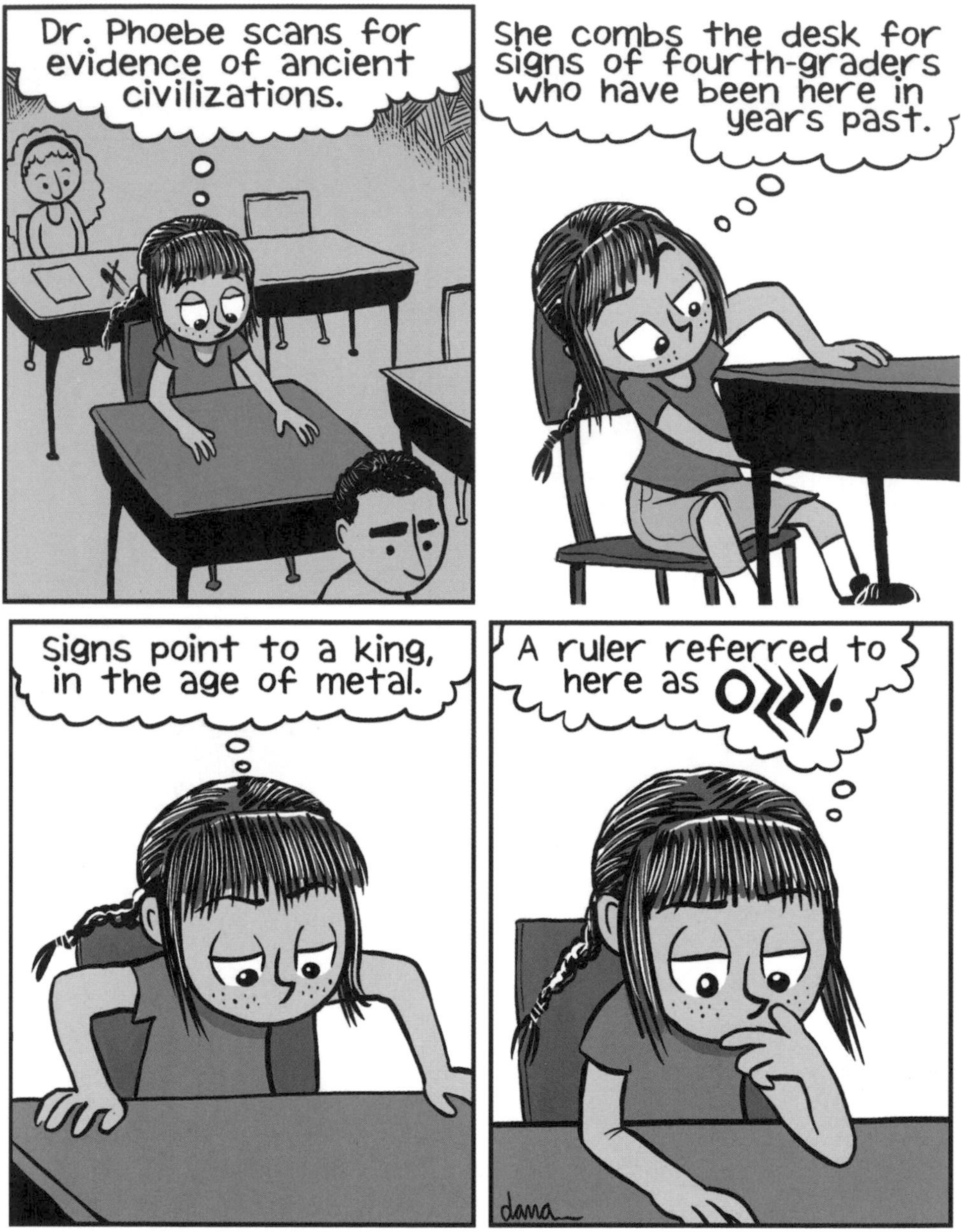
Dr. Phoebe scans for evidence of ancient civilizations.
She combs the desk for signs of fourth-graders who have been here in years past.
Signs point to a king, in the age of metal.
A ruler referred to here as OZZY.
dana

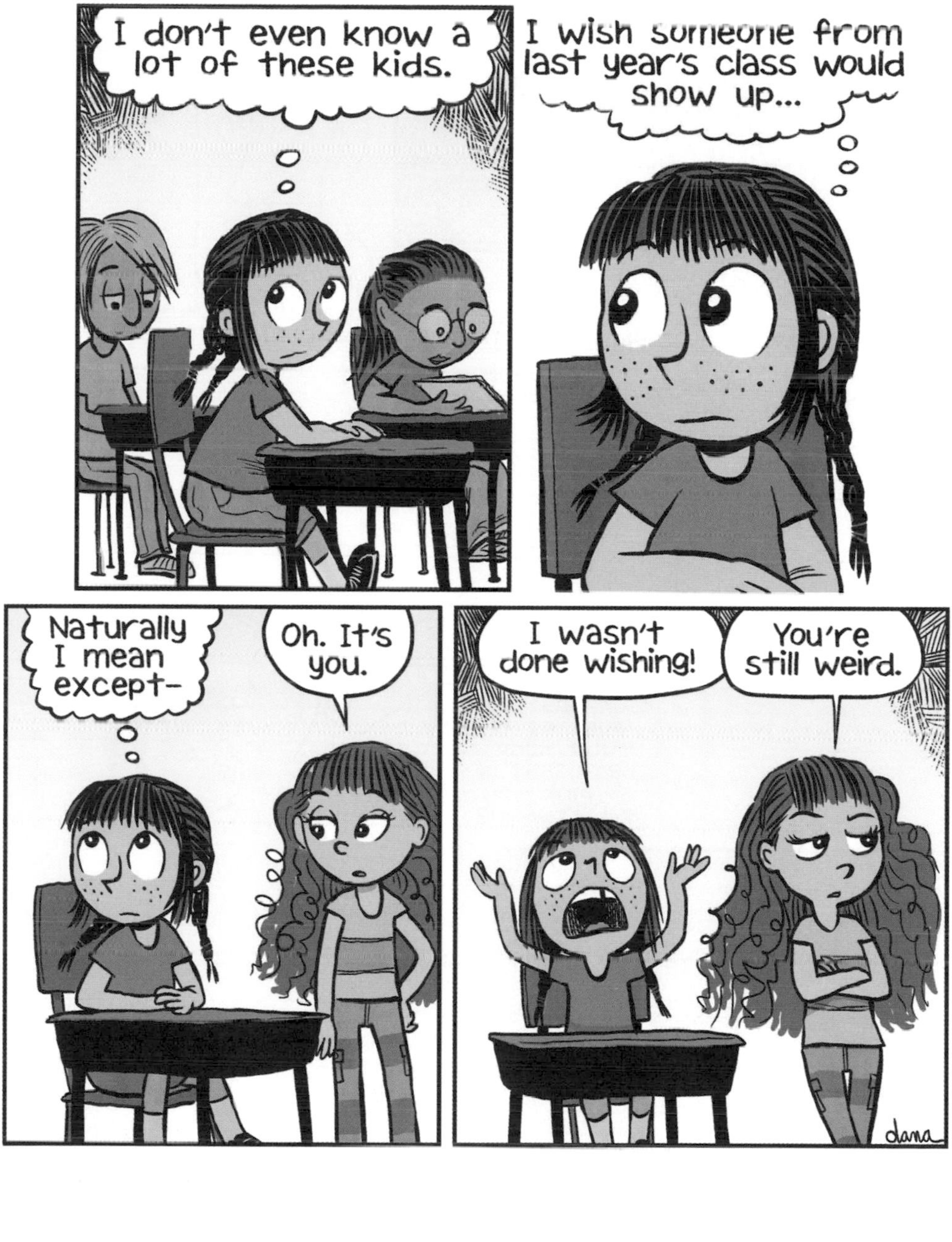
I don't even know a lot of these kids.
I wish someone from last year's class would show up...
Naturally I mean except-
Oh. It's you.
I wasn't done wishing!
You're still weird.
dana

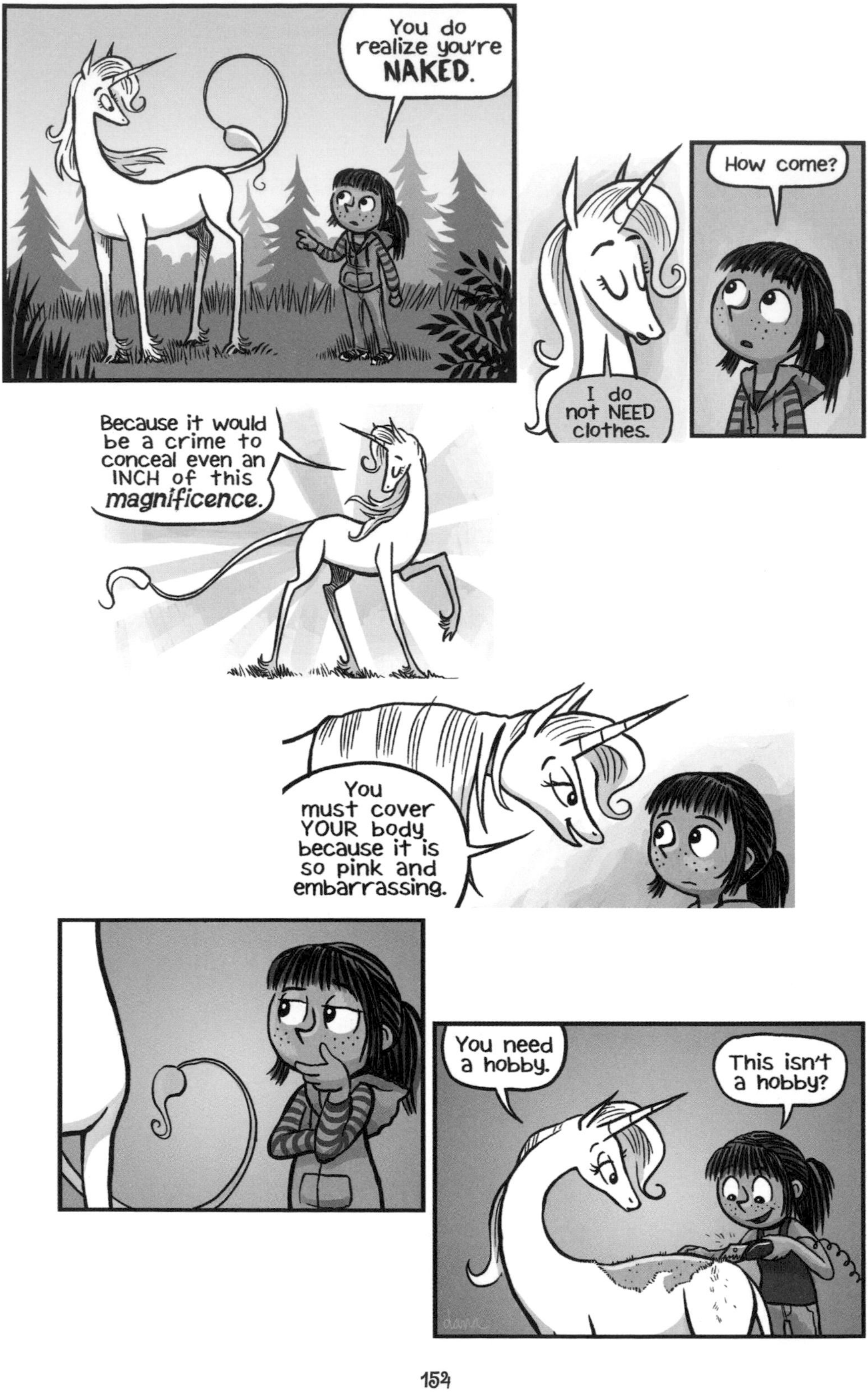
You do realize you're NAKED.
I do not NEED clothes.
How come?
Because it would be a crime to conceal even an INCH of this magnificence.
You must cover YOUR body because it is so pink and embarrassing.
You need a hobby.
This isn't a hobby?
dana

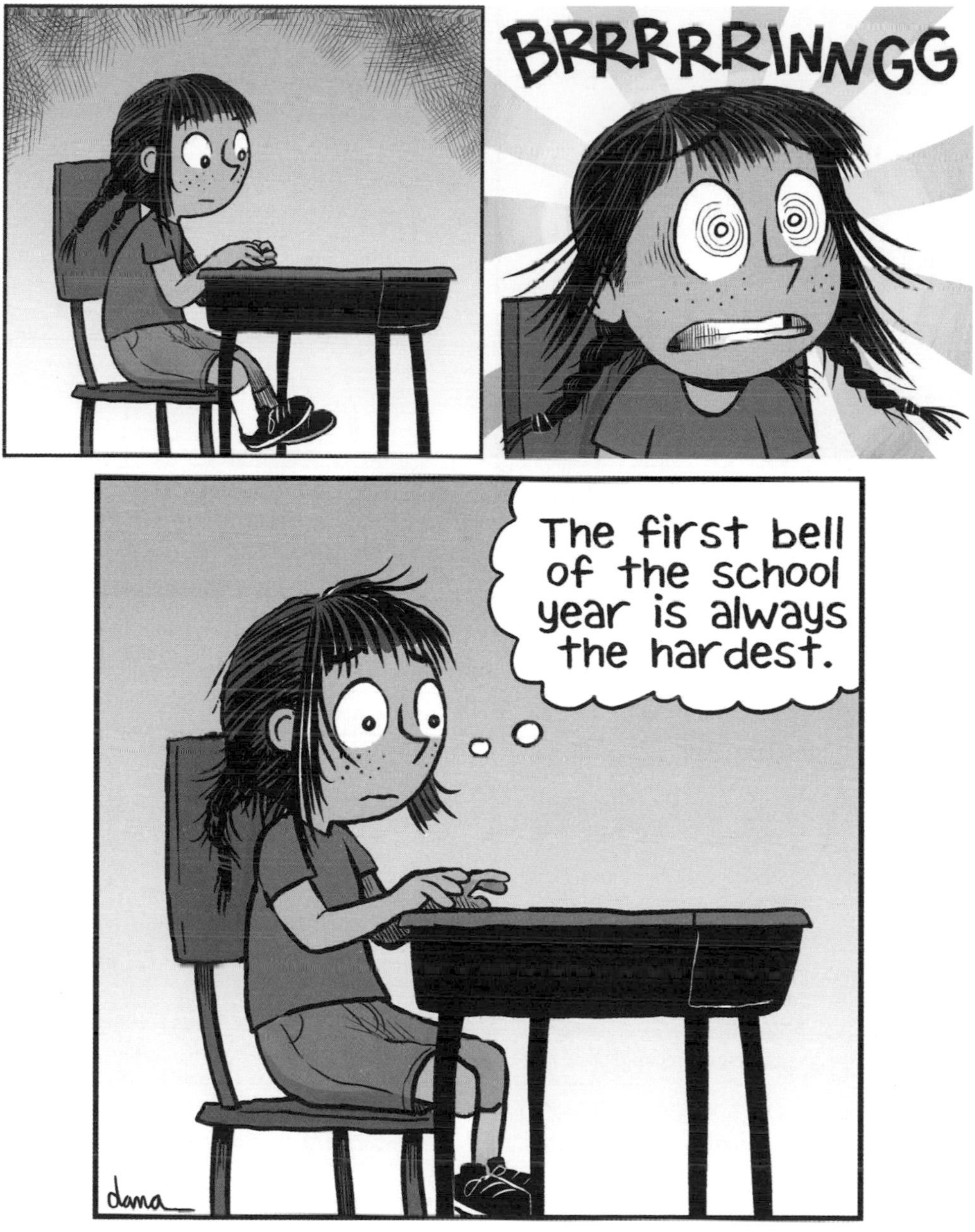
BRRRRRINNGG
The first bell of the school year is always the hardest.
dana

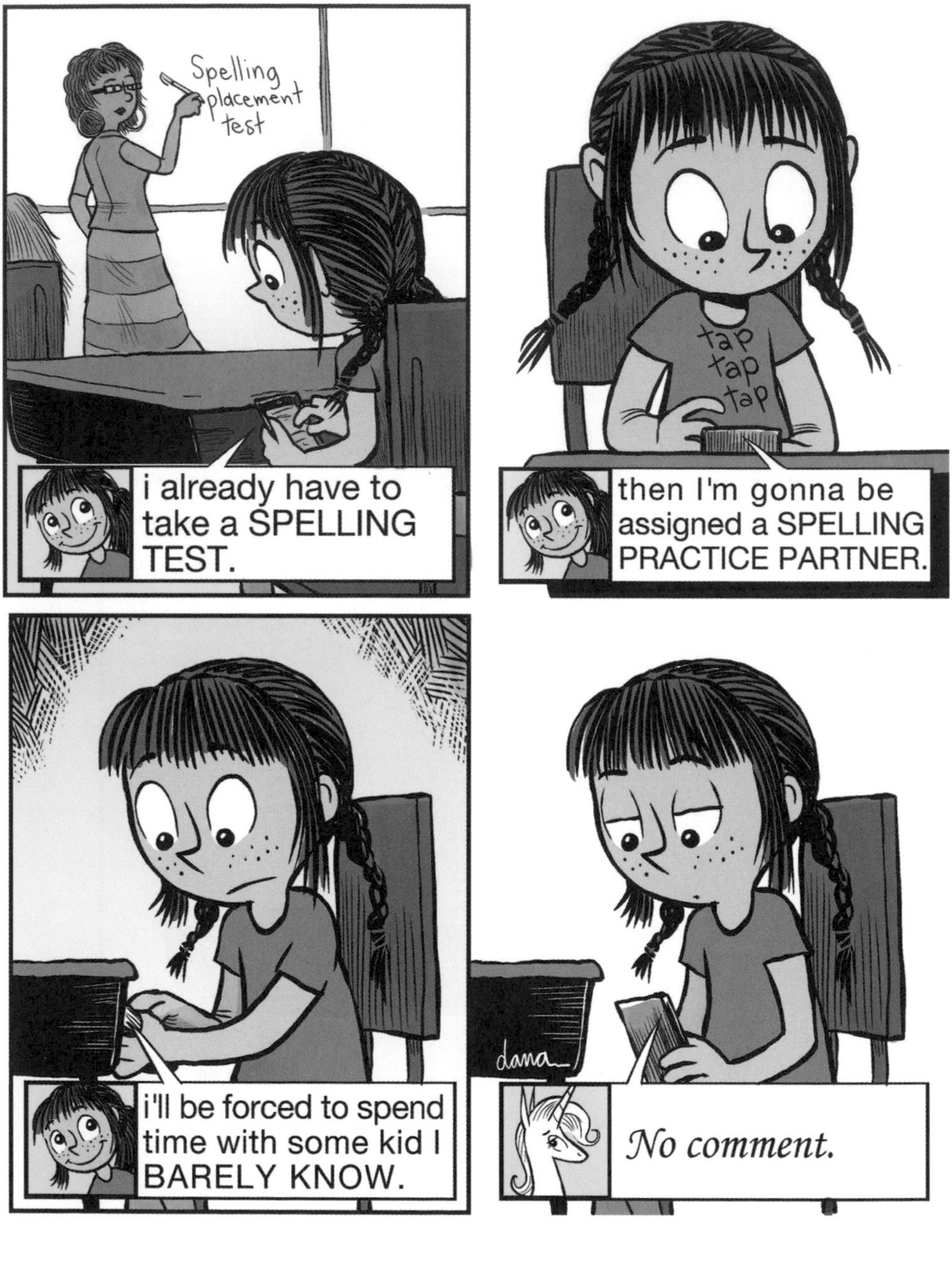
Spelling placement test
i already have to take a SPELLING TEST.
tap tap tap
then I'm gonna be assigned a SPELLING PRACTICE PARTNER.
i'll be forced to spend time with some kid I BARELY KNOW.
dana
No comment.

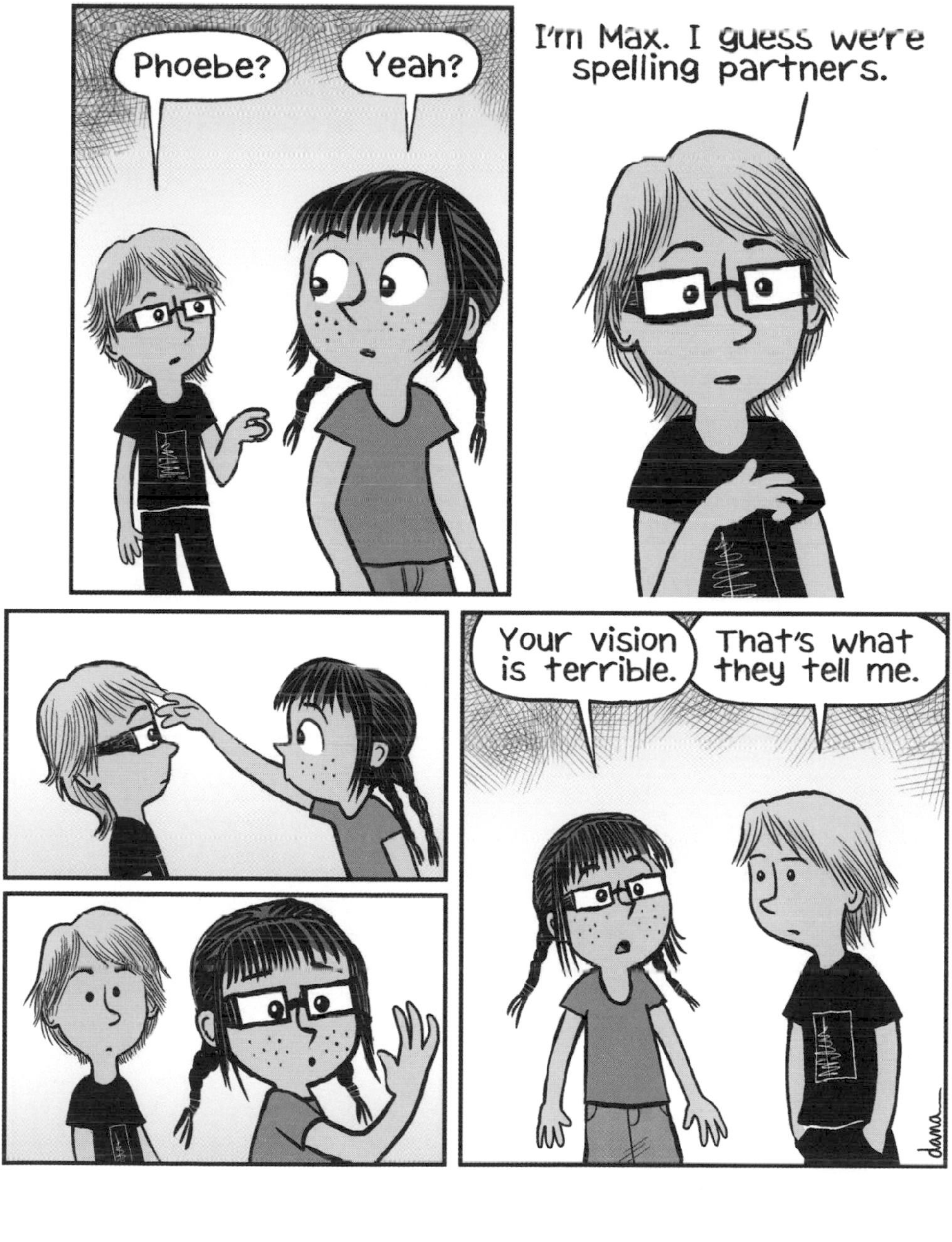
Phoebe?
Yeah?
I'm Max. I guess we're spelling partners.
Your vision is terrible.
That's what they tell me.
dana

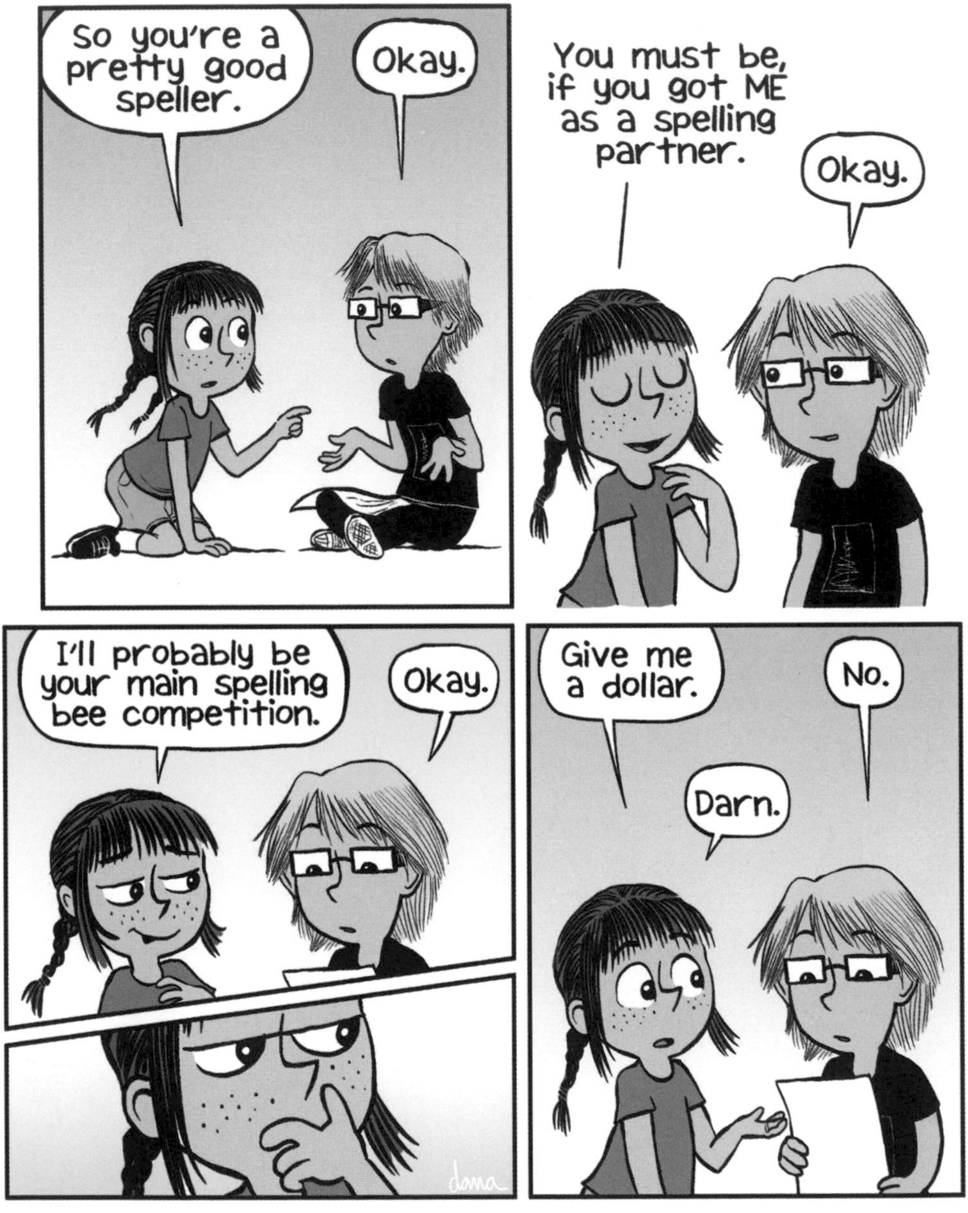
So you're a pretty good speller.
Okay.
You must be, if you got ME as a spelling partner.
Okay.
I'll probably be your main spelling bee competition.
Okay.
Give me a dollar.
No.
Darn.
dana

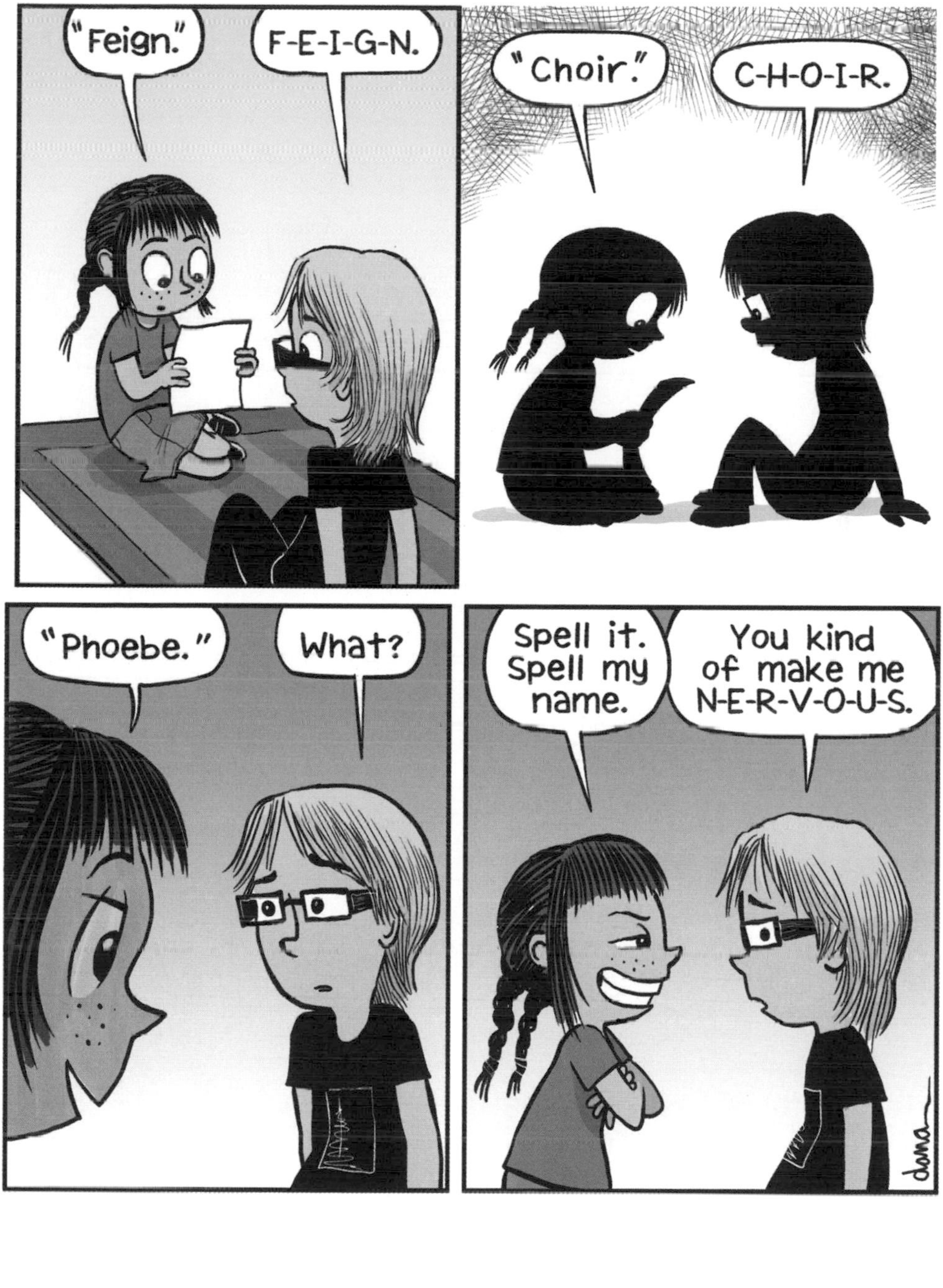
"Feign."
F-E-I-G-N.
"Choir."
C-H-O-I-R.
"Phoebe."
What?
Spell it. Spell my name.
You kind of make me N-E-R-V-O-U-S.
dana

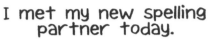

I met my new spelling partner today.

How did it go?

Great!

I...borrowed his glasses without asking, and then demanded he spell my name.

So NOT great.

Kind of dreadful, yeah.

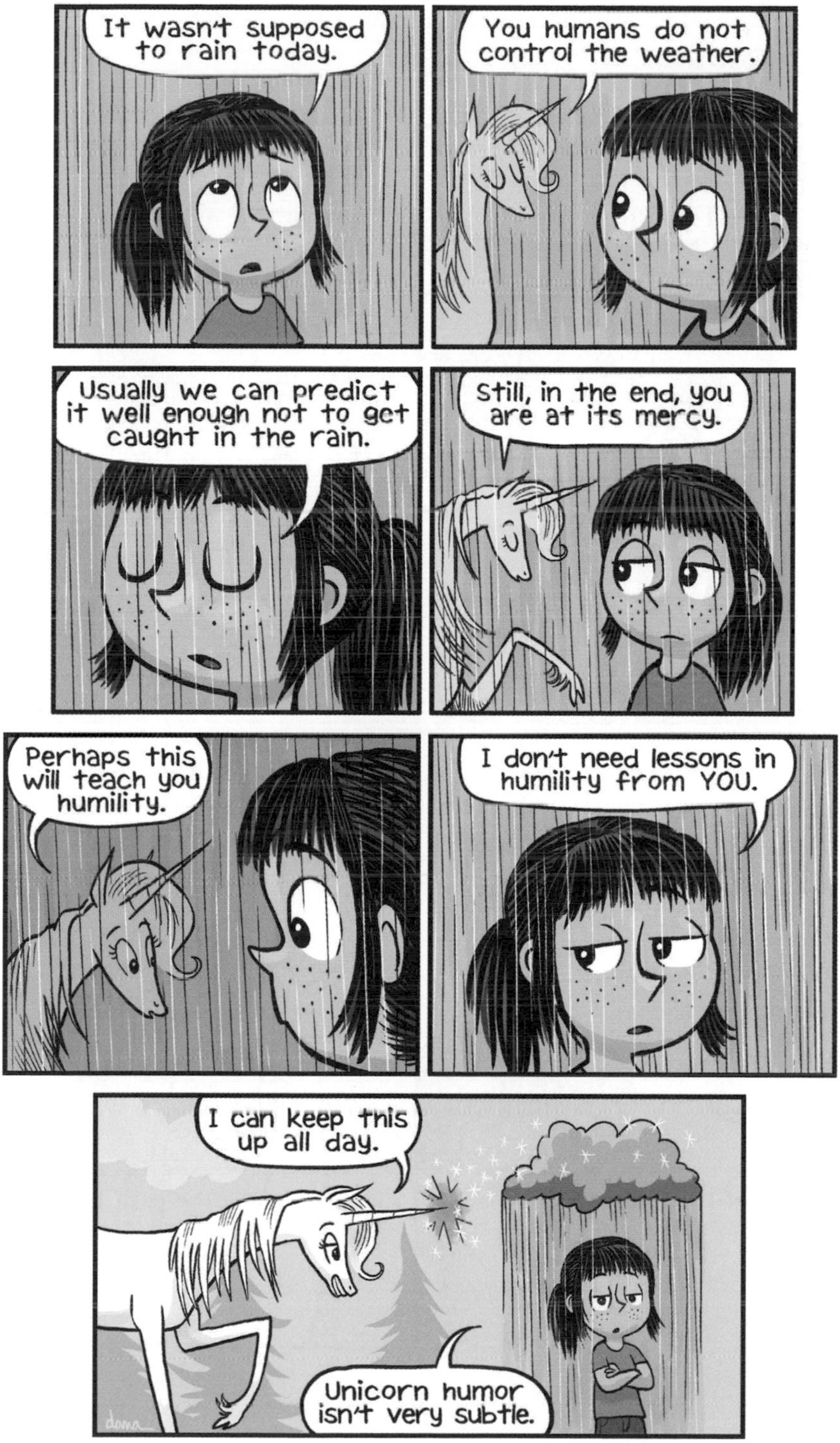

It wasn't supposed to rain today.
You humans do not control the weather.
Usually we can predict it well enough not to get caught in the rain.
Still, in the end, you are at its mercy.
Perhaps this will teach you humility.
I don't need lessons in humility from YOU.
I can keep this up all day.
Unicorn humor isn't very subtle.

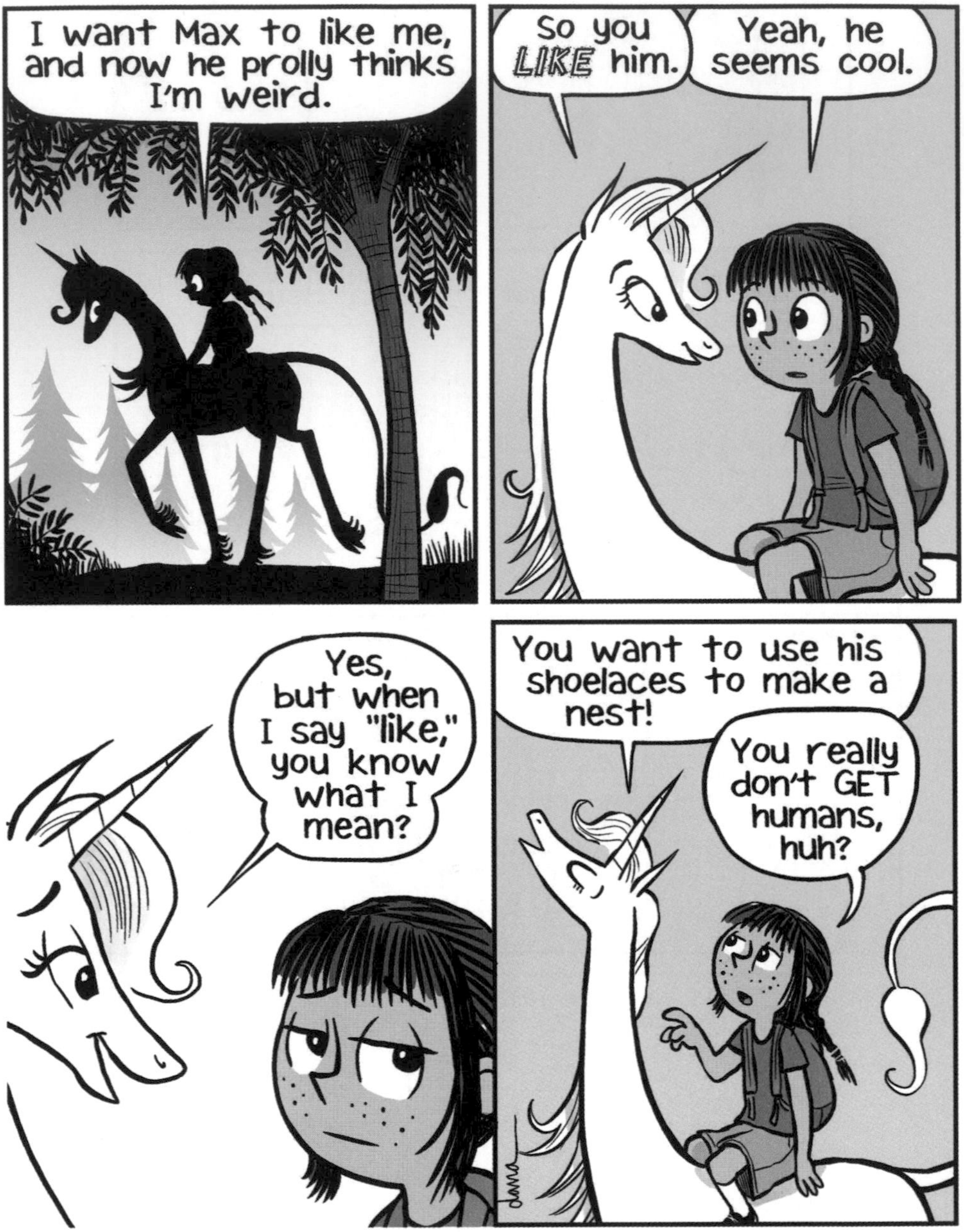
I want Max to like me, and now he prolly thinks I'm weird.
So you LIKE him.
Yeah, he seems cool.
Yes, but when I say "like," you know what I mean?
You want to use his shoelaces to make a nest!
You really don't GET humans, huh?

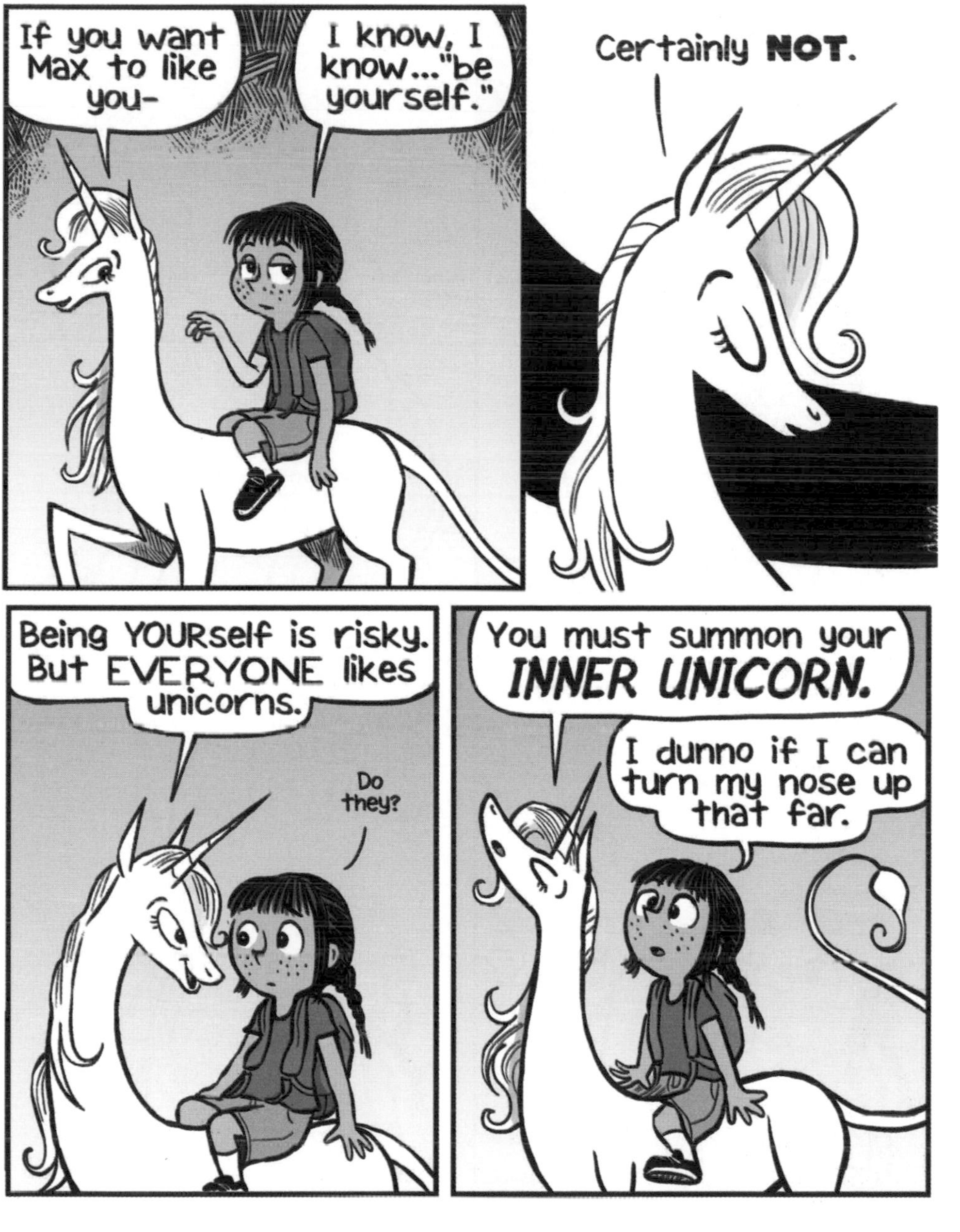

If you want Max to like you-
I know, I know..."be yourself."
Certainly NOT.
Being YOURself is risky. But EVERYONE likes unicorns.
Do they?
You must summon your INNER UNICORN.
I dunno if I can turn my nose up that far.

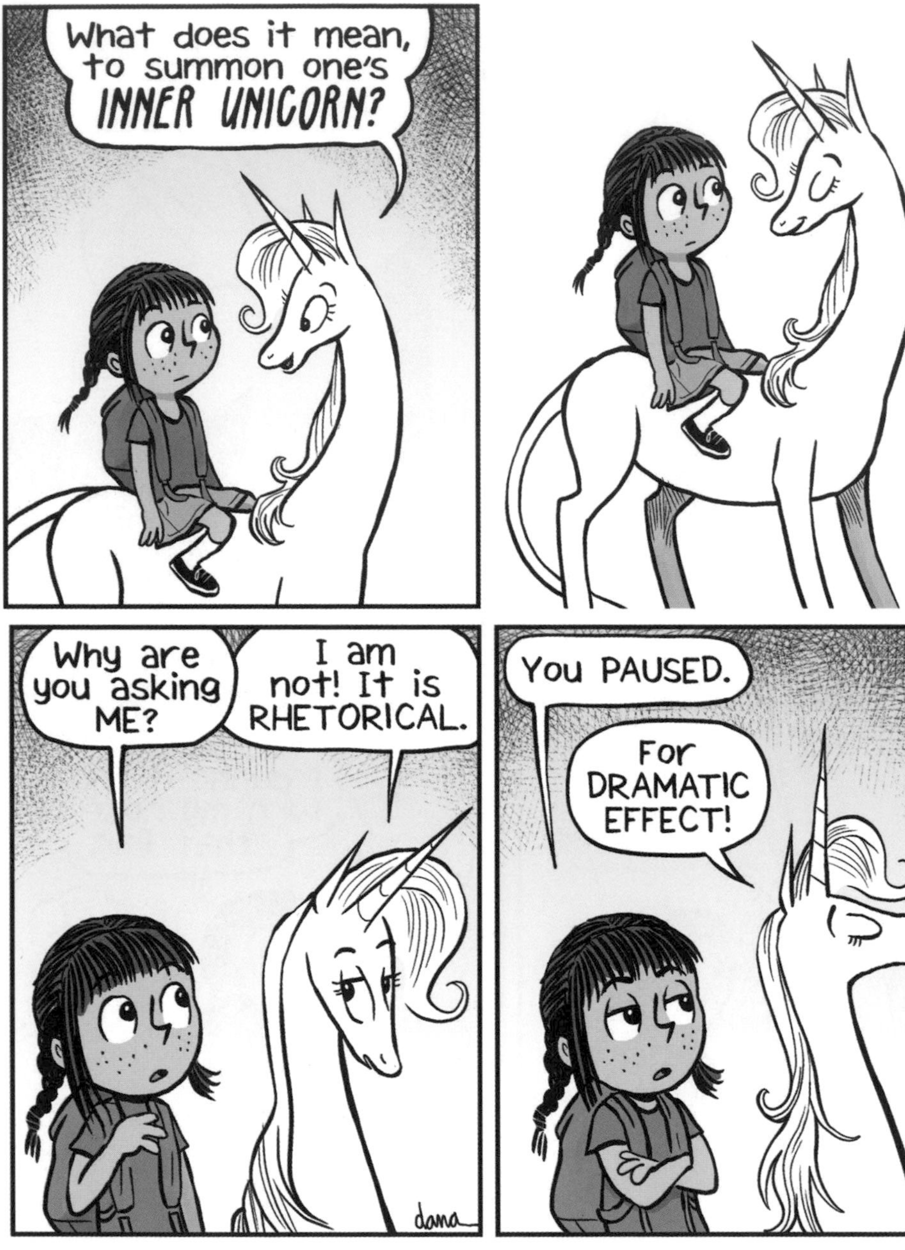
What does it mean, to summon one's INNER UNICORN?
Why are you asking ME?
I am not! It is RHETORICAL.
You PAUSED.
For DRAMATIC EFFECT!
dana

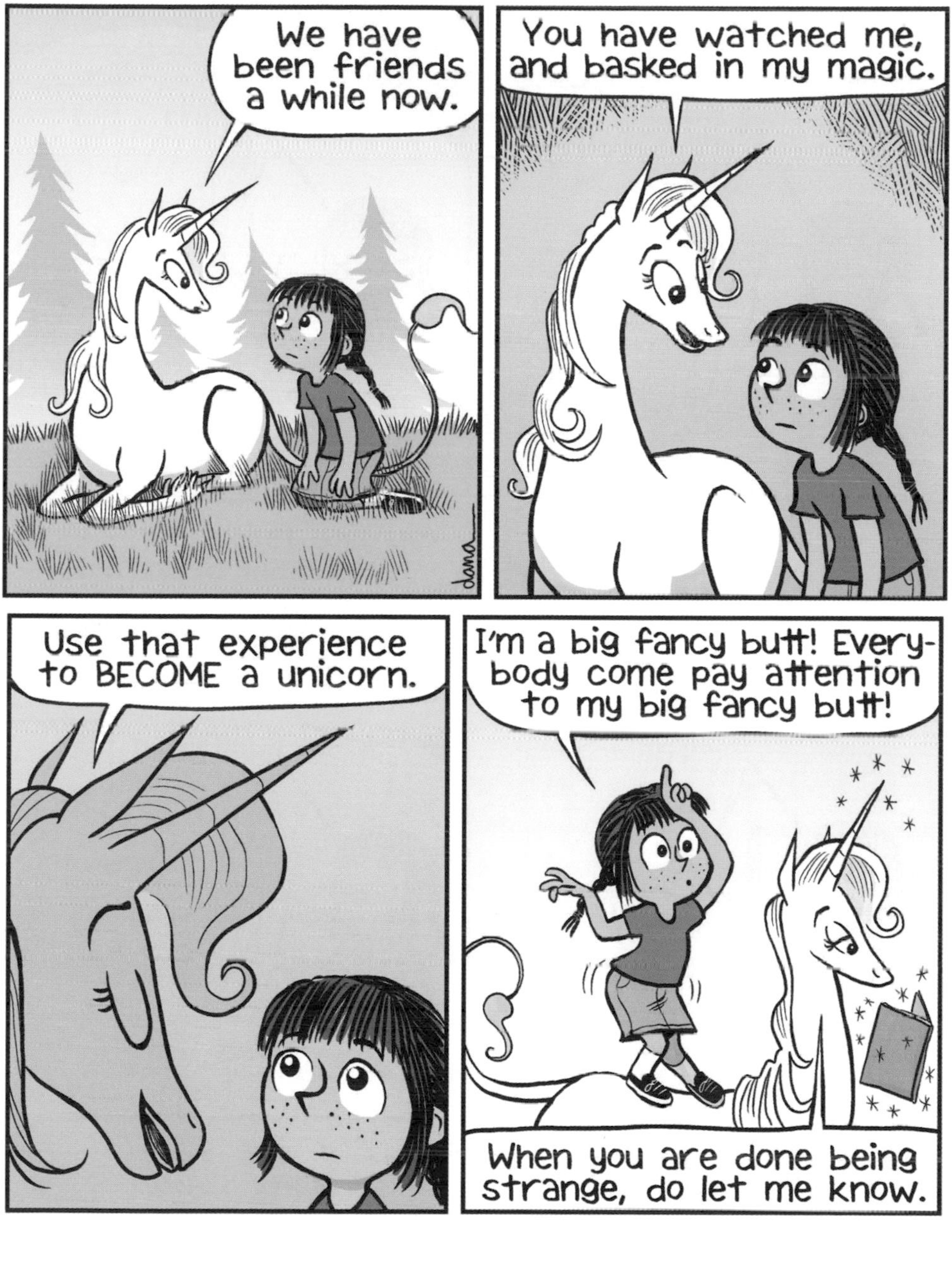
We have been friends a while now.
You have watched me, and basked in my magic.
Use that experience to BECOME a unicorn.
I'm a big fancy butt! Everybody come pay attention to my big fancy butt!
When you are done being strange, do let me know.

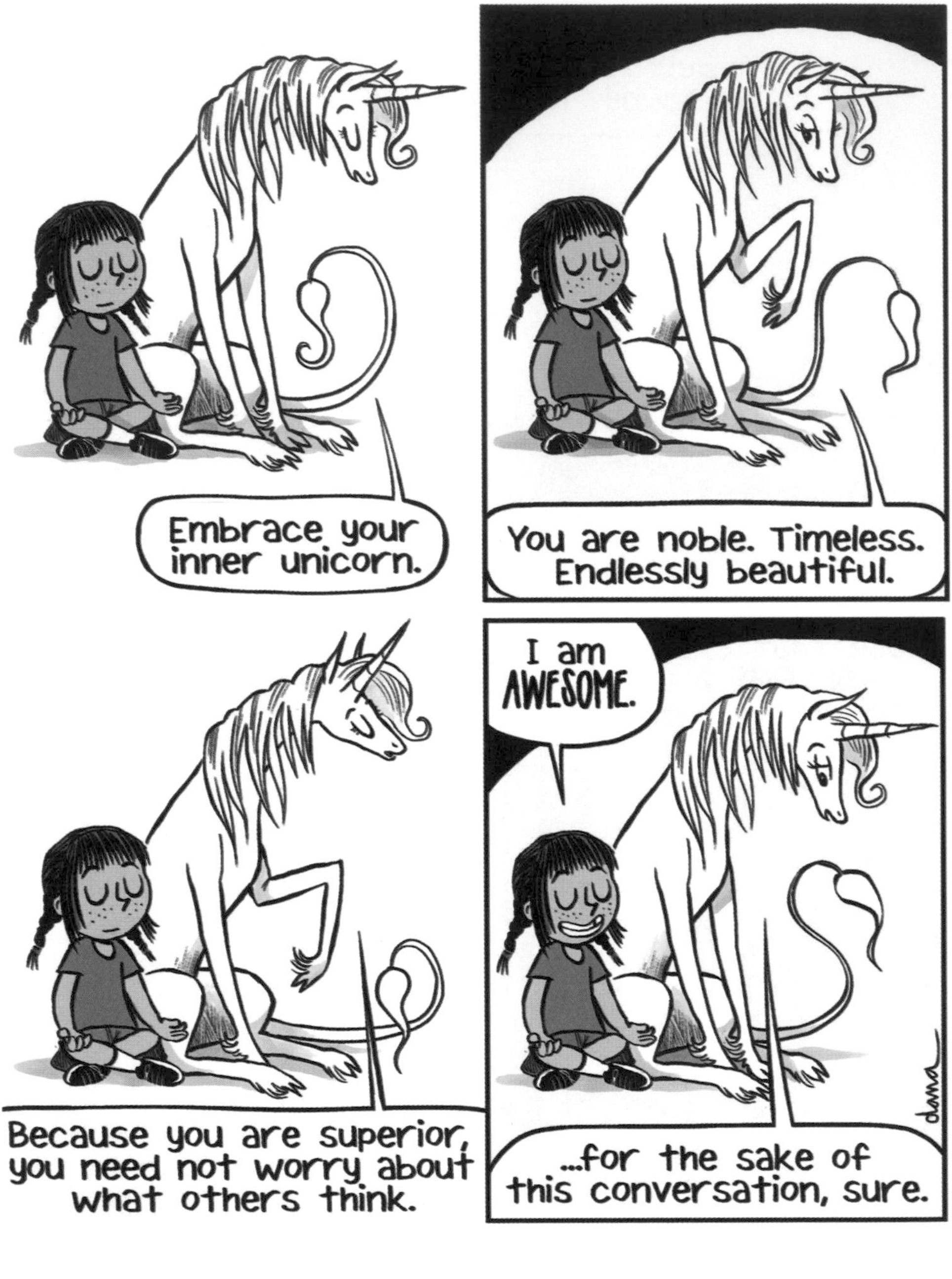
Embrace your inner unicorn.
You are noble. Timeless. Endlessly beautiful.
Because you are superior, you need not worry about what others think.
I am AWESOME.
...for the sake of this conversation, sure.
dana

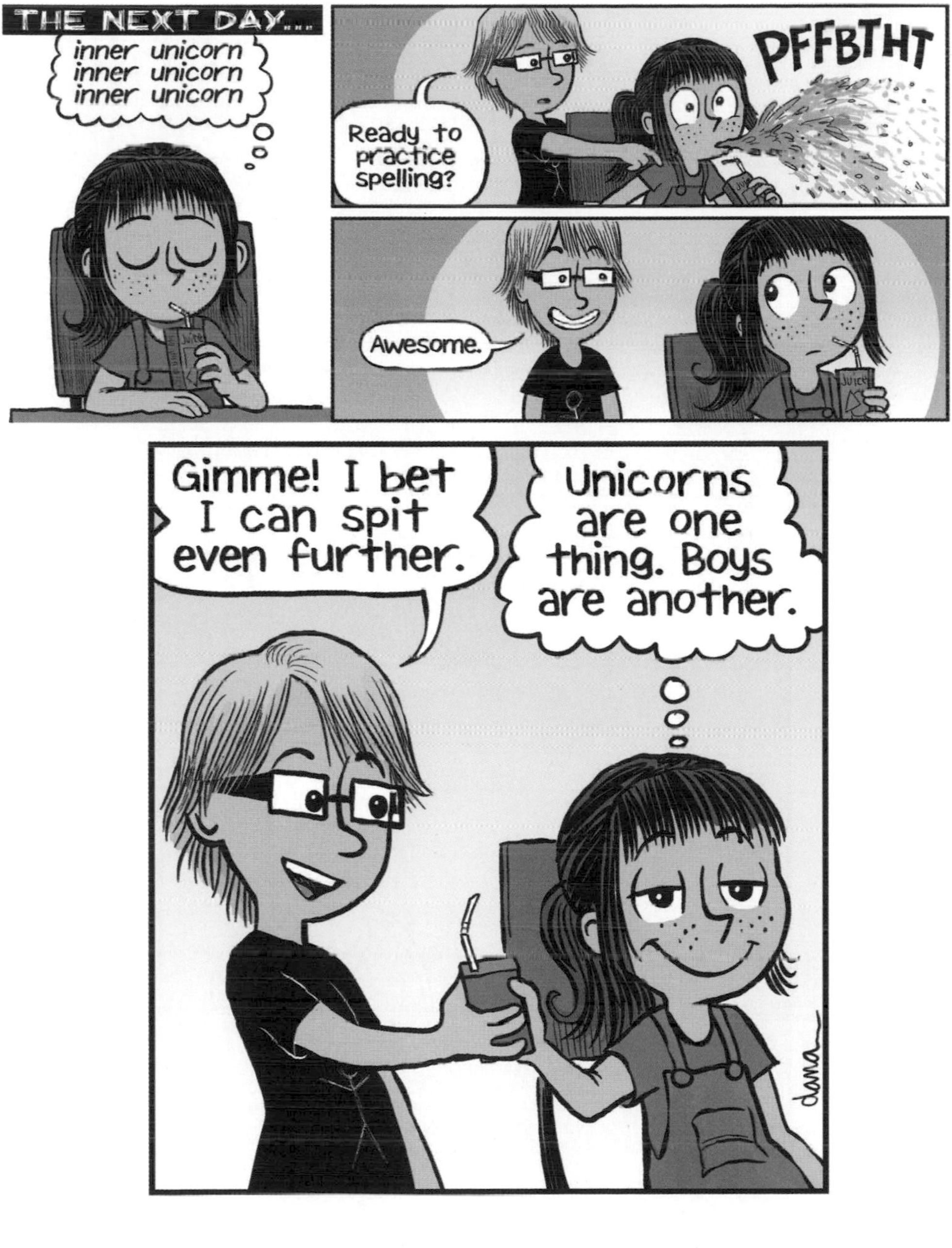
THE NEXT DAY....
inner unicorn inner unicorn inner unicorn
Ready to practice spelling?
PFFBTHT
Awesome.
Gimme! I bet I can spit even further.
Unicorns are one thing. Boys are another.
dana

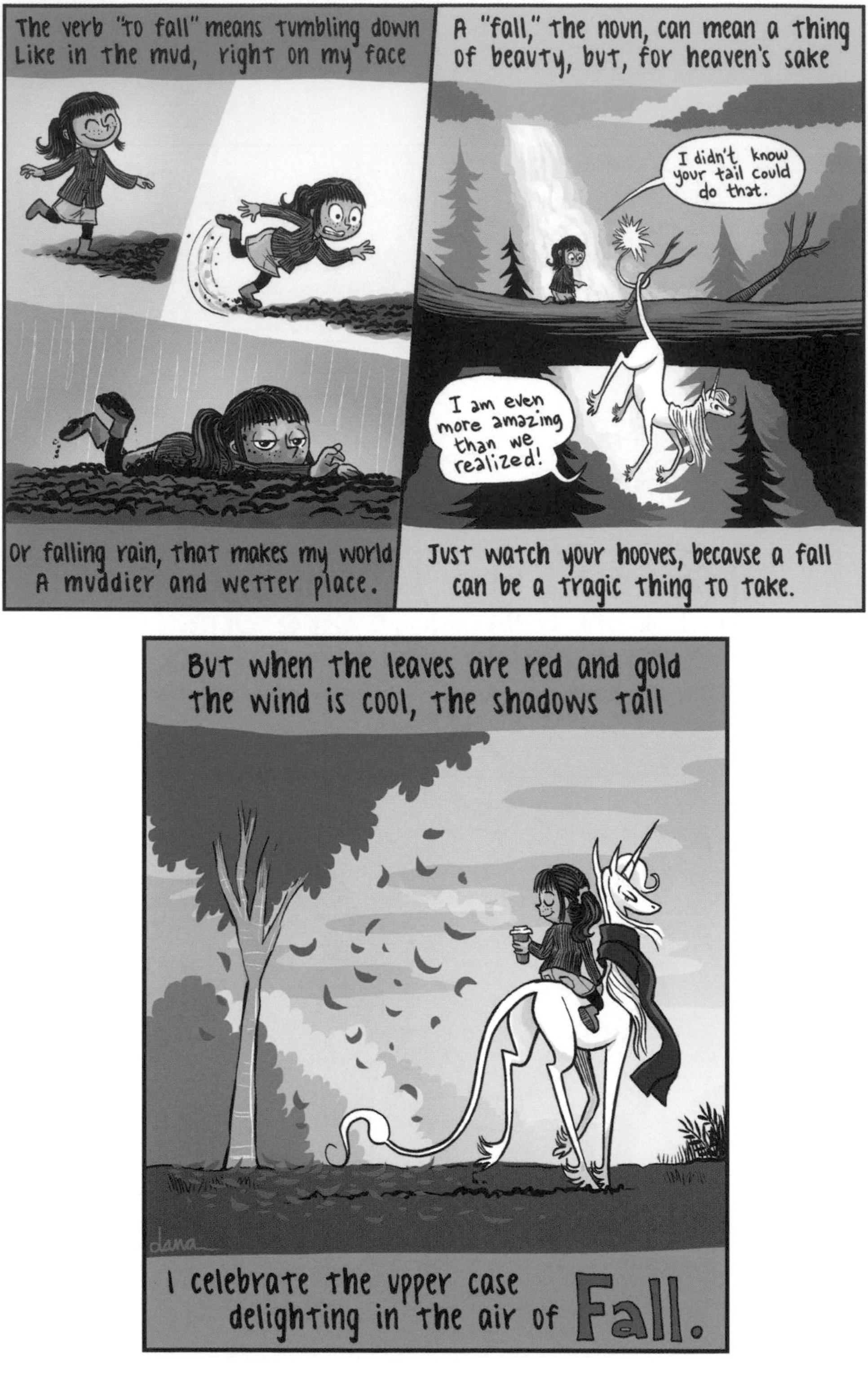

The verb "to fall" means tumbling down
Like in the mud, right on my face
Or falling rain, that makes my world
A muddier and wetter place.
A "fall," the noun, can mean a thing
of beauty, but, for heaven's sake
I didn't know your tail could do that.
I am even more amazing than we realized!
Just watch your hooves, because a fall
can be a tragic thing to take.
But when the leaves are red and gold
the wind is cool, the shadows tall
dana
I celebrate the upper case
delighting in the air of Fall.

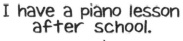

I have a piano lesson after school.

I'll be done with school, except WAIT! Instead of freedom, here's MORE school.

Just when I thought I was out, they pull me back in!

Is that a line from something?

Yeah, probably.

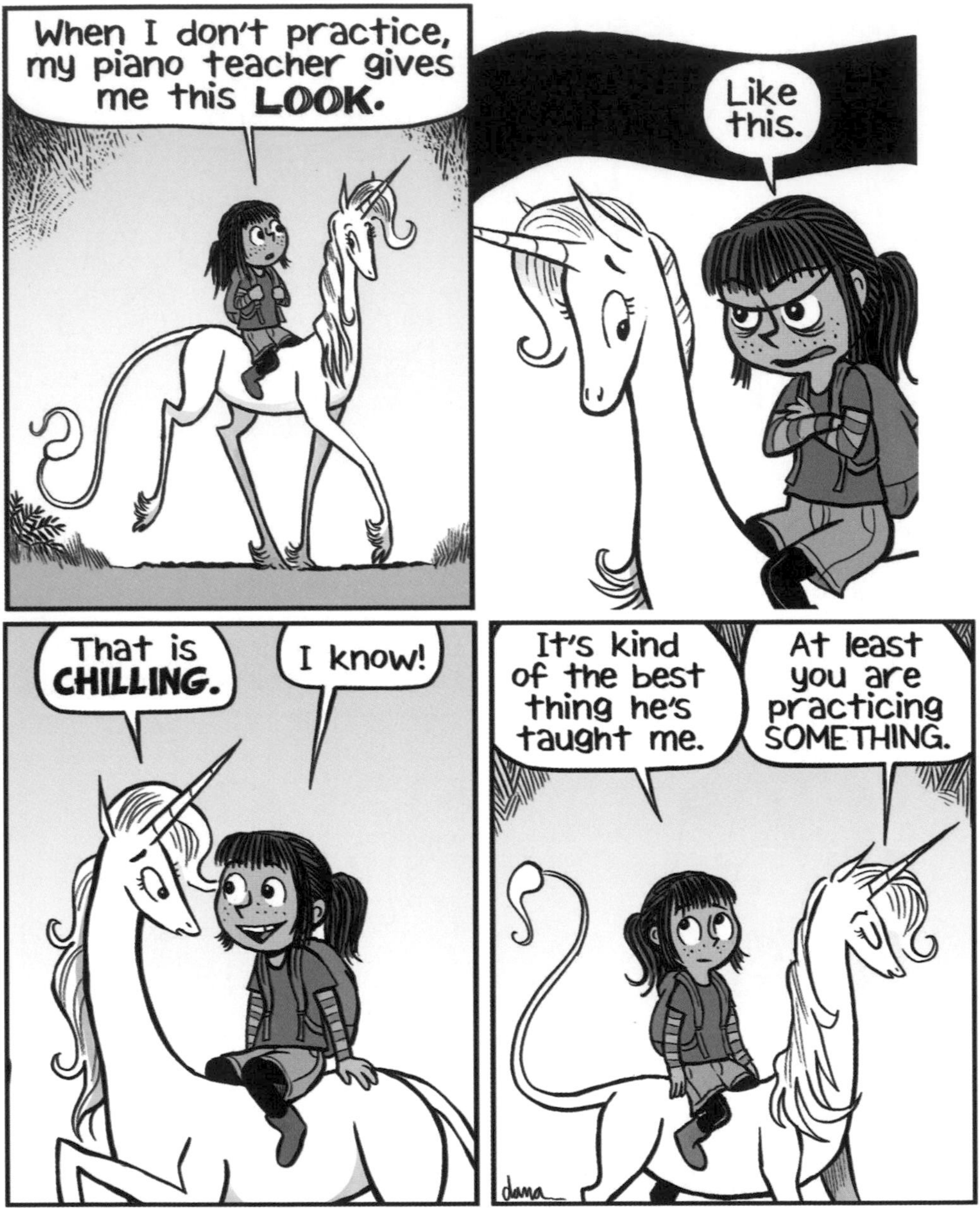
When I don't practice, my piano teacher gives me this LOOK.
Like this.
That is CHILLING.
I know!
It's kind of the best thing he's taught me.
At least you are practicing SOMETHING.
dana

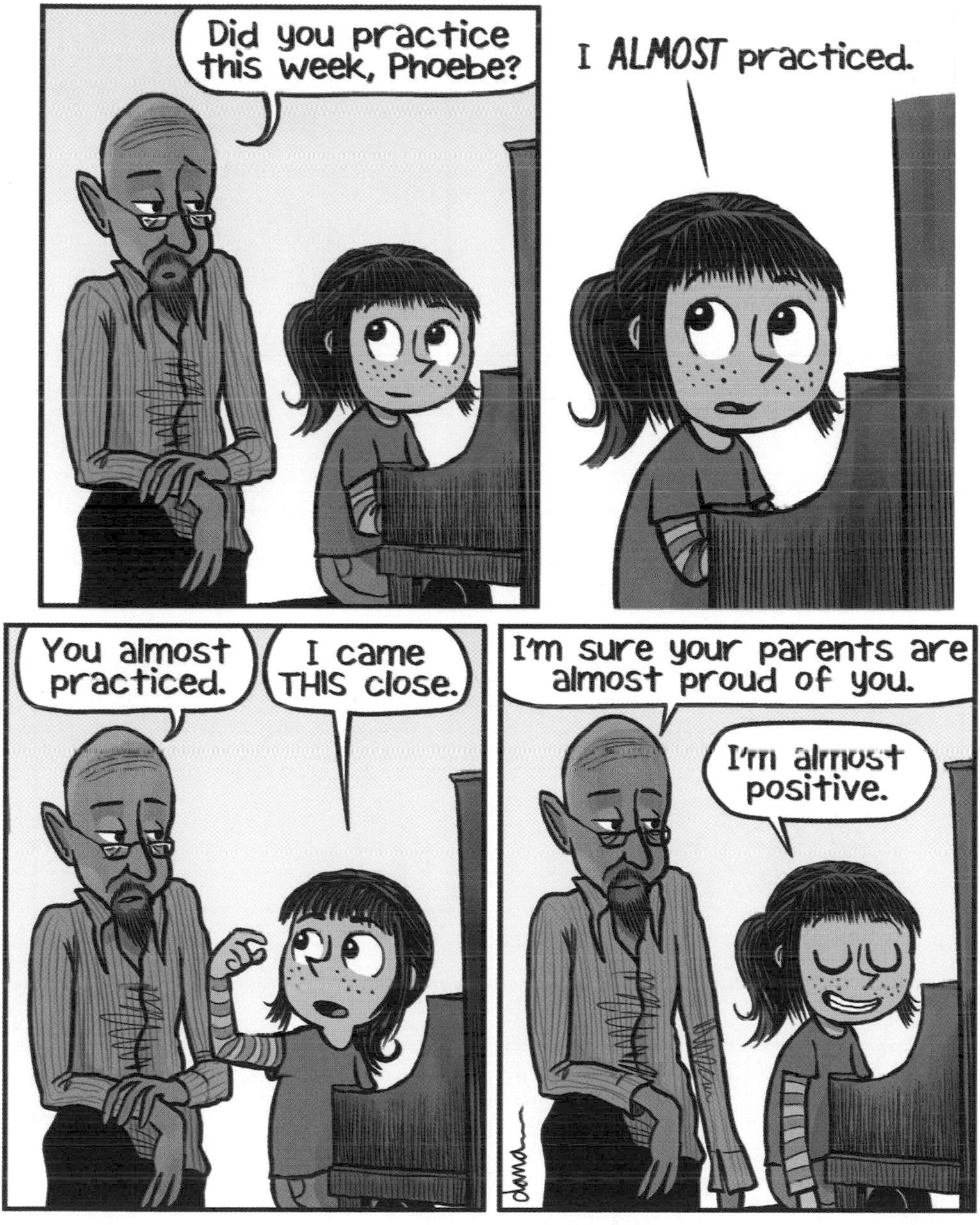
Did you practice this week, Phoebe?
I ALMOST practiced.
You almost practiced.
I came THIS close.
I'm sure your parents are almost proud of you.
I'm almost positive.

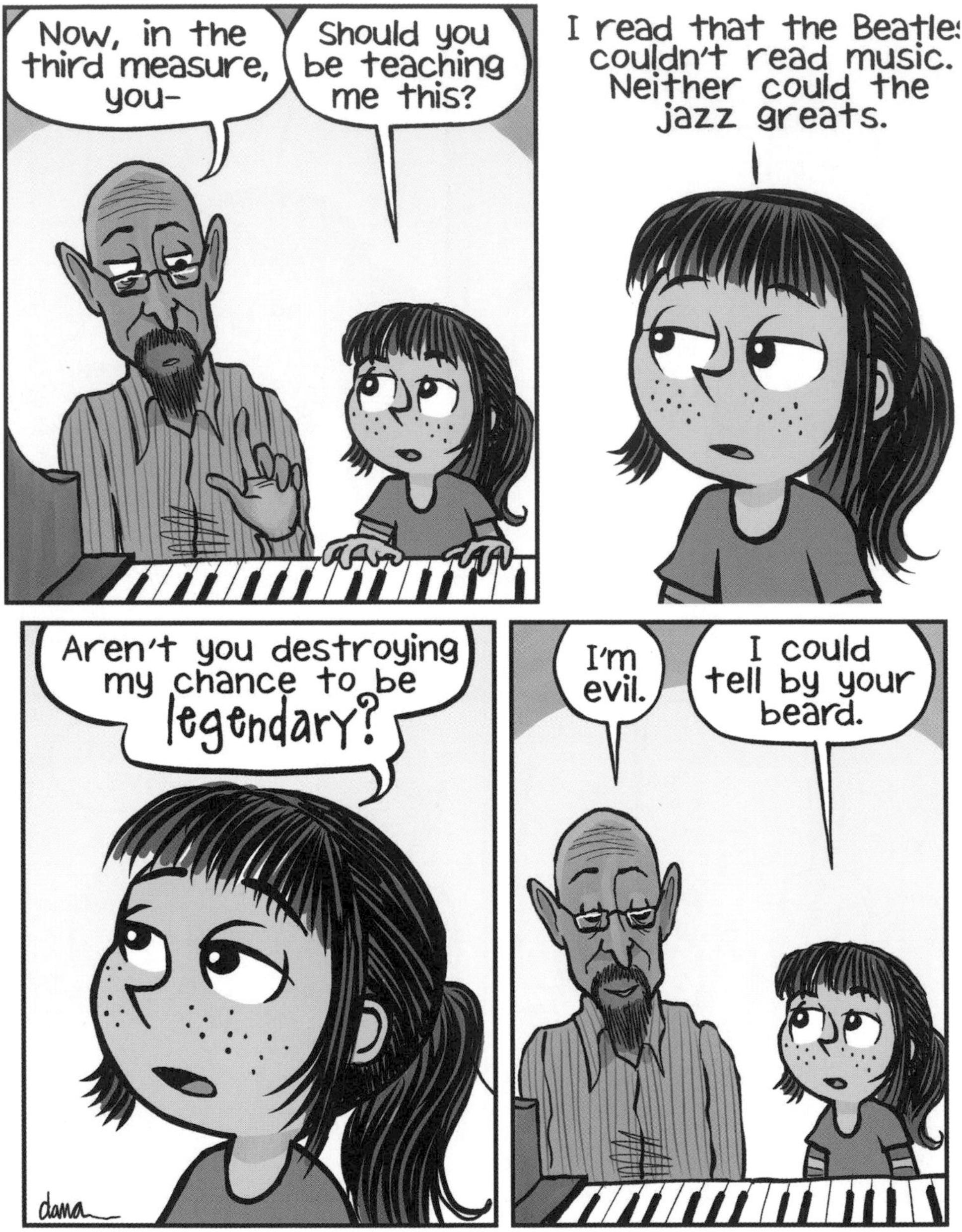
Now, in the third measure, you-
Should you be teaching me this?
I read that the Beatles couldn't read music. Neither could the jazz greats.
Aren't you destroying my chance to be legendary?
I'm evil.
I could tell by your beard.
dana

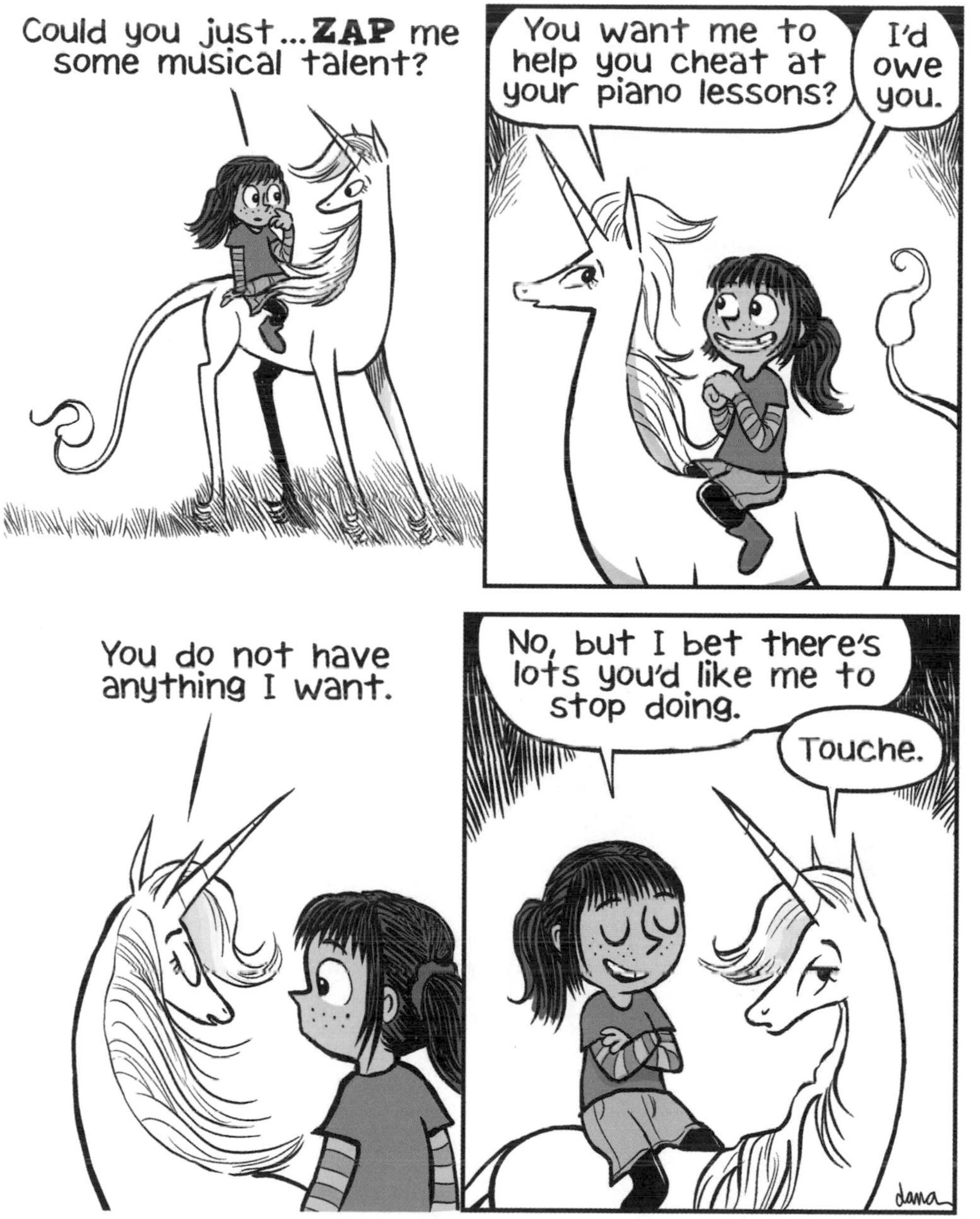
Could you just...ZAP me some musical talent?
You want me to help you cheat at your piano lessons?
I'd owe you.
You do not have anything I want.
No, but I bet there's lots you'd like me to stop doing.
Touche.
dana

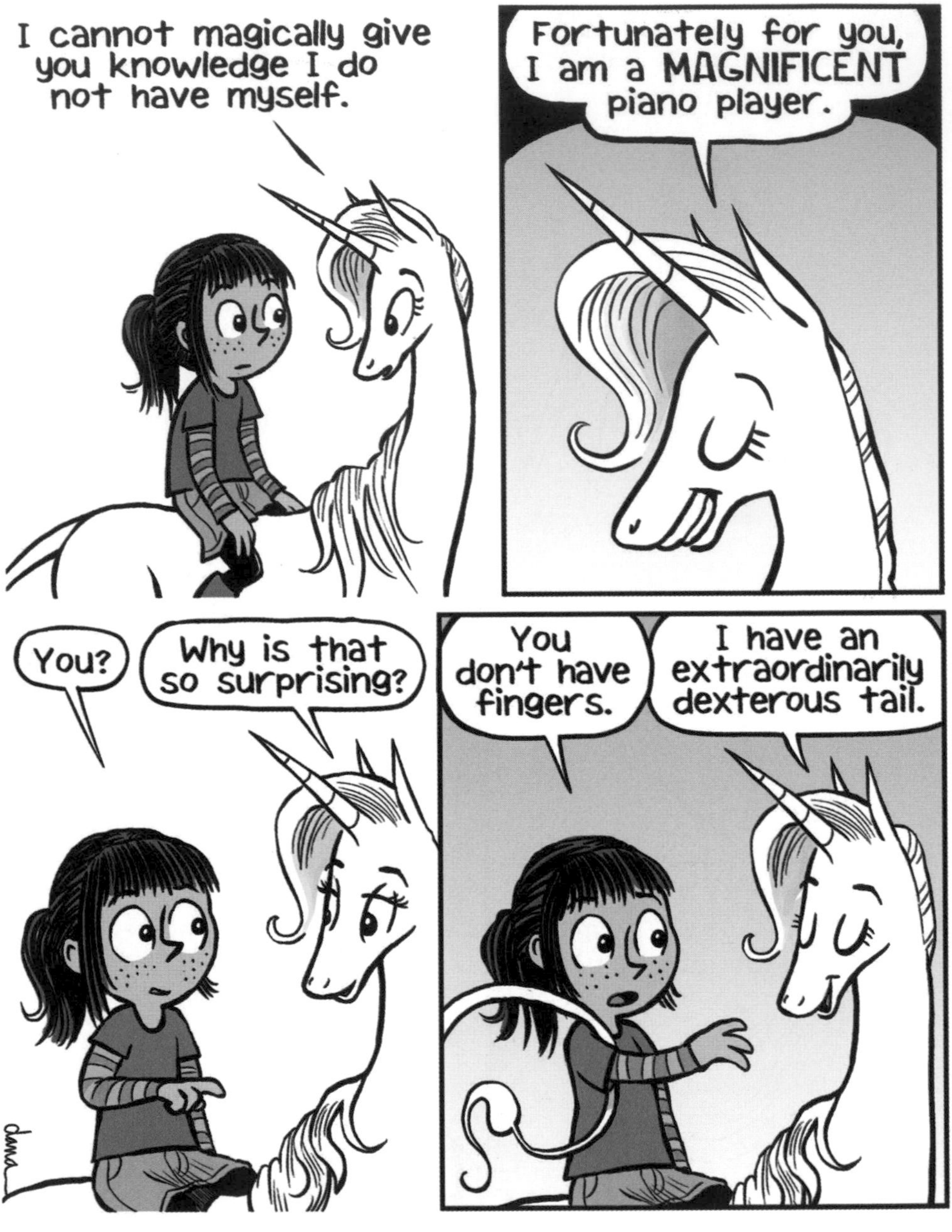
I cannot magically give you knowledge I do not have myself.
Fortunately for you, I am a MAGNIFICENT piano player.
You?
Why is that so surprising?
You don't have fingers.
I have an extraordinarily dexterous tail.
dana

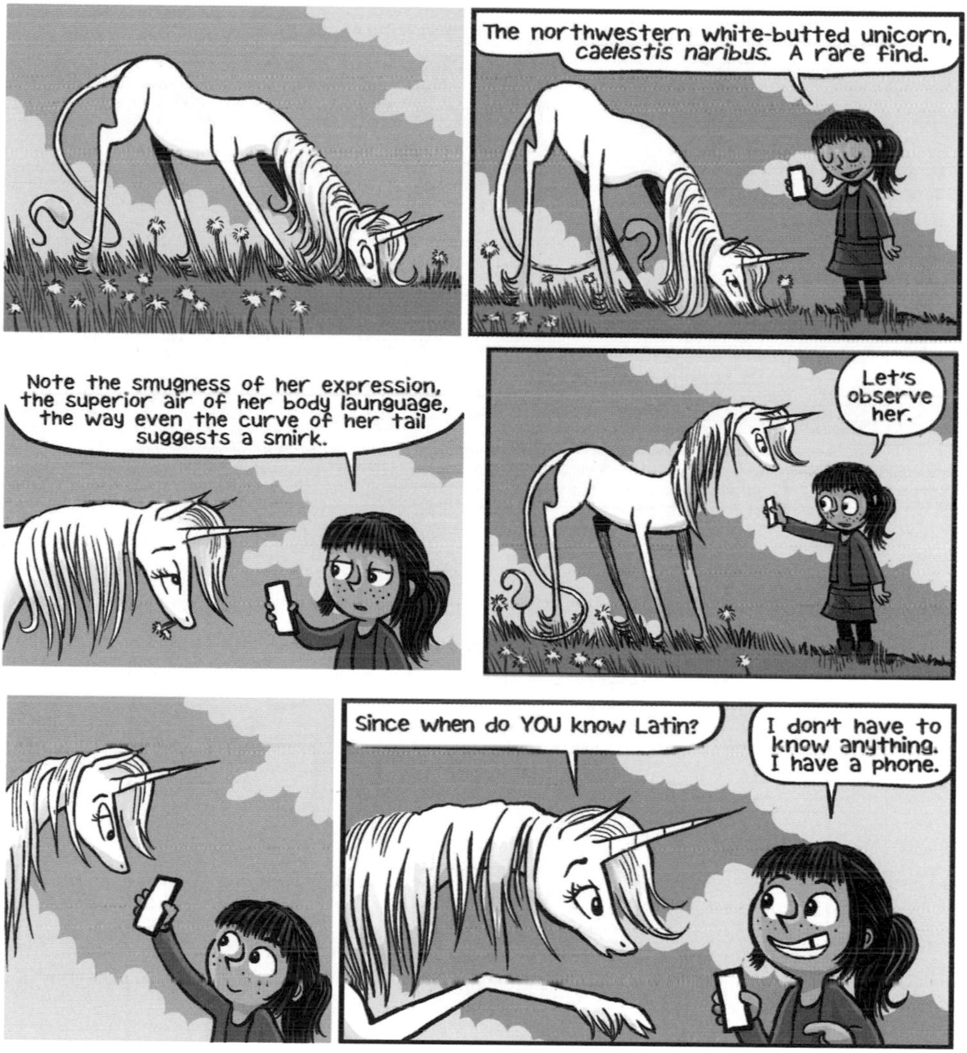

The northwestern white-butted unicorn, *caelestis naribus*. A rare find.
Note the smugness of her expression, the superior air of her body launguage, the way even the curve of her tail suggests a smirk.
Let's observe her.
Since when do YOU know Latin?
I don't have to know anything. I have a phone.

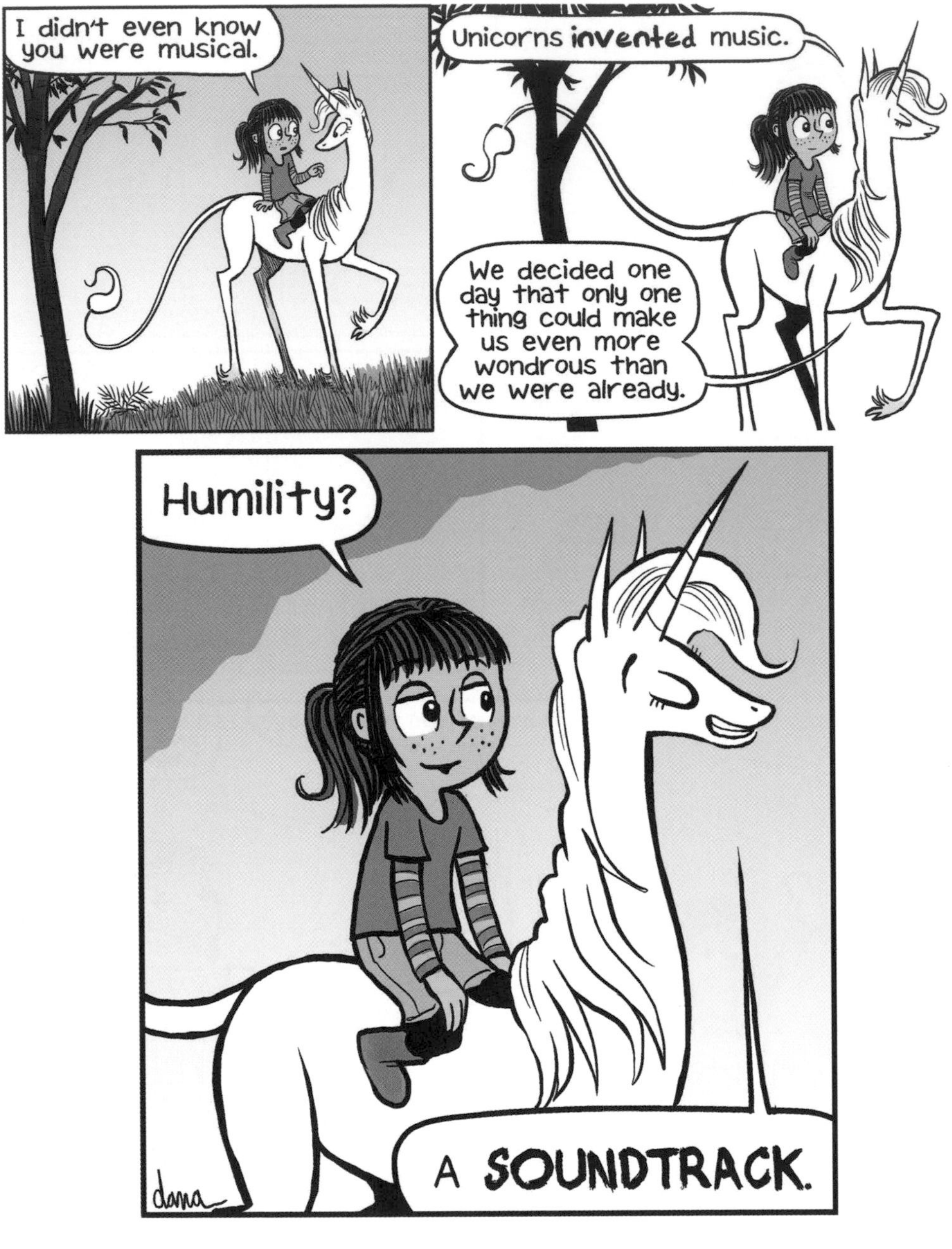
I didn't even know you were musical.
Unicorns **invented** music.
We decided one day that only one thing could make us even more wondrous than we were already.
Humility?
A **SOUNDTRACK.**
dana

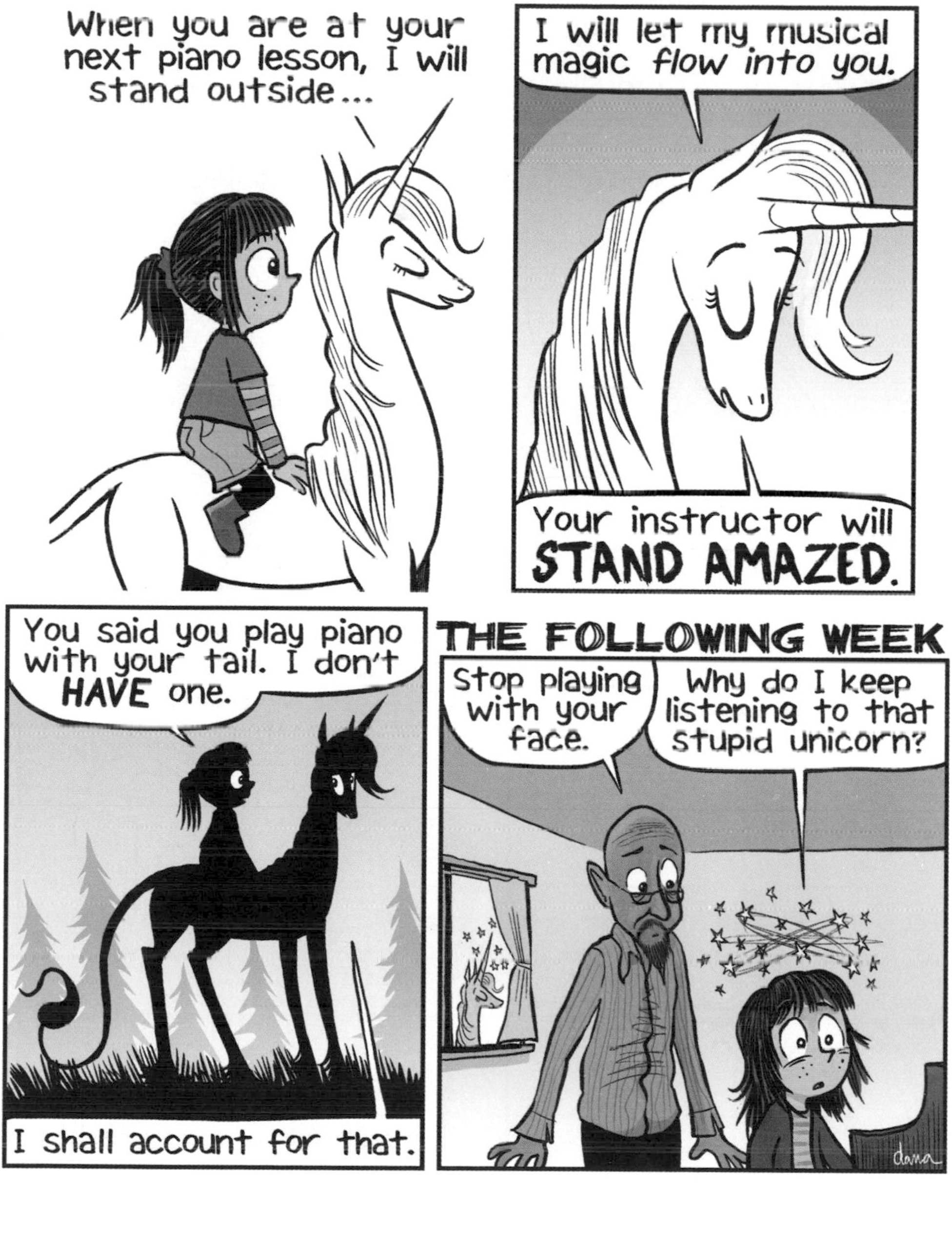
When you are at your next piano lesson, I will stand outside...
I will let my musical magic *flow into you.*
Your instructor will **STAND AMAZED.**
You said you play piano with your tail. I don't **HAVE** one.
I shall account for that.
THE FOLLOWING WEEK
Stop playing with your face.
Why do I keep listening to that stupid unicorn?
dana

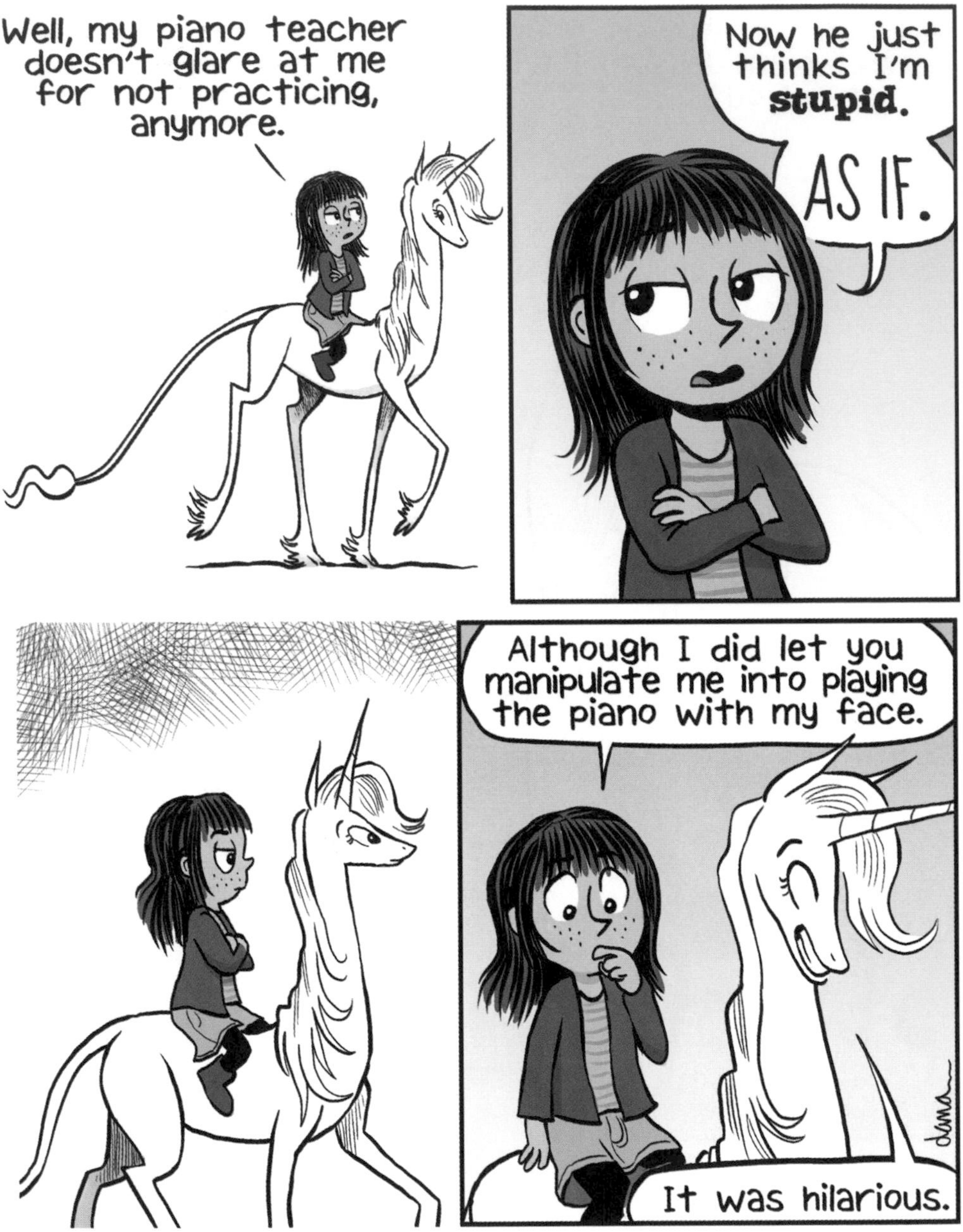
Well, my piano teacher doesn't glare at me for not practicing, anymore.
Now he just thinks I'm **stupid**.
AS IF.
Although I did let you manipulate me into playing the piano with my face.
It was hilarious.
dana

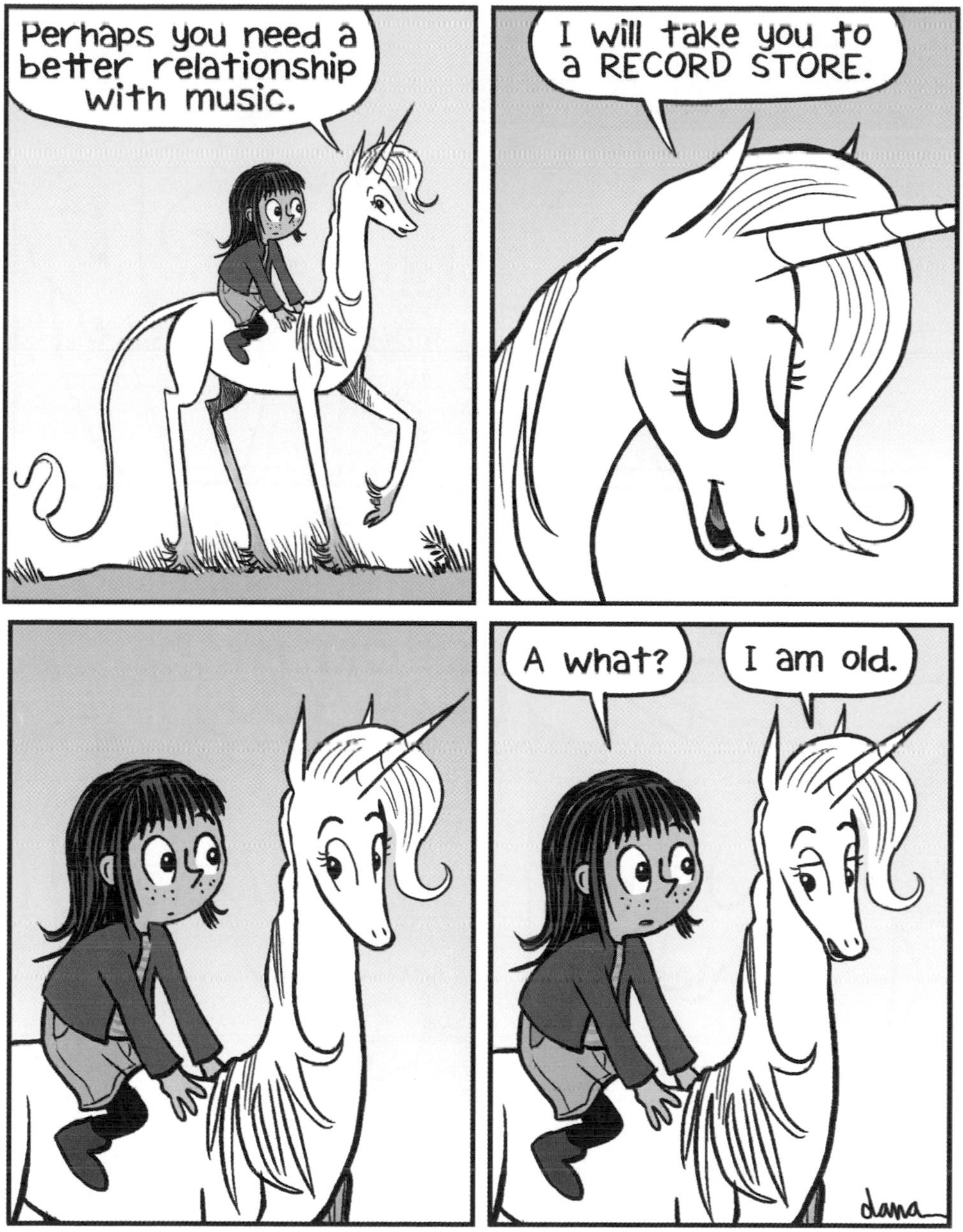
Perhaps you need a better relationship with music.
I will take you to a RECORD STORE.
A what?
I am old.
dana

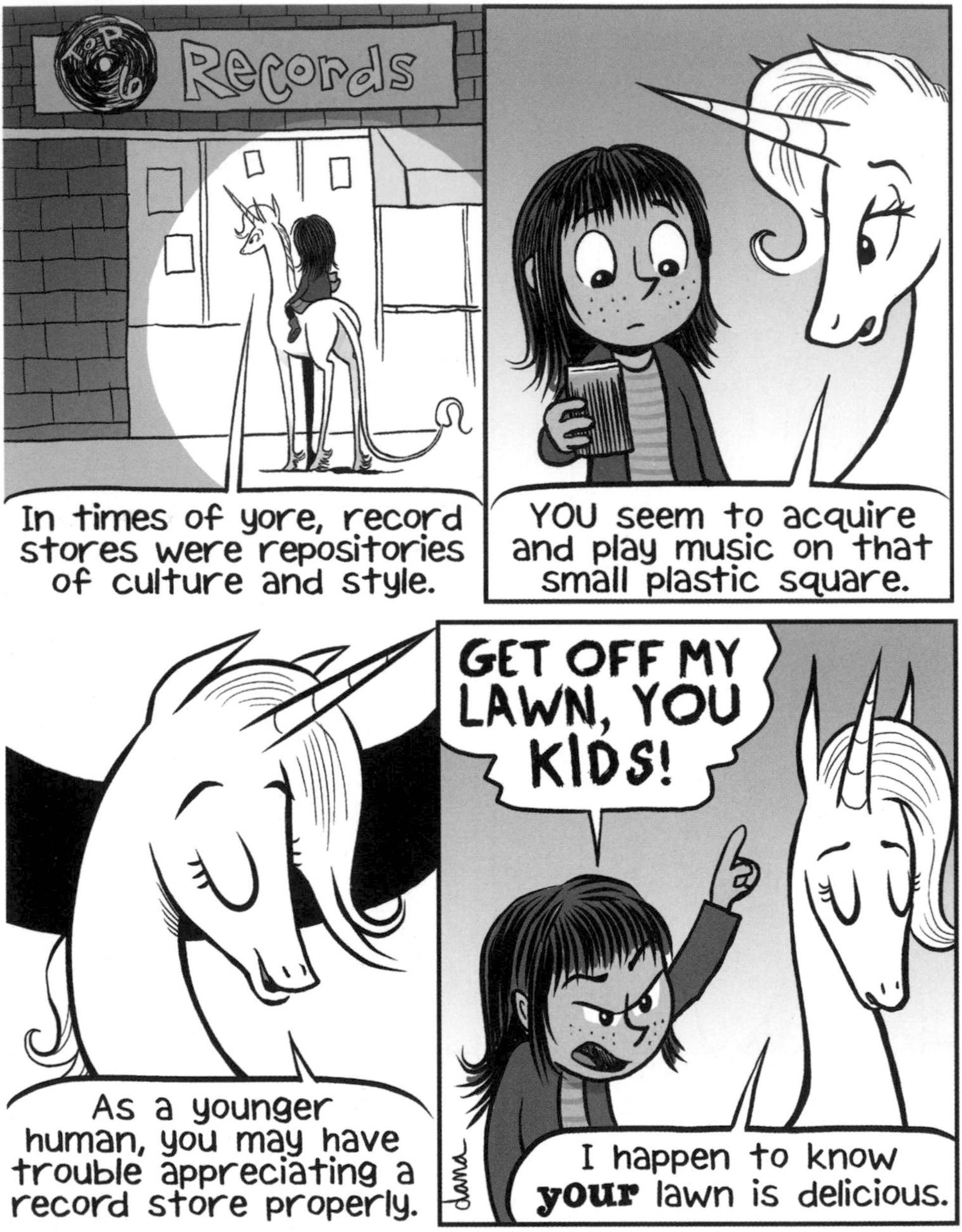
Records
In times of yore, record stores were repositories of culture and style.
YOU seem to acquire and play music on that small plastic square.
As a younger human, you may have trouble appreciating a record store properly.
GET OFF MY LAWN, YOU KIDS!
I happen to know **your** lawn is delicious.
dana

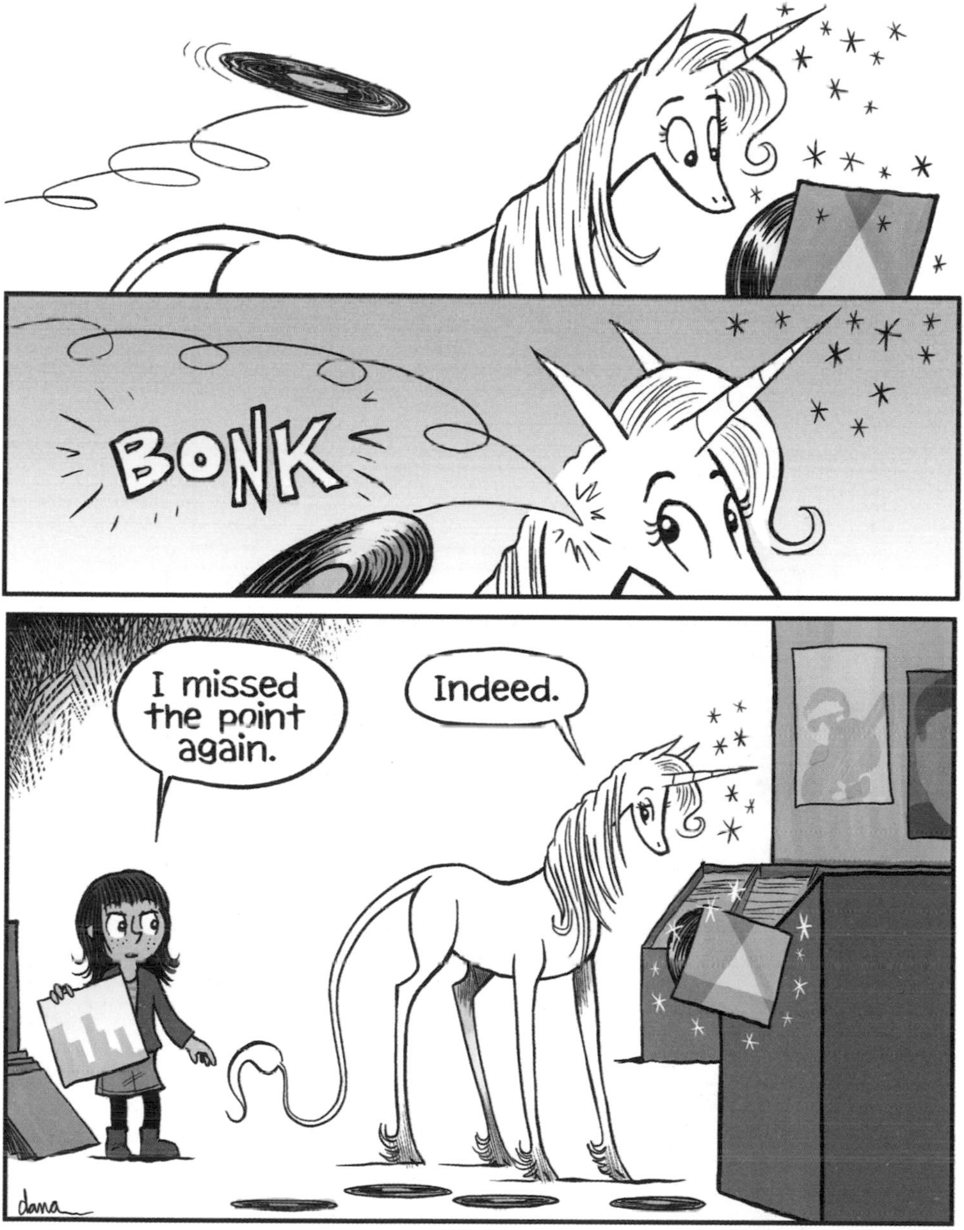
BONK
I missed the point again.
Indeed.
dana

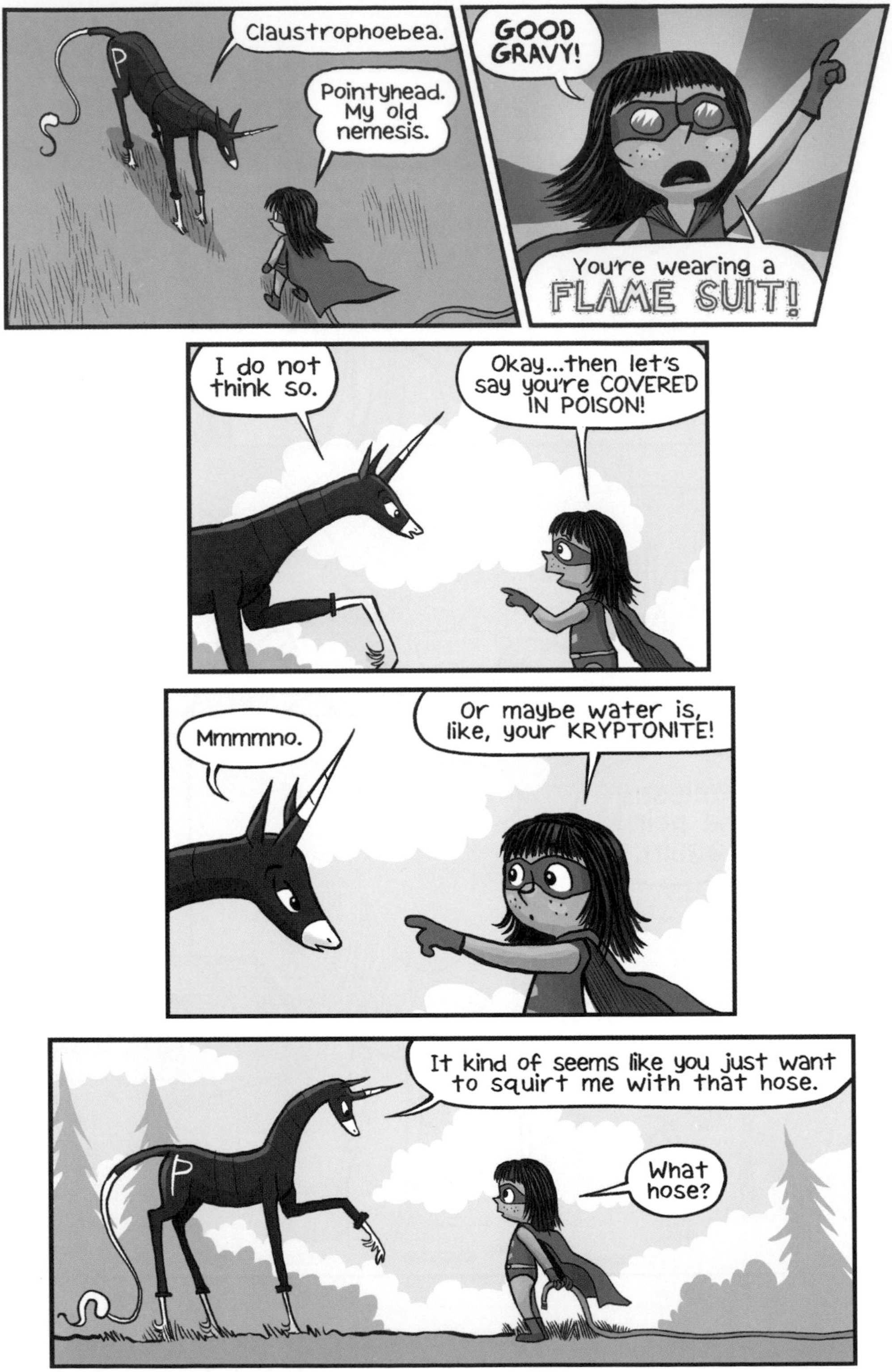
Claustrophoebea.
Pointyhead. My old nemesis.
GOOD GRAVY!
You're wearing a FLAME SUIT!
I do not think so.
Okay...then let's say you're COVERED IN POISON!
Mmmmno.
Or maybe water is, like, your KRYPTONITE!
It kind of seems like you just want to squirt me with that hose.
What hose?

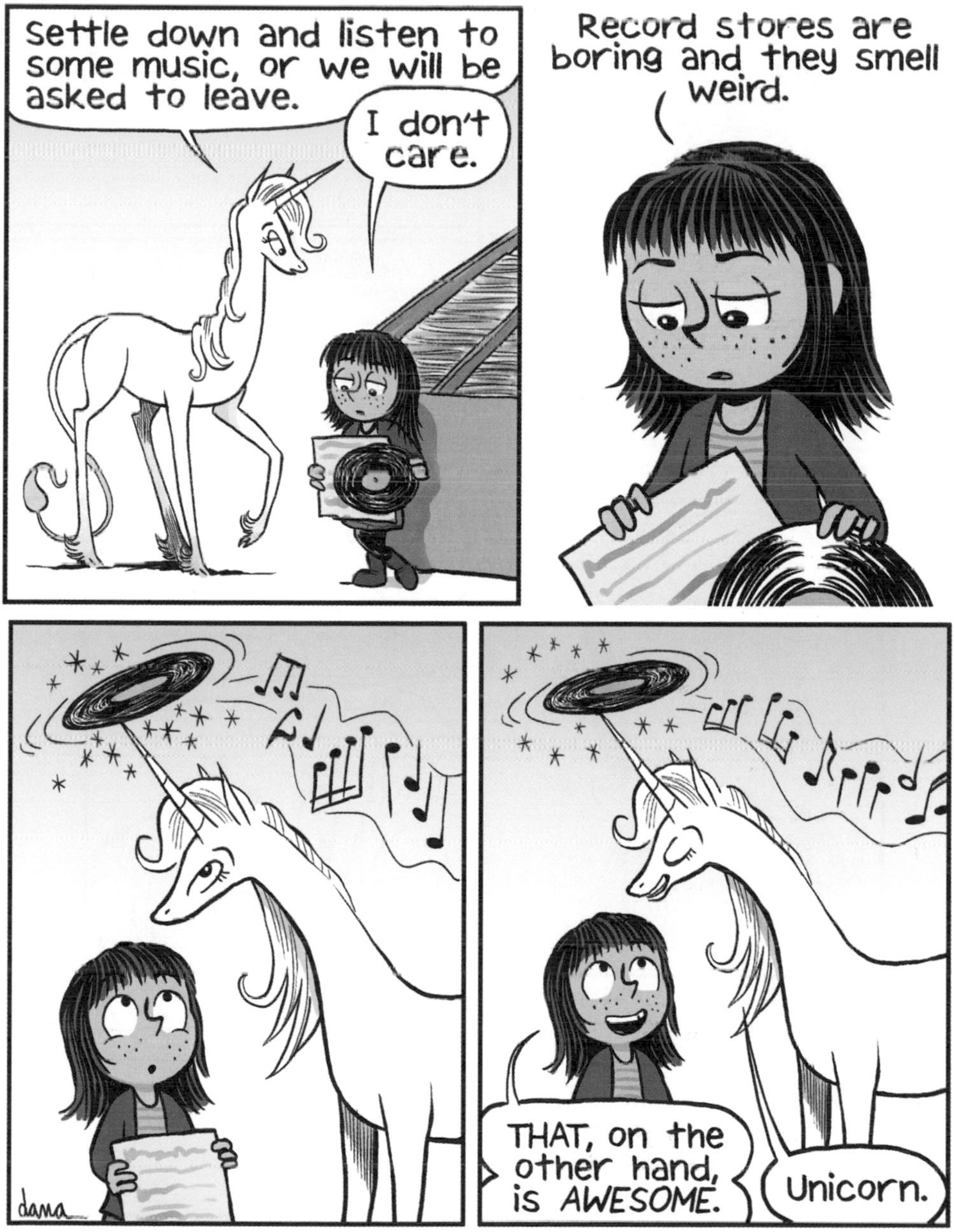
Settle down and listen to some music, or we will be asked to leave.
I don't care.
Record stores are boring and they smell weird.
THAT, on the other hand, is AWESOME.
Unicorn.

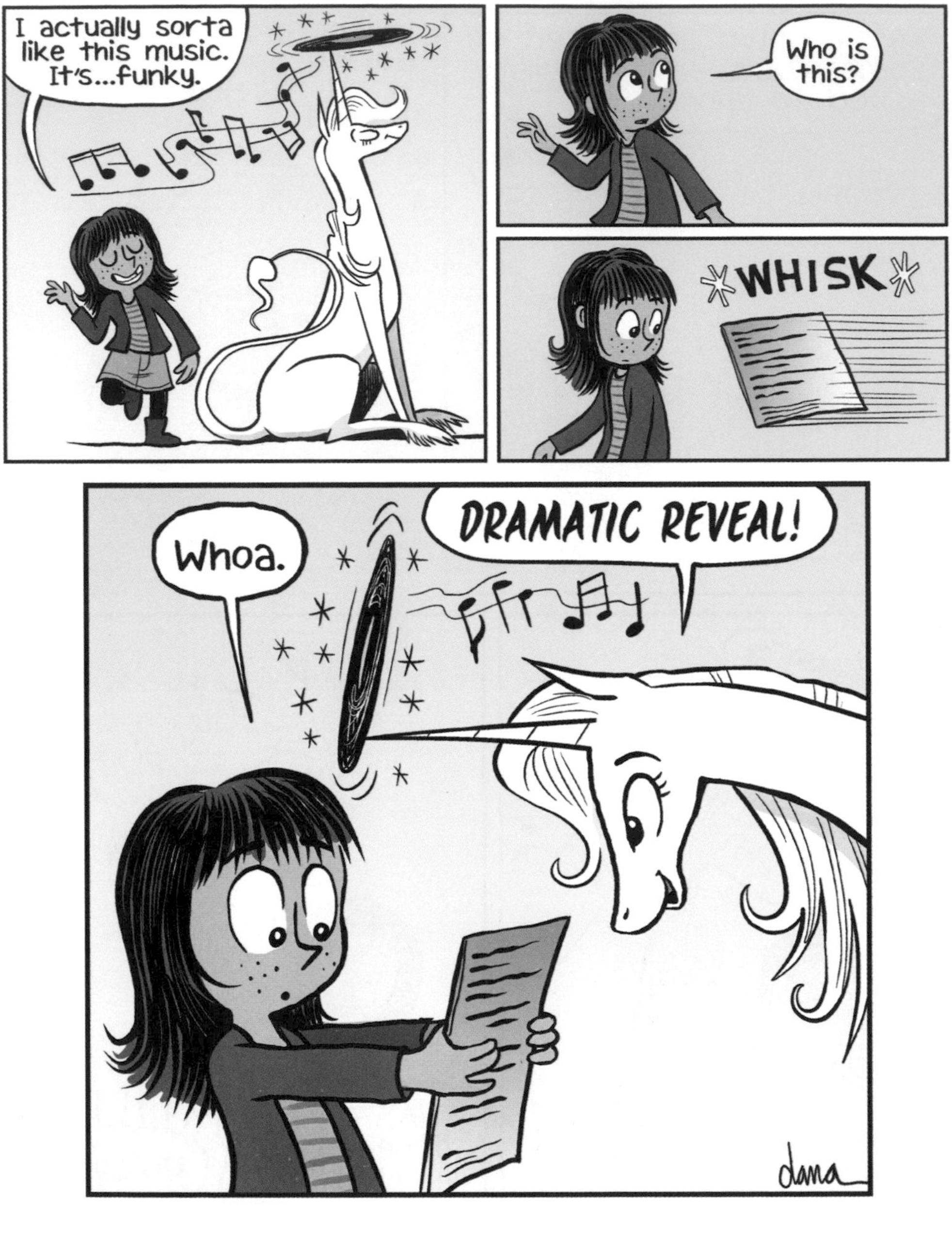
I actually sorta like this music. It's...funky.
Who is this?
WHISK
Whoa.
DRAMATIC REVEAL!
dana

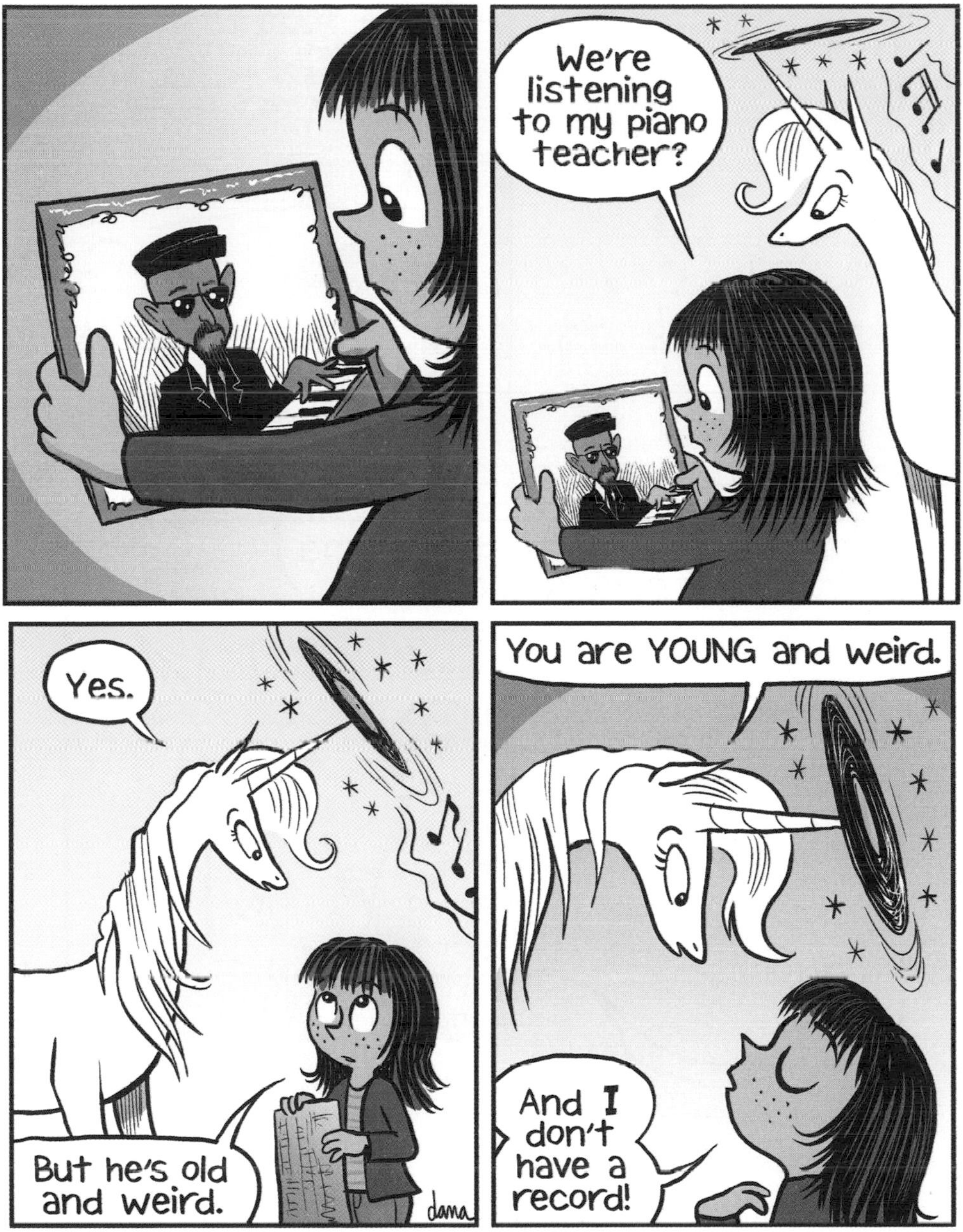
We're listening to my piano teacher?
Yes.
But he's old and weird.
You are YOUNG and weird.
And I don't have a record!
dana

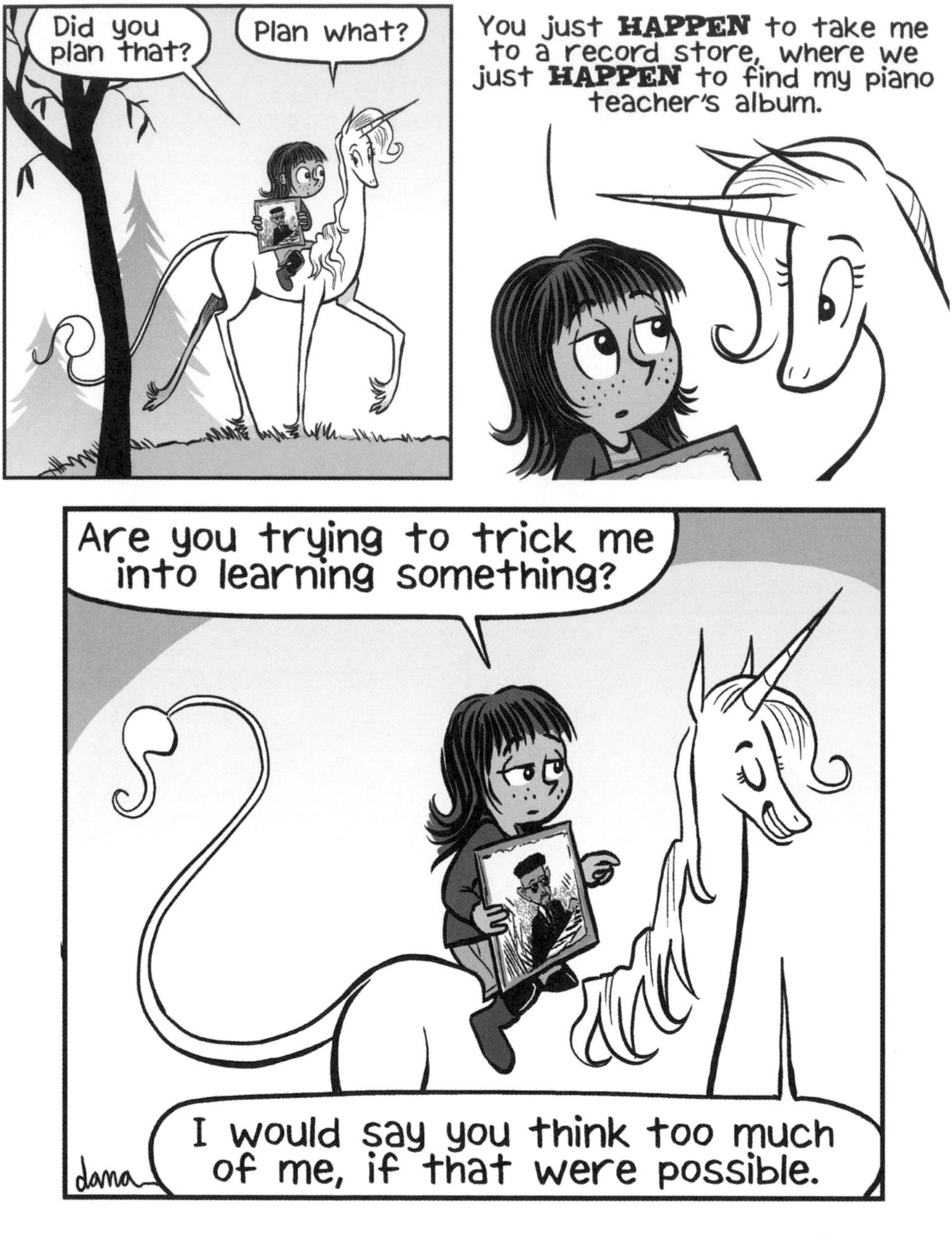
Did you plan that?
Plan what?
You just HAPPEN to take me to a record store, where we just HAPPEN to find my piano teacher's album.
Are you trying to trick me into learning something?
I would say you think too much of me, if that were possible.
dana

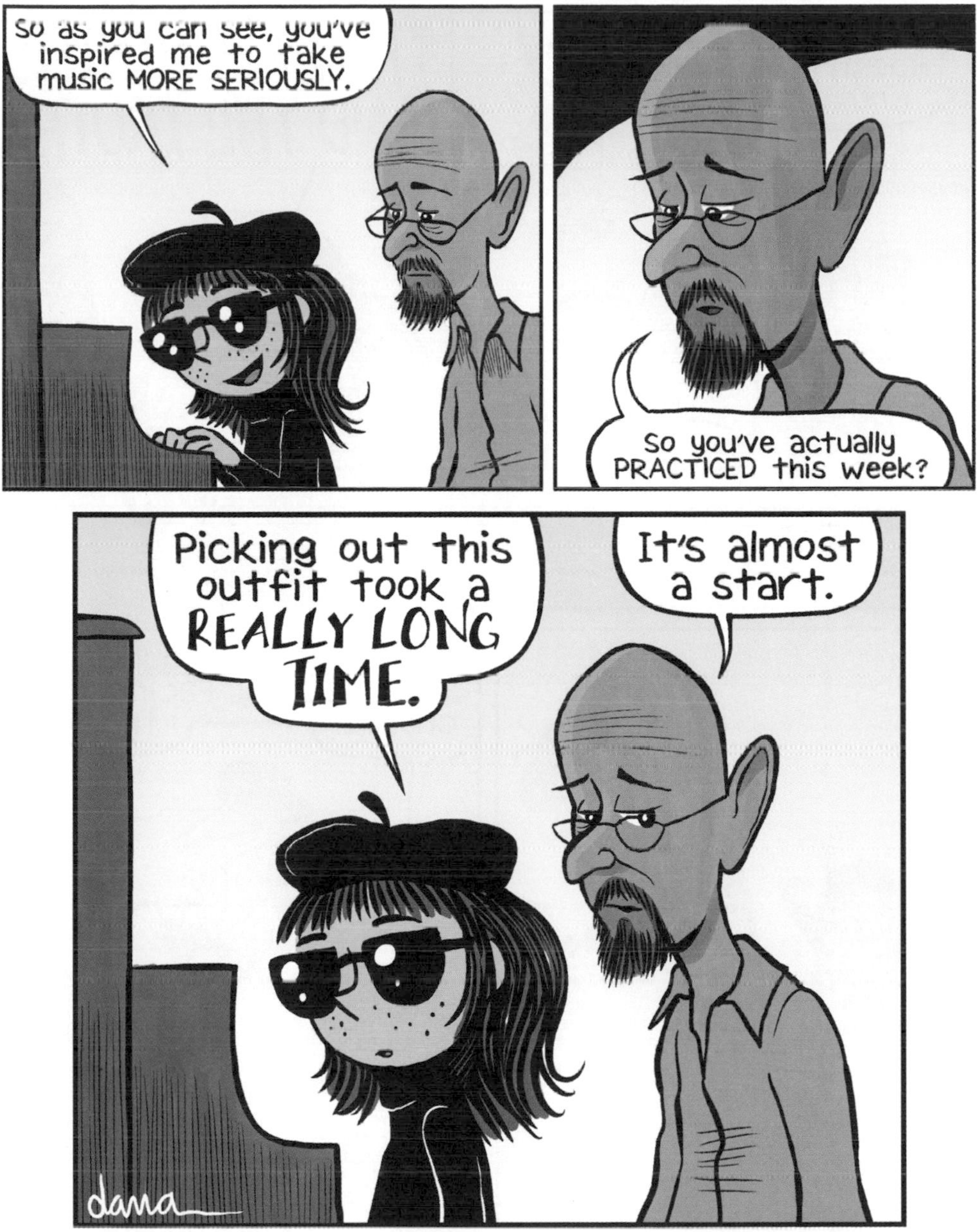
So as you can see, you've inspired me to take music MORE SERIOUSLY.
So you've actually PRACTICED this week?
Picking out this outfit took a REALLY LONG TIME.
It's almost a start.
dana

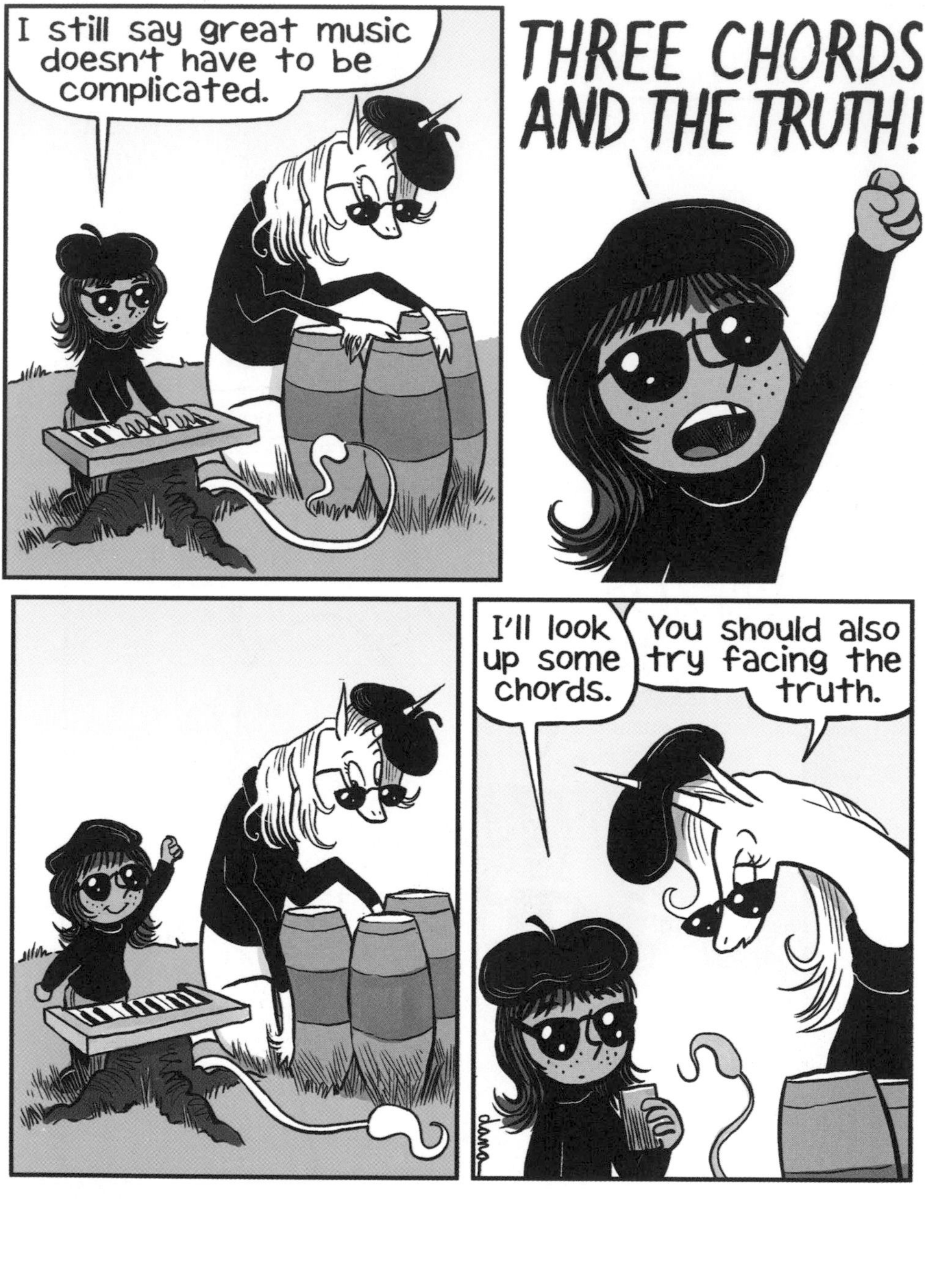

I still say great music doesn't have to be complicated.
THREE CHORDS AND THE TRUTH!
I'll look up some chords.
You should also try facing the truth.

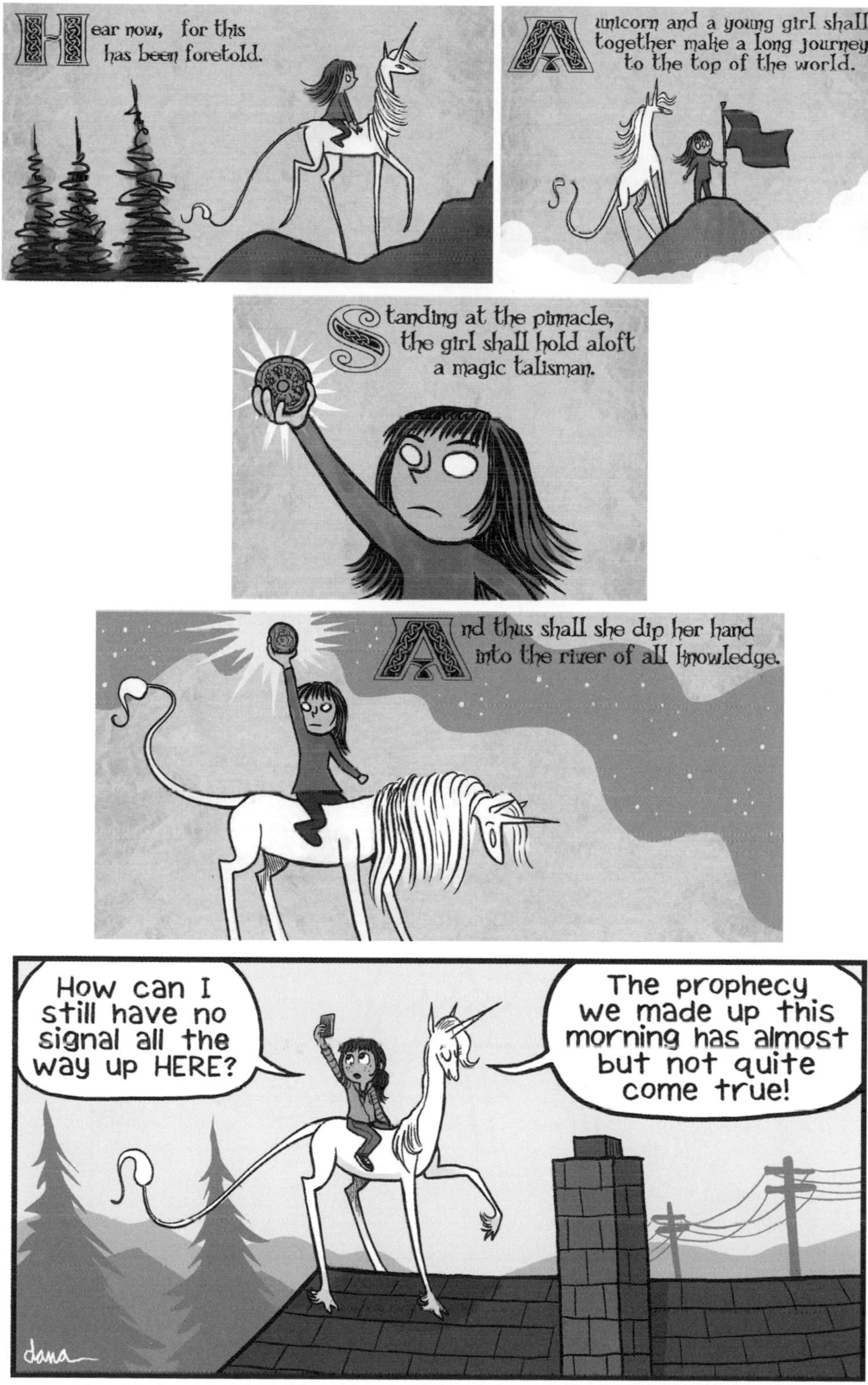
Hear now, for this has been foretold.
A unicorn and a young girl shall together make a long journey to the top of the world.
Standing at the pinnacle, the girl shall hold aloft a magic talisman.
And thus shall she dip her hand into the river of all knowledge.
How can I still have no signal all the way up HERE?
The prophecy we made up this morning has almost but not quite come true!
dana

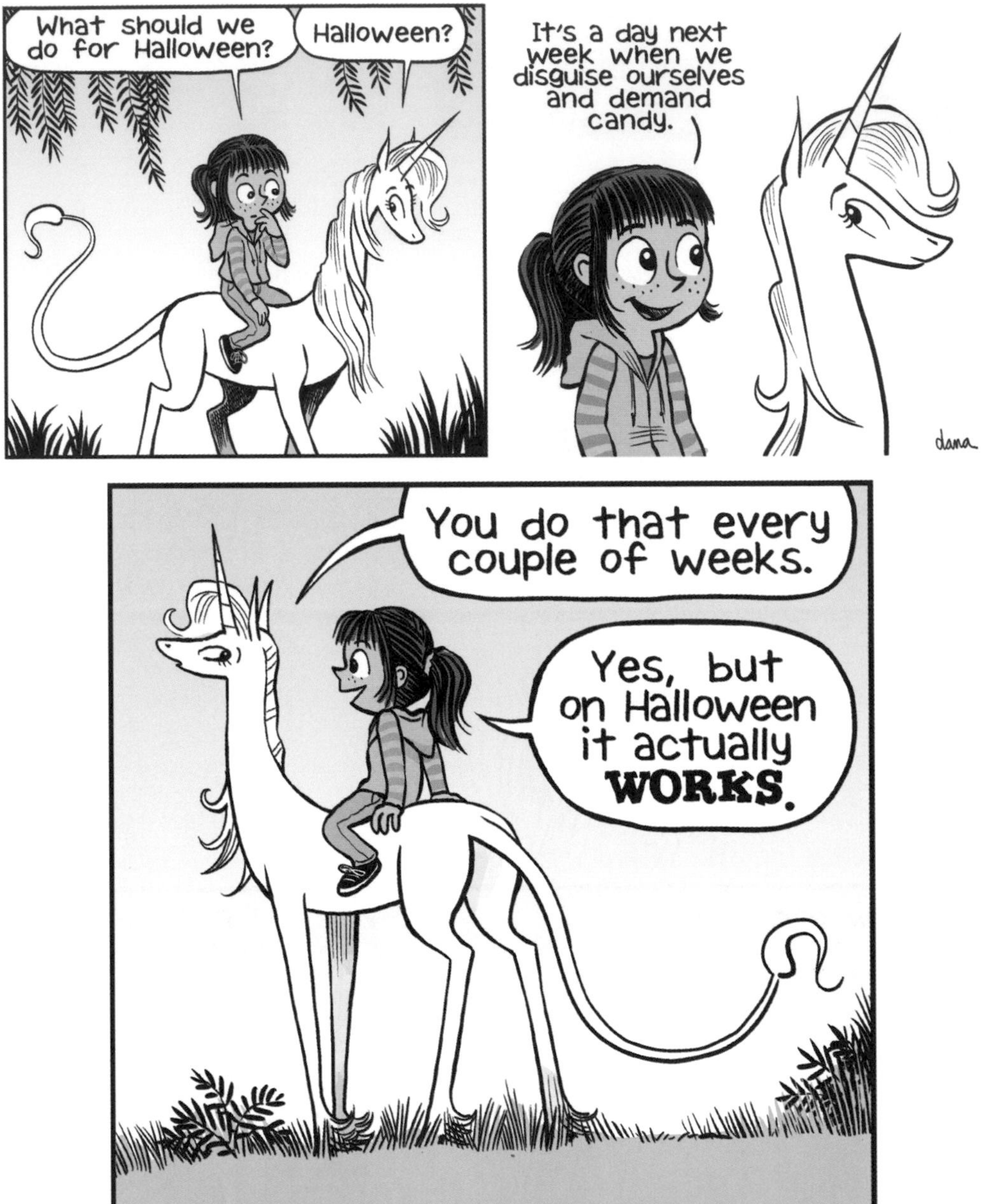
What should we do for Halloween?
Halloween?
It's a day next week when we disguise ourselves and demand candy.
dana
You do that every couple of weeks.
Yes, but on Halloween it actually **WORKS**.

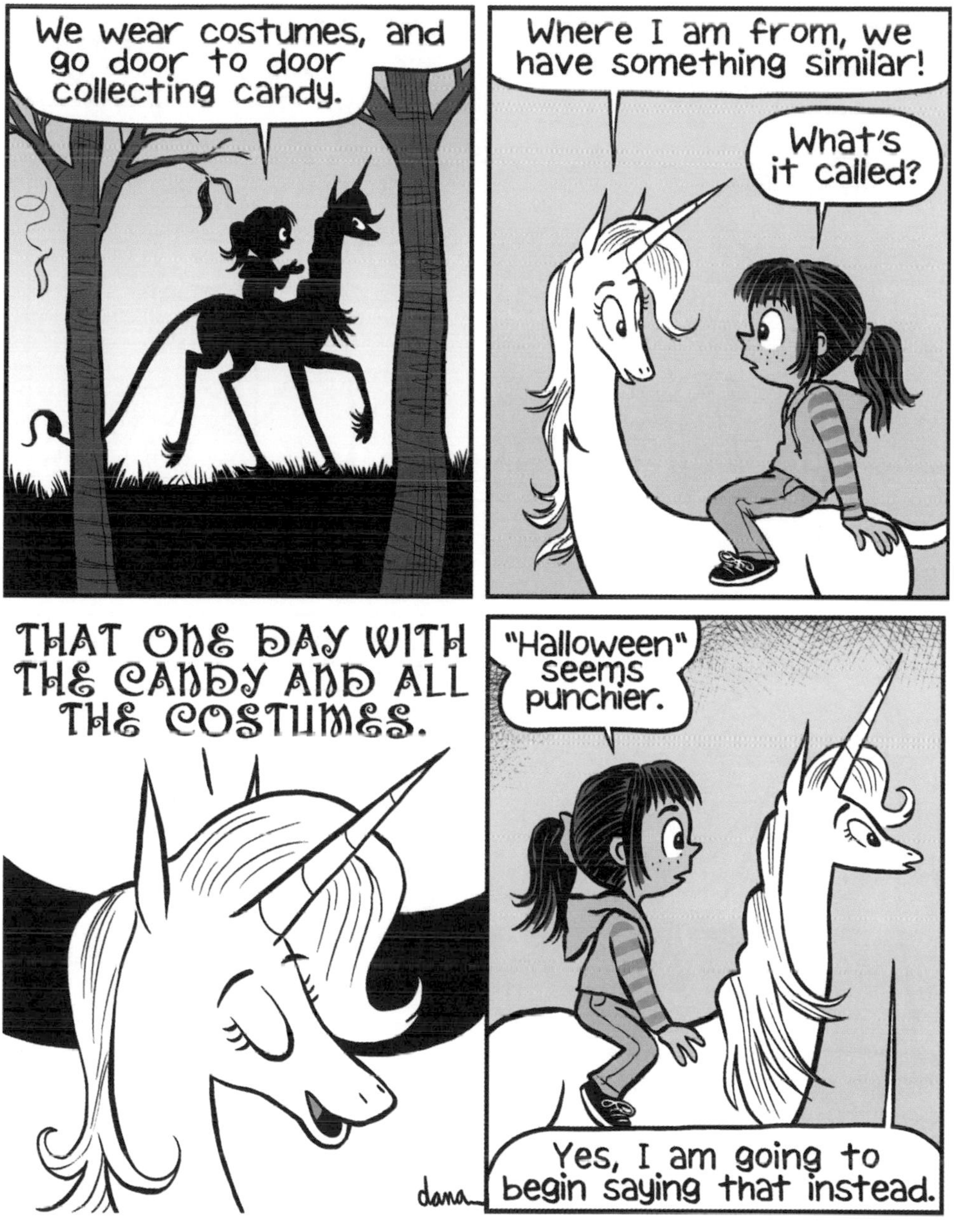
We wear costumes, and go door to door collecting candy.
Where I am from, we have something similar!
What's it called?
THAT ONE DAY WITH THE CANDY AND ALL THE COSTUMES.
"Halloween" seems punchier.
Yes, I am going to begin saying that instead.
dana

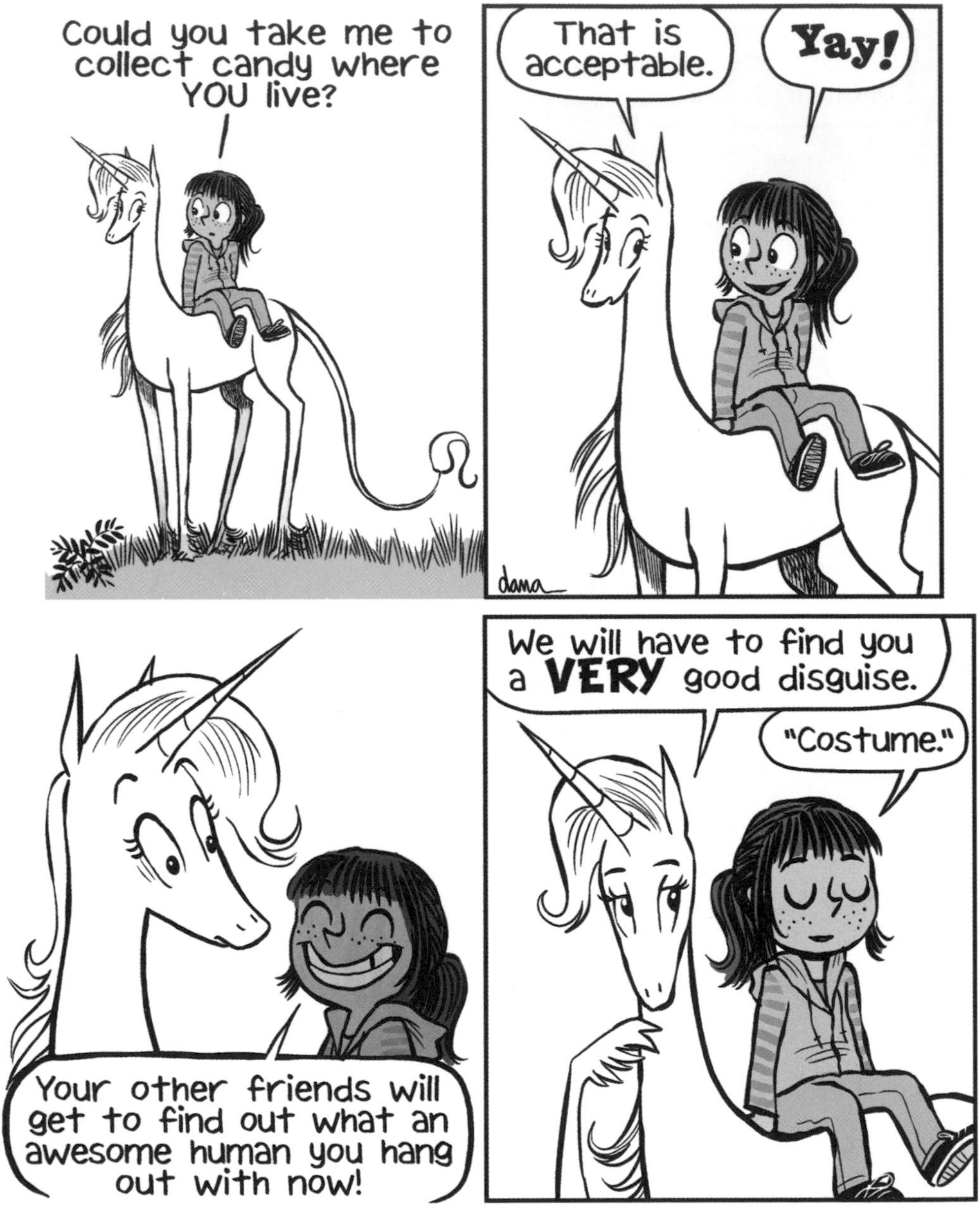
Could you take me to collect candy where YOU live?
That is acceptable.
Yay!
dana
Your other friends will get to find out what an awesome human you hang out with now!
We will have to find you a VERY good disguise.
"Costume."

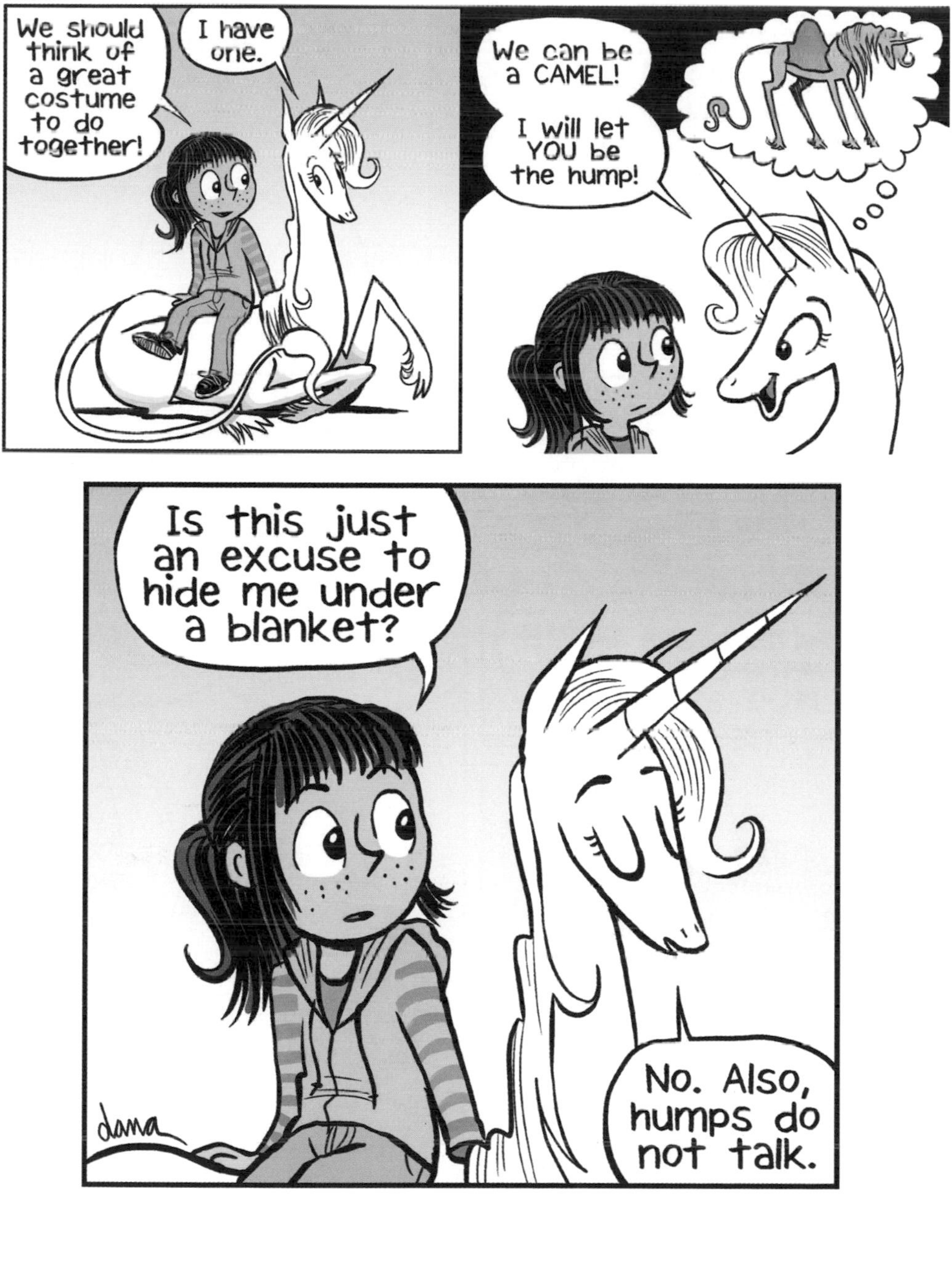
We should think of a great costume to do together!
I have one.
We can be a CAMEL!
I will let YOU be the hump!
Is this just an excuse to hide me under a blanket?
No. Also, humps do not talk.
dana

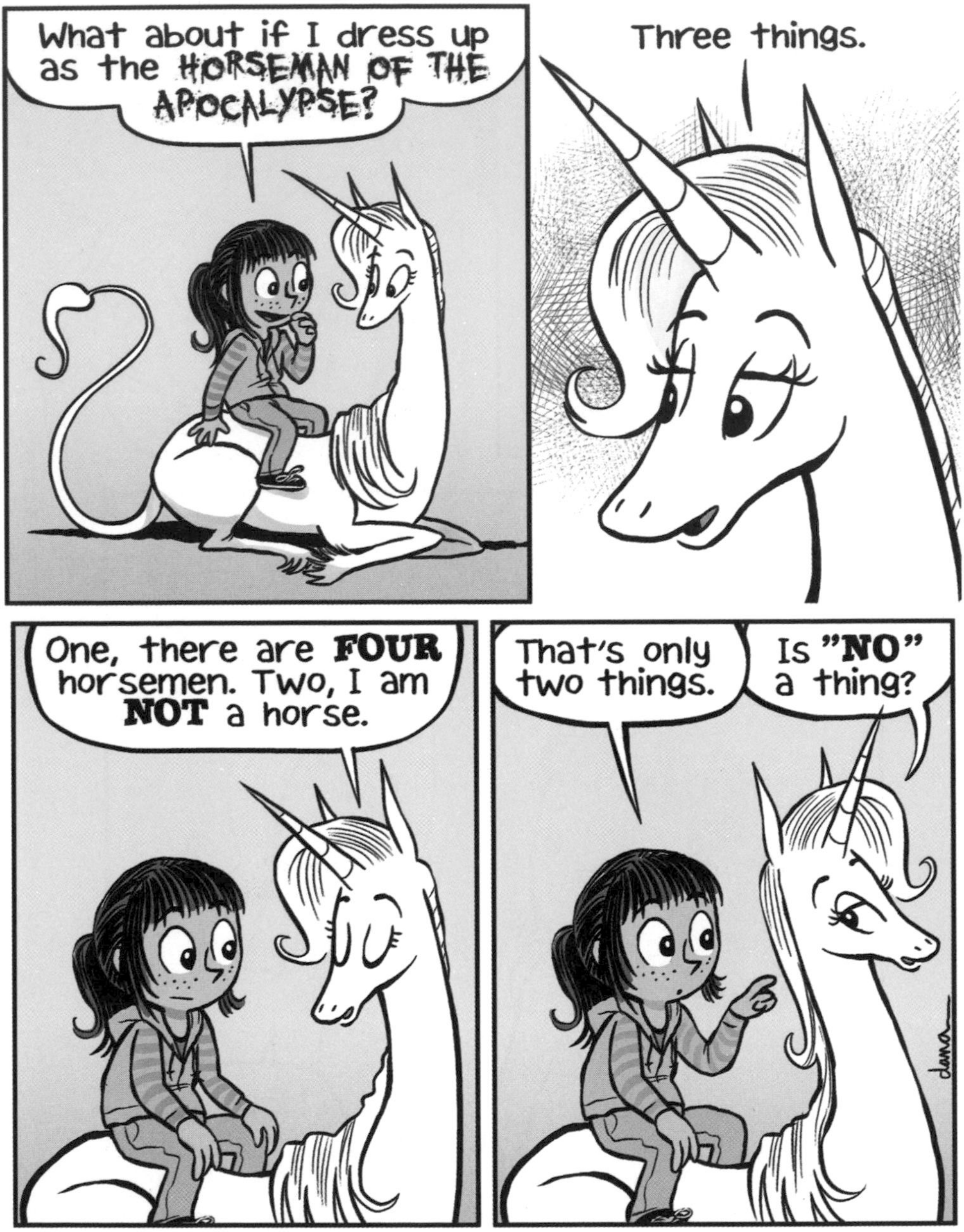
What about if I dress up as the HORSEMAN OF THE APOCALYPSE?
Three things.
One, there are **FOUR** horsemen. Two, I am **NOT** a horse.
That's only two things.
Is **"NO"** a thing?
dana

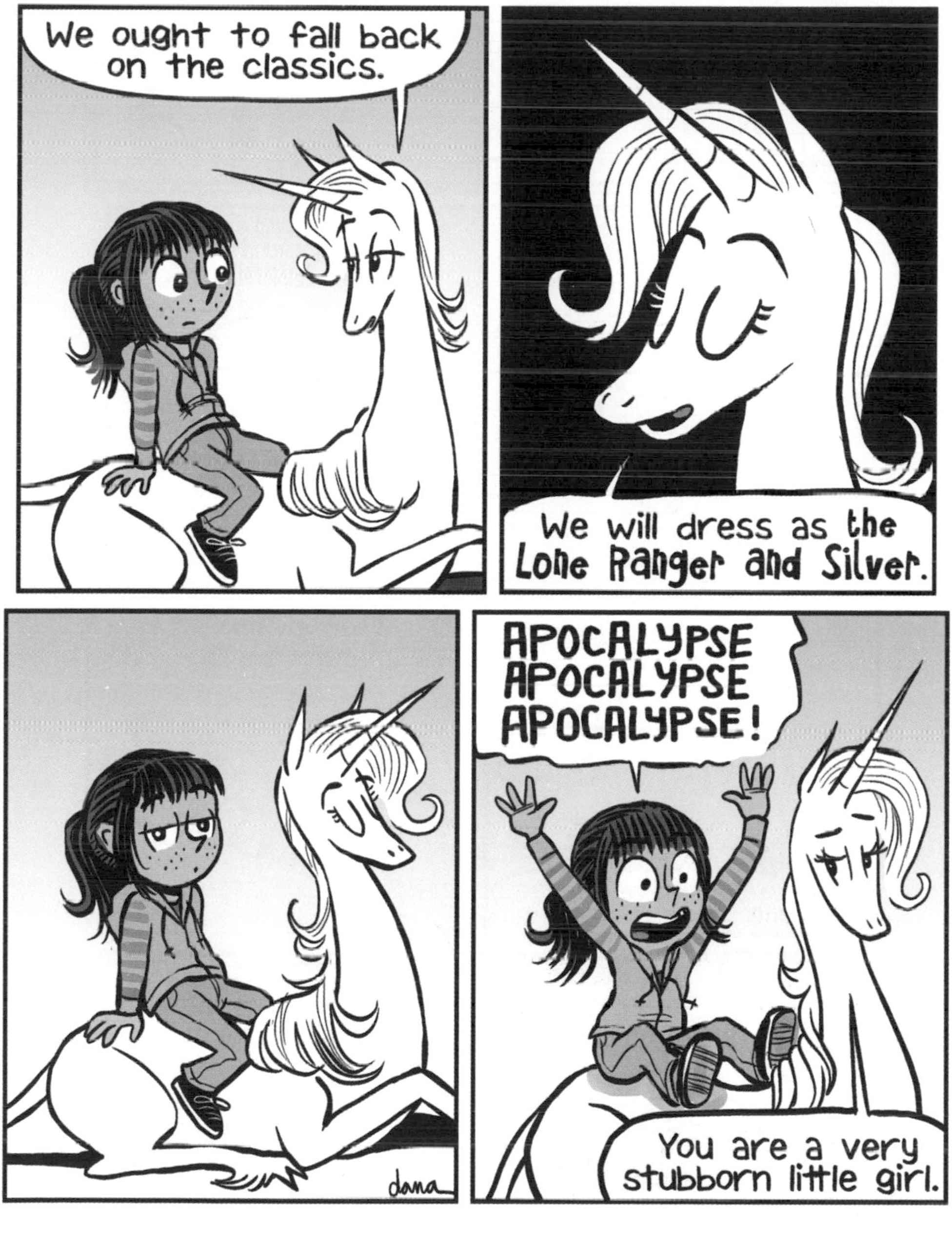

We ought to fall back on the classics.
We will dress as the Lone Ranger and Silver.
APOCALYPSE APOCALYPSE APOCALYPSE!
You are a very stubborn little girl.
dana

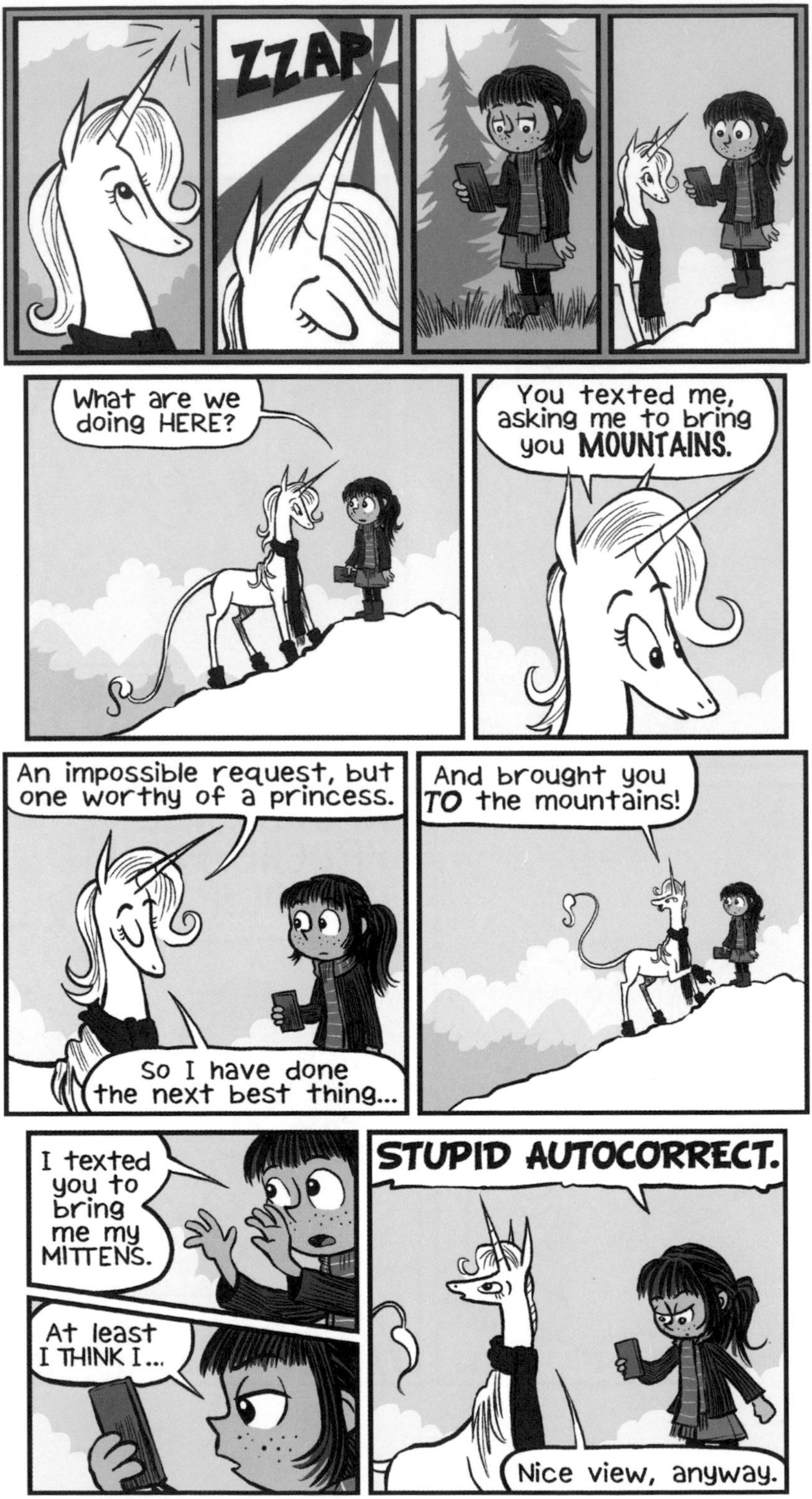

ZZAP
What are we doing HERE?
You texted me, asking me to bring you MOUNTAINS.
An impossible request, but one worthy of a princess.
So I have done the next best thing...
And brought you TO the mountains!
I texted you to bring me my MITTENS.
At least I THINK I...
STUPID AUTOCORRECT.
Nice view, anyway.

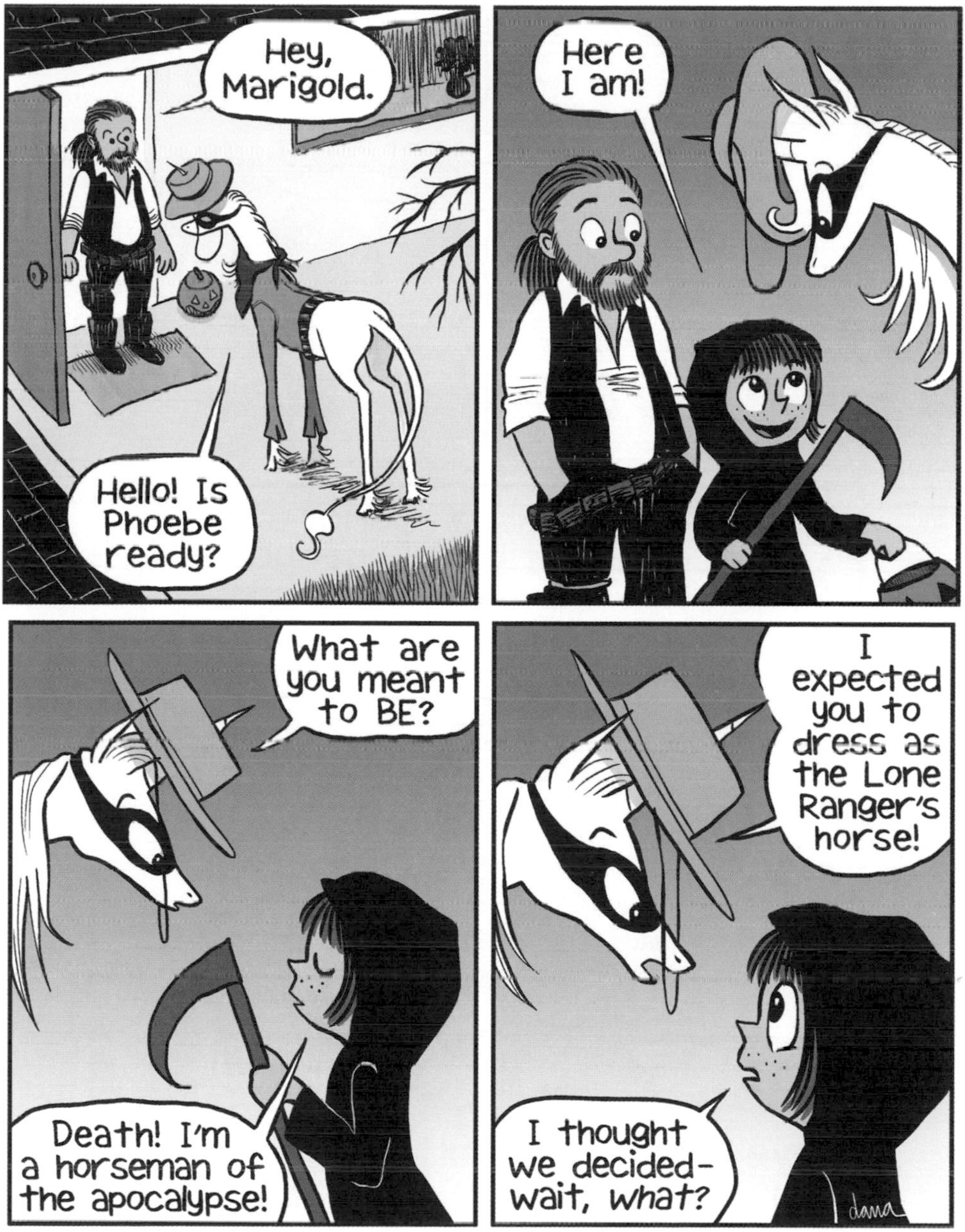
Hey, Marigold.
Hello! Is Phoebe ready?
Here I am!
What are you meant to BE?
Death! I'm a horseman of the apocalypse!
I expected you to dress as the Lone Ranger's horse!
I thought we decided- wait, what?
dana

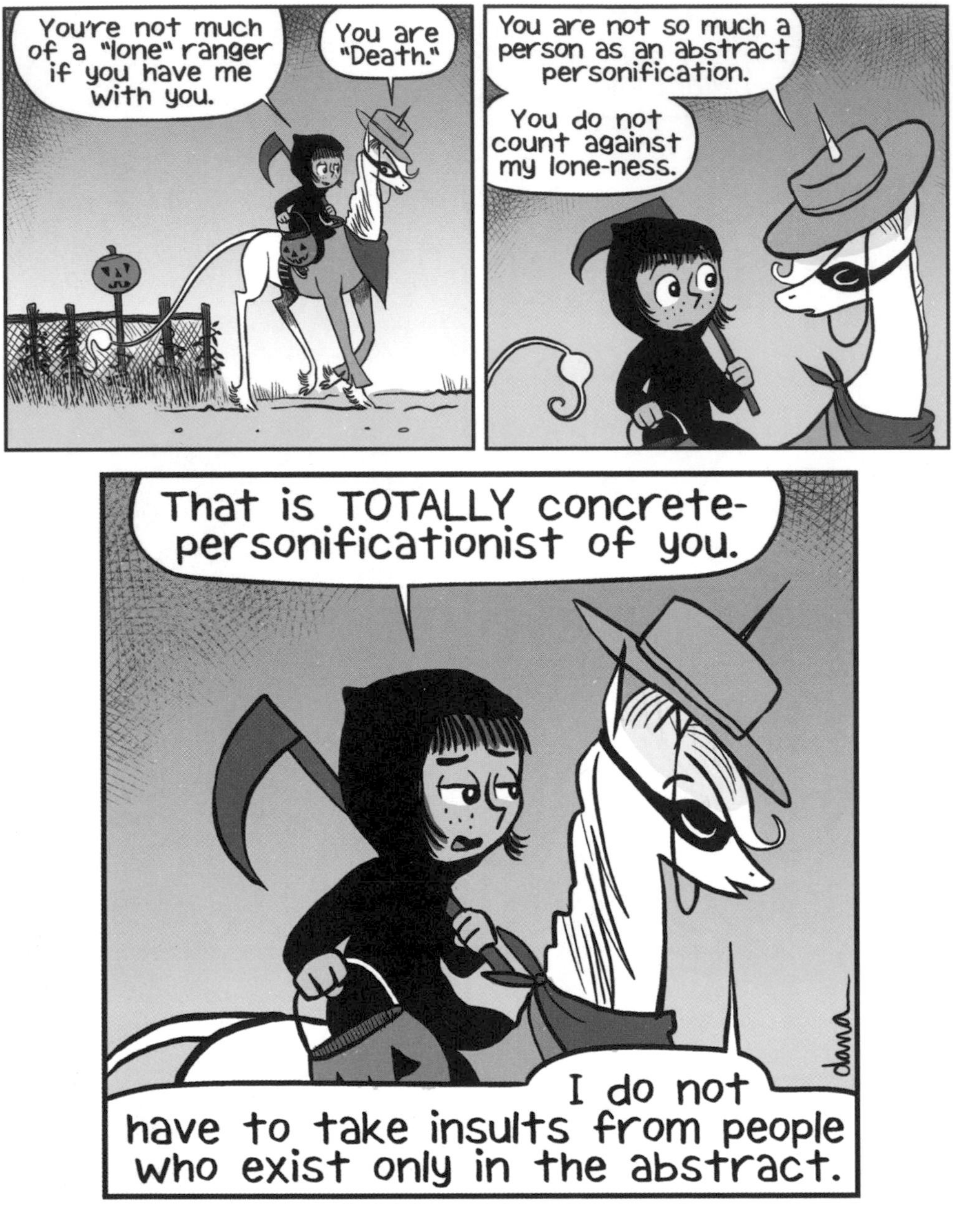
You're not much of a "lone" ranger if you have me with you.
You are "Death."
You are not so much a person as an abstract personification.
You do not count against my lone-ness.
That is TOTALLY concrete-personificationist of you.
I do not have to take insults from people who exist only in the abstract.
dana

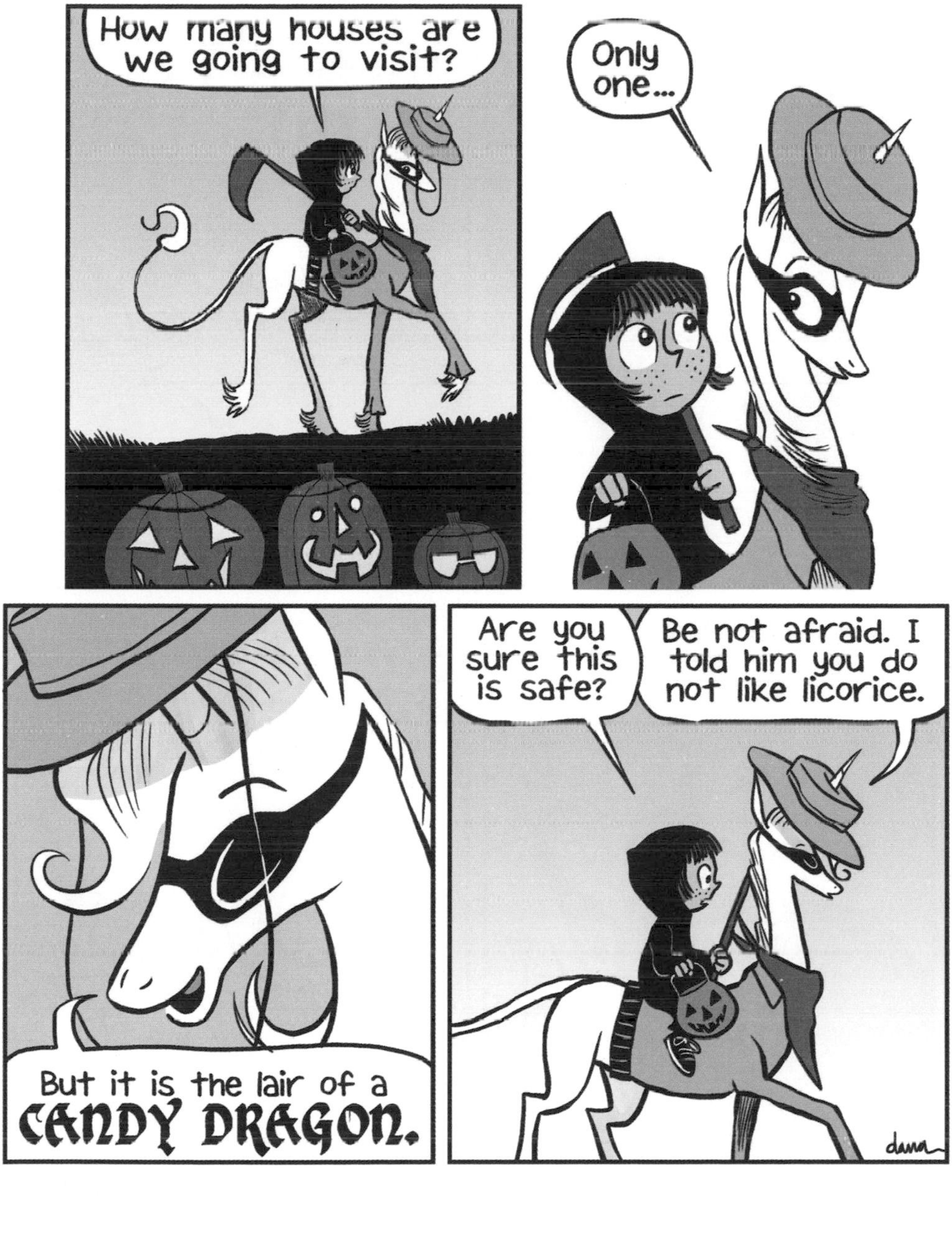
How many houses are we going to visit?
Only one...
But it is the lair of a
CANDY DRAGON.
Are you sure this is safe?
Be not afraid. I told him you do not like licorice.
dana

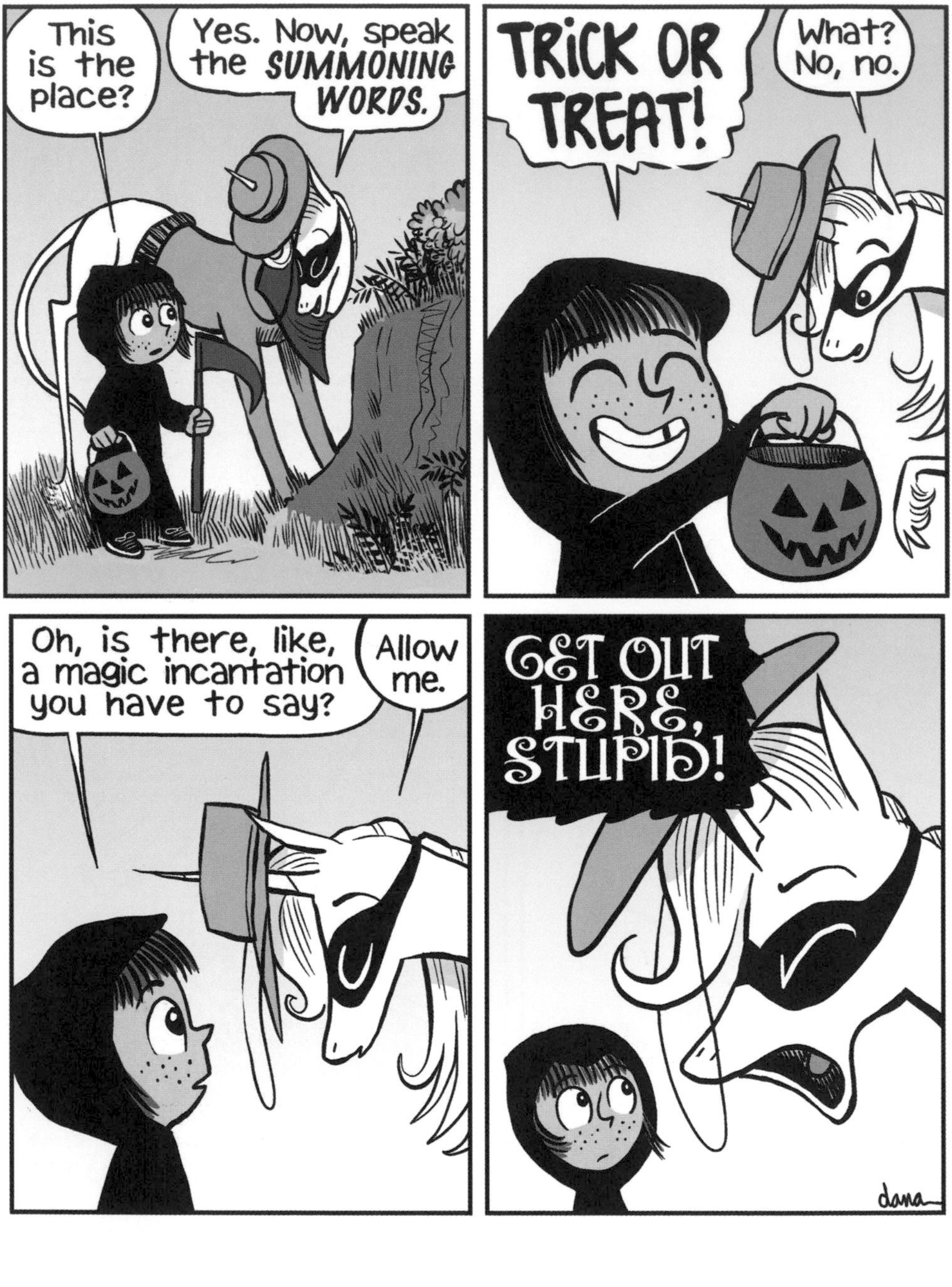
This is the place?
Yes. Now, speak the SUMMONING WORDS.
TRICK OR TREAT!
What? No, no.
Oh, is there, like, a magic incantation you have to say?
Allow me.
GET OUT HERE, STUPID!
dana

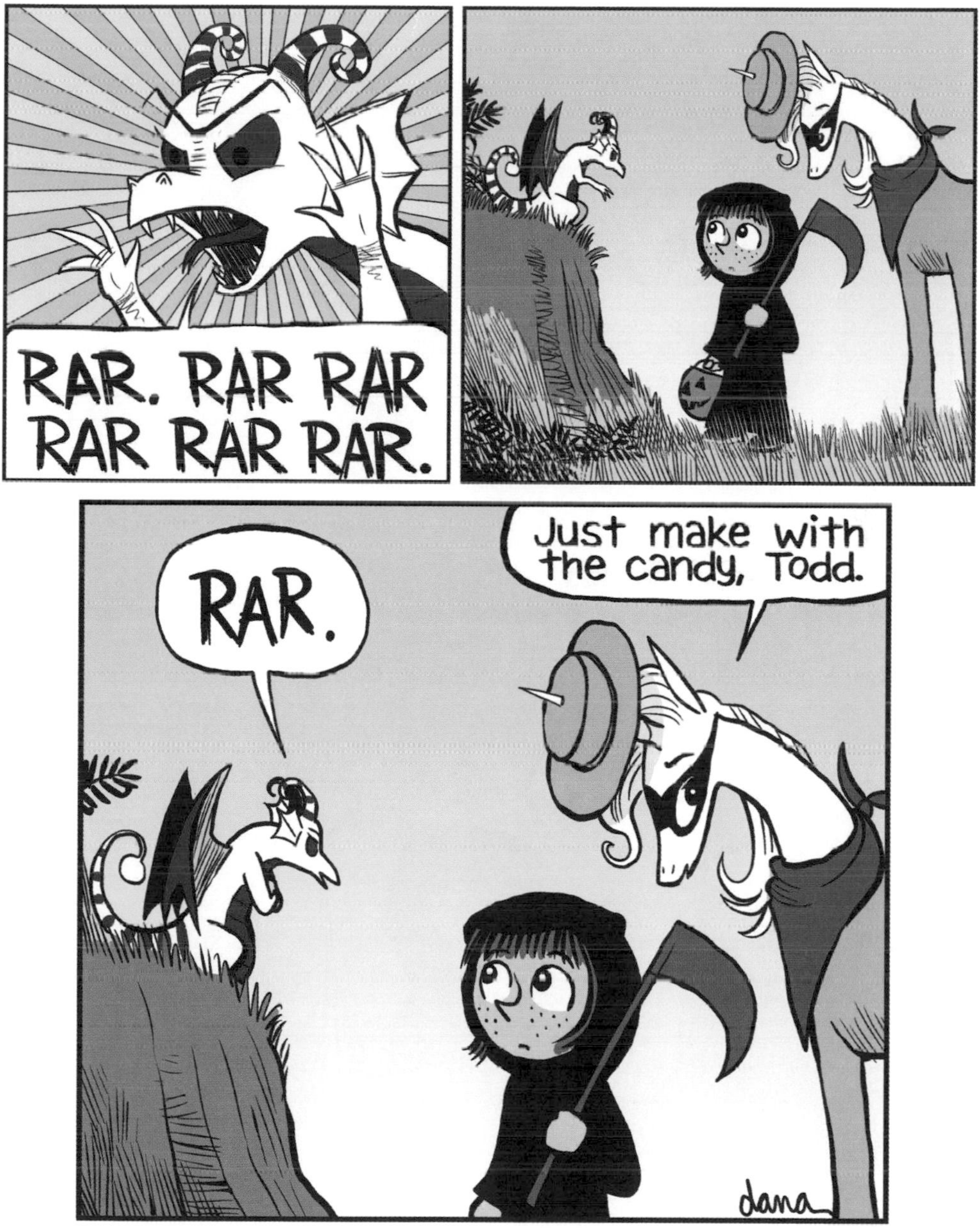
RAR. RAR RAR RAR RAR RAR.
RAR.
Just make with the candy, Todd.
dana

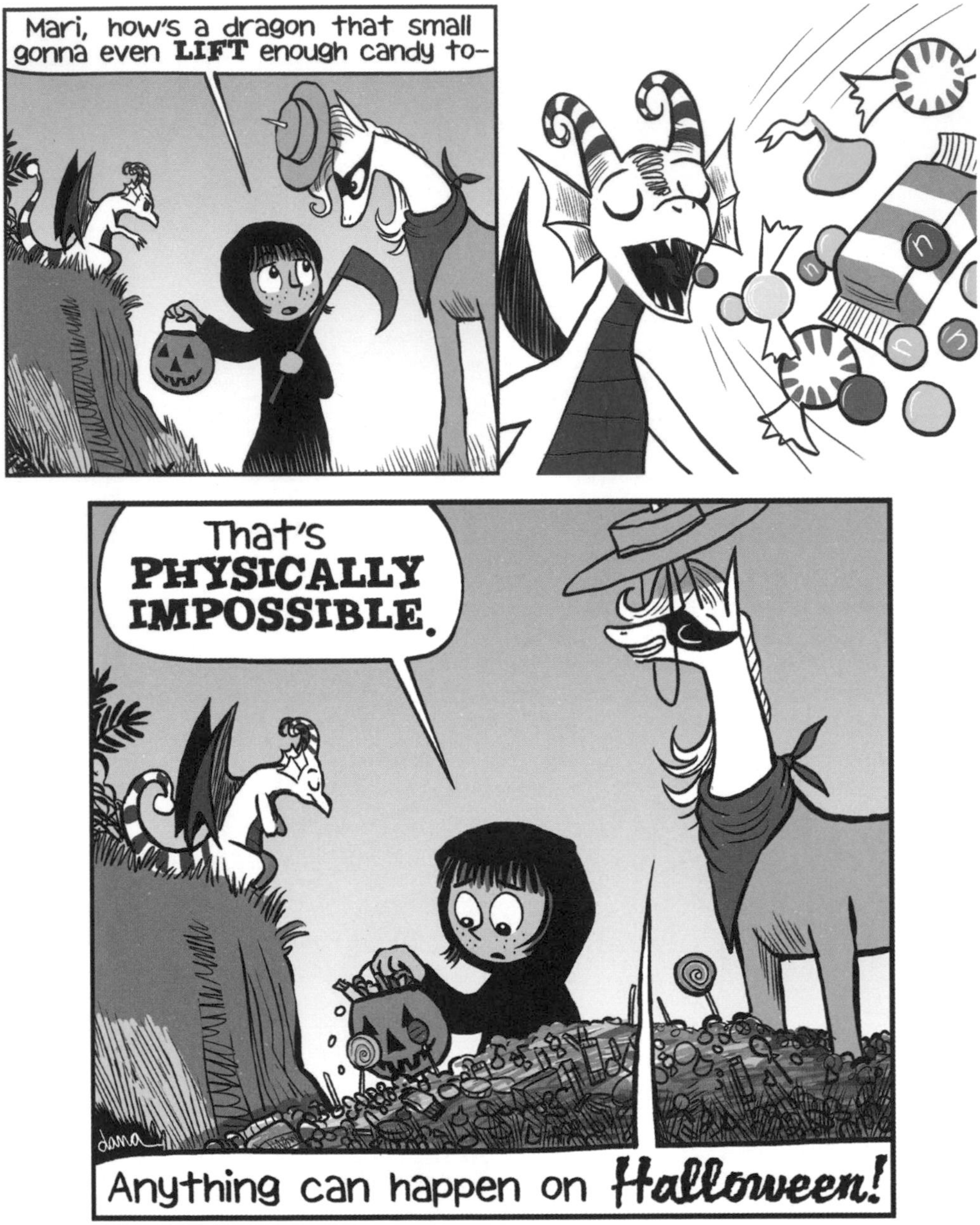
Mari, how's a dragon that small gonna even **LIFT** enough candy to-
That's **PHYSICALLY IMPOSSIBLE.**
dana
Anything can happen on *Halloween!*

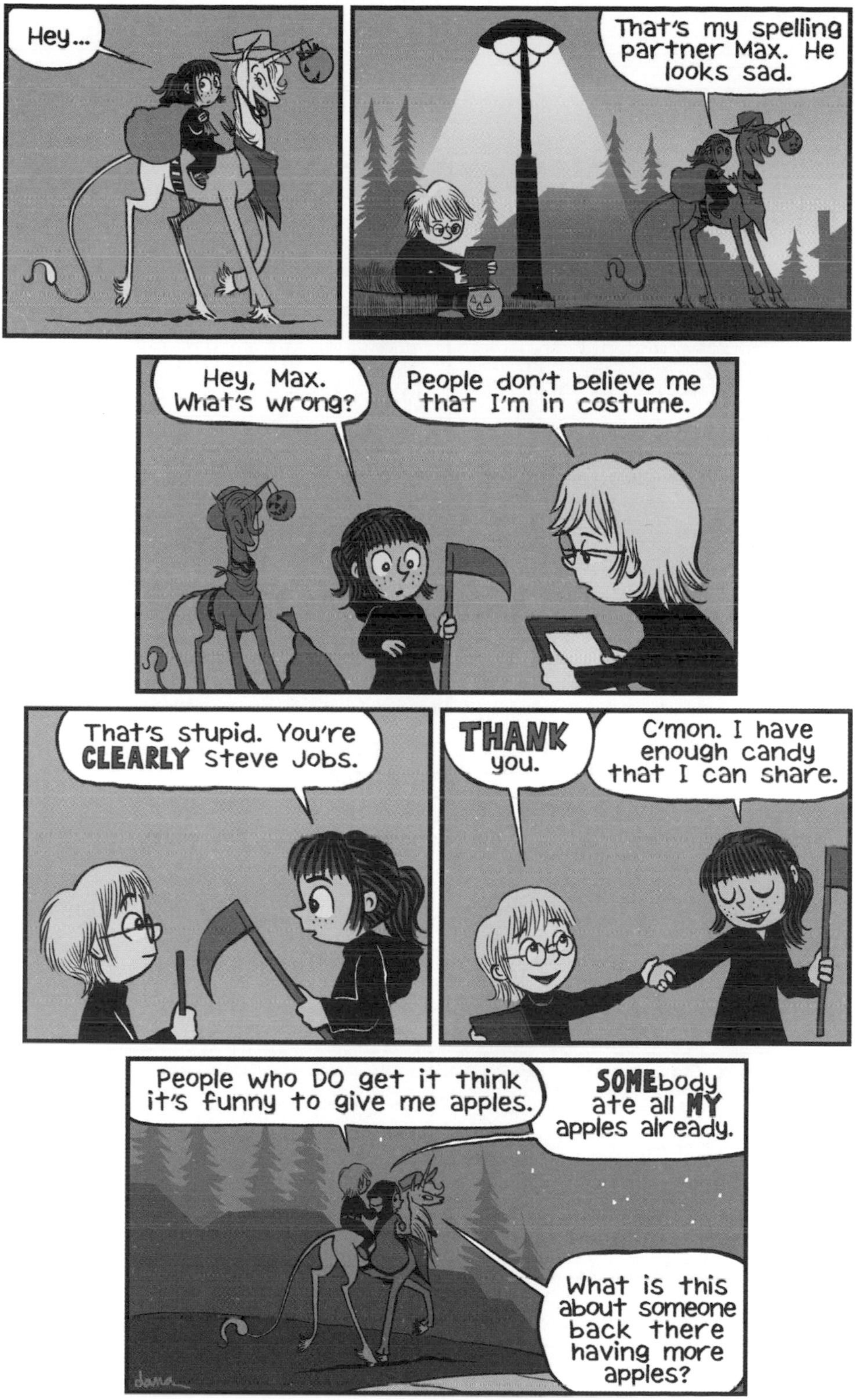
Hey...
That's my spelling partner Max. He looks sad.
Hey, Max. What's wrong?
People don't believe me that I'm in costume.
That's stupid. You're CLEARLY Steve Jobs.
THANK you.
C'mon. I have enough candy that I can share.
People who DO get it think it's funny to give me apples.
SOMEbody ate all MY apples already.
What is this about someone back there having more apples?
dana

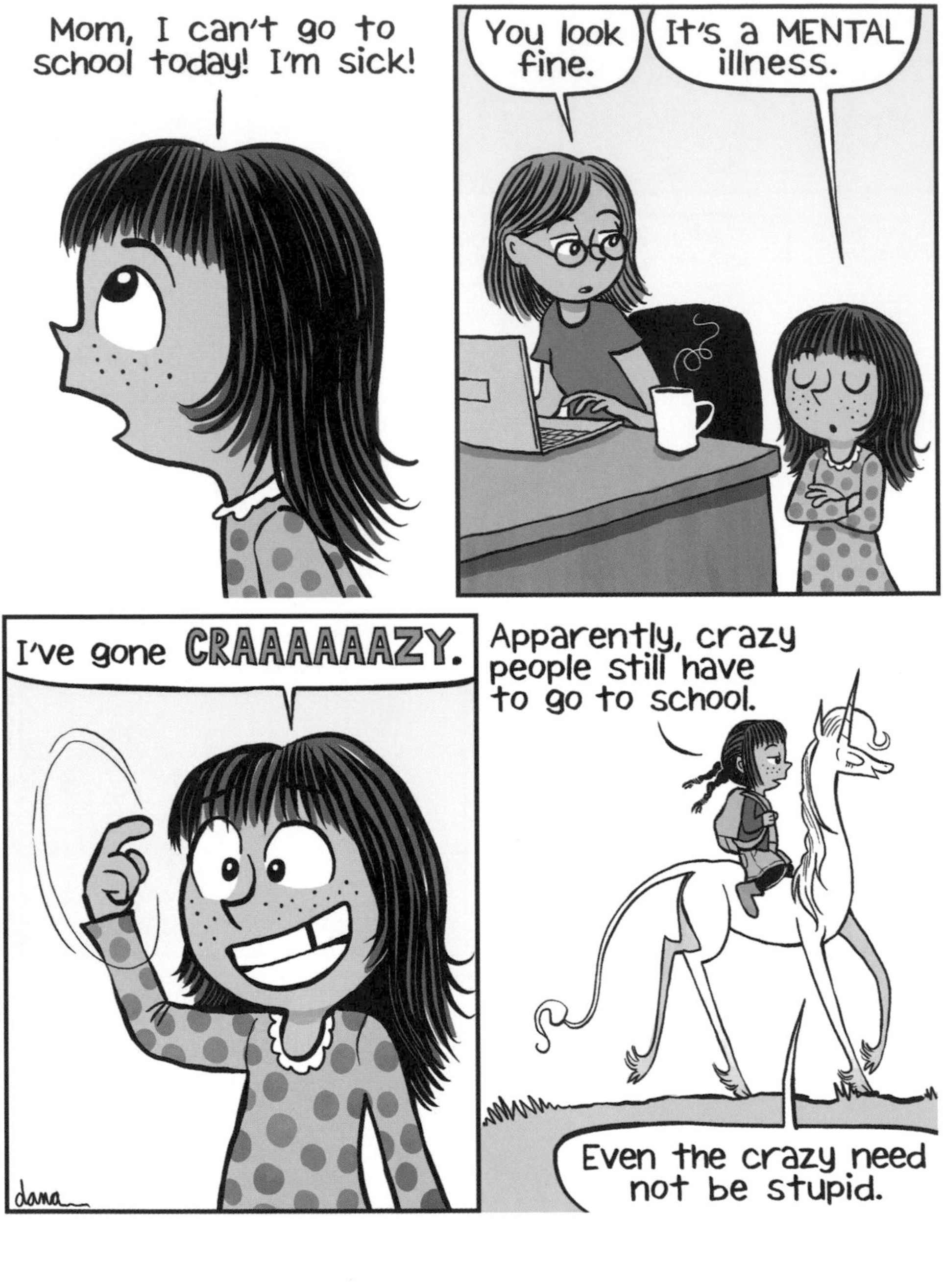
Mom, I can't go to school today! I'm sick!
You look fine.
It's a MENTAL illness.
I've gone CRAAAAAAAZY.
Apparently, crazy people still have to go to school.
Even the crazy need not be stupid.
dana

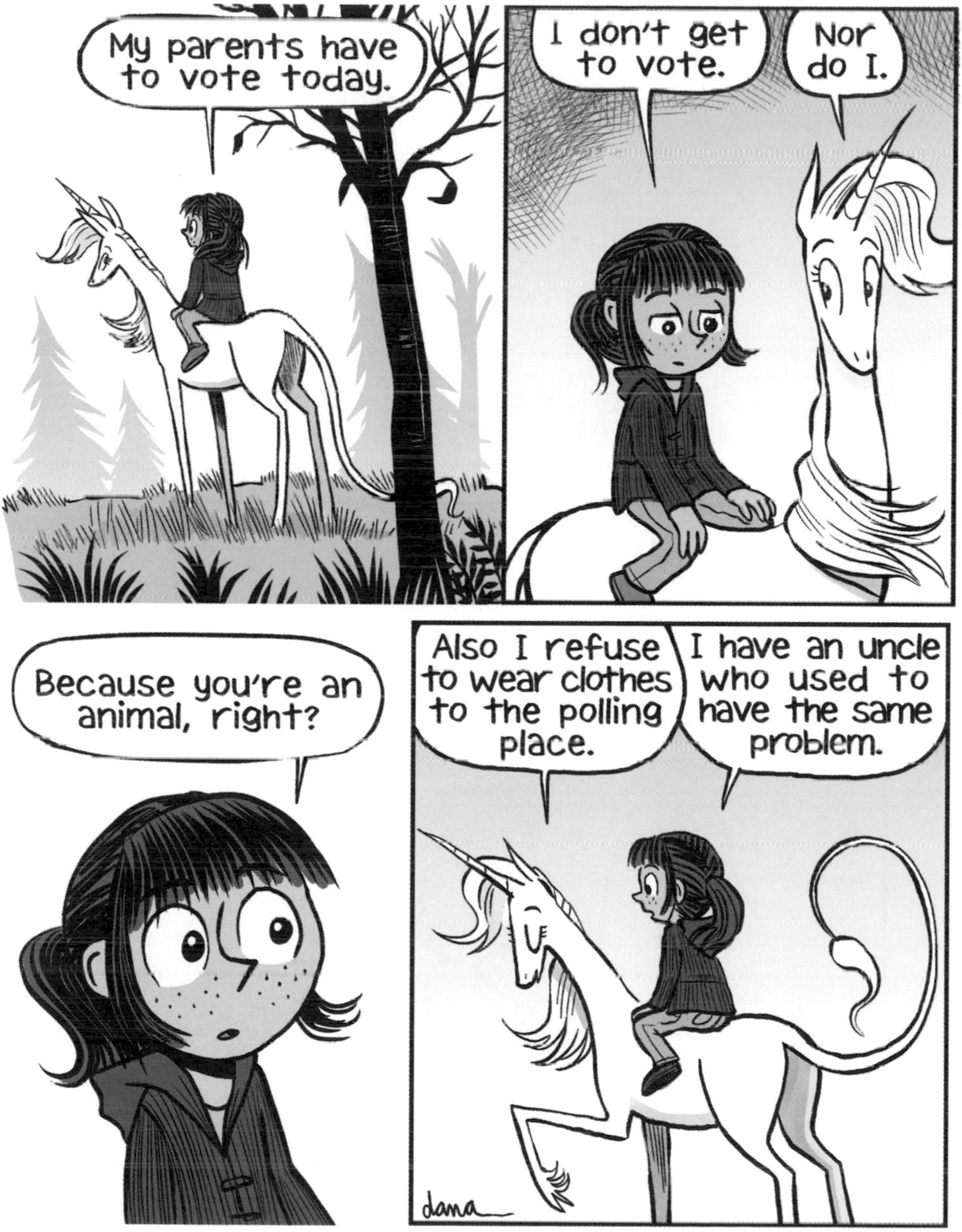
My parents have to vote today.
I don't get to vote.
Nor do I.
Because you're an animal, right?
Also I refuse to wear clothes to the polling place.
I have an uncle who used to have the same problem.
dana

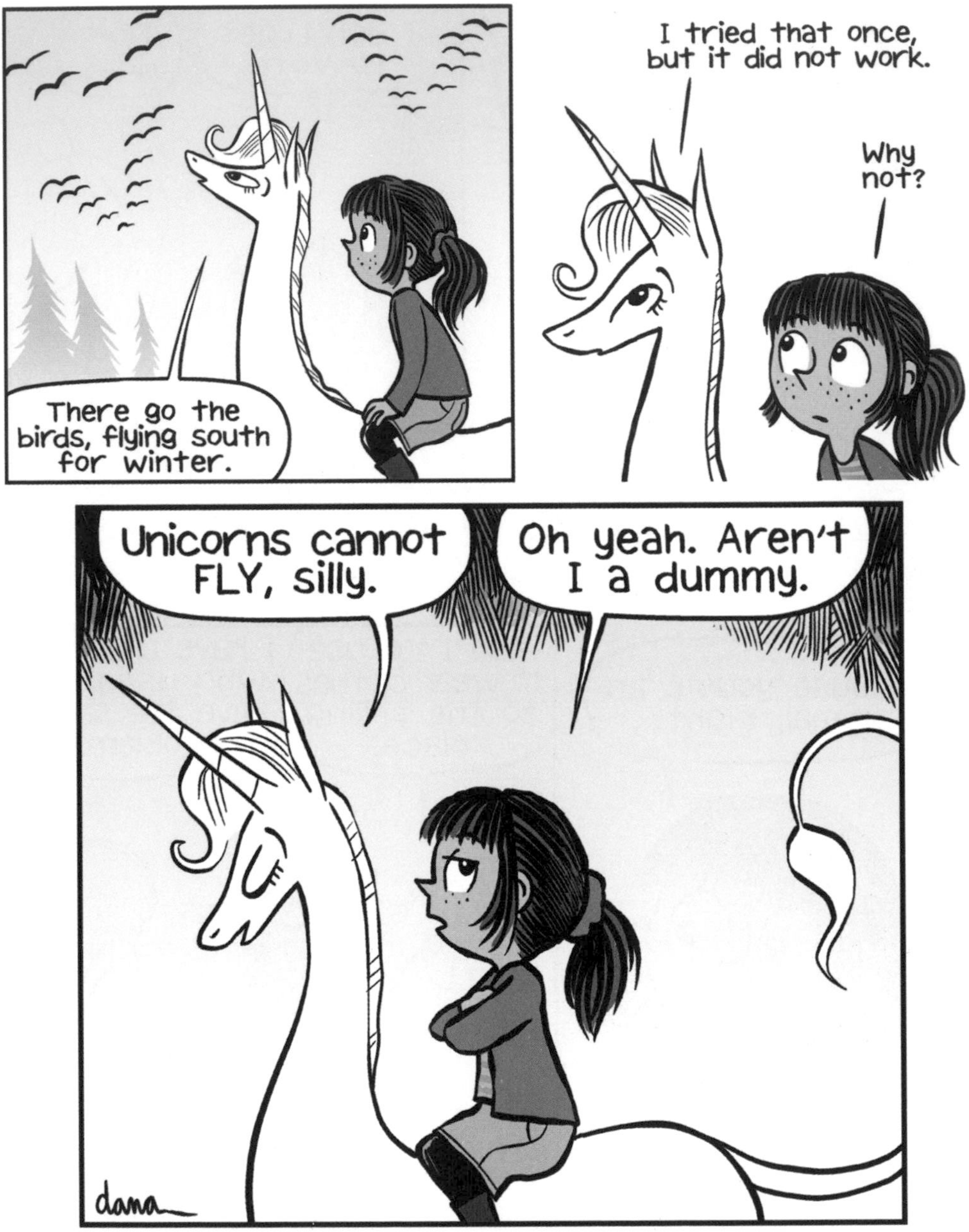
There go the birds, flying south for winter.
I tried that once, but it did not work.
Why not?
Unicorns cannot FLY, silly.
Oh yeah. Aren't I a dummy.
dana

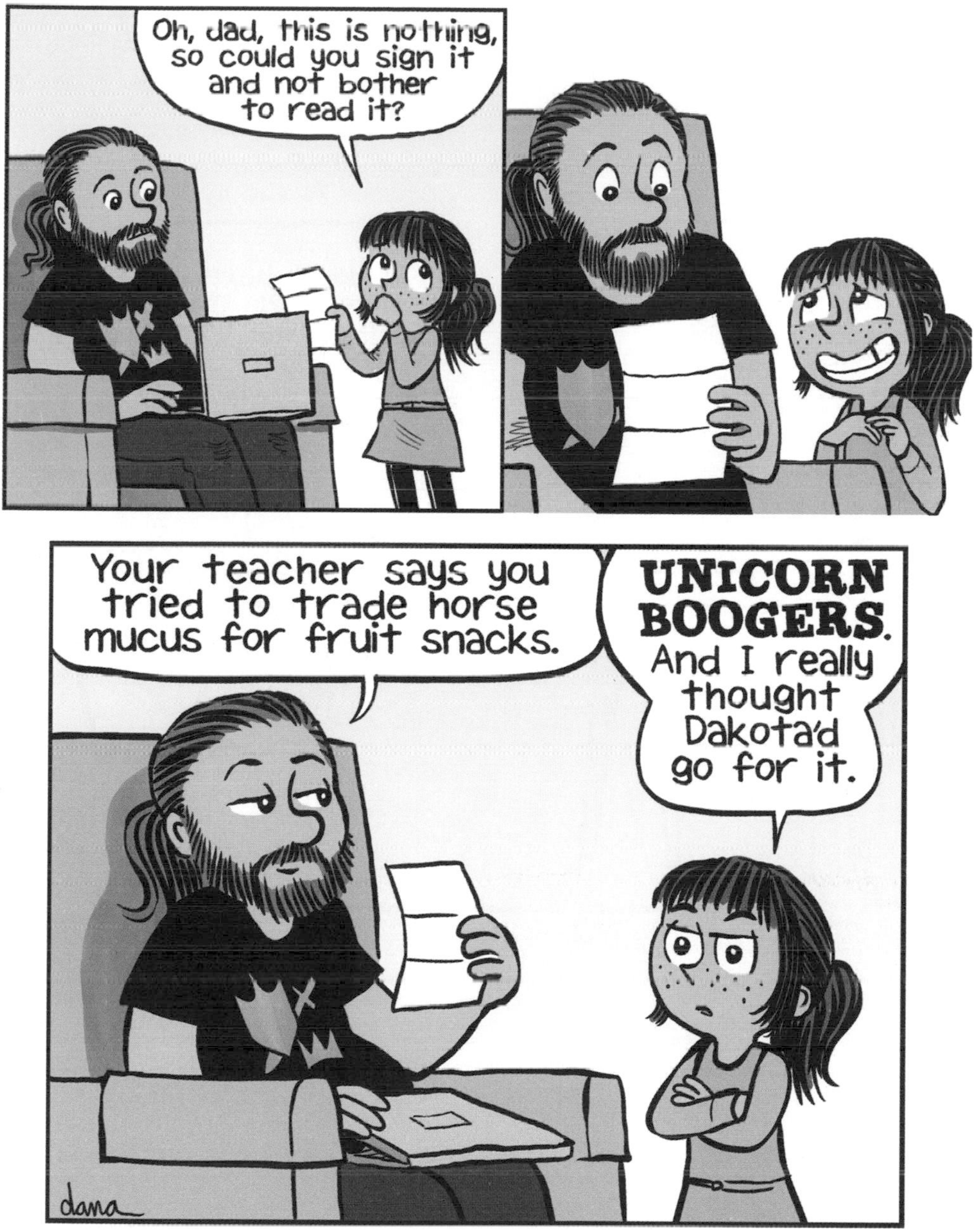
Oh, dad, this is nothing, so could you sign it and not bother to read it?
Your teacher says you tried to trade horse mucus for fruit snacks.
UNICORN BOOGERS. And I really thought Dakota'd go for it.
dana

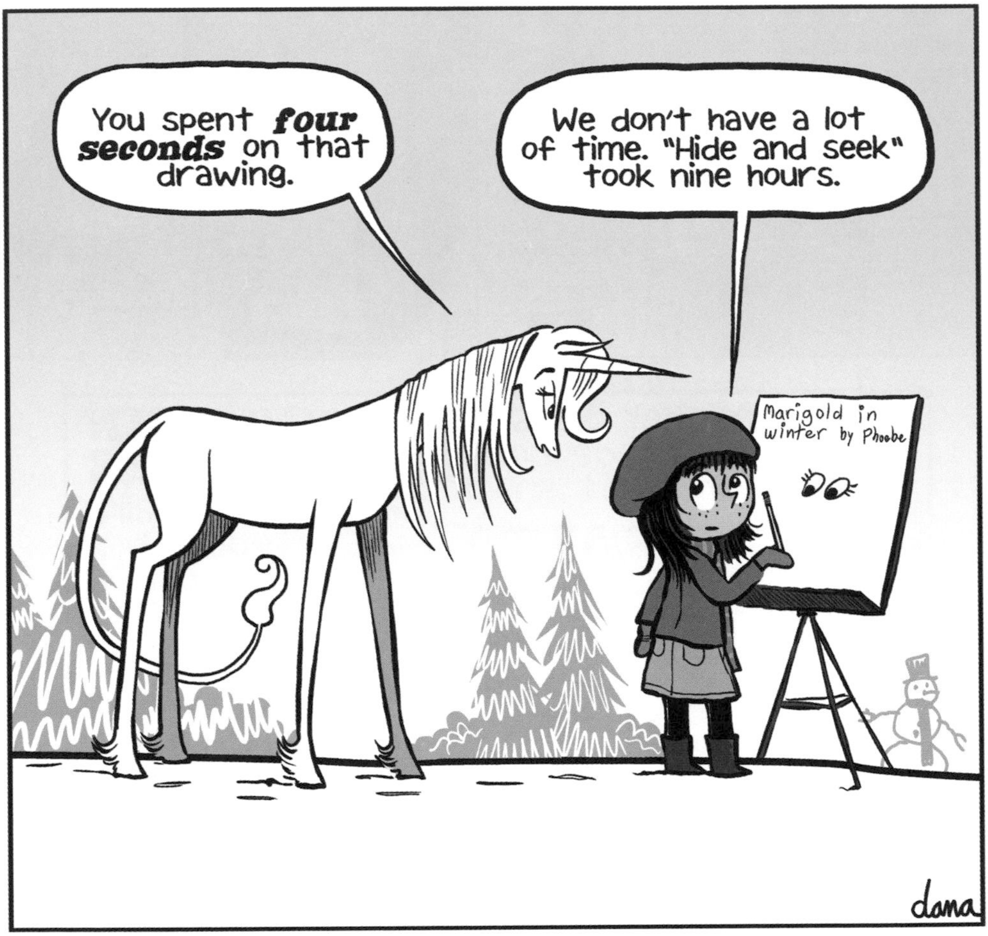
You spent **four seconds** on that drawing.
We don't have a lot of time. "Hide and seek" took nine hours.
Marigold in winter by Phoebe
dana

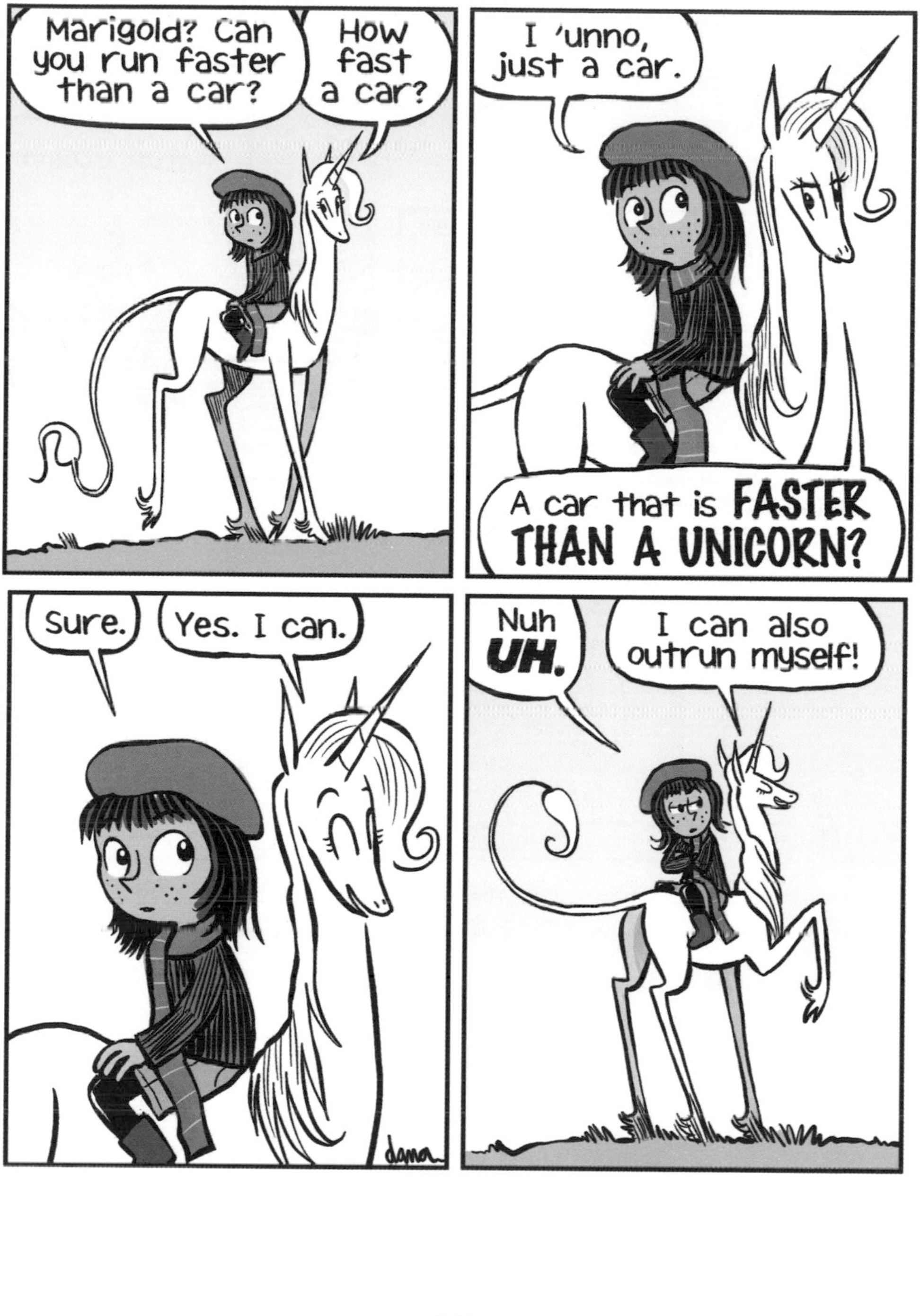
Marigold? Can you run faster than a car?
How fast a car?
I 'unno, just a car.
A car that is FASTER THAN A UNICORN?
Sure.
Yes. I can.
Nuh UH.
I can also outrun myself!
dana

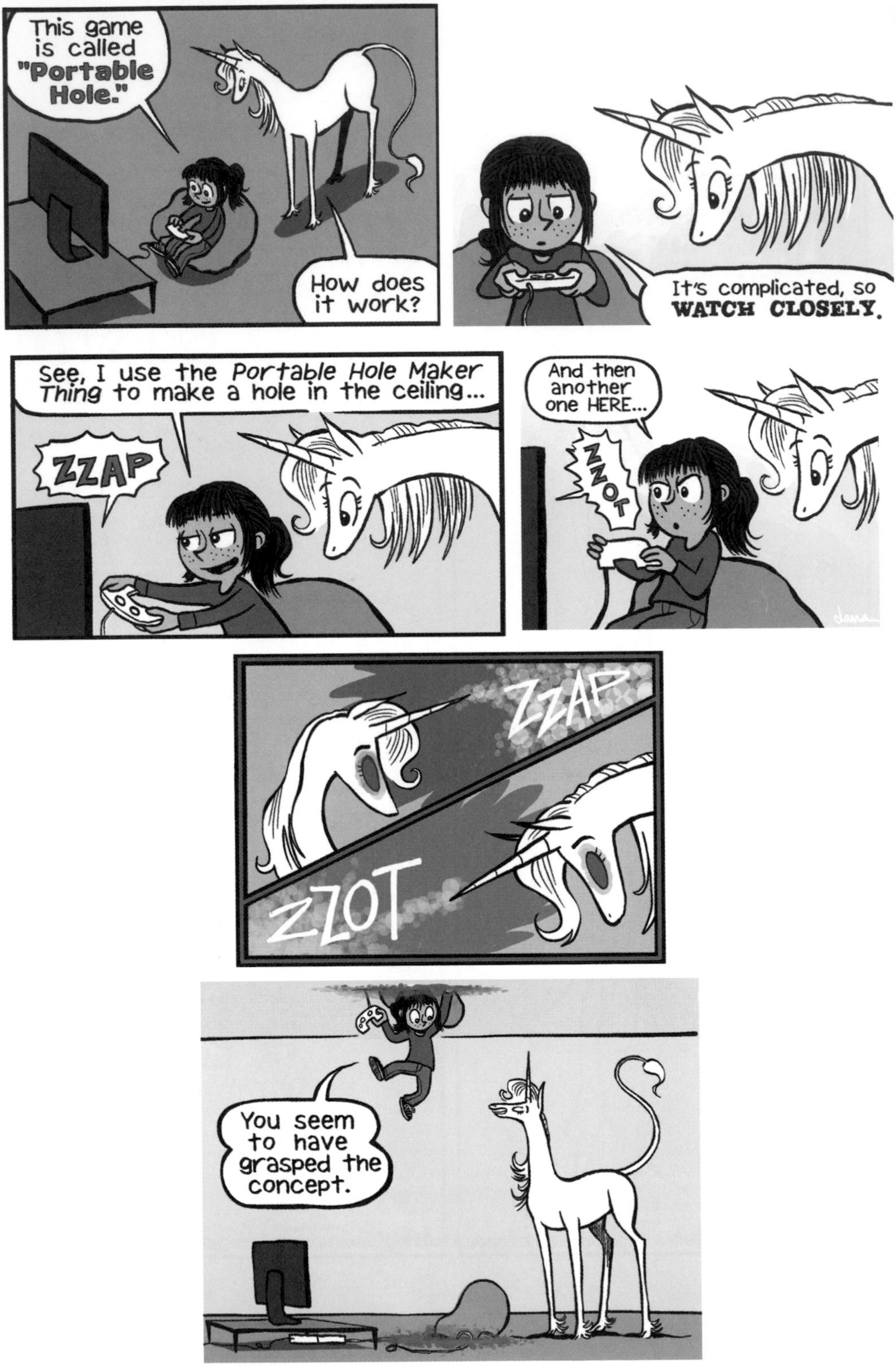
This game is called **"Portable Hole."**
How does it work?
It's complicated, so **WATCH CLOSELY.**
See, I use the *Portable Hole Maker Thing* to make a hole in the ceiling...
ZZAP
And then another one HERE...
ZZOT
ZZAP
ZZOT
You seem to have grasped the concept.

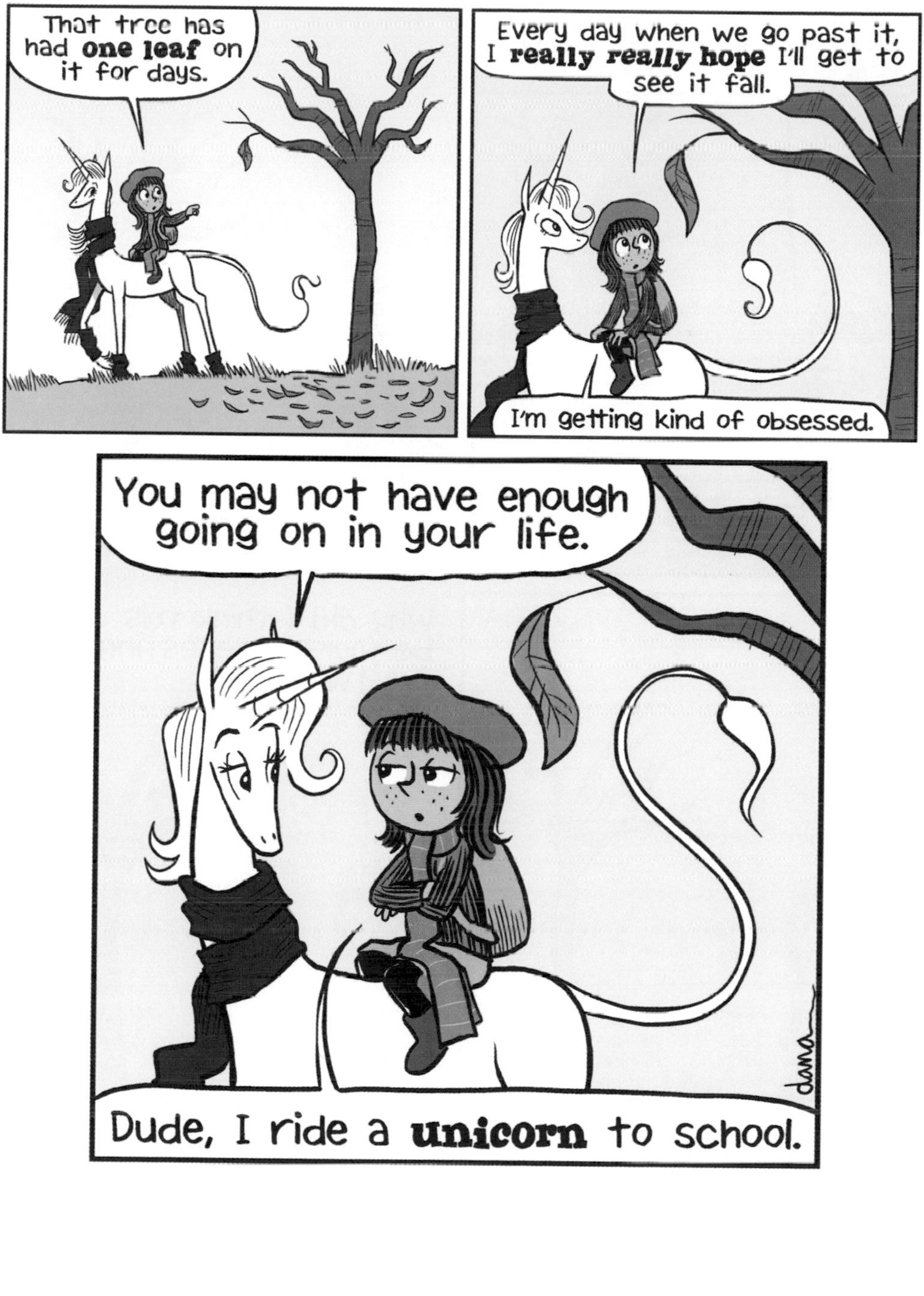
That tree has had **one leaf** on it for days.
Every day when we go past it, I **really *really* hope** I'll get to see it fall.
I'm getting kind of obsessed.
You may not have enough going on in your life.
Dude, I ride a **unicorn** to school.
dana

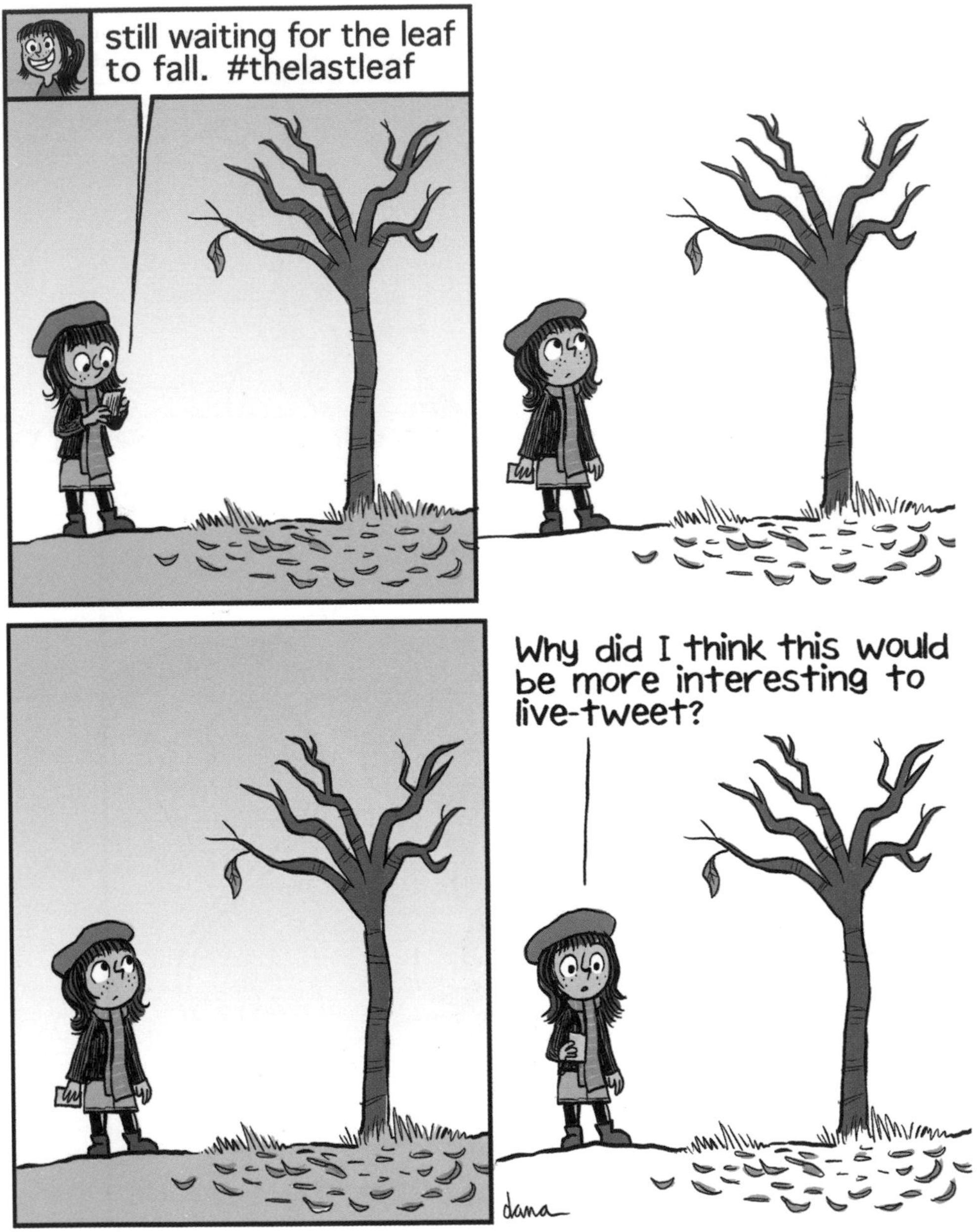
still waiting for the leaf to fall. #thelastleaf
Why did I think this would be more interesting to live-tweet?
dana

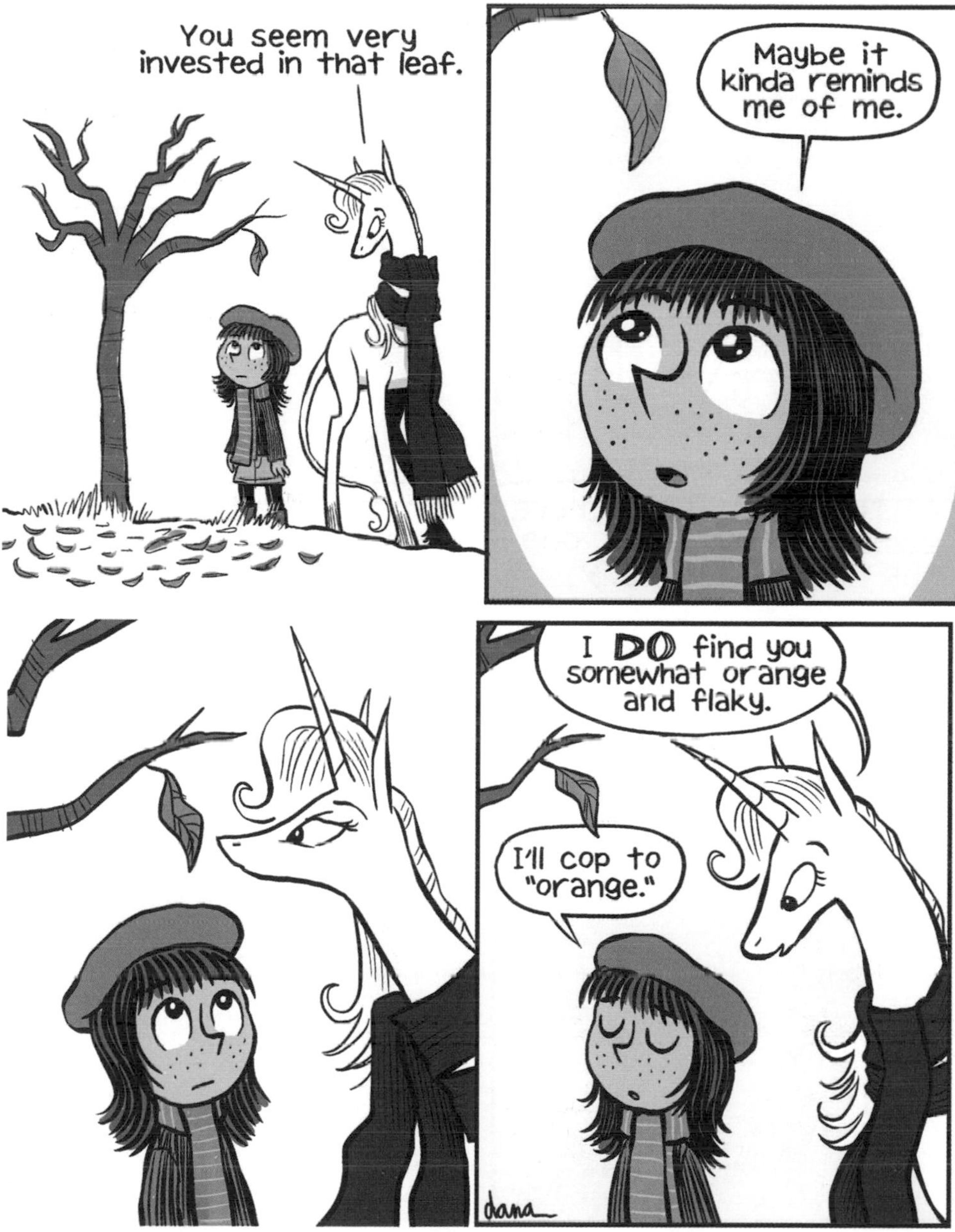
You seem very invested in that leaf.
Maybe it kinda reminds me of me.
I DO find you somewhat orange and flaky.
I'll cop to "orange."
dana

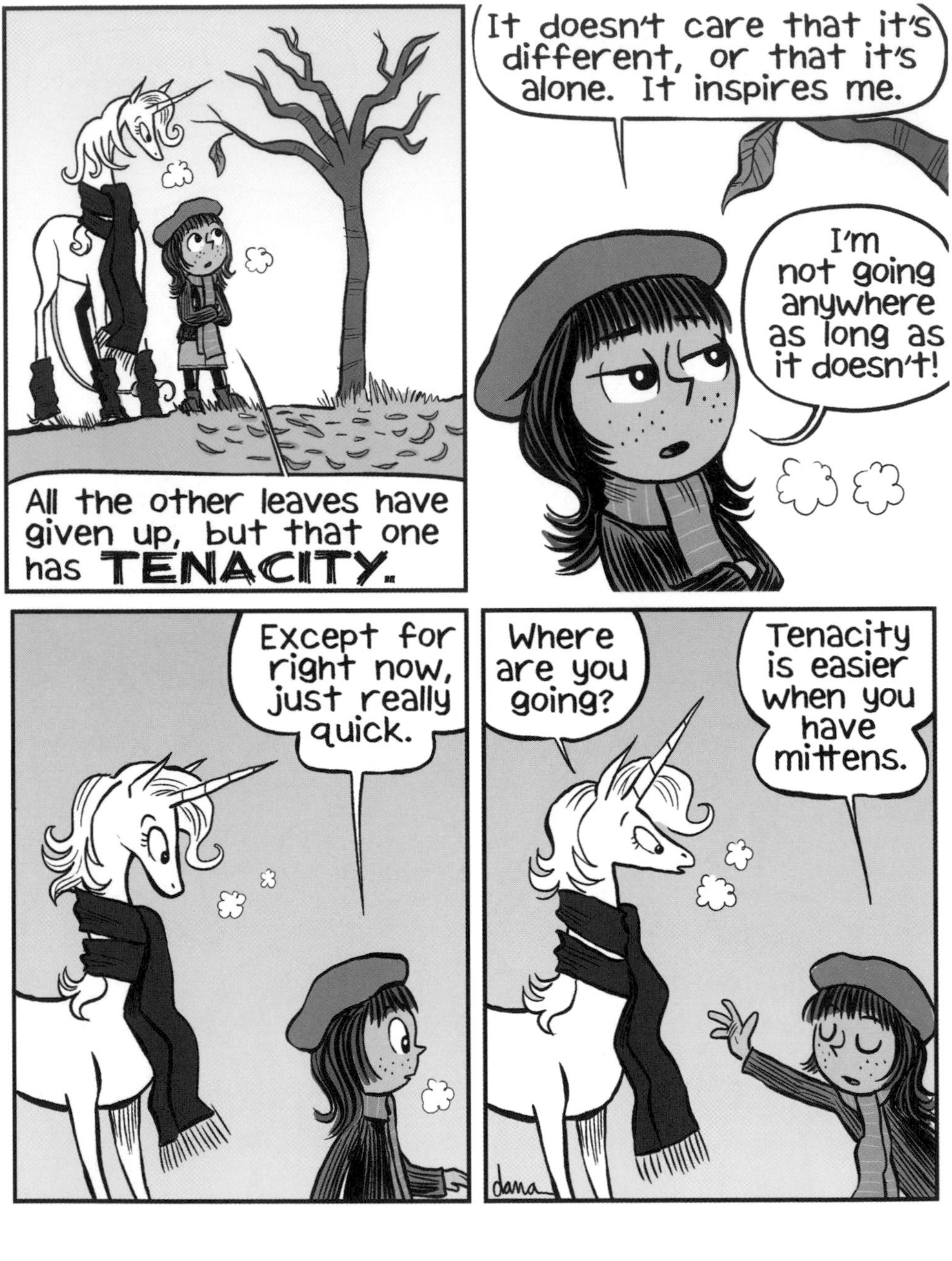
All the other leaves have given up, but that one has TENACITY.
It doesn't care that it's different, or that it's alone. It inspires me.
I'm not going anywhere as long as it doesn't!
Except for right now, just really quick.
Where are you going?
Tenacity is easier when you have mittens.
dana

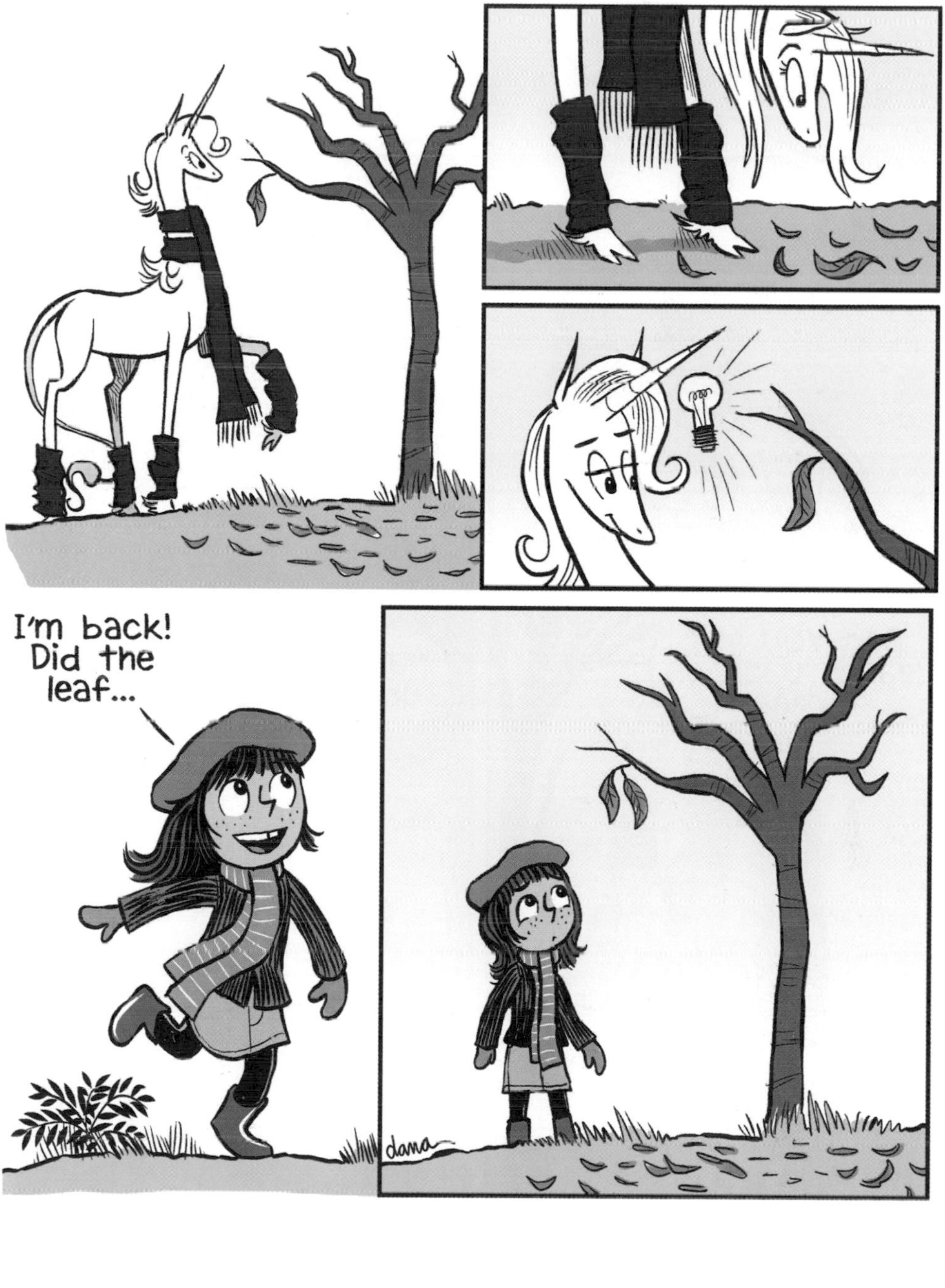
I'm back!
Did the
leaf...
dana

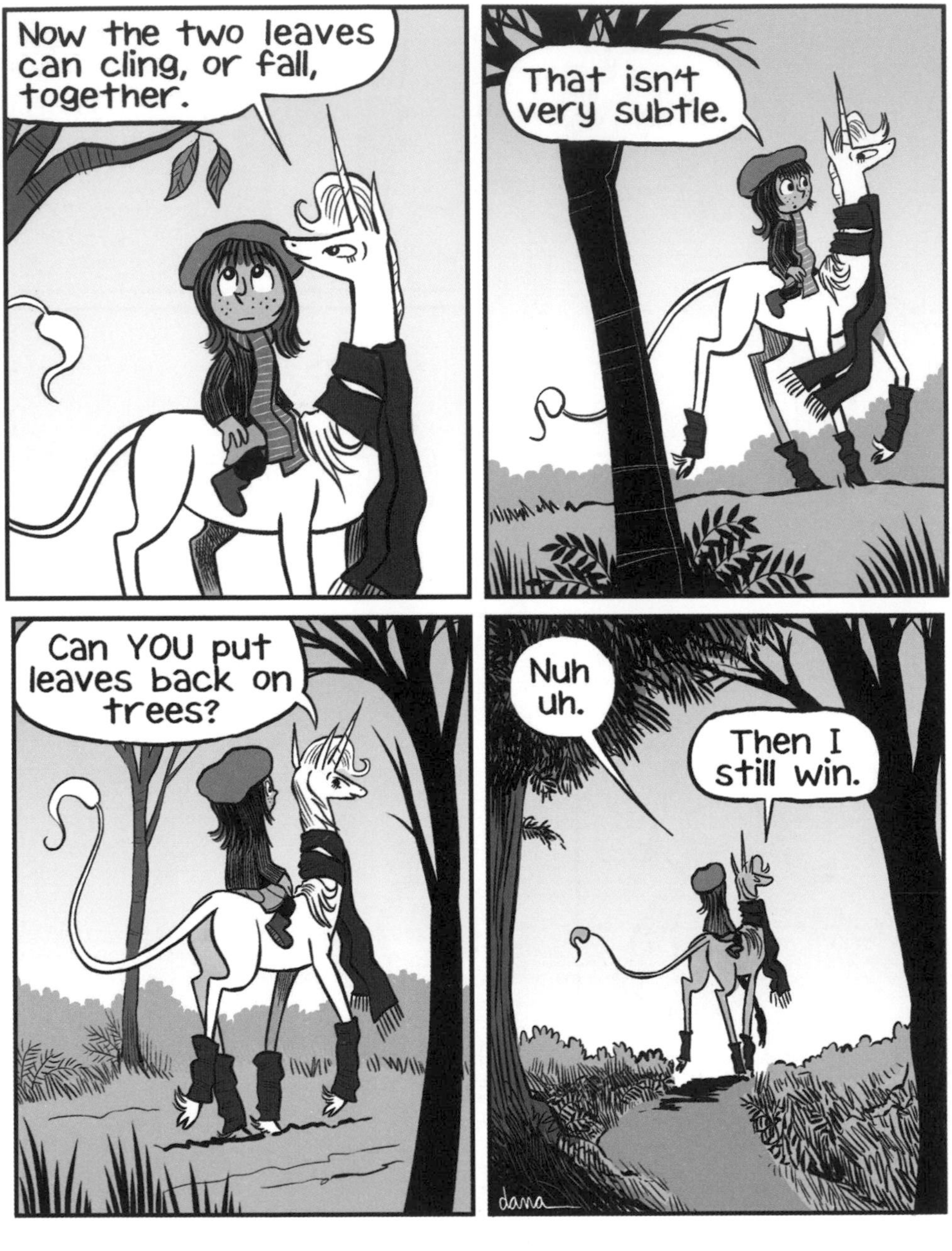
Now the two leaves can cling, or fall, together.
That isn't very subtle.
Can YOU put leaves back on trees?
Nuh uh.
Then I still win.
dana

PURRRRRR
PURRRR
hee hee
PURRRR
twitch
Can I help you?
You were PURRING.
Unicorns do NOT purr.
PURRRRRR
dana

How to Draw Marigold

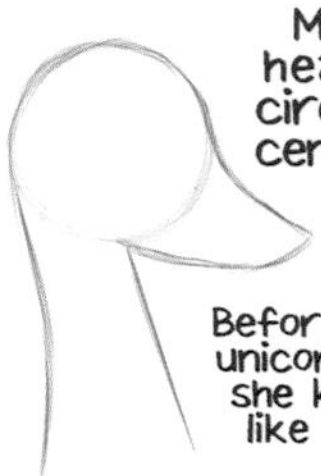

Marigold's head has a circle at the center of it.

Before I draw her unicorny features, she kind of looks like a dinosaur.

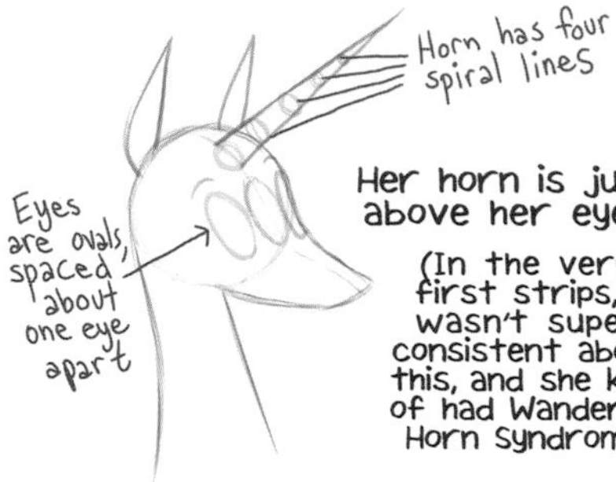
Horn has four spiral lines
Eyes are ovals, spaced about one eye apart

Her horn is just above her eyes.

(In the very first strips, I wasn't super consistent about this, and she kind of had Wandering Horn Syndrome.)

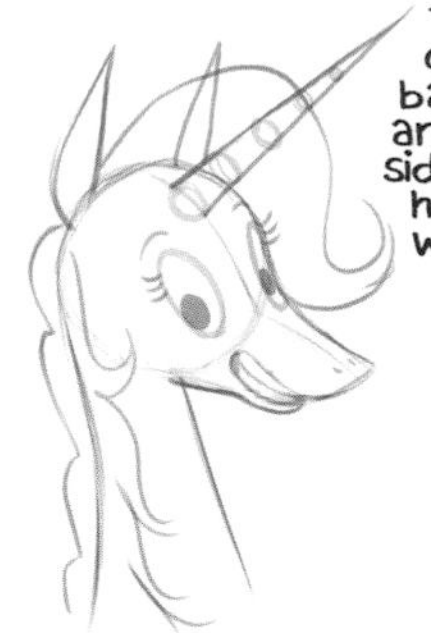

The front part of her mane is basically a swoop, and is on the far side of her head and horn no matter which way she's facing.

(It's magic.)

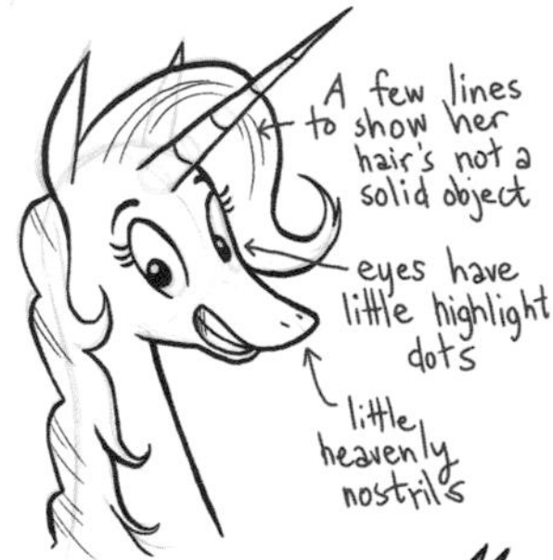
A few lines to show her hair's not a solid object
eyes have little highlight dots
little heavenly nostrils

Marigold is kind of swan-shaped, with a long slender neck.

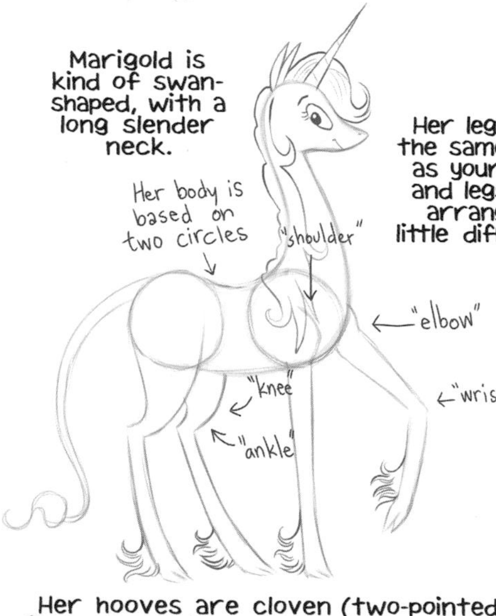
Her body is based on two circles
"shoulder"
"elbow"
"knee"
"wrist"
"ankle"

Her legs have the same joints as your arms and legs, just arranged a little differently.

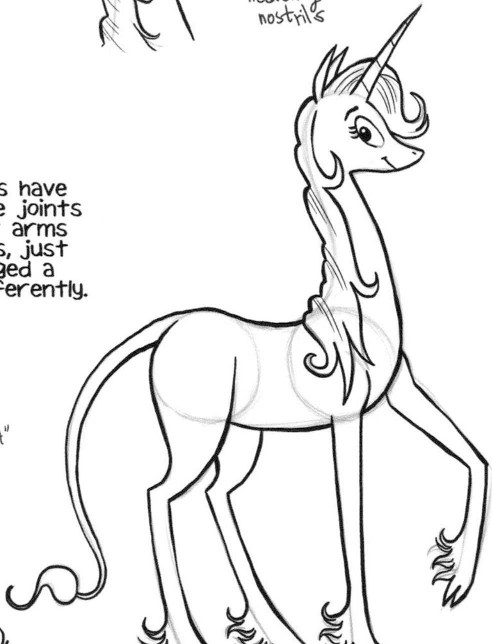

Her hooves are cloven (two-pointed), like a deer's. Also she has fluffy fetlocks.

How to Draw Phoebe

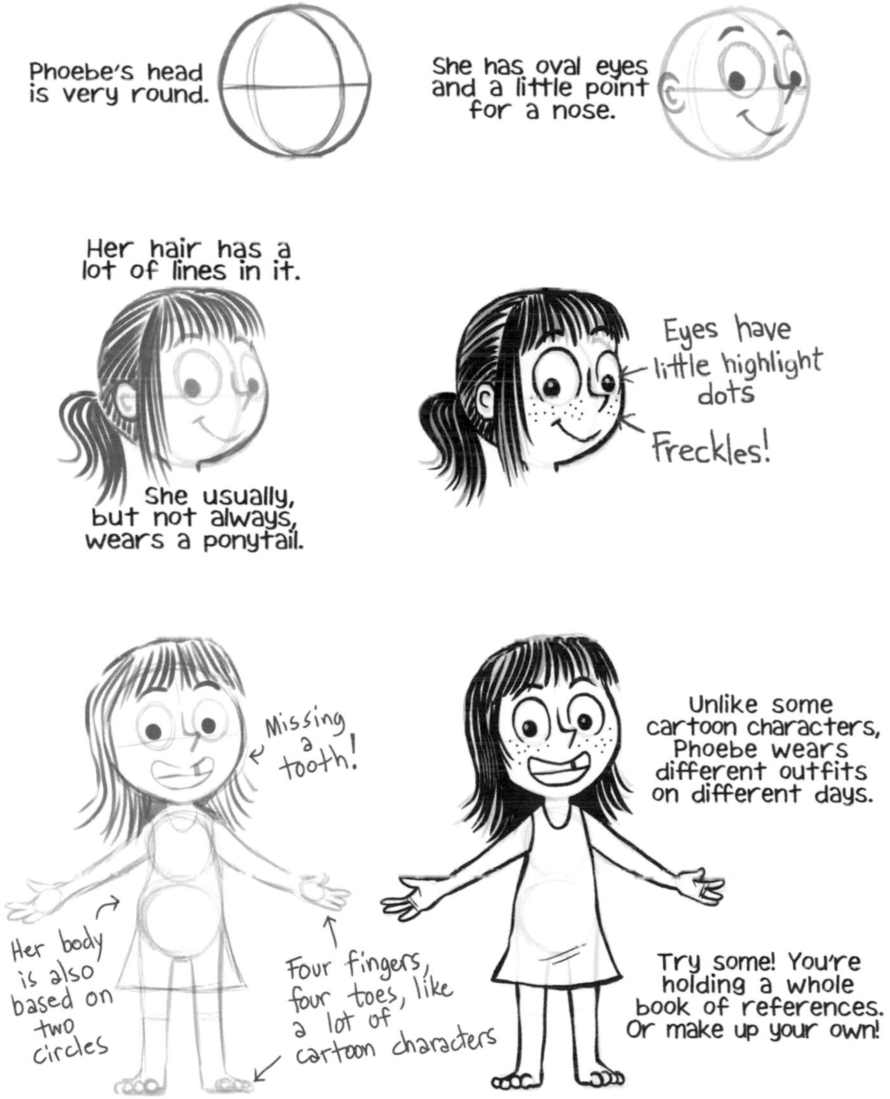

Phoebe's head is very round.
She has oval eyes and a little point for a nose.
Her hair has a lot of lines in it.
She usually, but not always, wears a ponytail.
Eyes have little highlight dots
Freckles!
Missing a tooth!
Her body is also based on two circles
Four fingers, four toes, like a lot of cartoon characters
Unlike some cartoon characters, Phoebe wears different outfits on different days.
Try some! You're holding a whole book of references. Or make up your own!

Make a Marigold Heavenly Nostrils Stick Puppet

MATERIALS: white cardboard or white paper plate; scissors; pencil; large craft stick; markers; glue; tape; yarn

INSTRUCTIONS:

 Photocopy or trace the picture of Marigold, below.

 Color the picture with markers.

 Cut out the picture and glue it on the cardboard or paper plate.

 Cut the cardboard or paper plate around the picture.

 Tape the picture to the craft stick.

 Glue yarn for mane.

Make an Animated Flip Book

Cartoonists create stories in cartoon panels. Often cartoonists are also animators. An animator must capture a broad range of movements in order for a cartoon to look continuous. Animation is possible because of a phenomenon called "persistence of vision," when a sequence of images moves past the eye fast enough, the brain fills in the missing parts so the subject appears to be moving.

MATERIALS: paper, index cards, or sticky notes; stapler and staples, paper clips, or brads; pencil or marker

INSTRUCTIONS:

 Cut at least 20 strips of paper to be the exact same size, or use alternative materials, such as index cards or sticky notes.

 Fasten the pages together with a staple, brad, or paperclip.

 Pick a subject—anything from a bouncing ball to a running Marigold or a shooting star.

 Draw three key images first: the first on page one, the last on page twenty, and the middle on page ten, then fill in the pages between the key images.

Make Unicorn Slumber Party Snack Mix

Marigold's favorite food might be luscious, tender grass, but snack mix is required at a slumber party! This is a yummy, easy-to-make treat.

INGREDIENTS: 1 bag Bugles (they look just like unicorn horns!), 1 bag cheddar fish crackers, 1 bag round pretzels, 1 cup nuts (either cashews or peanuts), 1 package ranch salad dressing mix, ½ cup vegetable oil

INSTRUCTIONS:

 Mix the vegetable oil with the dressing mix in a small bowl.

 Put the Bugles, crackers, pretzels, and nuts in a large bowl.

 Add the dressing mixture to the large bowl and mix.

 Store in airtight container or storage bags.

Fun Things to Know About Unicorns

Even though the unicorn is a fictitious animal, it is one of the official animals of Scotland and was used on the royal coat of arms of Scotland in medieval times. (The red lion shown in the shield on the crest is the other official animal.)

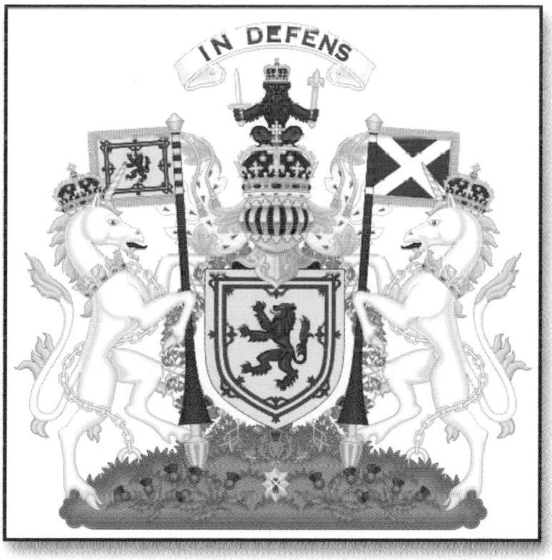
IN DEFENS

Lake Superior State University (through its Department of Natural Unicorns of the Unicorn Hunters) issues Questing Unicorn Licenses. Check it out at: www.lssu.edu/banished/uh_license.php.

Unicorns have appeared in folklore and art since ancient times in such different places as China, Greece, and France. One of the most famous depictions of unicorns is the *The Hunt of the Unicorn*, a series of seven tapestries that is in The Cloisters, which is part of The Metropolitan Museum of Art in New York. You can see them and learn more about them at: www.metmuseum.org/collections/search-the-collections/467642.

Create Your Own Cartoon Strip

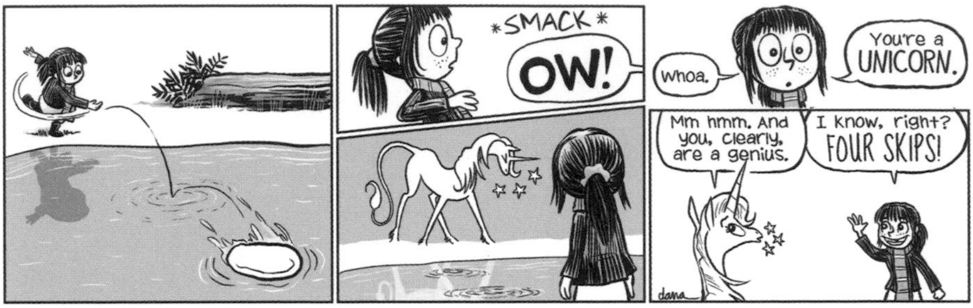
SMACK
OW!
Whoa.
You're a UNICORN.
Mm hmm. And you, clearly, are a genius.
I know, right? FOUR SKIPS!
dana

The comic strip *Phoebe and Her Unicorn* began when Phoebe met Marigold and they became friends. Think about how you met one of your favorite friends and draw a comic strip about it.

MATERIALS: blank piece of paper, pencil, markers, or colored pencils

INSTRUCTIONS:

1. Make three blank cartoon panels.

2. Look at the example above to see how Dana Simpson set the stage for the meeting and ended with the punch line.

3. Once you have decided on the story you want to tell, draw it in three panels. Remember, it should have a beginning, a middle, and an end.

4. In the first panel, give your comic strip a name.

> *"We'll be friends forever, won't we, Pooh?" asked Piglet. "Even longer," Pooh answered.*
>
> —Winnie the Pooh

Unicorn on a Roll

Another Phoebe and Her Unicorn Adventure

INTRODUCTION

i t was not long ago that if I suggested you should check out a clever, funny, sweet daily comic about a girl and her unicorn, I would have had to endure some eye rolls and serious questions about my maturity level.

But the times, they are a-changin'. Dana Simpson's *Phoebe and Her Unicorn* has arrived at just the right time to perpetuate an unprecedented shift in opinion and openness to the genuine thoughts, feelings, experiences—and humor—in the lives of authentic girls.

In modern media, women and girls are finally starting to be seen as regular plain old human beings. Fifty years ago—heck, fif*teen* years ago—almost any depiction of a young girl would be some sort of hyperidealized version of childhood femininity. Girls in comics and cartoons were either precocious little sprites; bossy, irritating nags; or ethereal, fragile beauties, even at their tender ages. They were characters created by observers and idealizers, and because of this vantage, the audience watched them from a distance. But the characterization of Phoebe is indicative of a very recent, very new, very refreshing change of perspective of who girls really are. Though she is a girl who has many interests that are the usual girlish things, she is relatable to all regardless of gender or age. We don't watch her from the cheap seats; we are right up there with her on the stage, flaws and all. She's not a little Kewpie doll to be protected or admired; rather, we see ourselves reflected back in her. She is not just every girl; she is every child. She is US.

Now let's talk Marigold Heavenly Nostrils. Vanity, the supposedly "feminine" personality flaw usually assigned to antagonists and villains, is turned on its head. Yes, Marigold is vain, but she is caring and attentive, she keeps her promises, and though she reminds us all that every creature is basically beneath her magical majesty, she certainly doesn't treat anyone that way. She is riddled with self-love and is utterly unapologetic. And couldn't we all stand to feel a little more free to love ourselves? Her vanity is not portrayed as a trait worthy of revile, but as something that makes her funny, fun to be around, and utterly endearing. Some would say these are some pretty essential qualities in a BFF.

And when paired together, these two very modern depictions of female archetypes not only demonstrate for us a heartwarming, true friendship—they show us a little of ourselves; a little of what we aspire to be; and, perhaps most important of all, they make us laugh.

So hopefully soon the days of rolling our eyes at little girls and their dreams of magic and unicorns will be gone. It's about time that all of us, like Dana, realized that little girls are onto something. That bringing a little magic into our world is all it takes to help us through the trials and tribulations of life. So sit back and enjoy—girl, boy, child, adult—*Phoebe and Her Unicorn* is for YOU.

— Lauren Faust
January 2015

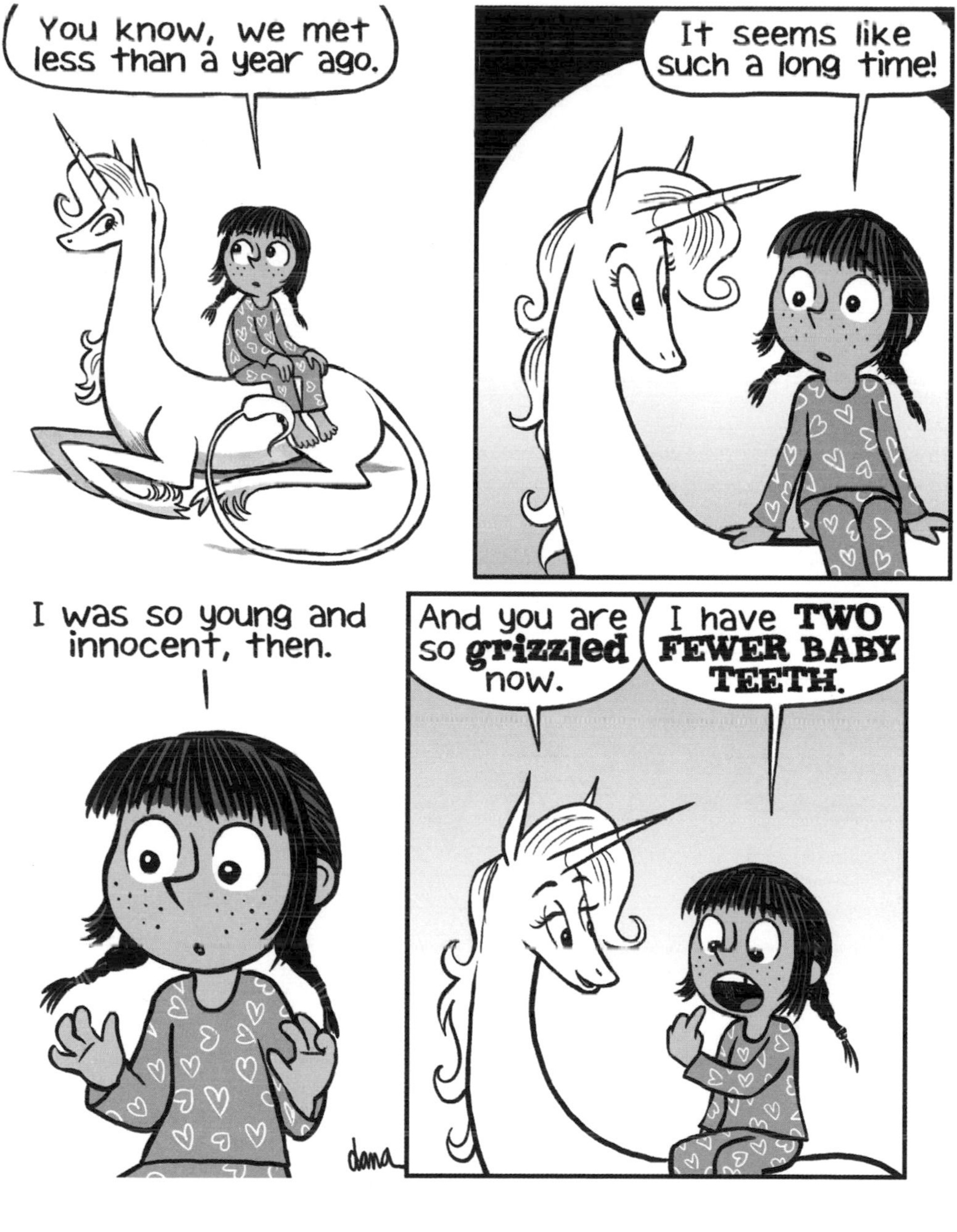
You know, we met less than a year ago.
It seems like such a long time!
I was so young and innocent, then.
And you are so **grizzled** now.
I have **TWO FEWER BABY TEETH.**
dana

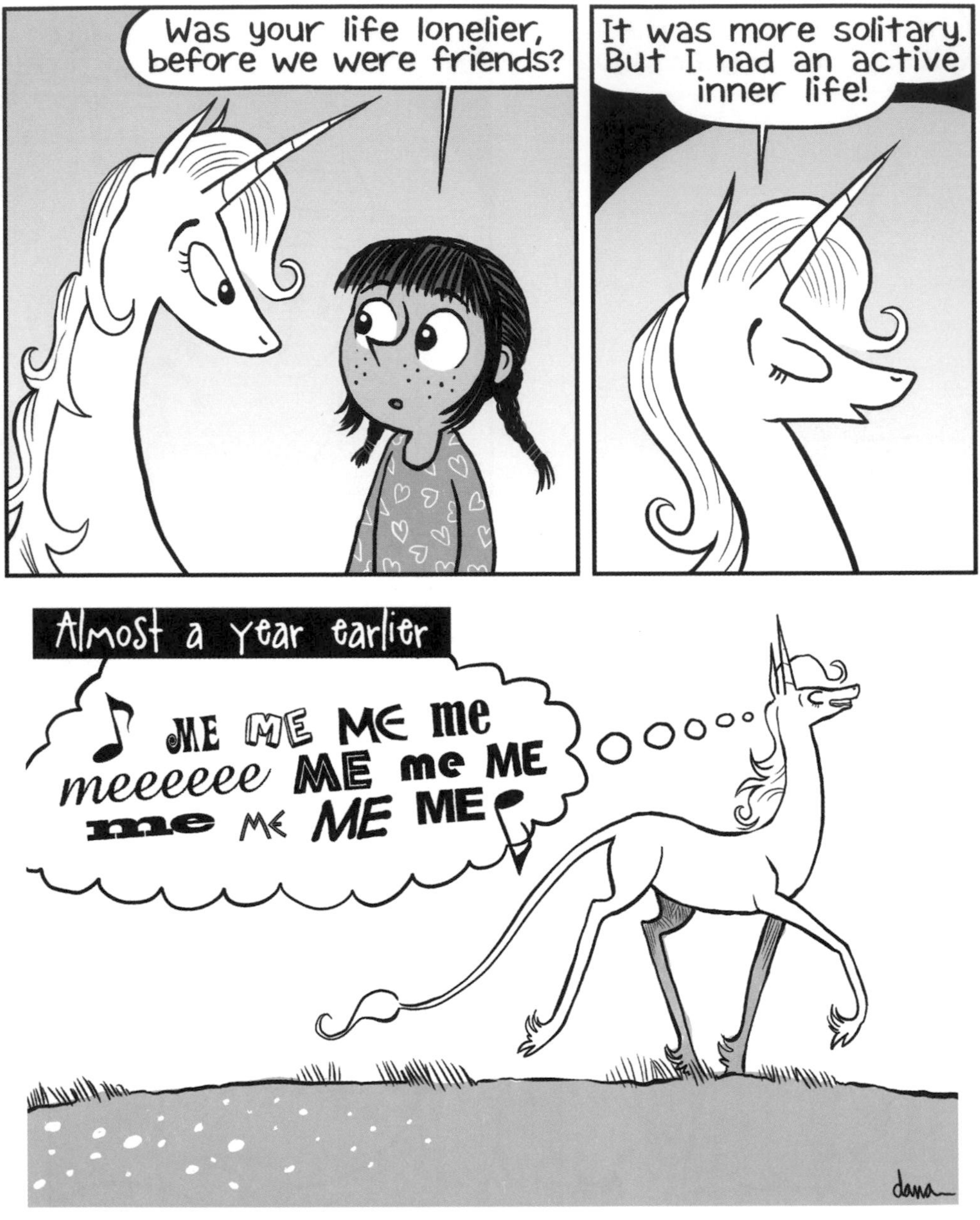
Was your life lonelier, before we were friends?
It was more solitary. But I had an active inner life!
Almost a year earlier
ME ME ME me meeeeee ME me ME me ME ME ME
dana

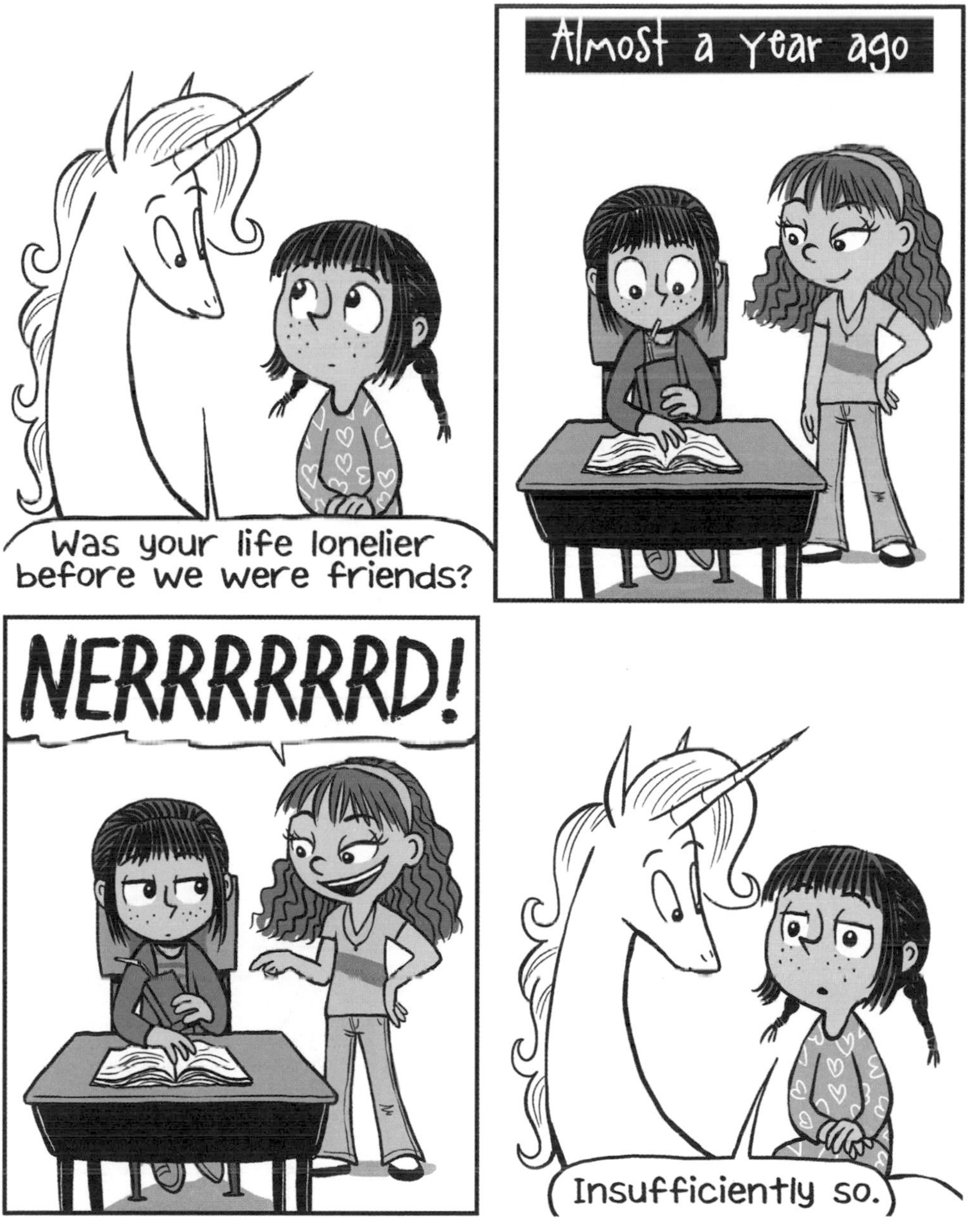
Was your life lonelier before we were friends?
Almost a year ago
NERRRRRRD!
Insufficiently so.

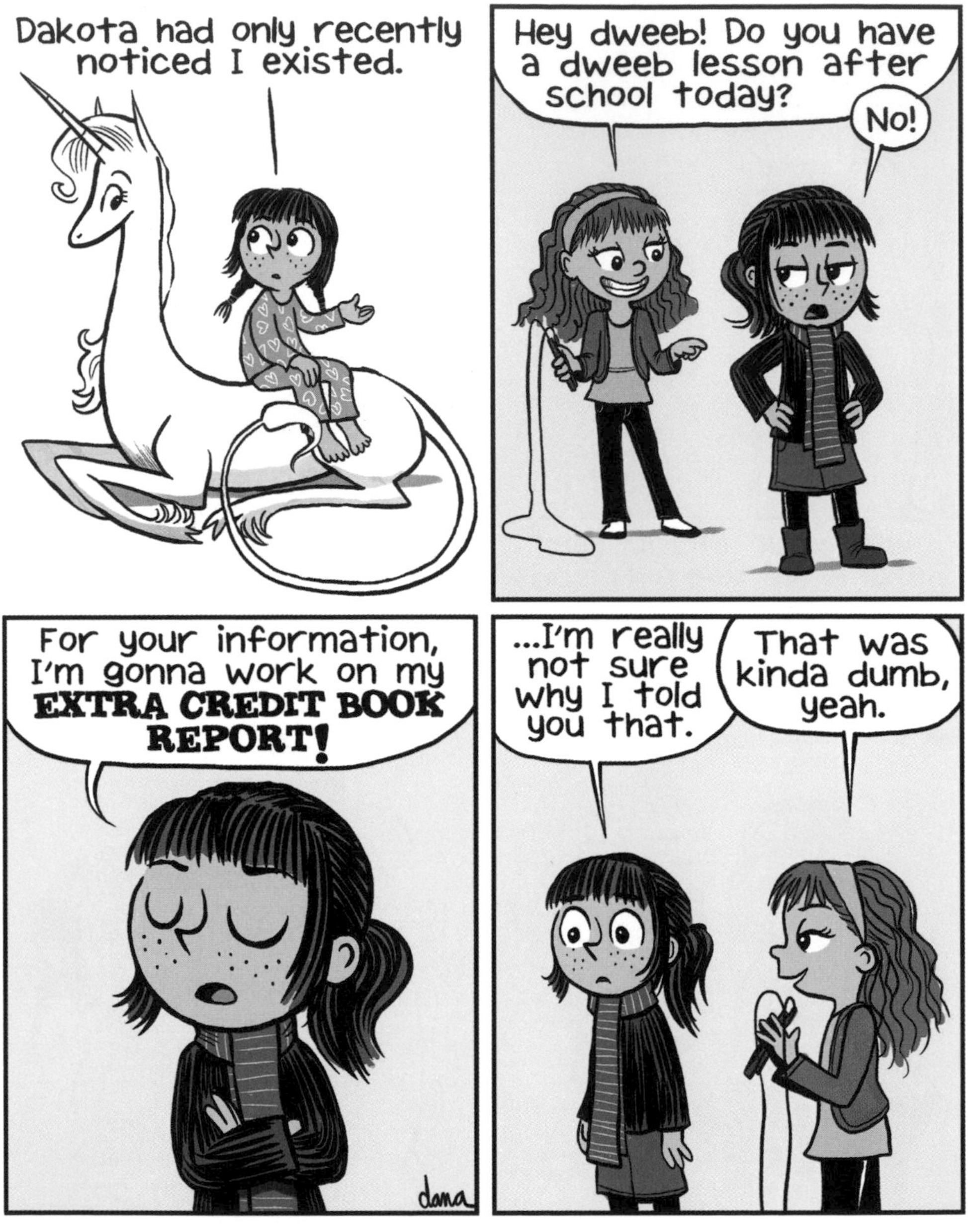
Dakota had only recently noticed I existed.
Hey dweeb! Do you have a dweeb lesson after school today?
No!
For your information, I'm gonna work on my **EXTRA CREDIT BOOK REPORT!**
...I'm really not sure why I told you that.
That was kinda dumb, yeah.
dana

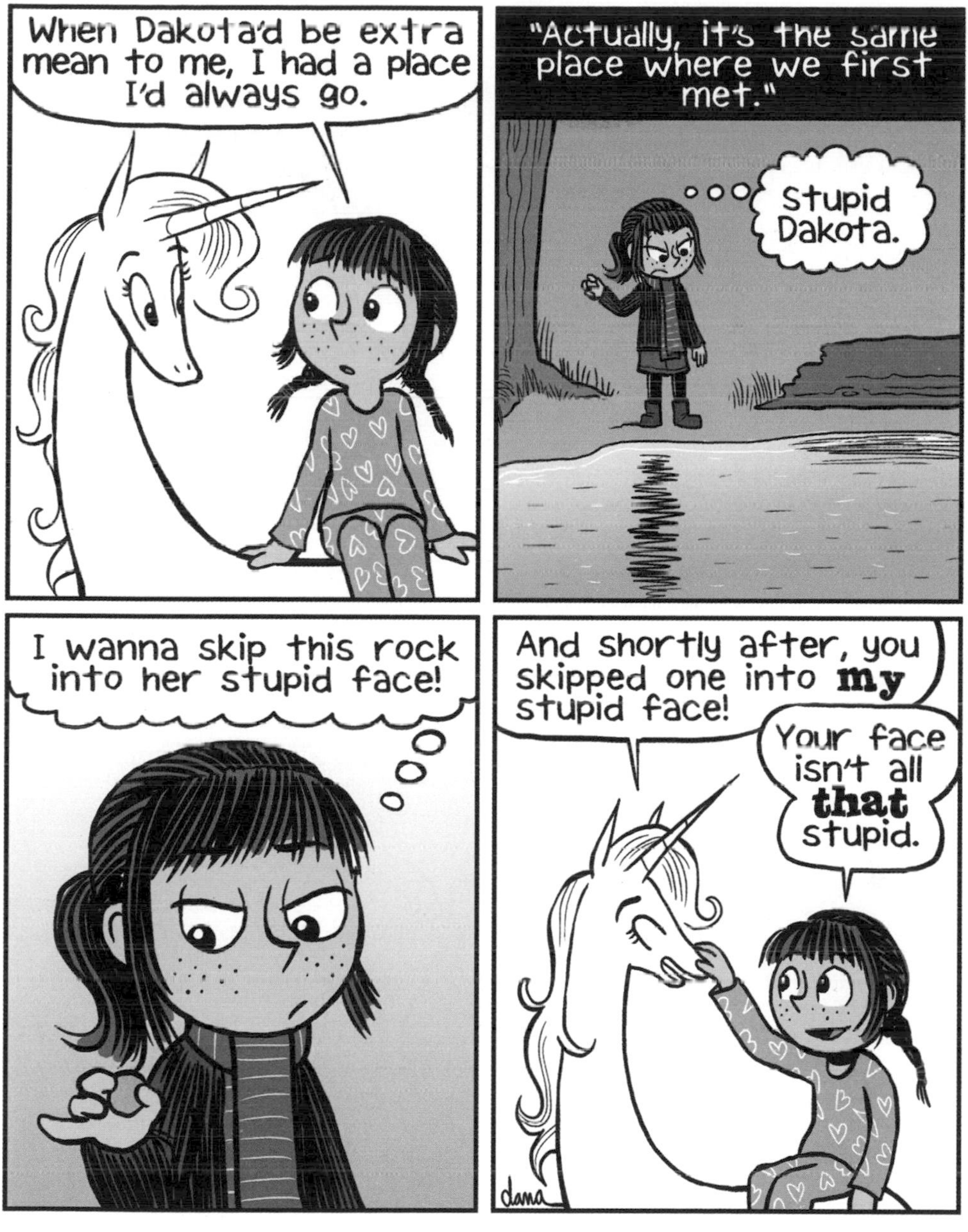
When Dakota'd be extra mean to me, I had a place I'd always go.
"Actually, it's the same place where we first met."
Stupid Dakota.
I wanna skip this rock into her stupid face!
And shortly after, you skipped one into **my** stupid face!
Your face isn't all **that** stupid.
dana

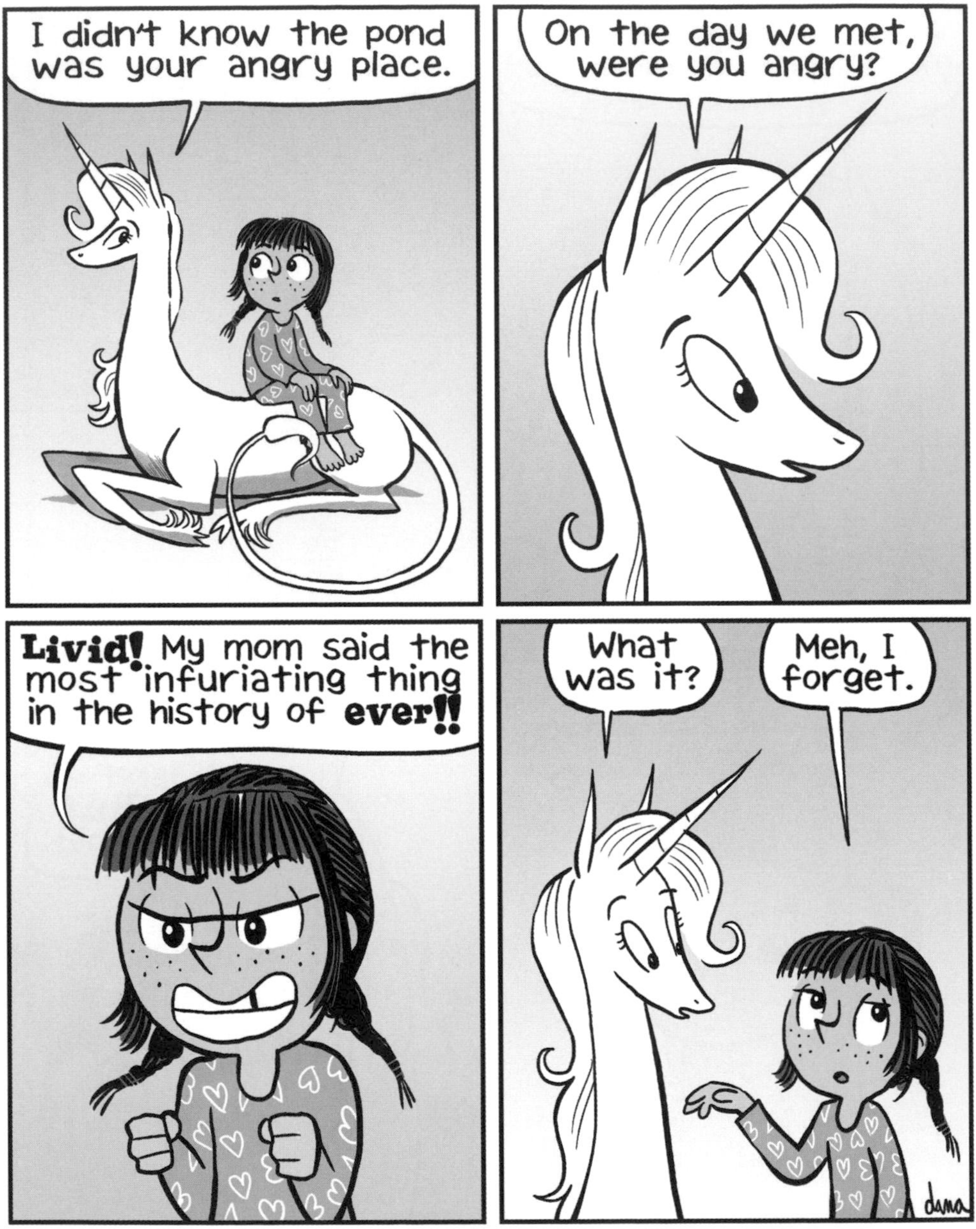
I didn't know the pond was your angry place.
On the day we met, were you angry?
Livid! My mom said the most infuriating thing in the history of ever!!
What was it?
Meh, I forget.
dana

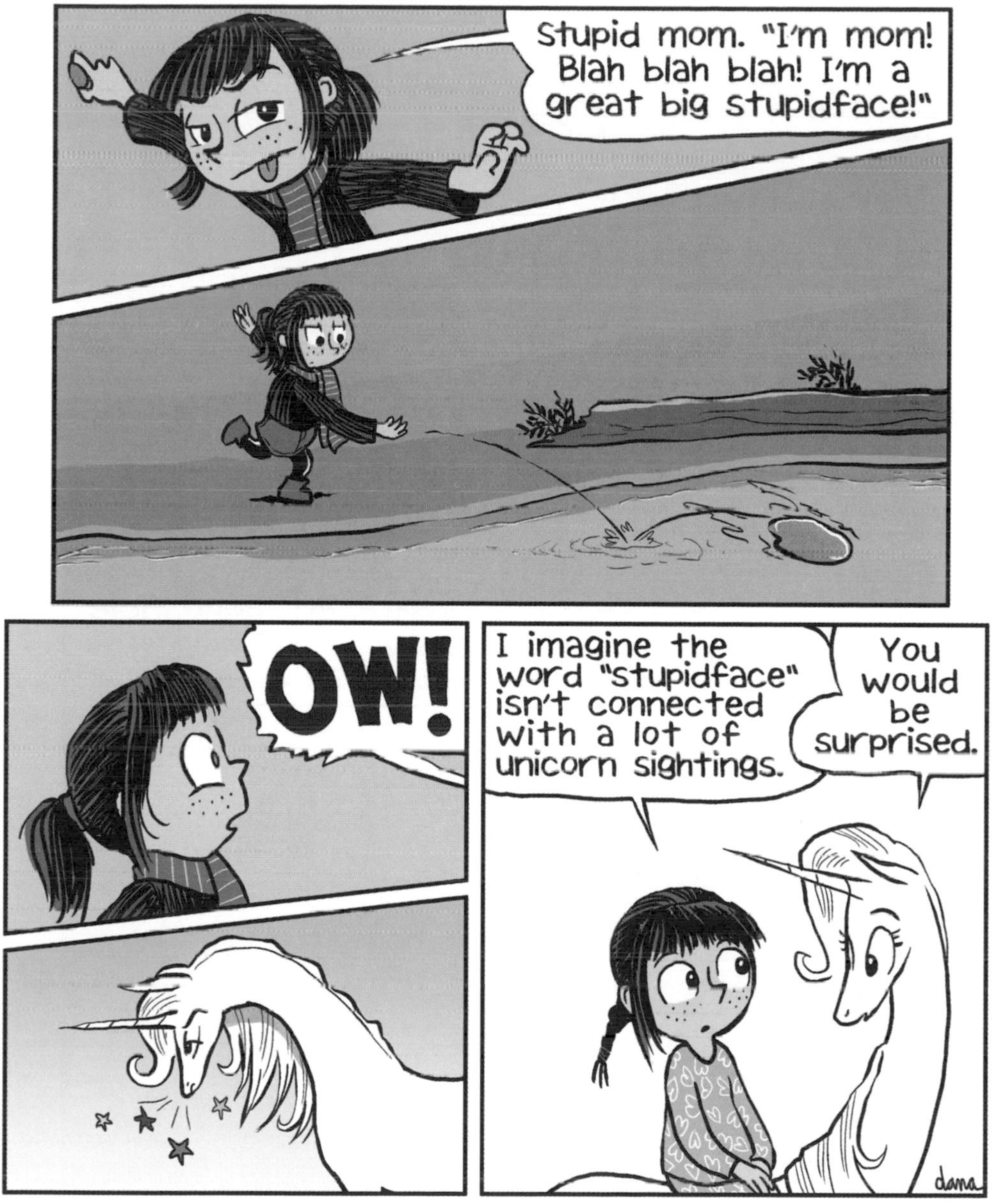
Stupid mom. "I'm mom! Blah blah blah! I'm a great big stupidface!"
OW!
I imagine the word "stupidface" isn't connected with a lot of unicorn sightings.
You would be surprised.
dana

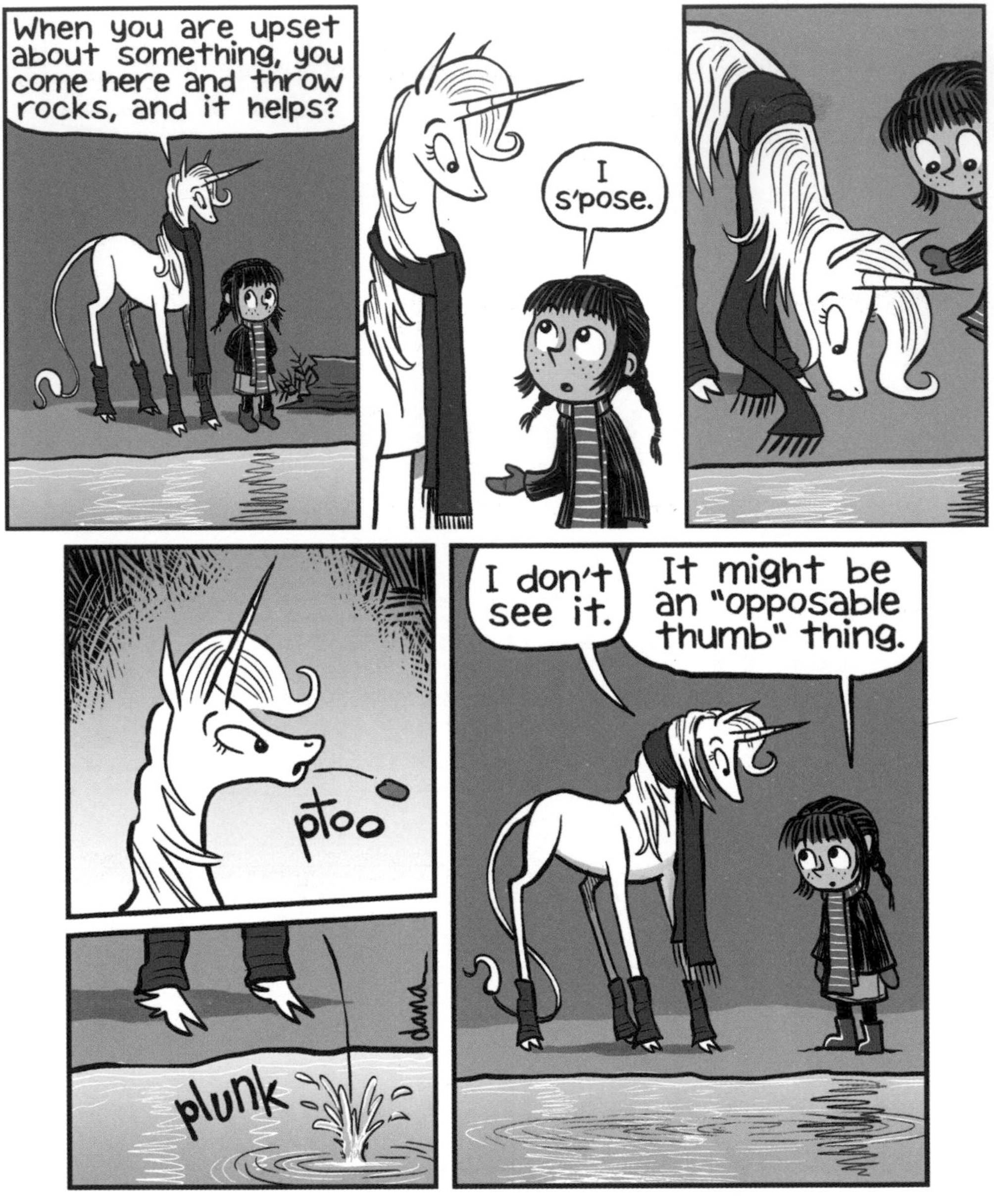

When you are upset about something, you come here and throw rocks, and it helps?
I s'pose.
ptoo
plunk
dana
I don't see it.
It might be an "opposable thumb" thing.

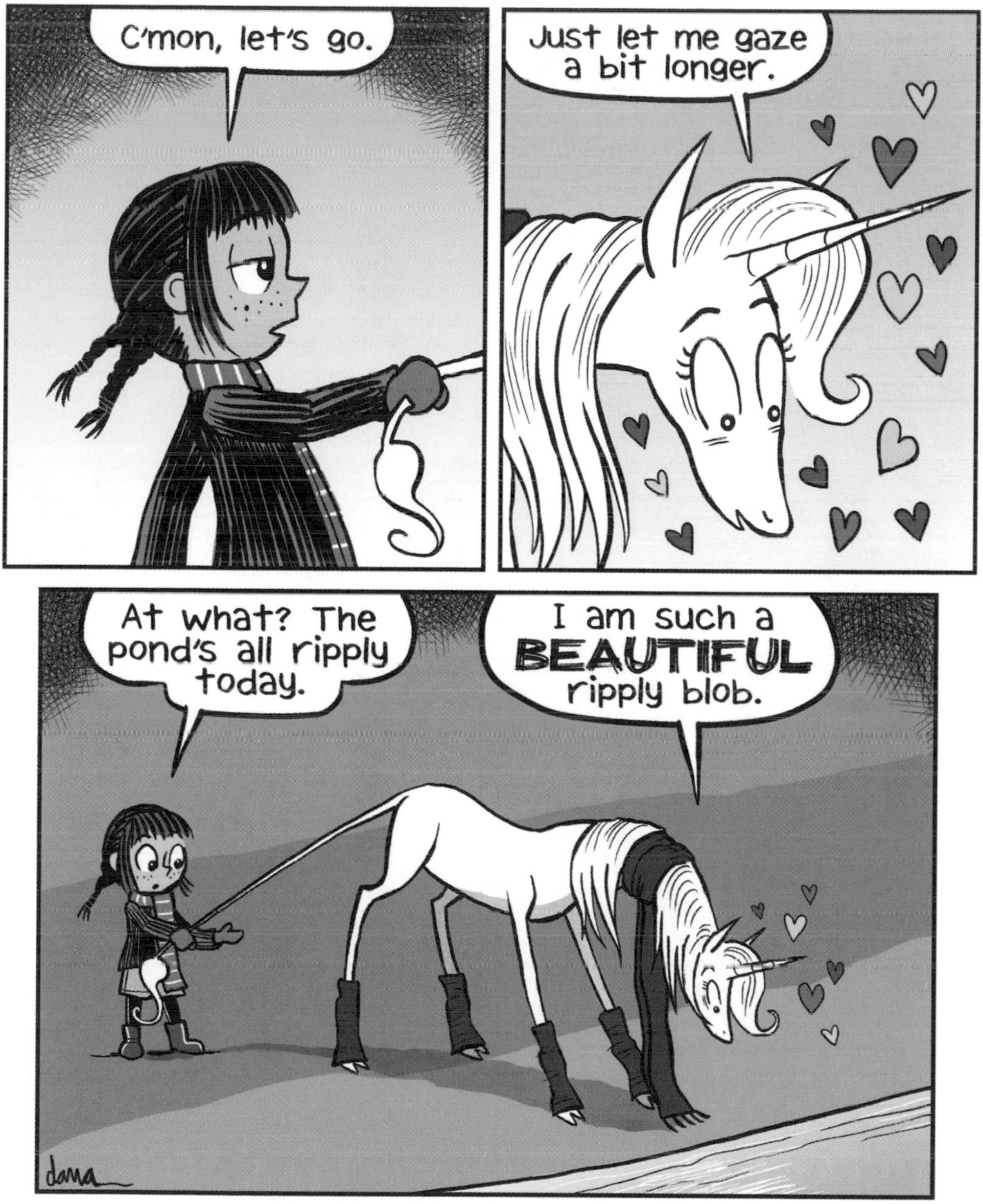
C'mon, let's go.
Just let me gaze a bit longer.
At what? The pond's all ripply today.
I am such a **BEAUTIFUL** ripply blob.
dana

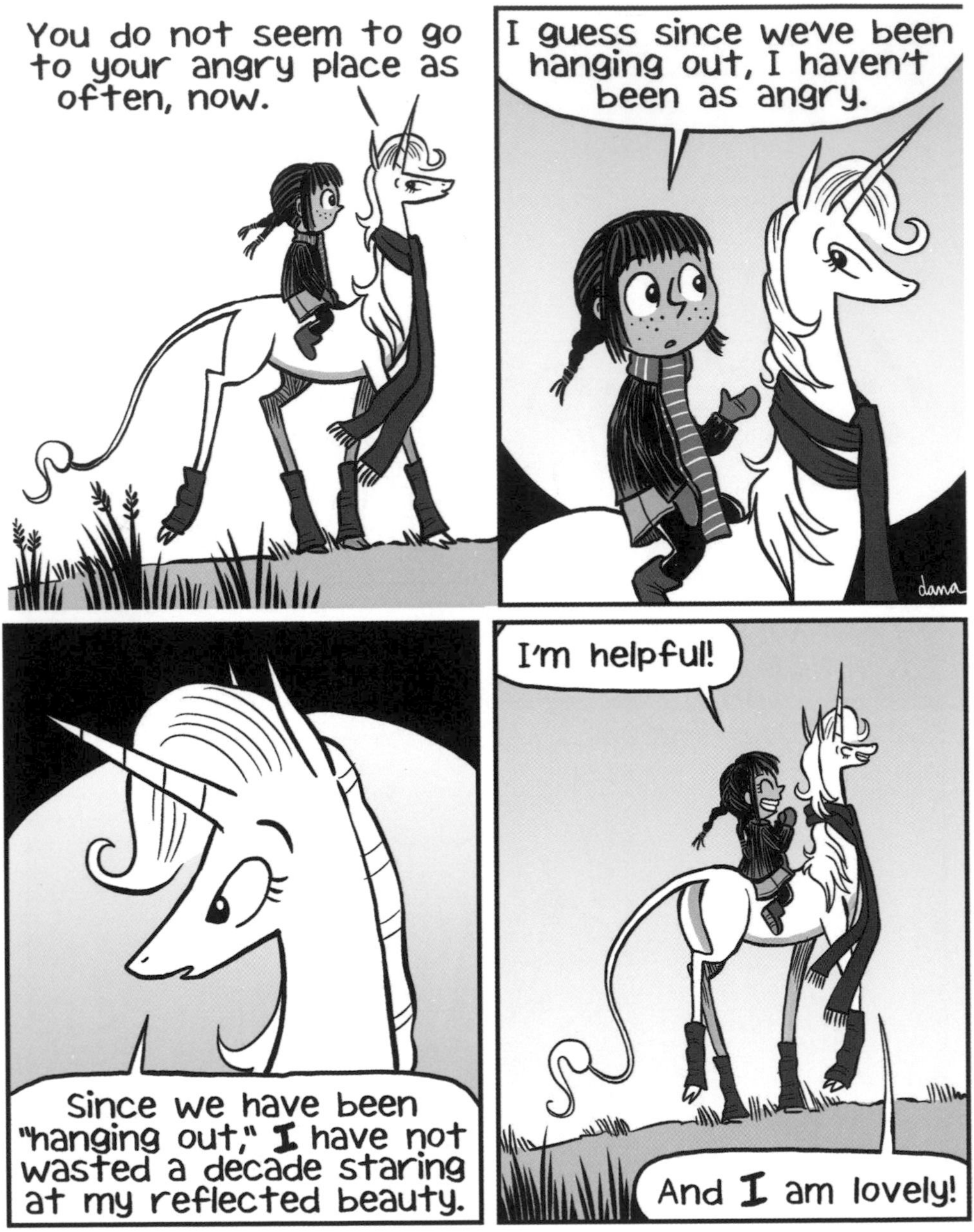
You do not seem to go to your angry place as often, now.
I guess since we've been hanging out, I haven't been as angry.
dana
Since we have been "hanging out," I have not wasted a decade staring at my reflected beauty.
I'm helpful!
And I am lovely!

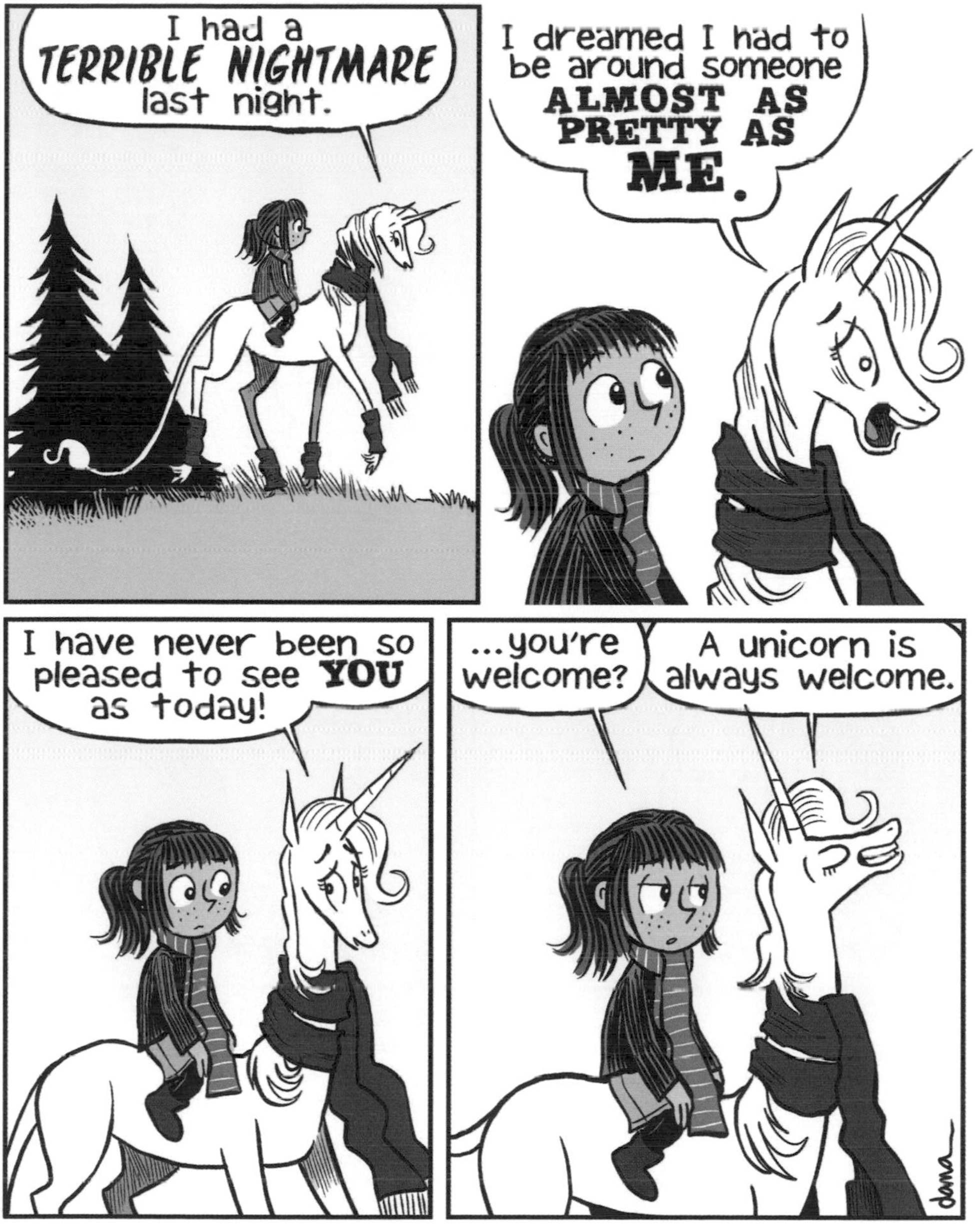
I had a TERRIBLE NIGHTMARE last night.
I dreamed I had to be around someone ALMOST AS PRETTY AS ME.
I have never been so pleased to see YOU as today!
...you're welcome?
A unicorn is always welcome.
dana

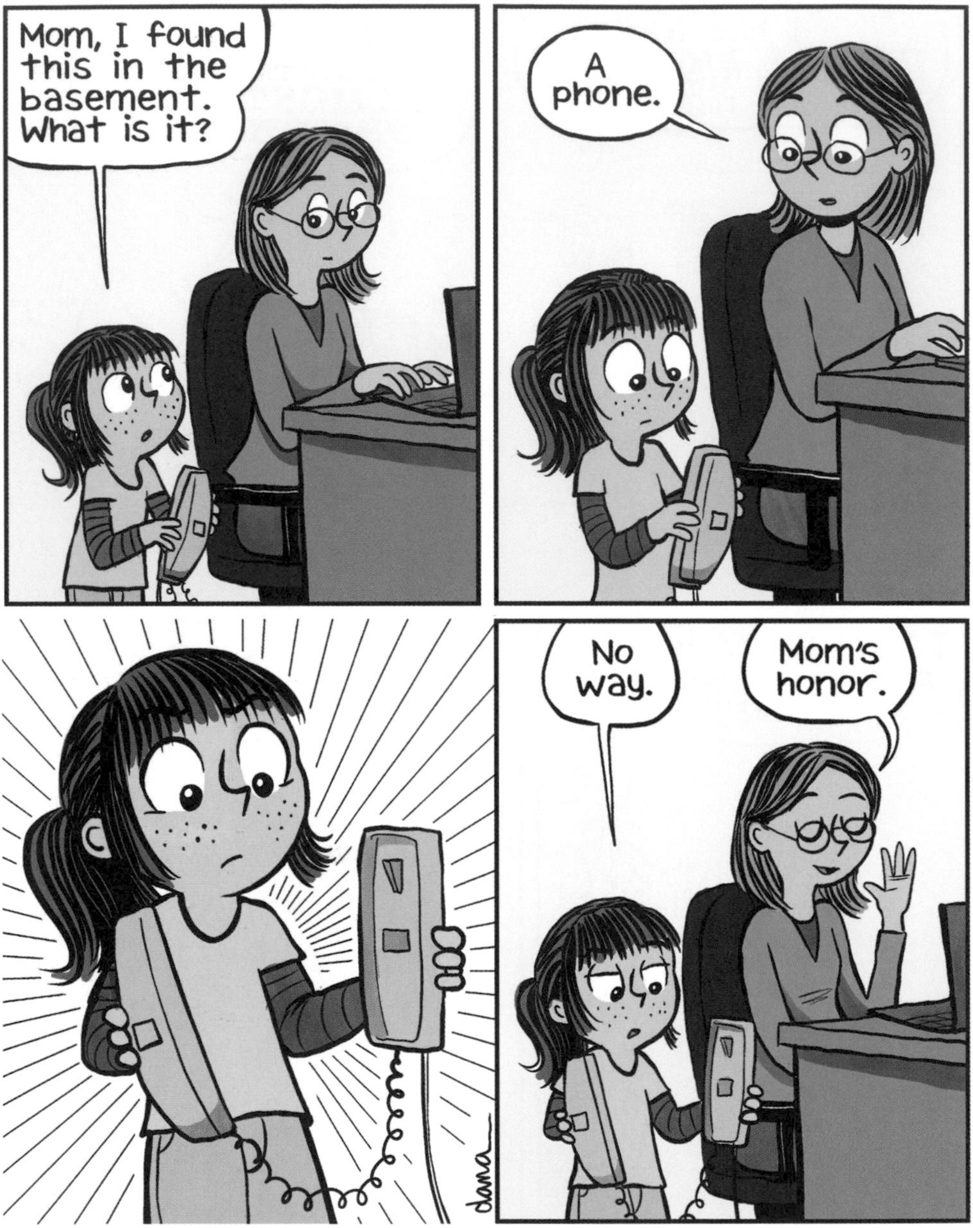
Mom, I found this in the basement. What is it?
A phone.
No way.
Mom's honor.
dana

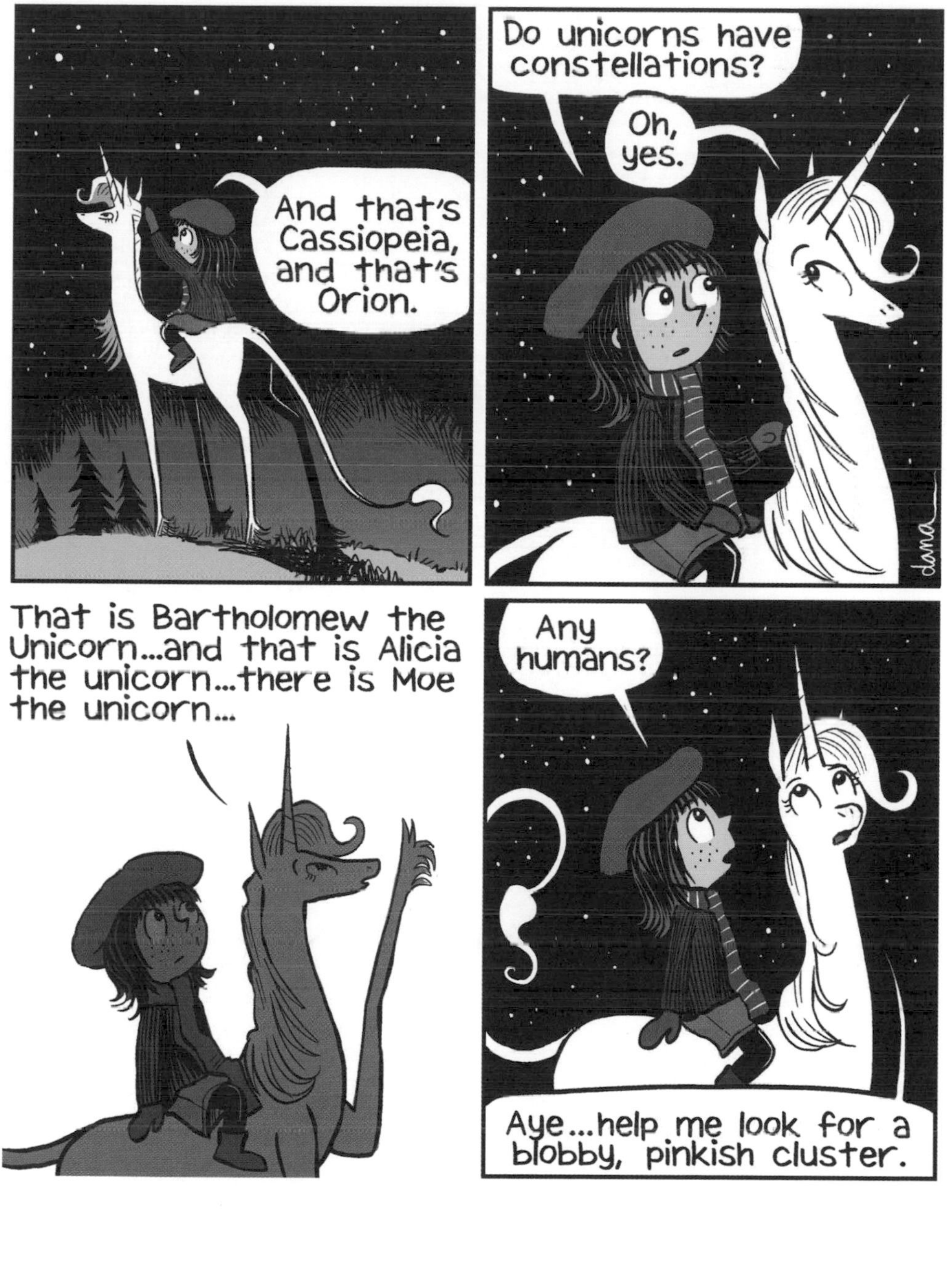
And that's Cassiopeia, and that's Orion.
Do unicorns have constellations?
Oh, yes.
dana
That is Bartholomew the Unicorn...and that is Alicia the unicorn...there is Moe the unicorn...
Any humans?
Aye...help me look for a blobby, pinkish cluster.

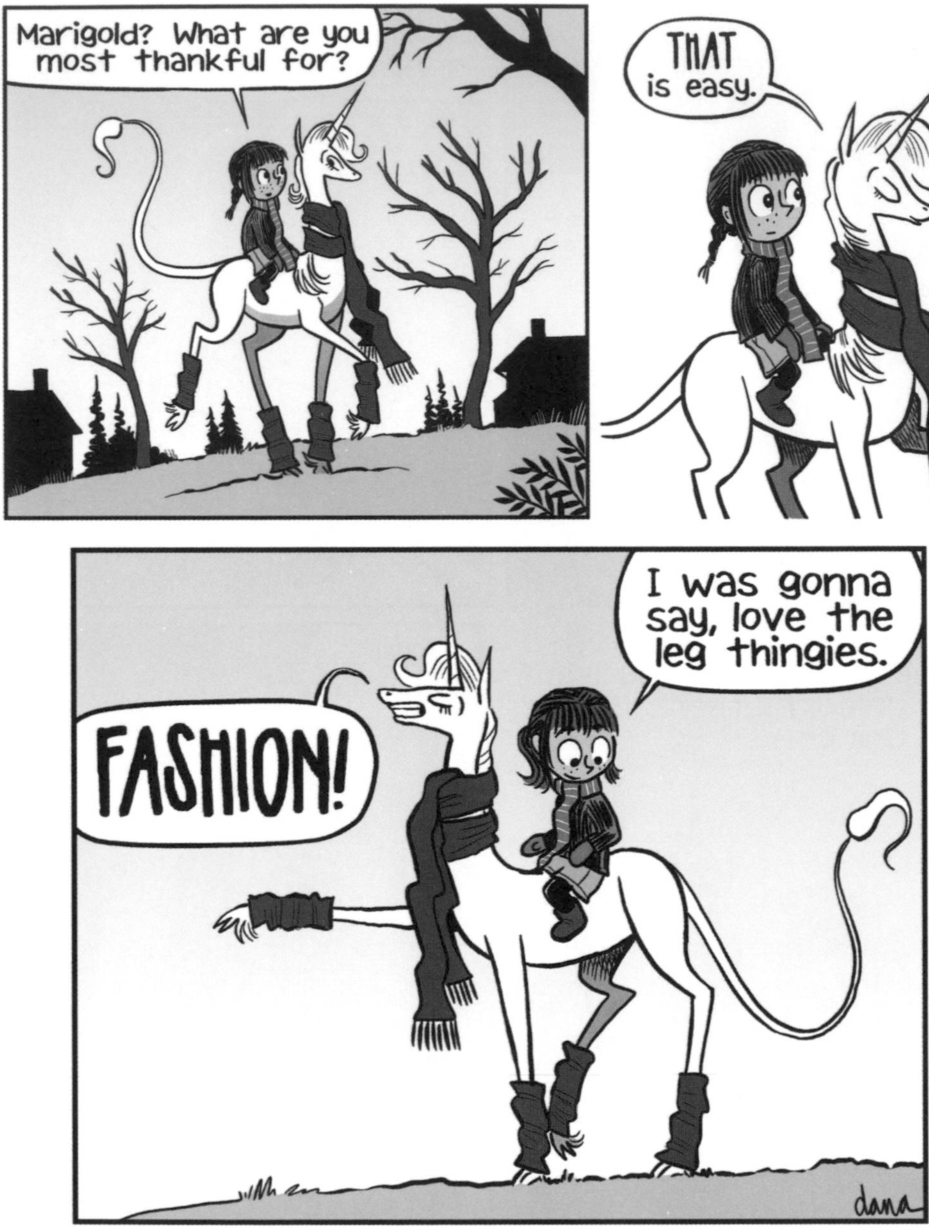
Marigold? What are you most thankful for?
THAT is easy.
I was gonna say, love the leg thingies.
FASHION!
dana

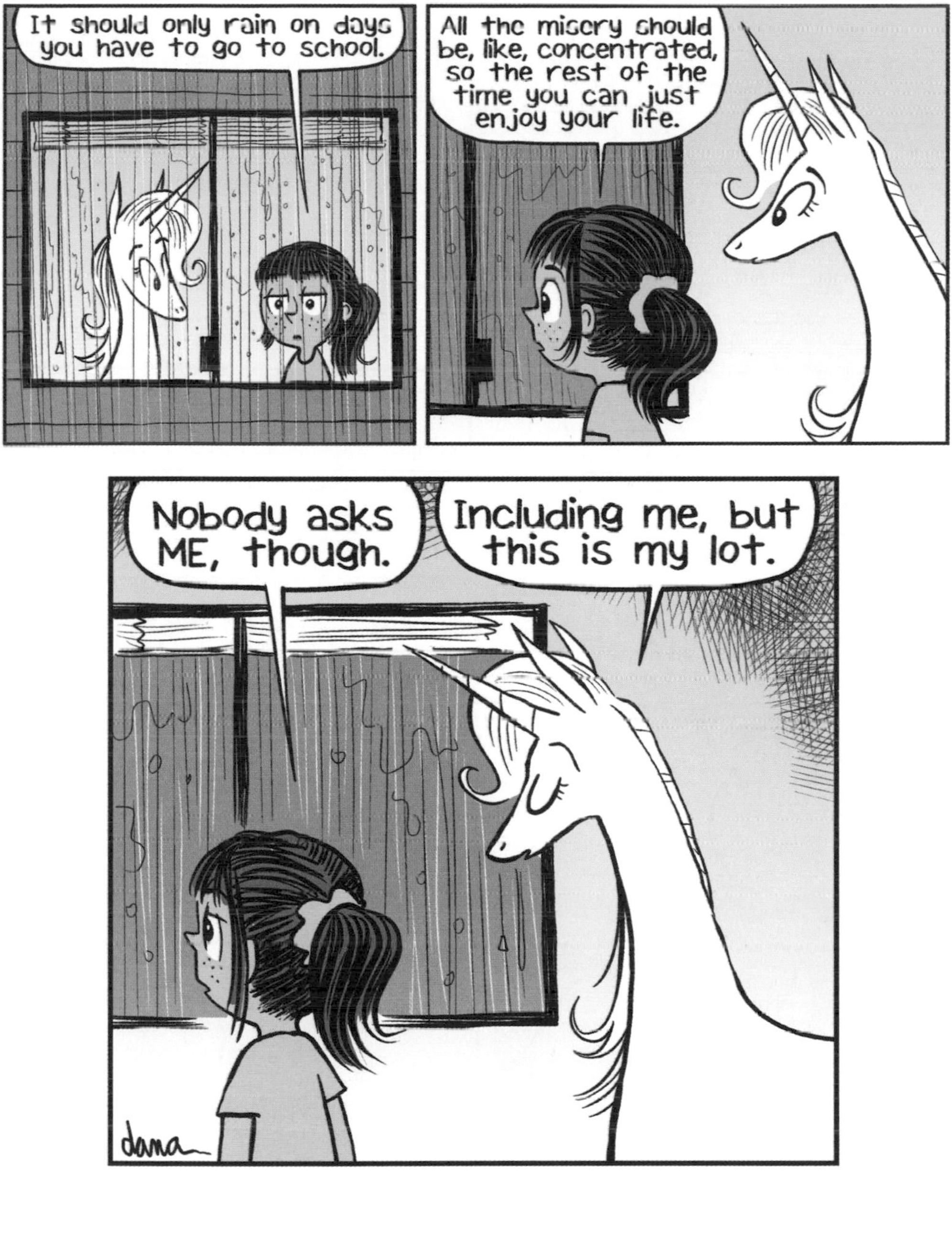
It should only rain on days you have to go to school.
All the misery should be, like, concentrated, so the rest of the time you can just enjoy your life.
Nobody asks ME, though.
Including me, but this is my lot.
dana

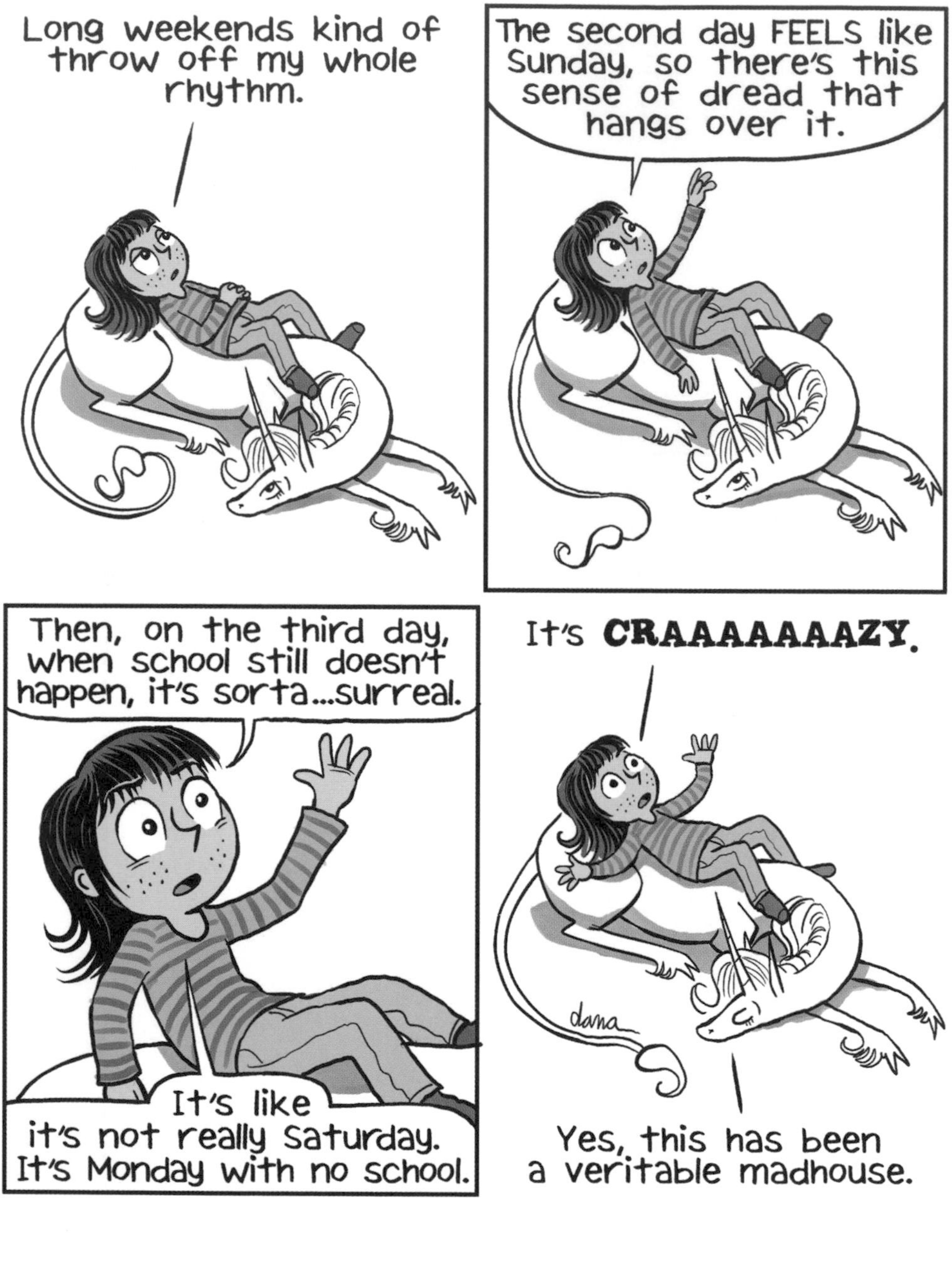

Long weekends kind of throw off my whole rhythm.
The second day FEELS like Sunday, so there's this sense of dread that hangs over it.
Then, on the third day, when school still doesn't happen, it's sorta...surreal.
It's like it's not really Saturday. It's Monday with no school.
It's CRAAAAAAAAZY.
Yes, this has been a veritable madhouse.
dana

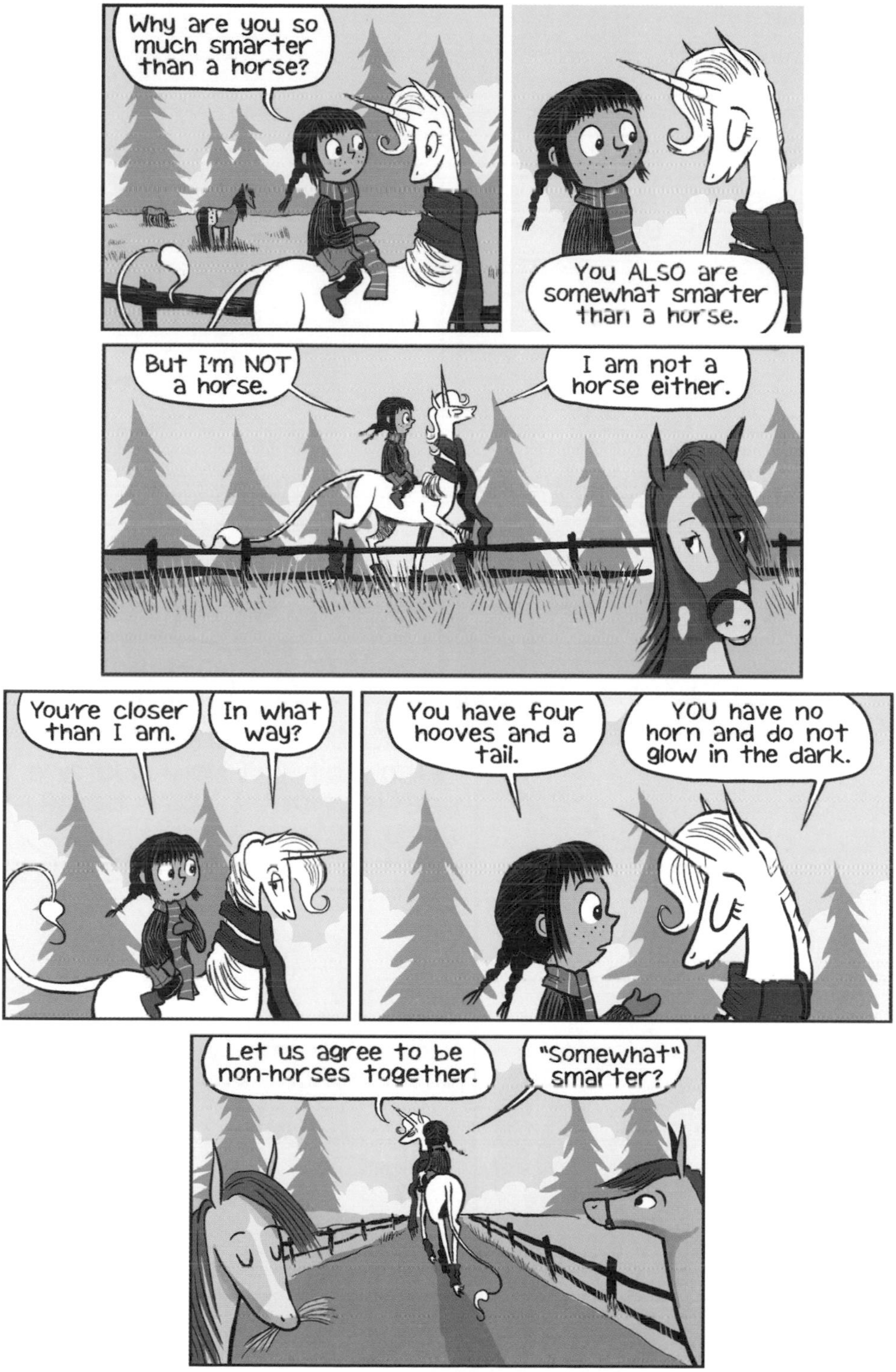

Why are you so much smarter than a horse?
You ALSO are somewhat smarter than a horse.
But I'm NOT a horse.
I am not a horse either.
You're closer than I am.
In what way?
You have four hooves and a tail.
YOU have no horn and do not glow in the dark.
Let us agree to be non-horses together.
"Somewhat" smarter?

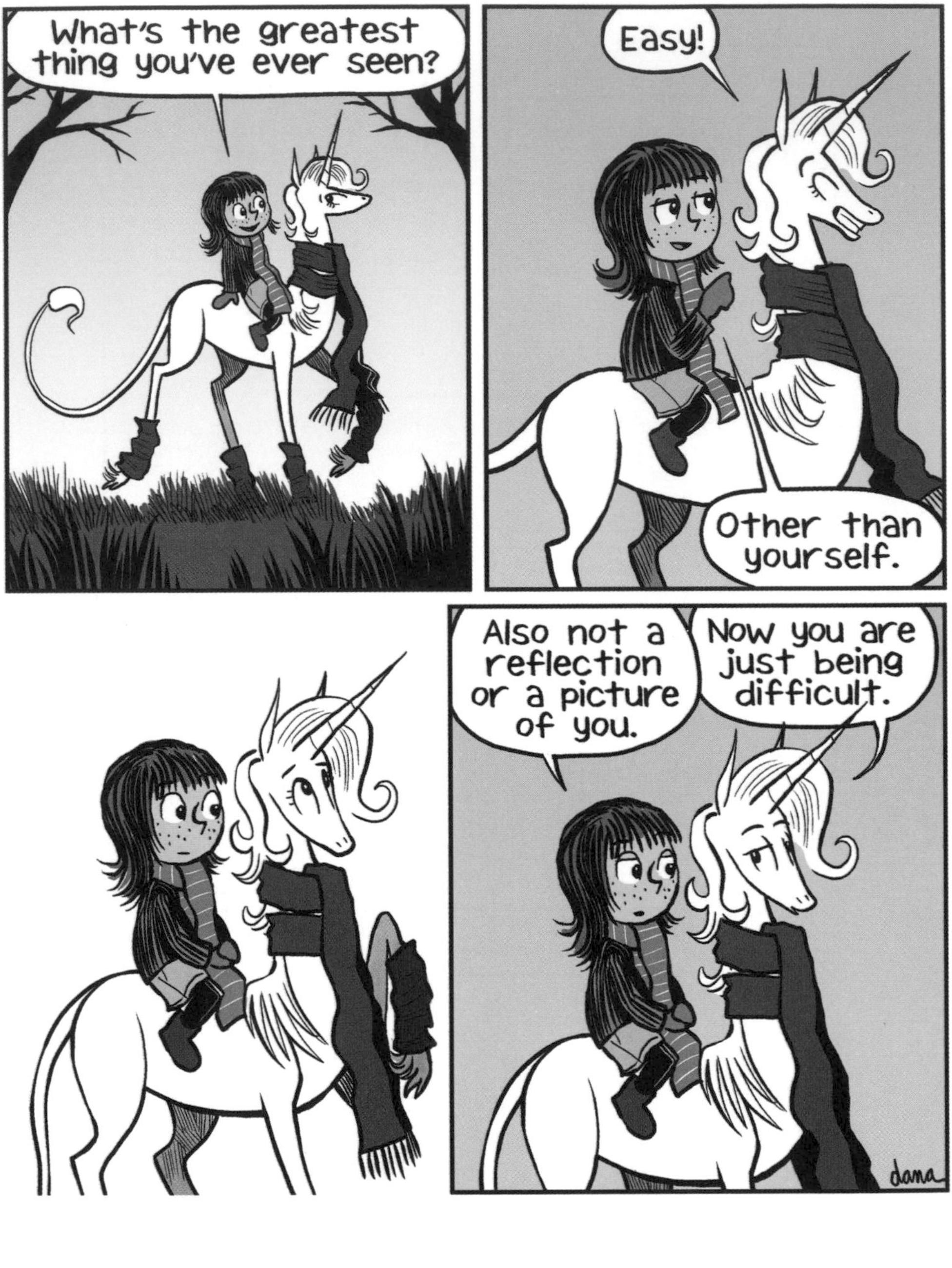
What's the greatest thing you've ever seen?
Easy!
Other than yourself.
Also not a reflection or a picture of you.
Now you are just being difficult.
dana

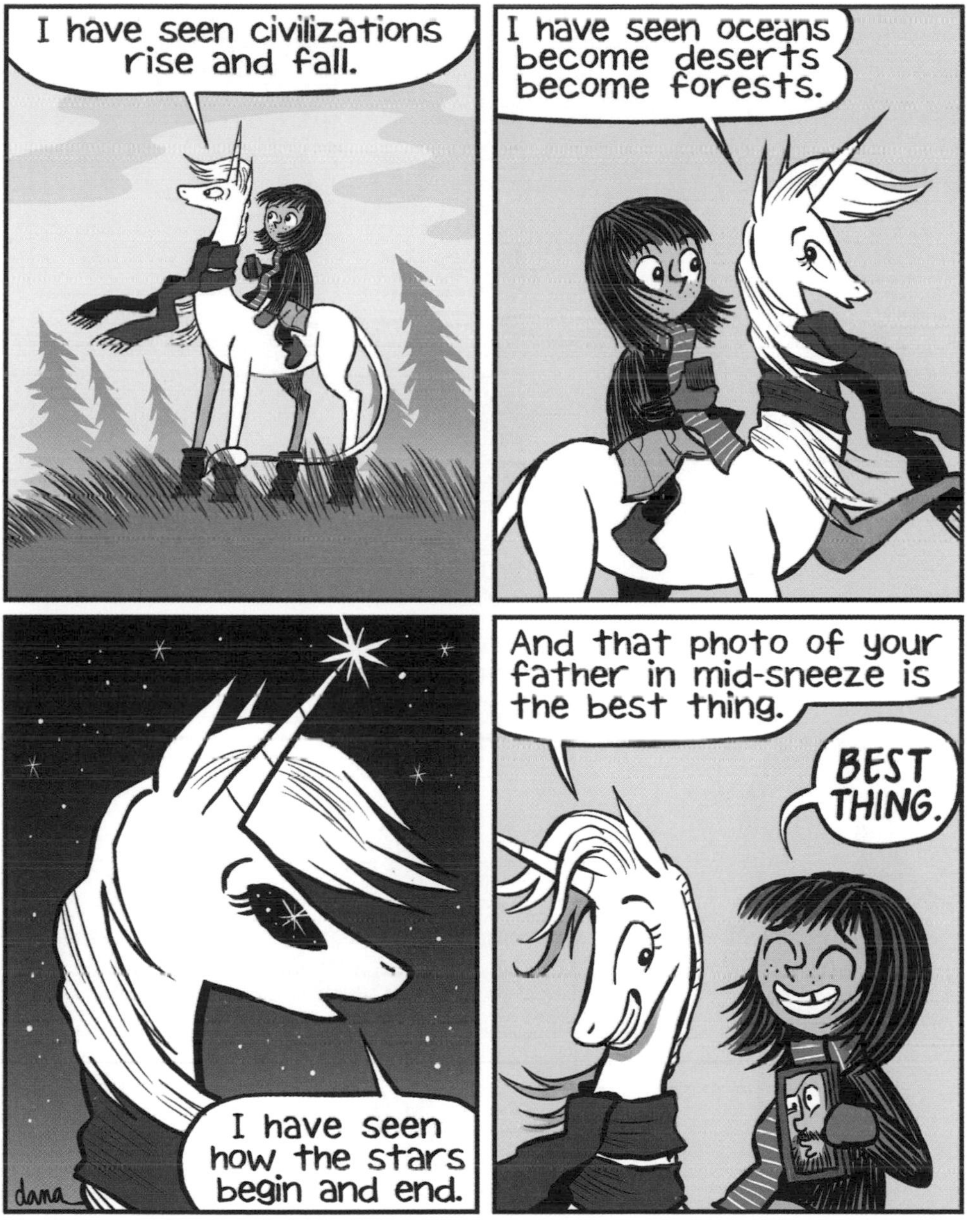
I have seen civilizations rise and fall.
I have seen oceans become deserts become forests.
I have seen how the stars begin and end.
dana
And that photo of your father in mid-sneeze is the best thing.
BEST THING.

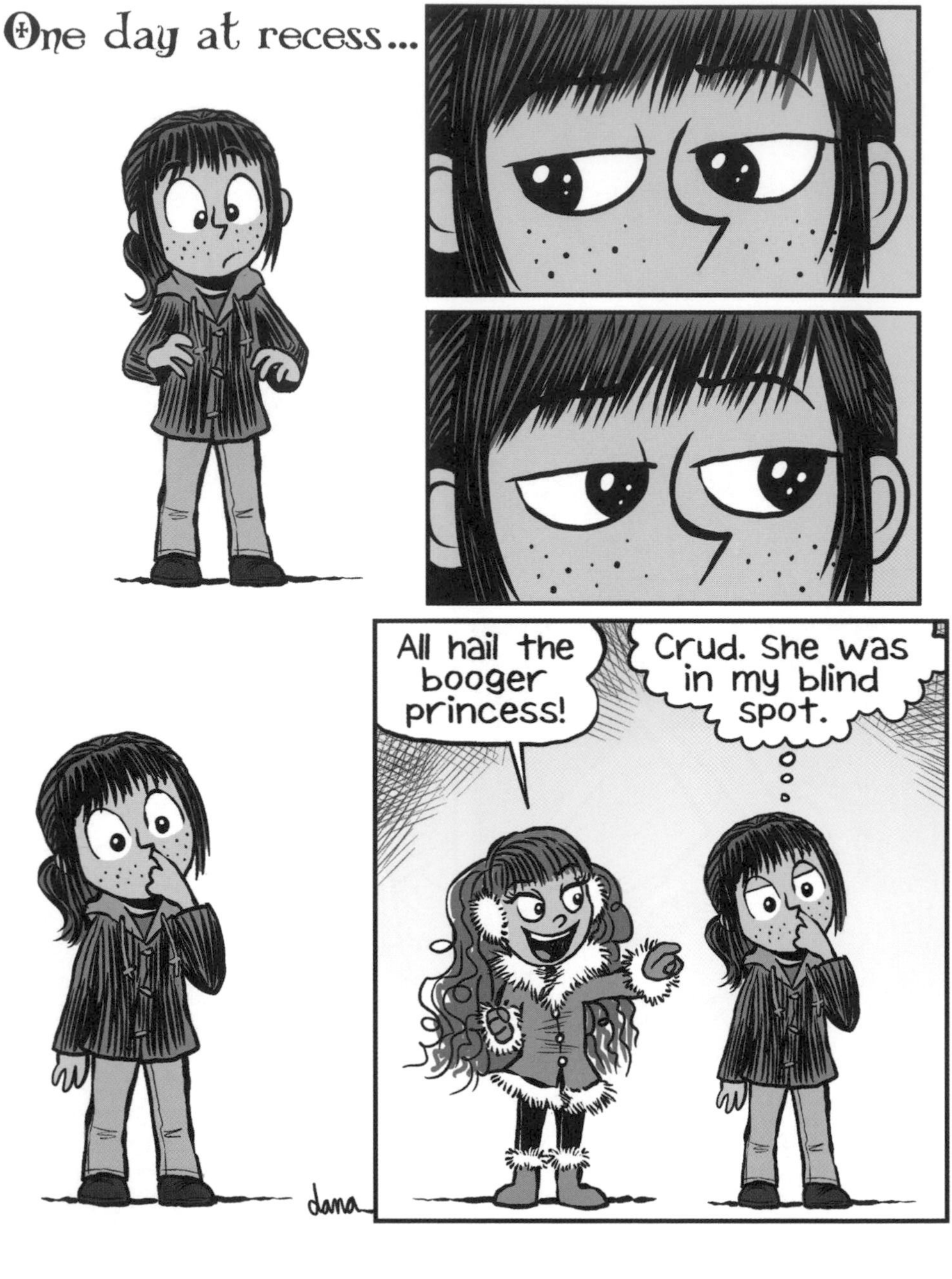
One day at recess...
All hail the booger princess!
Crud. She was in my blind spot.

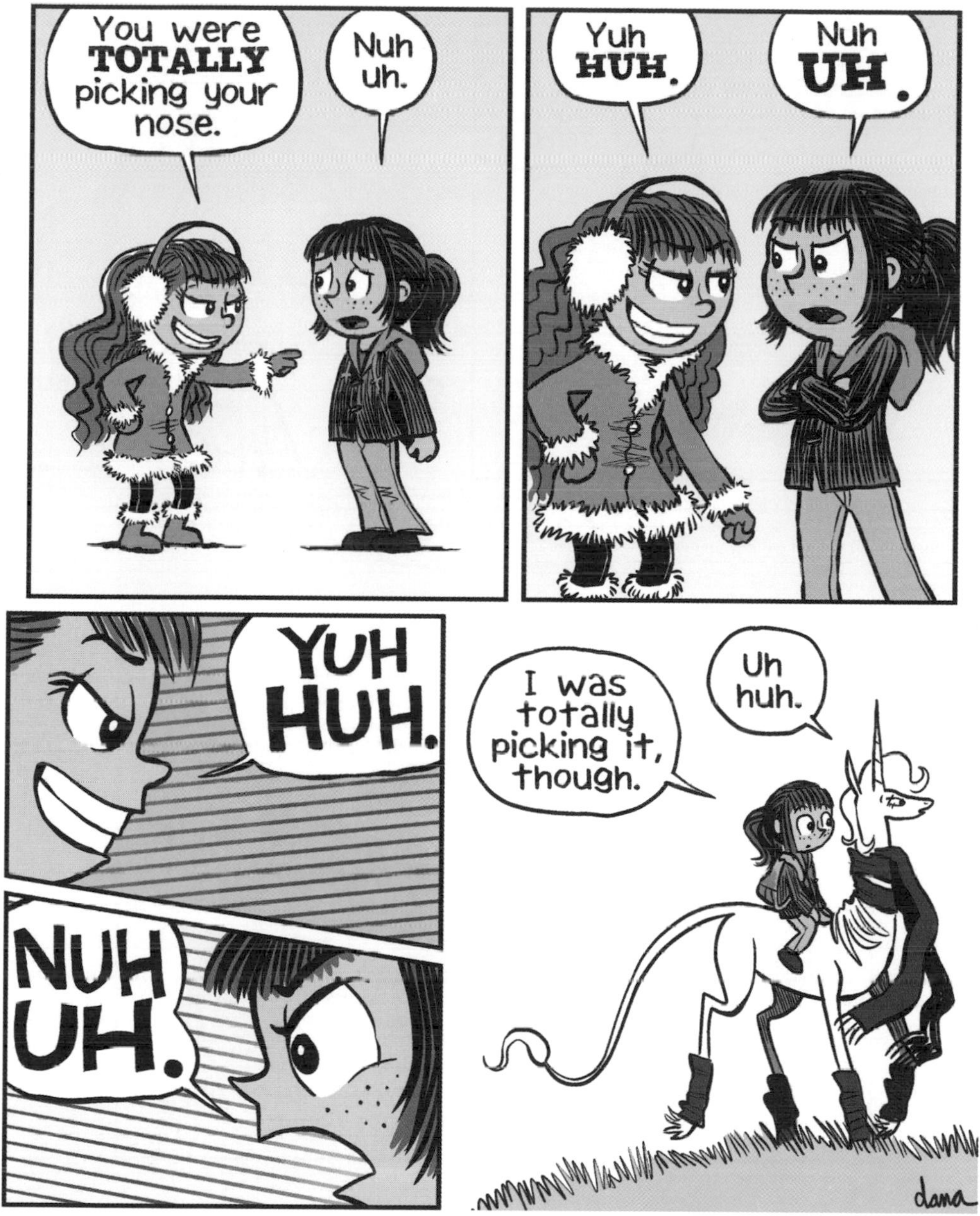
You were **TOTALLY** picking your nose.
Nuh uh.
Yuh **HUH**.
Nuh **UH**.
YUH HUH.
NUH UH.
I was totally picking it, though.
Uh huh.
dana

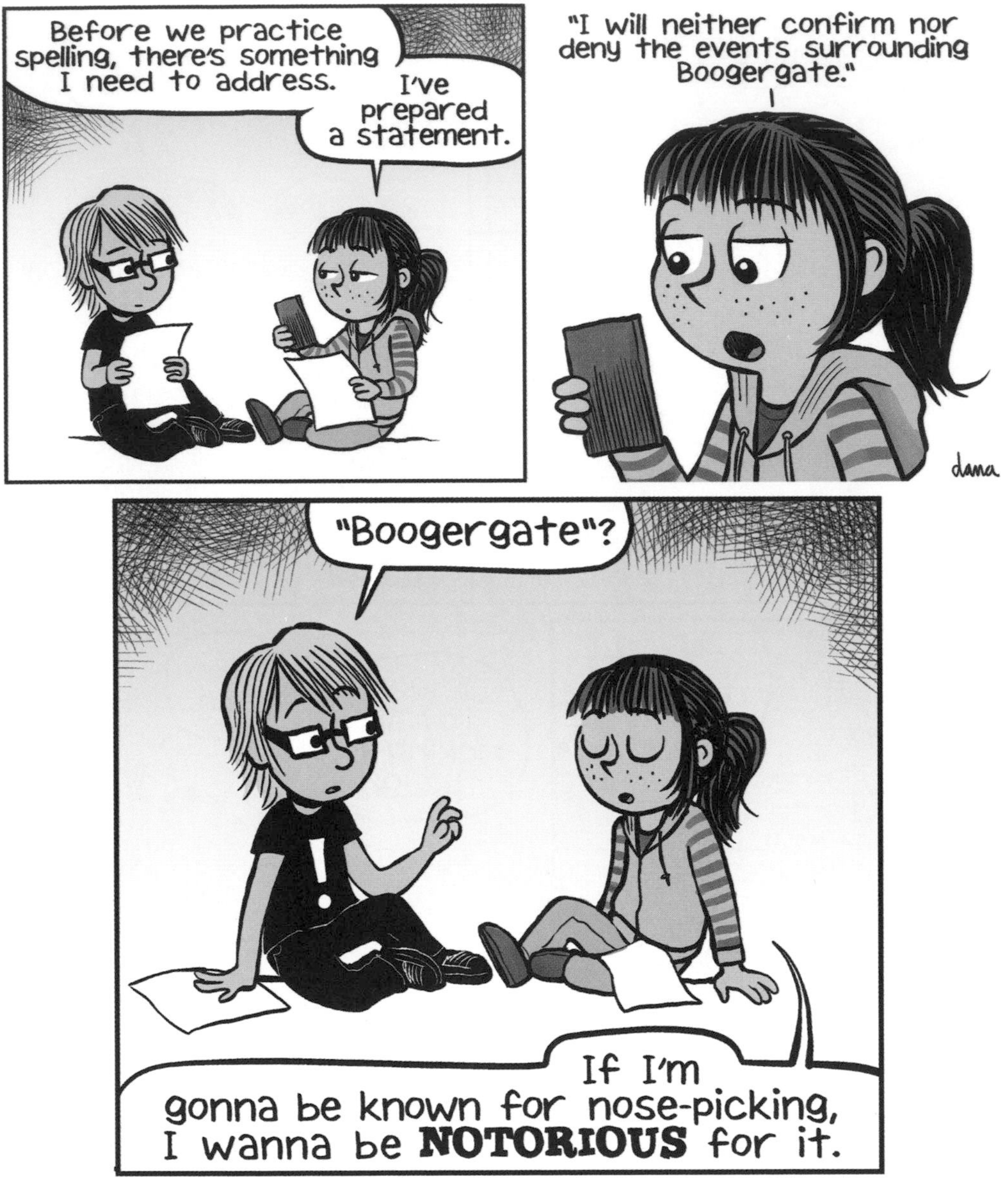
Before we practice spelling, there's something I need to address.
I've prepared a statement.
"I will neither confirm nor deny the events surrounding Boogergate."
dana
"Boogergate"?
If I'm gonna be known for nose-picking, I wanna be NOTORIOUS for it.

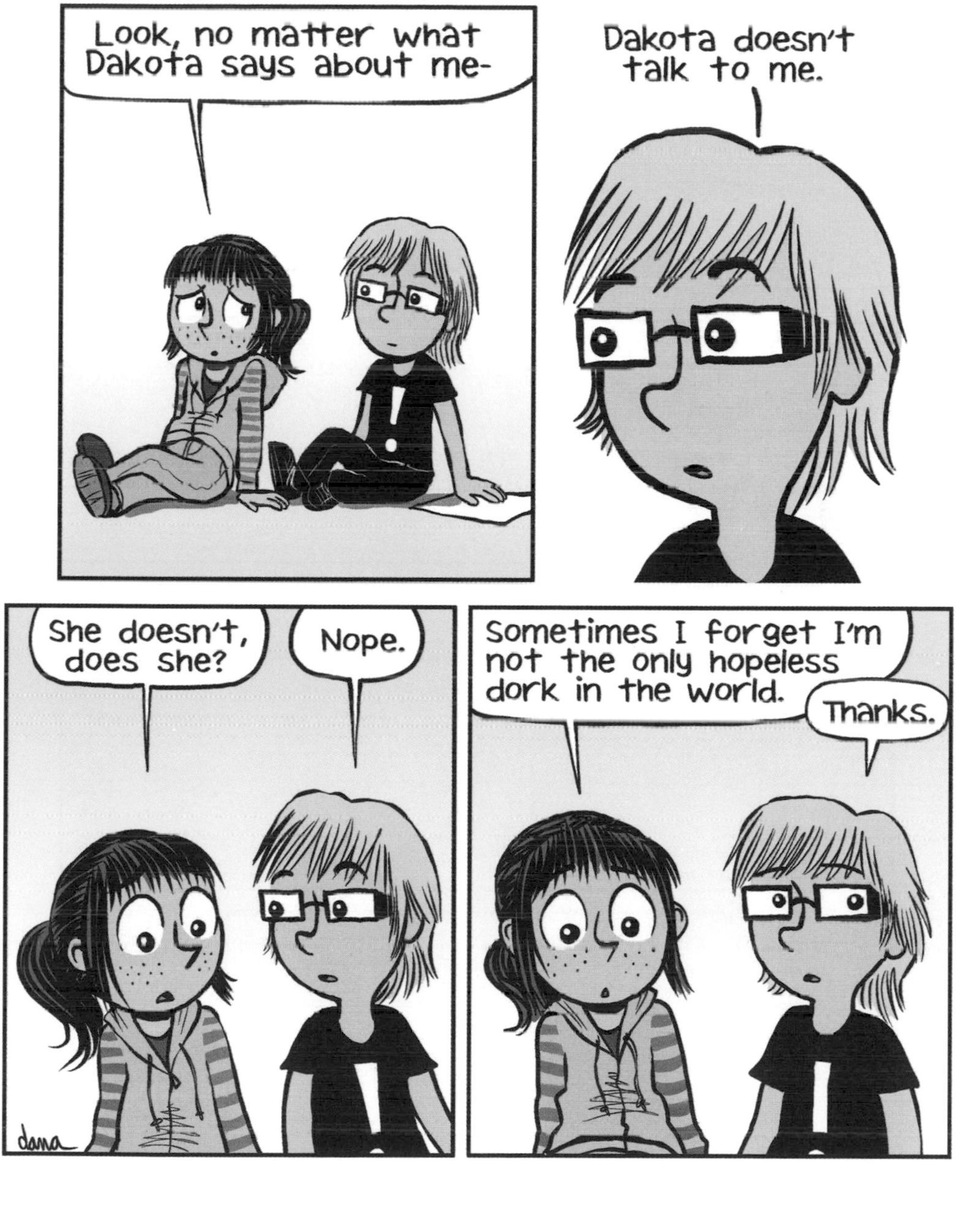
Look, no matter what Dakota says about me-
Dakota doesn't talk to me.
She doesn't, does she?
Nope.
Sometimes I forget I'm not the only hopeless dork in the world.
Thanks.
dana

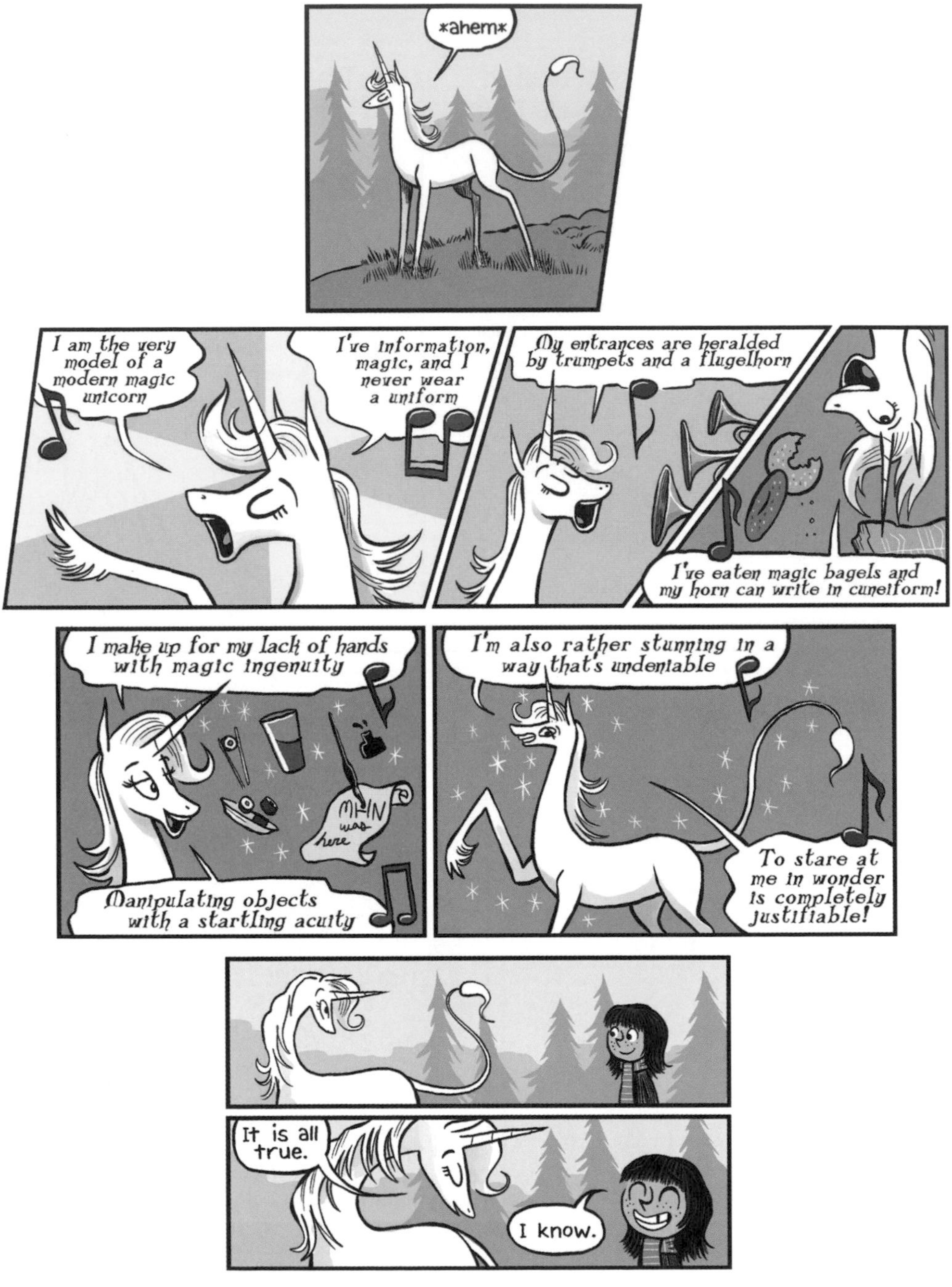

ahem
I am the very model of a modern magic unicorn
I've information, magic, and I never wear a uniform
My entrances are heralded by trumpets and a flugelhorn
I've eaten magic bagels and my horn can write in cuneiform!
I make up for my lack of hands with magic ingenuity
Manipulating objects with a startling acuity
I'm also rather stunning in a way that's undeniable
To stare at me in wonder is completely justifiable!
It is all true.
I know.

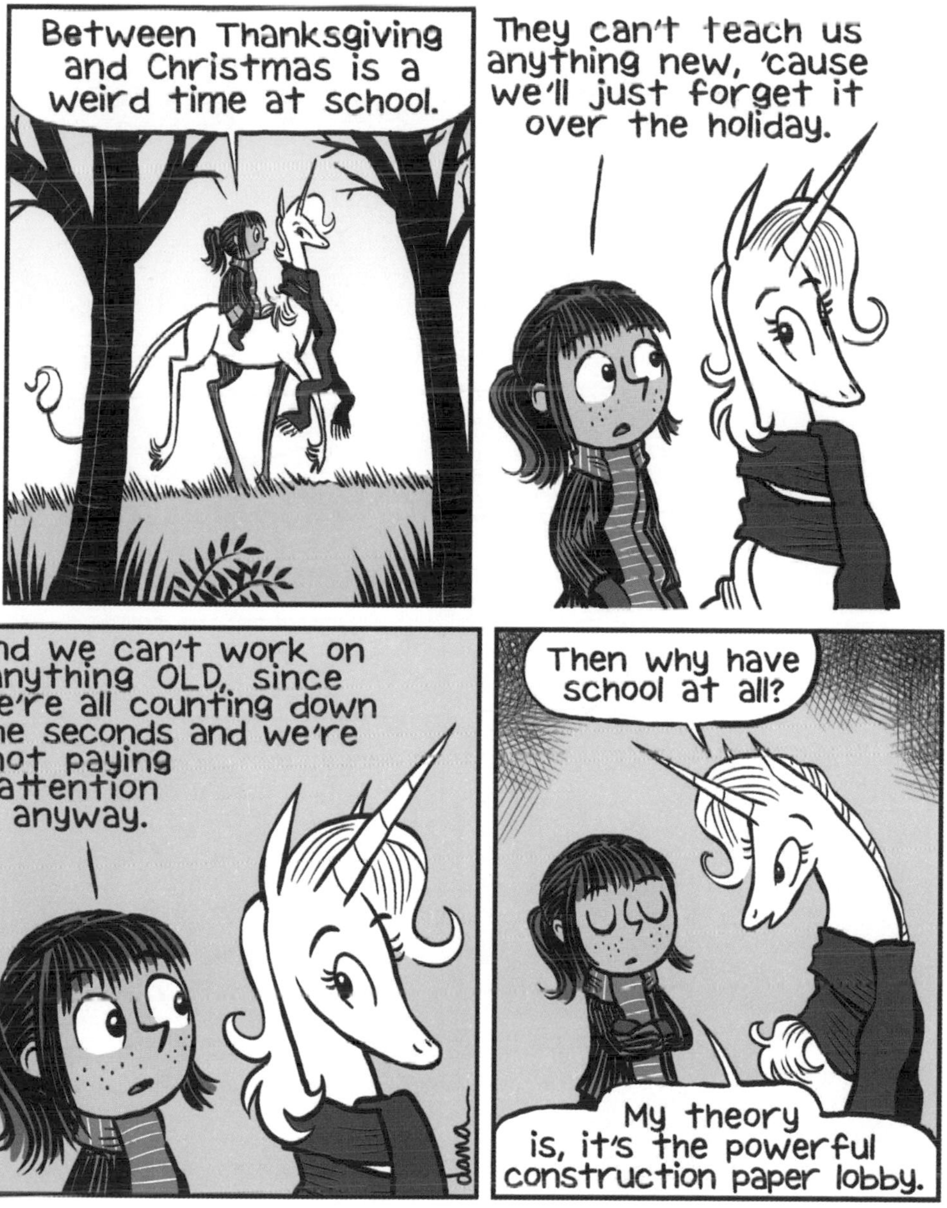
Between Thanksgiving and Christmas is a weird time at school.
They can't teach us anything new, 'cause we'll just forget it over the holiday.
And we can't work on anything OLD, since we're all counting down the seconds and we're not paying attention anyway.
dana
Then why have school at all?
My theory is, it's the powerful construction paper lobby.

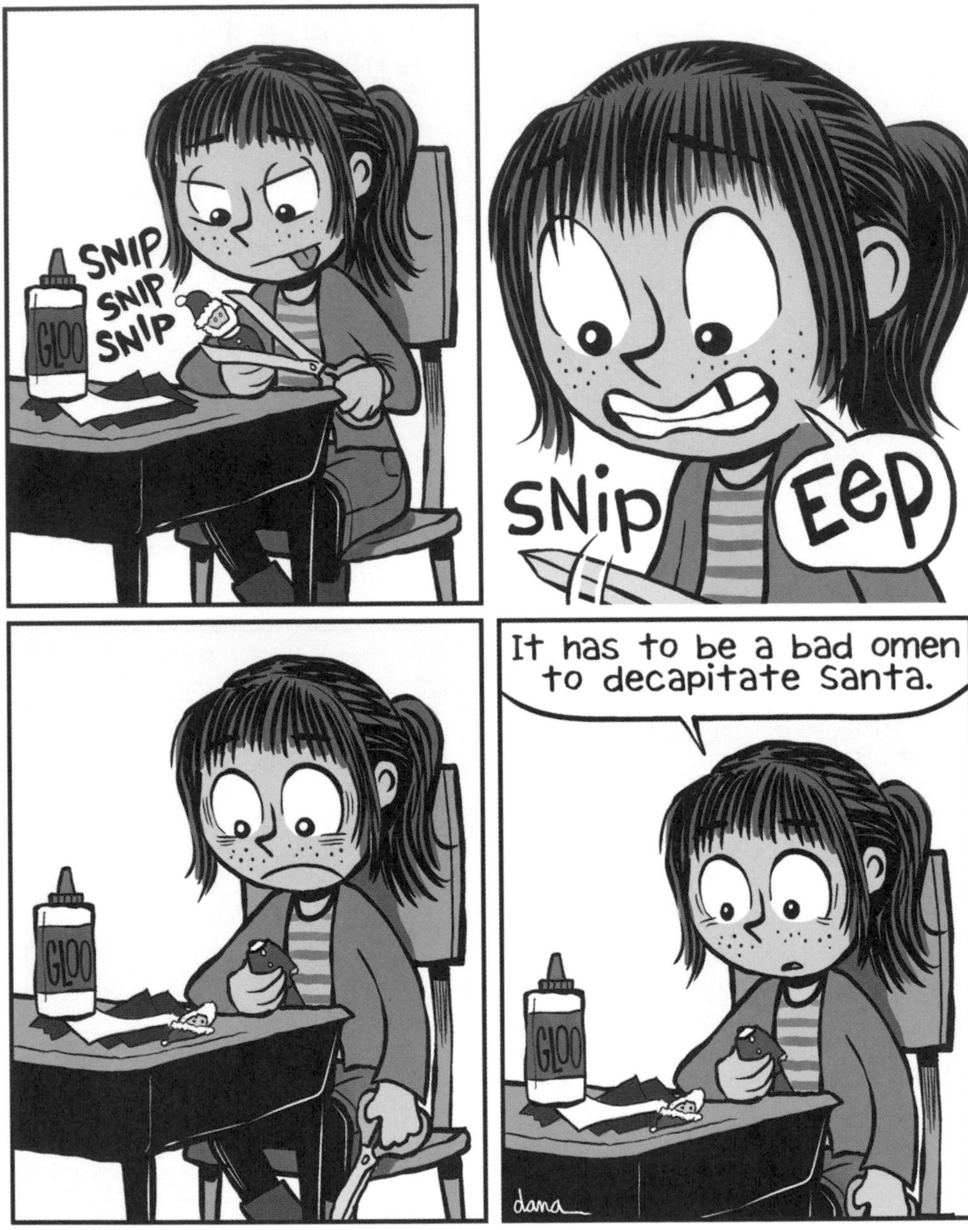
SNIP
SNIP
SNIP
GLOO
SNip
EEP
GLOO
It has to be a bad omen to decapitate Santa.
GLOO
dana

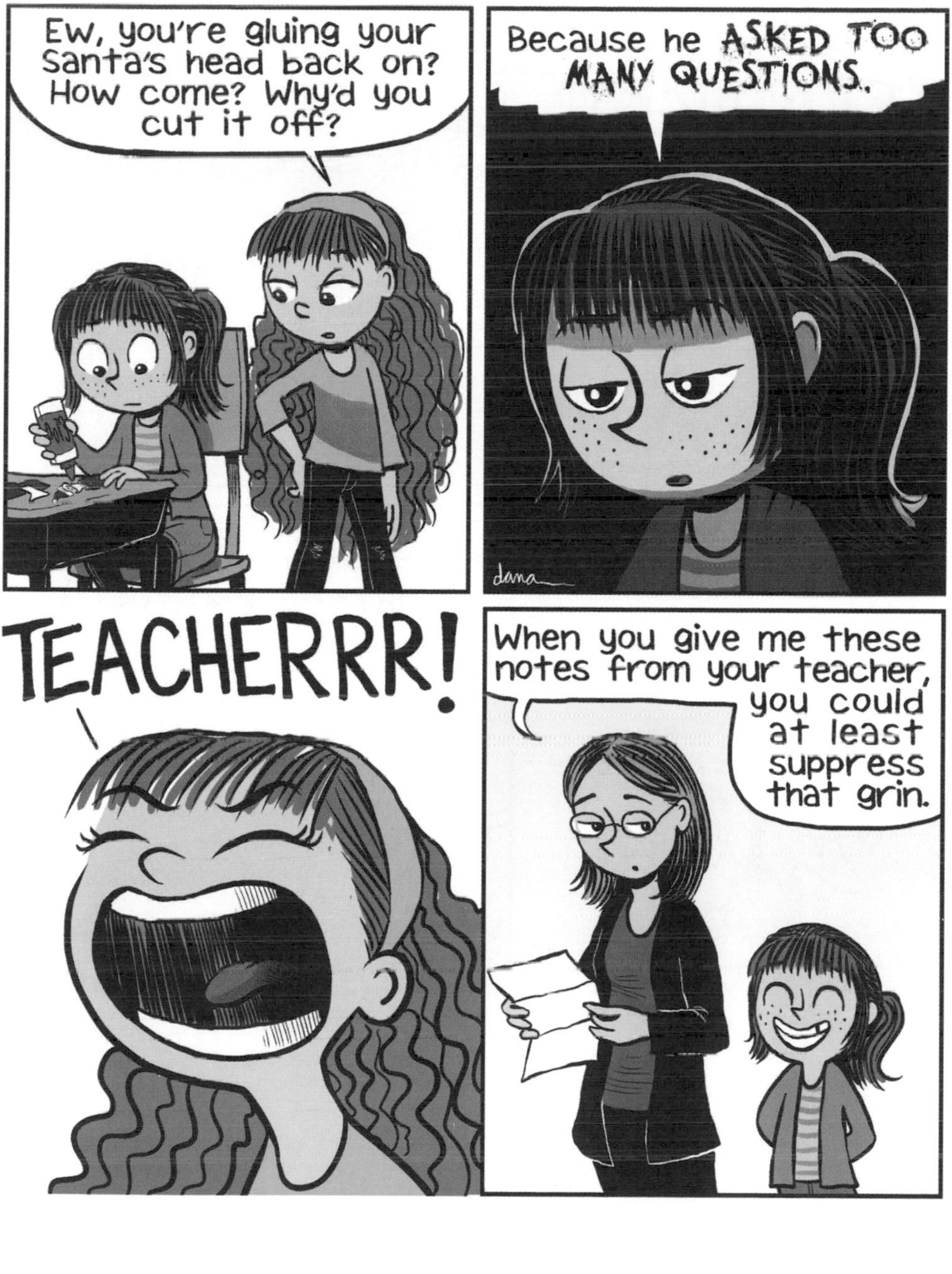
Ew, you're gluing your Santa's head back on? How come? Why'd you cut it off?
Because he ASKED TOO MANY QUESTIONS.
dana
TEACHERRR!
When you give me these notes from your teacher, you could at least suppress that grin.

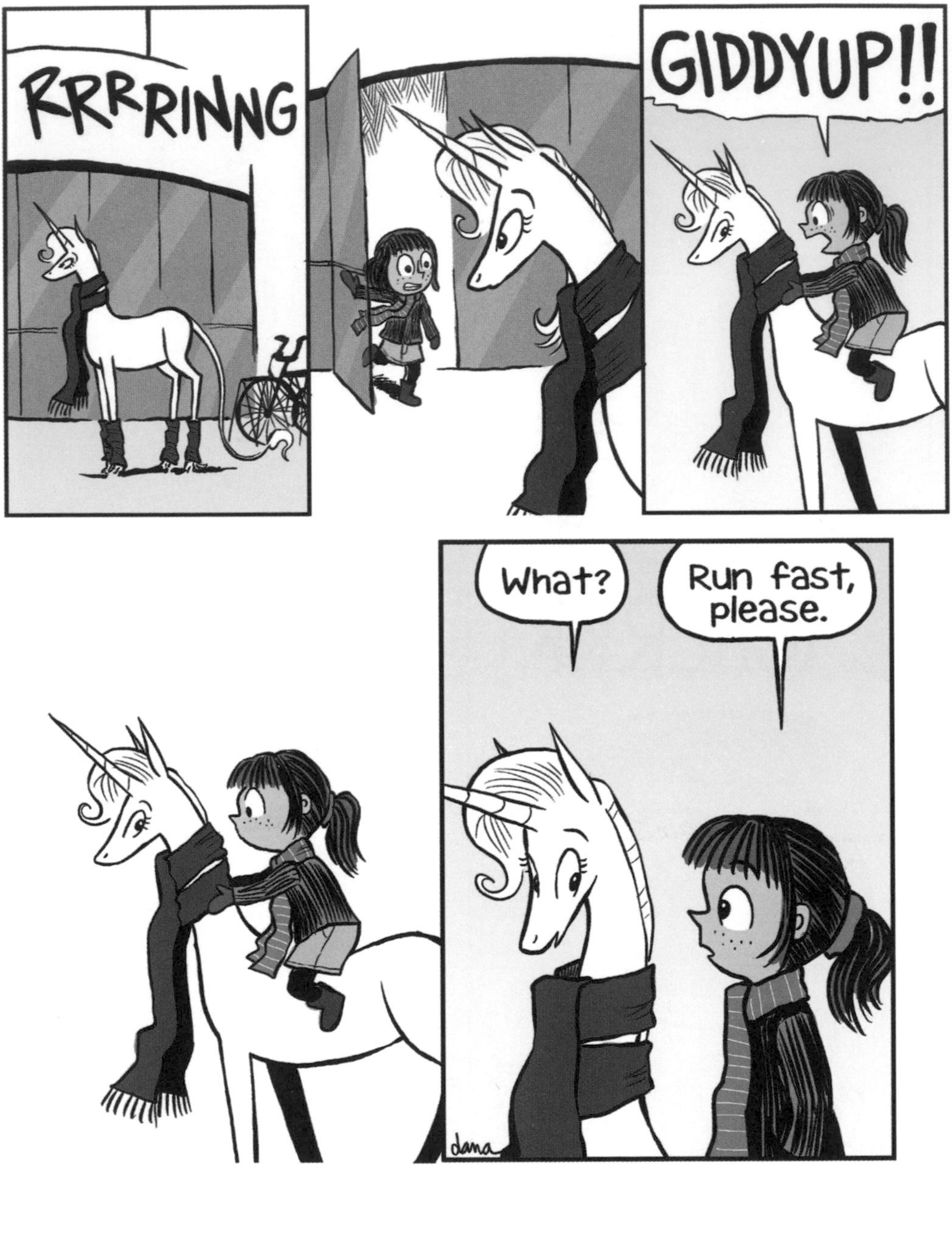
RRRRINNG
GIDDYUP!!
What?
Run fast, please.
dana

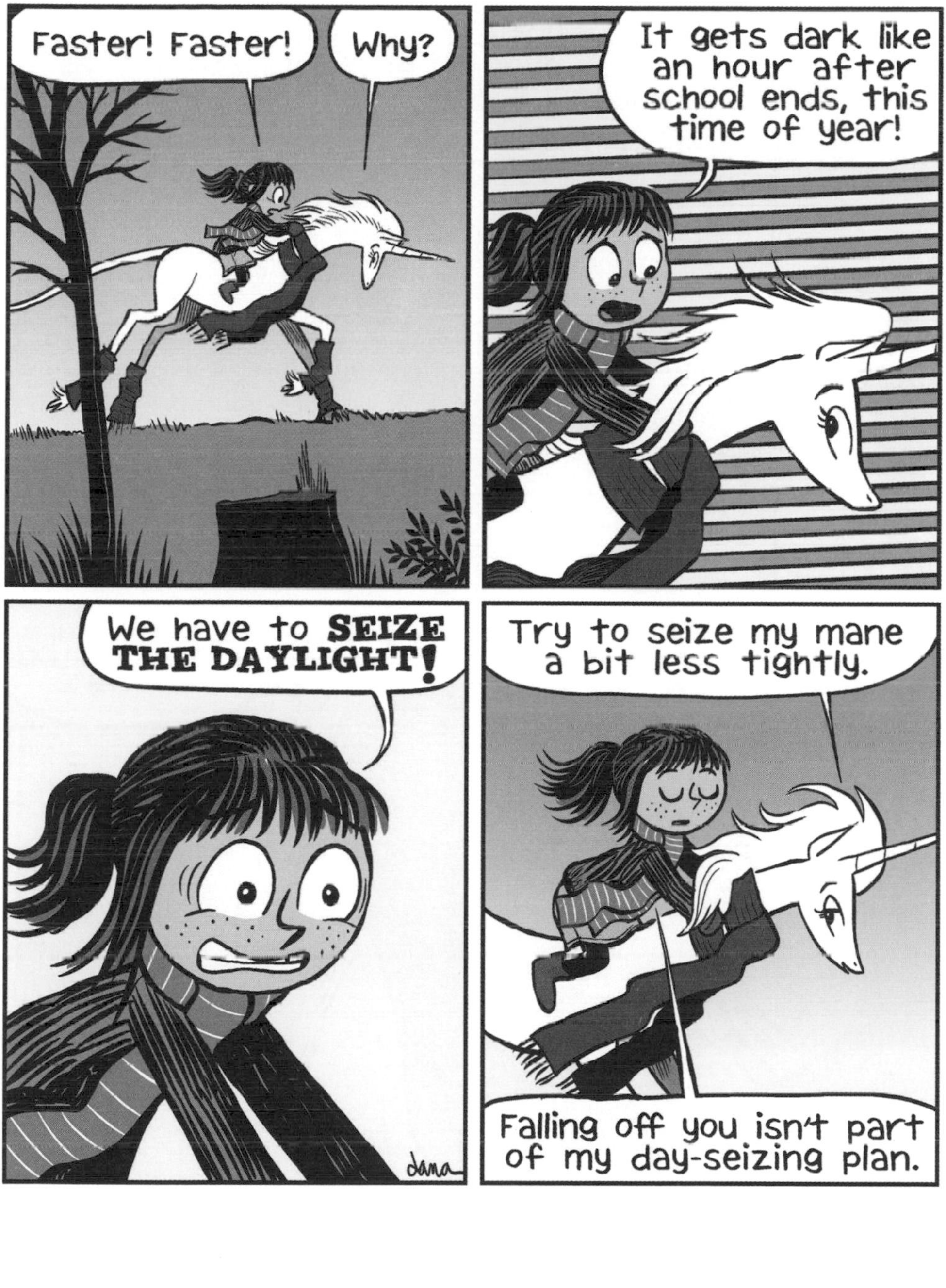
Faster! Faster!
Why?
It gets dark like an hour after school ends, this time of year!
We have to **SEIZE THE DAYLIGHT!**
Try to seize my mane a bit less tightly.
Falling off you isn't part of my day-seizing plan.
dana

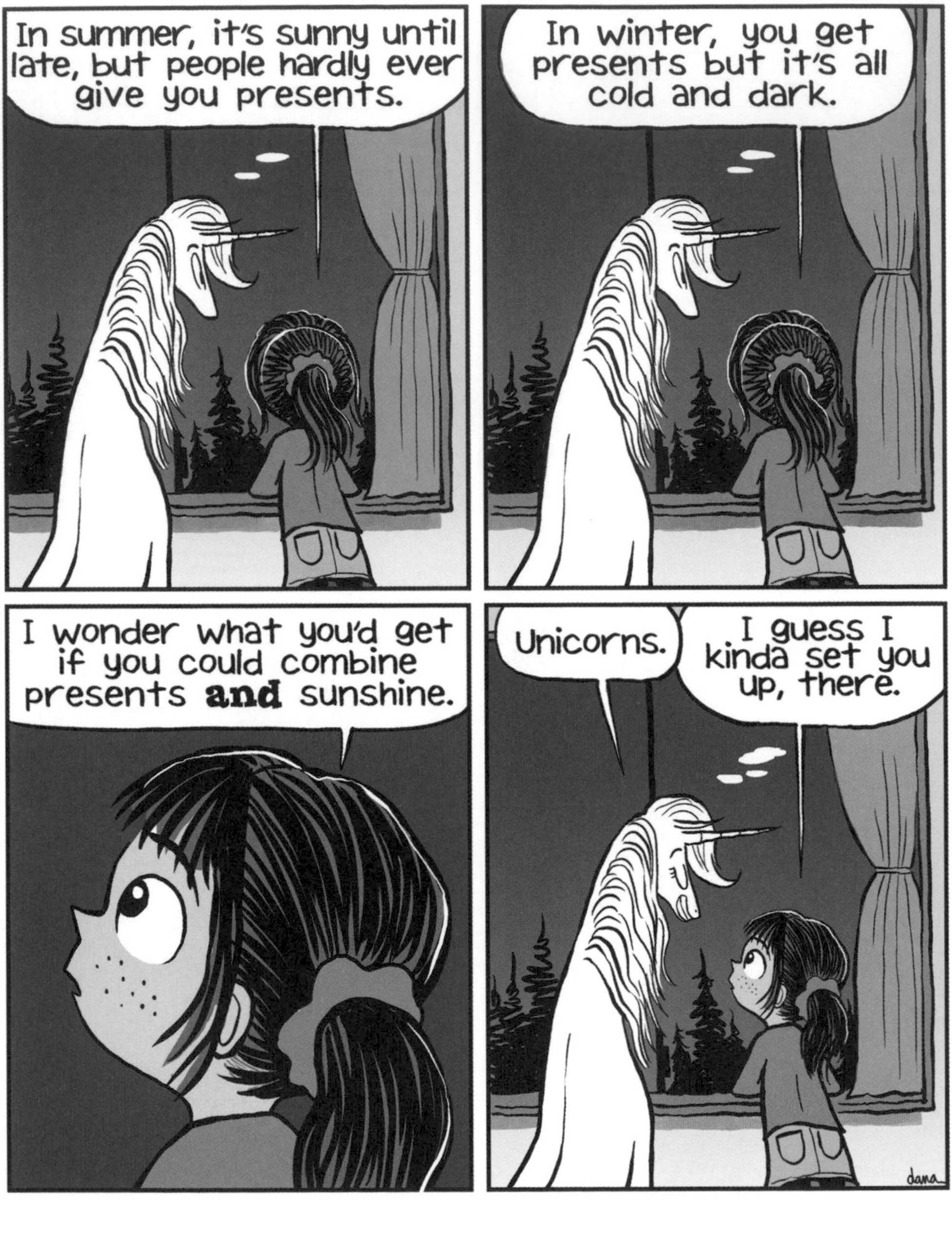
In summer, it's sunny until late, but people hardly ever give you presents.
In winter, you get presents but it's all cold and dark.
I wonder what you'd get if you could combine presents **and** sunshine.
Unicorns.
I guess I kinda set you up, there.
dana

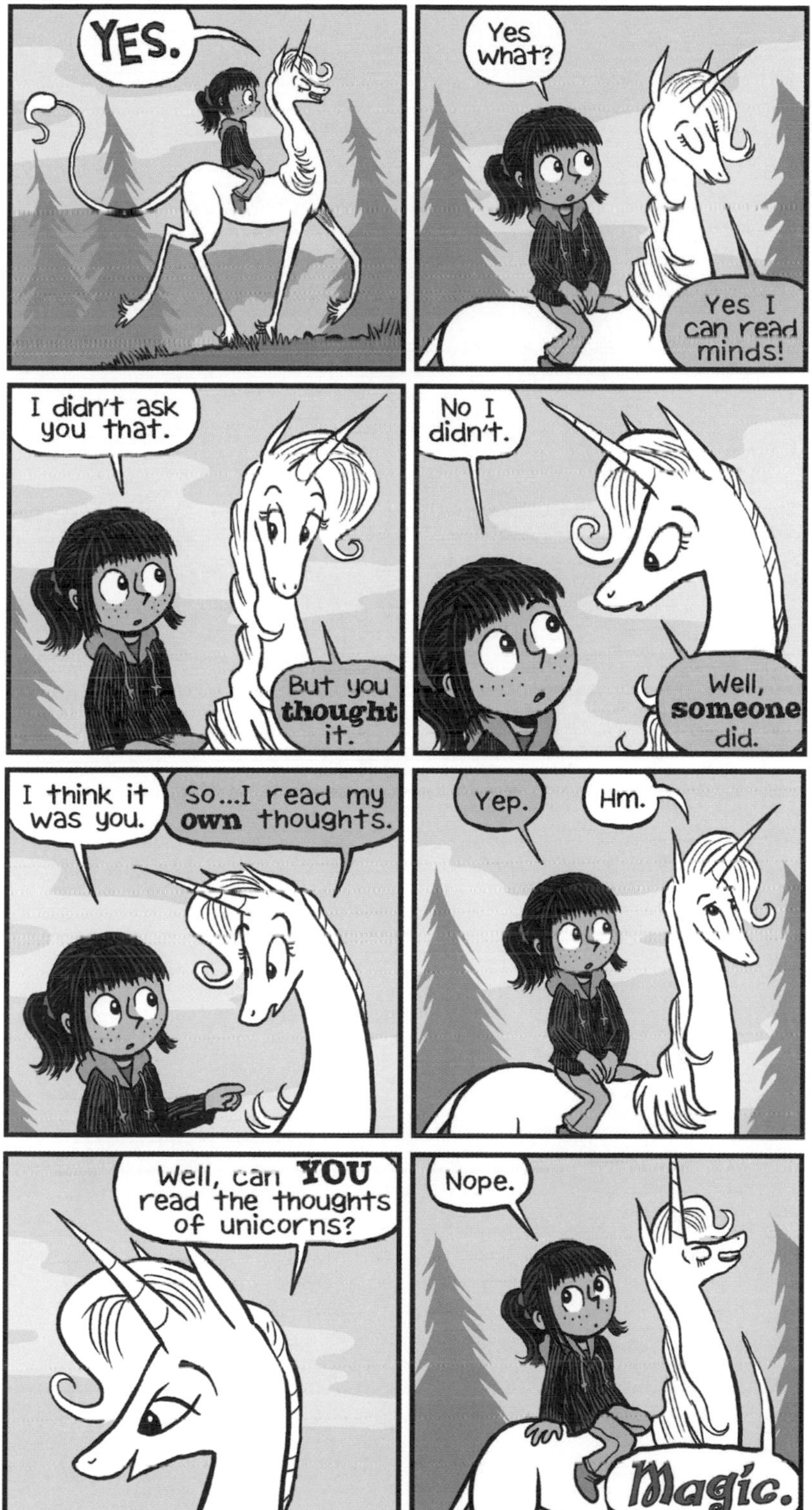
YES.
Yes what?
Yes I can read minds!
I didn't ask you that.
But you **thought** it.
No I didn't.
Well, **someone** did.
I think it was you.
So...I read my **own** thoughts.
Yep.
Hm.
Well, can **YOU** read the thoughts of unicorns?
Nope.
Magic.

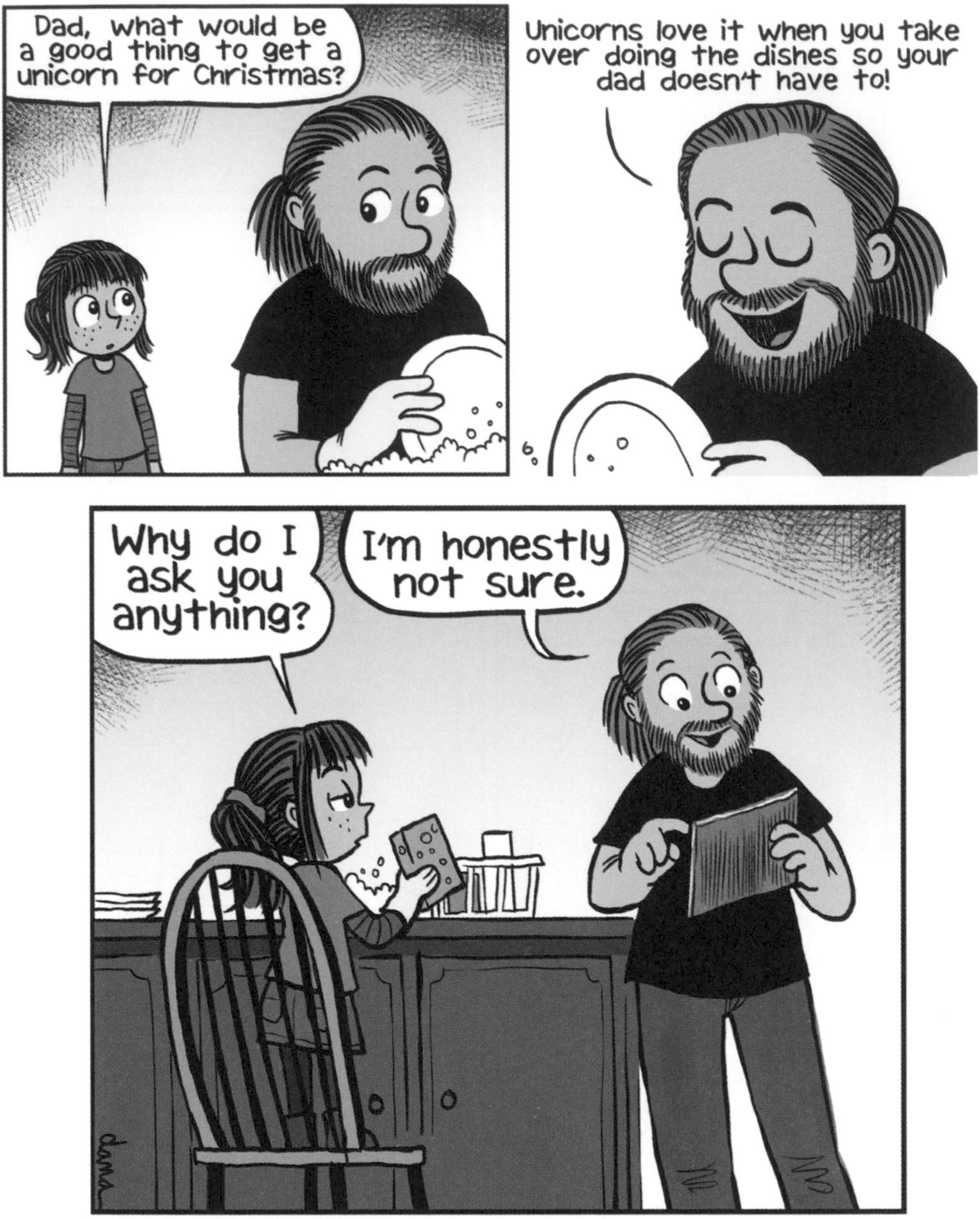
Dad, what would be a good thing to get a unicorn for Christmas?
Unicorns love it when you take over doing the dishes so your dad doesn't have to!
Why do I ask you anything?
I'm honestly not sure.
dana

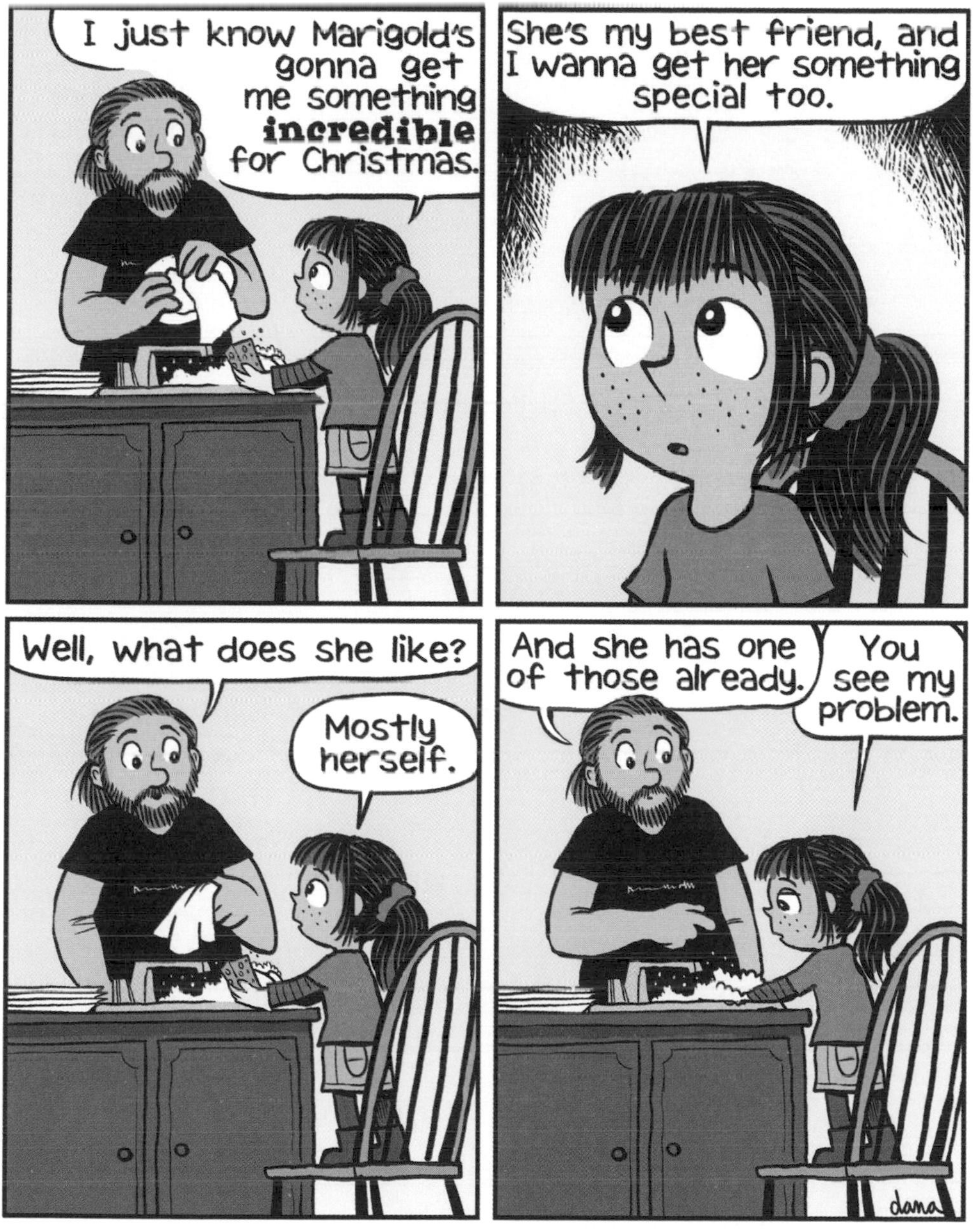
I just know Marigold's gonna get me something **incredible** for Christmas.
She's my best friend, and I wanna get her something special too.
Well, what does she like?
Mostly herself.
And she has one of those already.
You see my problem.
dana

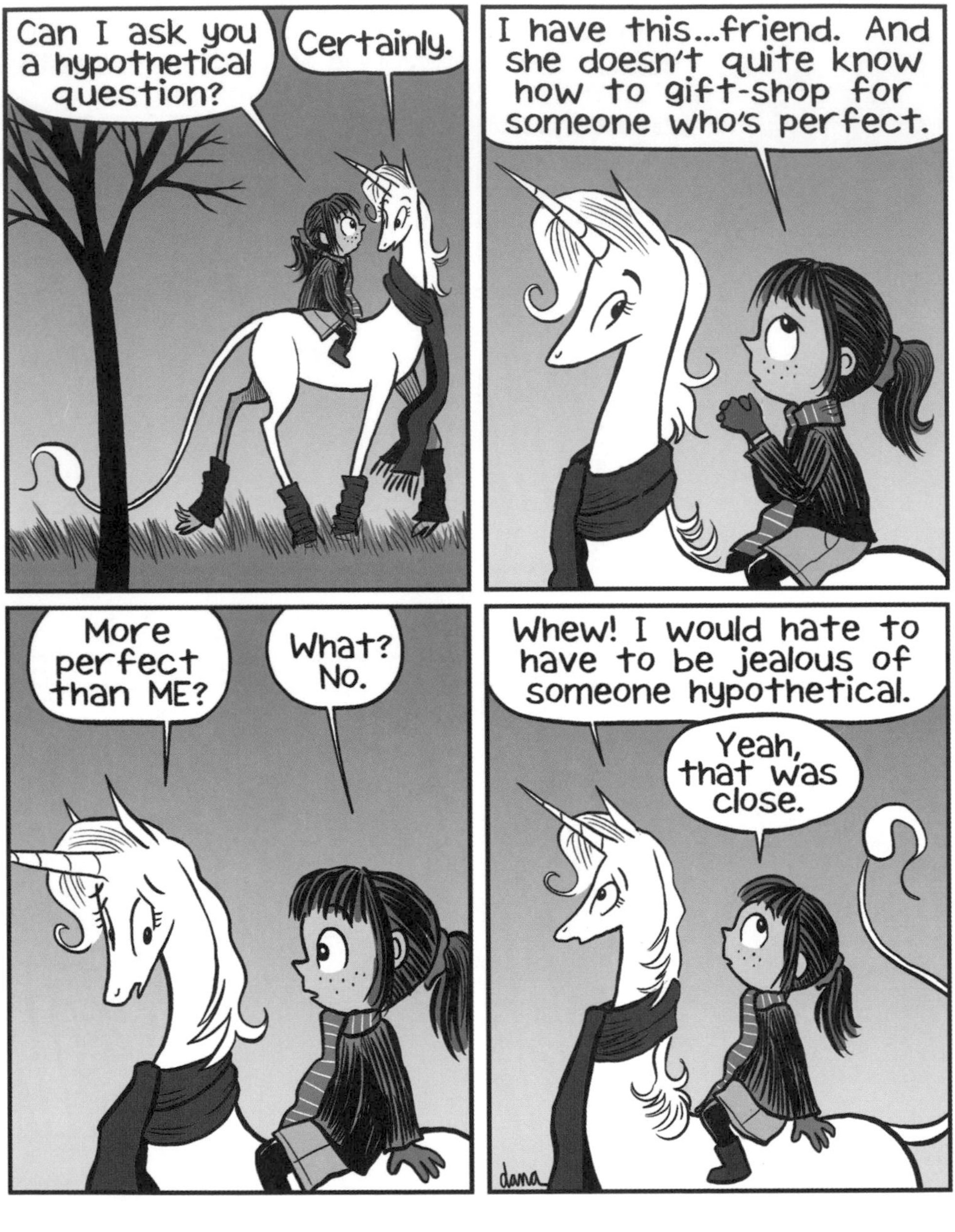
Can I ask you a hypothetical question?
Certainly.
I have this...friend. And she doesn't quite know how to gift-shop for someone who's perfect.
More perfect than ME?
What? No.
Whew! I would hate to have to be jealous of someone hypothetical.
Yeah, that was close.
dana

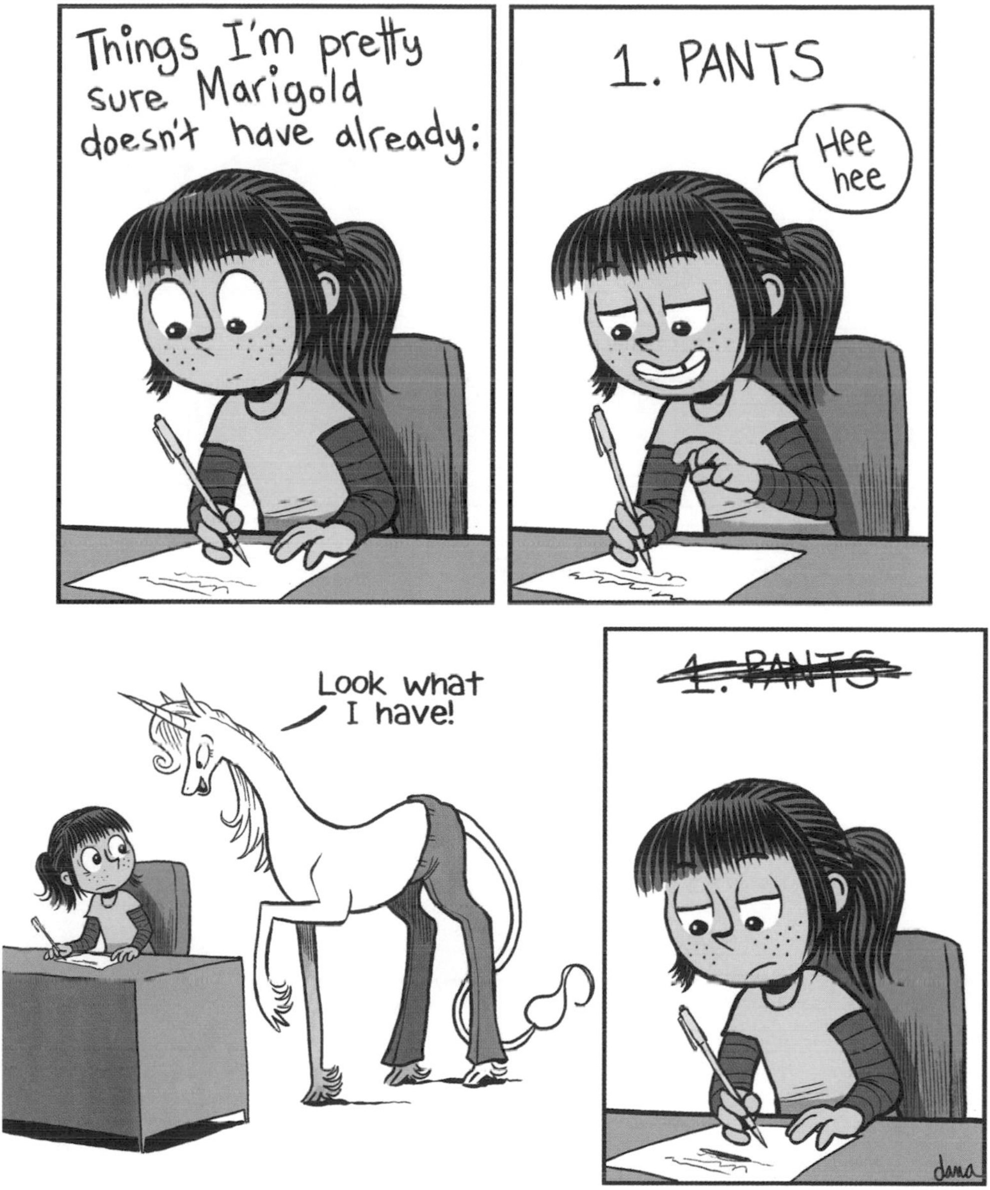
Things I'm pretty sure Marigold doesn't have already:
1. PANTS
Hee hee
Look what I have!
1. PANTS
dana

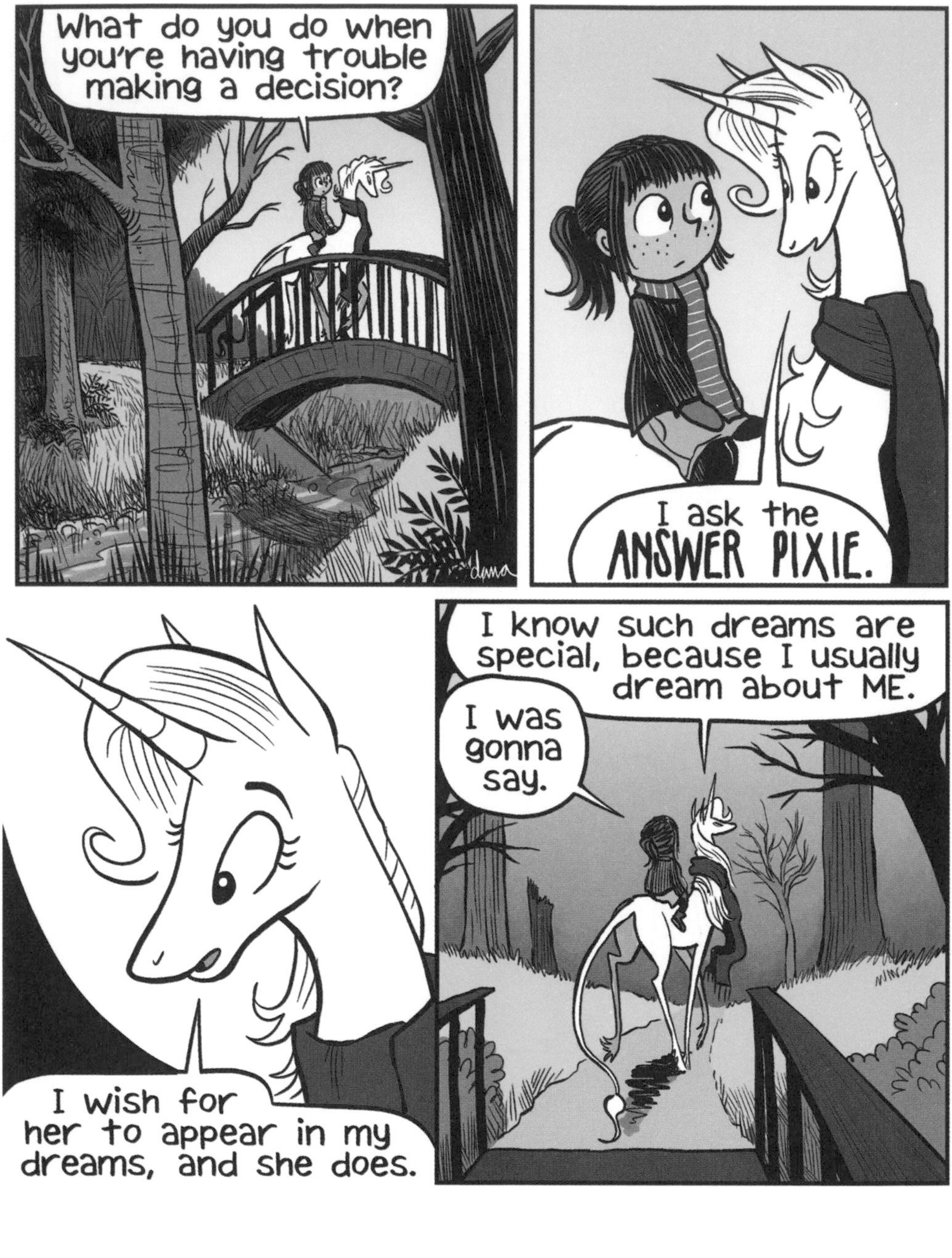
What do you do when you're having trouble making a decision?
I ask the ANSWER PIXIE.
I wish for her to appear in my dreams, and she does.
I know such dreams are special, because I usually dream about ME.
I was gonna say.

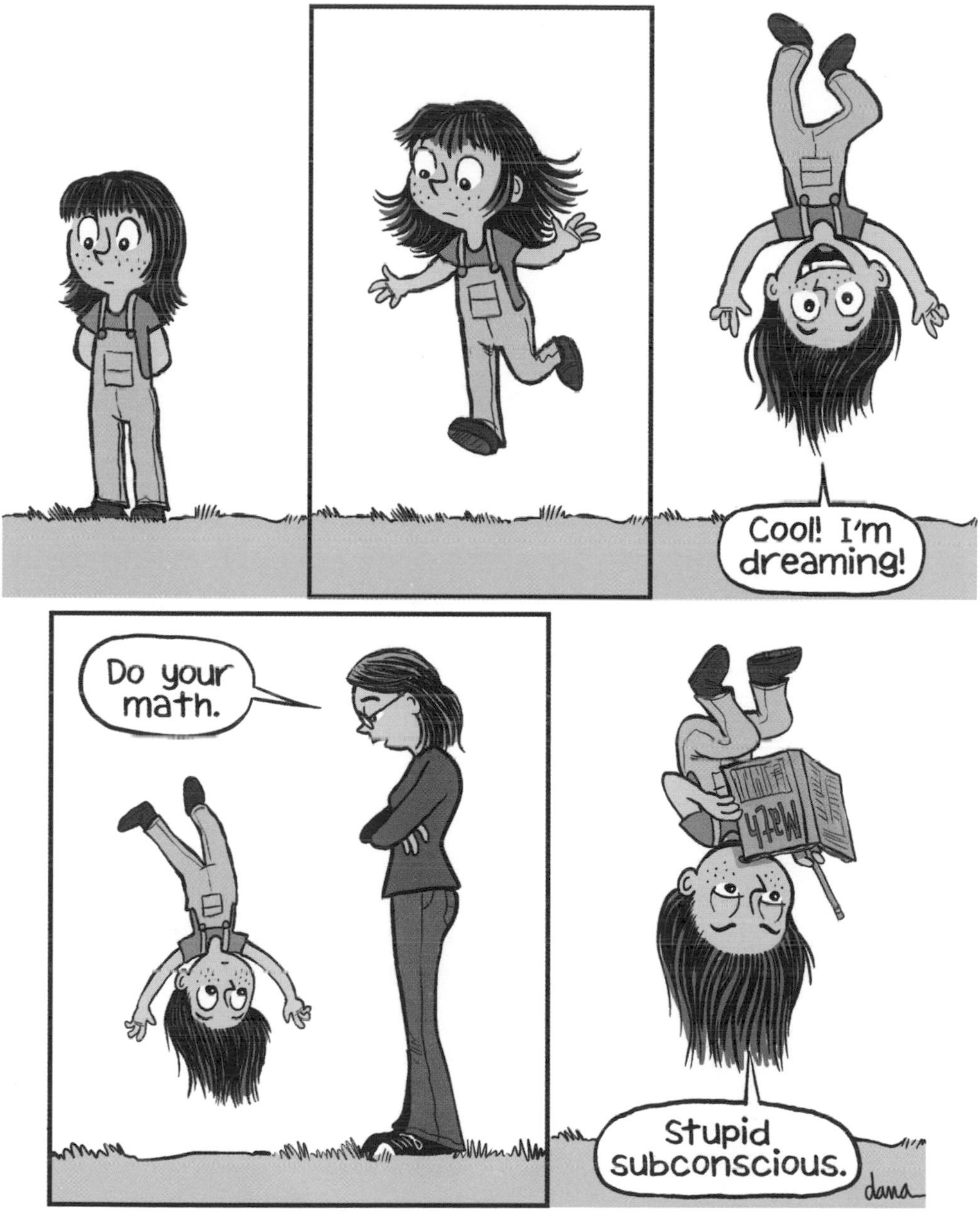

Cool! I'm dreaming!
Do your math.
Math
Stupid subconscious.
dana

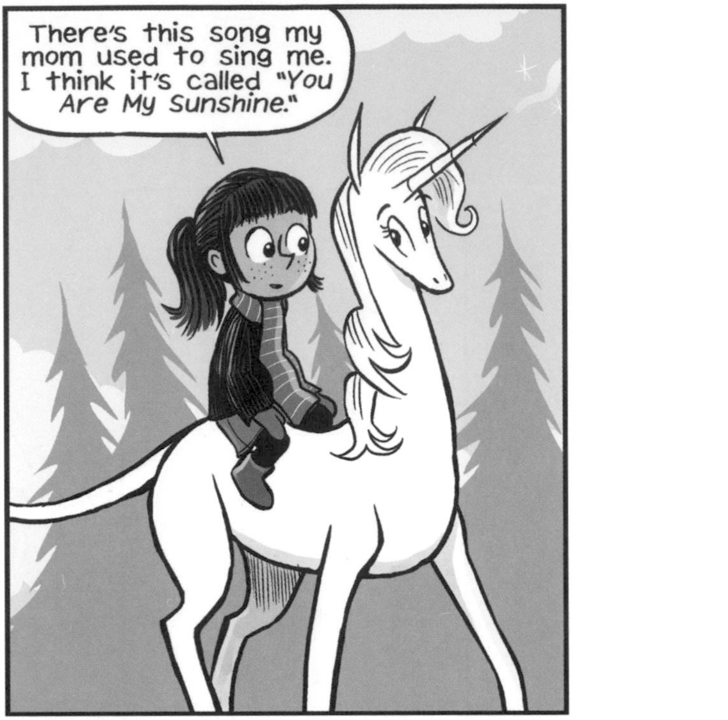
There's this song my mom used to sing me. I think it's called "You Are My Sunshine."

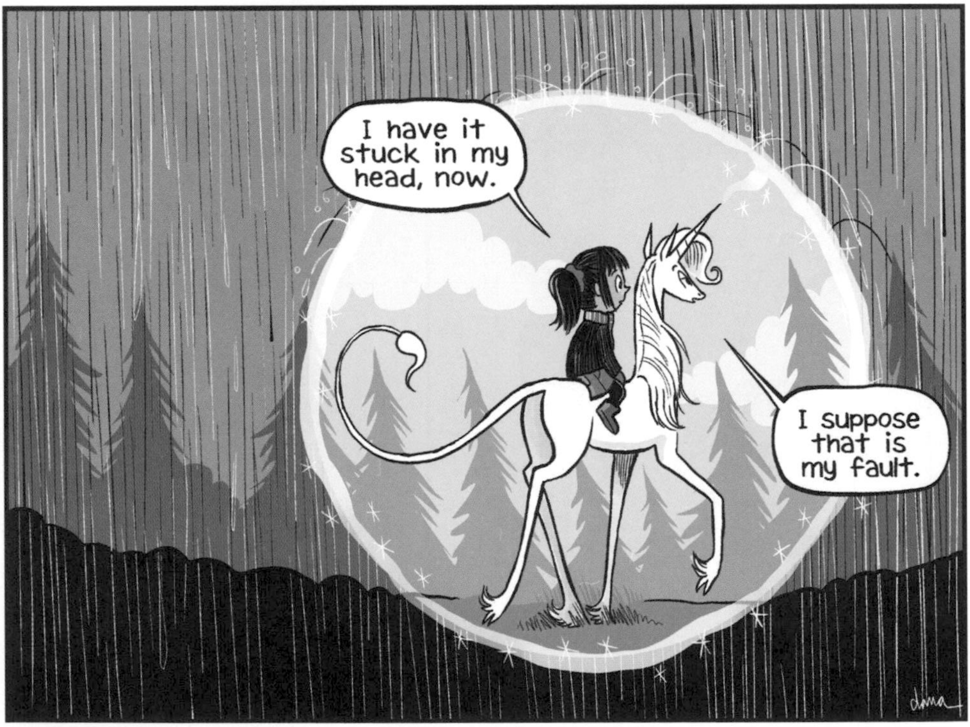
I have it stuck in my head, now.
I suppose that is my fault.

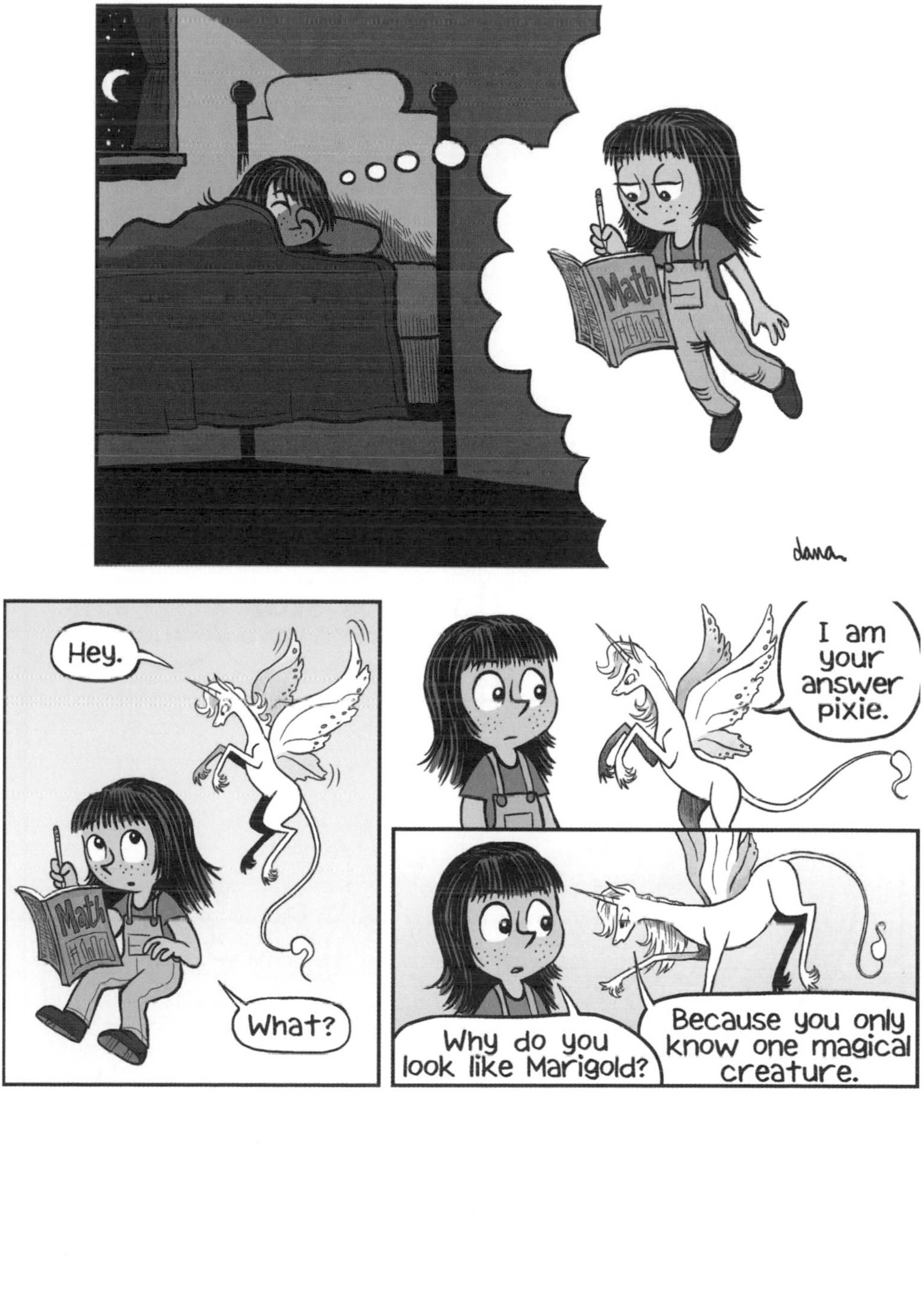
dana
Hey.
What?
I am your answer pixie.
Why do you look like Marigold?
Because you only know one magical creature.

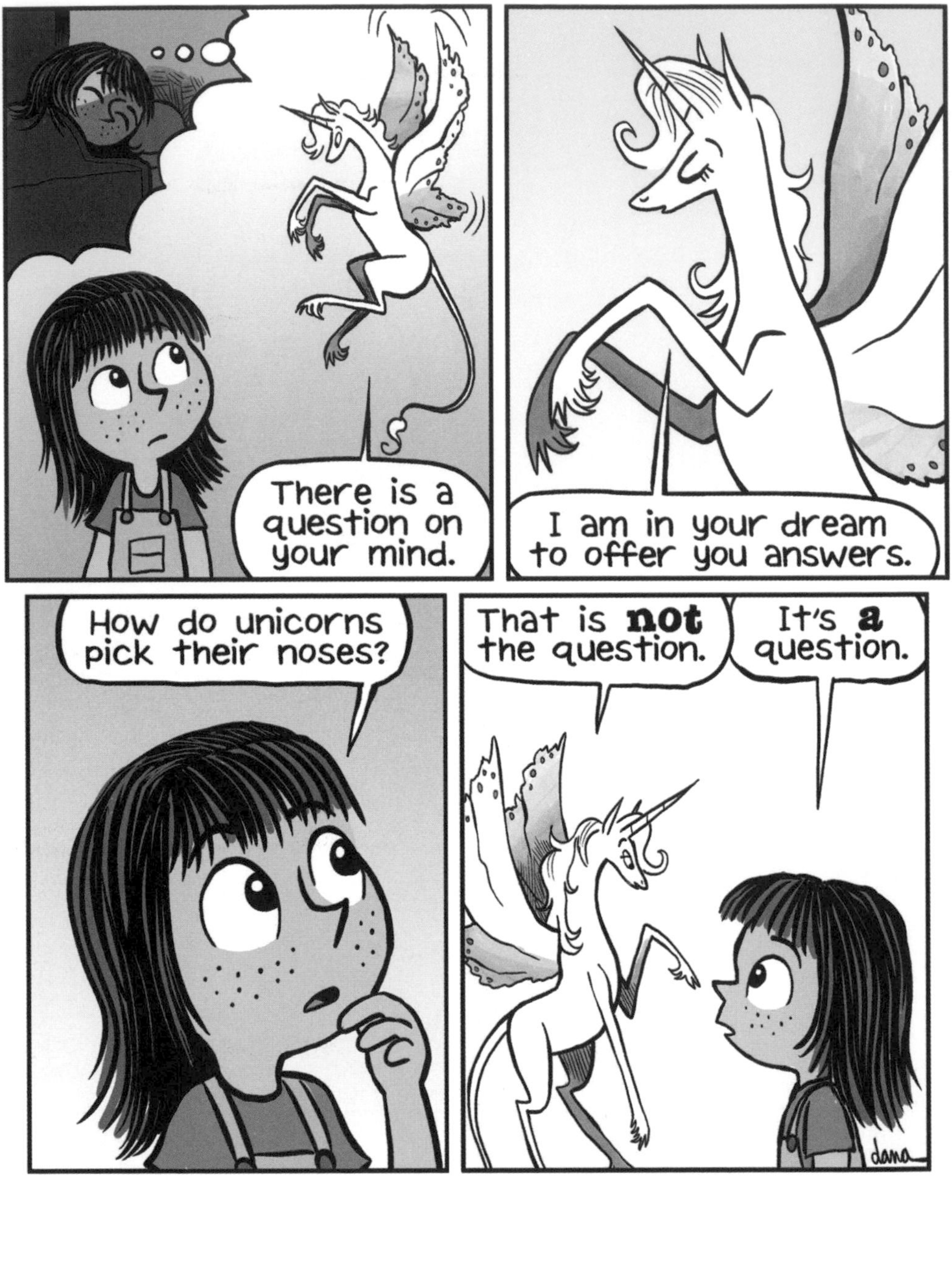
There is a question on your mind.
I am in your dream to offer you answers.
How do unicorns pick their noses?
That is **not** the question.
It's **a** question.
dana

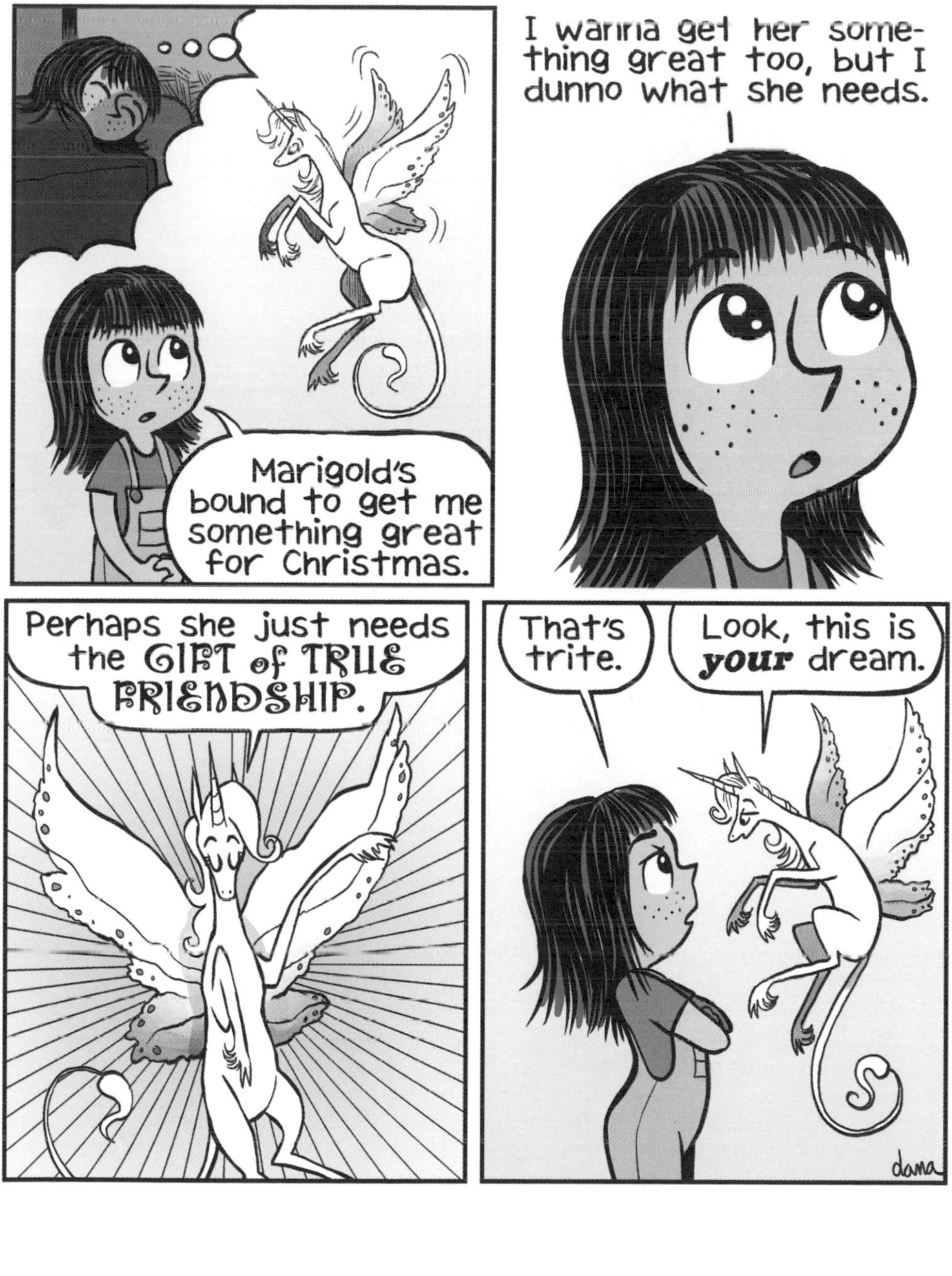
Marigold's bound to get me something great for Christmas.
I wanna get her something great too, but I dunno what she needs.
Perhaps she just needs the GIFT of TRUE FRIENDSHIP.
That's trite.
Look, this is *your* dream.
dana

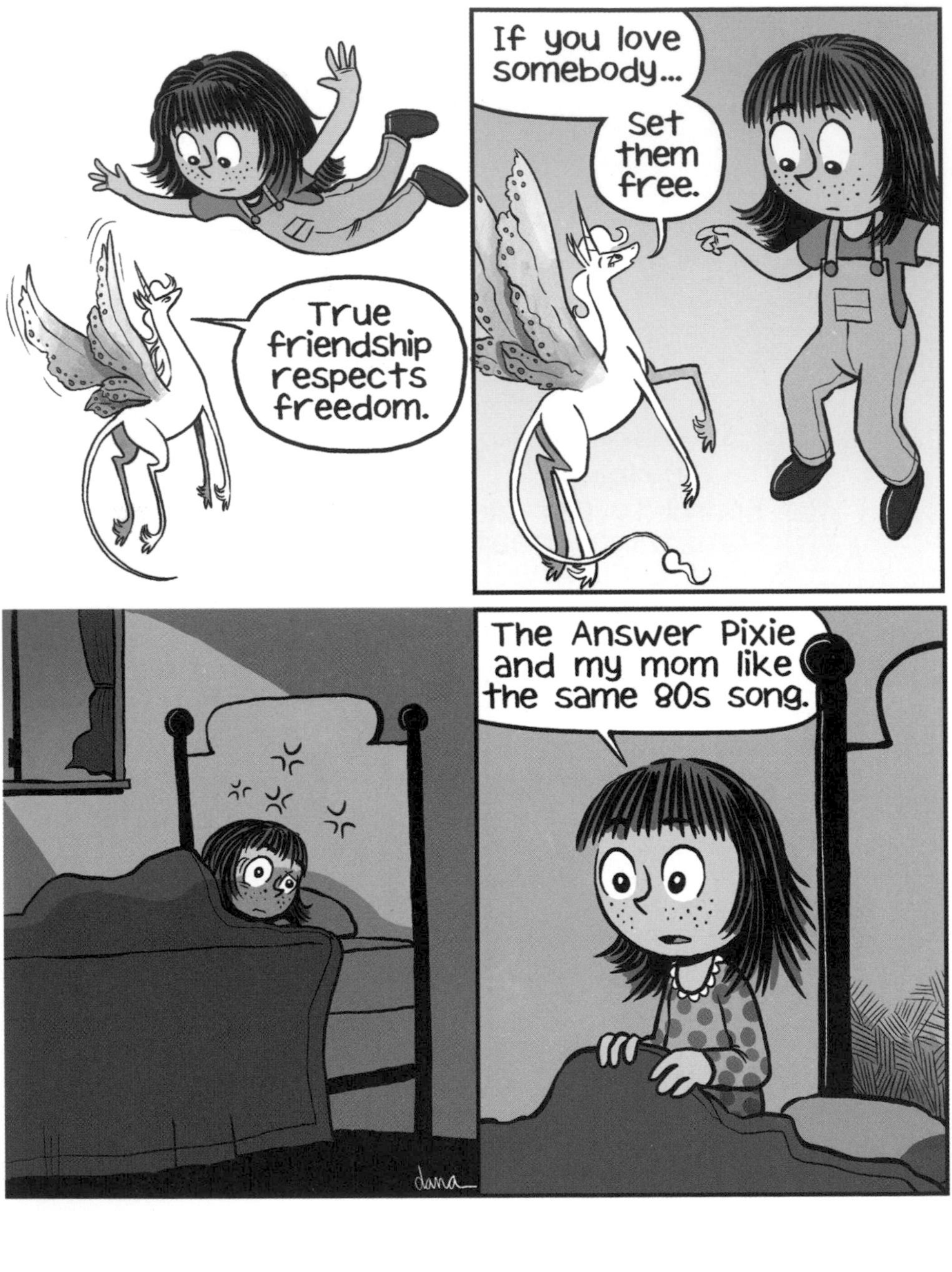
True friendship respects freedom.
If you love somebody...
Set them free.
The Answer Pixie and my mom like the same 80s song.
dana

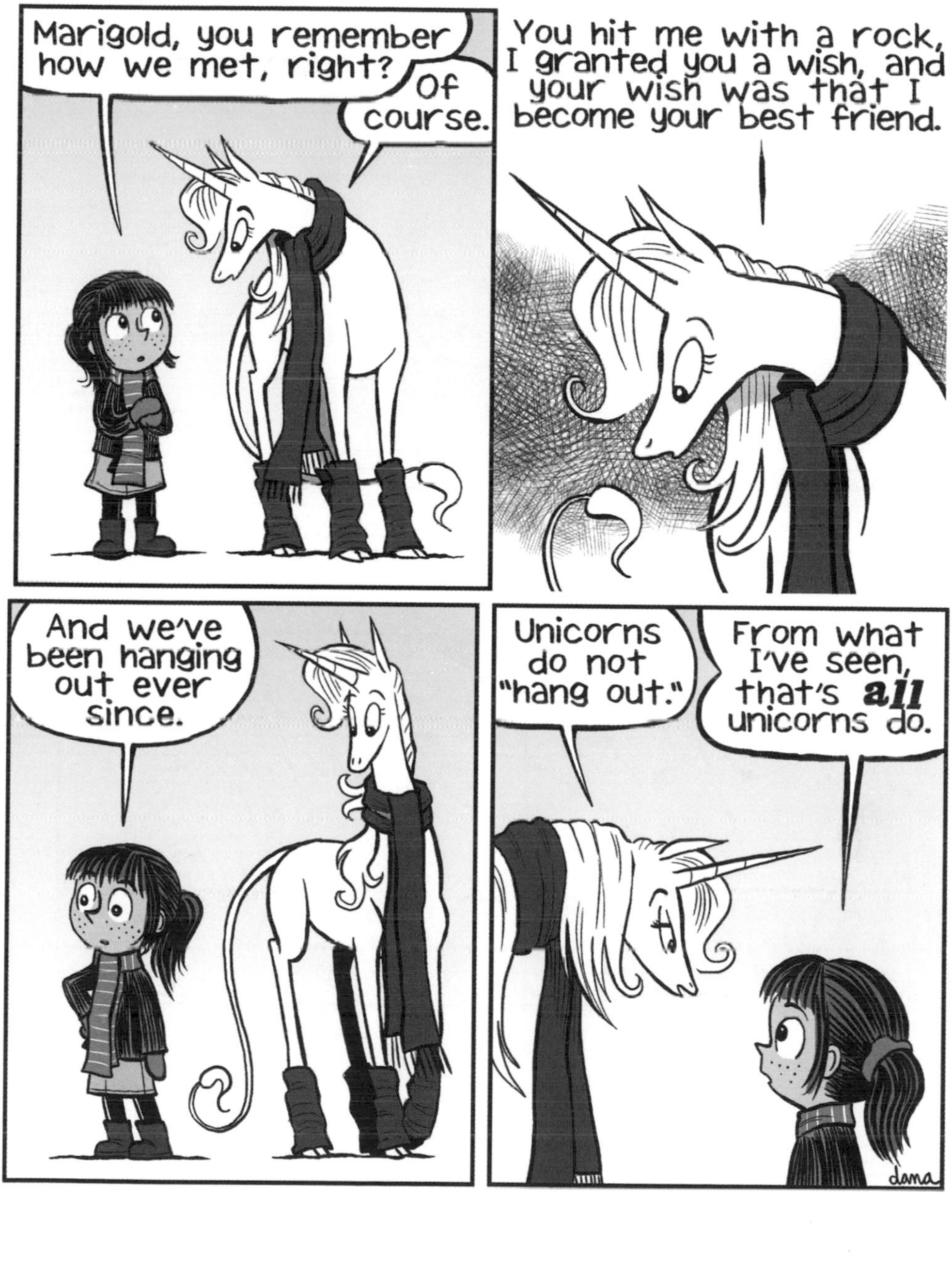
Marigold, you remember how we met, right?
Of course.
You hit me with a rock, I granted you a wish, and your wish was that I become your best friend.
And we've been hanging out ever since.
Unicorns do not "hang out."
From what I've seen, that's **all** unicorns do.
dana

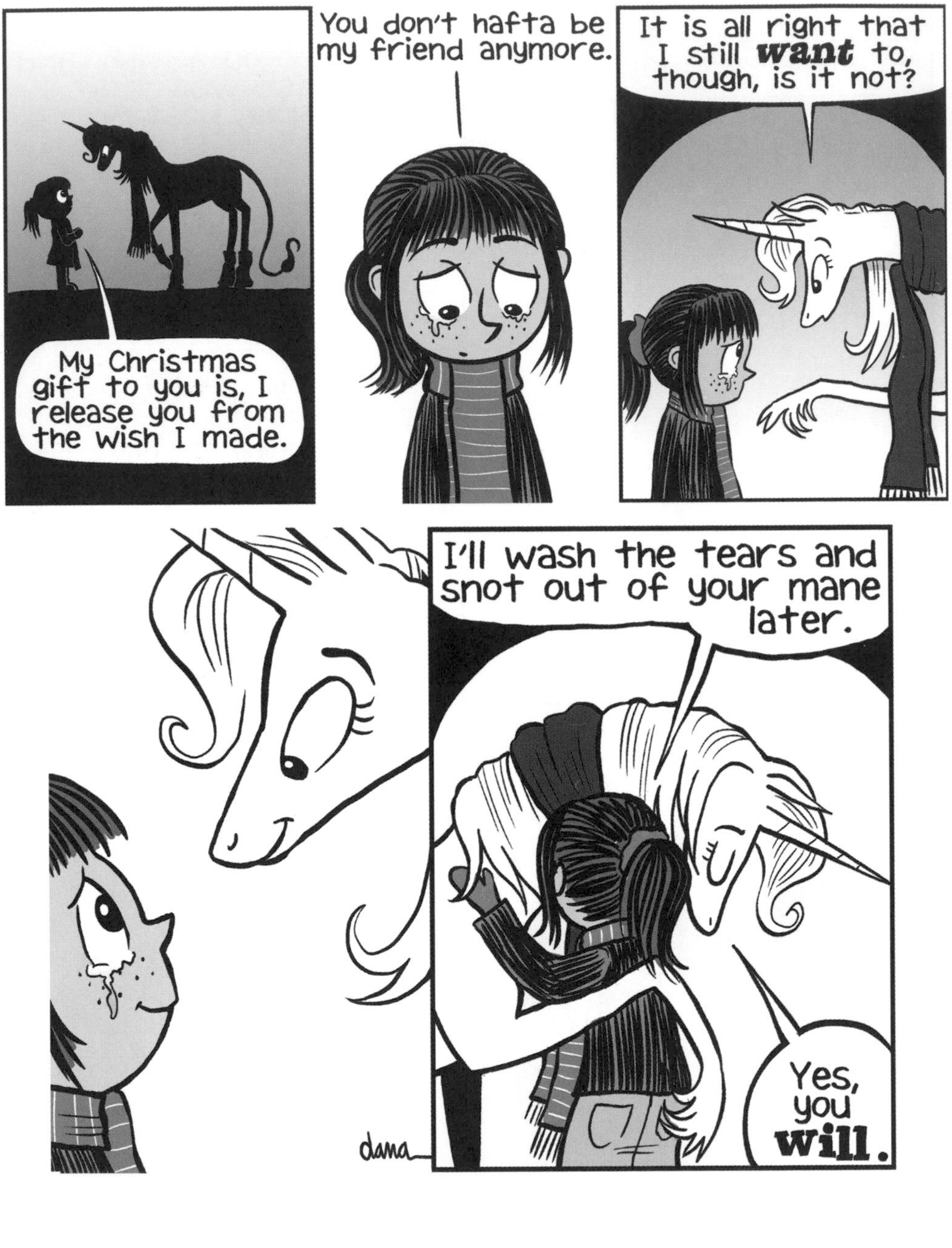
My Christmas gift to you is, I release you from the wish I made.
You don't hafta be my friend anymore.
It is all right that I still **want** to, though, is it not?
I'll wash the tears and snot out of your mane later.
Yes, you **will**.
dana

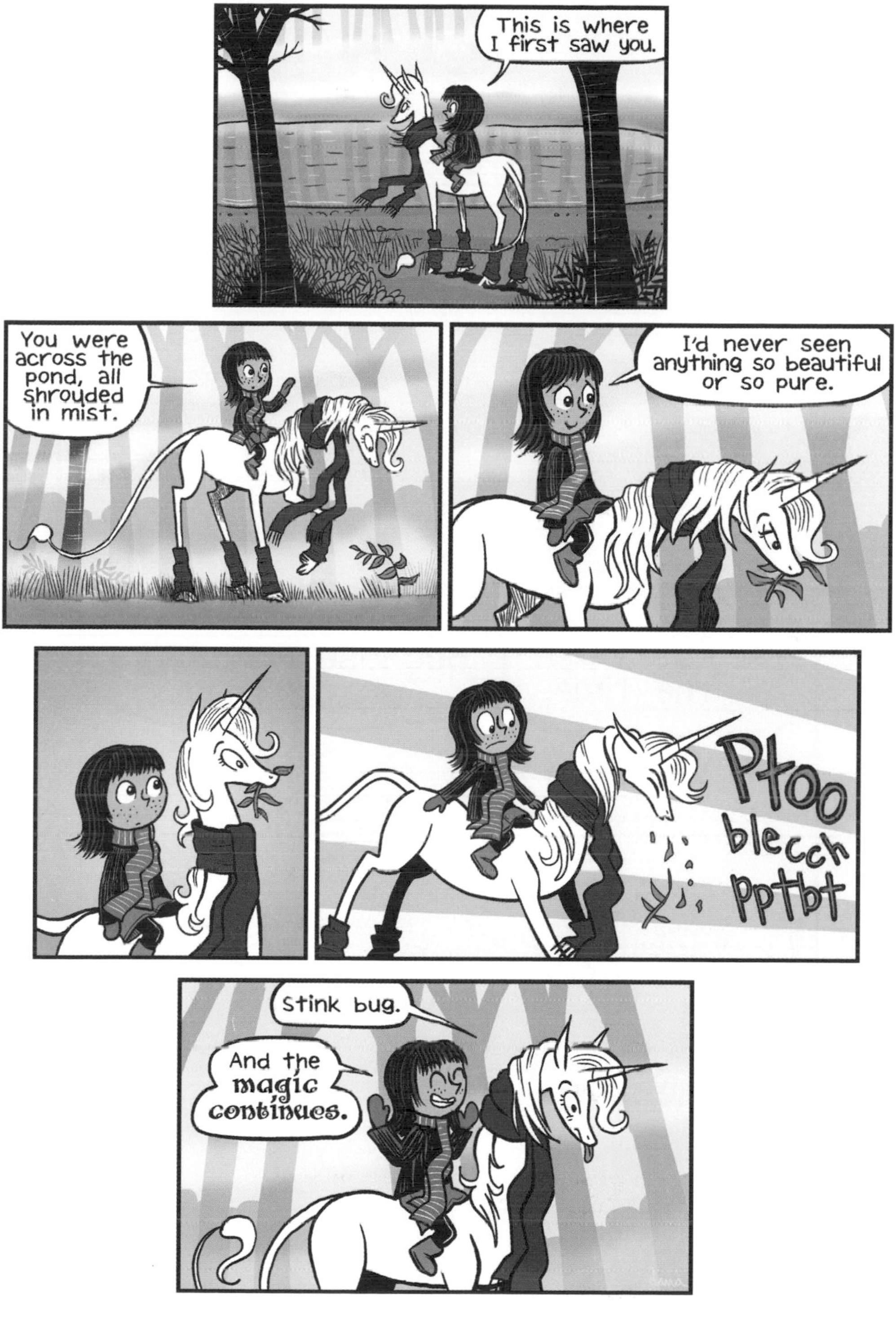
This is where I first saw you.
You were across the pond, all shrouded in mist.
I'd never seen anything so beautiful or so pure.
Ptoo
blecch
pptbt
Stink bug.
And the magic continues.

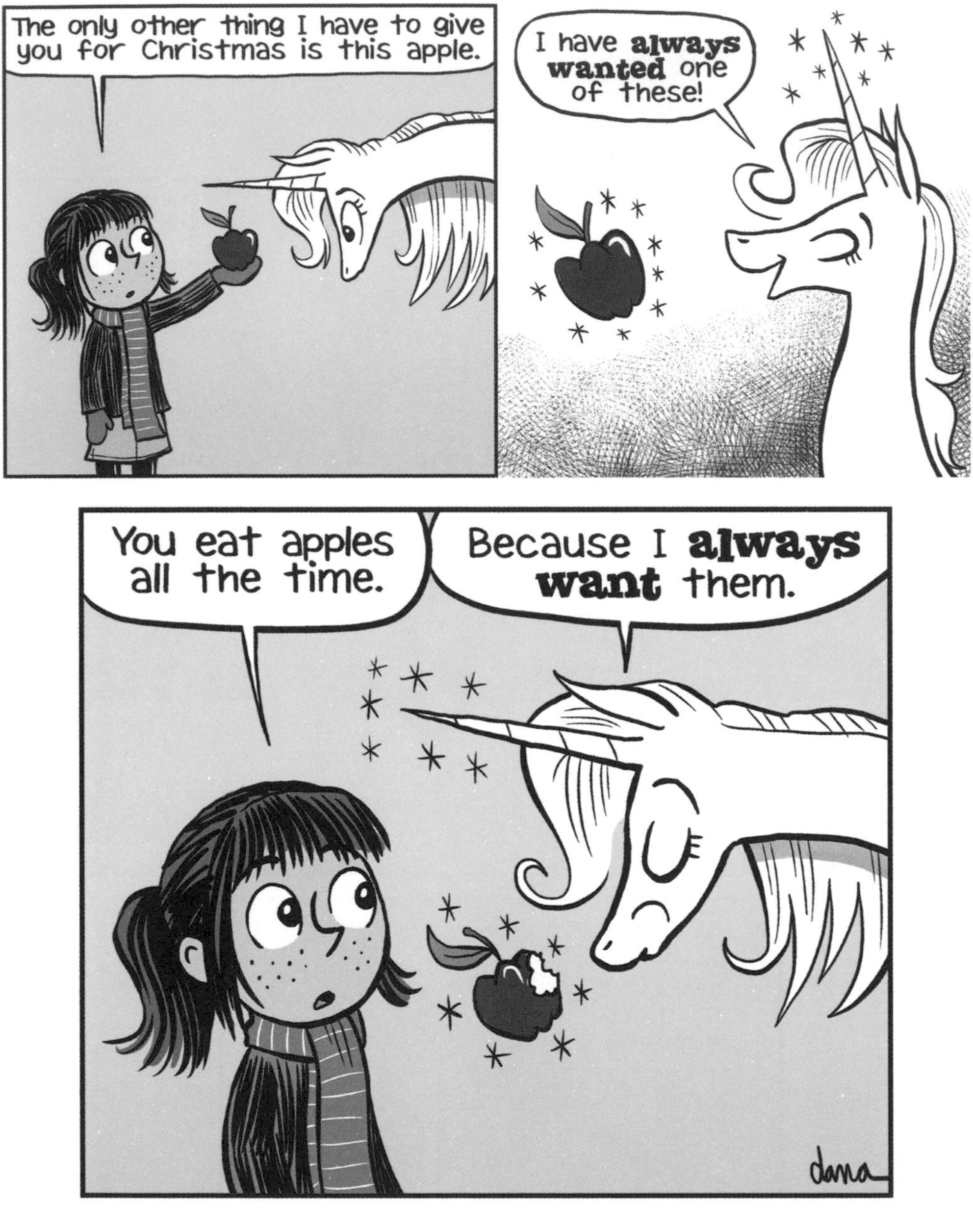
The only other thing I have to give you for Christmas is this apple.
I have **always wanted** one of these!
You eat apples all the time.
Because I **always want** them.
dana

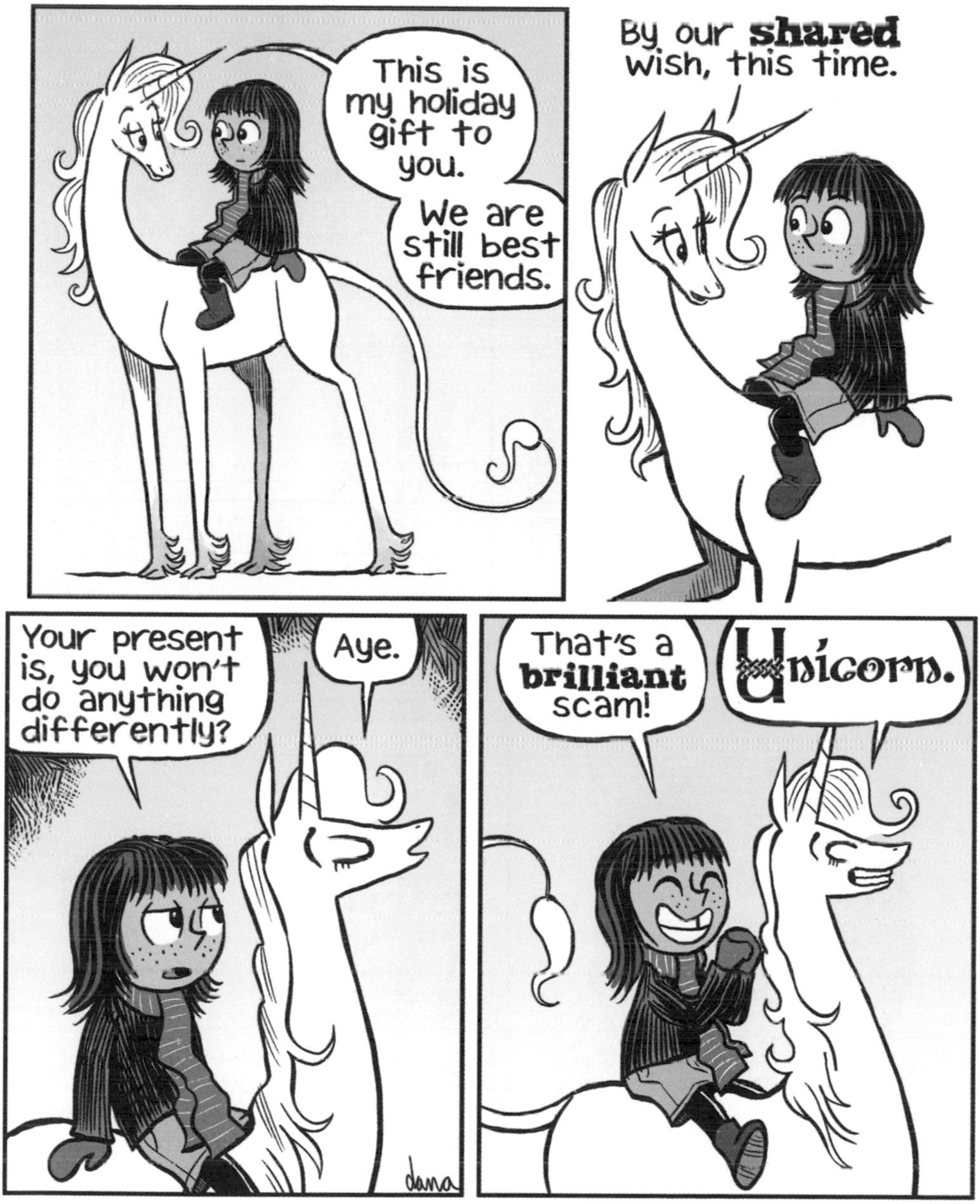
This is my holiday gift to you.
We are still best friends.
By our shared wish, this time.
Your present is, you won't do anything differently?
Aye.
That's a brilliant scam!
Unicorn.
dana

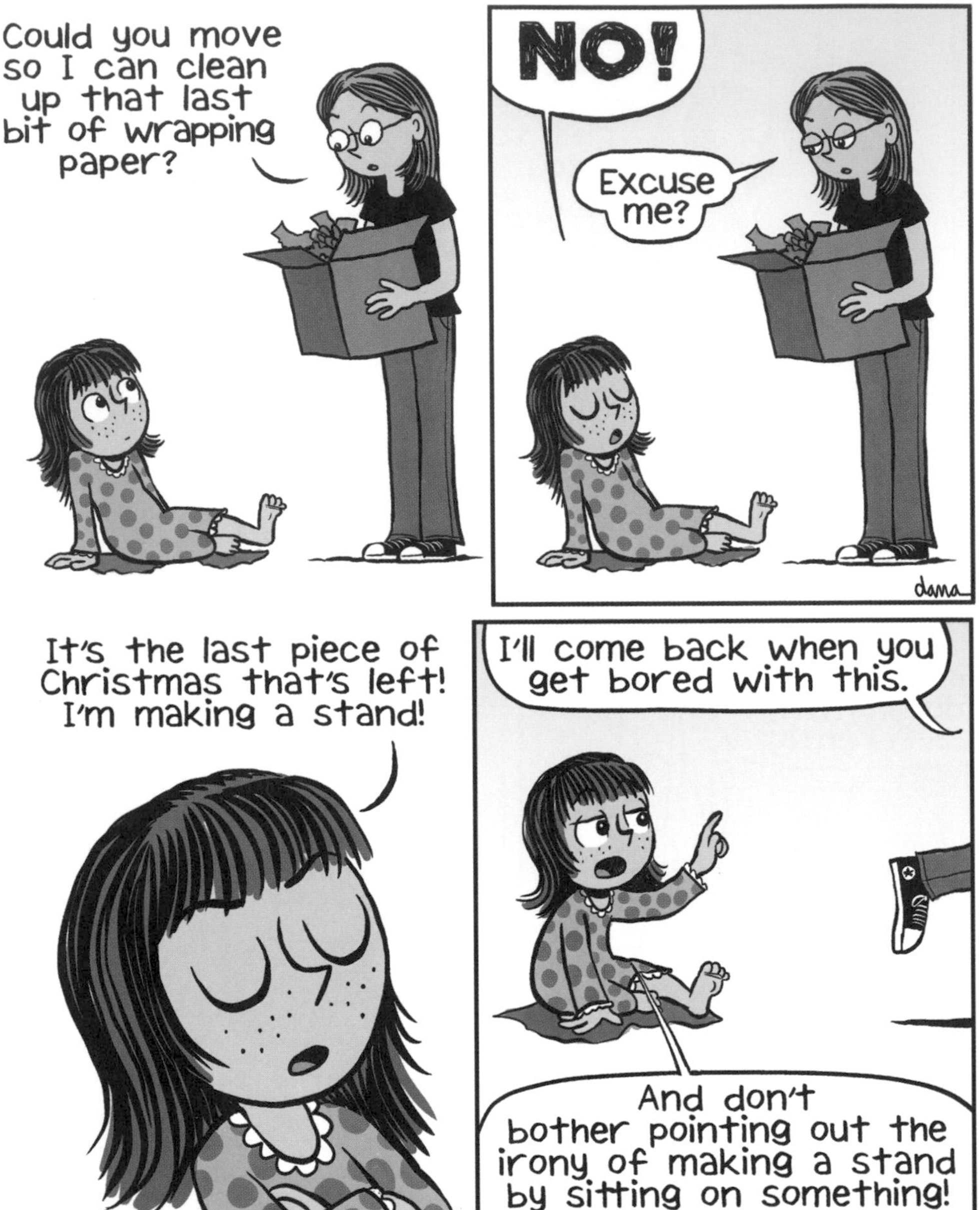
Could you move so I can clean up that last bit of wrapping paper?
NO!
Excuse me?
dana
It's the last piece of Christmas that's left! I'm making a stand!
I'll come back when you get bored with this.
And don't bother pointing out the irony of making a stand by sitting on something!

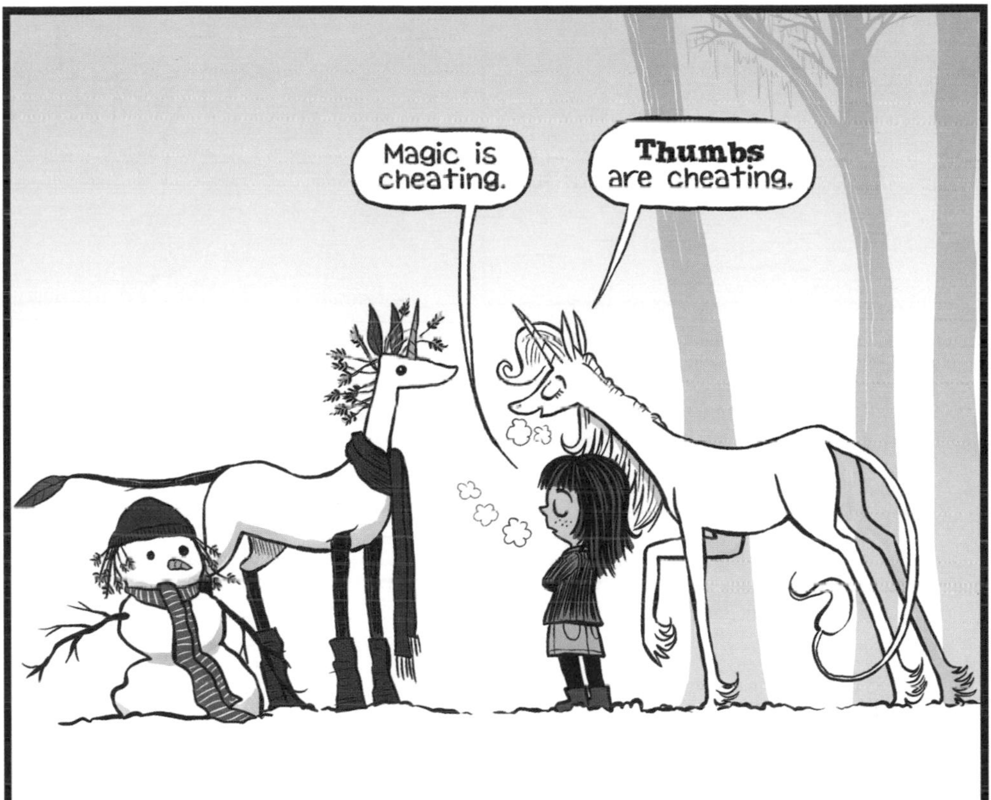
Magic is cheating.
Thumbs are cheating.
dana

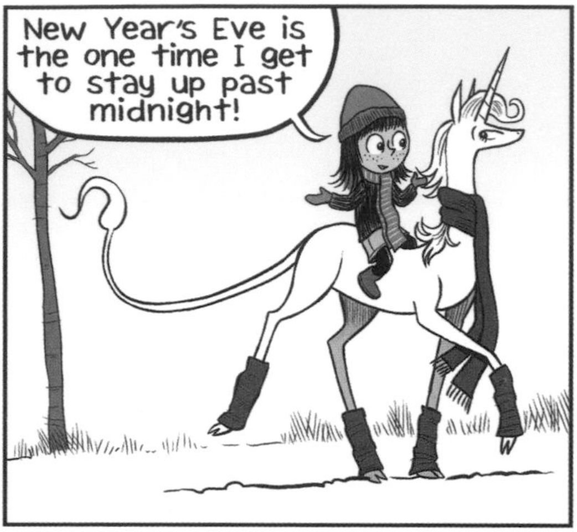
New Year's Eve is the one time I get to stay up past midnight!

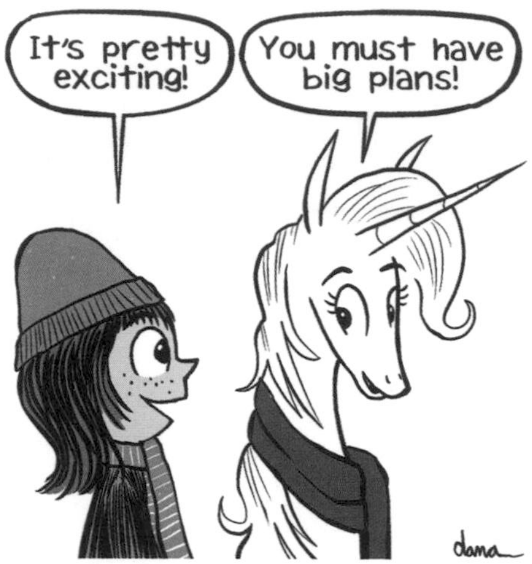
It's pretty exciting!
You must have big plans!
dana

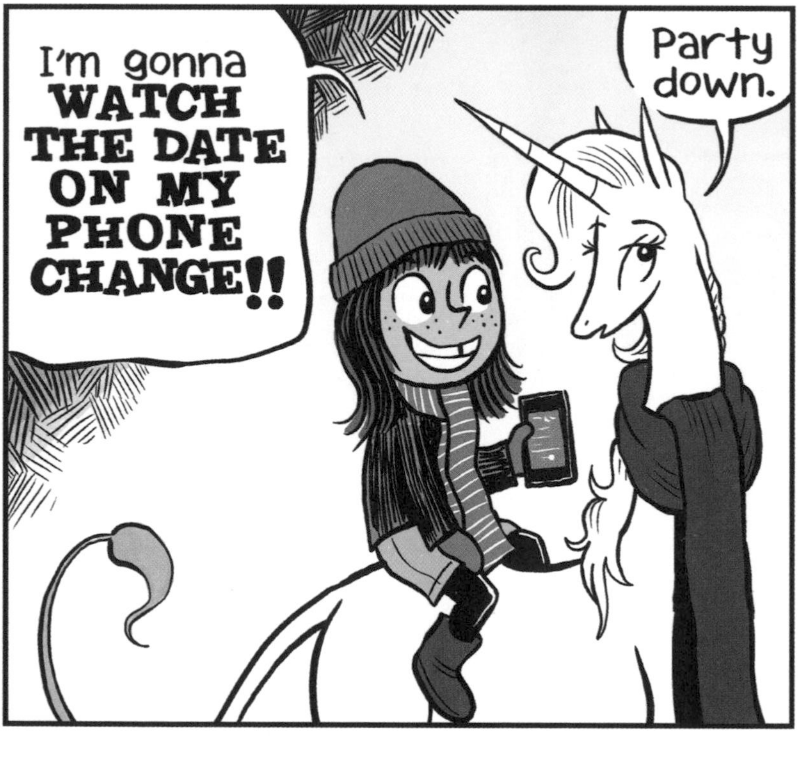
I'm gonna WATCH THE DATE ON MY PHONE CHANGE!!
Party down.

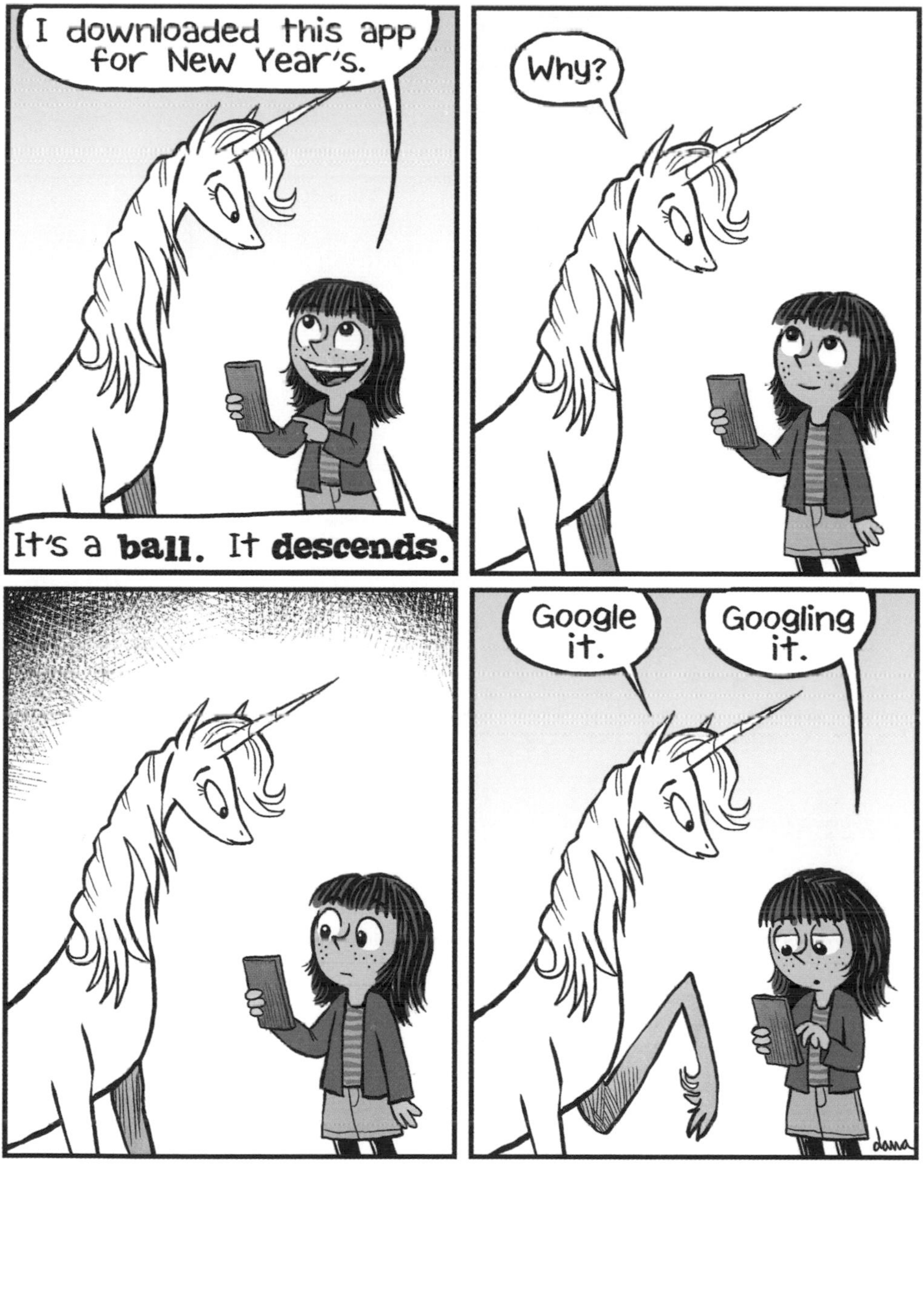
I downloaded this app for New Year's.
It's a **ball**. It **descends**.
Why?
Google it.
Googling it.
dana

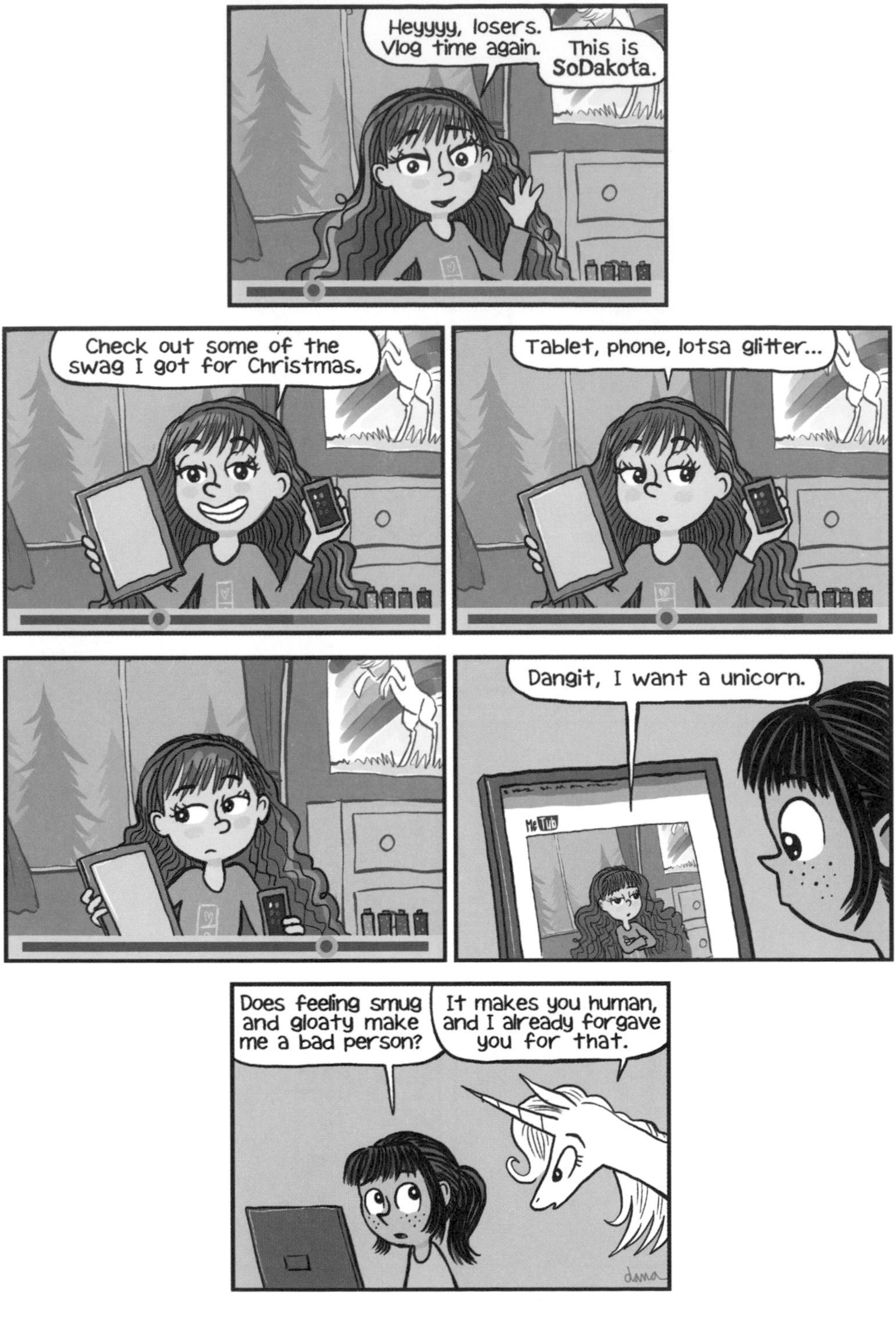
Heyyyy, losers. Vlog time again.
This is SoDakota.
Check out some of the swag I got for Christmas.
Tablet, phone, lotsa glitter...
Dangit, I want a unicorn.
MeTub
Does feeling smug and gloaty make me a bad person?
It makes you human, and I already forgave you for that.
dana

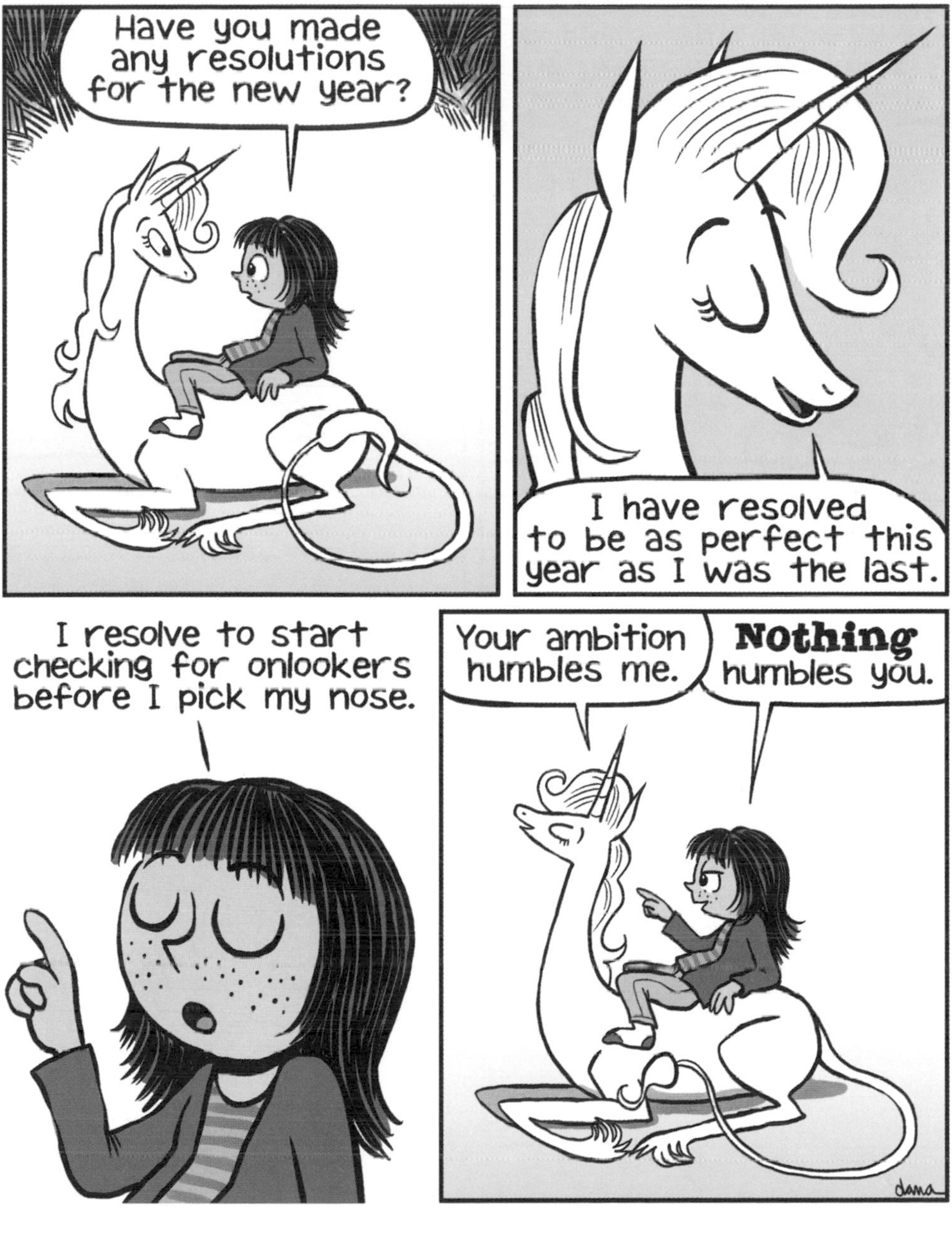
Have you made any resolutions for the new year?
I have resolved to be as perfect this year as I was the last.
I resolve to start checking for onlookers before I pick my nose.
Your ambition humbles me.
Nothing humbles you.
dana

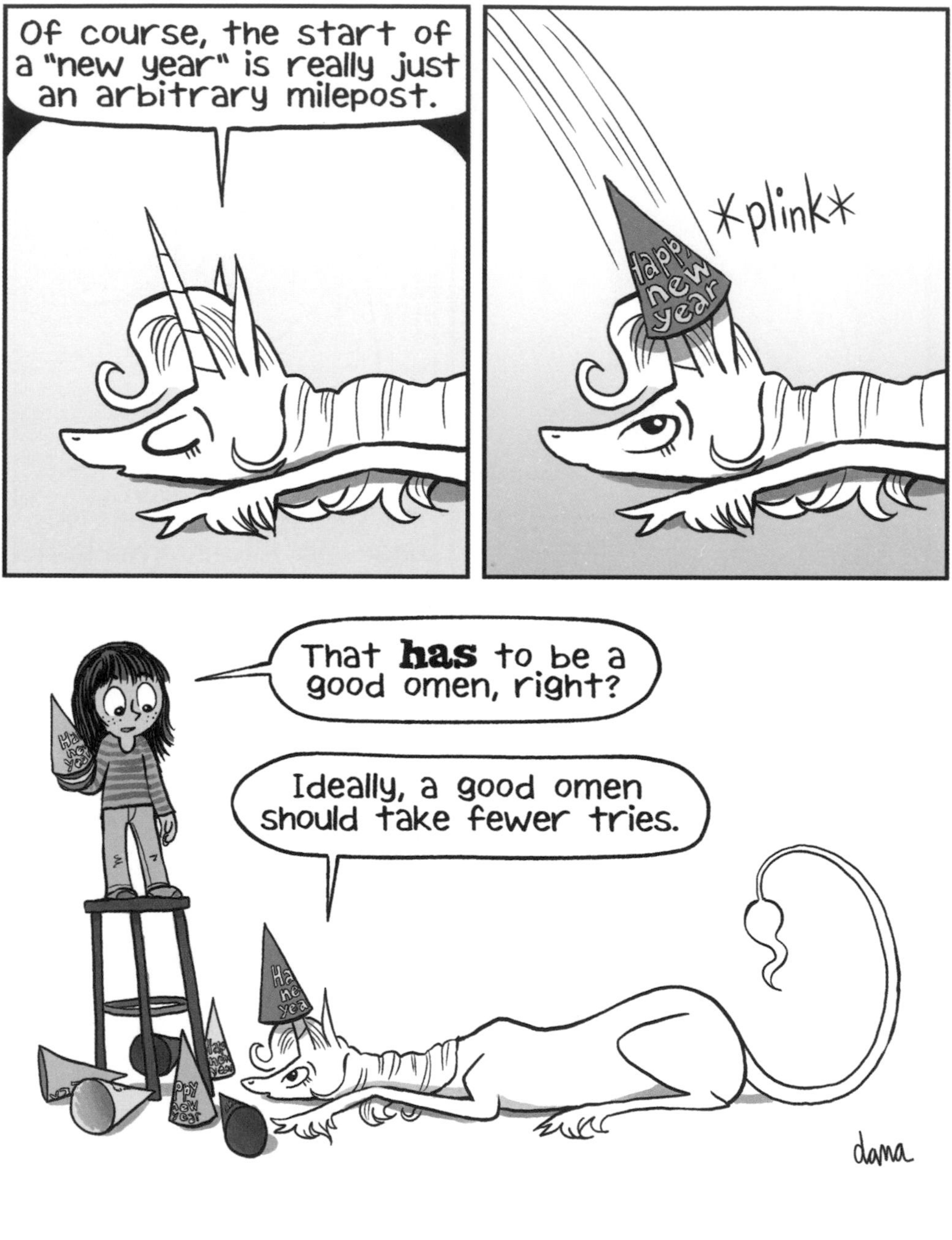
Of course, the start of a "new year" is really just an arbitrary milepost.
plink
That **has** to be a good omen, right?
Ideally, a good omen should take fewer tries.
dana

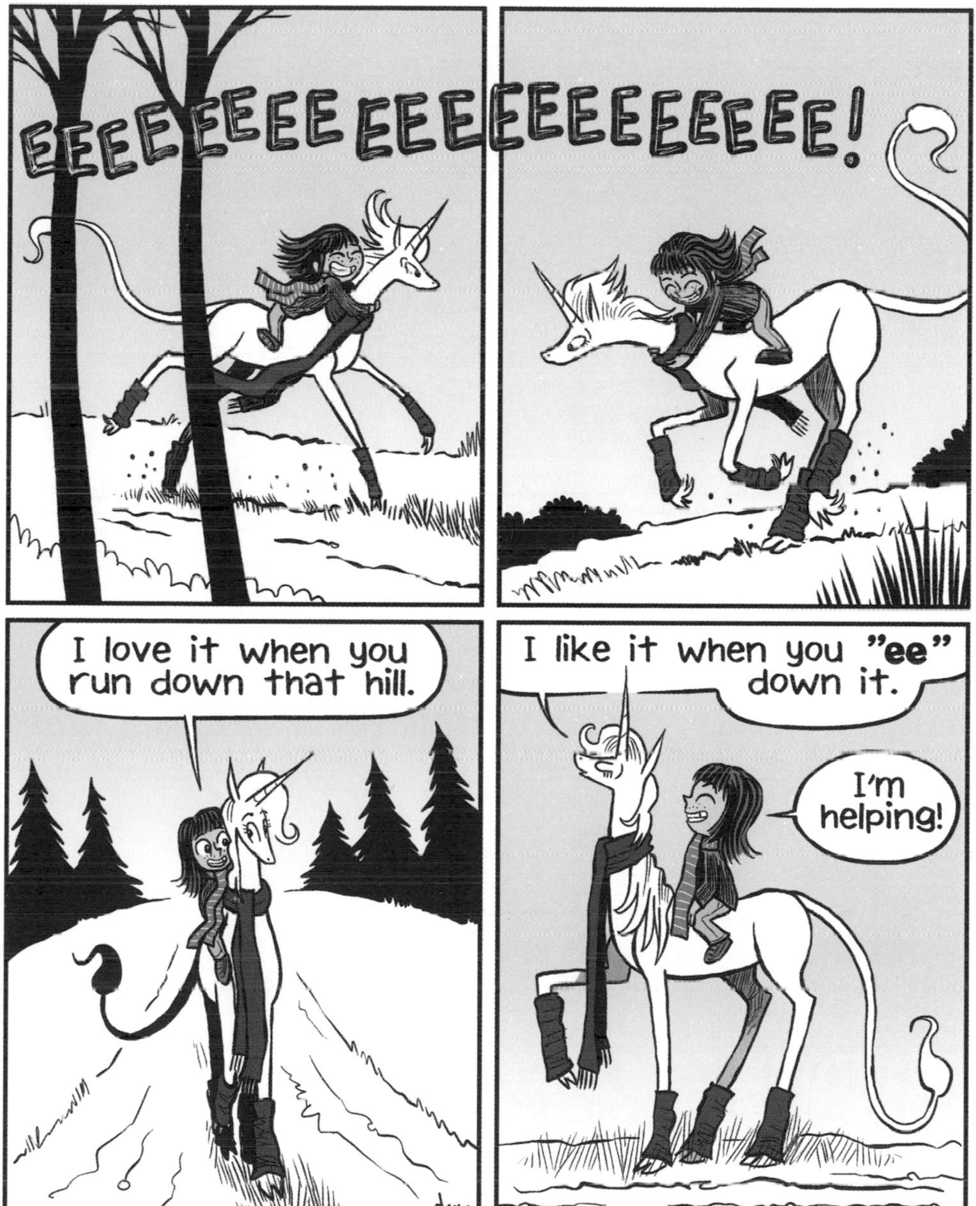
EEEEEEEEEEEEEEEEEEEEE!
I love it when you run down that hill.
I like it when you "ee" down it.
I'm helping!
dana

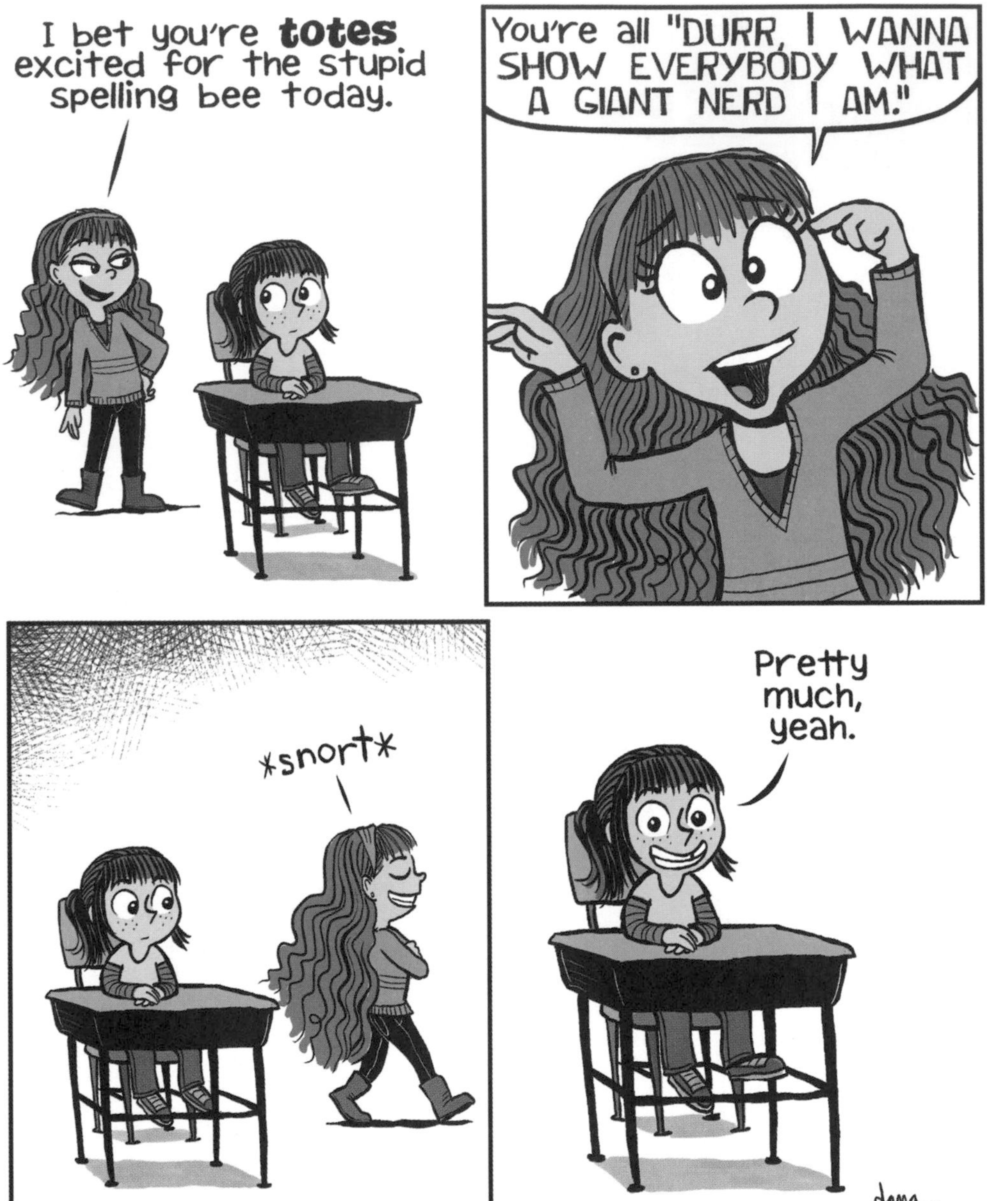
I bet you're **totes** excited for the stupid spelling bee today.
You're all "DURR, I WANNA SHOW EVERYBODY WHAT A GIANT NERD I AM."
snort
Pretty much, yeah.
dana

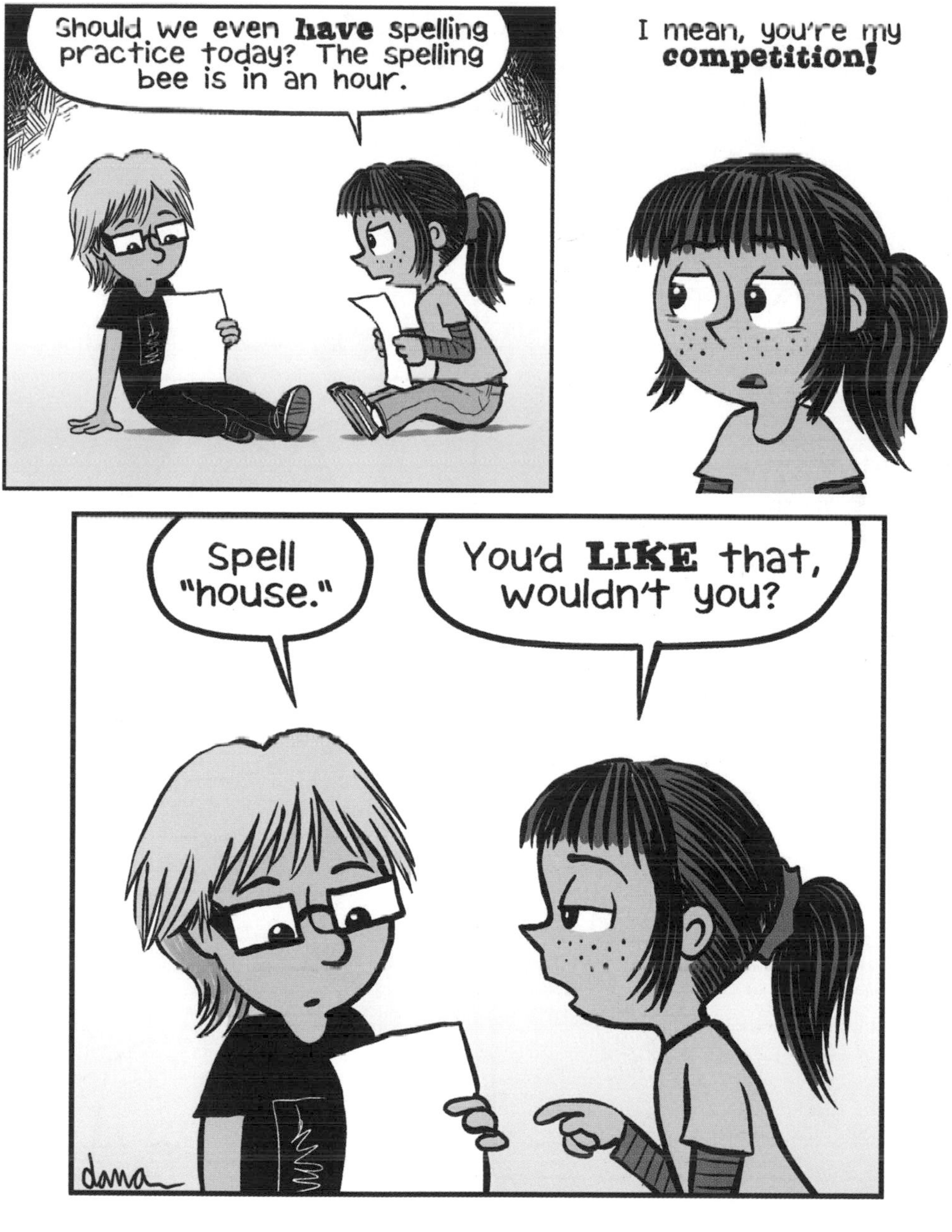
Should we even **have** spelling practice today? The spelling bee is in an hour.
I mean, you're my **competition!**
Spell "house."
You'd **LIKE** that, wouldn't you?
dana

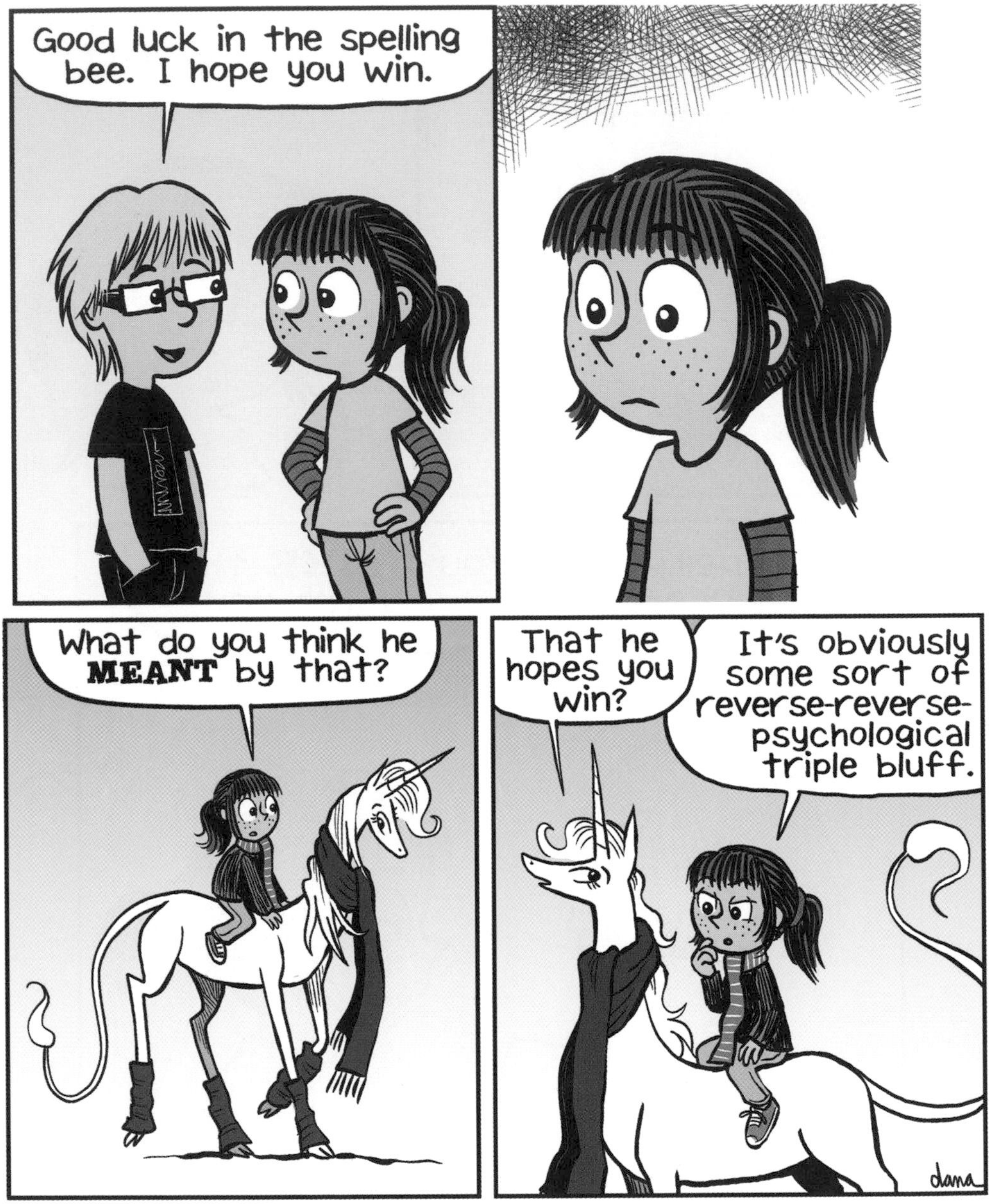
Good luck in the spelling bee. I hope you win.
What do you think he **MEANT** by that?
That he hopes you win?
It's obviously some sort of reverse-reverse-psychological triple bluff.
dana

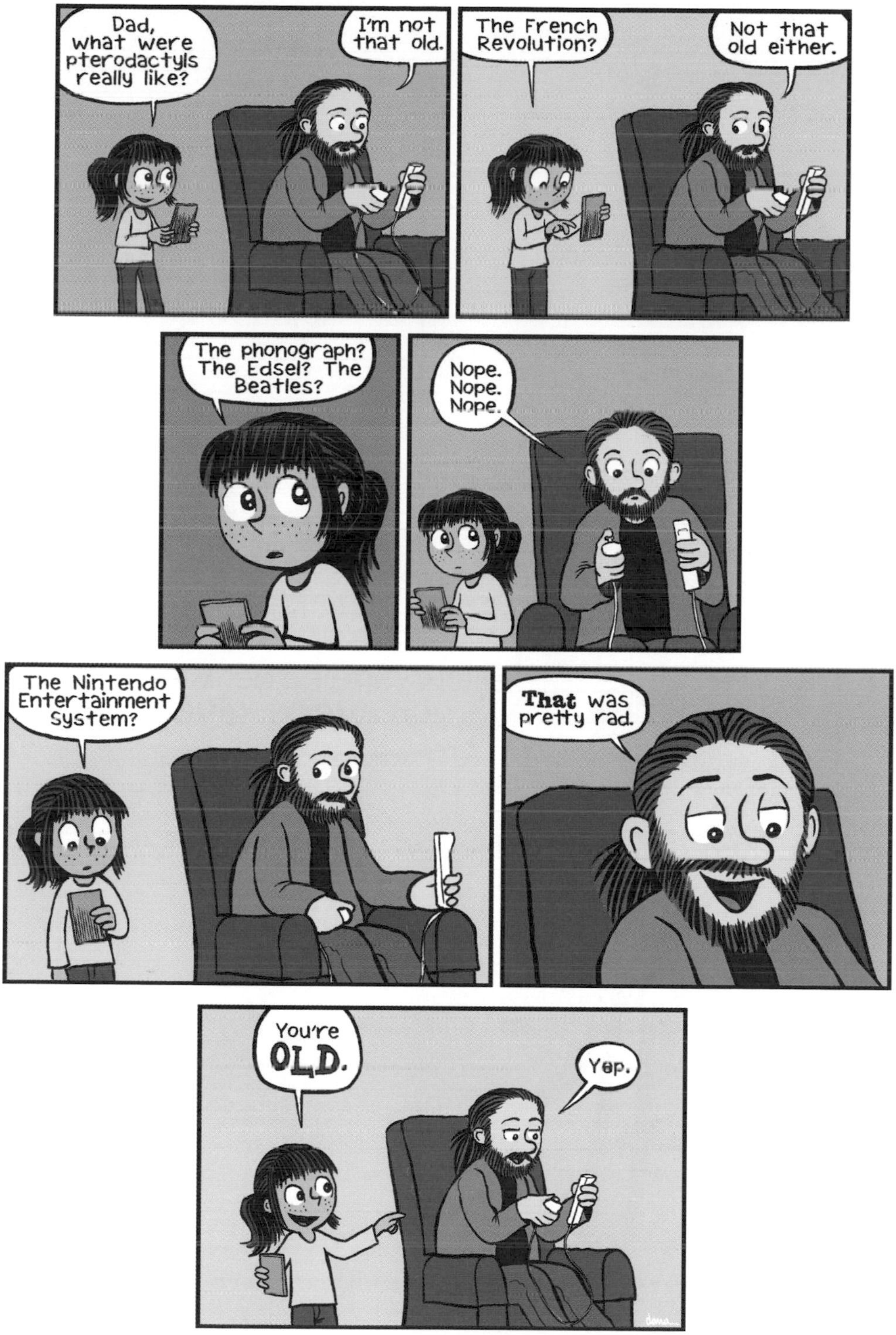
Dad, what were pterodactyls really like?
I'm not that old.
The French Revolution?
Not that old either.
The phonograph? The Edsel? The Beatles?
Nope. Nope. Nope.
The Nintendo Entertainment System?
That was pretty rad.
You're **OLD.**
Yep.

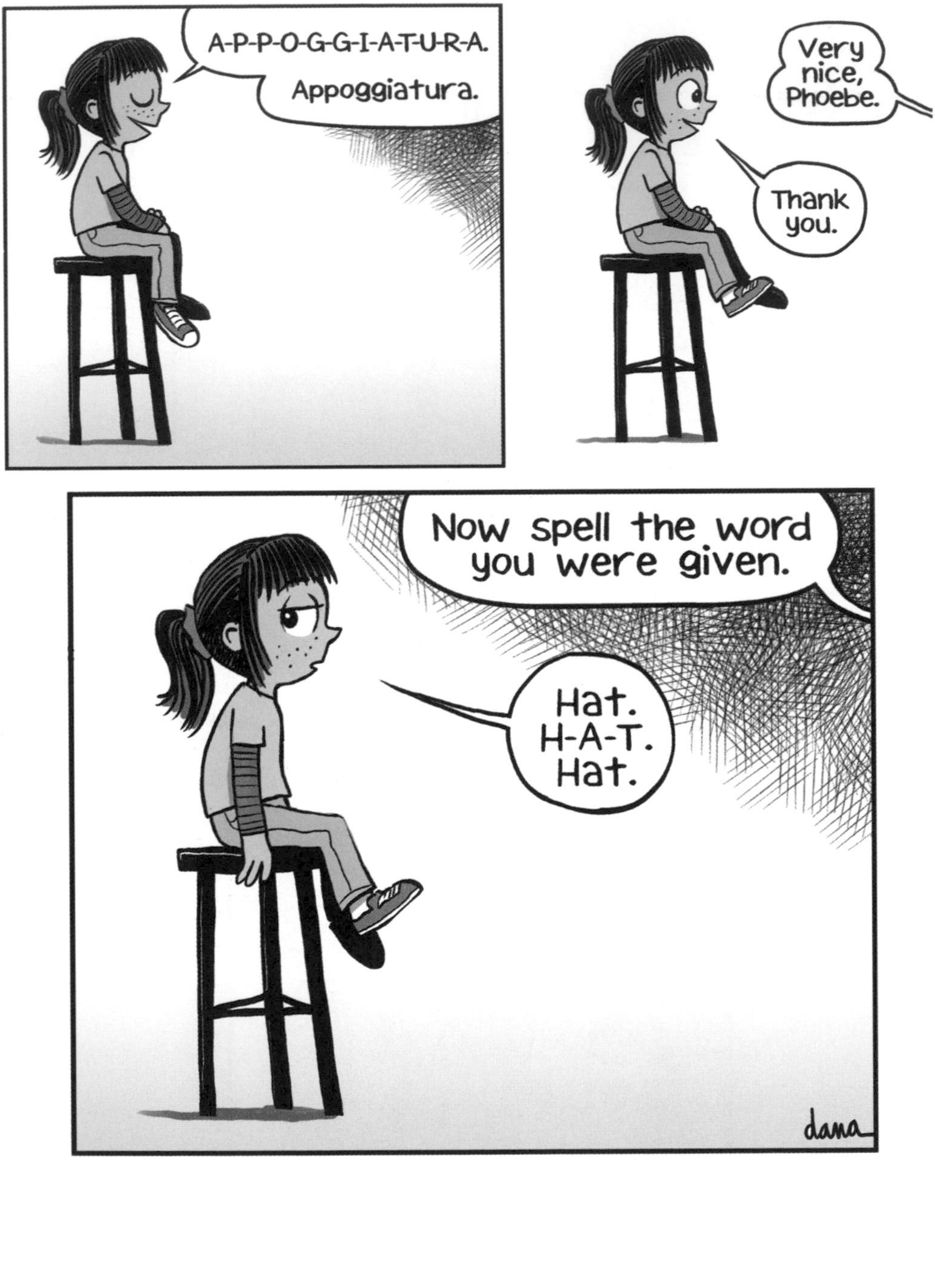
A-P-P-O-G-G-I-A-T-U-R-A.
Appoggiatura.
Very nice, Phoebe.
Thank you.
Now spell the word you were given.
Hat. H-A-T. Hat.
dana

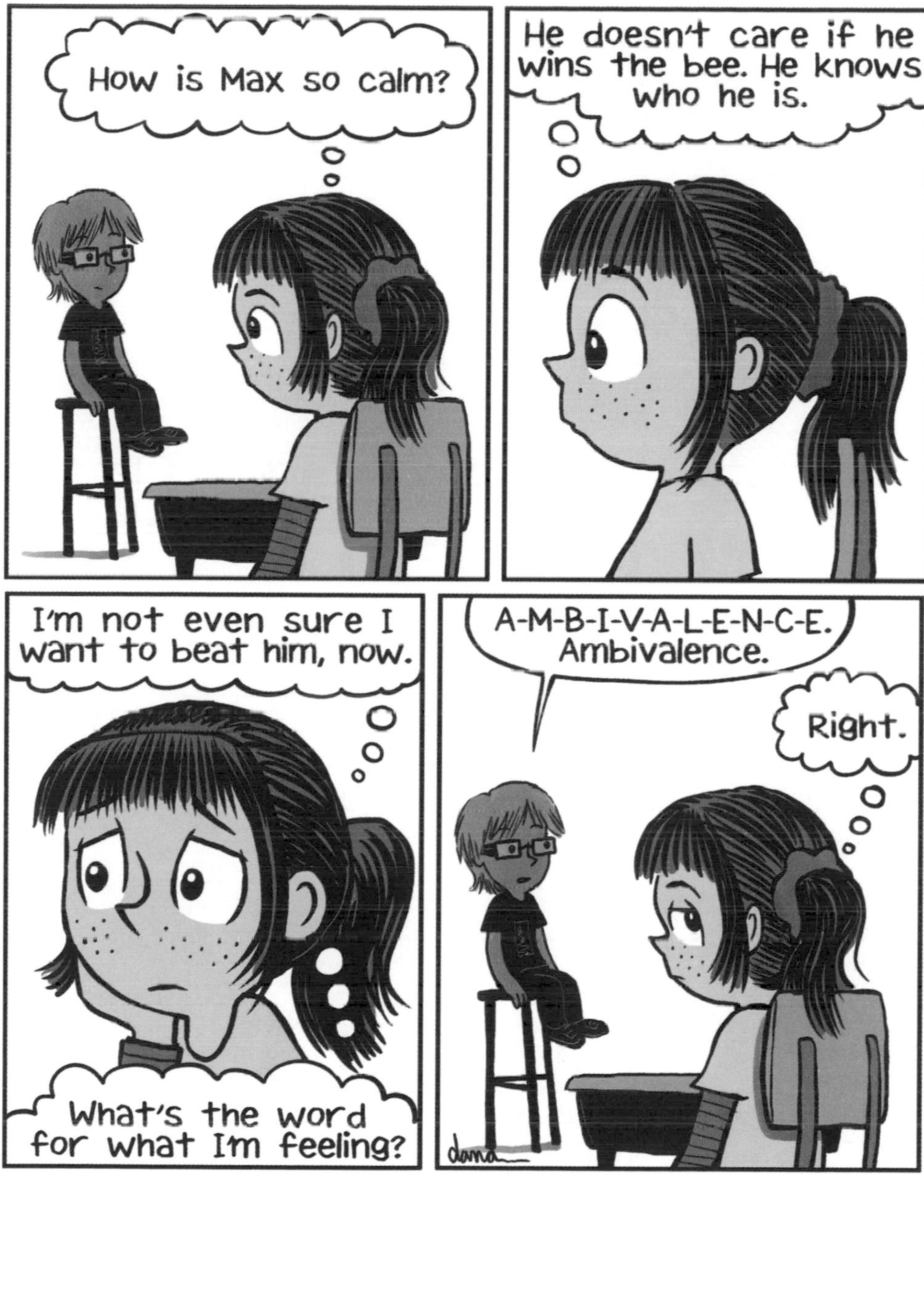
How is Max so calm?
He doesn't care if he wins the bee. He knows who he is.
I'm not even sure I want to beat him, now.
What's the word for what I'm feeling?
A-M-B-I-V-A-L-E-N-C-E. Ambivalence.
Right.
dana

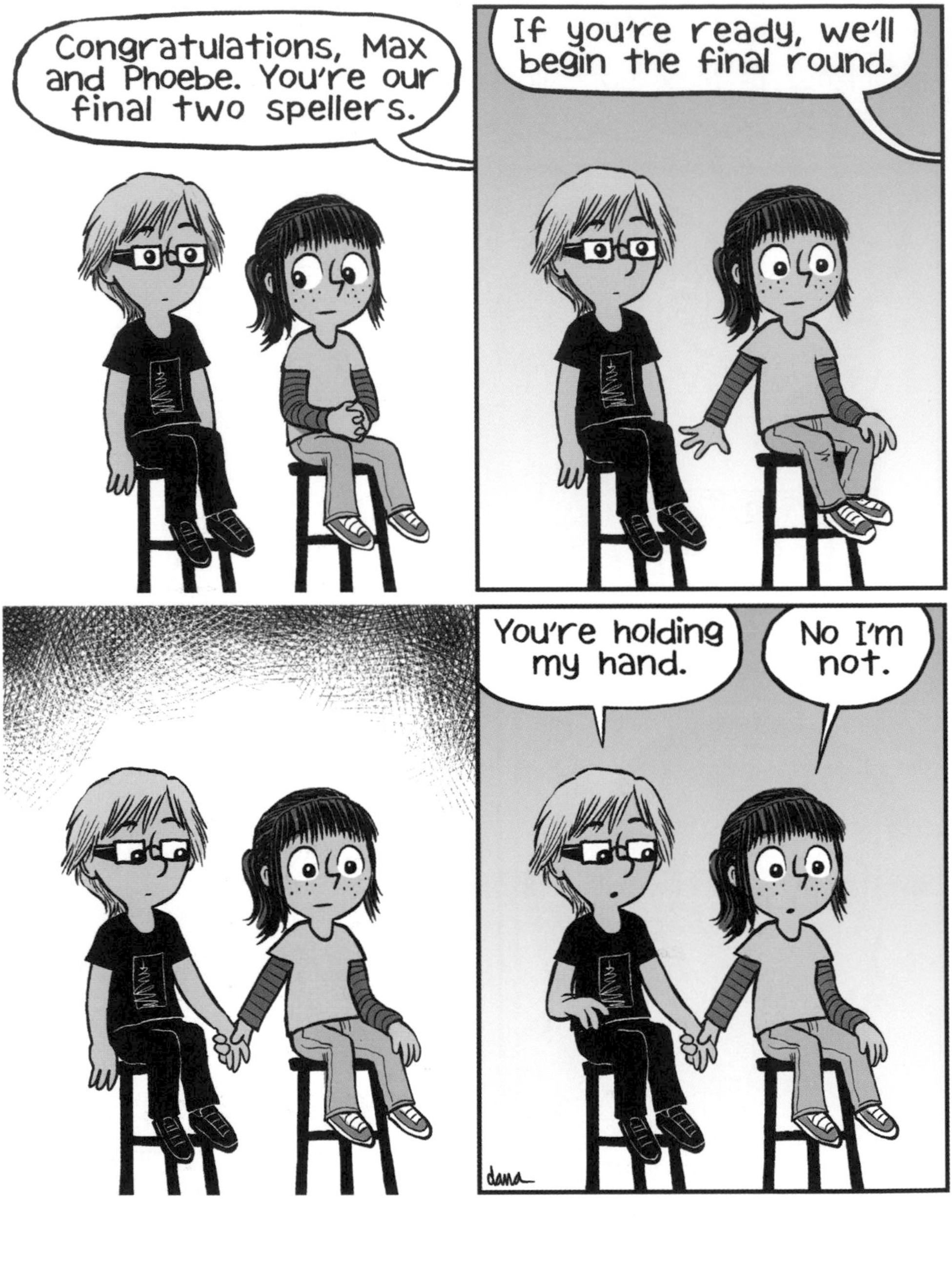
Congratulations, Max and Phoebe. You're our final two spellers.
If you're ready, we'll begin the final round.
You're holding my hand.
No I'm not.
dana

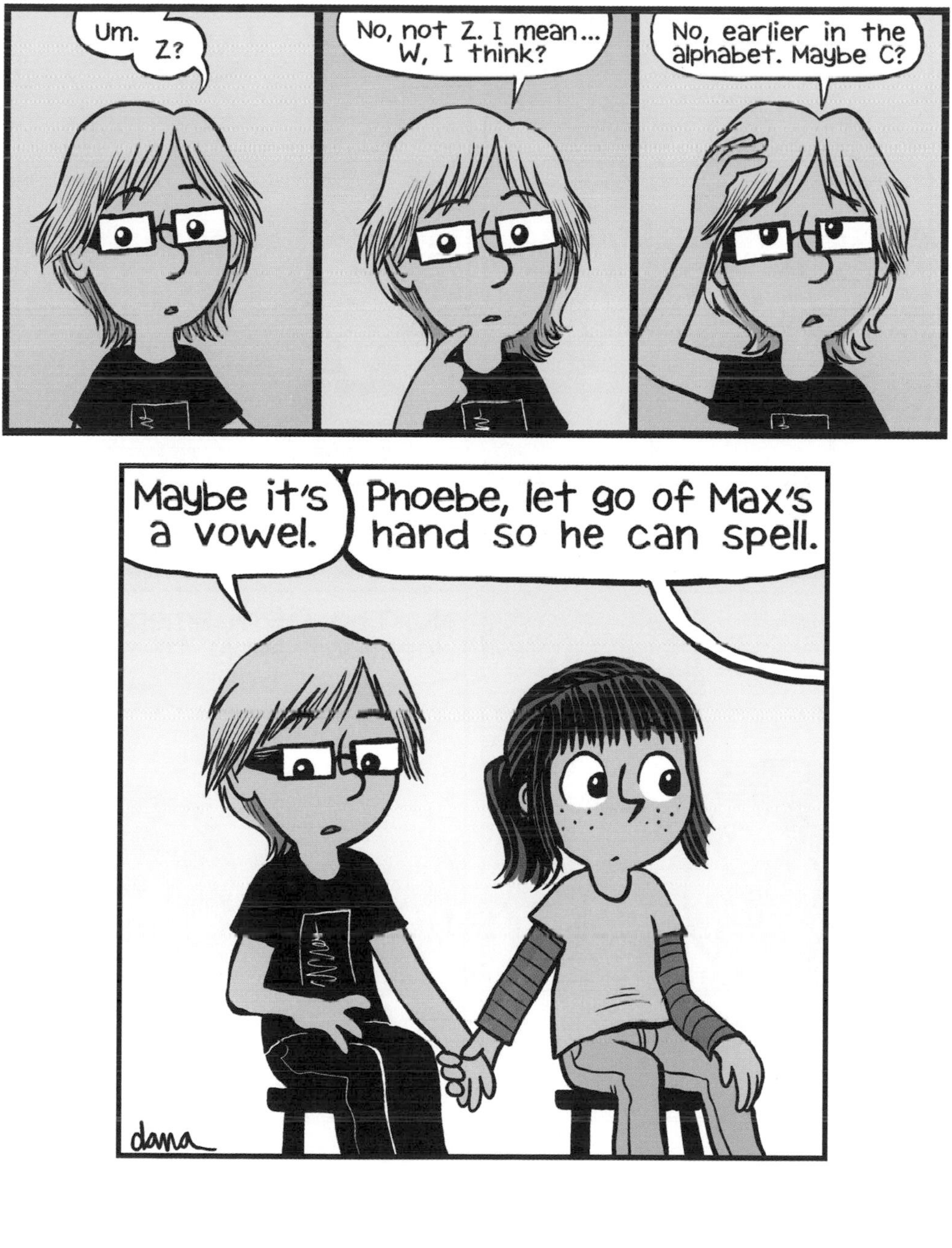
Um. Z?
No, not Z. I mean... W, I think?
No, earlier in the alphabet. Maybe C?
Maybe it's a vowel.
Phoebe, let go of Max's hand so he can spell.
dana

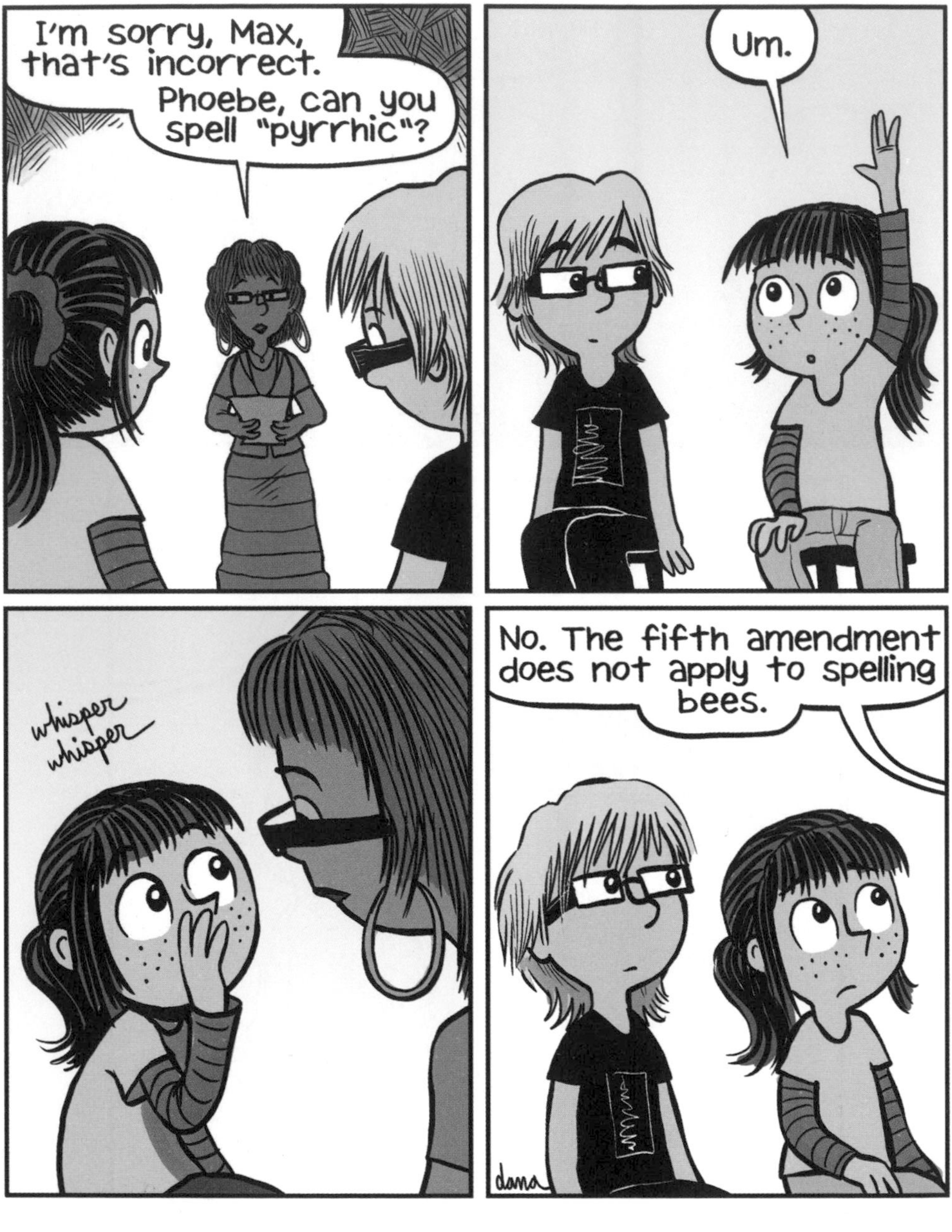
I'm sorry, Max, that's incorrect.
Phoebe, can you spell "pyrrhic"?
Um.
whisper whisper
No. The fifth amendment does not apply to spelling bees.
dana

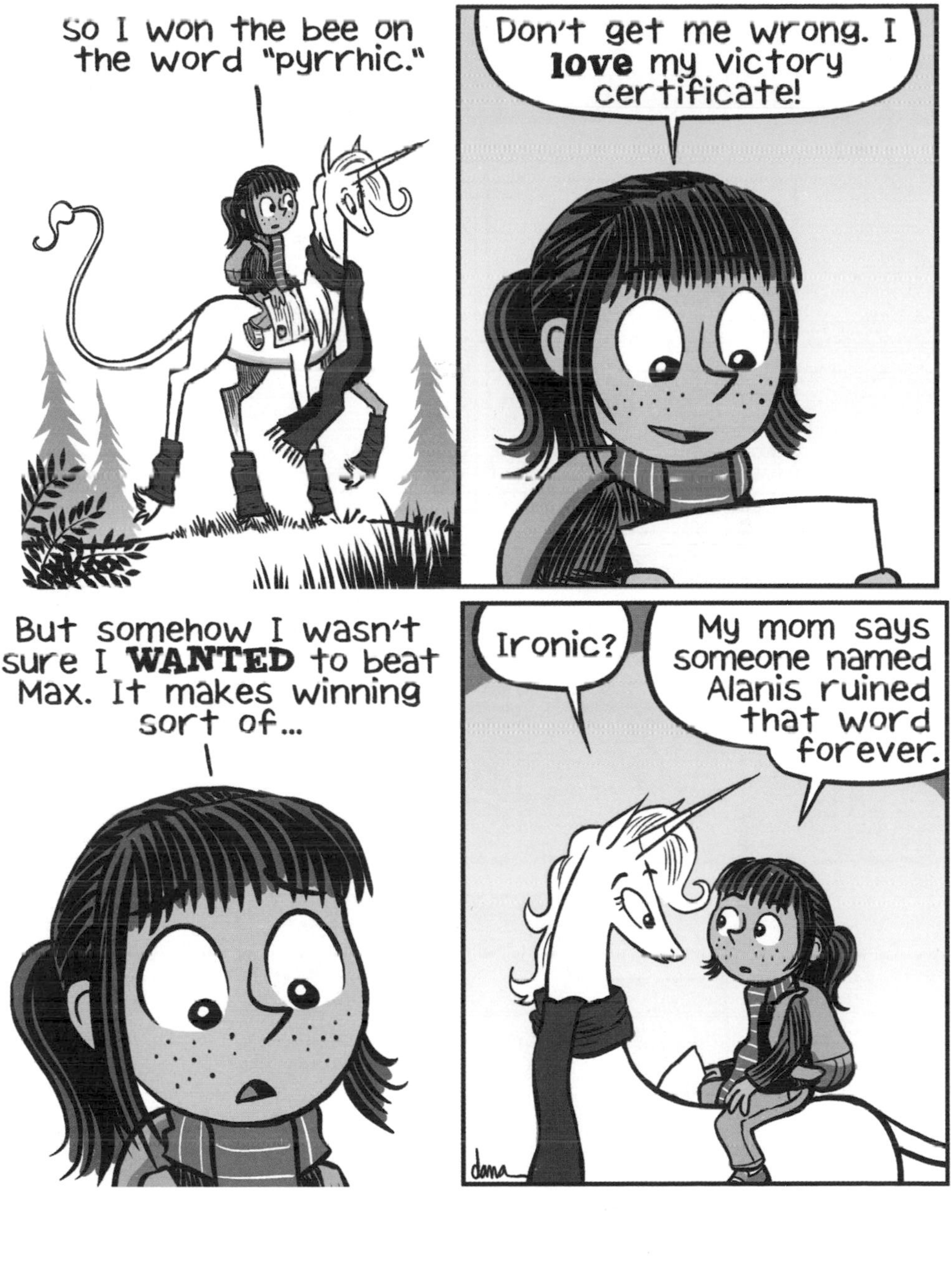
So I won the bee on the word "pyrrhic."
Don't get me wrong. I **love** my victory certificate!
But somehow I wasn't sure I **WANTED** to beat Max. It makes winning sort of...
Ironic?
My mom says someone named Alanis ruined that word forever.
dana

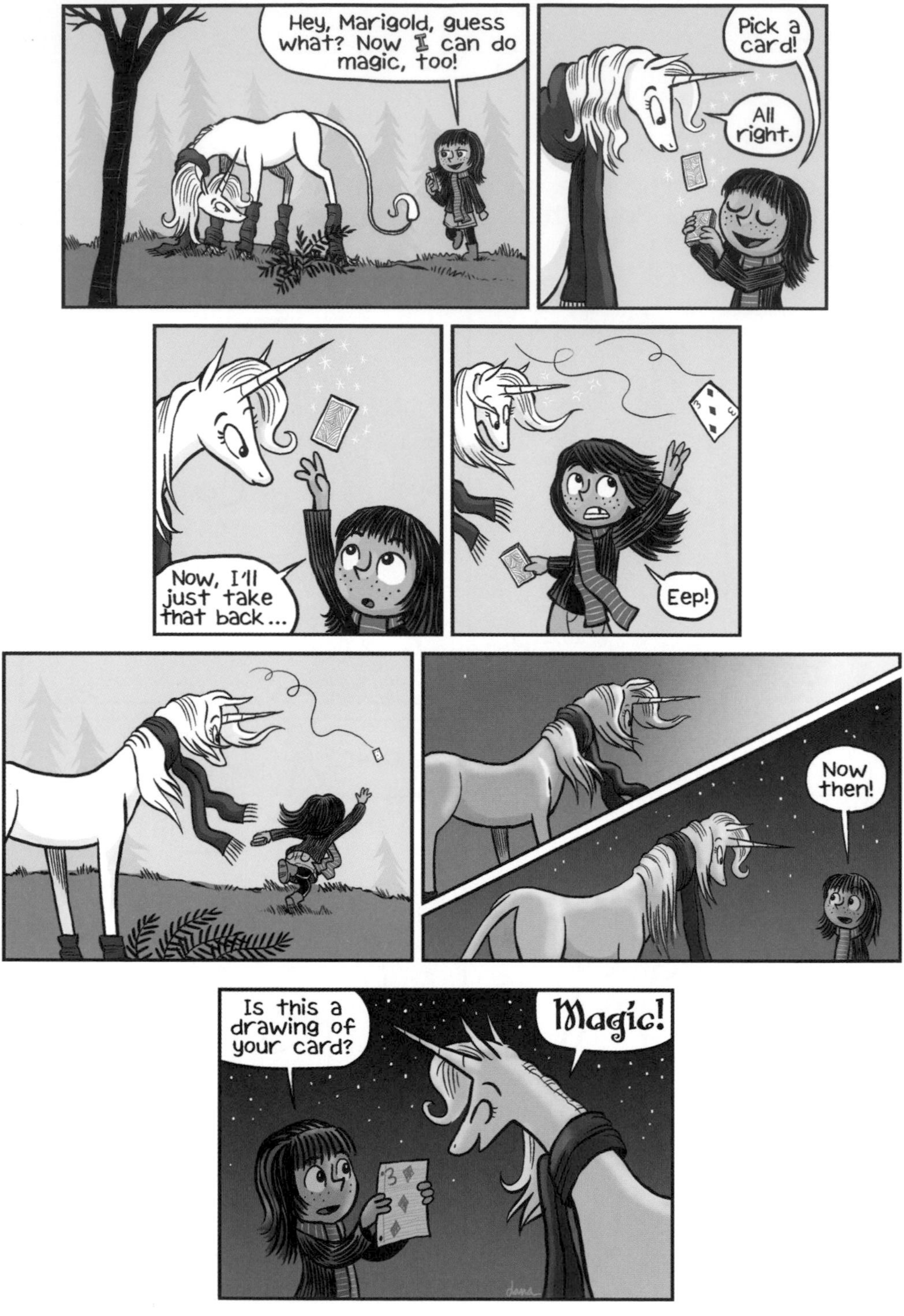
Hey, Marigold, guess what? Now I can do magic, too!
Pick a card!
All right.
Now, I'll just take that back...
Eep!
Now then!
Is this a drawing of your card?
Magic!

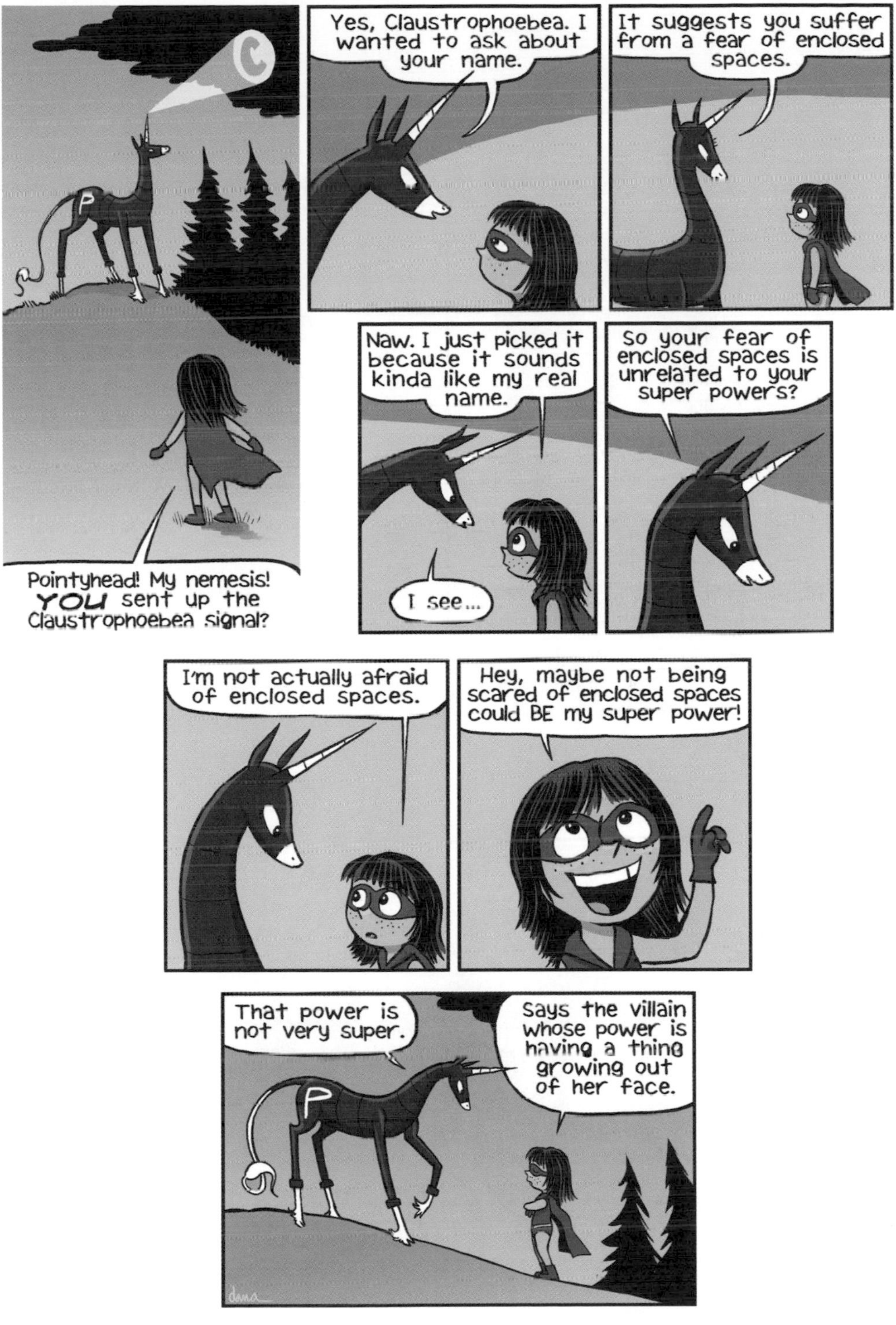
Pointyhead! My nemesis! YOU sent up the Claustrophoebea signal?
Yes, Claustrophoebea. I wanted to ask about your name.
It suggests you suffer from a fear of enclosed spaces.
Naw. I just picked it because it sounds kinda like my real name.
I see...
So your fear of enclosed spaces is unrelated to your super powers?
I'm not actually afraid of enclosed spaces.
Hey, maybe not being scared of enclosed spaces could BE my super power!
That power is not very super.
Says the villain whose power is having a thing growing out of her face.

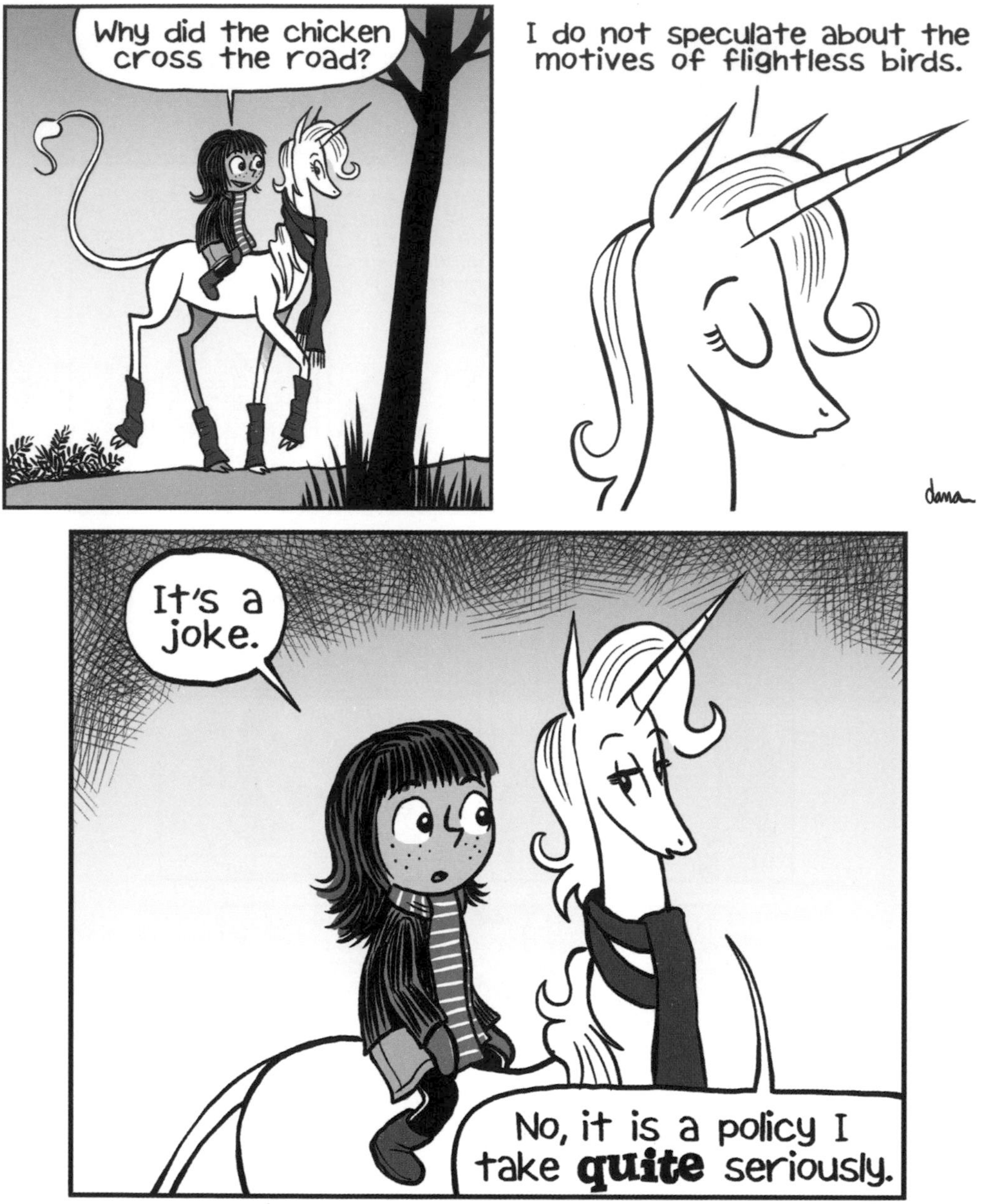
Why did the chicken cross the road?
I do not speculate about the motives of flightless birds.
dana
It's a joke.
No, it is a policy I take **quite** seriously.

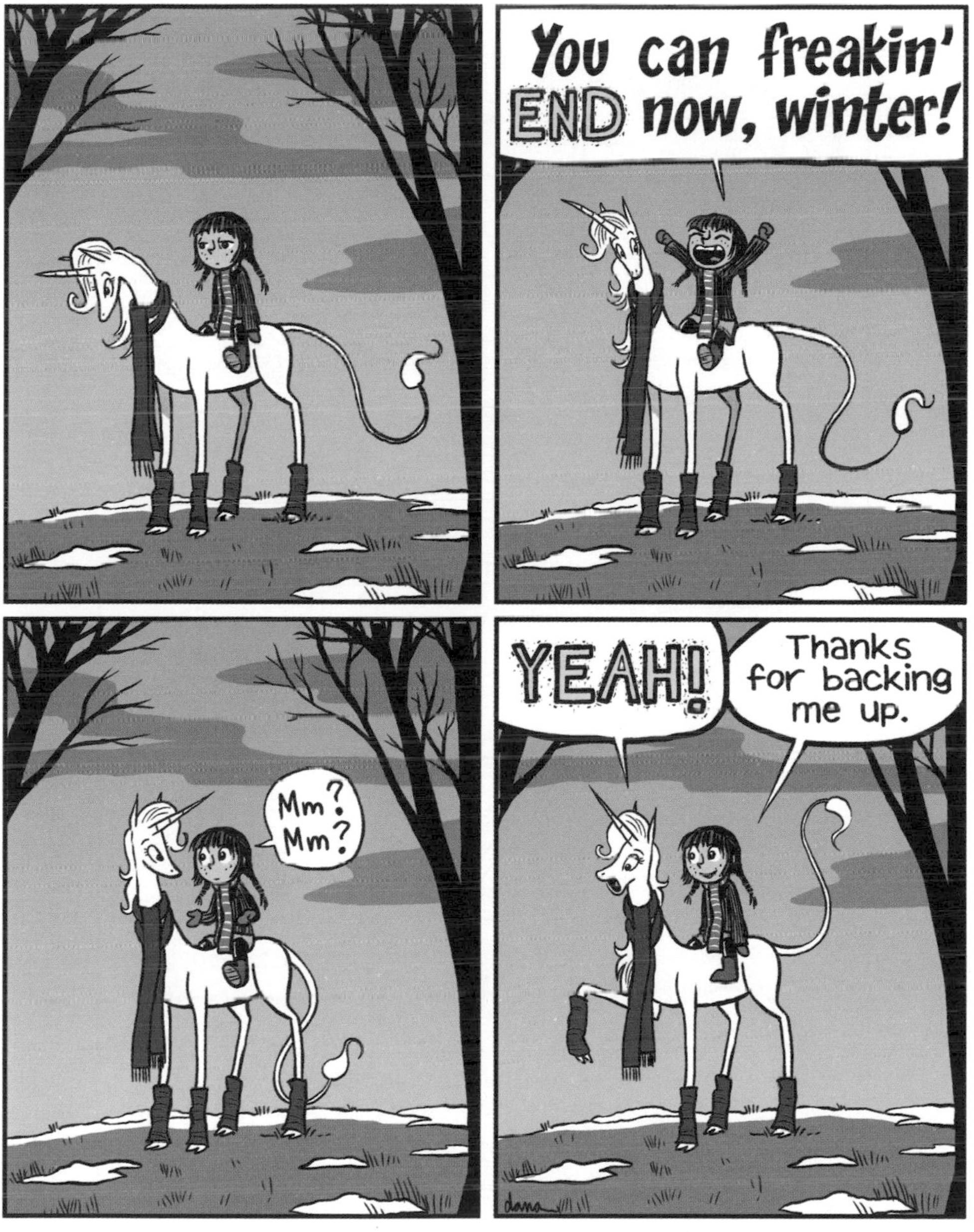
You can freakin' END now, winter!
Mm? Mm?
YEAH!
Thanks for backing me up.
dana

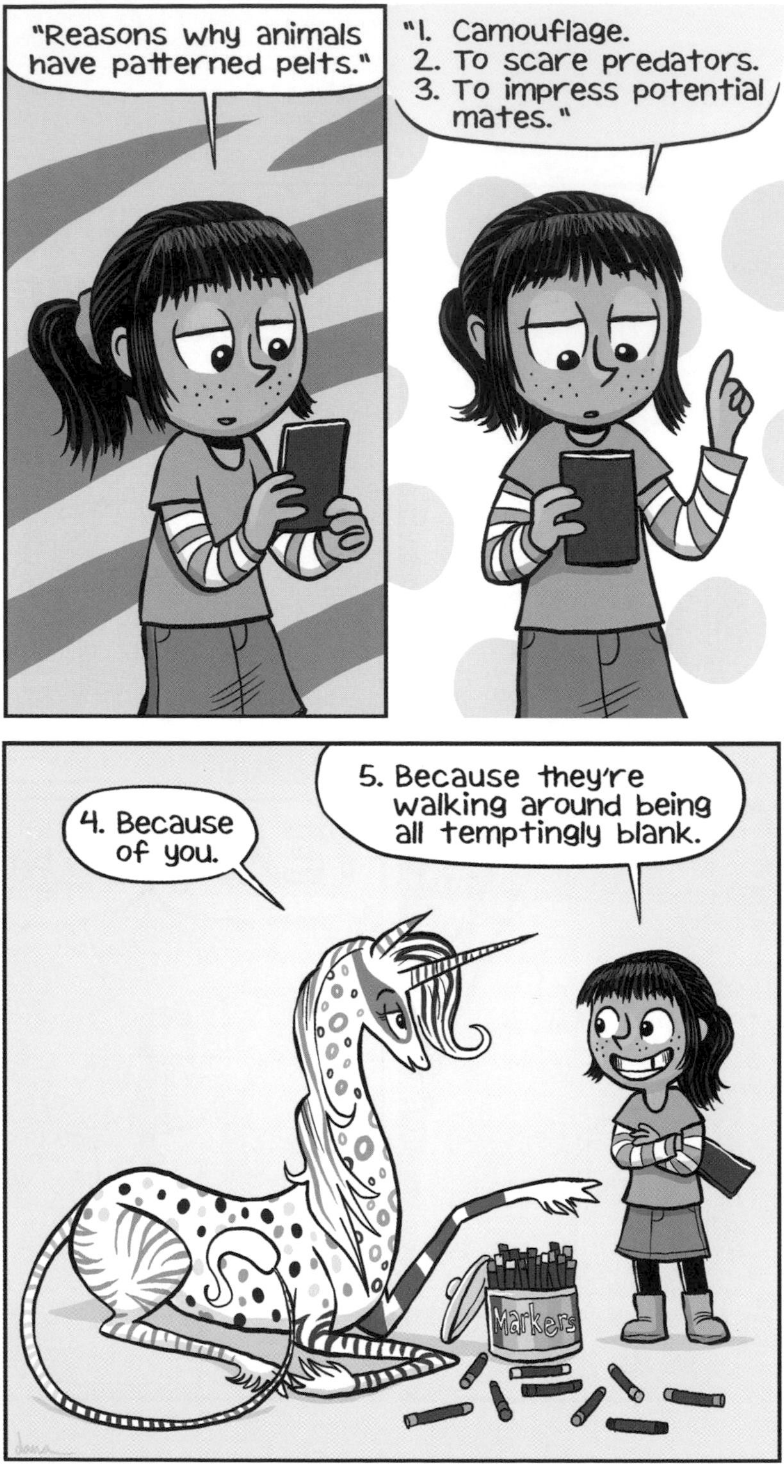
"Reasons why animals have patterned pelts."
"1. Camouflage.
2. To scare predators.
3. To impress potential mates."
4. Because of you.
5. Because they're walking around being all temptingly blank.
Markers
dana

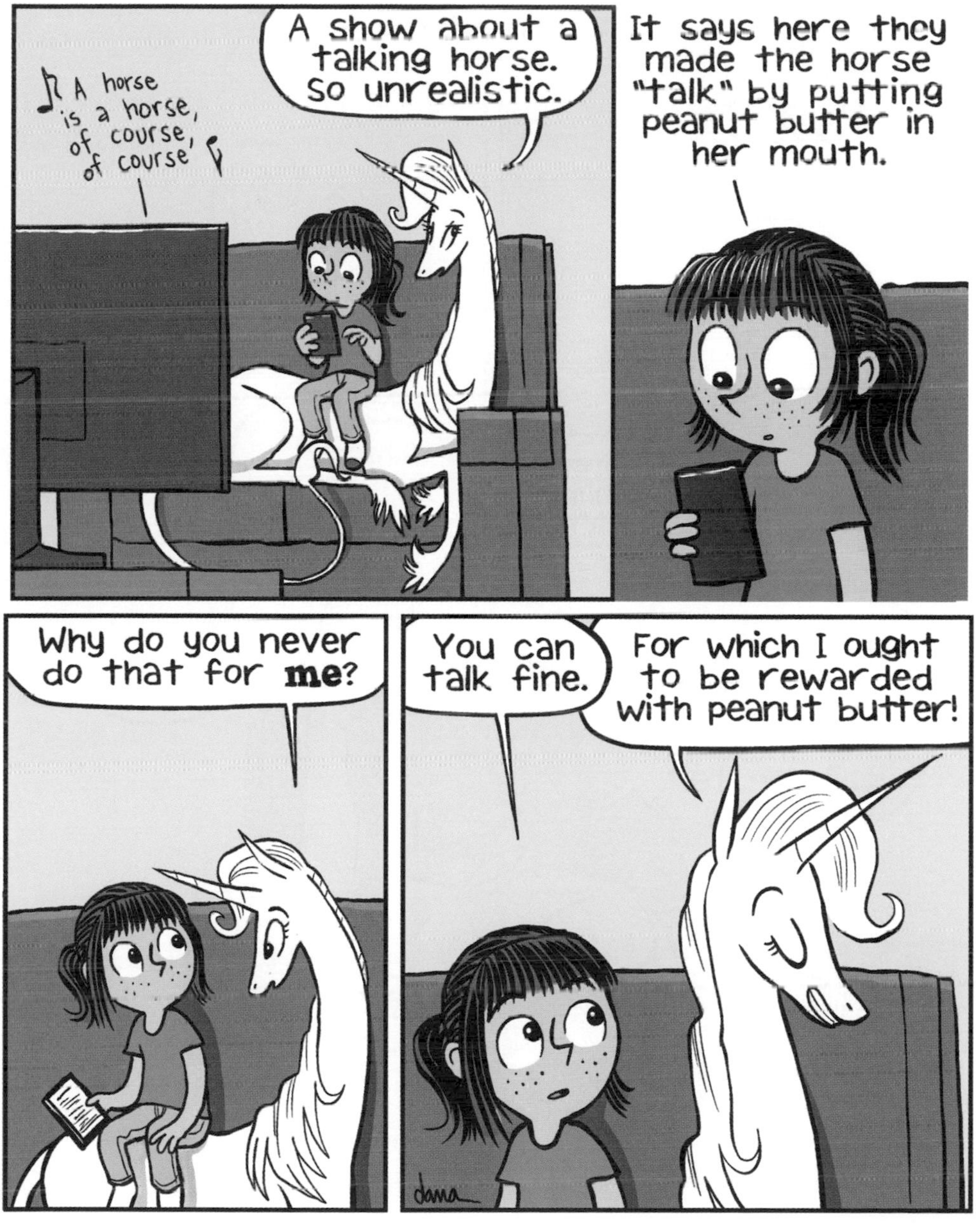

A horse is a horse, of course, of course
A show about a talking horse. So unrealistic.
It says here they made the horse "talk" by putting peanut butter in her mouth.
Why do you never do that for **me**?
You can talk fine.
For which I ought to be rewarded with peanut butter!
dana

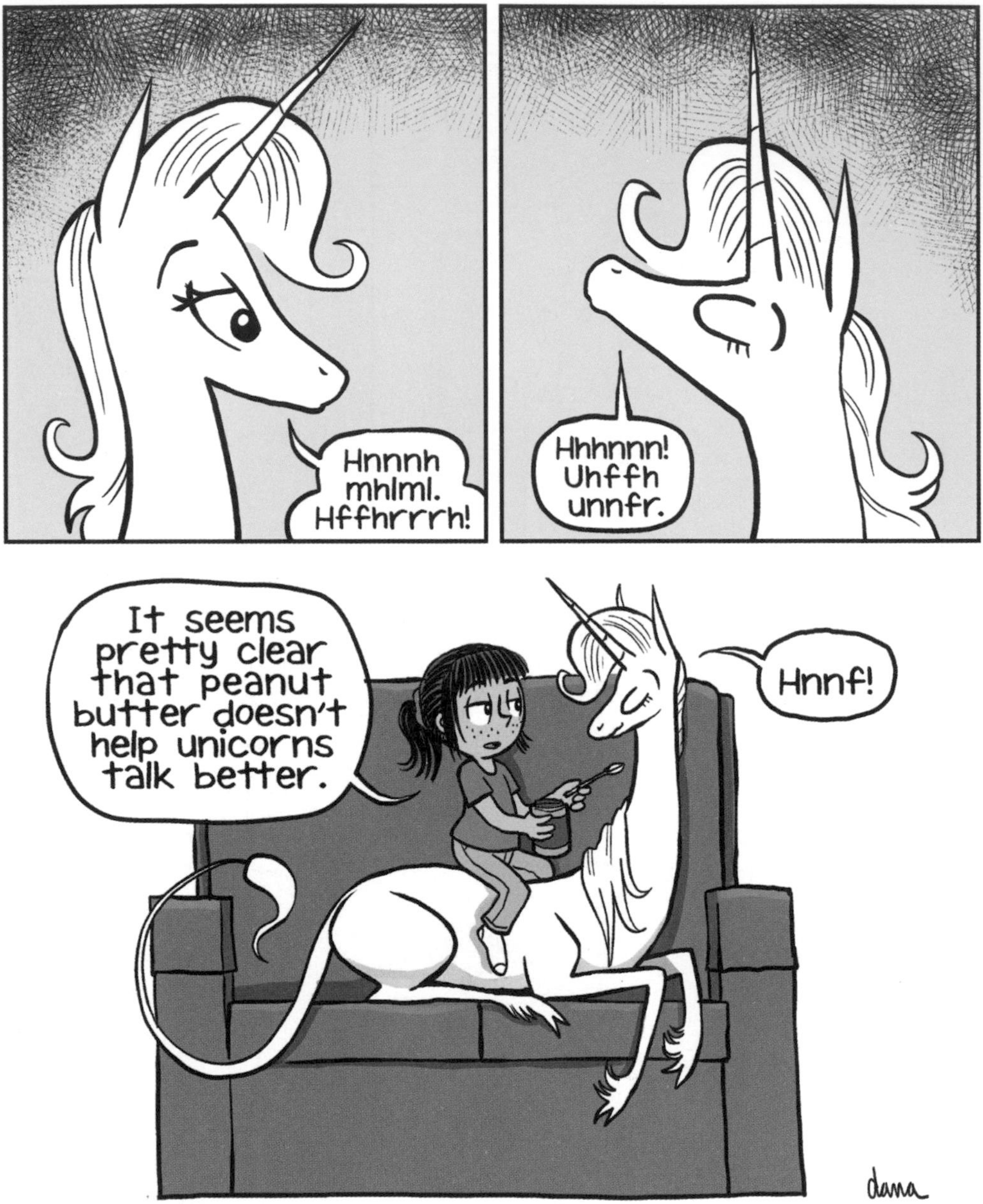
Hnnnh mhlml. Hffhrrrh!
Hhhnnn! Uhffh unnfr.
It seems pretty clear that peanut butter doesn't help unicorns talk better.
Hnnf!
dana

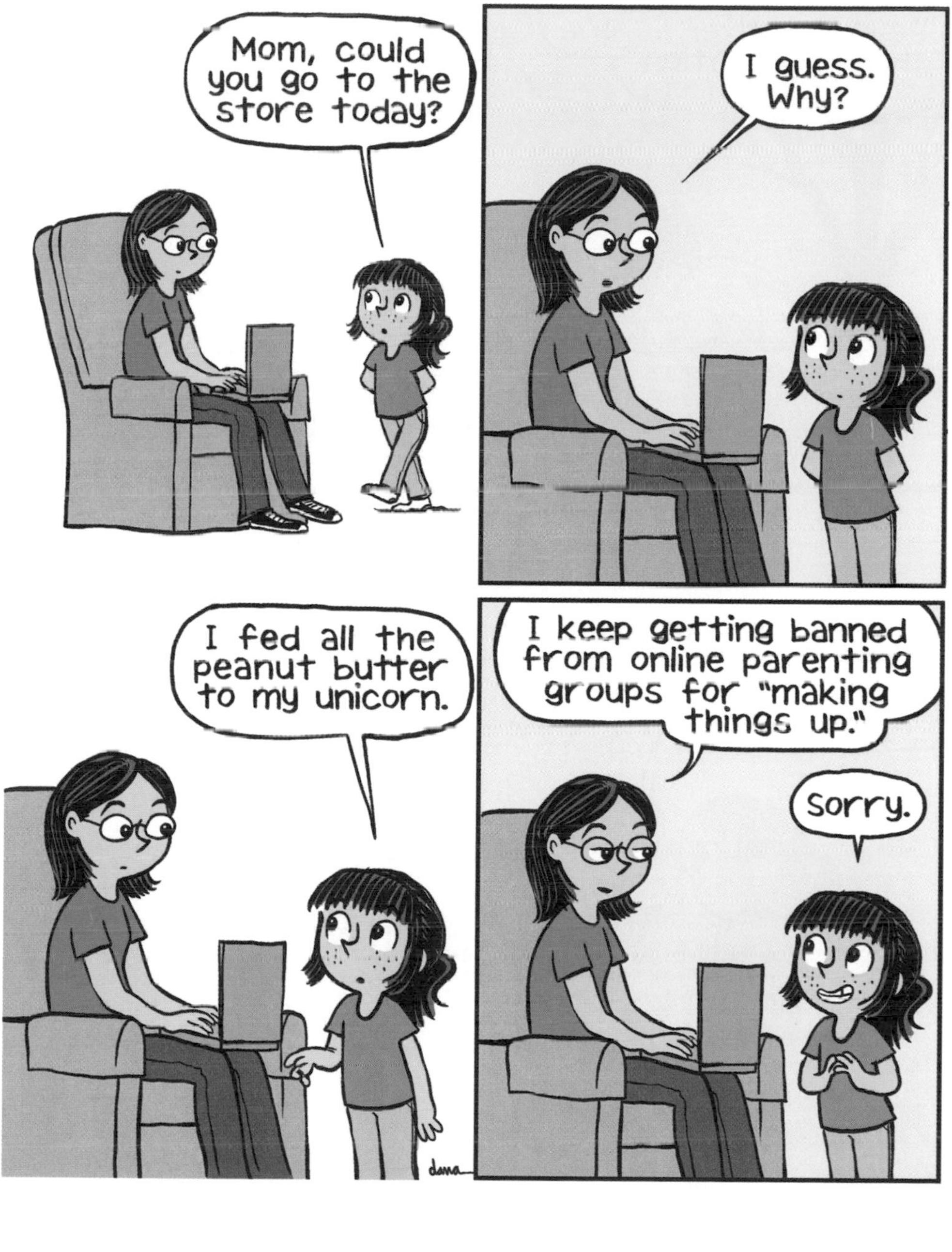
Mom, could you go to the store today?
I guess. Why?
I fed all the peanut butter to my unicorn.
I keep getting banned from online parenting groups for "making things up."
Sorry.
dana

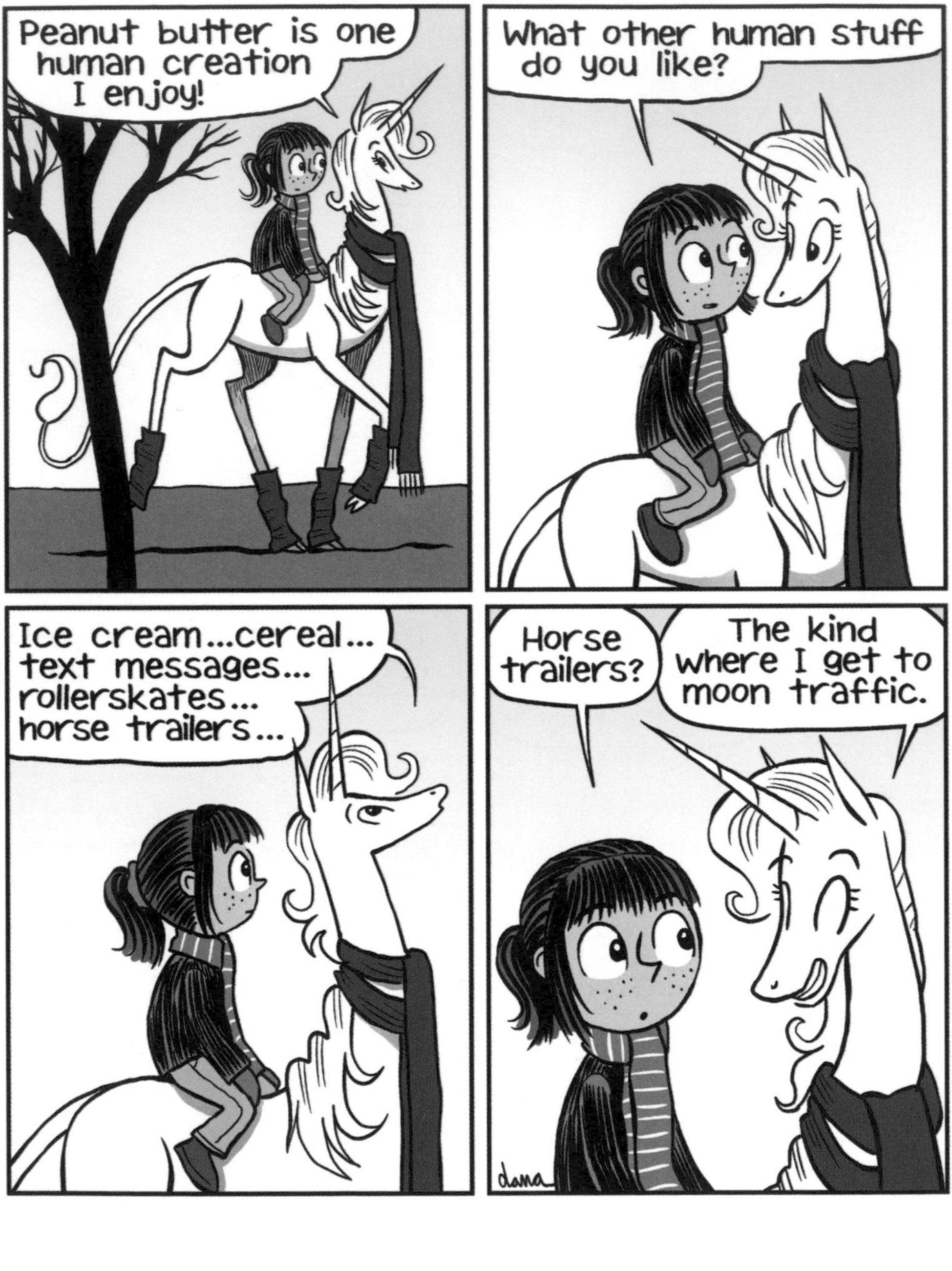
Peanut butter is one human creation I enjoy!
What other human stuff do you like?
Ice cream...cereal... text messages... rollerskates... horse trailers...
Horse trailers?
The kind where I get to moon traffic.
dana

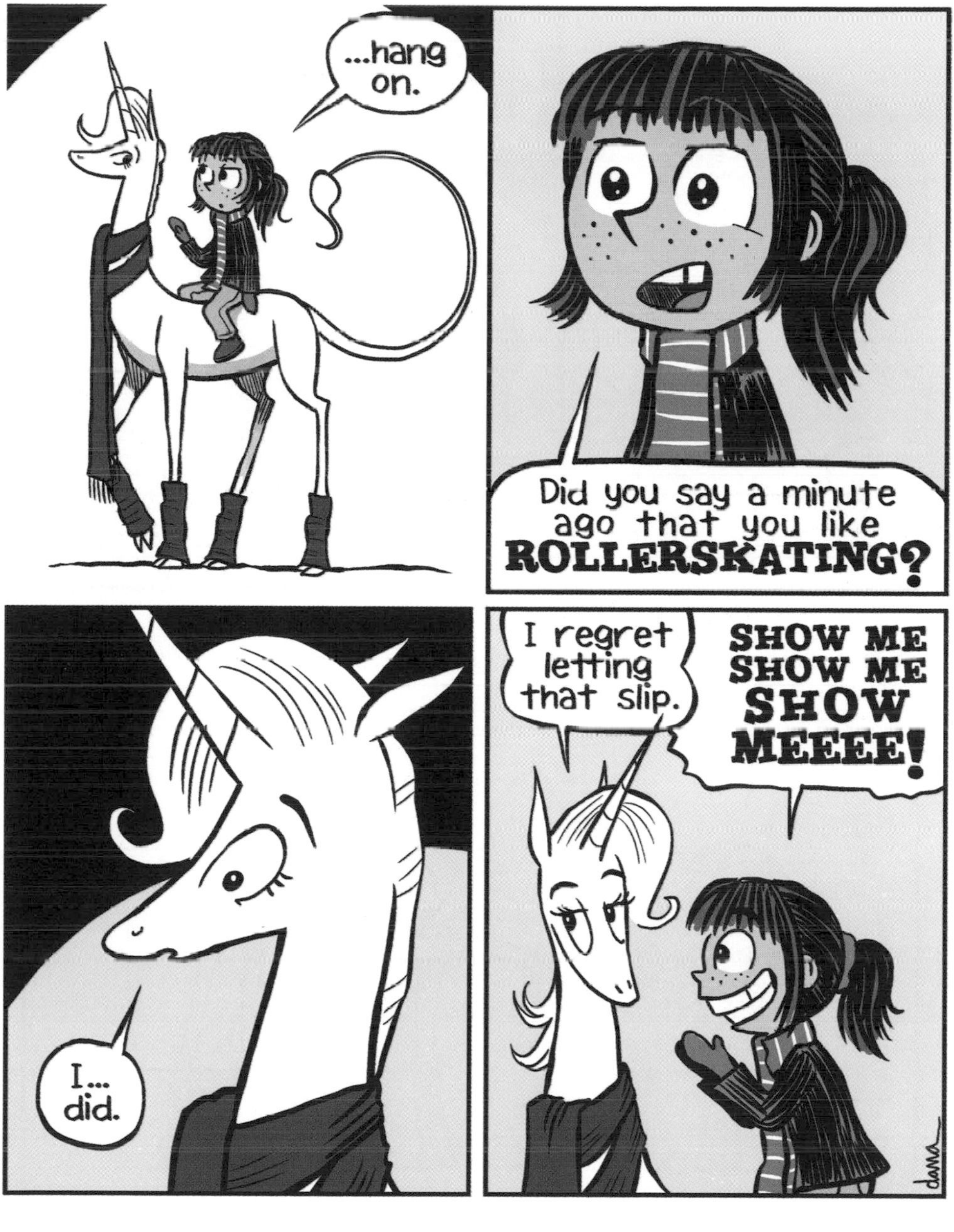
...hang on.
Did you say a minute ago that you like ROLLERSKATING?
I... did.
I regret letting that slip.
SHOW ME SHOW ME SHOW MEEEE!
dana

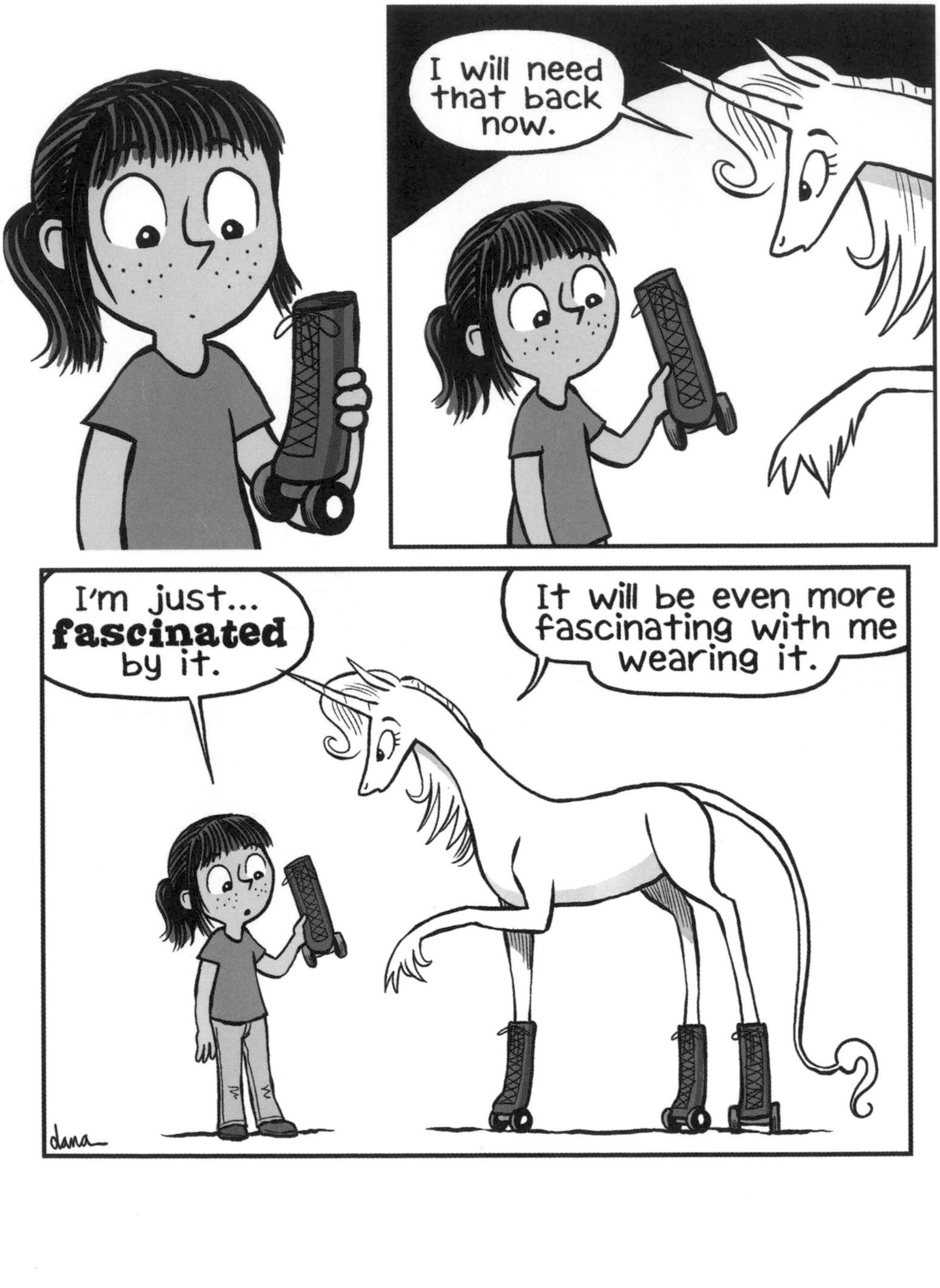
I will need that back now.
I'm just... **fascinated** by it.
It will be even more fascinating with me wearing it.
dana

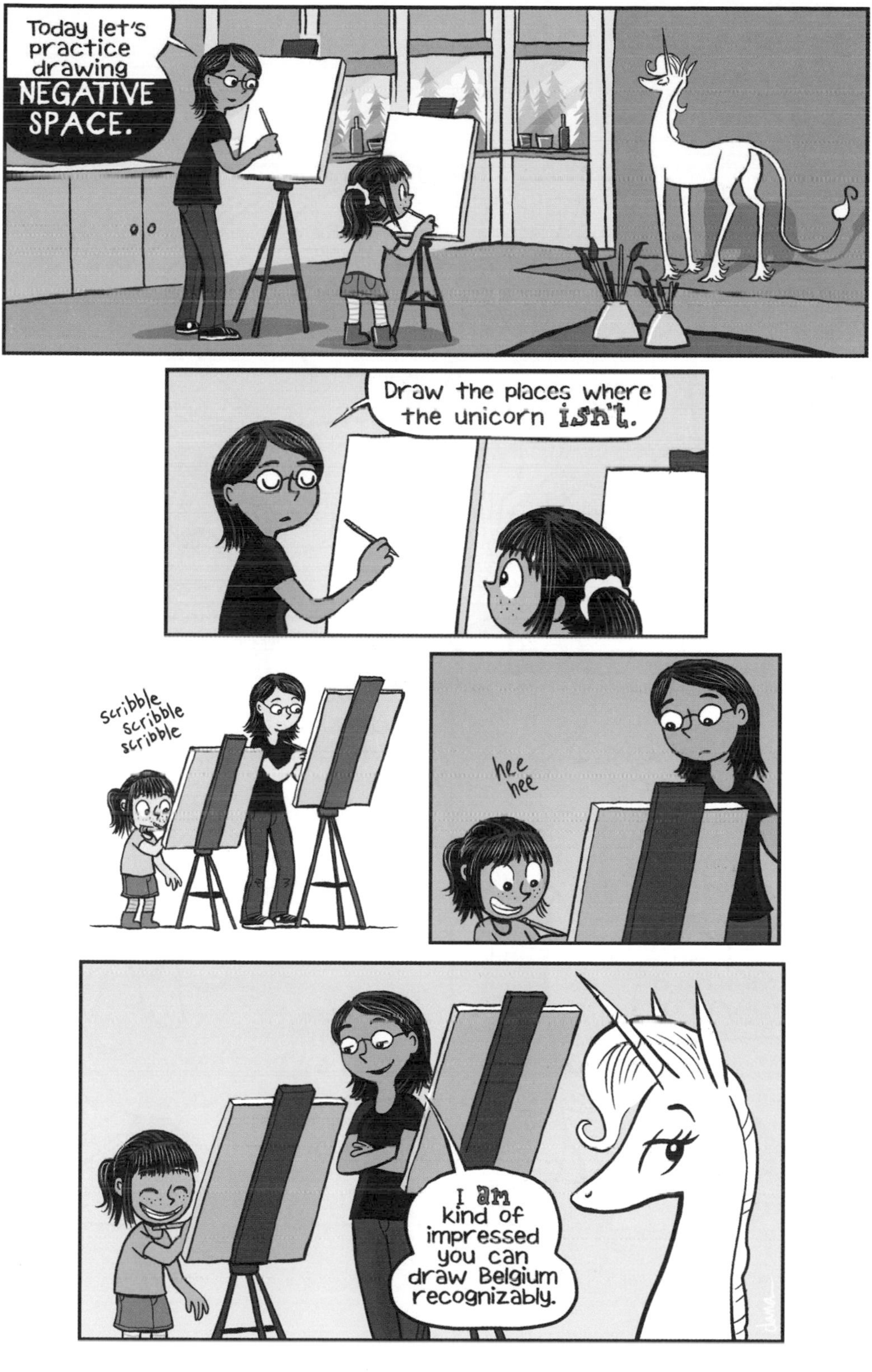
Today let's practice drawing NEGATIVE SPACE.
Draw the places where the unicorn isn't.
scribble scribble scribble
hee hee
I am kind of impressed you can draw Belgium recognizably.

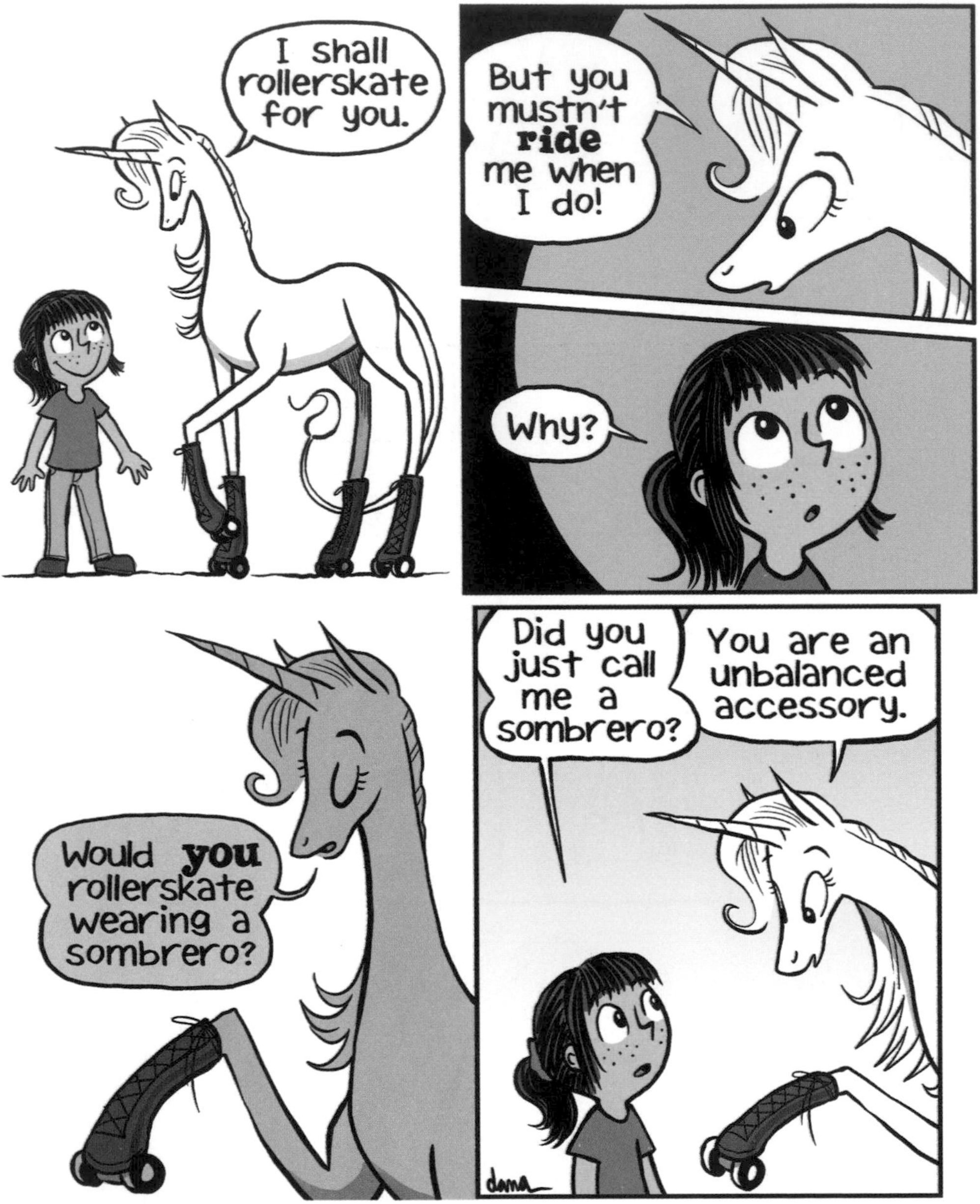
I shall rollerskate for you.
But you mustn't **ride** me when I do!
Why?
Would **you** rollerskate wearing a sombrero?
Did you just call me a sombrero?
You are an unbalanced accessory.
dana

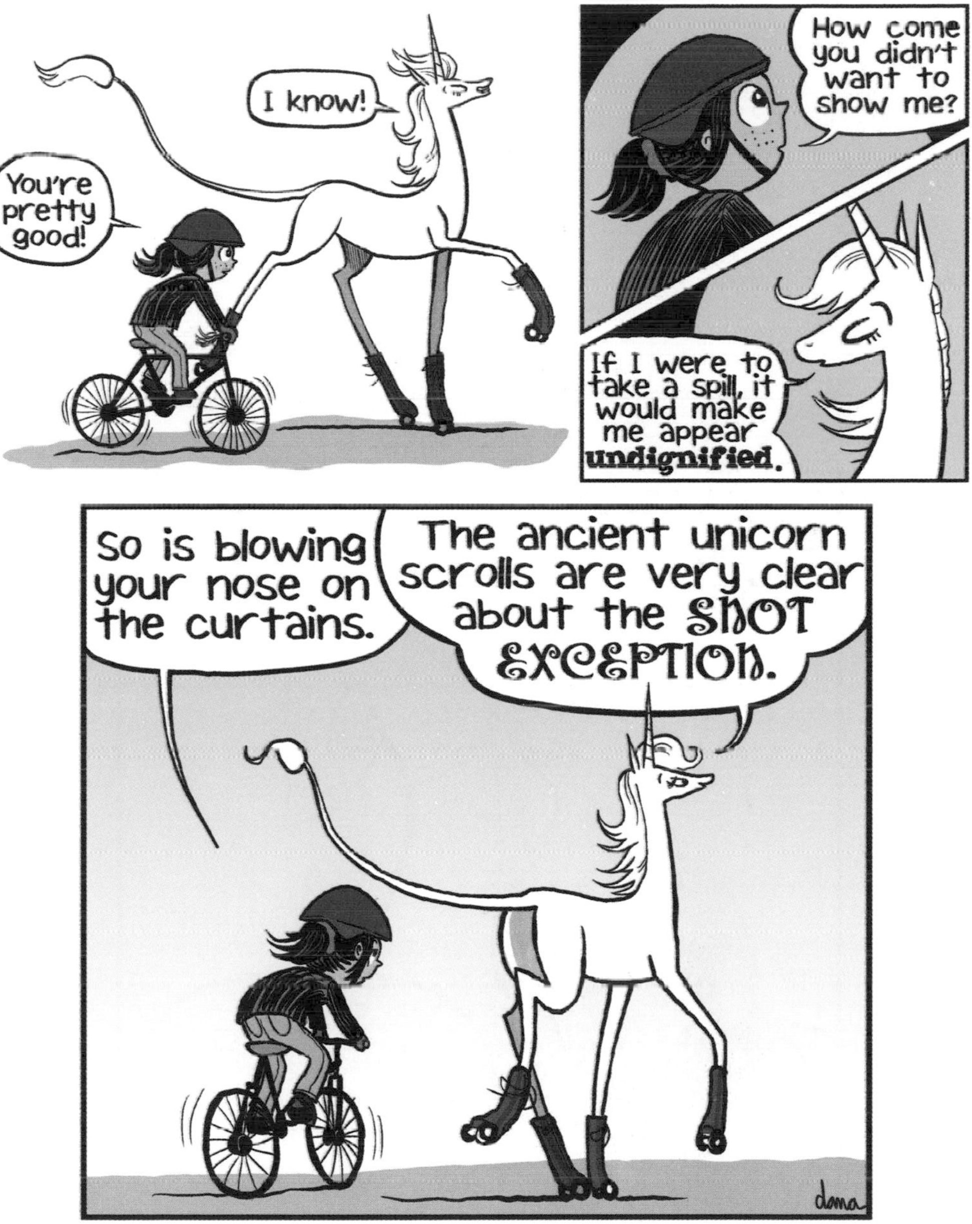
I know!
You're pretty good!
How come you didn't want to show me?
If I were to take a spill, it would make me appear **undignified**.
The ancient unicorn scrolls are very clear about the SNOT EXCEPTION.
So is blowing your nose on the curtains.
dana

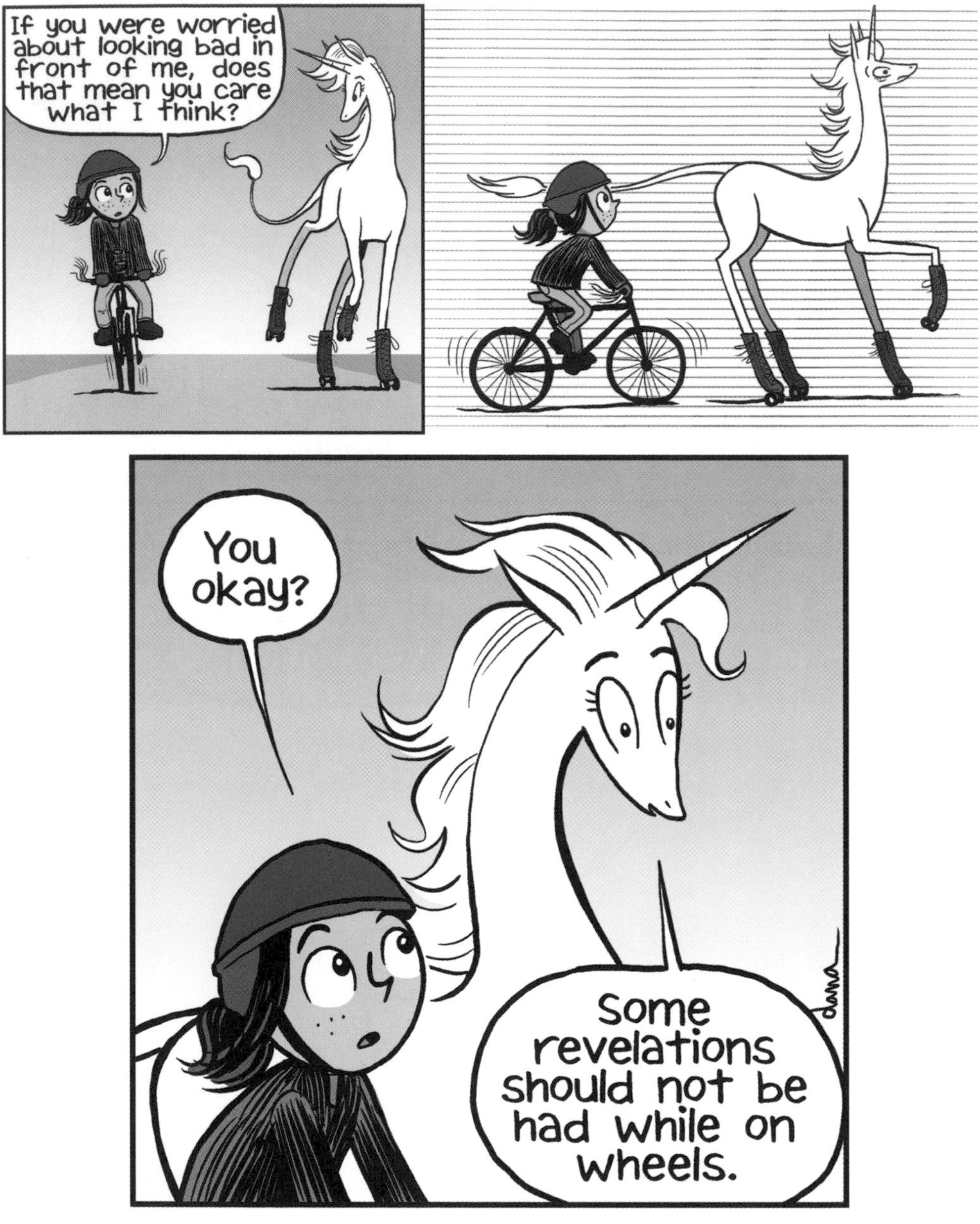
If you were worried about looking bad in front of me, does that mean you care what I think?
You okay?
Some revelations should not be had while on wheels.
dana

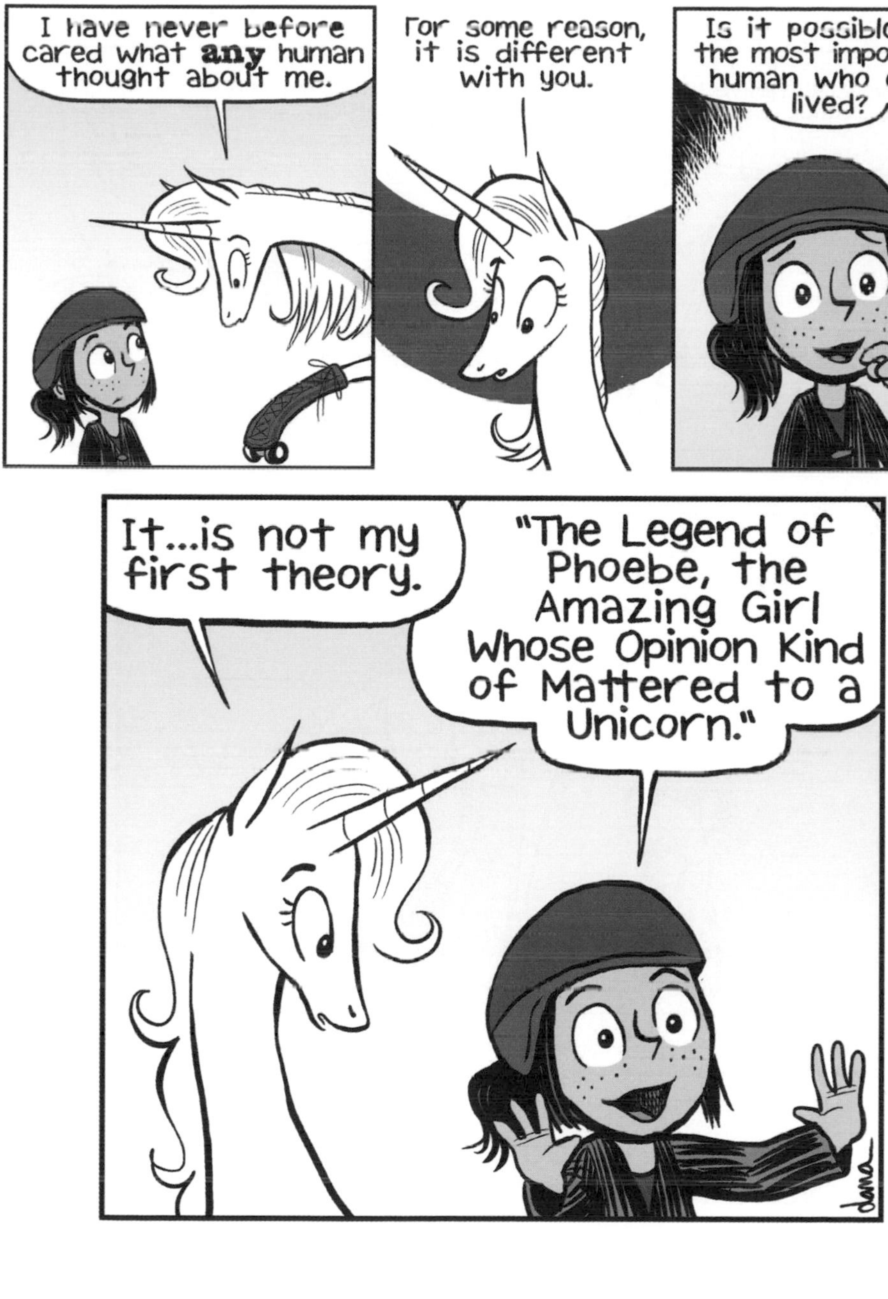
I have never before cared what **any** human thought about me.
For some reason, it is different with you.
Is it possible I'm the most important human who ever lived?
It...is not my first theory.
"The Legend of Phoebe, the Amazing Girl Whose Opinion Kind of Mattered to a Unicorn."
dana

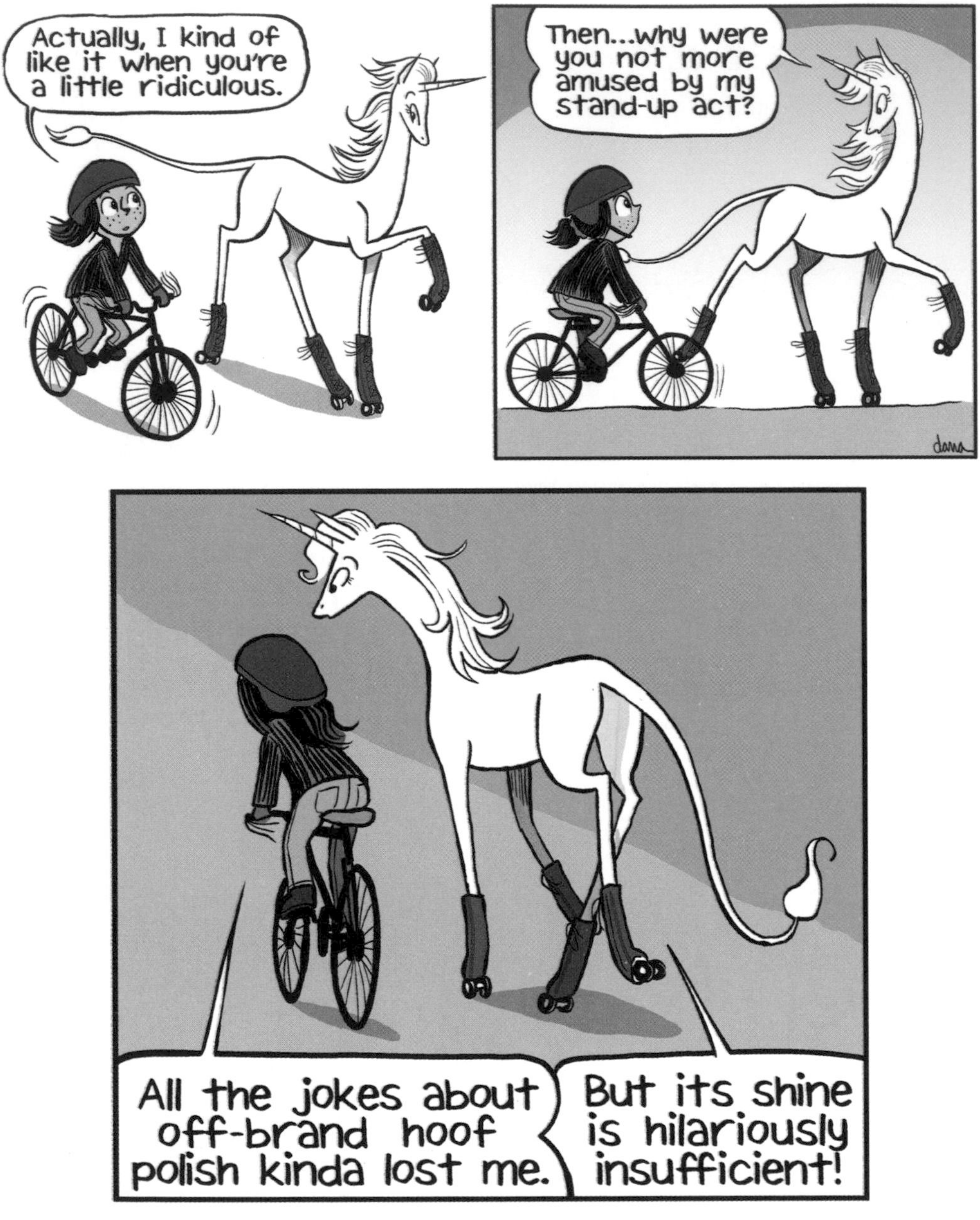
Actually, I kind of like it when you're a little ridiculous.
Then...why were you not more amused by my stand-up act?
All the jokes about off-brand hoof polish kinda lost me.
But its shine is hilariously insufficient!

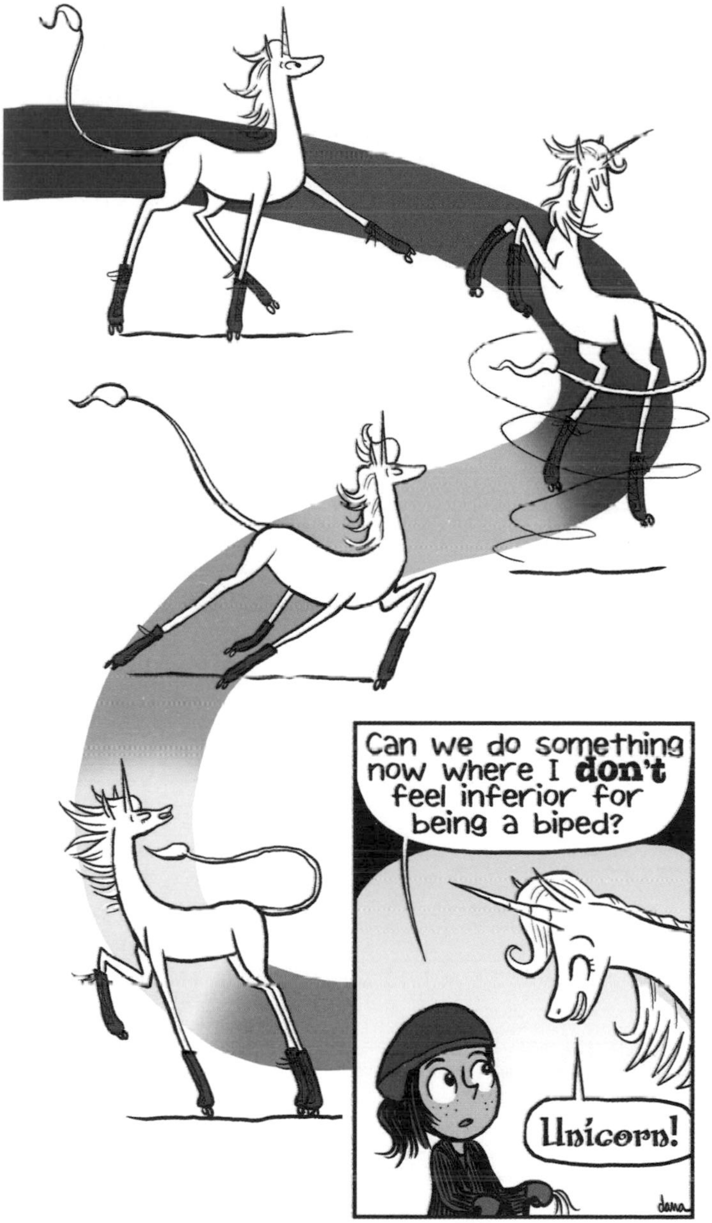
Can we do something now where I **don't** feel inferior for being a biped?
Unicorn!
dana

Go, Boysenberry Swirl, and open the gates of Glitter City!

Why are you giving orders?

'Cause I'm playing Princess Sunbeam.

In **real** unicorn government, "Princess" is strictly a ceremonial position.

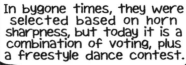

The QUORUM of the POINTIEST makes most of the **real** decisions.

In bygone times, they were selected based on horn sharpness, but today it is a combination of voting, plus a freestyle dance contest.

Also the gates are over on your side.

I should open them then.

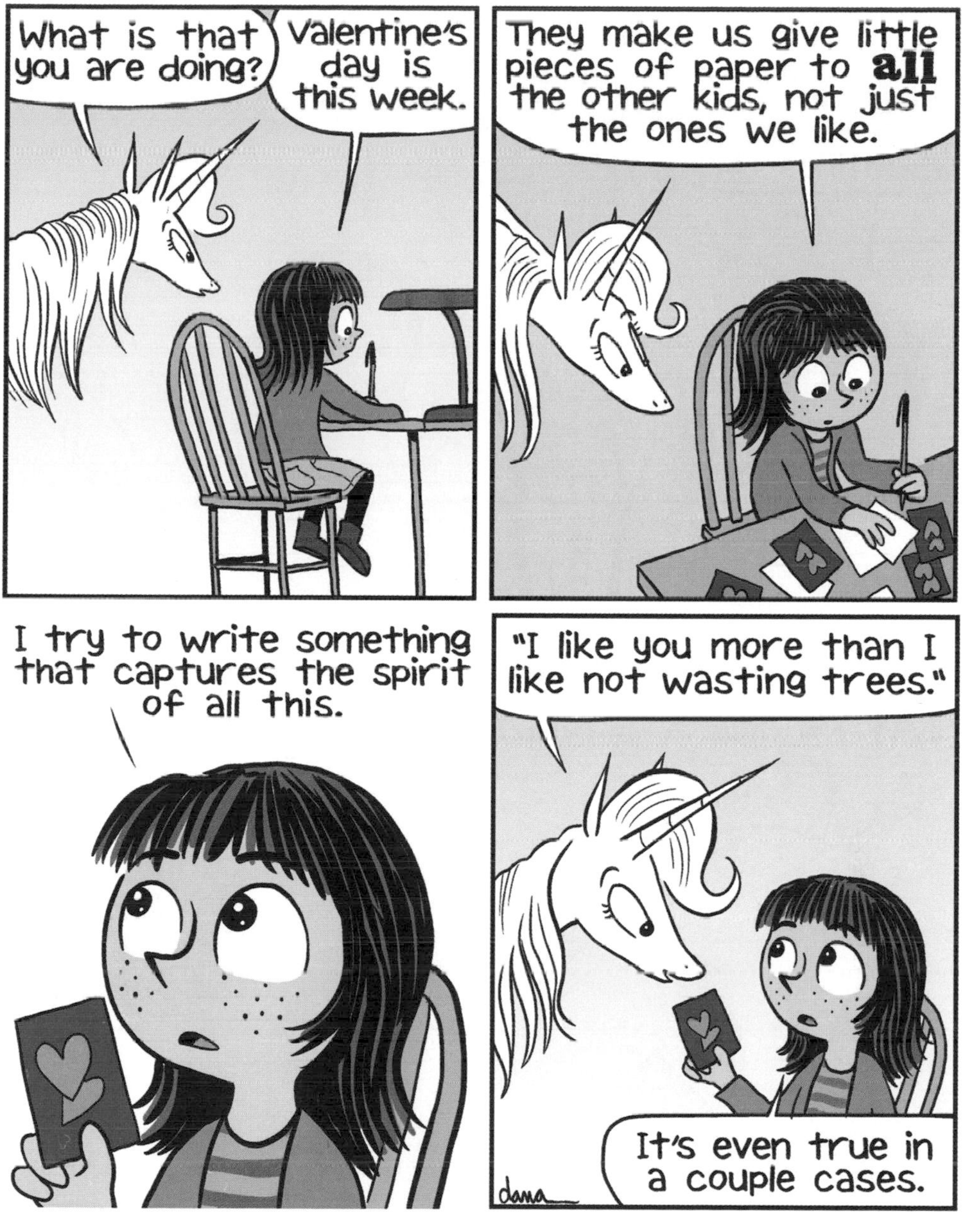
What is that you are doing?
Valentine's day is this week.
They make us give little pieces of paper to **all** the other kids, not just the ones we like.
I try to write something that captures the spirit of all this.
"I like you more than I like not wasting trees."
It's even true in a couple cases.
dana

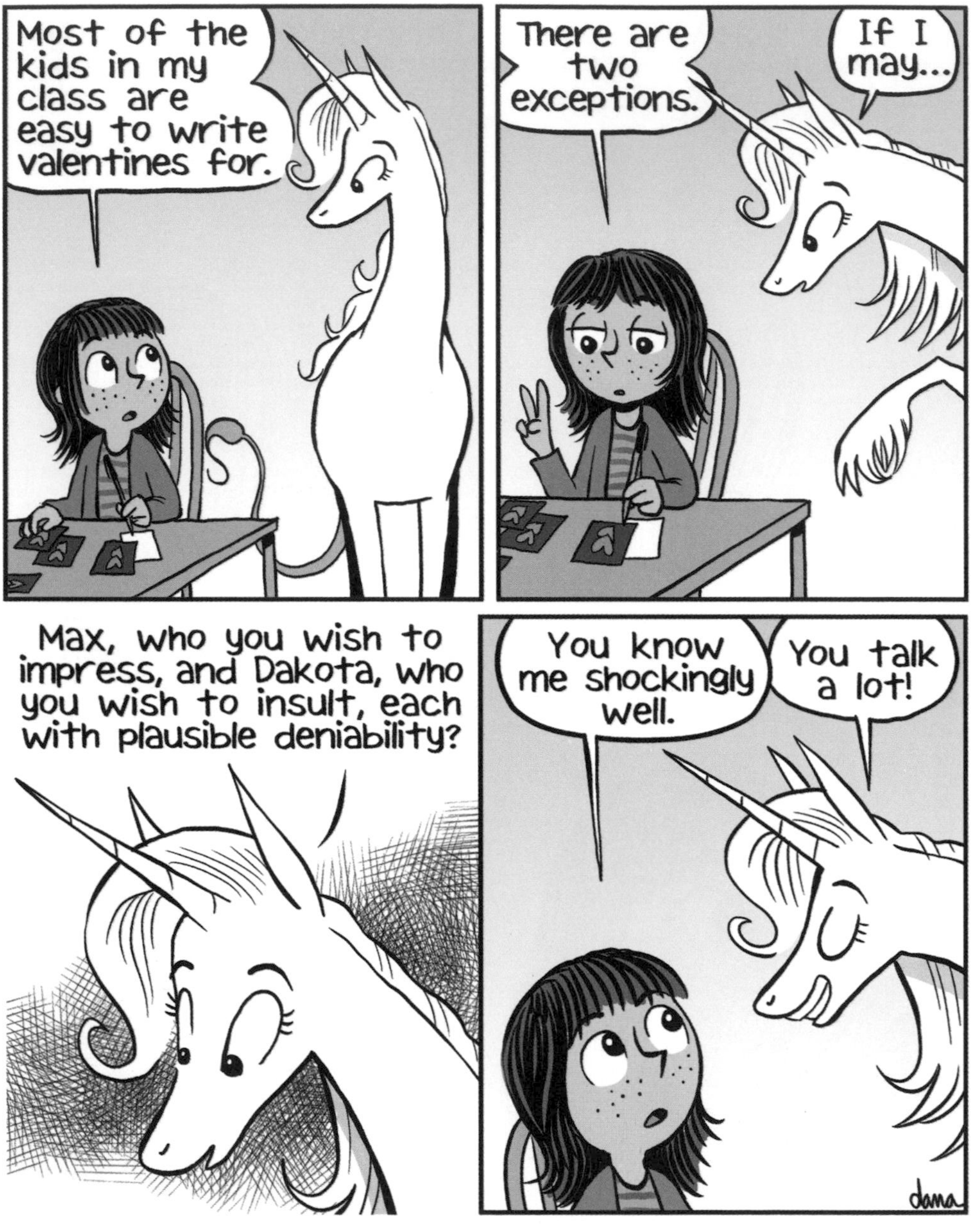
Most of the kids in my class are easy to write valentines for.
There are two exceptions.
If I may...
Max, who you wish to impress, and Dakota, who you wish to insult, each with plausible deniability?
You know me shockingly well.
You talk a lot!
dana

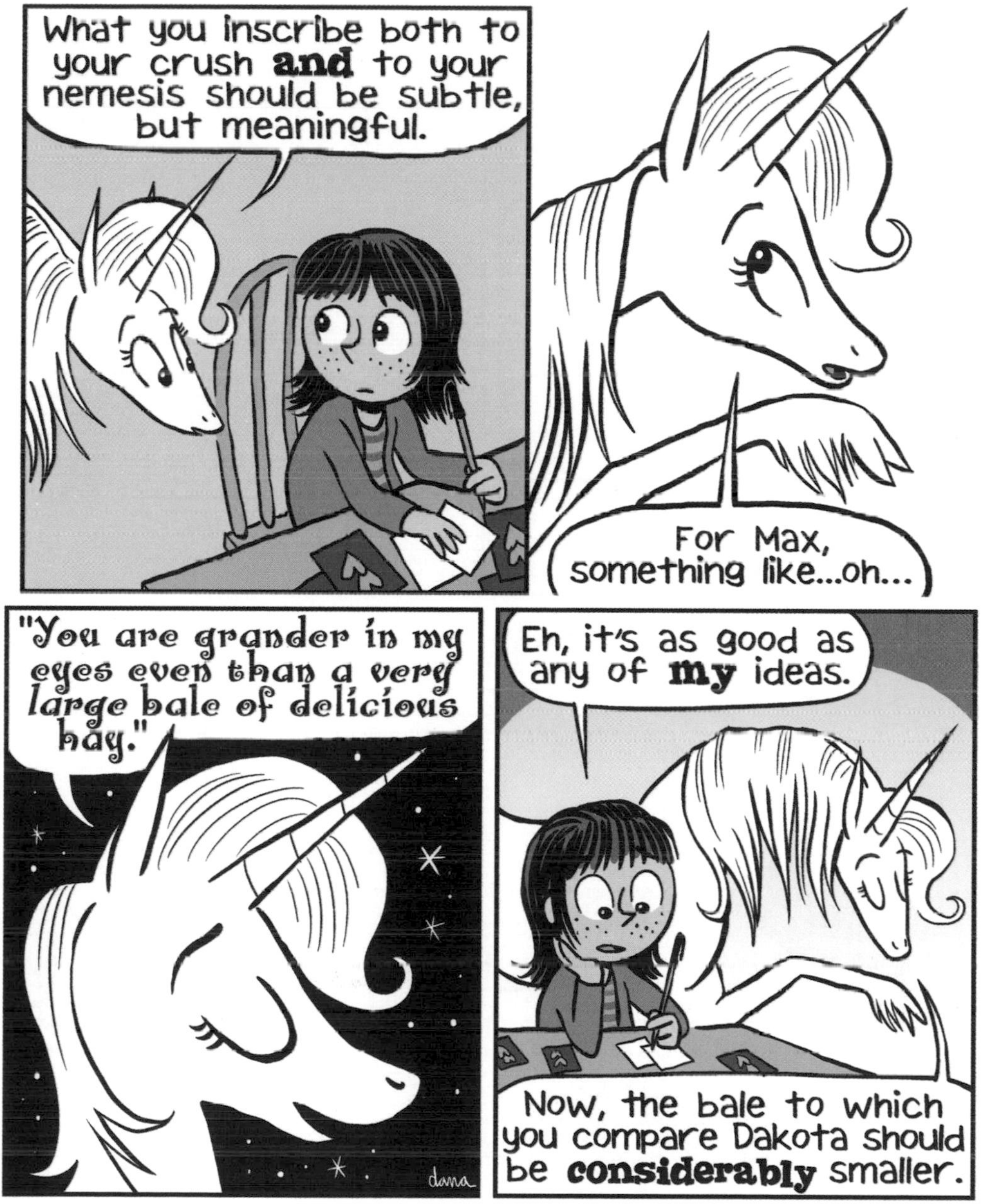
What you inscribe both to your crush **and** to your nemesis should be subtle, but meaningful.
For Max, something like...oh...
"You are grander in my eyes even than a very large bale of delicious hay."
dana
Eh, it's as good as any of **my** ideas.
Now, the bale to which you compare Dakota should be **considerably** smaller.

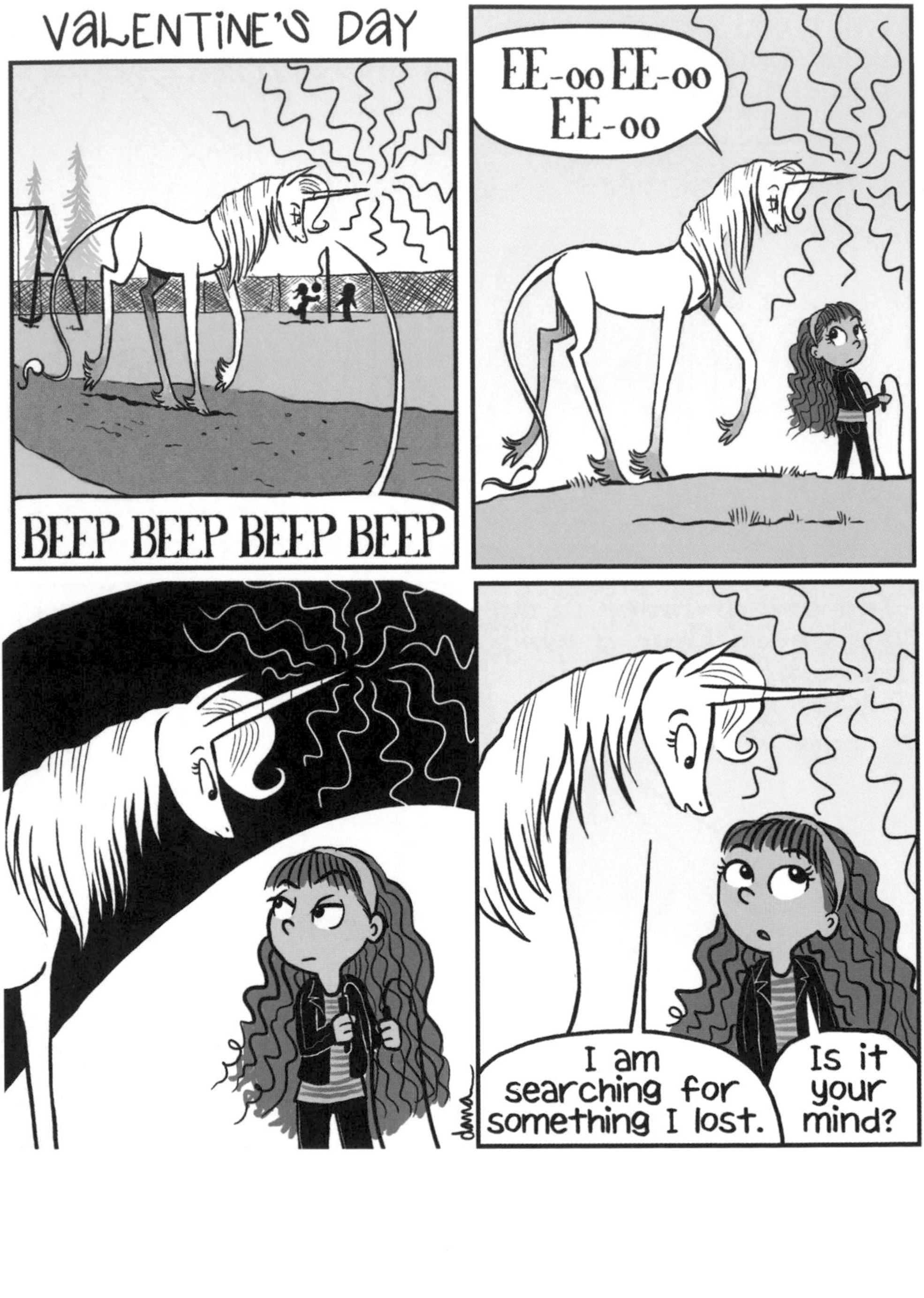
VALENTINE'S DAY
BEEP BEEP BEEP BEEP
EE-oo EE-oo EE-oo
I am searching for something I lost.
Is it your mind?
dana

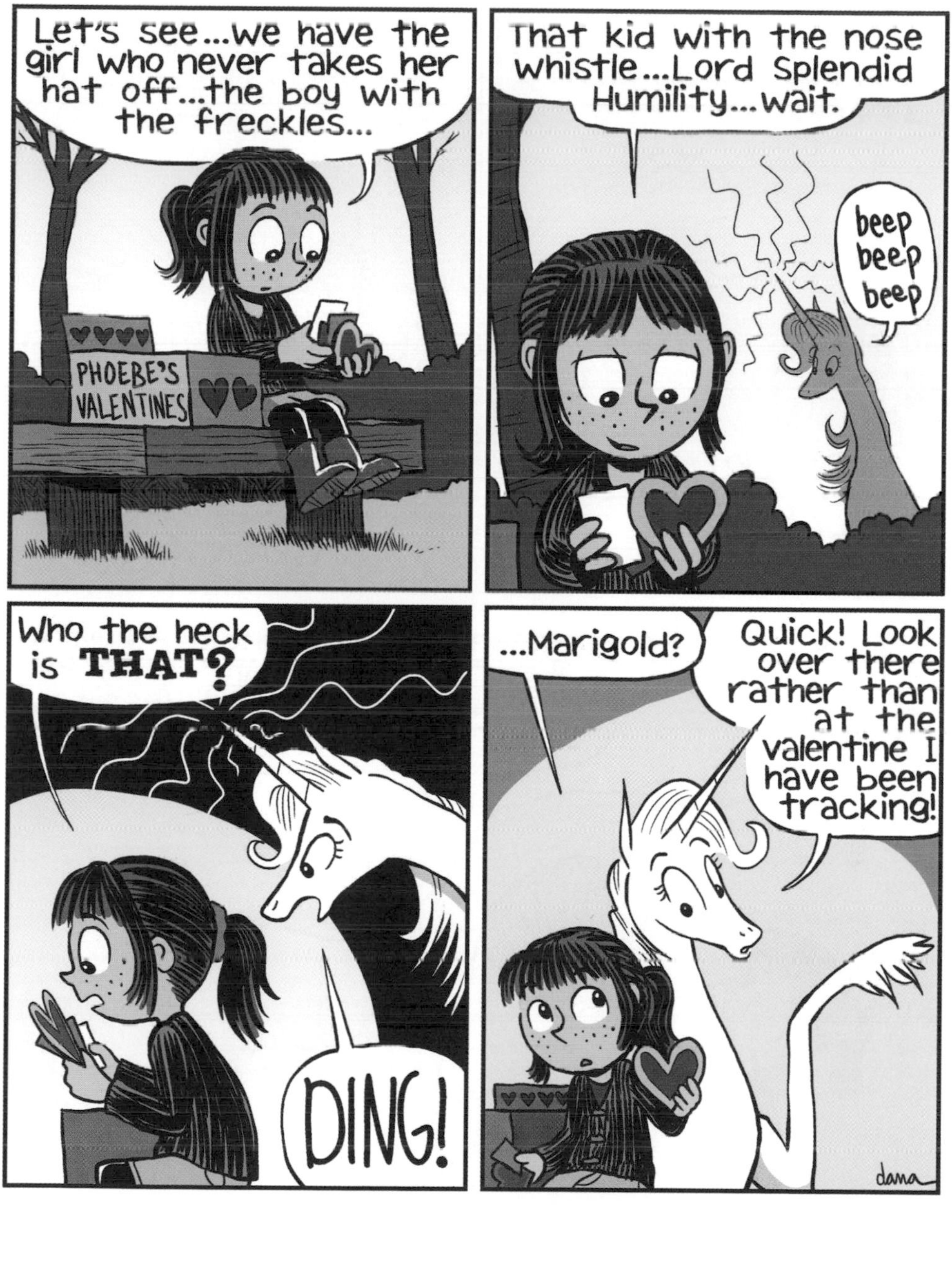
Let's see...we have the girl who never takes her hat off...the boy with the freckles...
PHOEBE'S VALENTINES
That kid with the nose whistle...Lord Splendid Humility...wait.
beep beep beep
Who the heck is **THAT?**
DING!
...Marigold?
Quick! Look over there rather than at the valentine I have been tracking!
dana

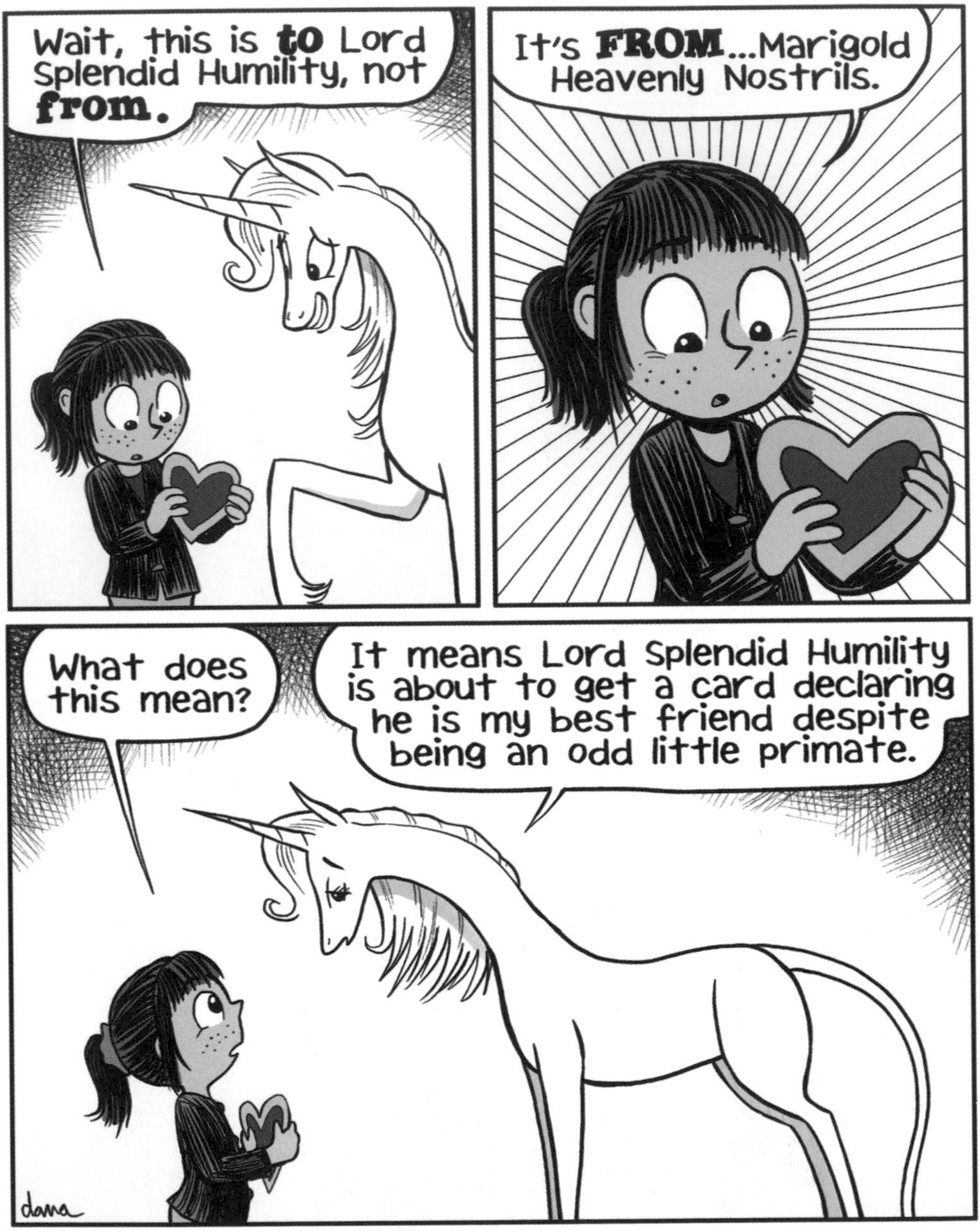
Wait, this is to Lord Splendid Humility, not from.
It's FROM...Marigold Heavenly Nostrils.
What does this mean?
It means Lord Splendid Humility is about to get a card declaring he is my best friend despite being an odd little primate.
dana

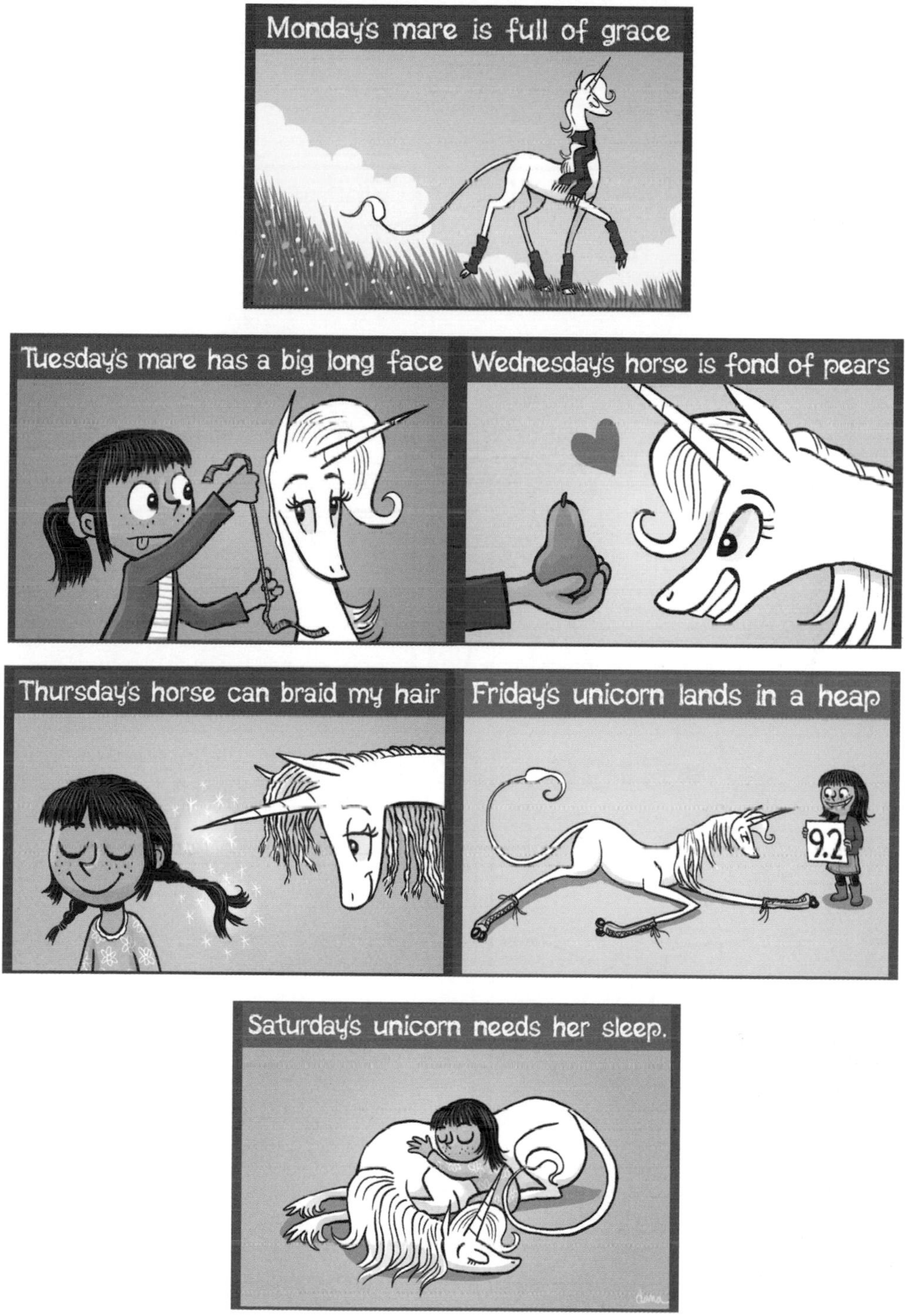
Monday's mare is full of grace
Tuesday's mare has a big long face
Wednesday's horse is fond of pears
Thursday's horse can braid my hair
Friday's unicorn lands in a heap
9.2
Saturday's unicorn needs her sleep.

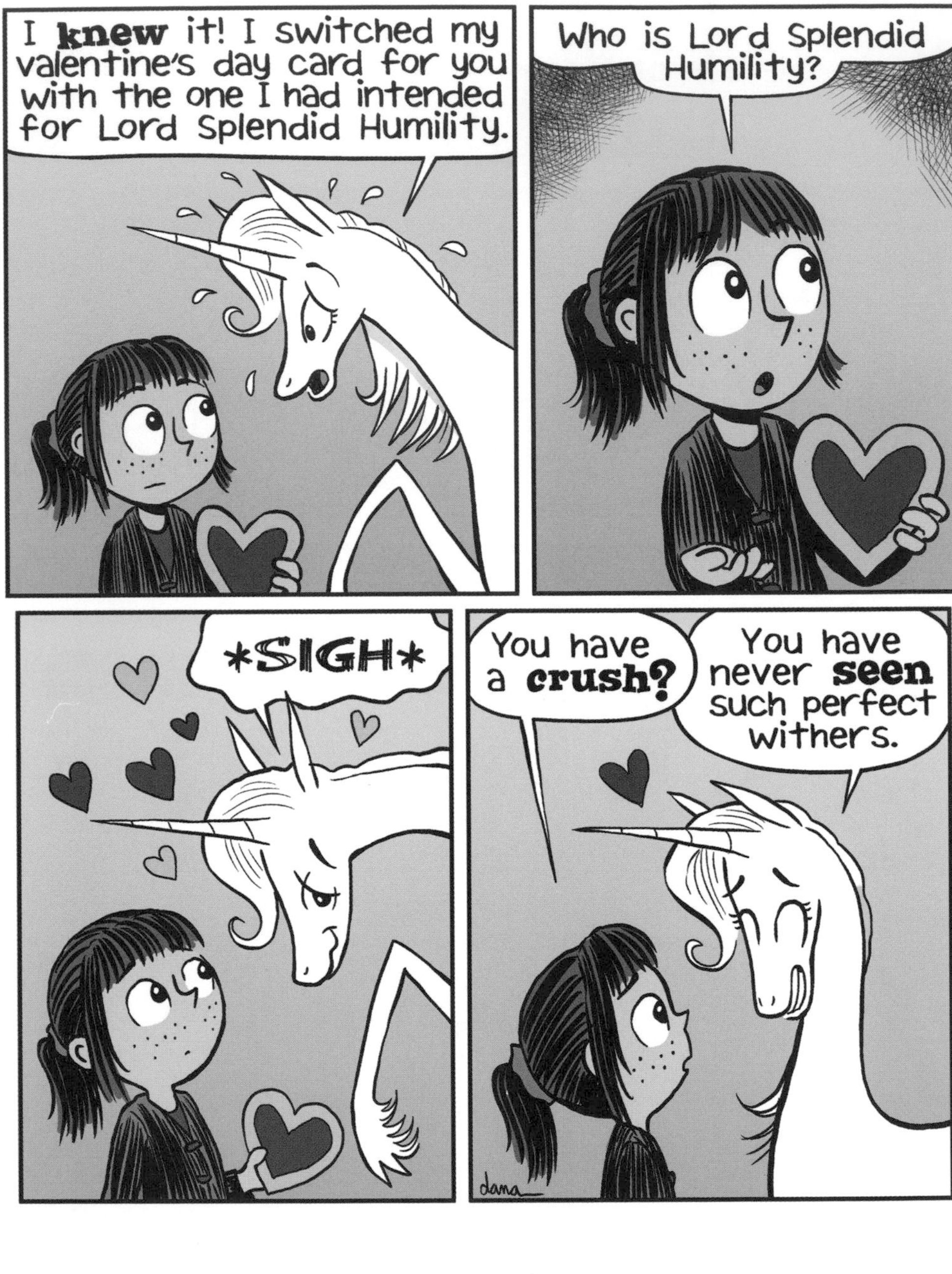
I **knew** it! I switched my valentine's day card for you with the one I had intended for Lord Splendid Humility.
Who is Lord Splendid Humility?
SIGH
You have a **crush?**
You have never **seen** such perfect withers.
dana

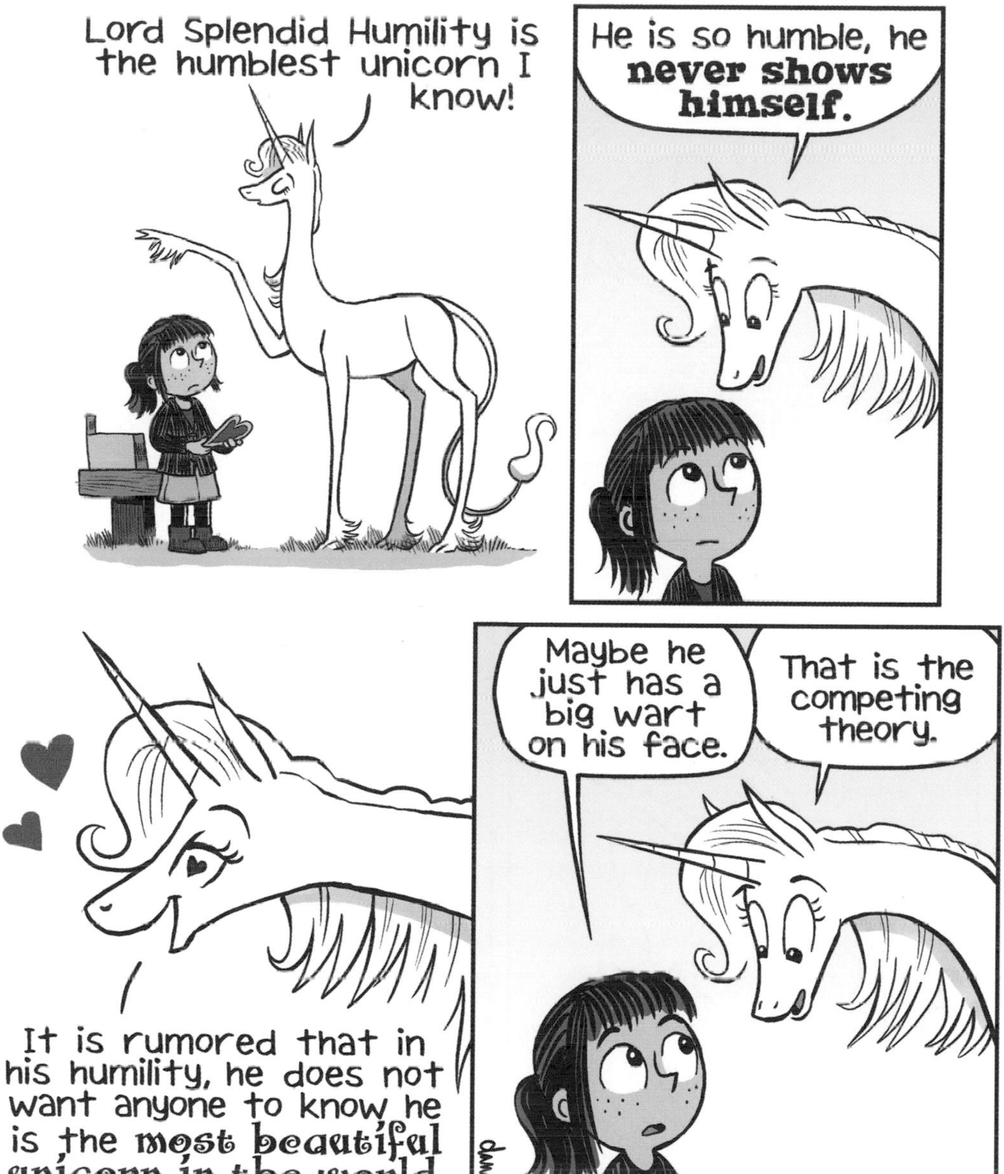

Lord Splendid Humility is the humblest unicorn I know!
He is so humble, he **never shows himself**.
It is rumored that in his humility, he does not want anyone to know he is the most beautiful unicorn in the world.
Maybe he just has a big wart on his face.
That is the competing theory.
dana

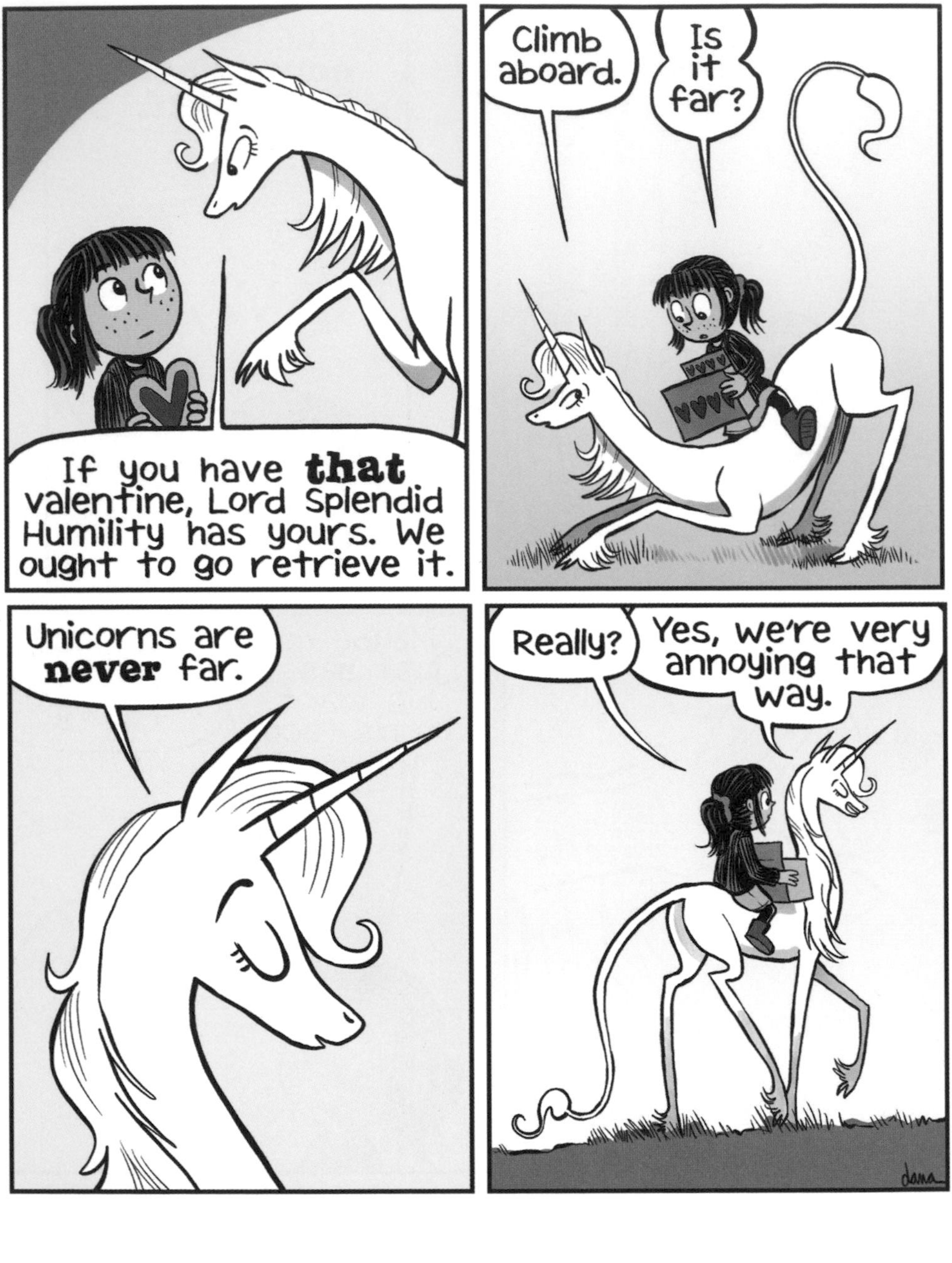

If you have **that** valentine, Lord Splendid Humility has yours. We ought to go retrieve it.
Climb aboard.
Is it far?
Unicorns are **never** far.
Really?
Yes, we're very annoying that way.
dana

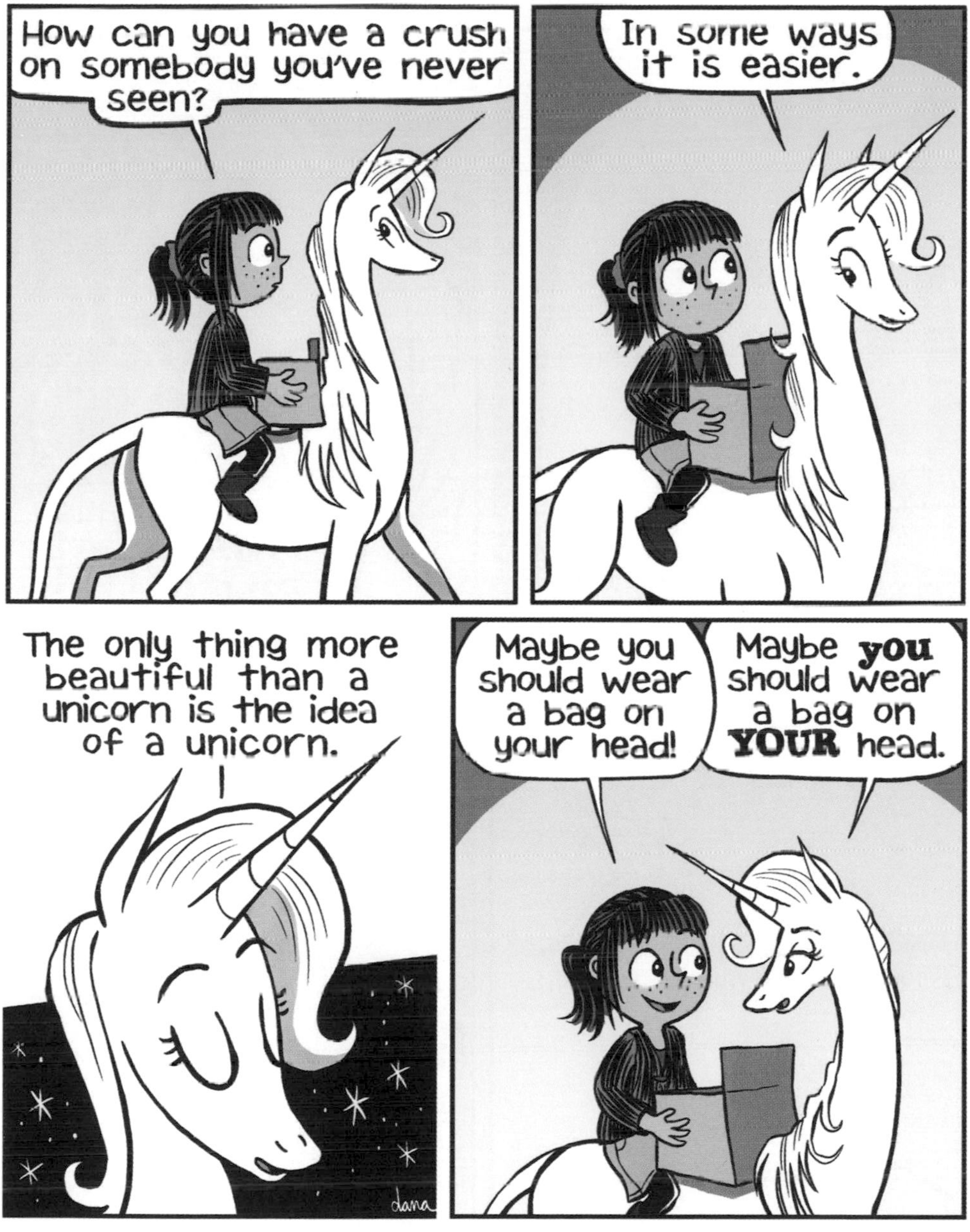
How can you have a crush on somebody you've never seen?
In some ways it is easier.
The only thing more beautiful than a unicorn is the idea of a unicorn.
Maybe you should wear a bag on your head!
Maybe **you** should wear a bag on **YOUR** head.
dana

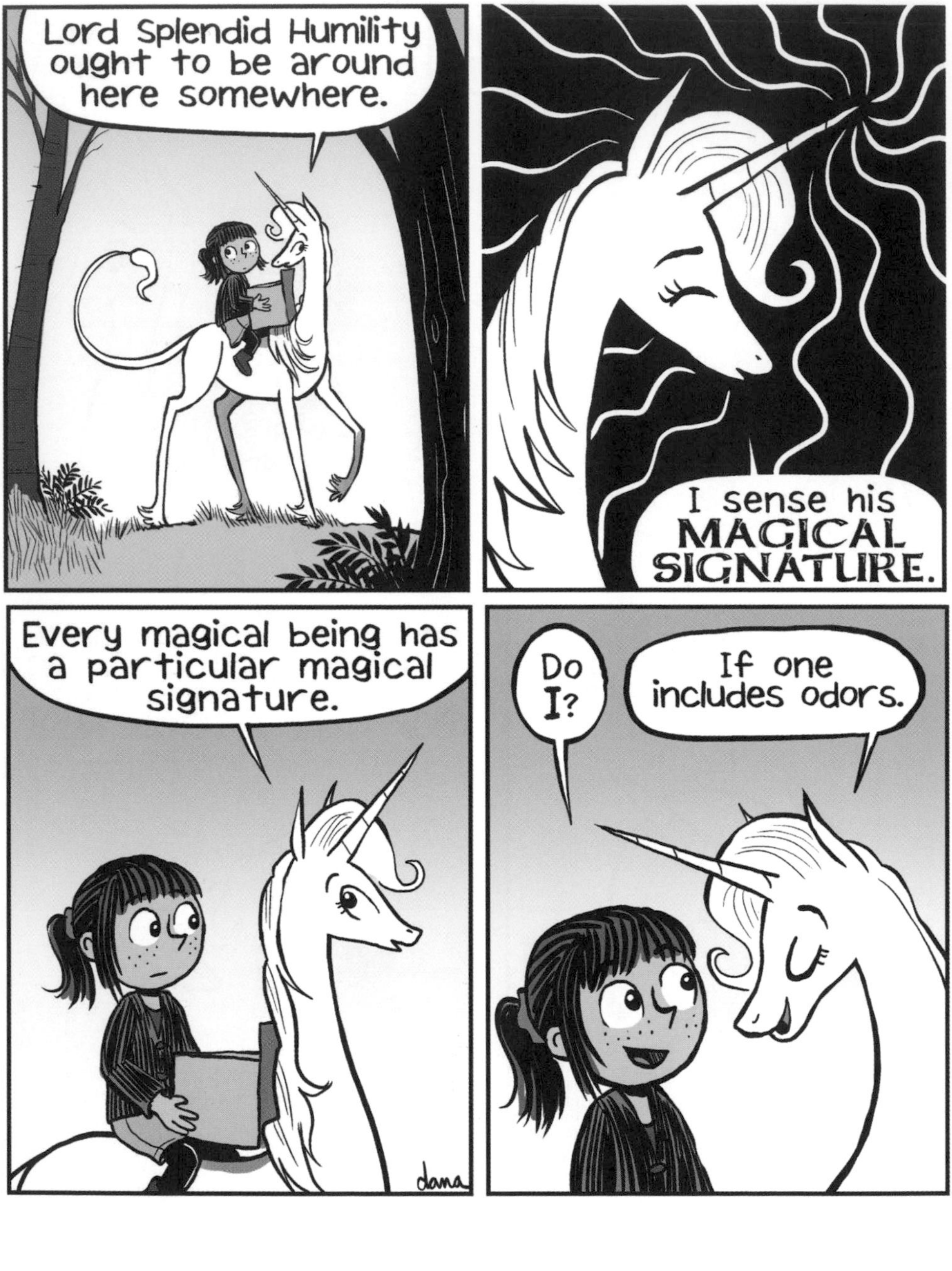

Lord Splendid Humility ought to be around here somewhere.
I sense his MAGICAL SIGNATURE.
Every magical being has a particular magical signature.
dana
Do I?
If one includes odors.

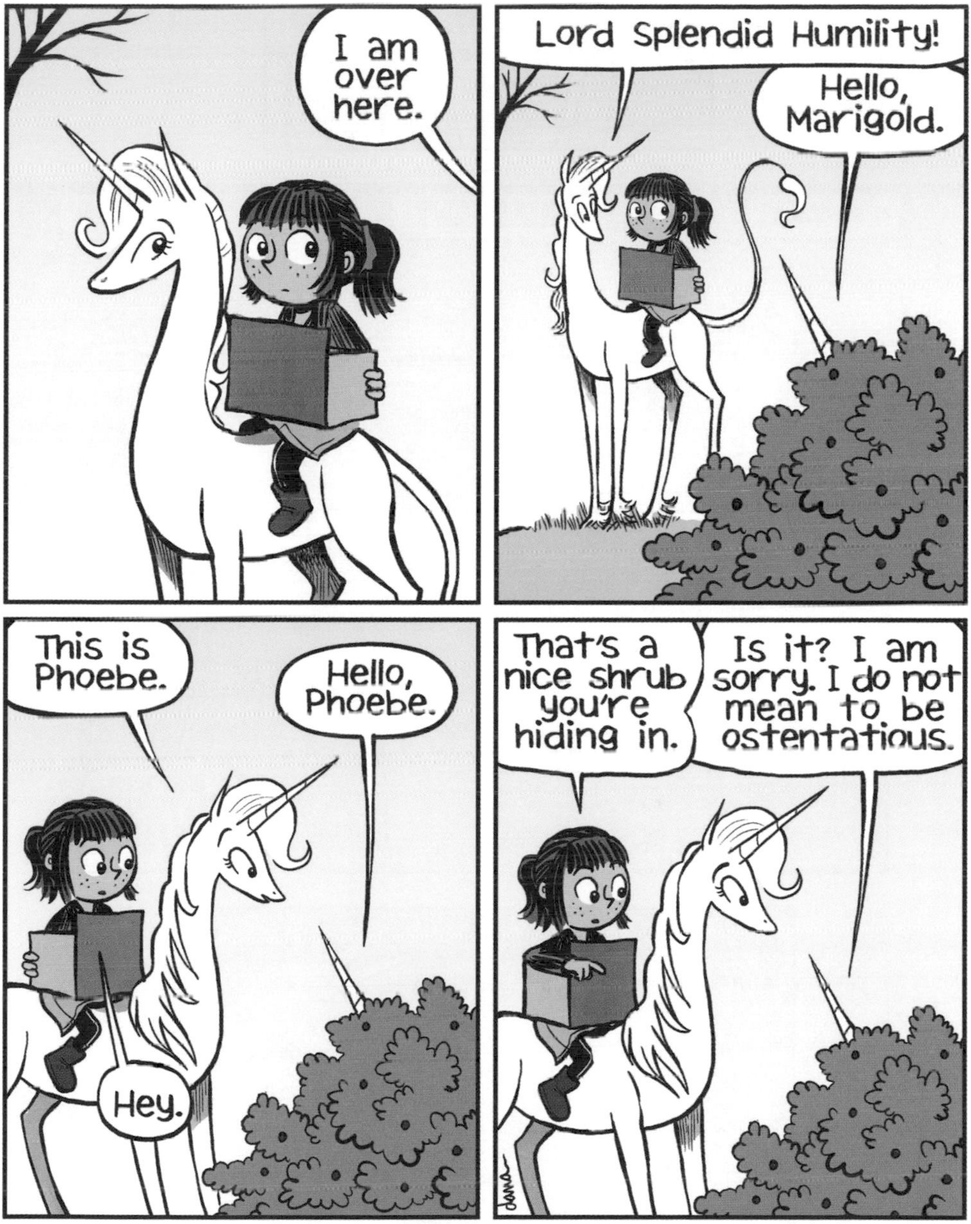
I am over here.
Lord Splendid Humility!
Hello, Marigold.
This is Phoebe.
Hello, Phoebe.
Hey.
That's a nice shrub you're hiding in.
Is it? I am sorry. I do not mean to be ostentatious.
dana

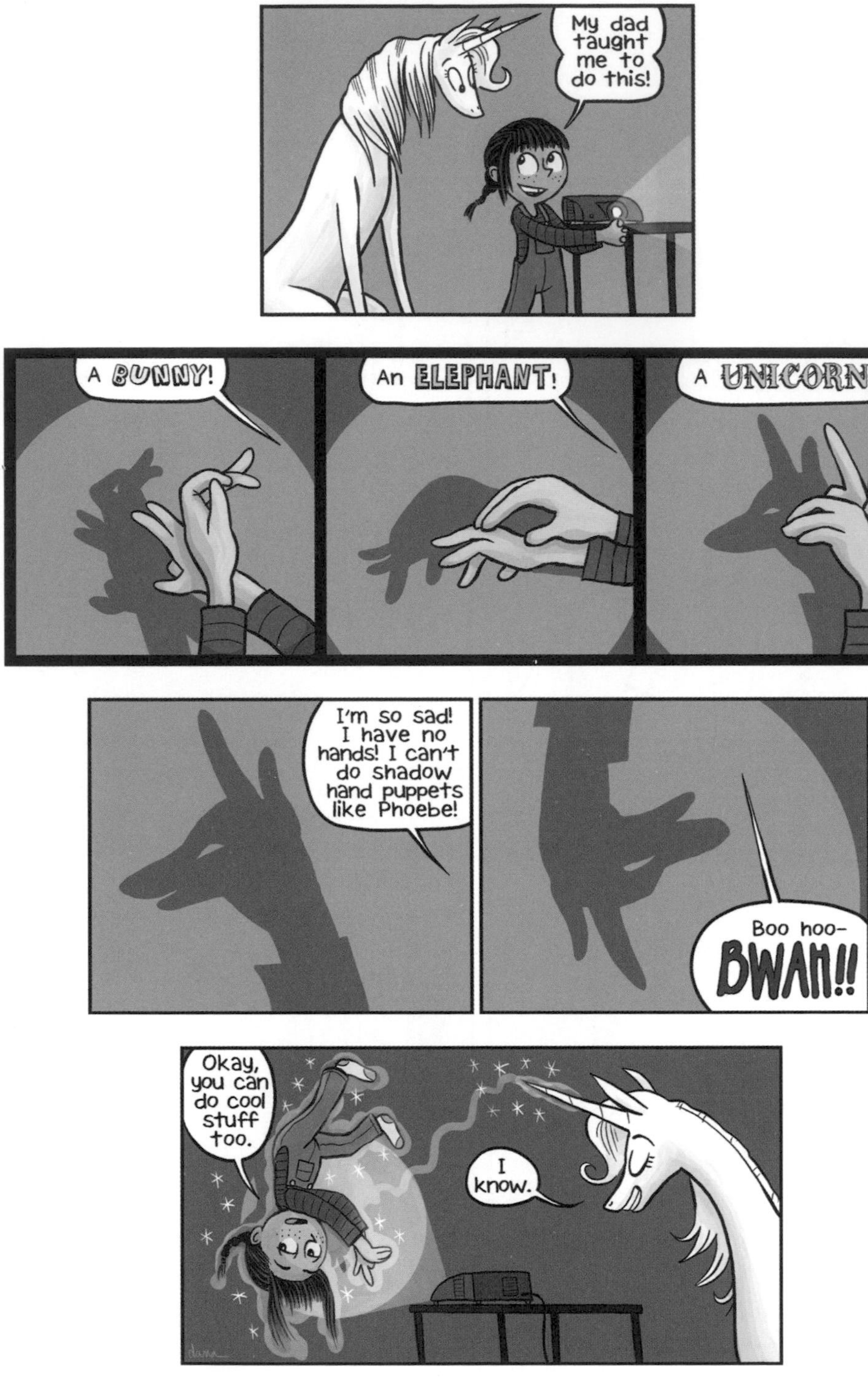
My dad taught me to do this!
A BUNNY!
An ELEPHANT!
A UNICORN!
I'm so sad! I have no hands! I can't do shadow hand puppets like Phoebe!
Boo hoo-
BWAH!!
Okay, you can do cool stuff too.
I know.

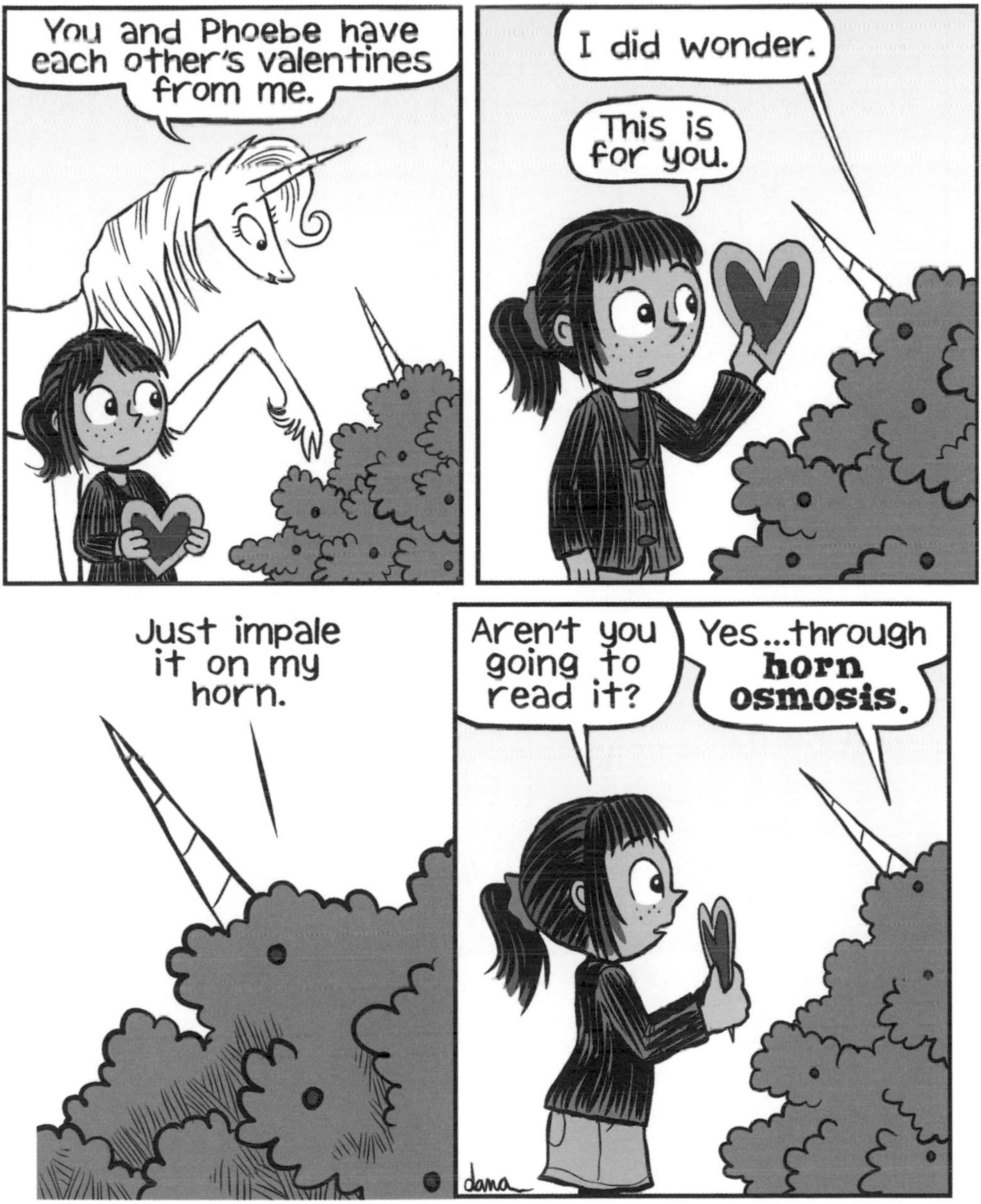
You and Phoebe have each other's valentines from me.
I did wonder.
This is for you.
Just impale it on my horn.
Aren't you going to read it?
Yes...through **horn osmosis**.
dana

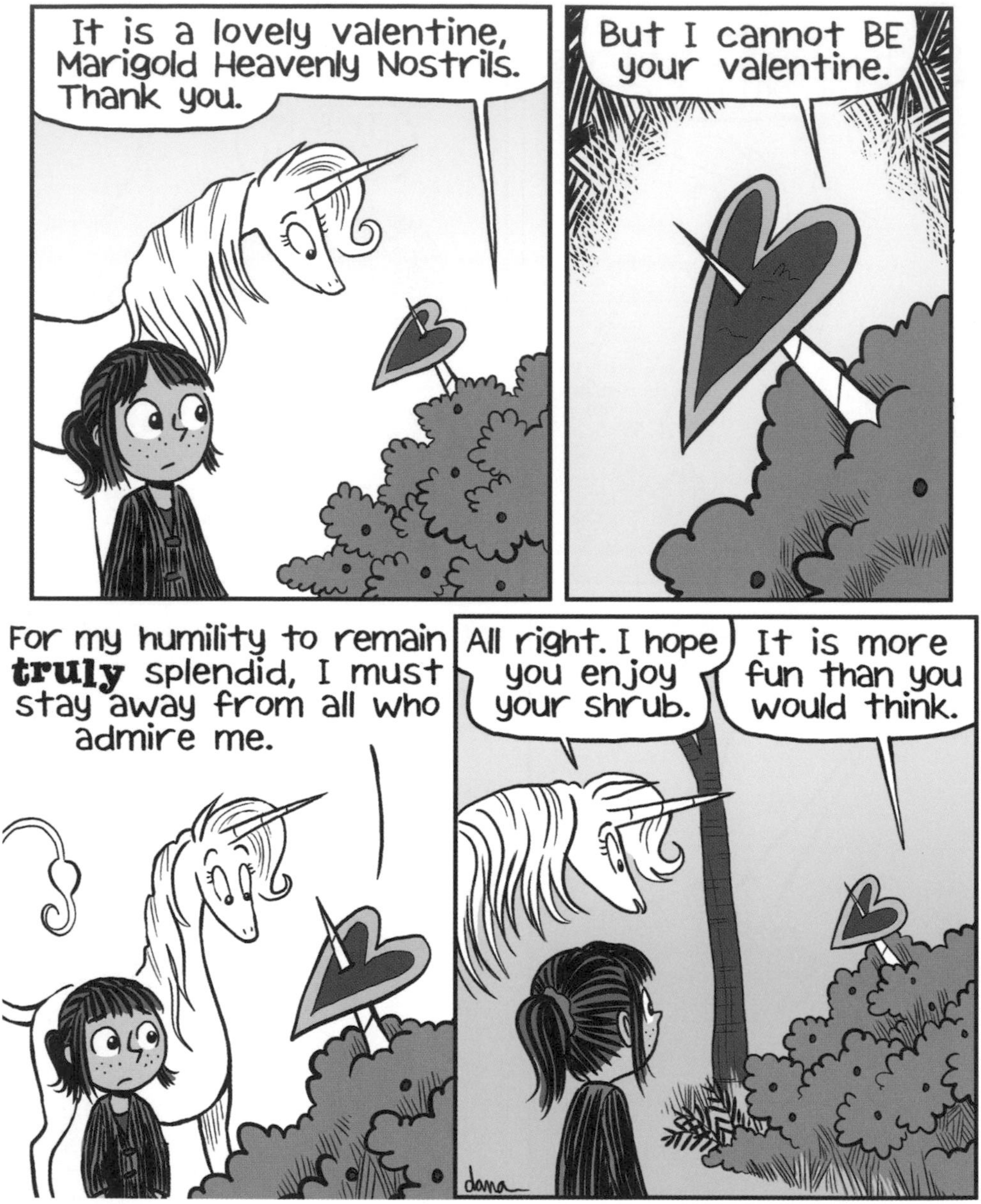
It is a lovely valentine, Marigold Heavenly Nostrils. Thank you.
But I cannot BE your valentine.
For my humility to remain **truly** splendid, I must stay away from all who admire me.
All right. I hope you enjoy your shrub.
It is more fun than you would think.
dana

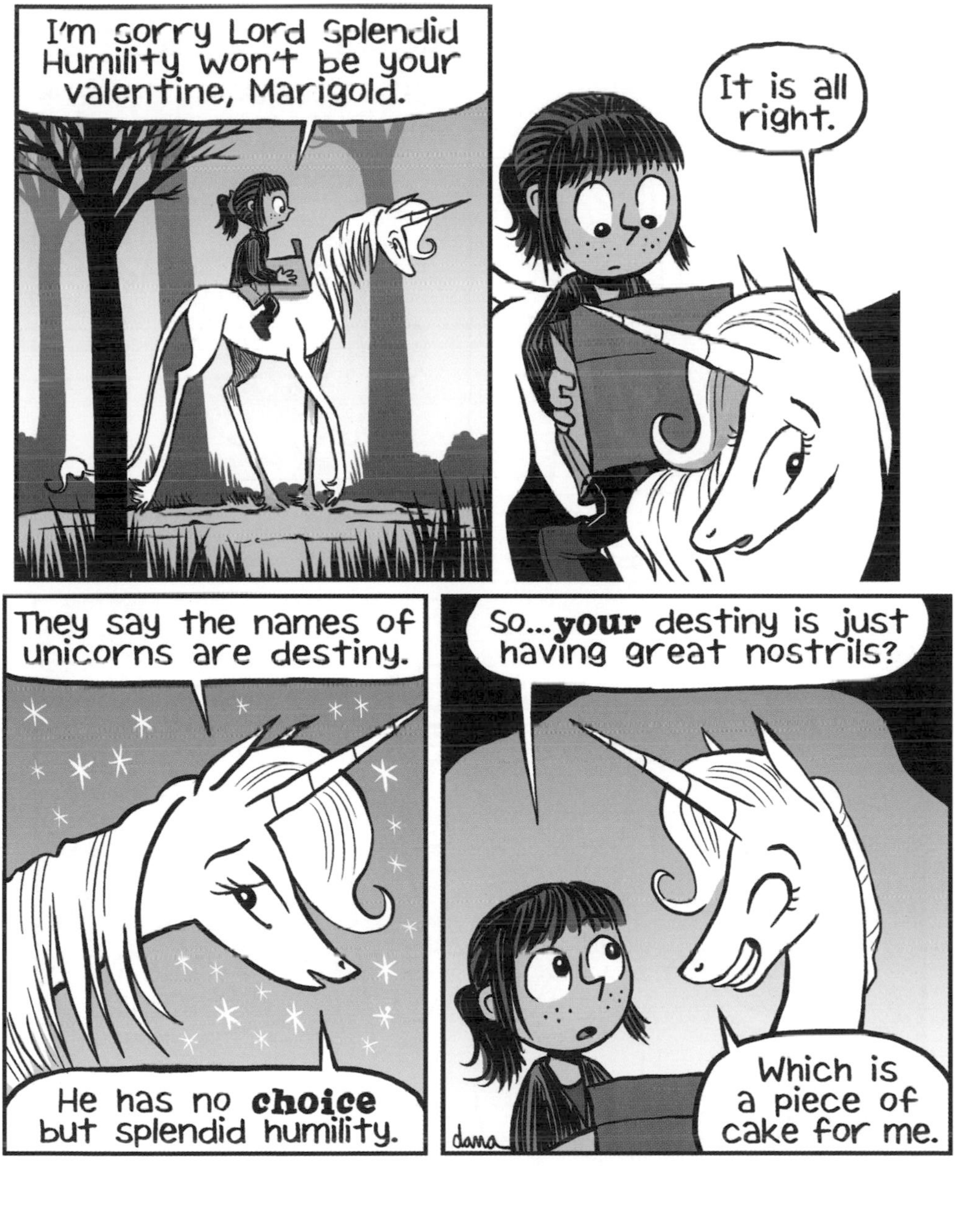
I'm sorry Lord Splendid Humility won't be your valentine, Marigold.
It is all right.
They say the names of unicorns are destiny.
He has no **choice** but splendid humility.
So...**your** destiny is just having great nostrils?
Which is a piece of cake for me.
dana

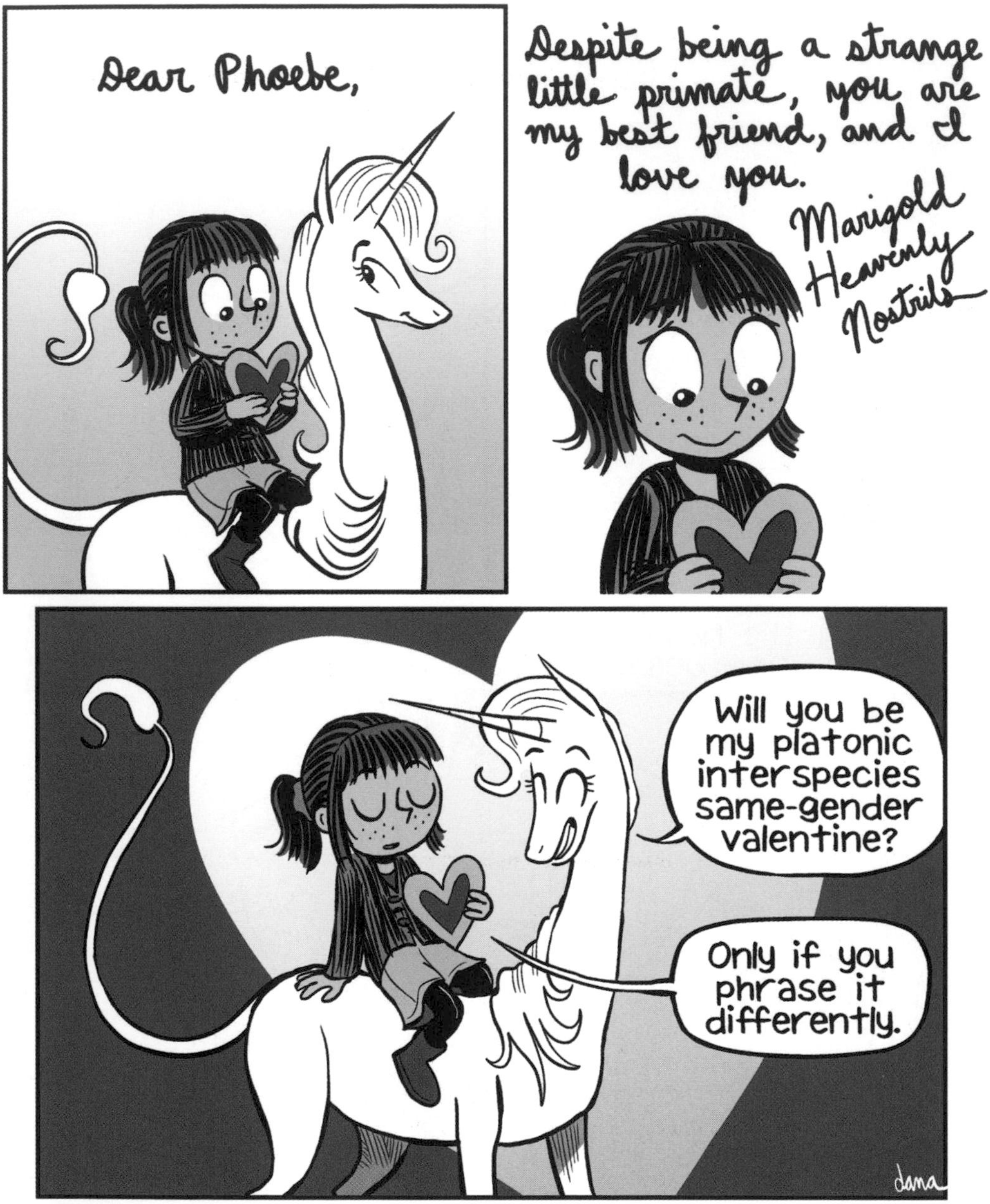
Dear Phoebe,
Despite being a strange little primate, you are my best friend, and I love you.
Marigold Heavenly Nostrils
Will you be my platonic interspecies same-gender valentine?
Only if you phrase it differently.
dana

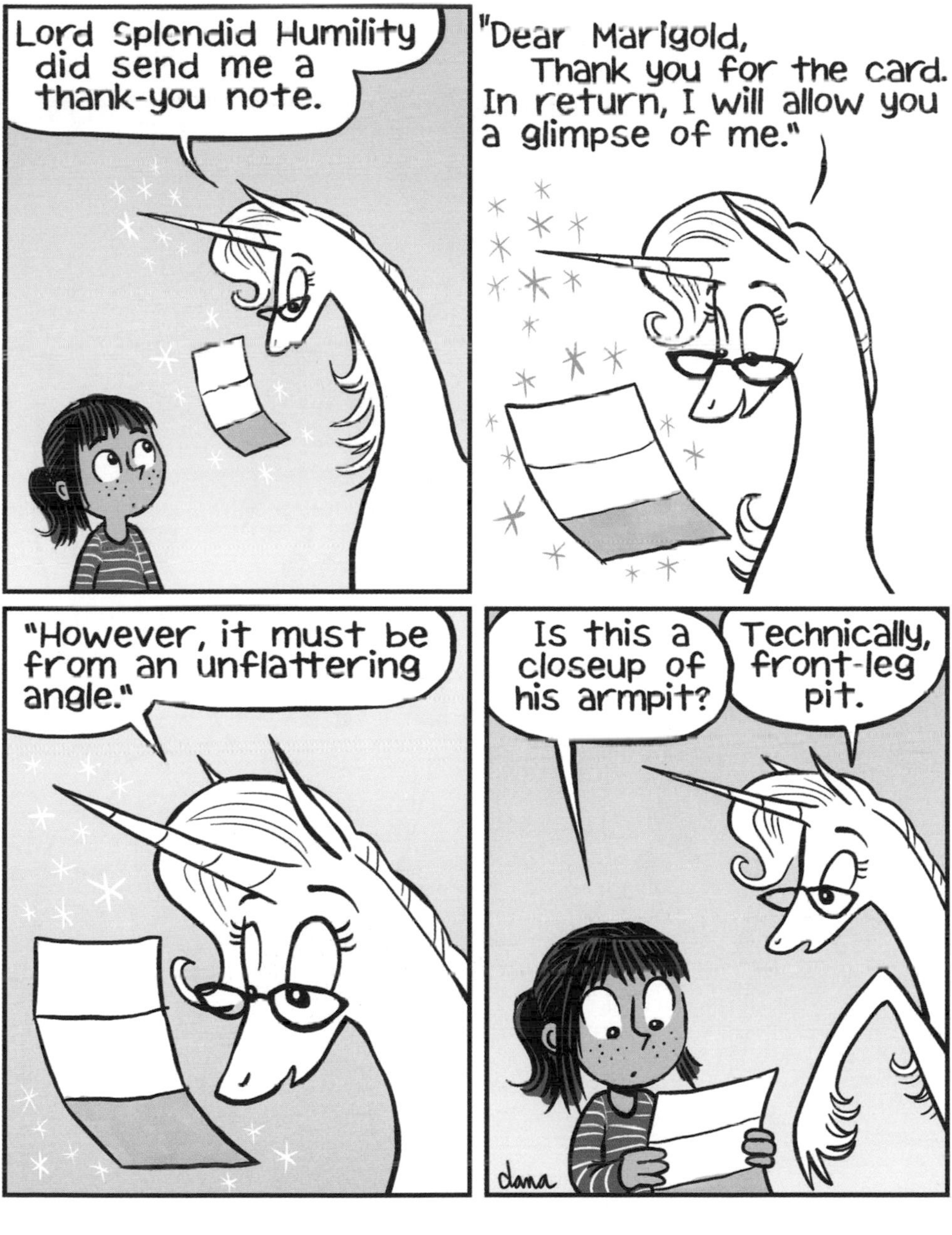
Lord Splendid Humility did send me a thank-you note.
"Dear Marigold,
Thank you for the card. In return, I will allow you a glimpse of me."
"However, it must be from an unflattering angle."
Is this a closeup of his armpit?
Technically, front-leg pit.
dana

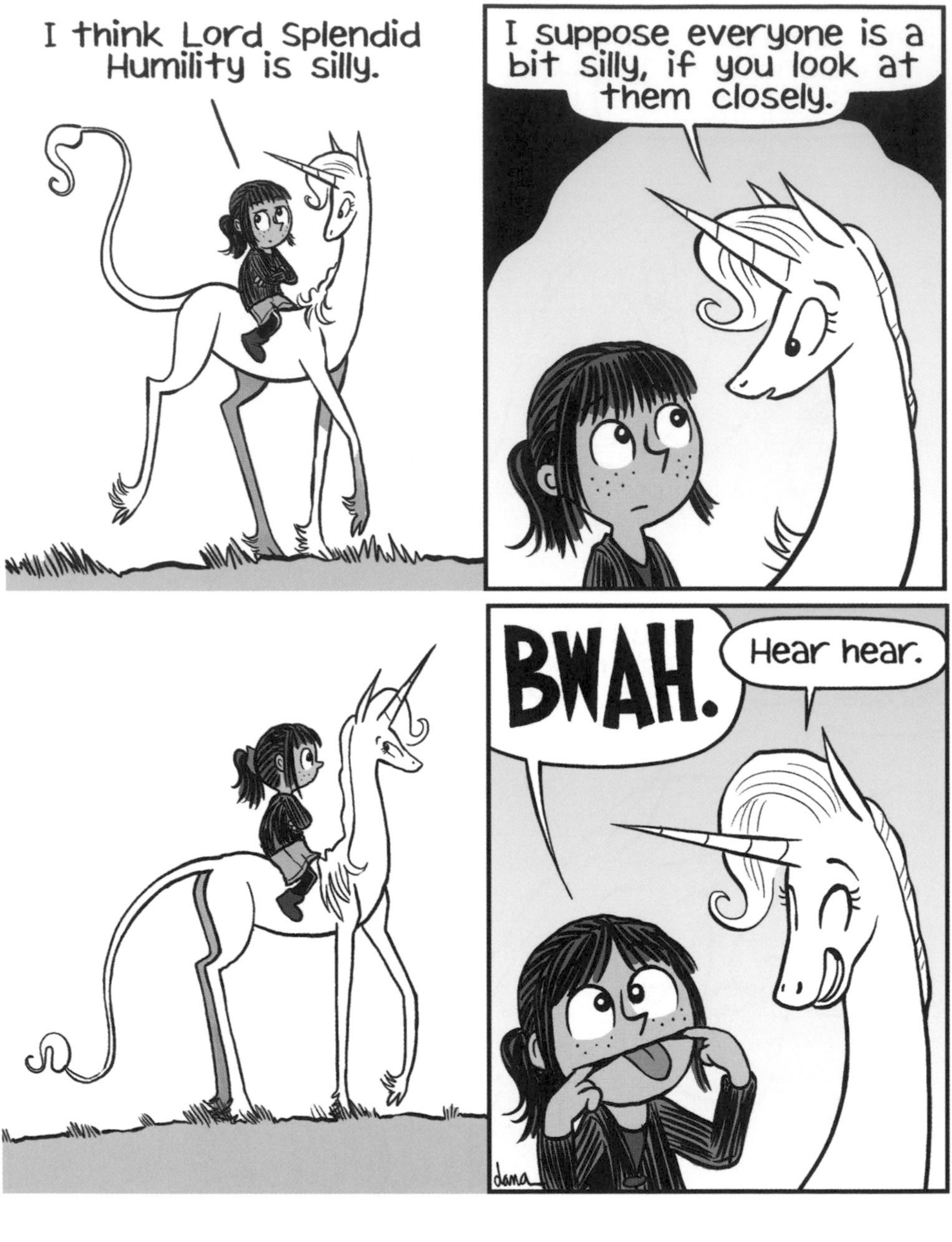
I think Lord Splendid Humility is silly.
I suppose everyone is a bit silly, if you look at them closely.
BWAH.
Hear hear.
dana

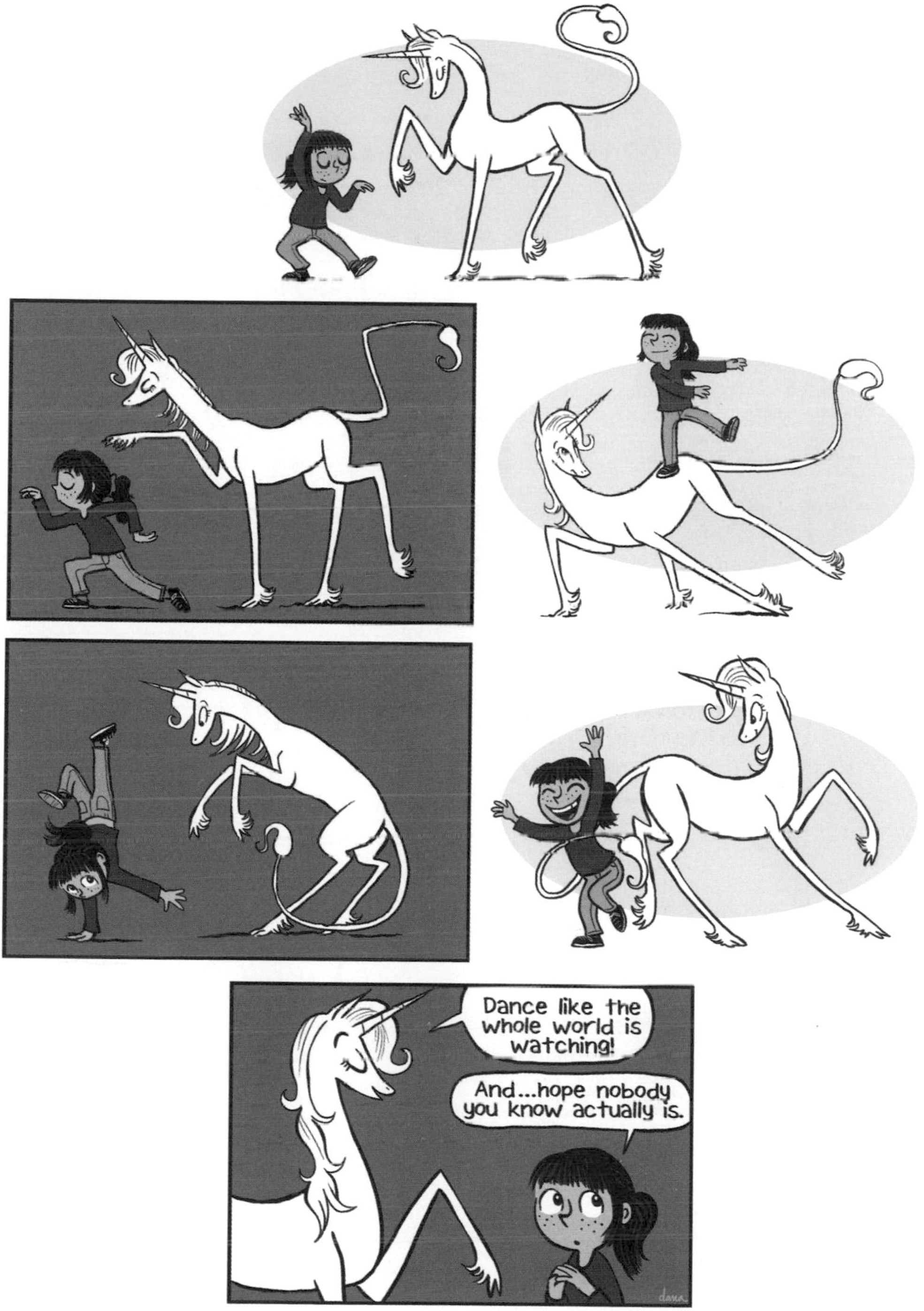
Dance like the whole world is watching!
And...hope nobody you know actually is.
dana

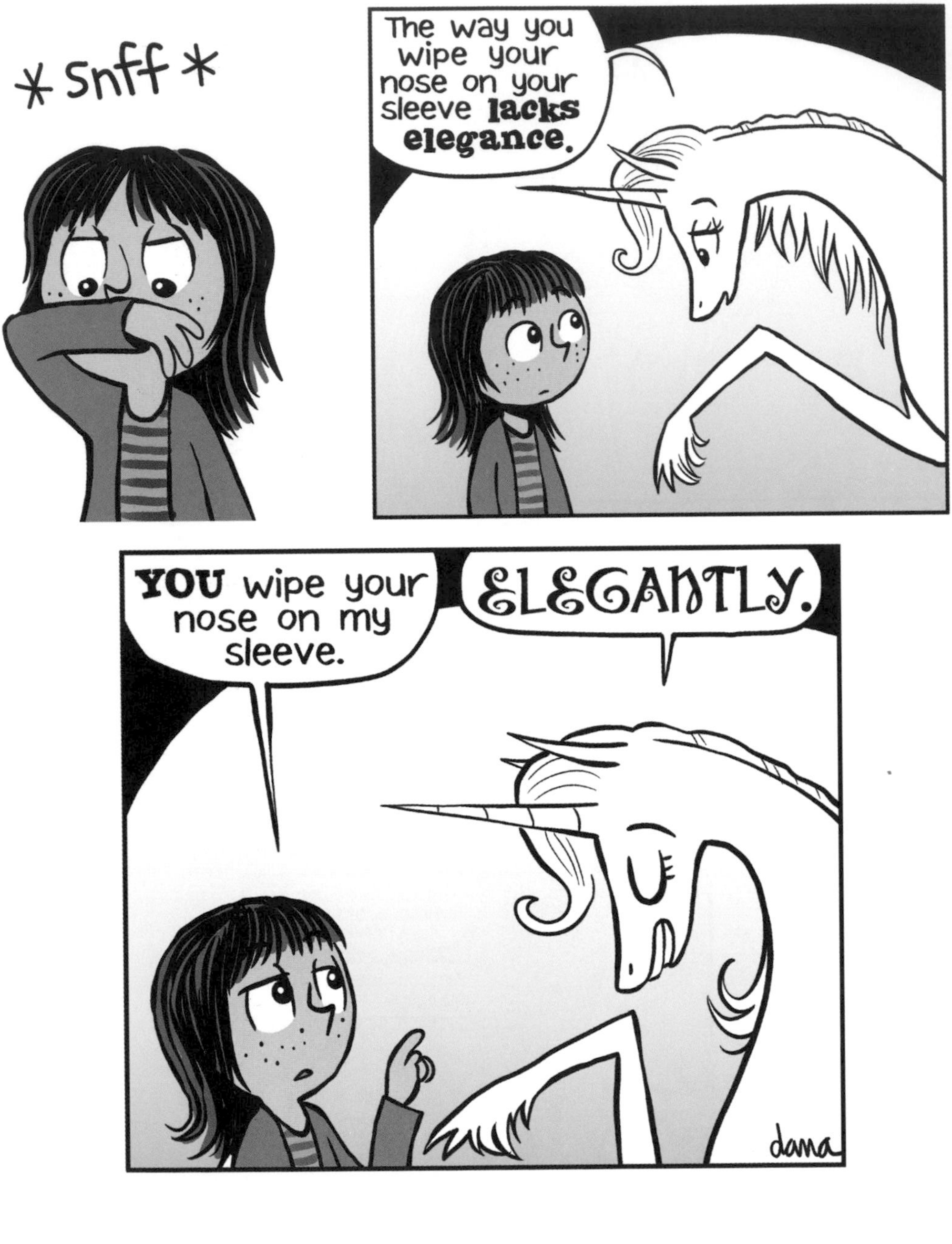
snff
The way you wipe your nose on your sleeve **lacks elegance.**
YOU wipe your nose on my sleeve.
ELEGANTLY.
dana

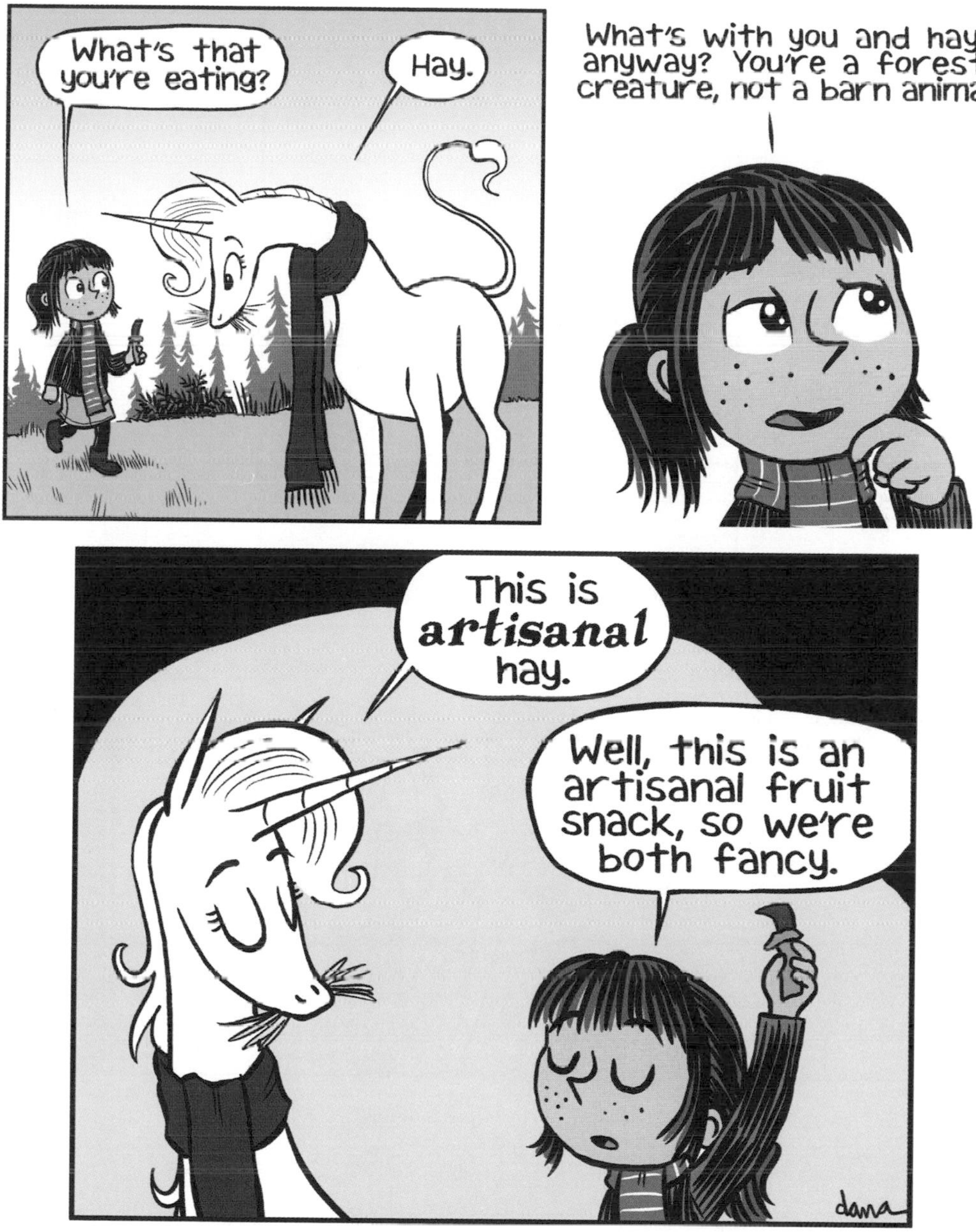
What's that you're eating?
Hay.
What's with you and hay, anyway? You're a forest creature, not a barn animal.
This is **artisanal** hay.
Well, this is an artisanal fruit snack, so we're both fancy.
dana

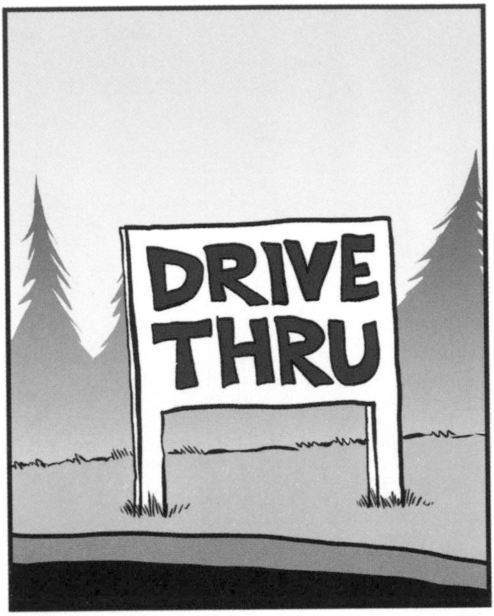
DRIVE THRU

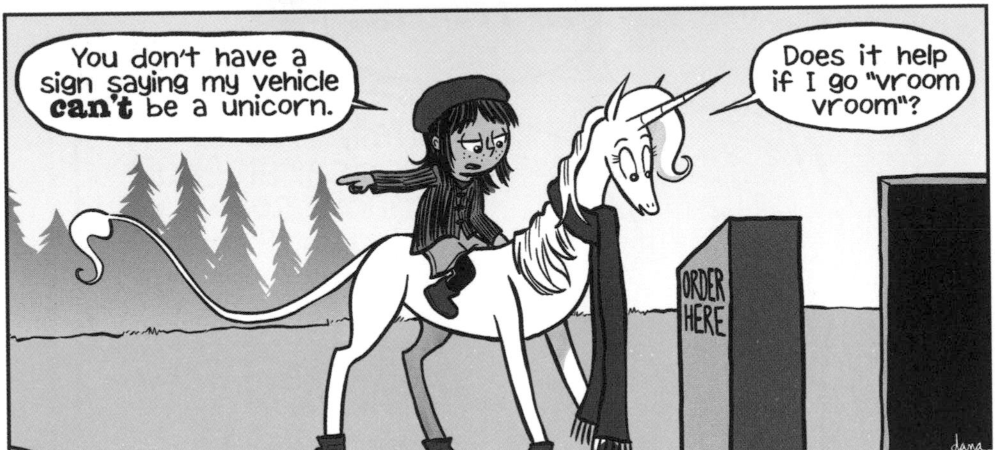
You don't have a sign saying my vehicle **can't** be a unicorn.
Does it help if I go "vroom vroom"?
ORDER HERE
dana

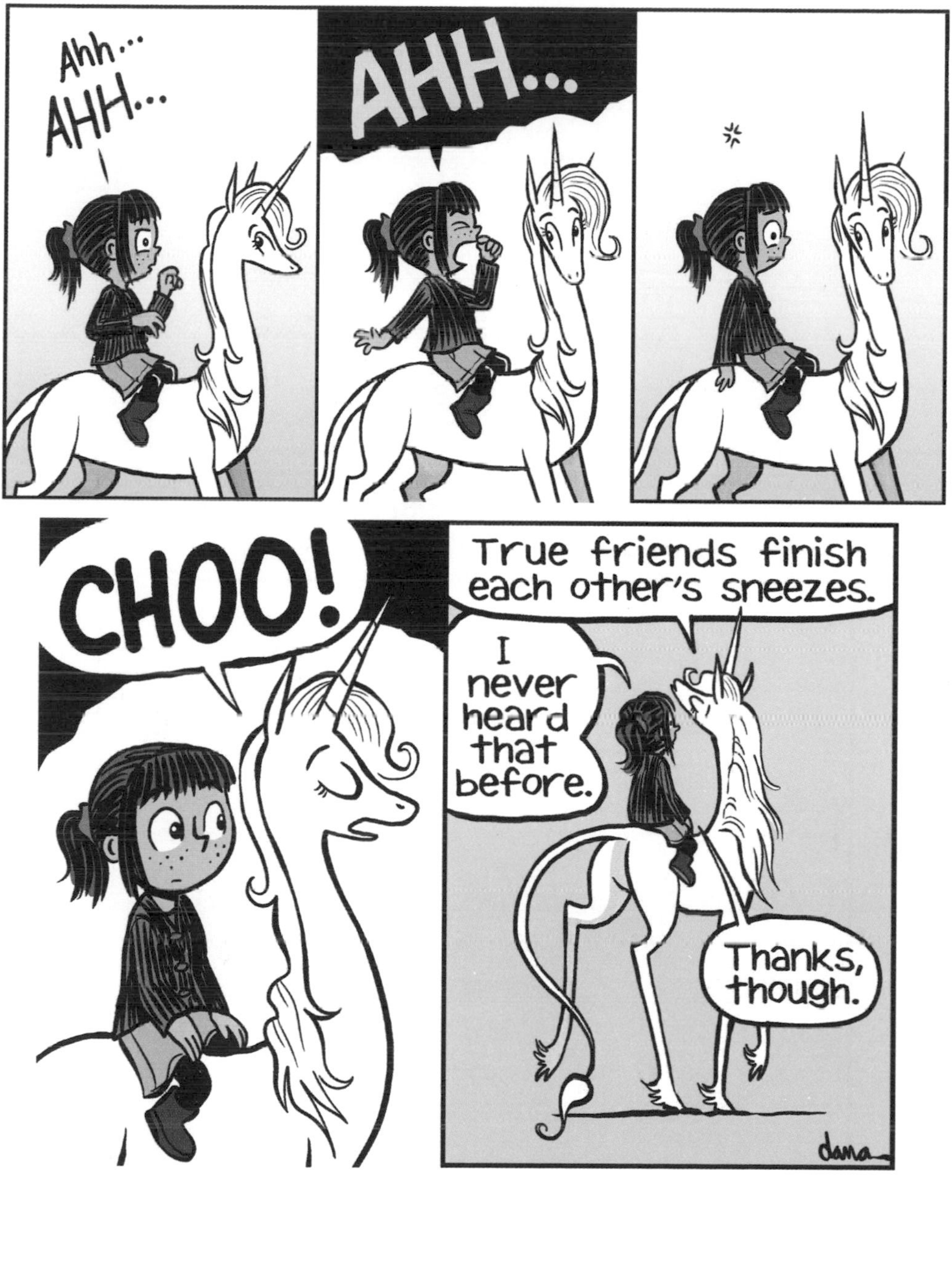
Ahh...
AHH...
AHH...
CHOO!
True friends finish each other's sneezes.
I never heard that before.
Thanks, though.
dana

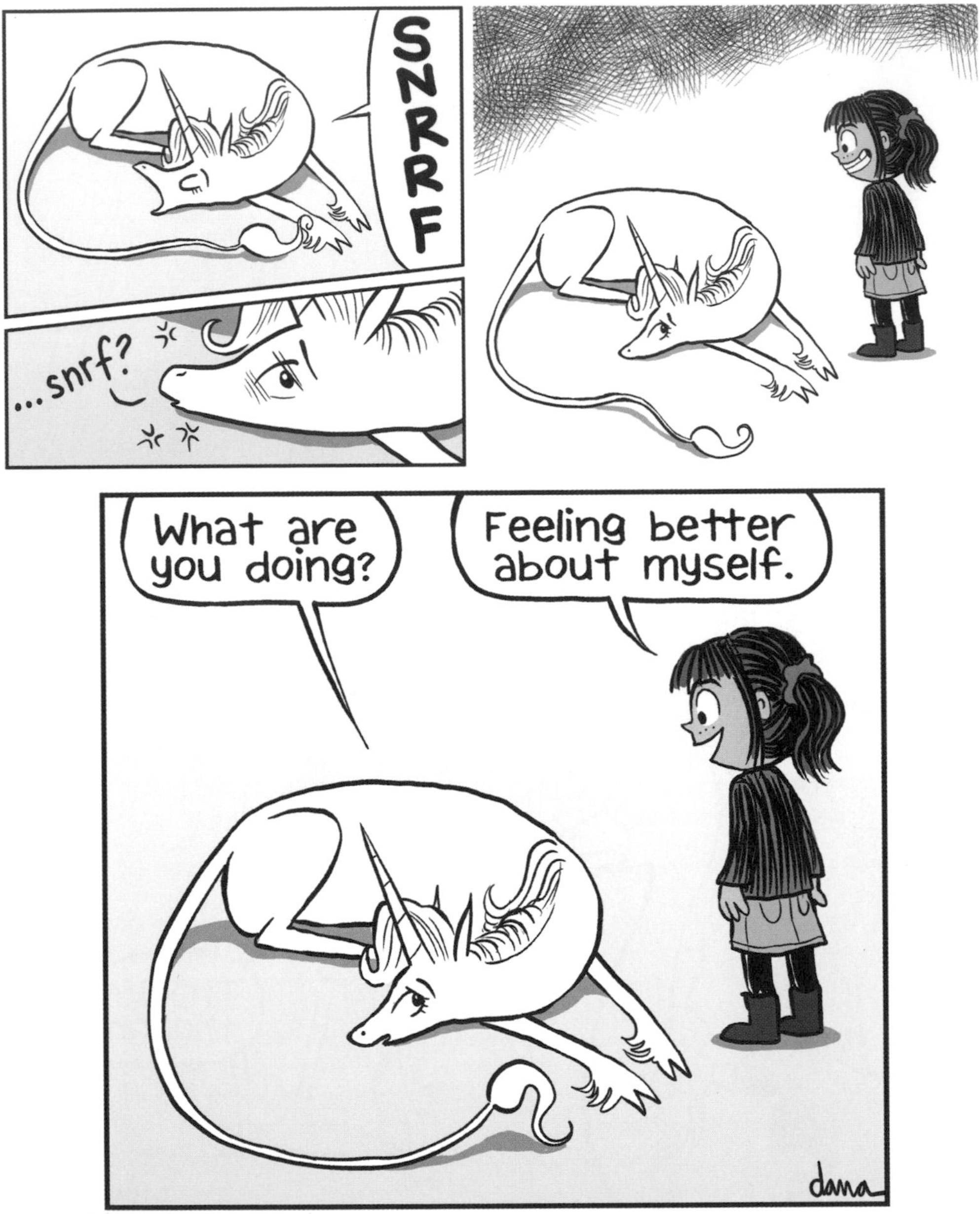
SNRRF
...snrf?
What are you doing?
Feeling better about myself.
dana

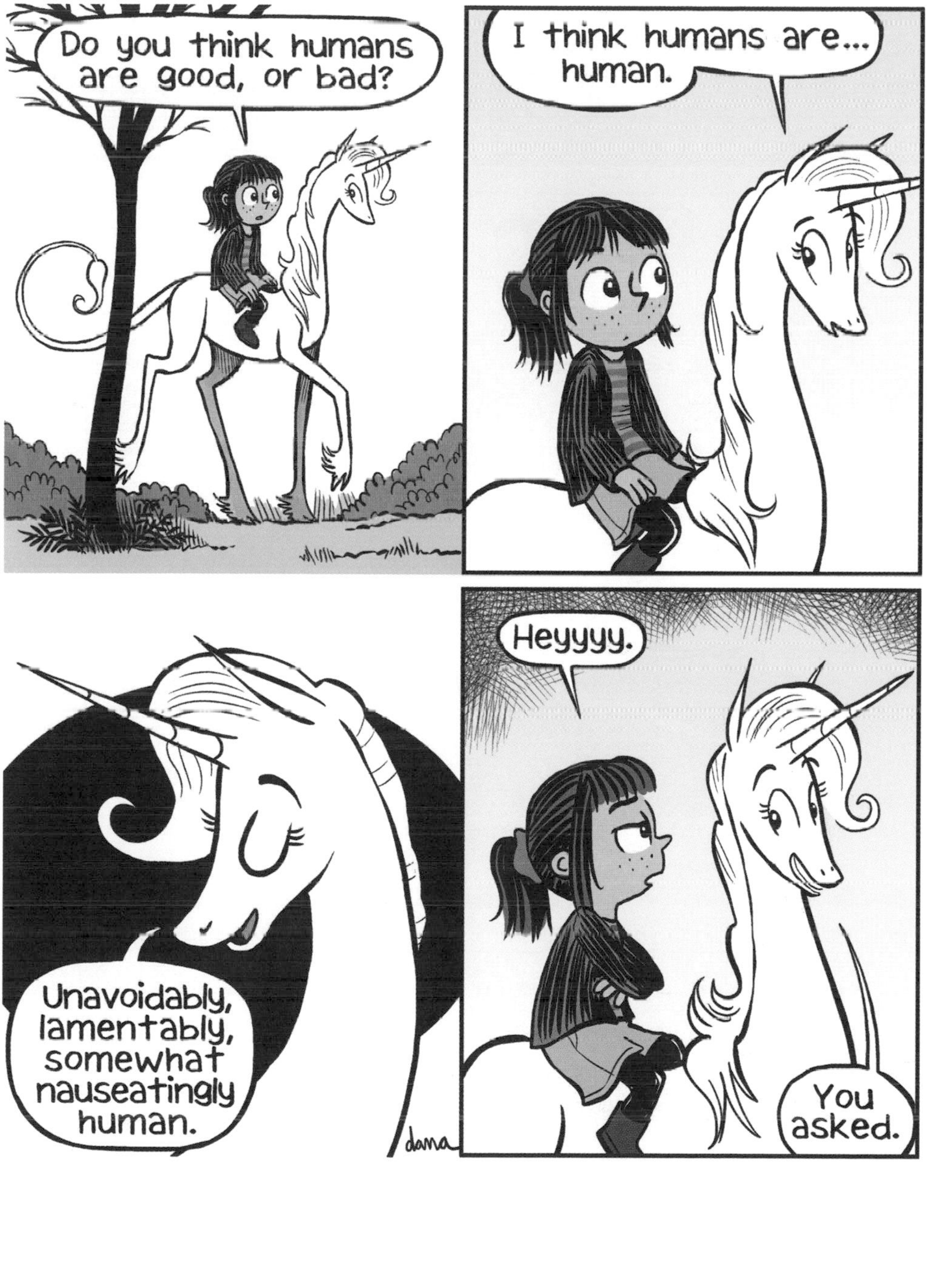
Do you think humans are good, or bad?
I think humans are... human.
Unavoidably, lamentably, somewhat nauseatingly human.
Heyyyy.
You asked.
dana

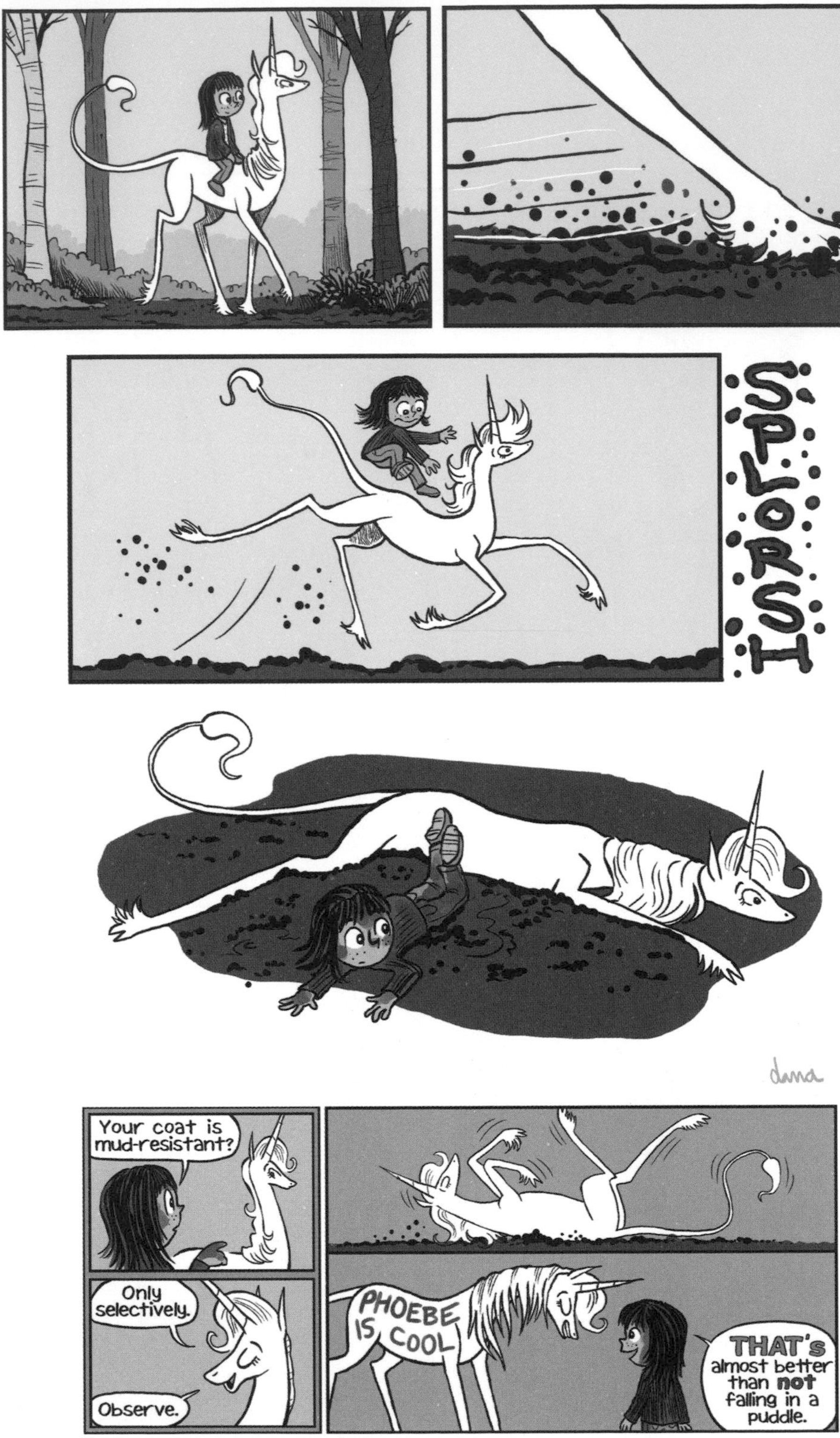
SPLORSH
dana
Your coat is mud-resistant?
Only selectively.
Observe.
PHOEBE IS COOL
THAT's almost better than not falling in a puddle.

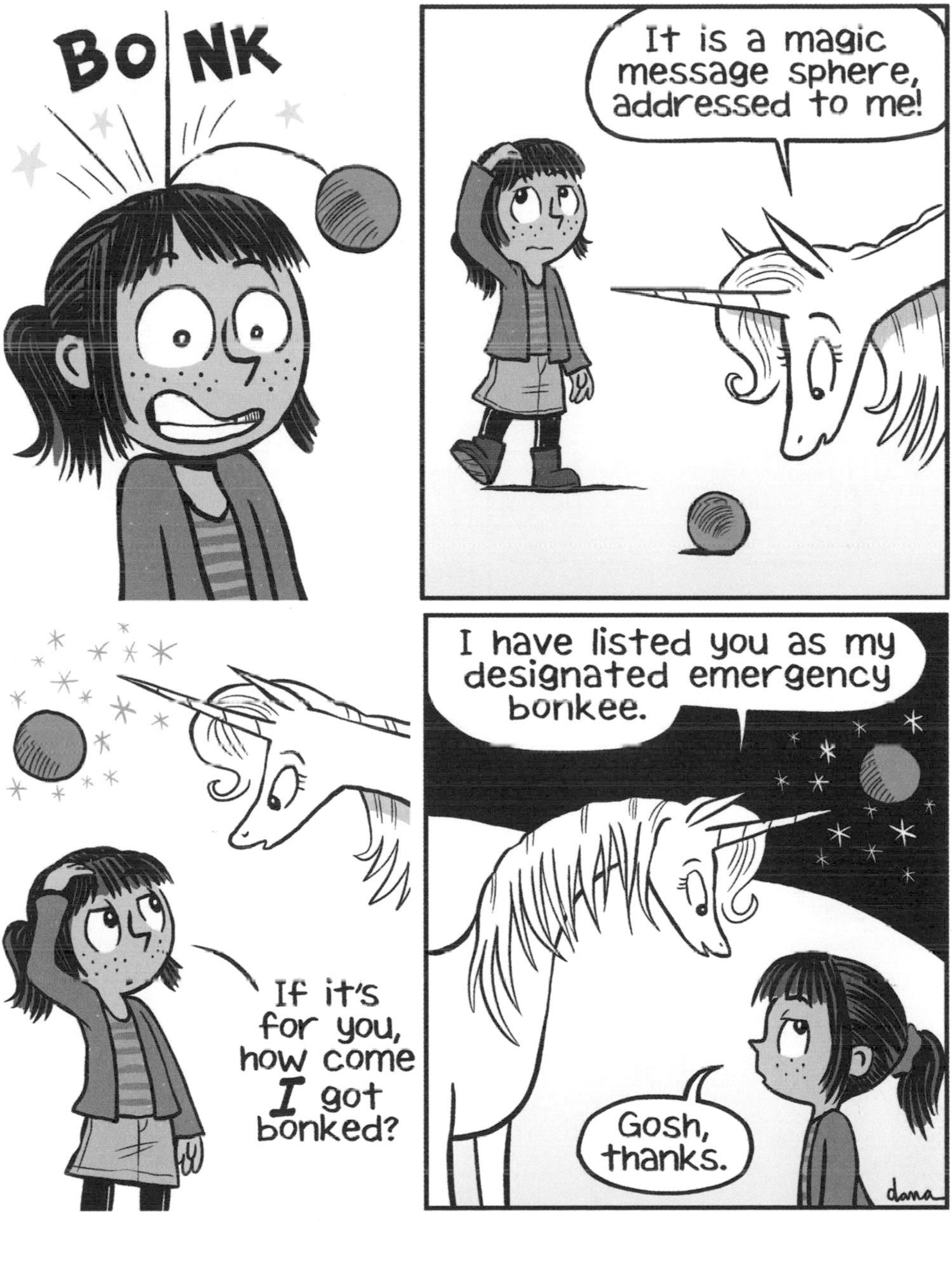
BONK
It is a magic message sphere, addressed to me!
If it's for you, how come I got bonked?
I have listed you as my designated emergency bonkee.
Gosh, thanks.
dana

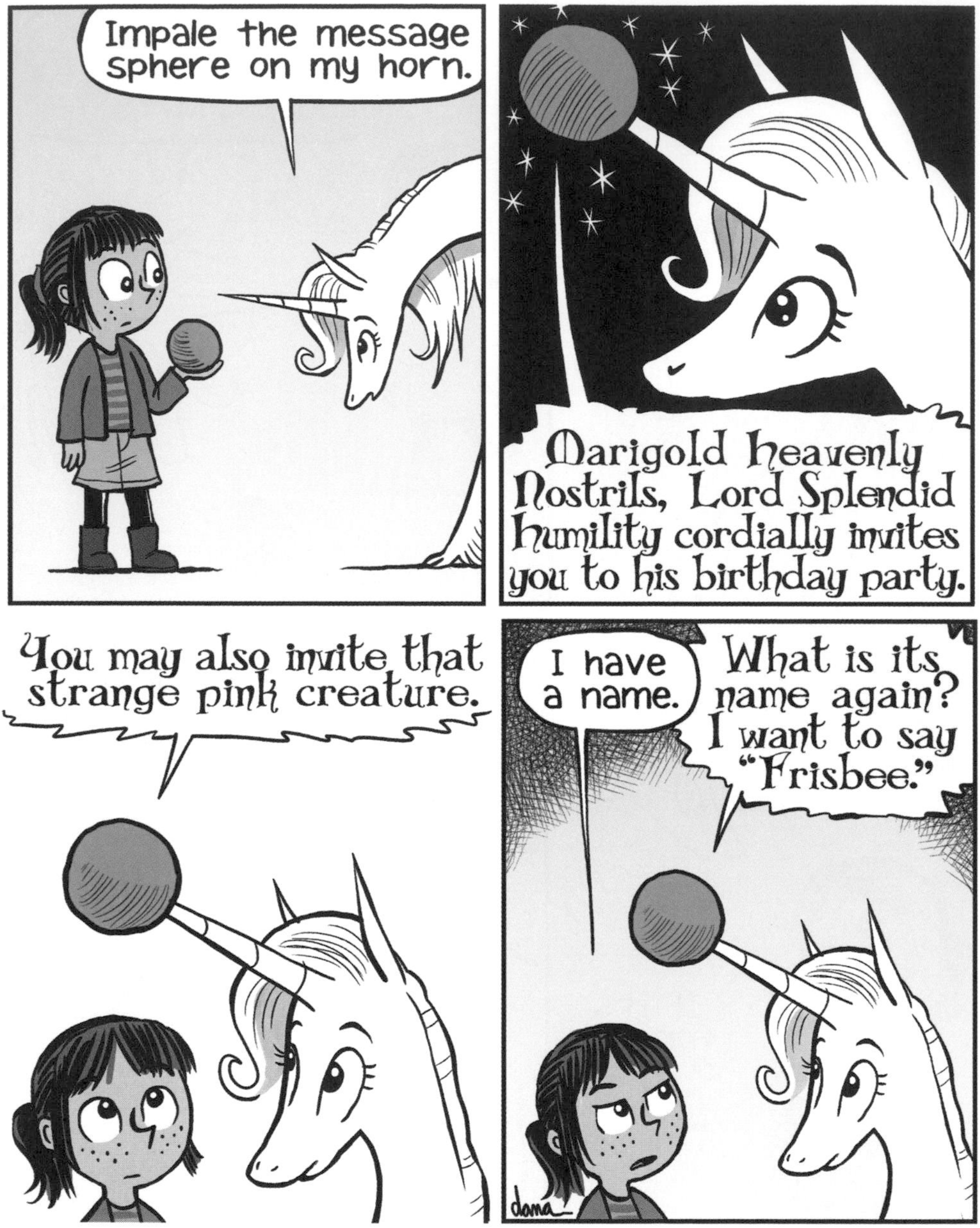
Impale the message sphere on my horn.
Marigold Heavenly Nostrils, Lord Splendid Humility cordially invites you to his birthday party.
You may also invite that strange pink creature.
What is its name again? I want to say "Frisbee."
I have a name.
dana

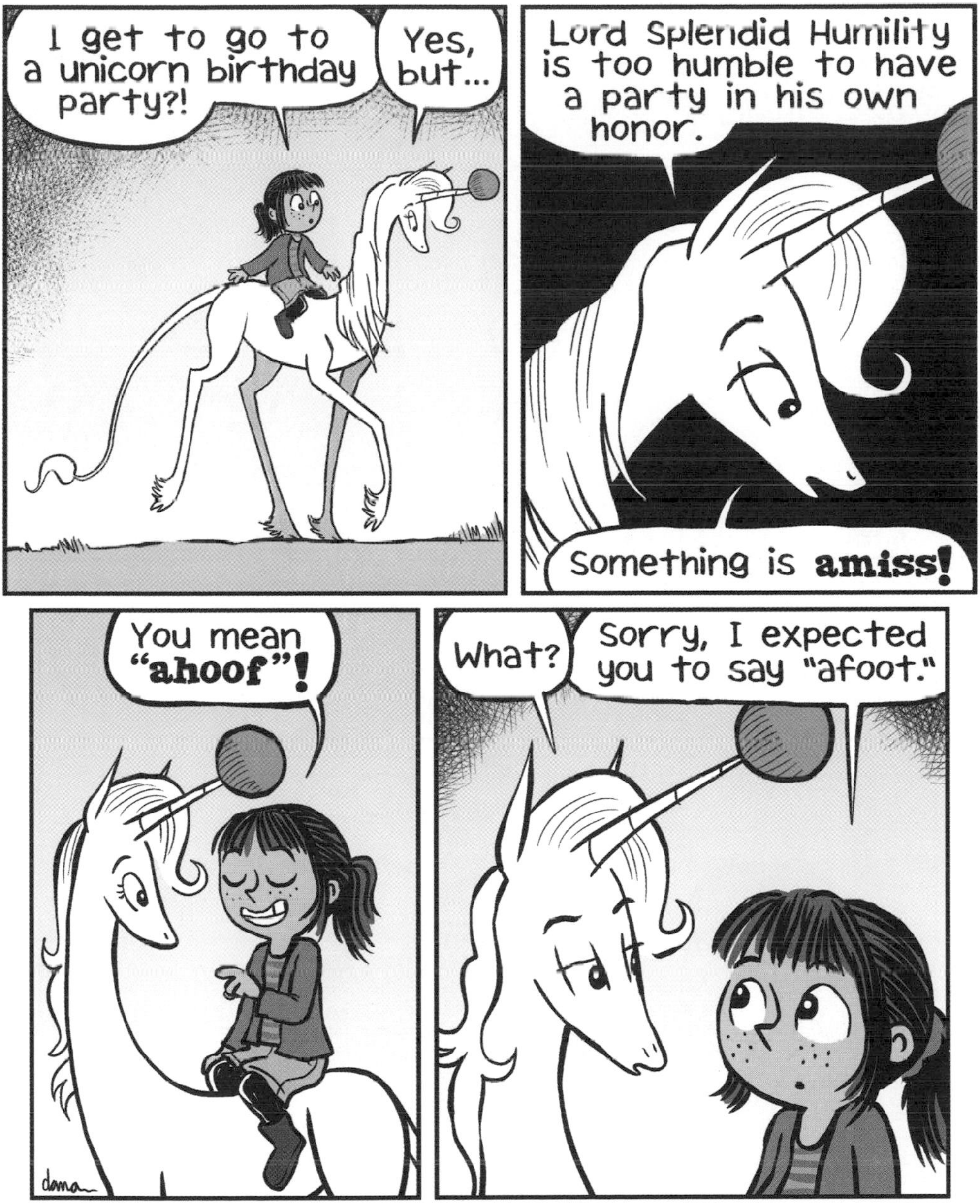
I get to go to a unicorn birthday party?!
Yes, but...
Lord Splendid Humility is too humble to have a party in his own honor.
Something is **amiss!**
You mean "**ahoof**"!
What?
Sorry, I expected you to say "afoot."
dana

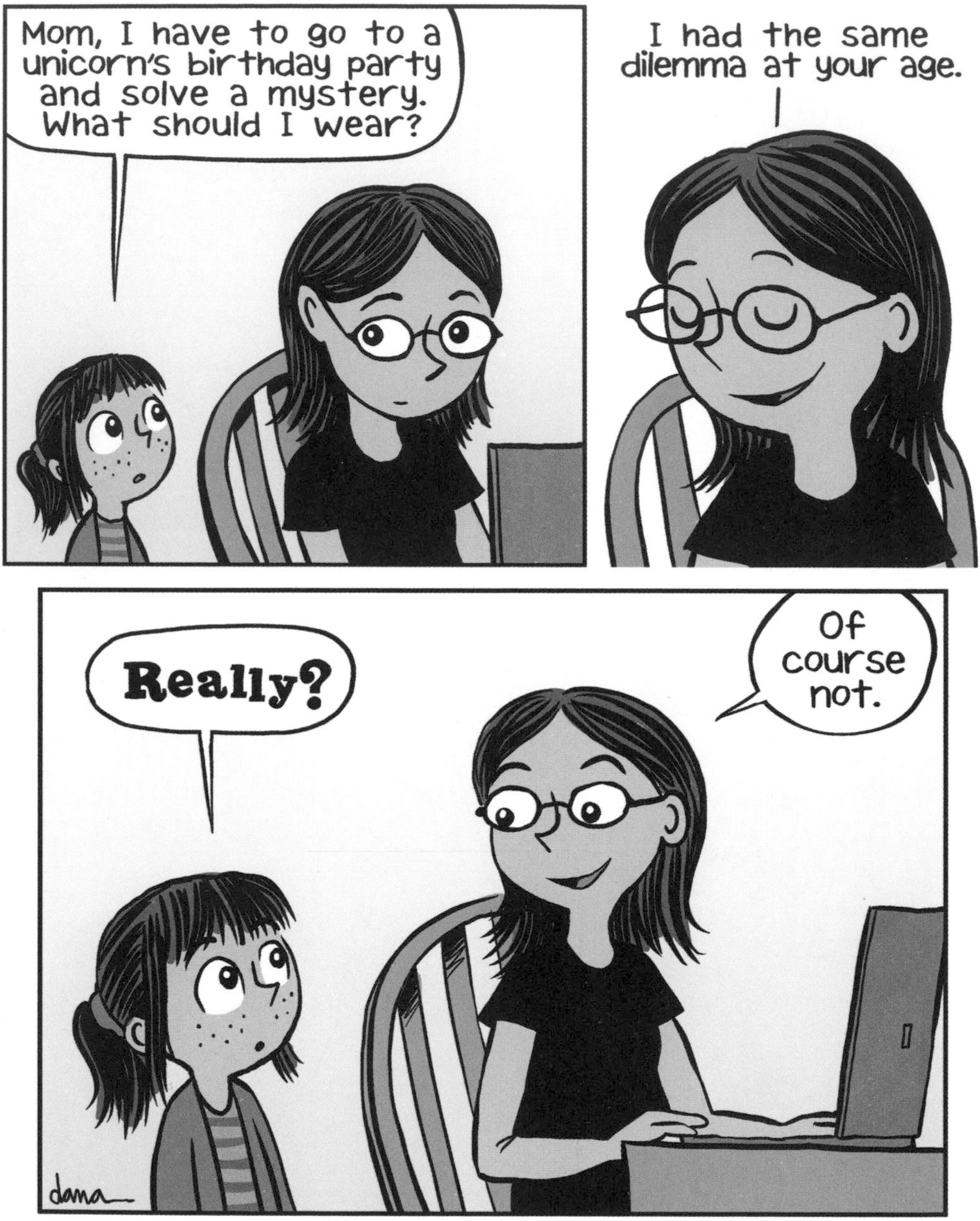
Mom, I have to go to a unicorn's birthday party and solve a mystery. What should I wear?
I had the same dilemma at your age.
Really?
Of course not.
dana

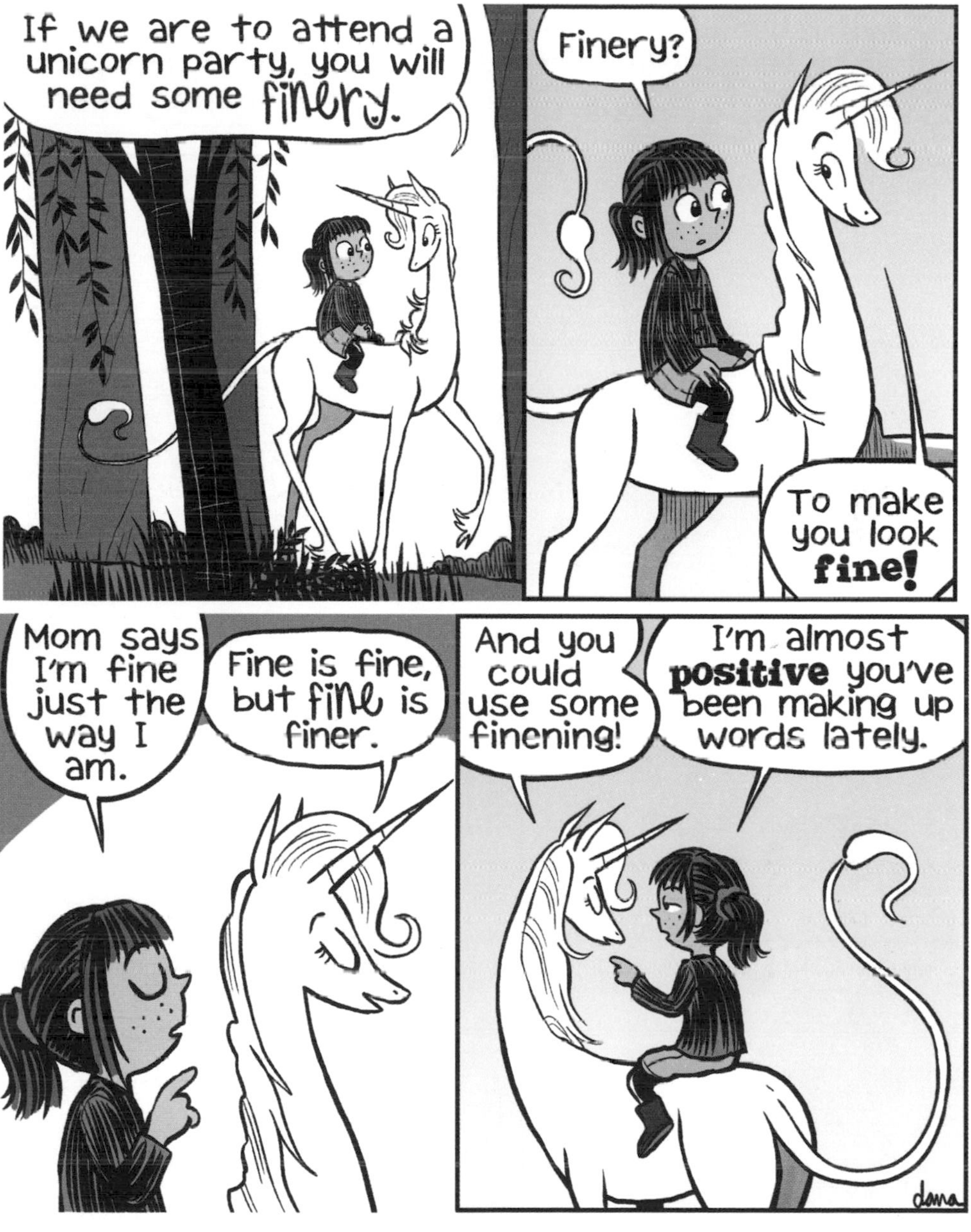
If we are to attend a unicorn party, you will need some finery.
Finery?
To make you look fine!
Mom says I'm fine just the way I am.
Fine is fine, but fine is finer.
And you could use some finening!
I'm almost positive you've been making up words lately.
dana

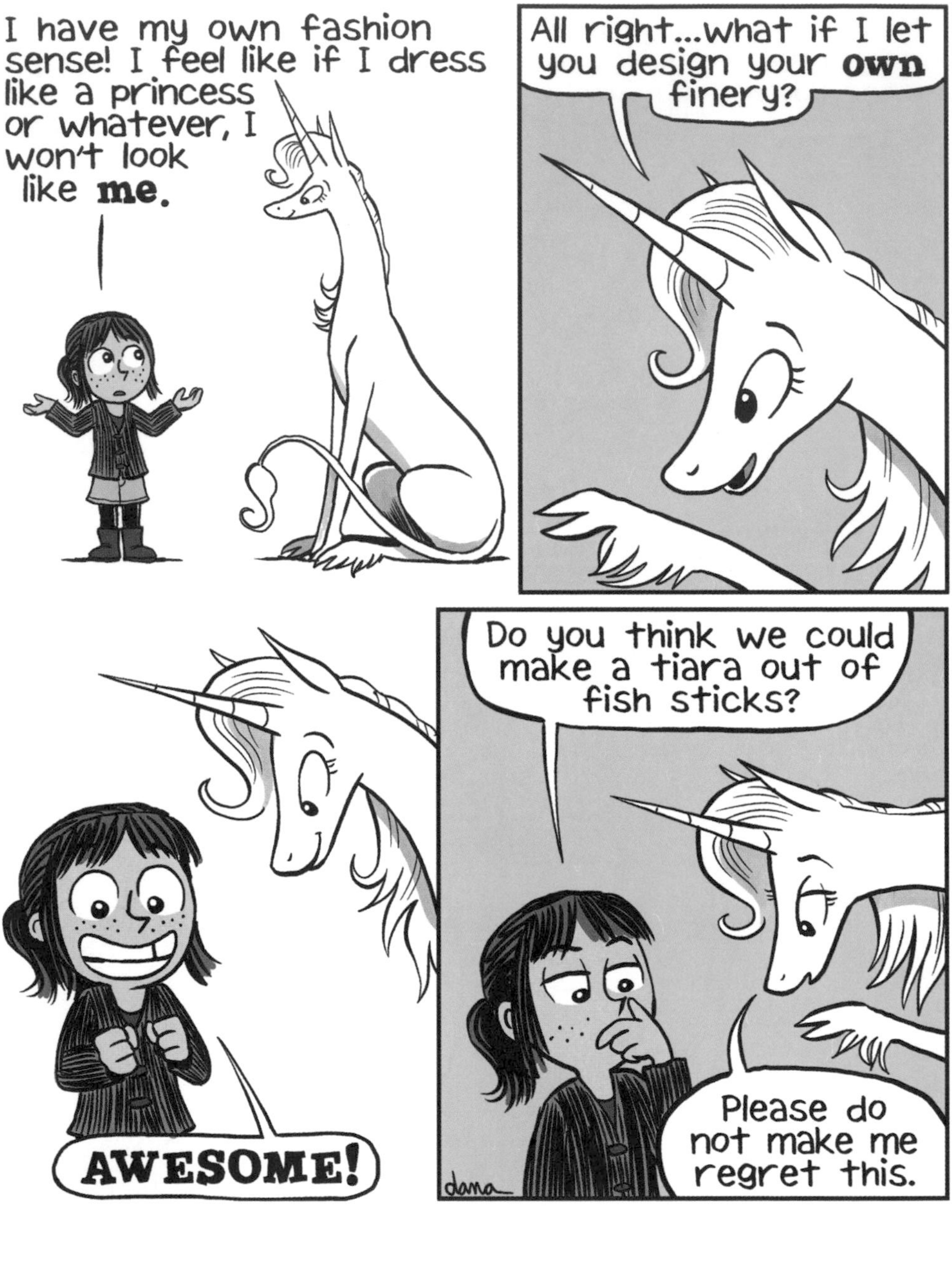
I have my own fashion sense! I feel like if I dress like a princess or whatever, I won't look like **me**.
All right...what if I let you design your **own** finery?
AWESOME!
Do you think we could make a tiara out of fish sticks?
Please do not make me regret this.
dana

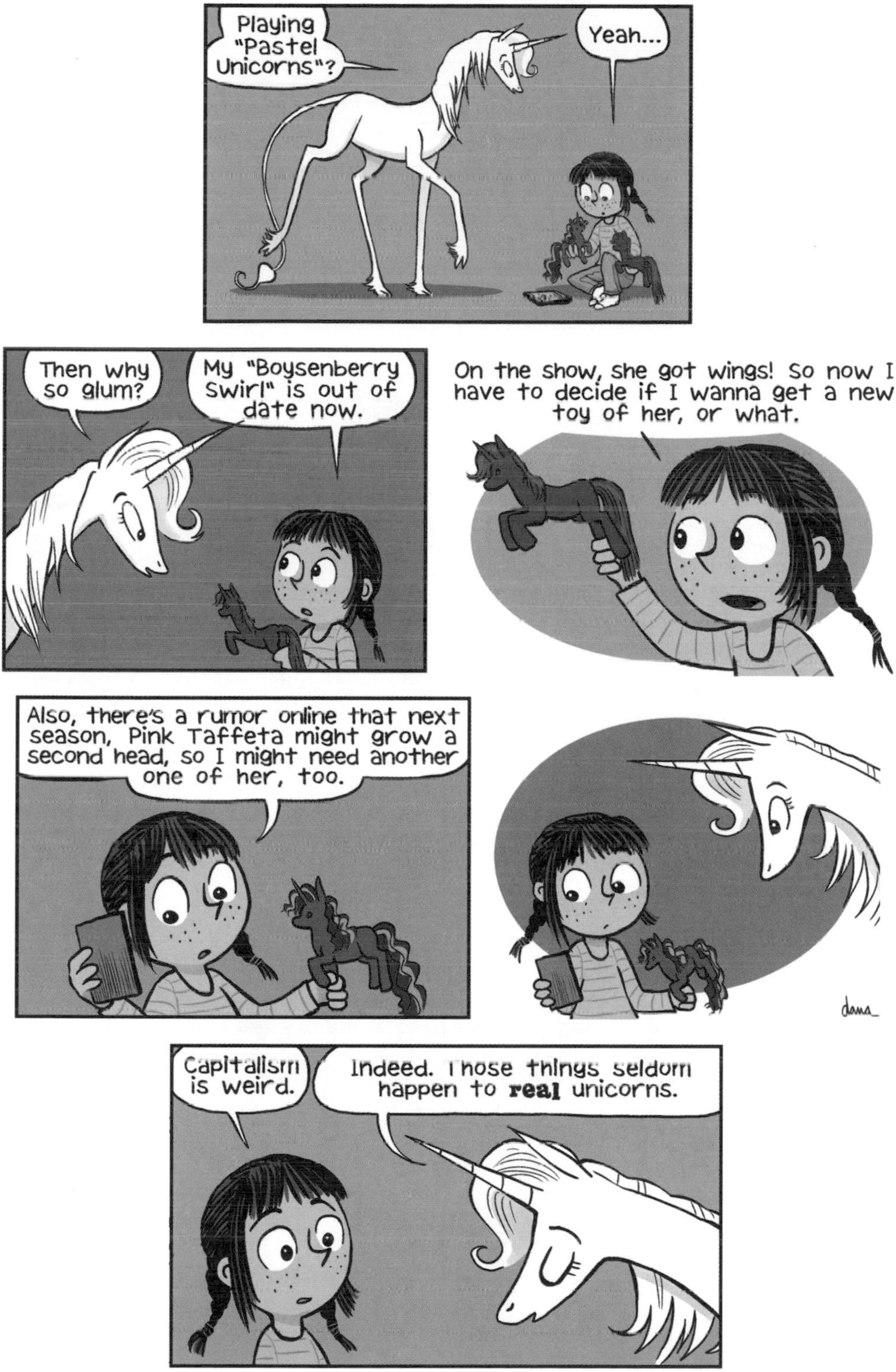
Playing "Pastel Unicorns"?
Yeah...
Then why so glum?
My "Boysenberry Swirl" is out of date now.
On the show, she got wings! So now I have to decide if I wanna get a new toy of her, or what.
Also, there's a rumor online that next season, Pink Taffeta might grow a second head, so I might need another one of her, too.
dana
Capitalism is weird.
Indeed. Those things seldom happen to **real** unicorns.

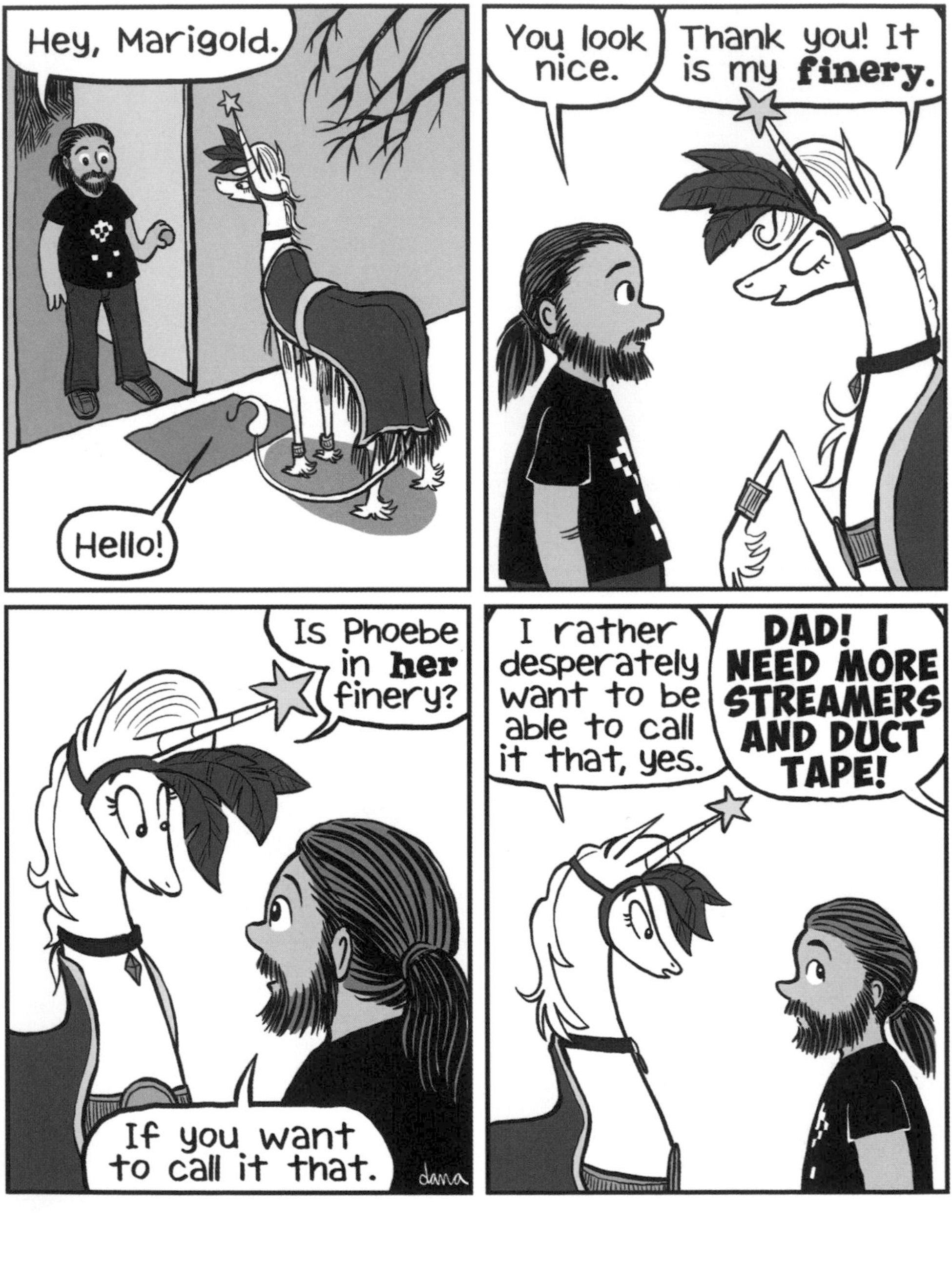
Hey, Marigold.
Hello!
You look nice.
Thank you! It is my **finery**.
Is Phoebe in **her** finery?
If you want to call it that.
I rather desperately want to be able to call it that, yes.
DAD! I NEED MORE STREAMERS AND DUCT TAPE!
dana

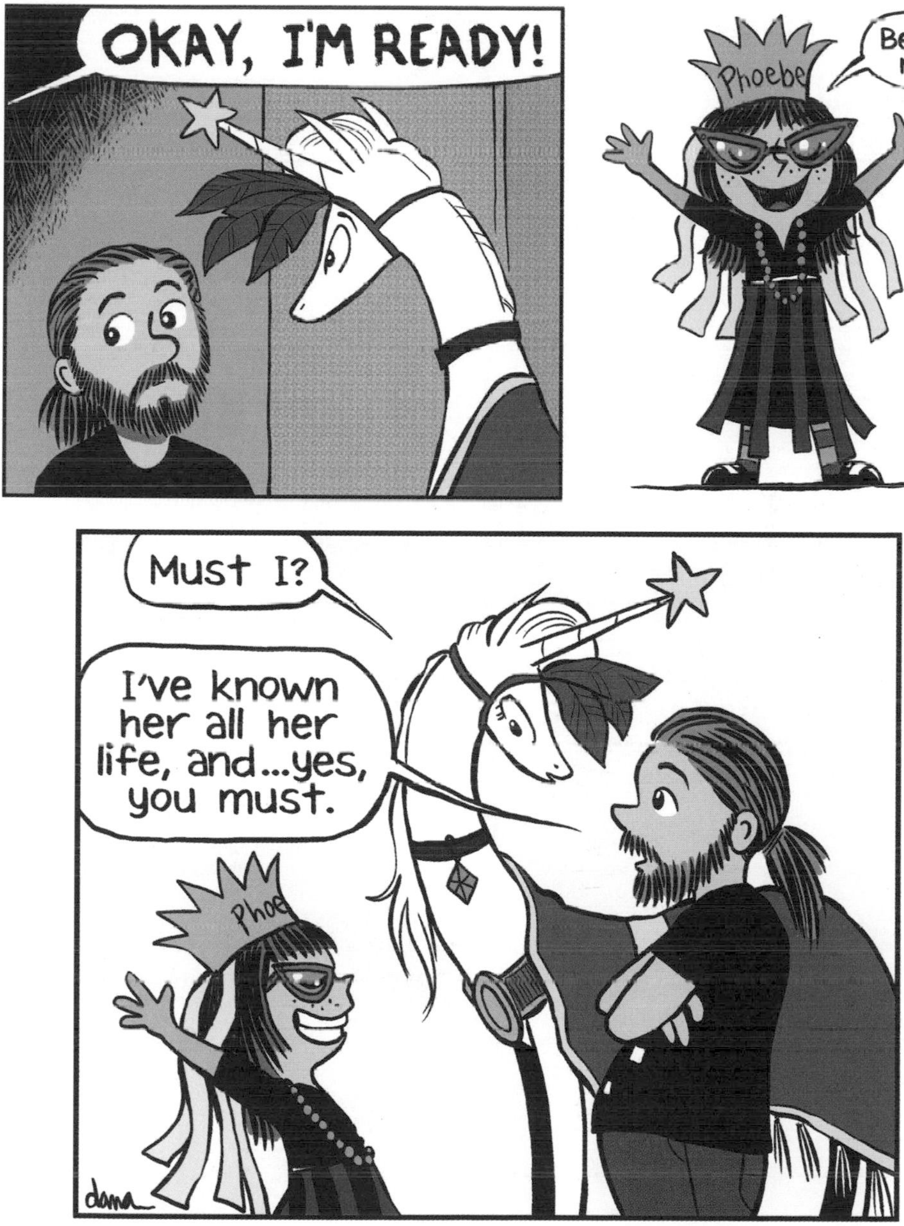
OKAY, I'M READY!
Phoebe
Behold me!
Must I?
I've known her all her life, and...yes, you must.
Phoe
dana

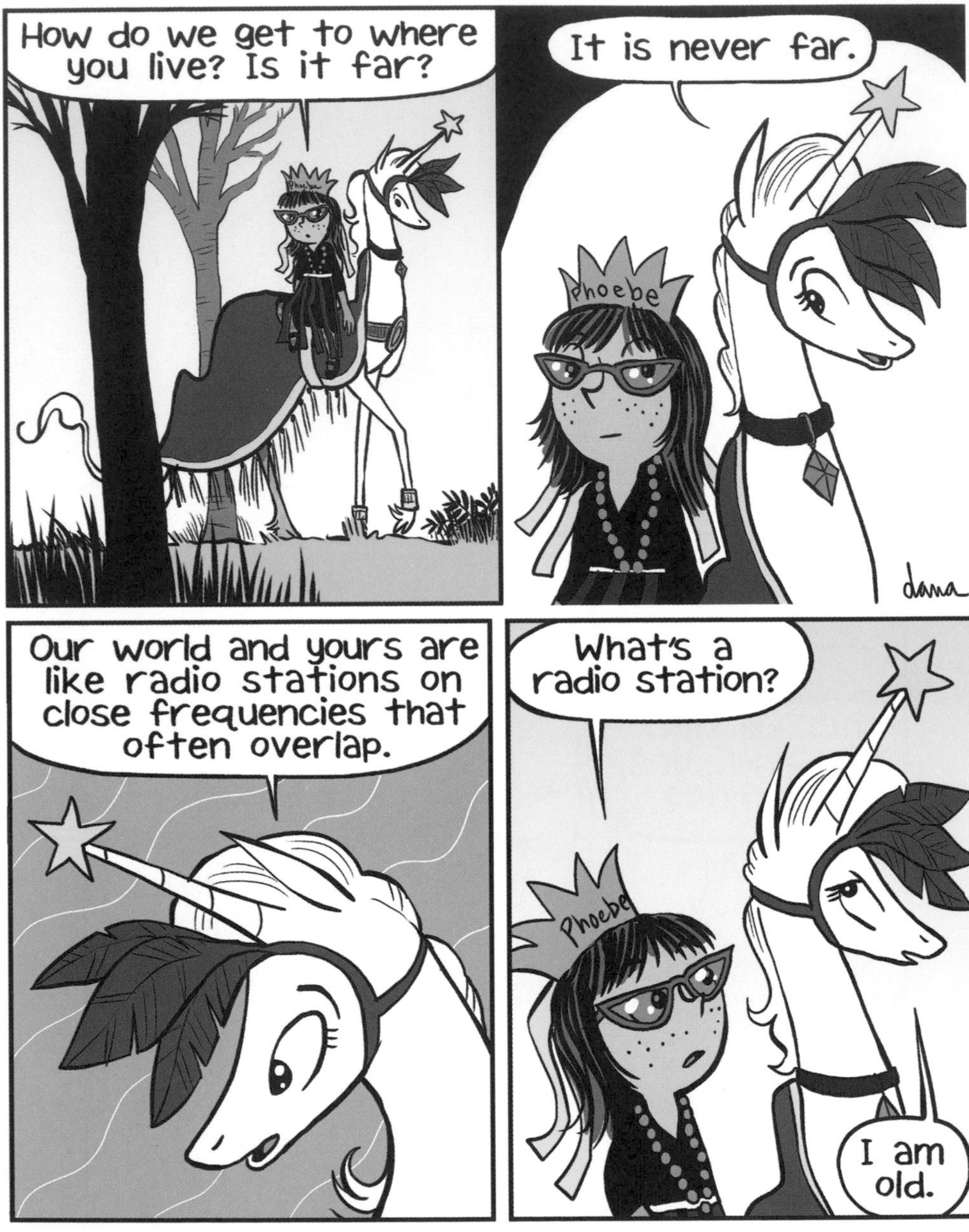
How do we get to where you live? Is it far?
Phoebe
It is never far.
Phoebe
dana
Our world and yours are like radio stations on close frequencies that often overlap.
What's a radio station?
Phoebe
I am old.

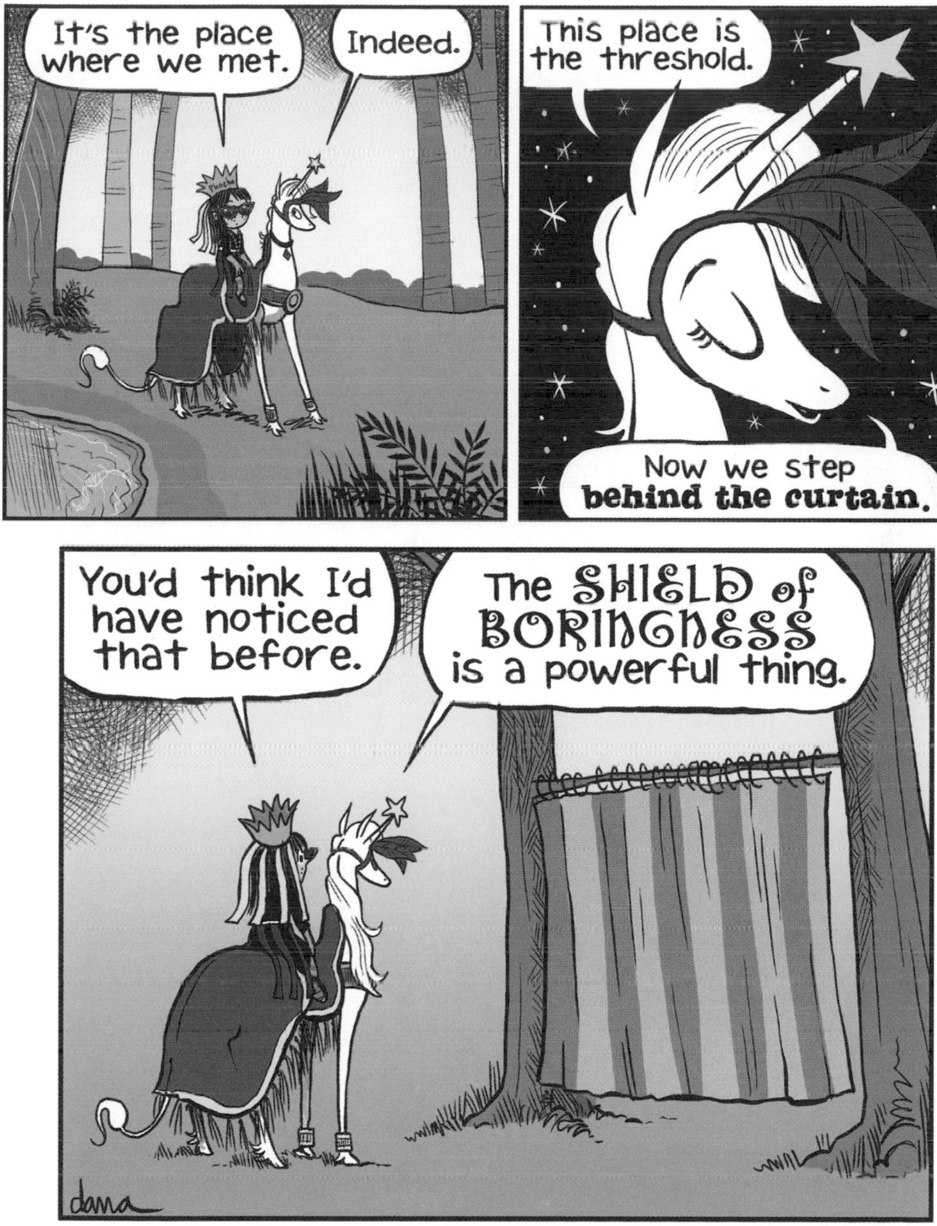
It's the place where we met.
Indeed.
This place is the threshold.
Now we step **behind the curtain.**
You'd think I'd have noticed that before.
The SHIELD of BORINGNESS is a powerful thing.
dana

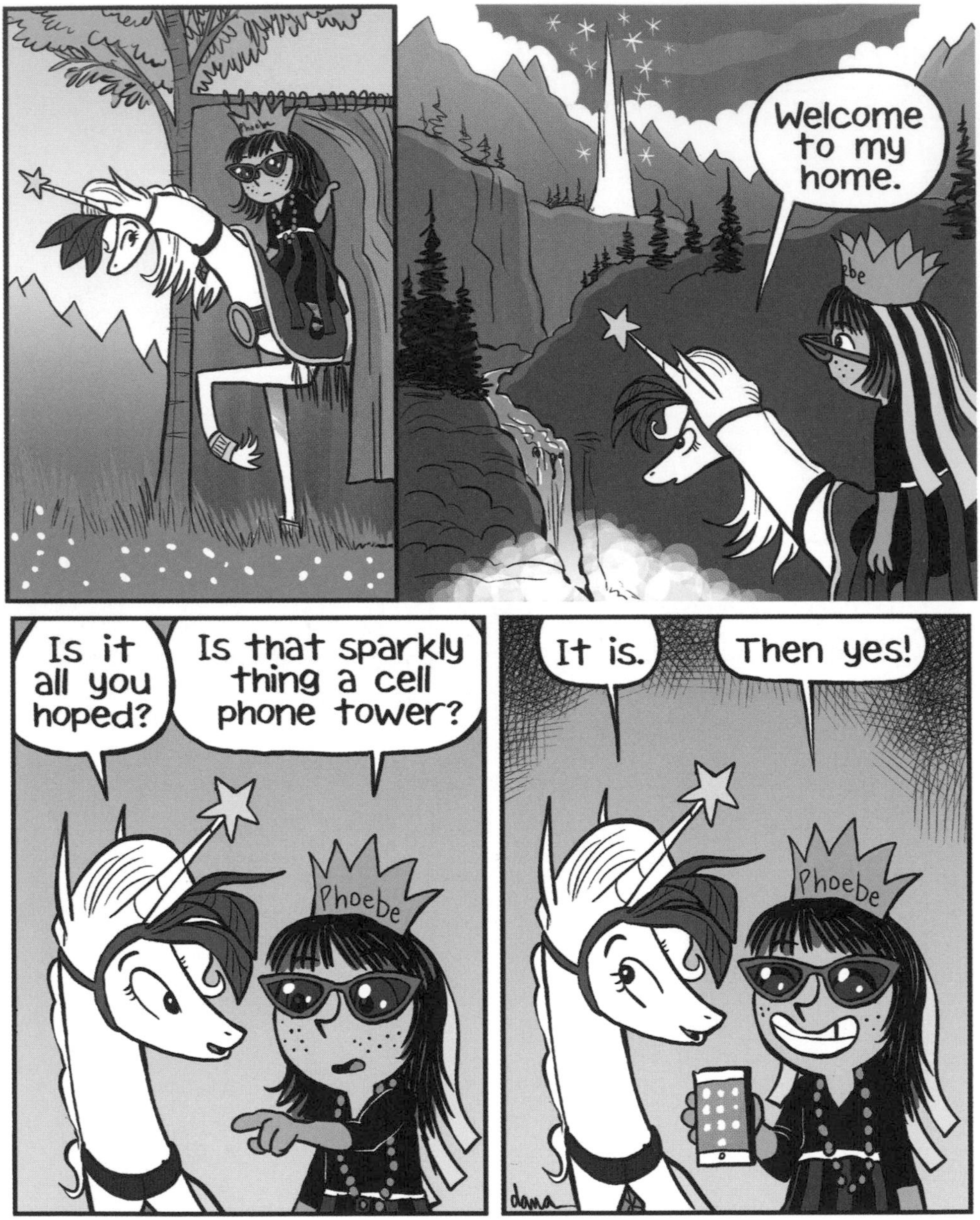

Phoebe
Welcome to my home.
Is it all you hoped?
Is that sparkly thing a cell phone tower?
Phoebe
It is.
Then yes!
Phoebe
dana

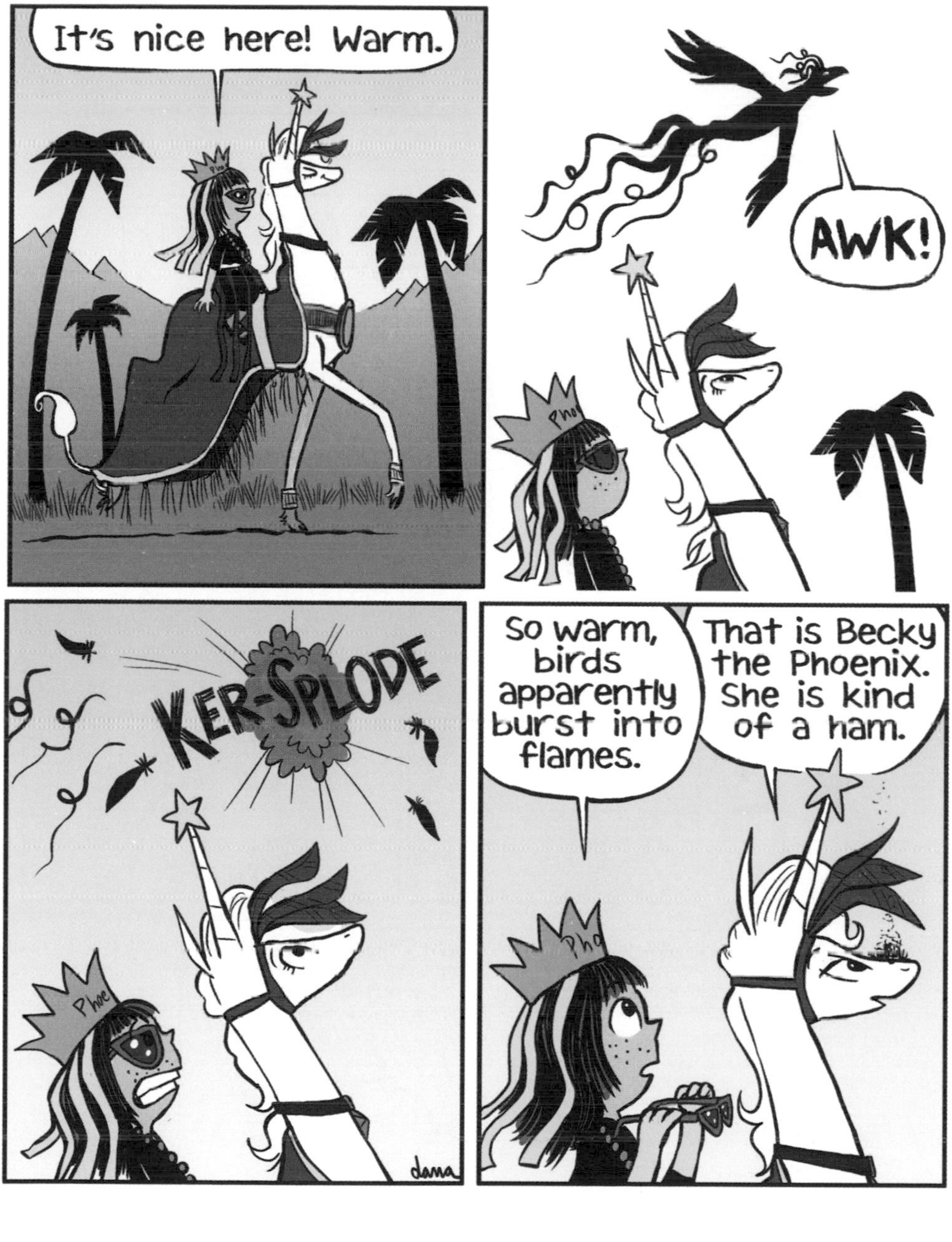
It's nice here! Warm.
Pho
AWK!
Pho
KER-SPLODE
Phoe
So warm, birds apparently burst into flames.
That is Becky the Phoenix. She is kind of a ham.
Pho
dana

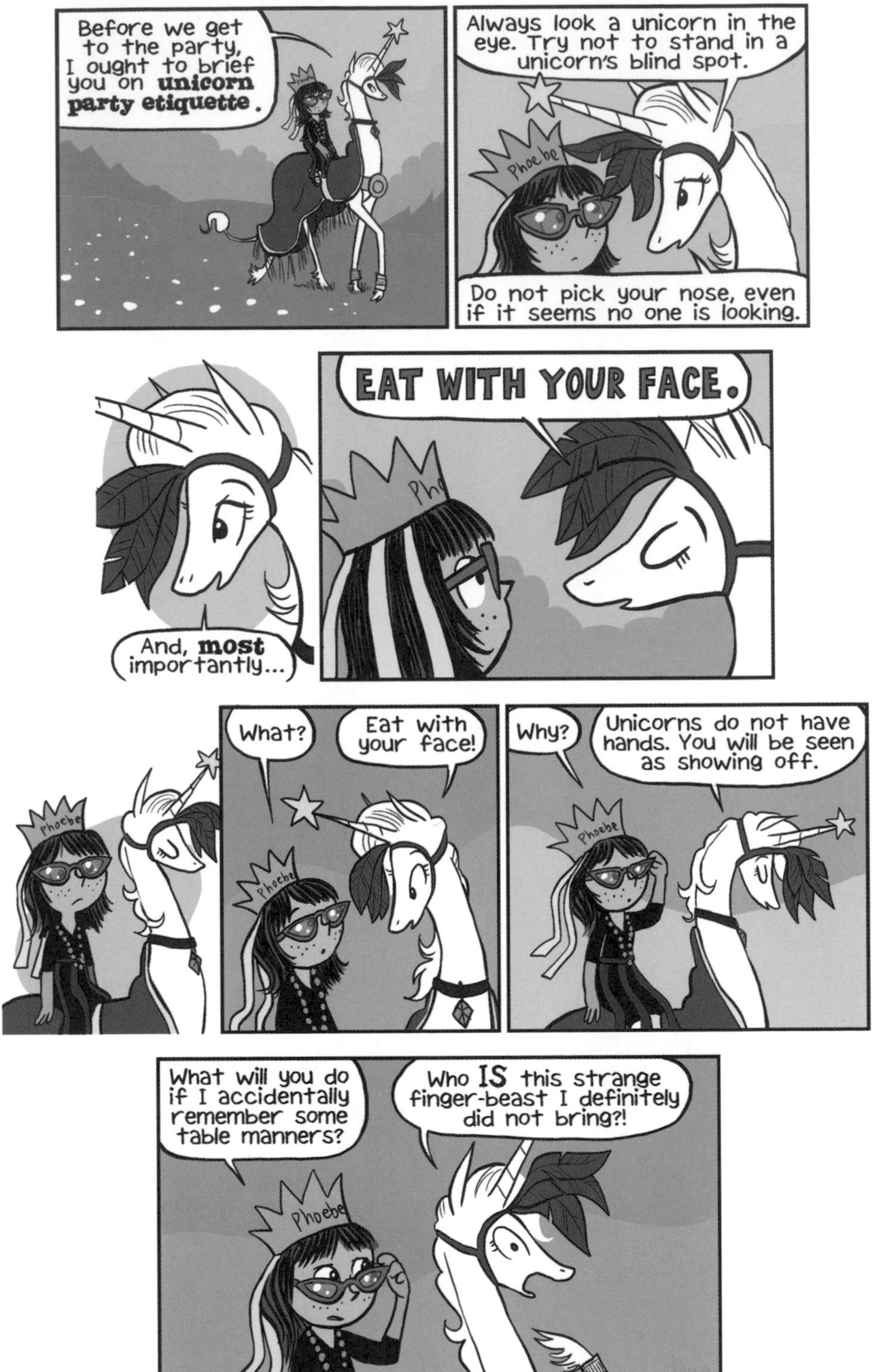
Before we get to the party, I ought to brief you on **unicorn party etiquette**.
Always look a unicorn in the eye. Try not to stand in a unicorn's blind spot.
Do not pick your nose, even if it seems no one is looking.
And, **most** importantly...
EAT WITH YOUR FACE.
What?
Eat with your face!
Why?
Unicorns do not have hands. You will be seen as showing off.
What will you do if I accidentally remember some table manners?
Who IS this strange finger-beast I definitely did not bring?!

This is it.
Phoebe
By the shores of Shimmering Cove, the unicorns gather.
That's poetic.
Phoebe
It used to be "Yak Odor Cove," but we changed it.
dana

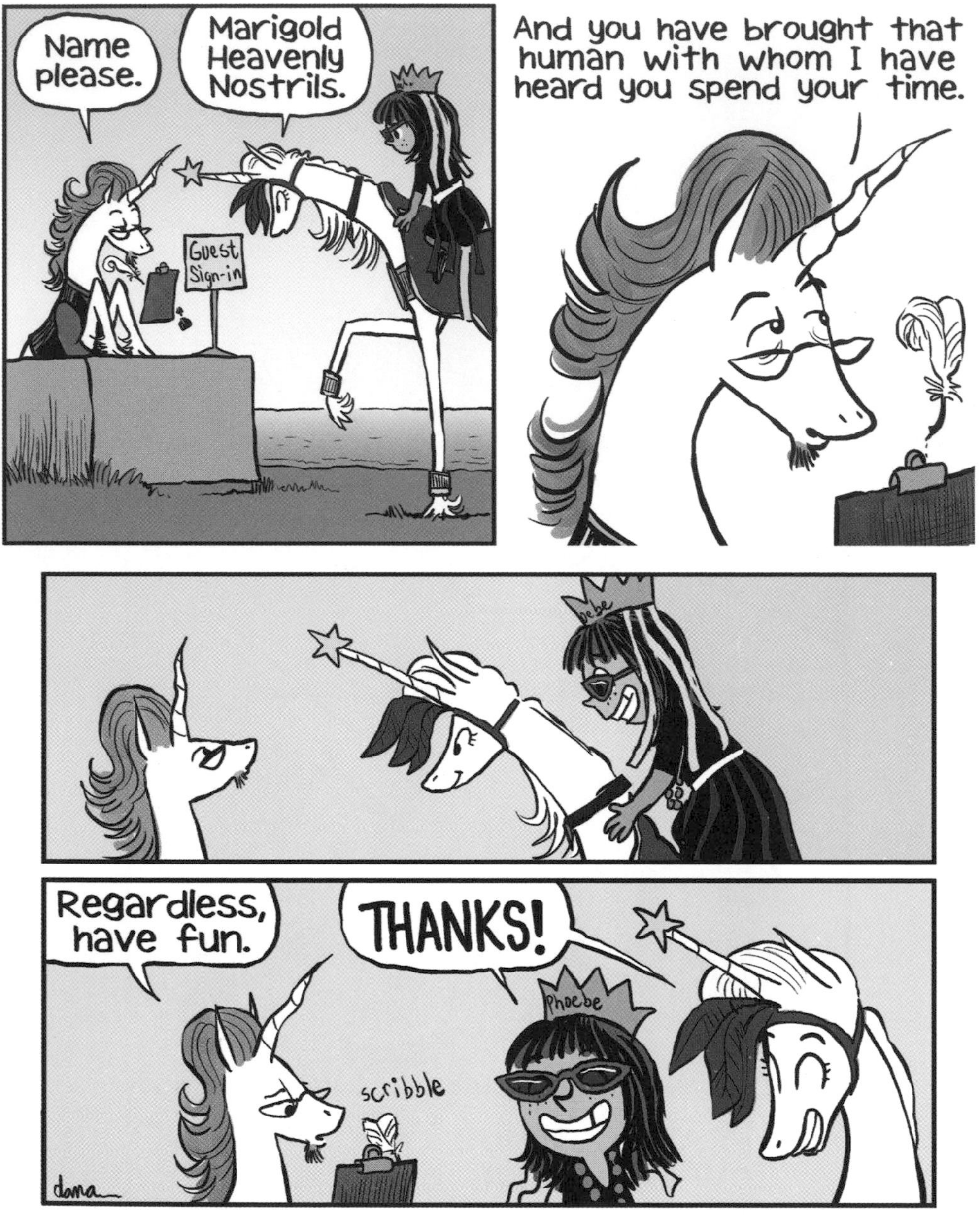

Name please.
Marigold Heavenly Nostrils.
Guest Sign-in
And you have brought that human with whom I have heard you spend your time.
Regardless, have fun.
THANKS!
Phoebe
scribble

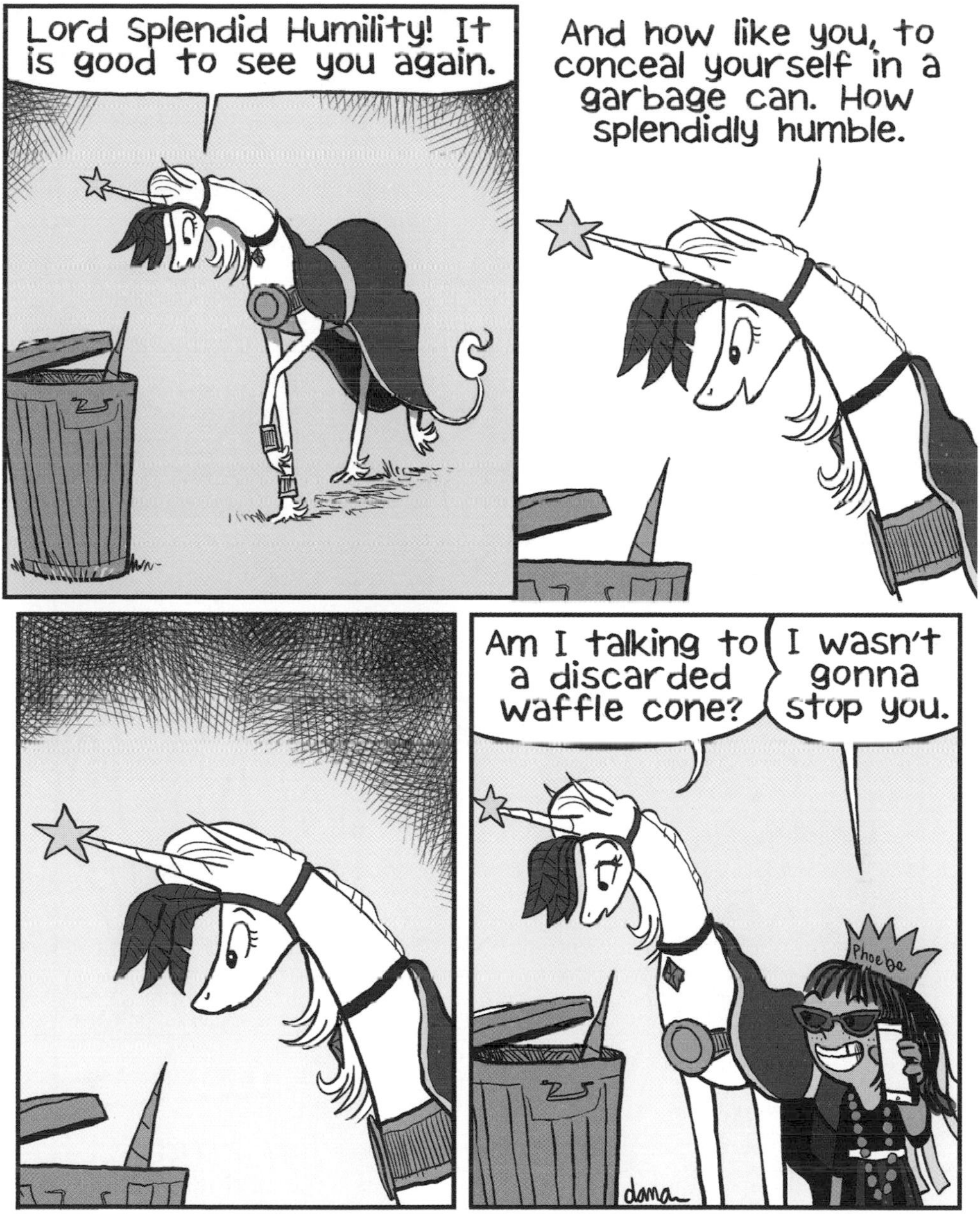
Lord Splendid Humility! It is good to see you again.
And how like you, to conceal yourself in a garbage can. How splendidly humble.
Am I talking to a discarded waffle cone?
I wasn't gonna stop you.
Phoebe
dana

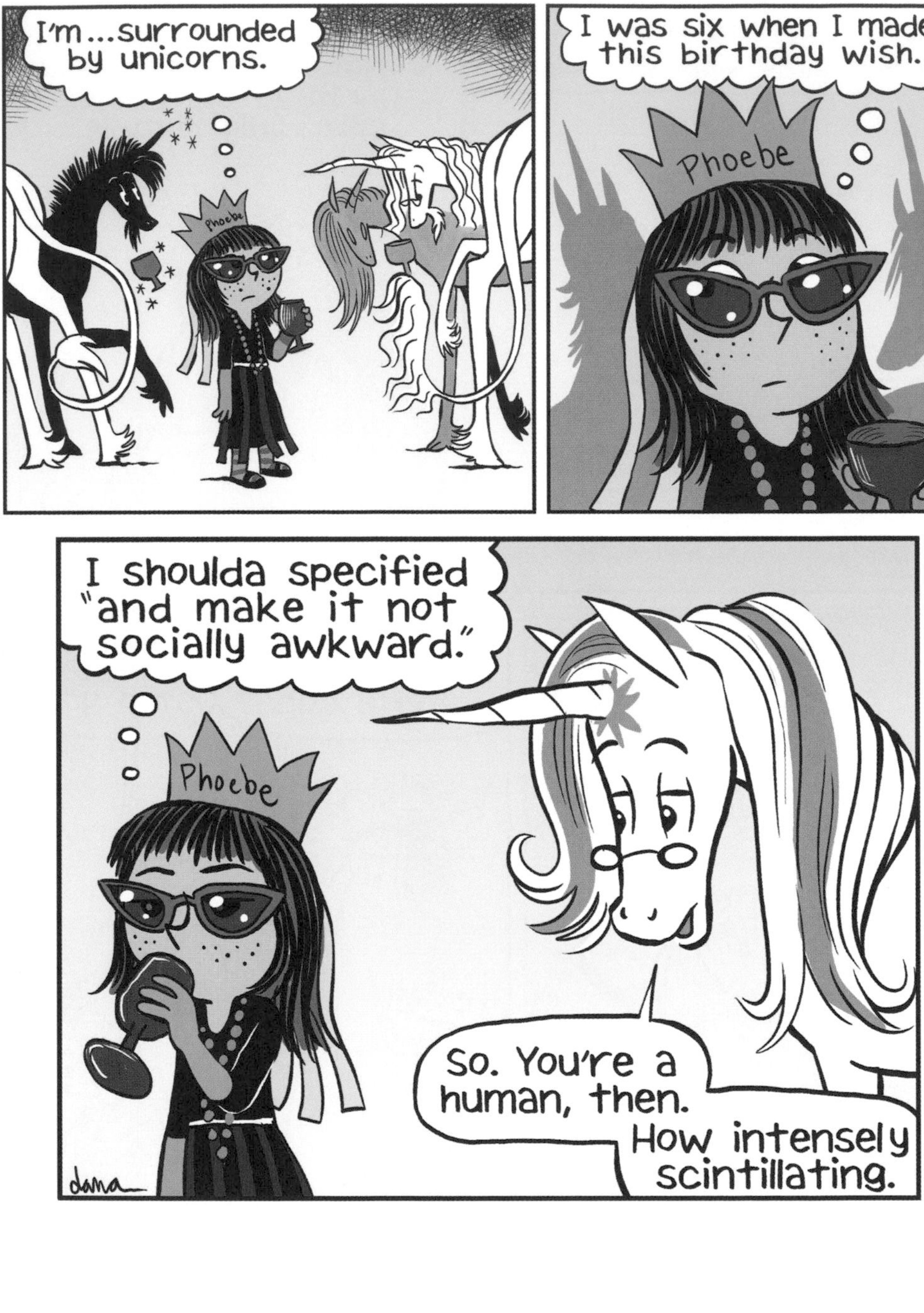
I'm...surrounded by unicorns.
Phoebe
I was six when I made this birthday wish.
Phoebe
I shoulda specified "and make it not socially awkward."
Phoebe
So. You're a human, then.
How intensely scintillating.
dana

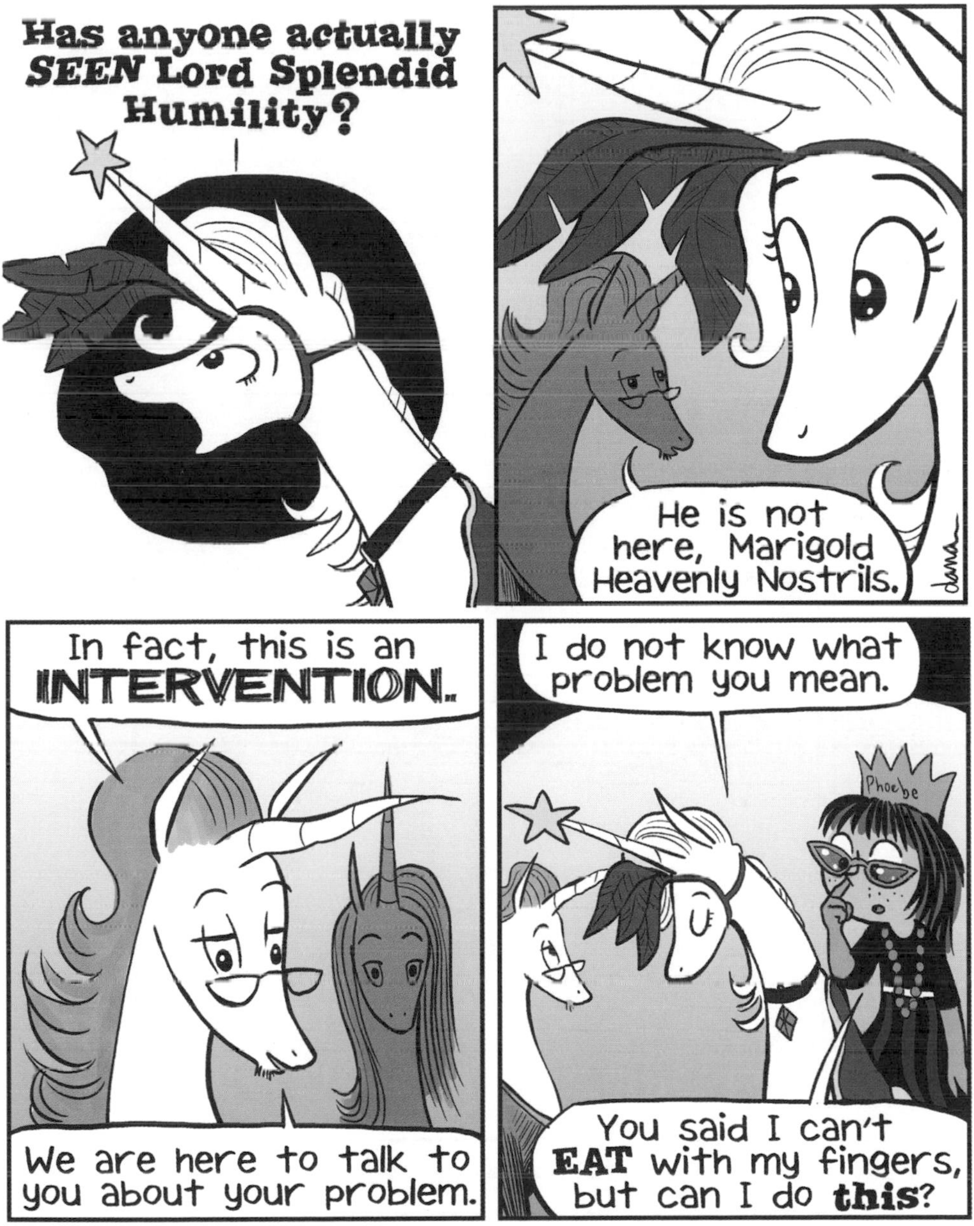

Has anyone actually SEEN Lord Splendid Humility?
He is not here, Marigold Heavenly Nostrils.
dana
In fact, this is an INTERVENTION.
We are here to talk to you about your problem.
I do not know what problem you mean.
Phoebe
You said I can't EAT with my fingers, but can I do this?

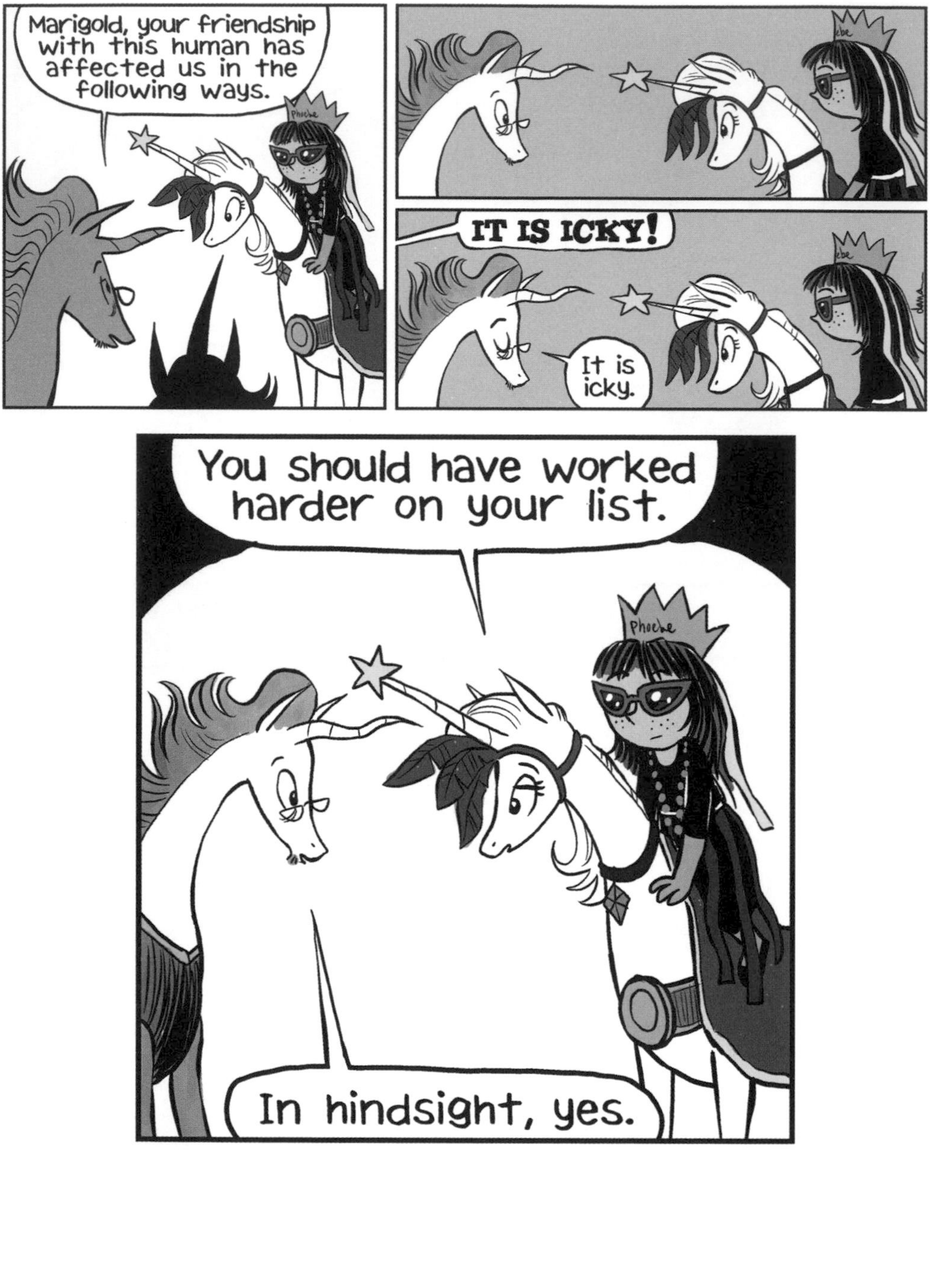
Marigold, your friendship with this human has affected us in the following ways.
IT IS ICKY!
It is icky.
You should have worked harder on your list.
Phoebe
In hindsight, yes.

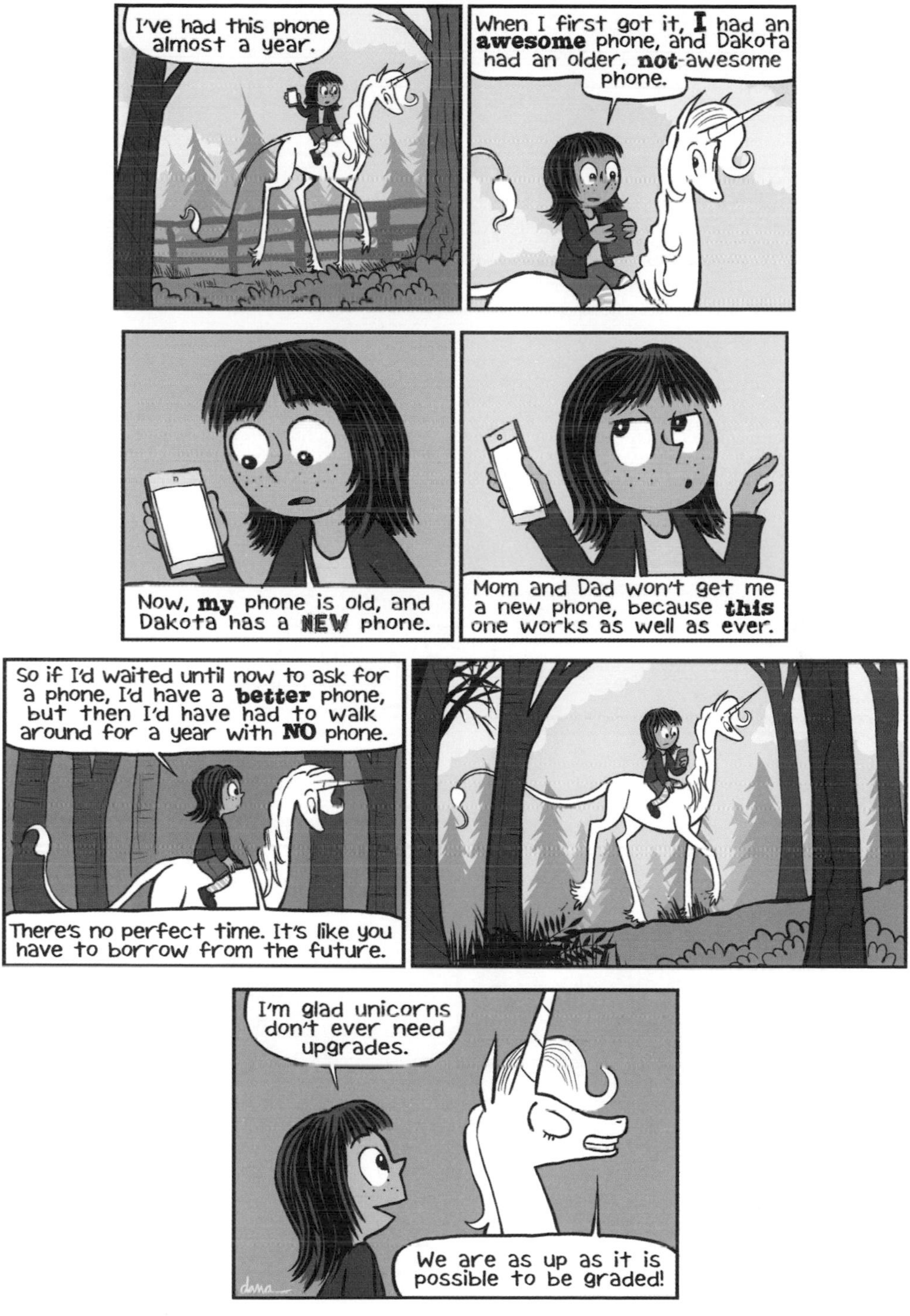
I've had this phone almost a year.
When I first got it, I had an awesome phone, and Dakota had an older, not-awesome phone.
Now, my phone is old, and Dakota has a NEW phone.
Mom and Dad won't get me a new phone, because this one works as well as ever.
So if I'd waited until now to ask for a phone, I'd have a better phone, but then I'd have had to walk around for a year with NO phone.
There's no perfect time. It's like you have to borrow from the future.
I'm glad unicorns don't ever need upgrades.
We are as up as it is possible to be graded!
dana

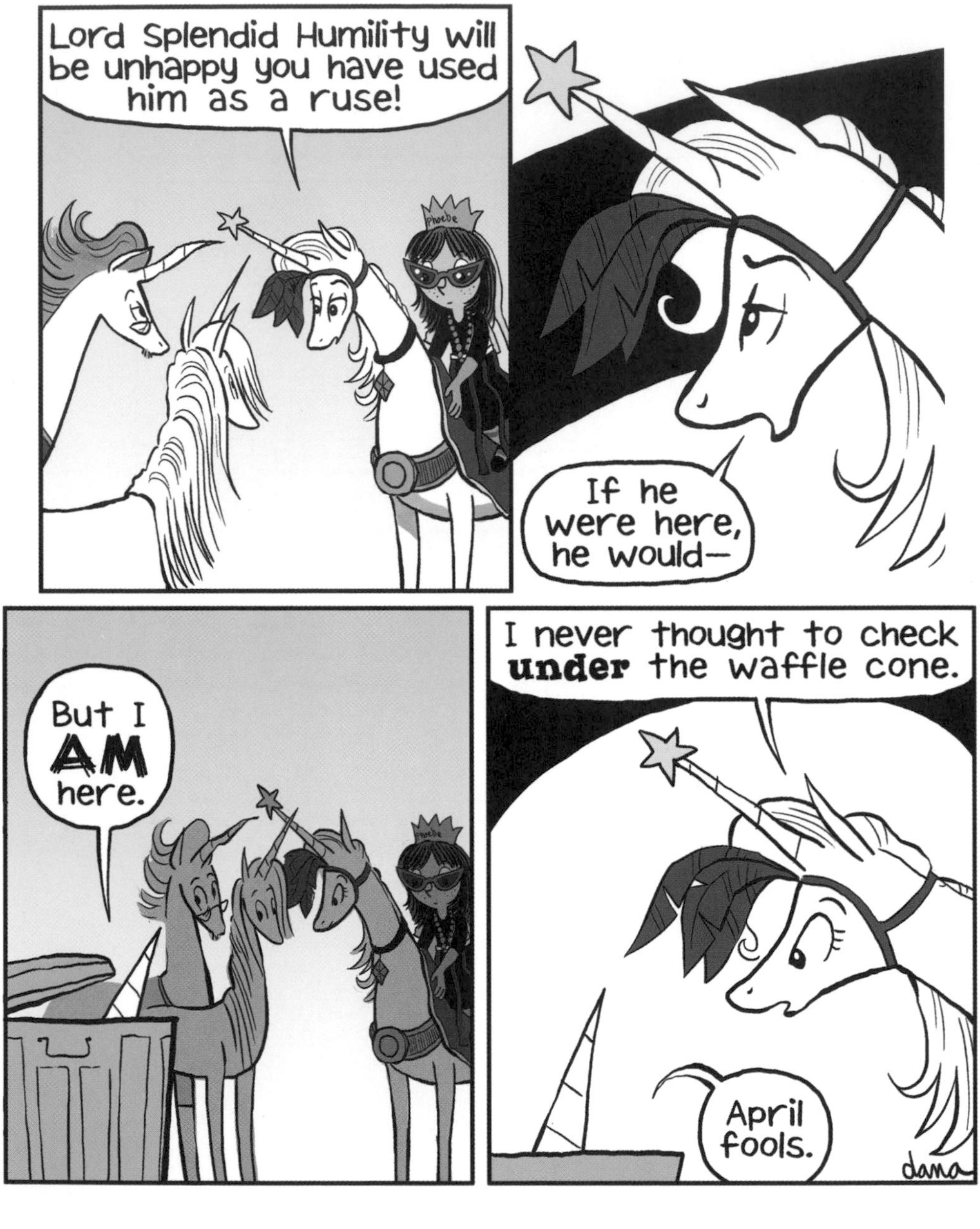
Lord Splendid Humility will be unhappy you have used him as a ruse!
Phoebe
If he were here, he would—
But I AM here.
Phoebe
I never thought to check **under** the waffle cone.
April fools.
dana

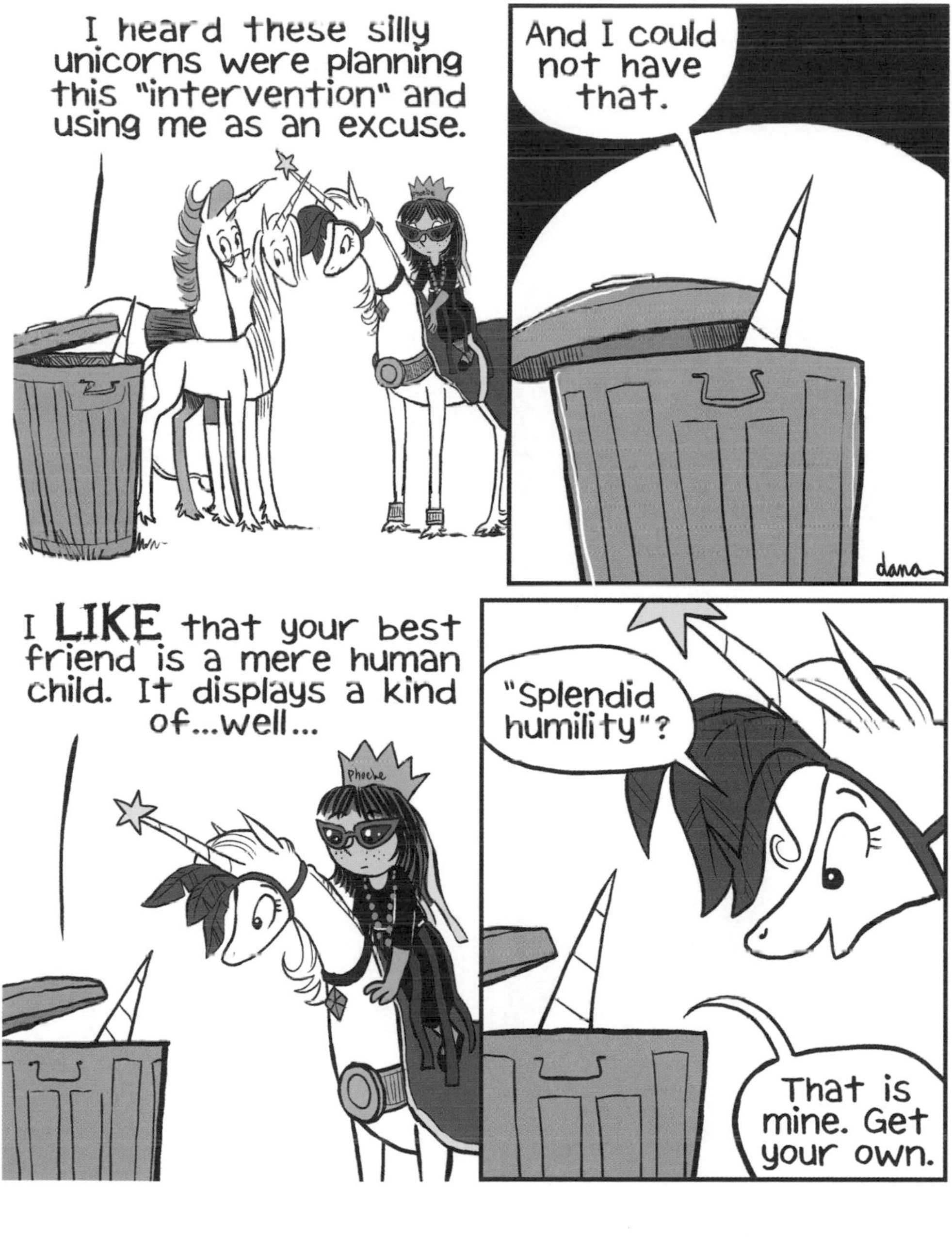
I heard these silly unicorns were planning this "intervention" and using me as an excuse.
And I could not have that.
dana
I LIKE that your best friend is a mere human child. It displays a kind of...well...
Phoebe
"Splendid humility"?
That is mine. Get your own.

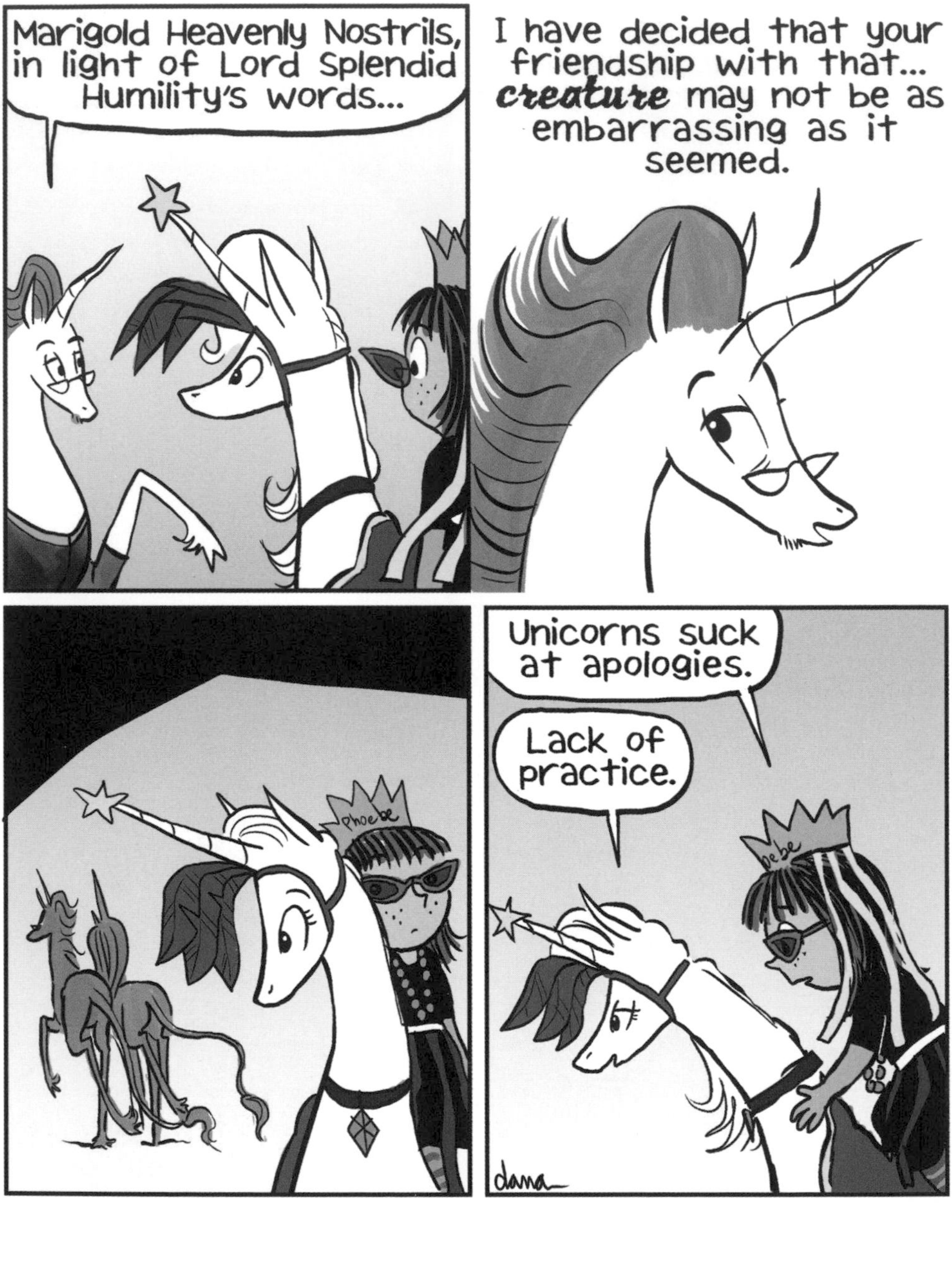
Marigold Heavenly Nostrils, in light of Lord Splendid Humility's words...
I have decided that your friendship with that... *creature* may not be as embarrassing as it seemed.
phoebe
Unicorns suck at apologies.
Lack of practice.
dana

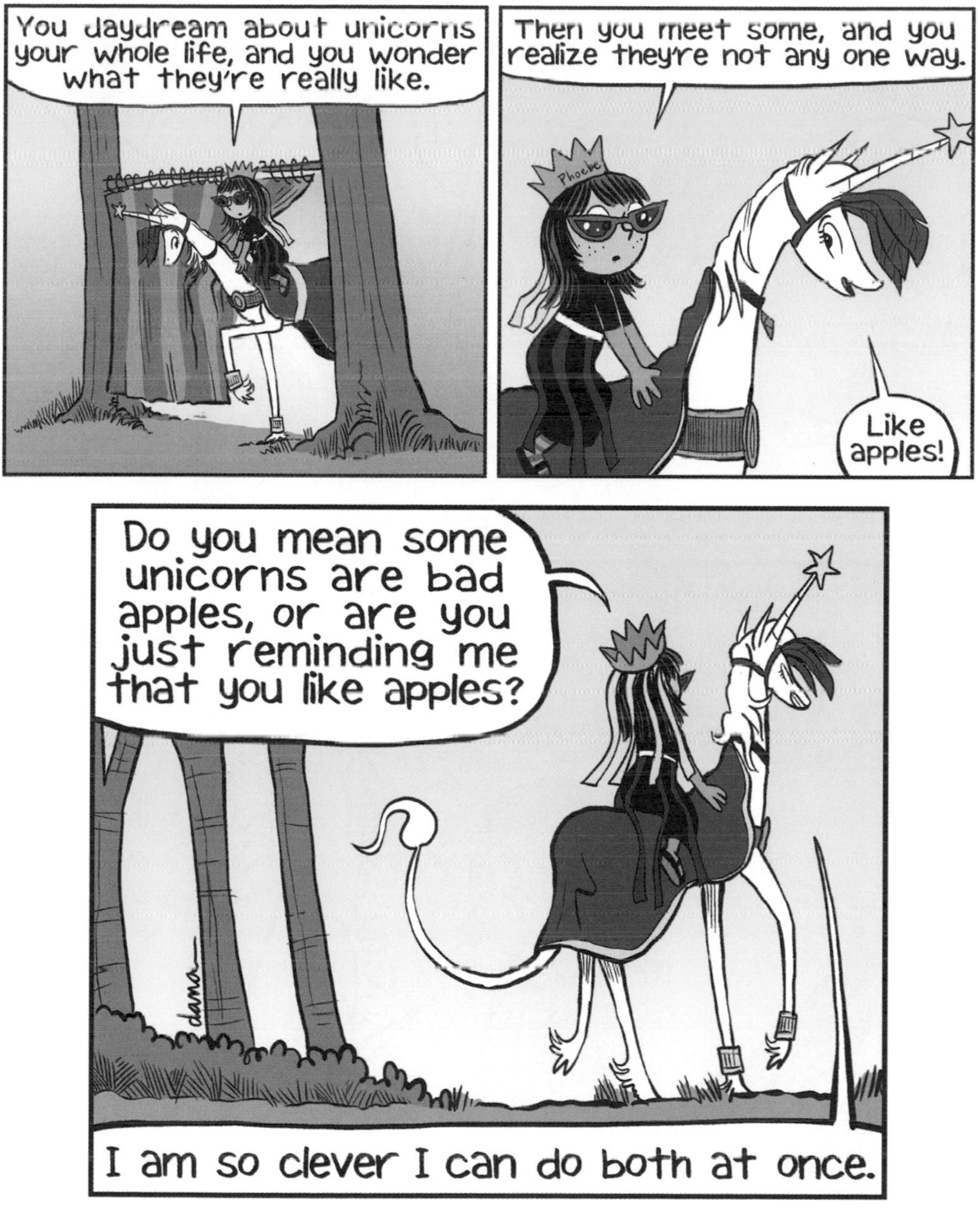

You daydream about unicorns your whole life, and you wonder what they're really like.
Then you meet some, and you realize they're not any one way.
Phoebe
Like apples!
Do you mean some unicorns are bad apples, or are you just reminding me that you like apples?
dana
I am so clever I can do both at once.

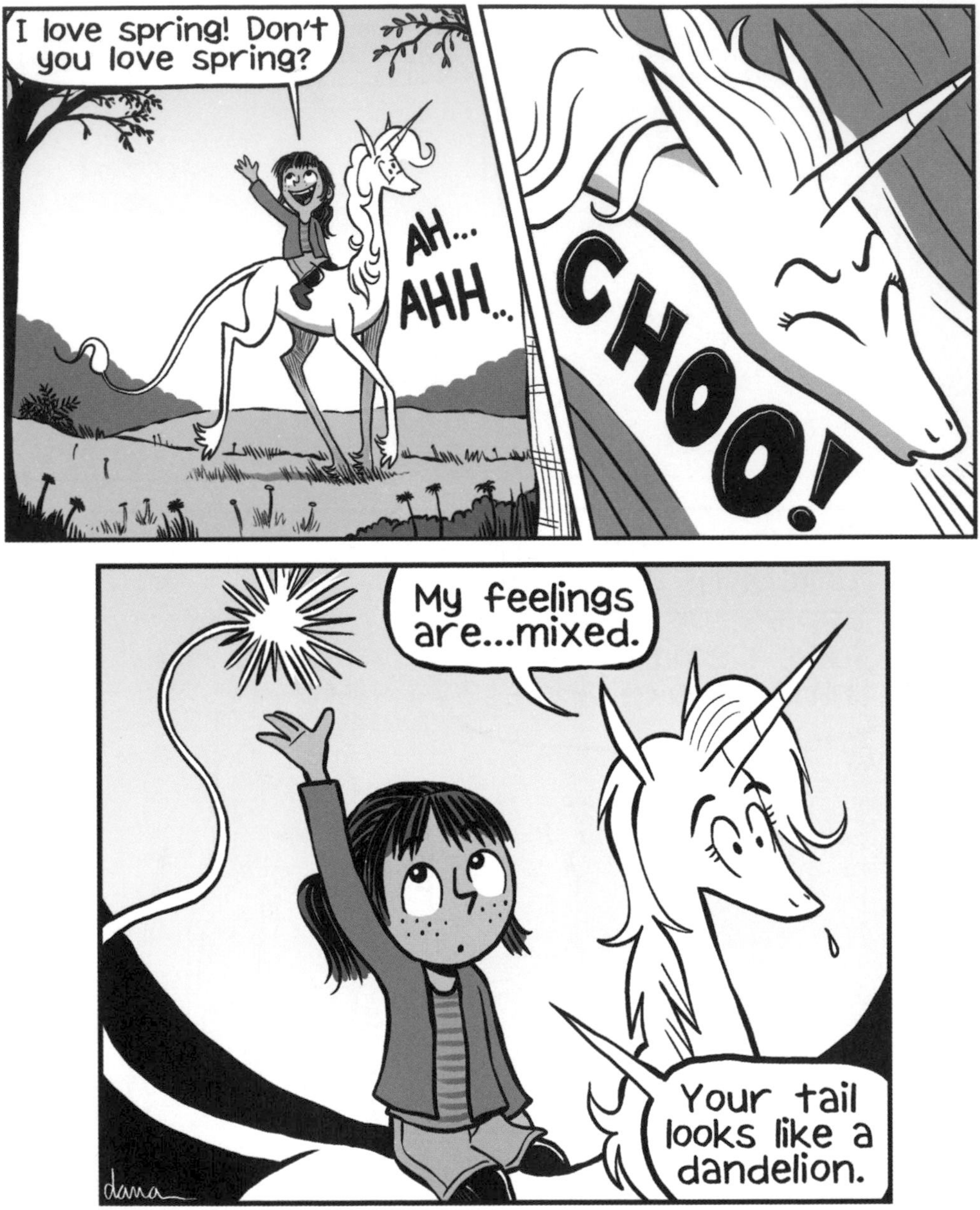
I love spring! Don't you love spring?
AH... AHH...
CHOO!
My feelings are...mixed.
Your tail looks like a dandelion.
dana

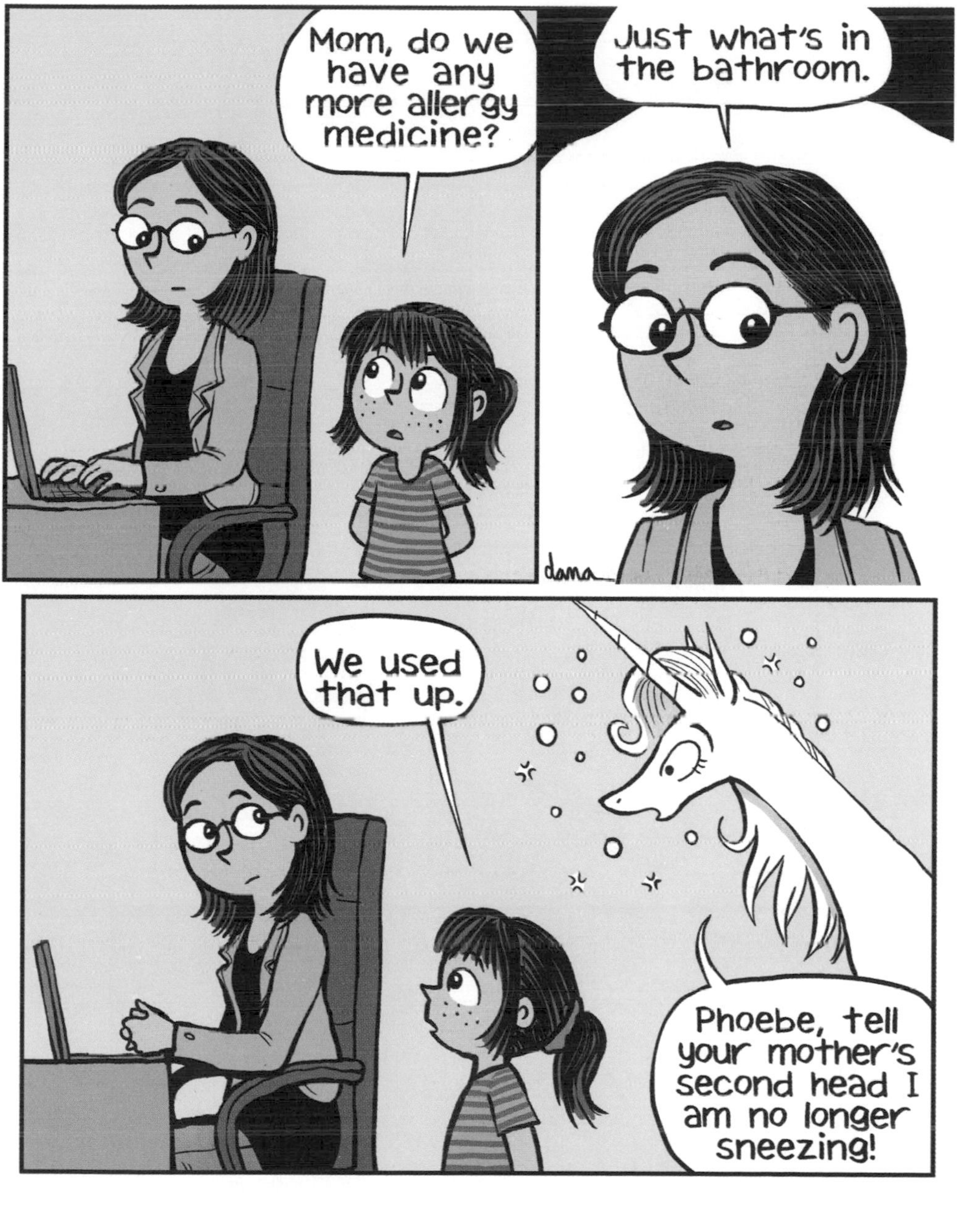
Mom, do we have any more allergy medicine?
Just what's in the bathroom.
dana
We used that up.
Phoebe, tell your mother's second head I am no longer sneezing!

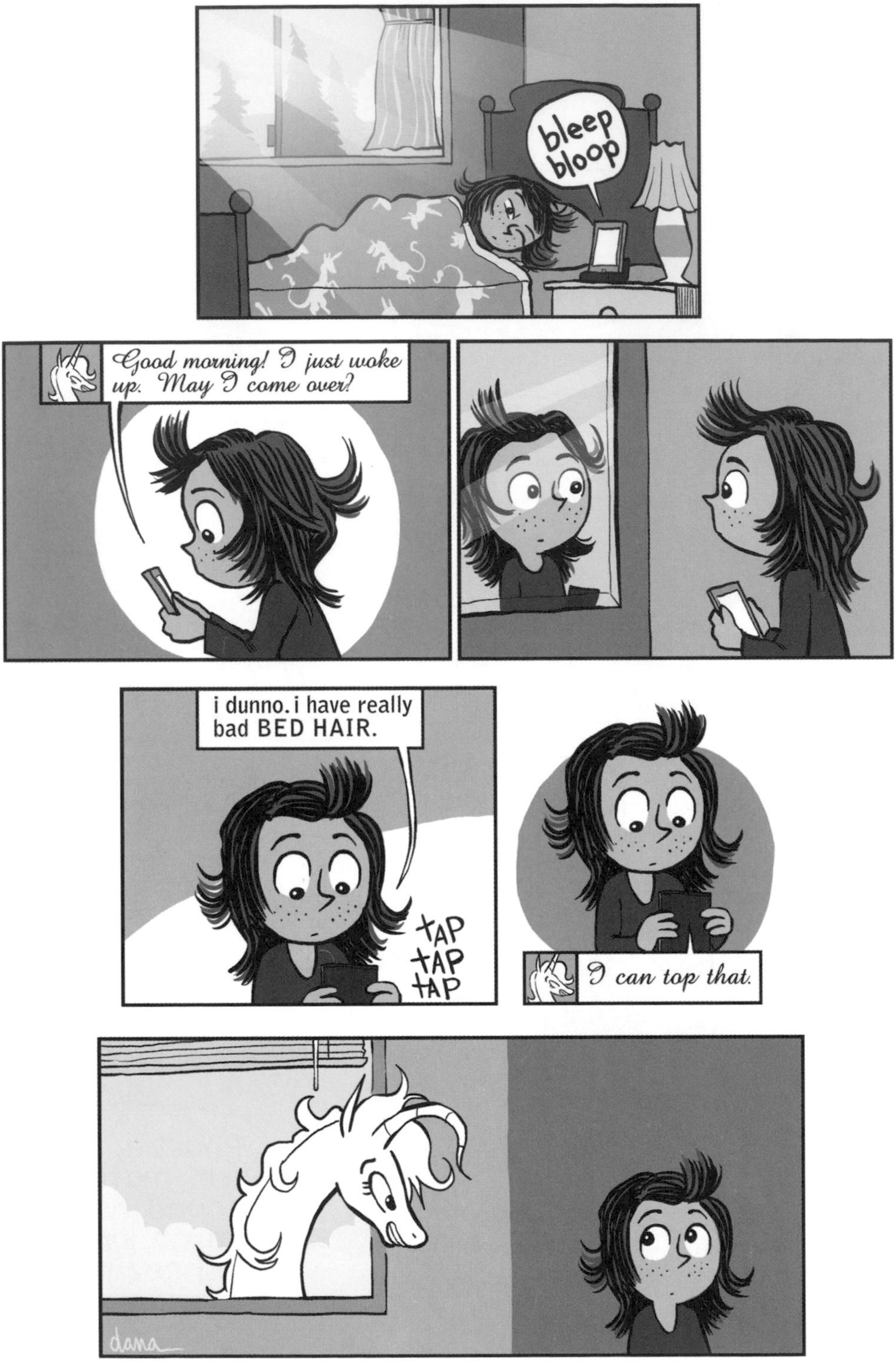
bleep
bloop
Good morning! I just woke up. May I come over?
i dunno. i have really bad BED HAIR.
tAP
tAP
tAP
I can top that.
dana

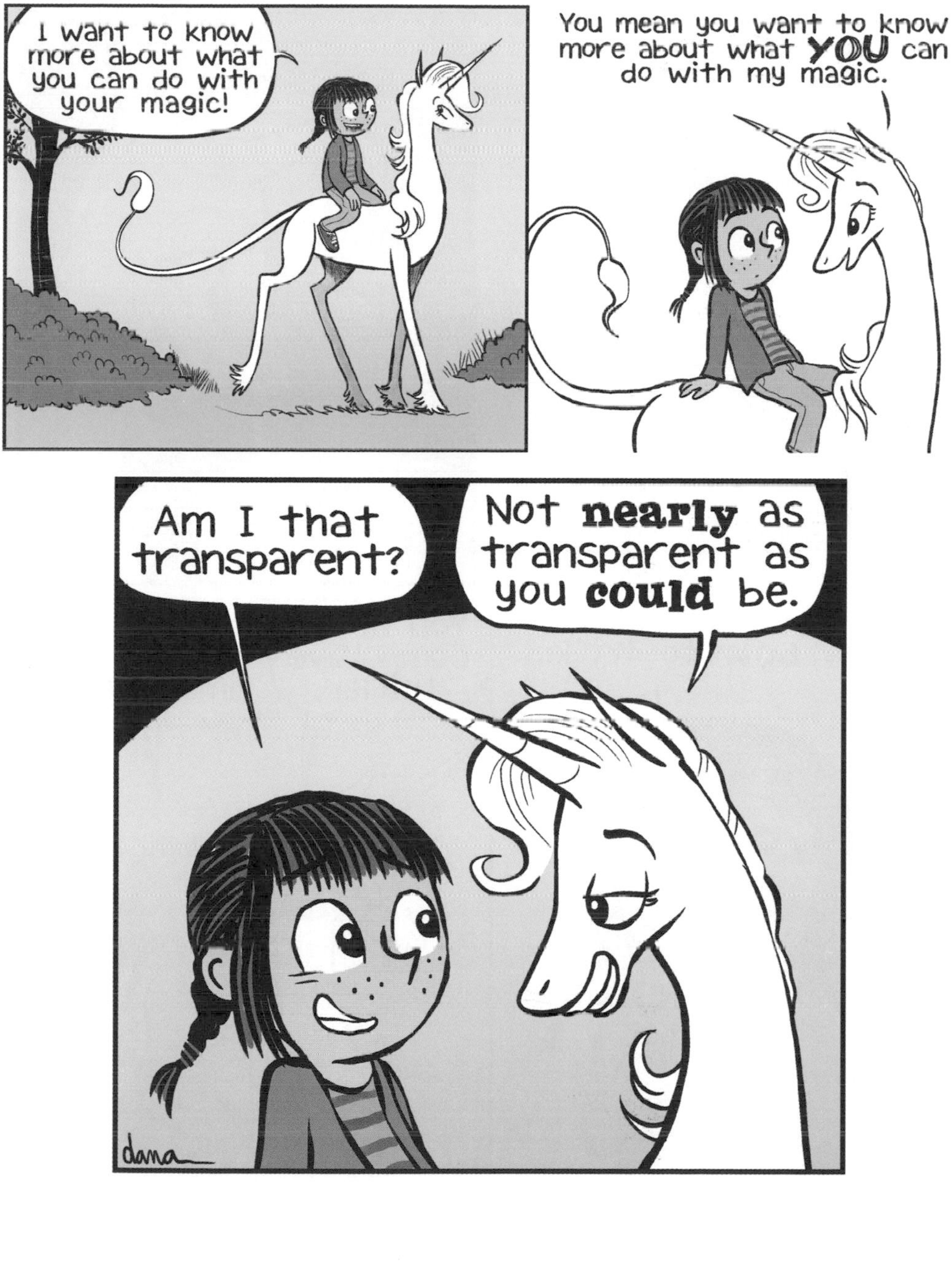
I want to know more about what you can do with your magic!
You mean you want to know more about what YOU can do with my magic.
Am I that transparent?
Not nearly as transparent as you could be.
dana

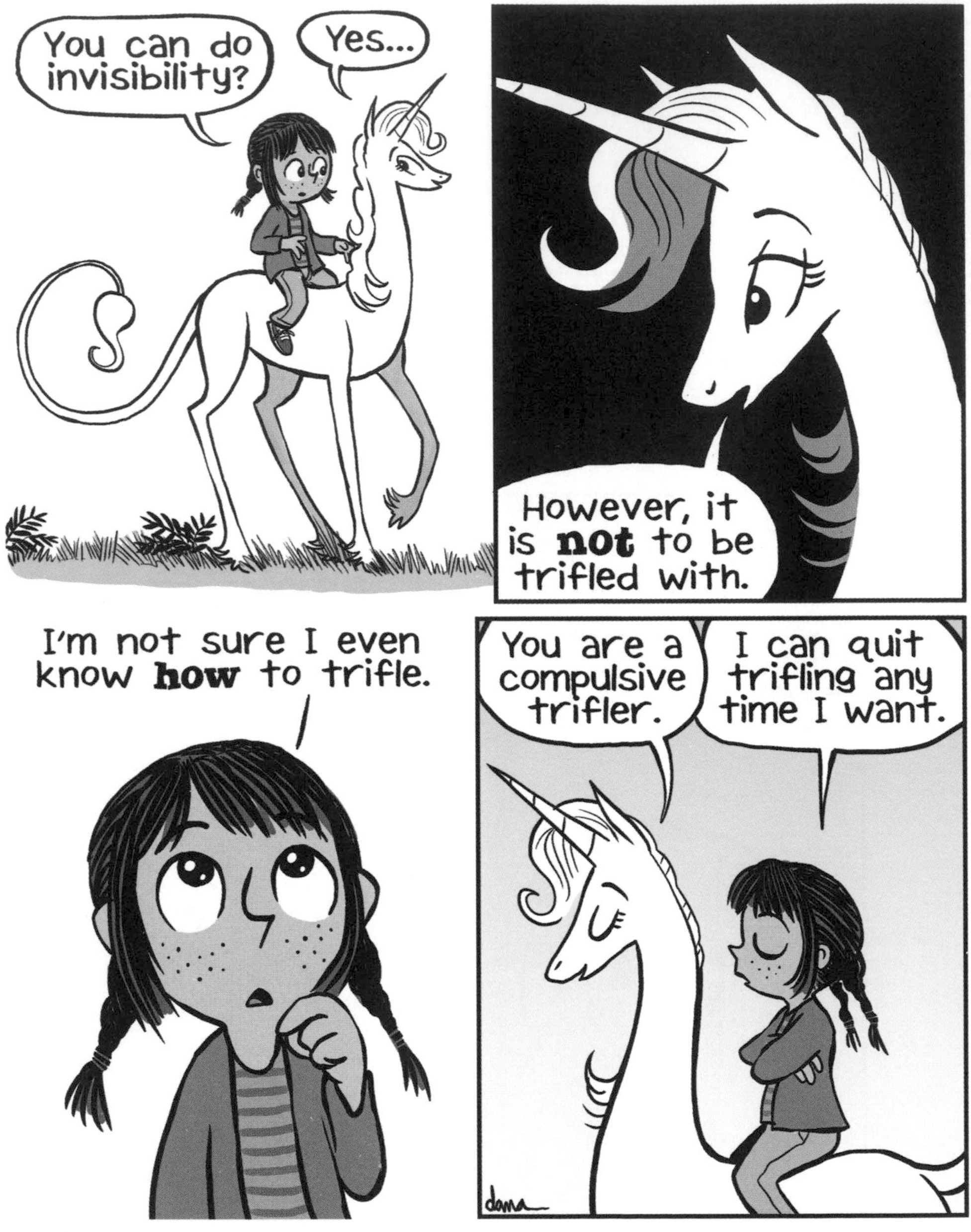
You can do invisibility?
Yes...
However, it is **not** to be trifled with.
I'm not sure I even know **how** to trifle.
You are a compulsive trifler.
I can quit trifling any time I want.
dana

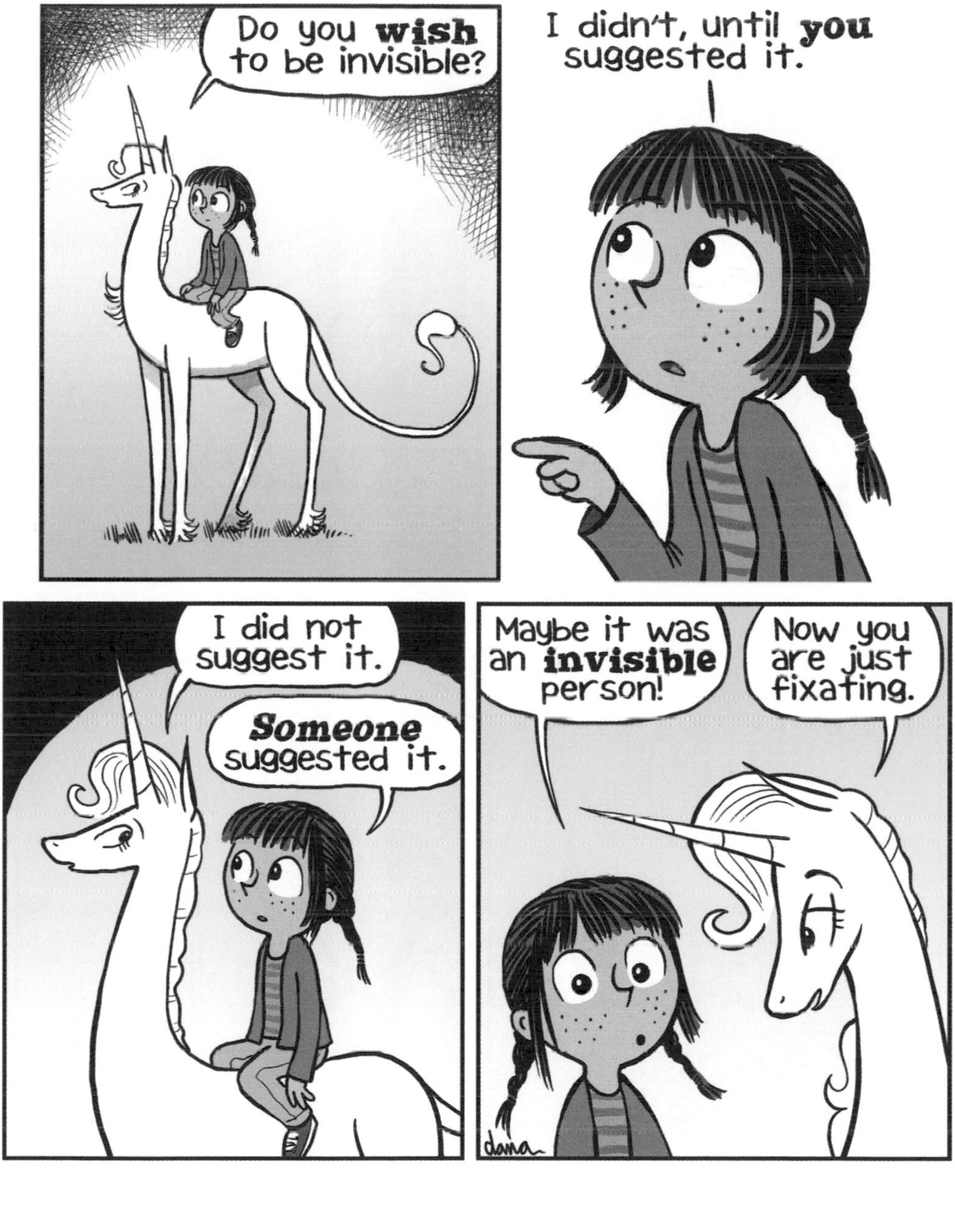
Do you **wish** to be invisible?
I didn't, until **you** suggested it.
I did not suggest it.
Someone suggested it.
Maybe it was an **invisible** person!
Now you are just fixating.
dana

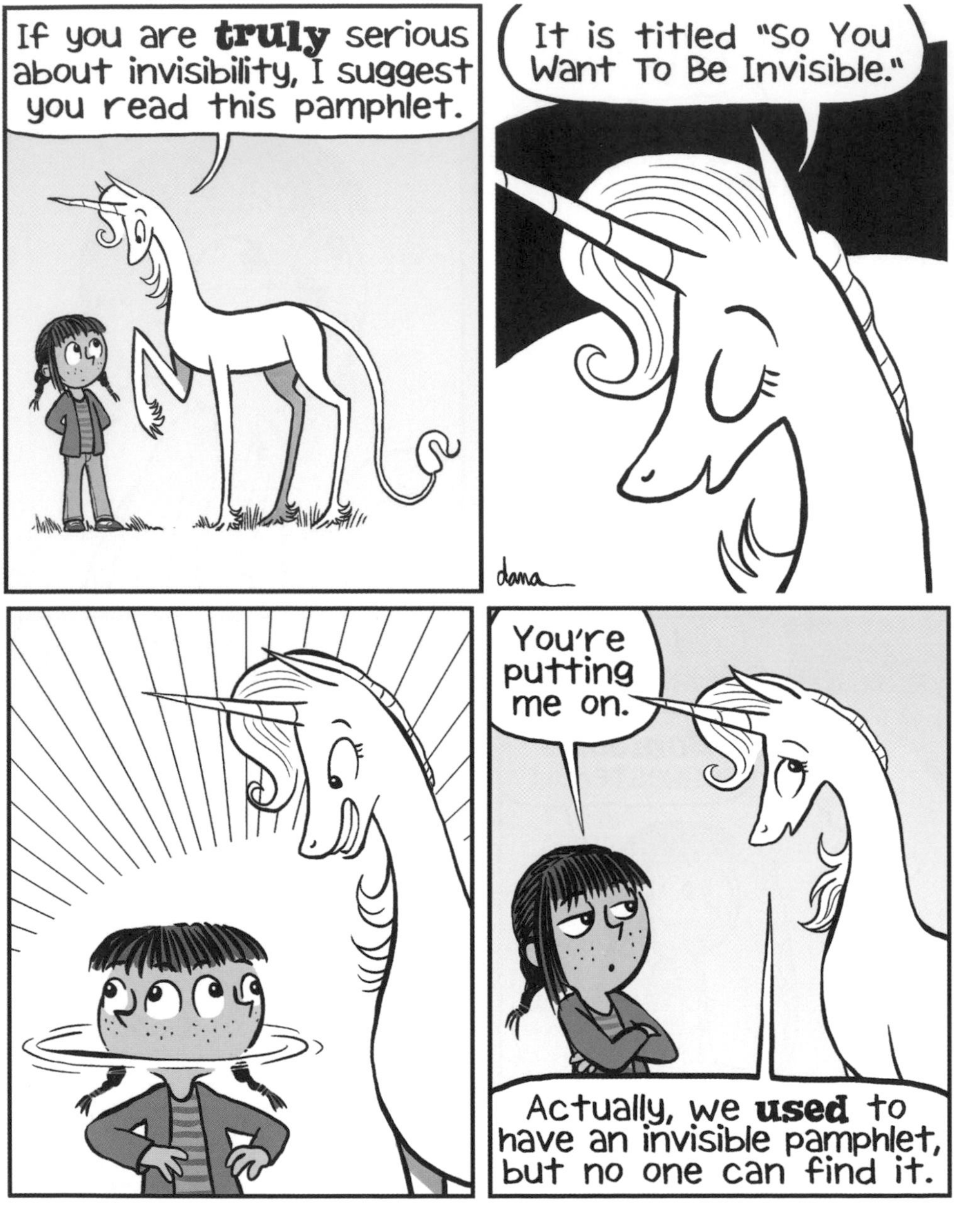

If you are **truly** serious about invisibility, I suggest you read this pamphlet.
It is titled "So You Want To Be Invisible."
dana
You're putting me on.
Actually, we **used** to have an invisible pamphlet, but no one can find it.

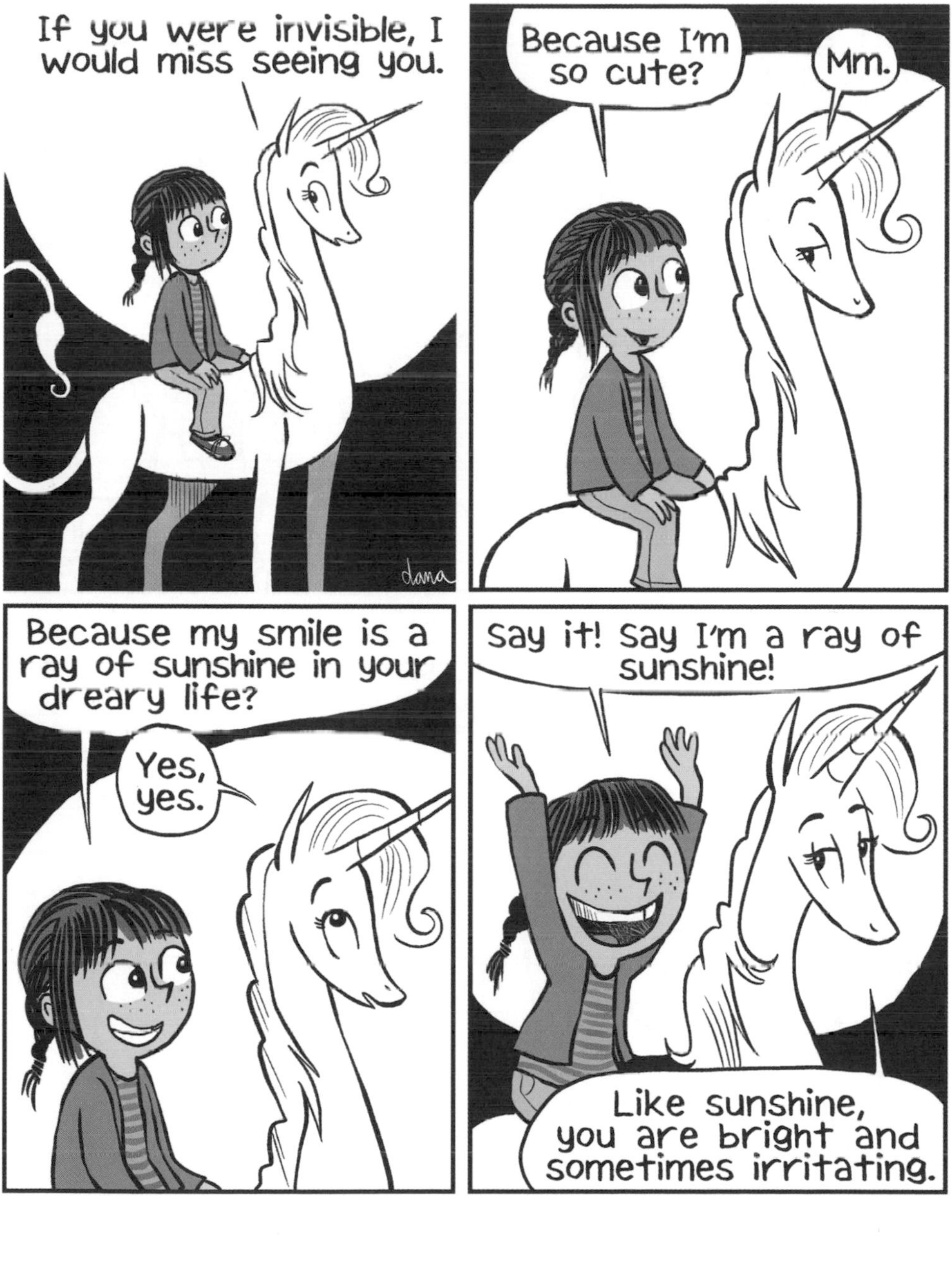
If you were invisible, I would miss seeing you.
Because I'm so cute?
Mm.
Because my smile is a ray of sunshine in your dreary life?
Yes, yes.
Say it! Say I'm a ray of sunshine!
Like sunshine, you are bright and sometimes irritating.
dana

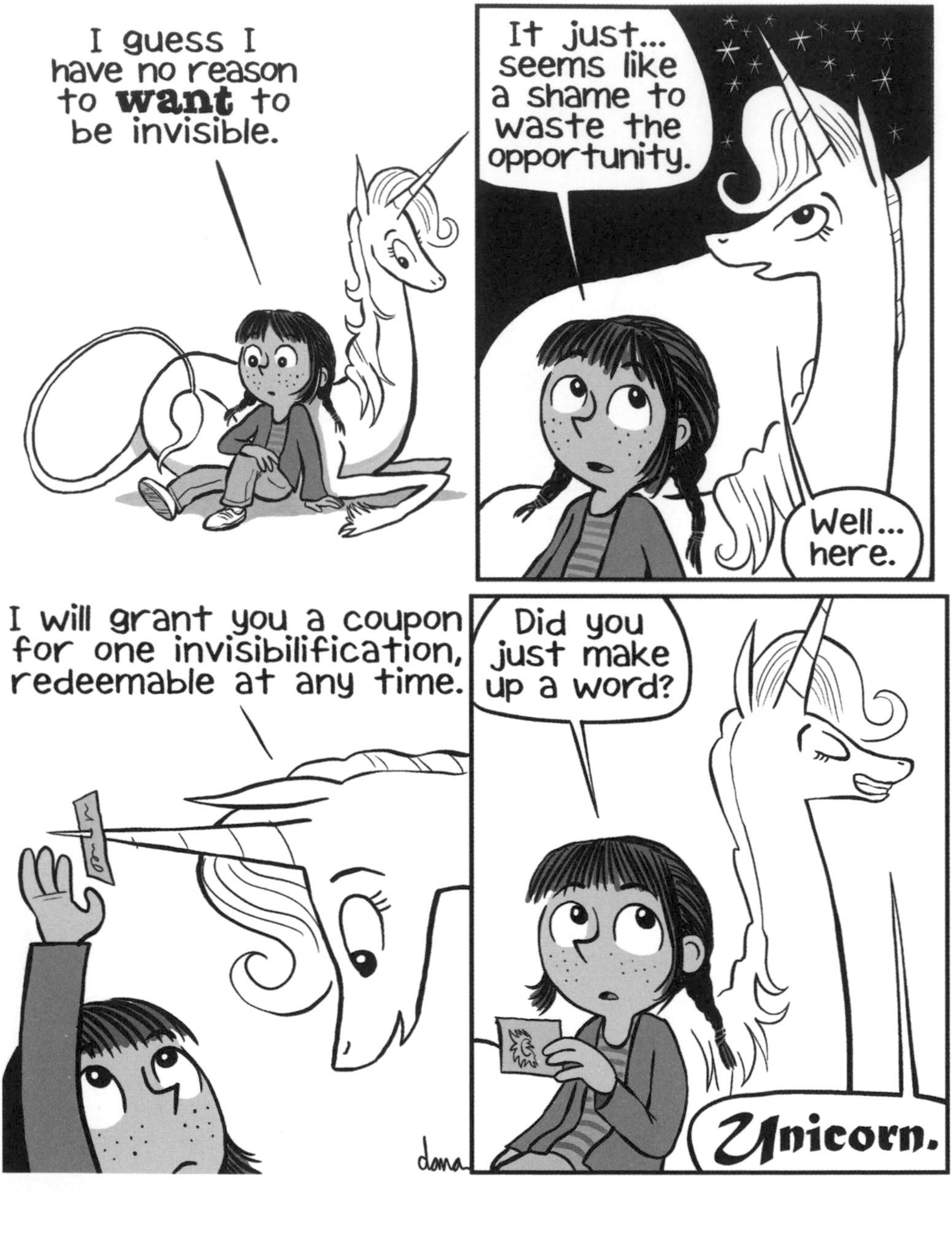

I guess I have no reason to **want** to be invisible.
It just... seems like a shame to waste the opportunity.
Well... here.
I will grant you a coupon for one invisibilification, redeemable at any time.
Did you just make up a word?
Unicorn.
dana

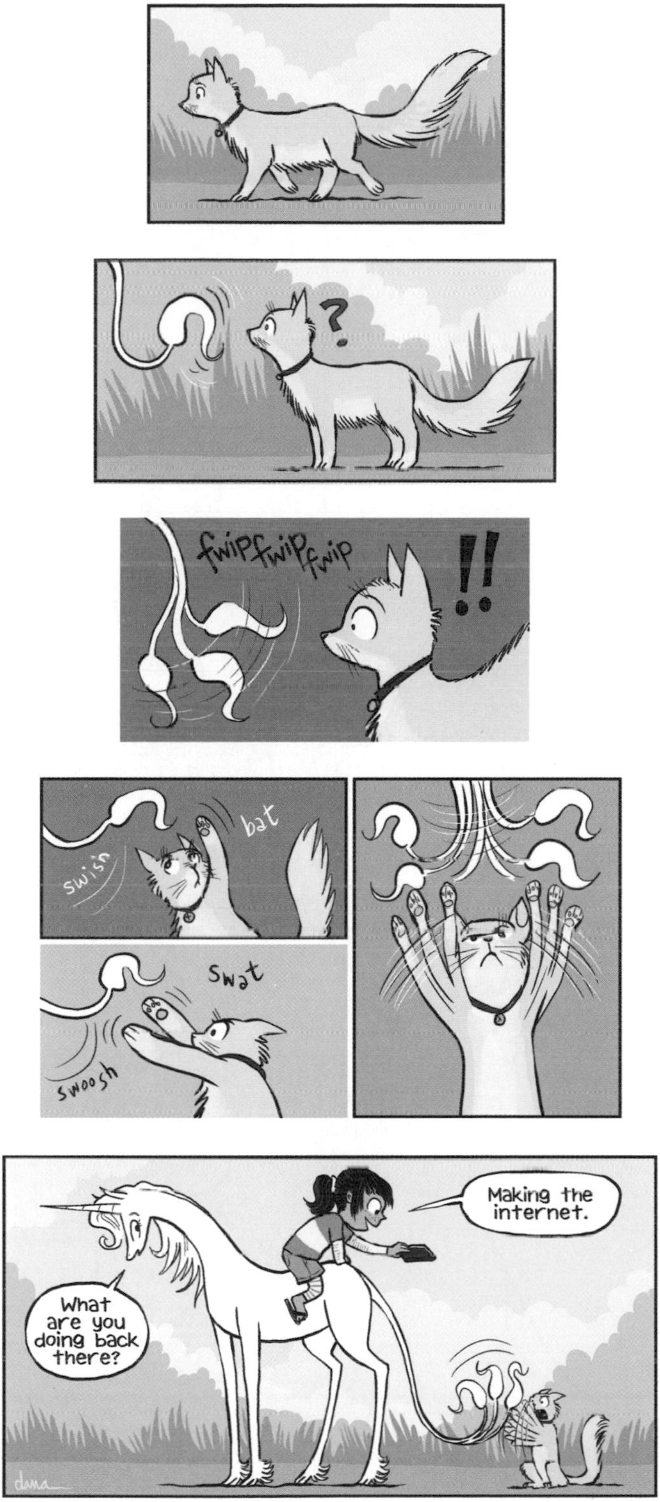
?
fwipfwipfwip
!!
swish
bat
swat
swoosh
What are you doing back there?
Making the internet.

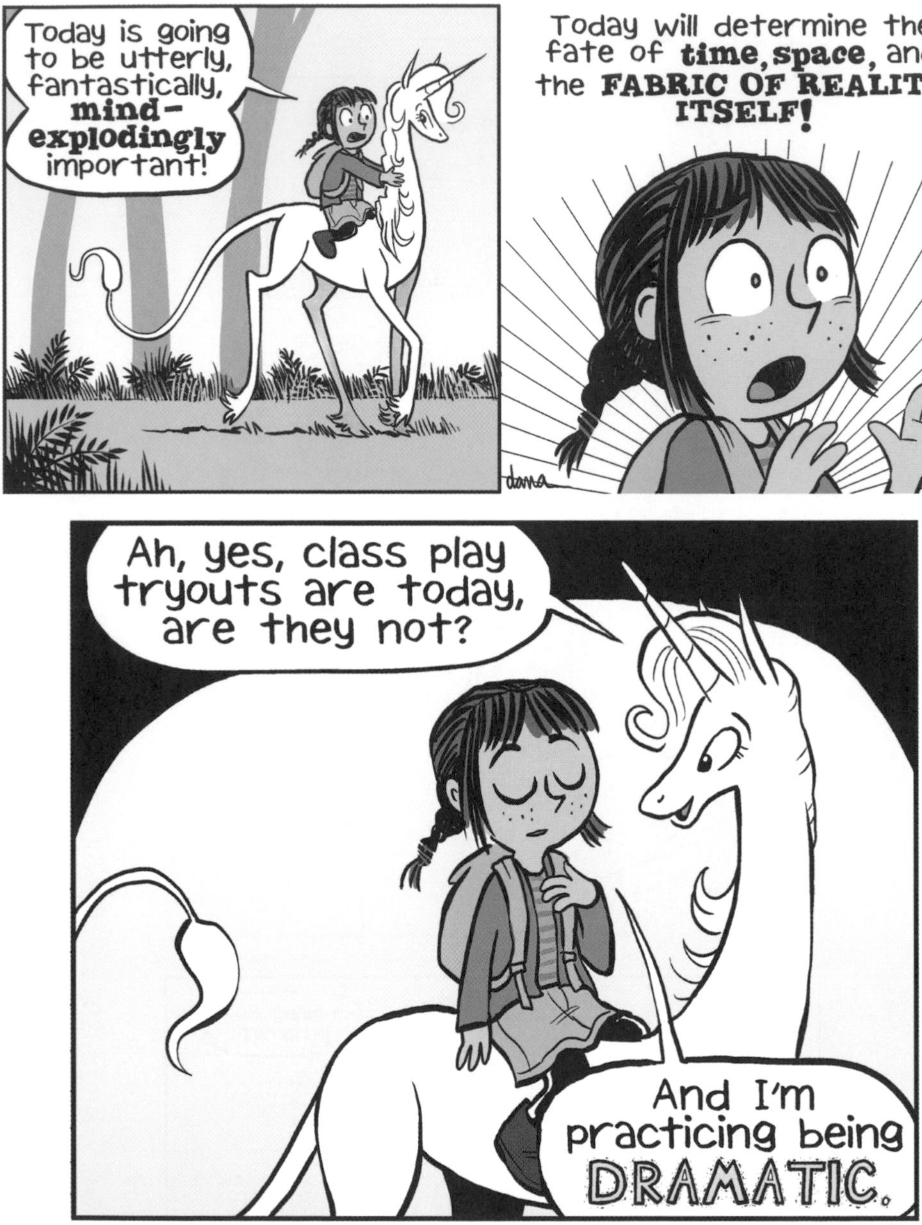
Today is going to be utterly, fantastically, **mind-explodingly** important!
Today will determine the fate of **time, space,** and the **FABRIC OF REALITY ITSELF!**
Ah, yes, class play tryouts are today, are they not?
And I'm practicing being DRAMATIC.

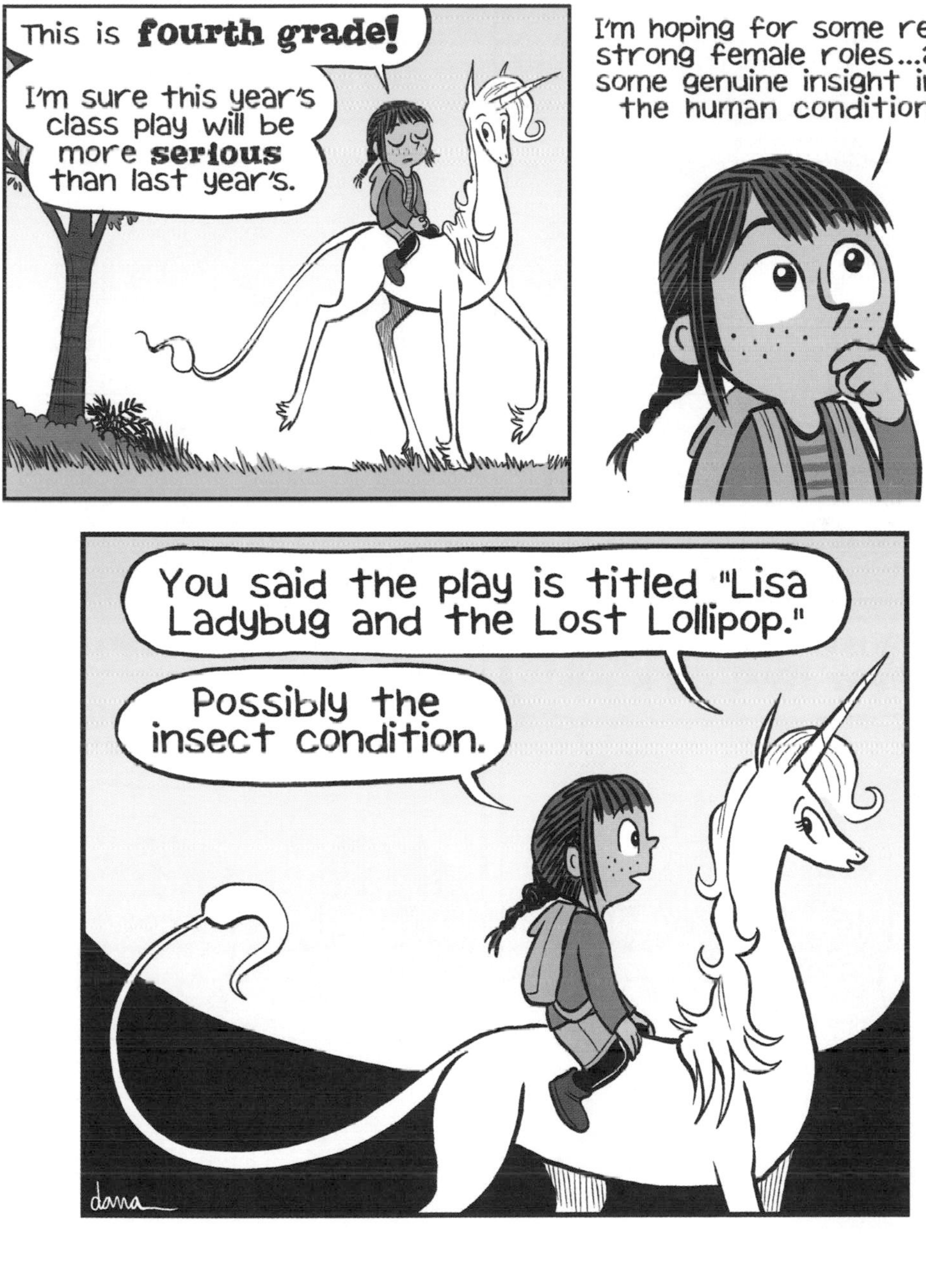
This is fourth grade!
I'm sure this year's class play will be more serious than last year's.
I'm hoping for some really strong female roles...and some genuine insight into the human condition.
You said the play is titled "Lisa Ladybug and the Lost Lollipop."
Possibly the insect condition.
dana

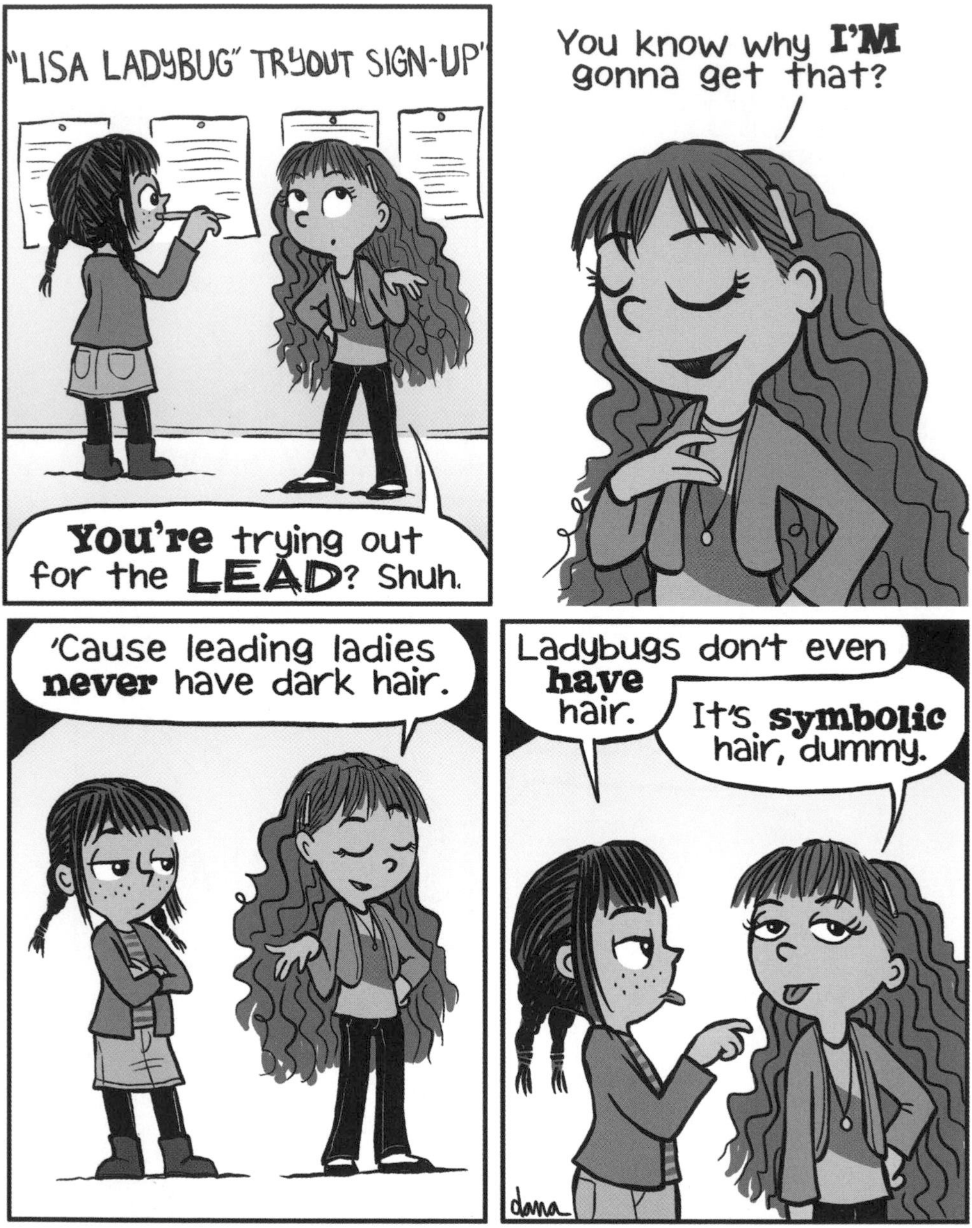
"LISA LADYBUG" TRYOUT SIGN-UP"
You're trying out for the LEAD? Shuh.
You know why I'M gonna get that?
'Cause leading ladies never have dark hair.
Ladybugs don't even have hair.
It's symbolic hair, dummy.
dana

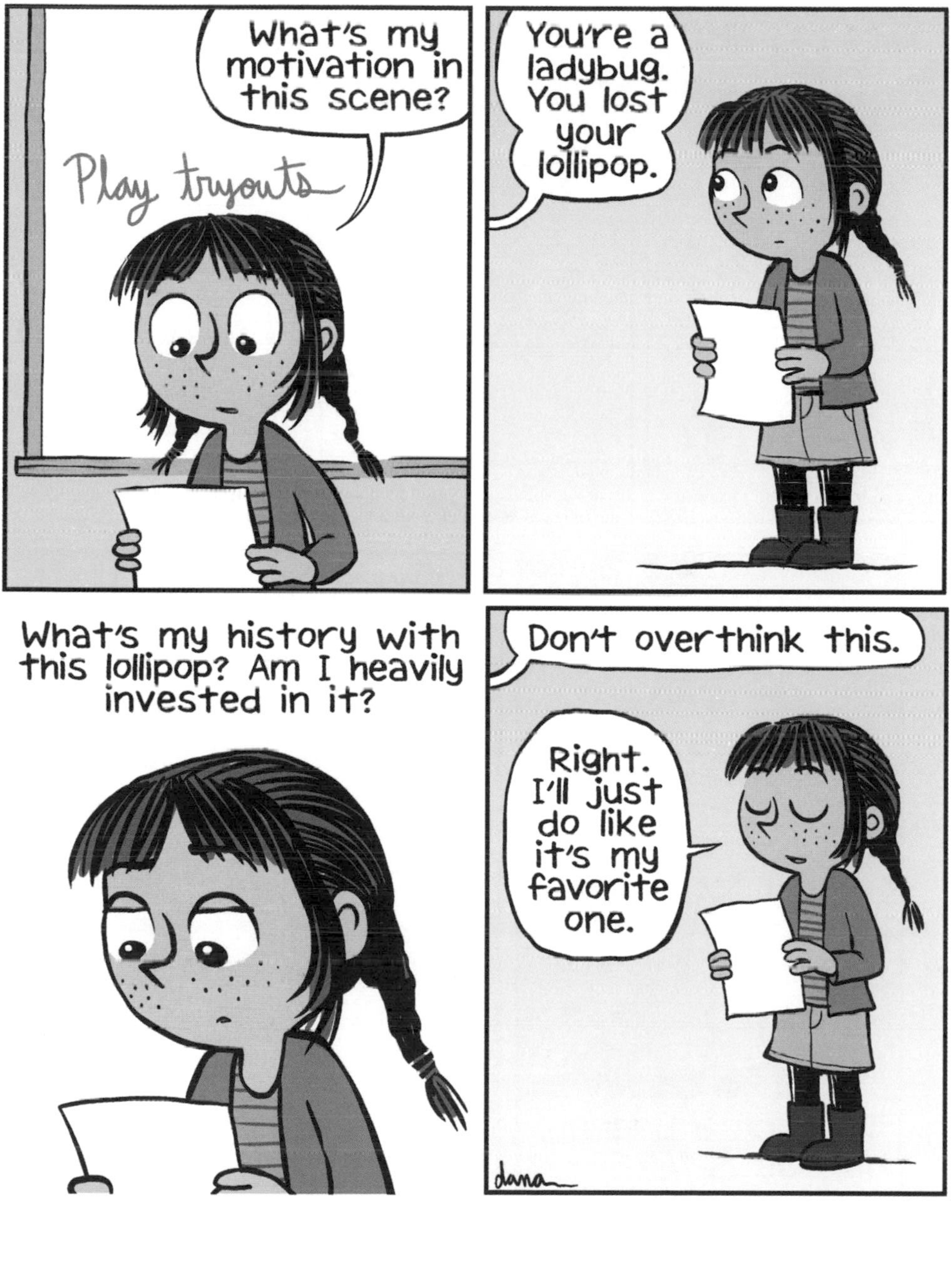
Play tryouts
What's my motivation in this scene?
You're a ladybug. You lost your lollipop.
What's my history with this lollipop? Am I heavily invested in it?
Don't overthink this.
Right. I'll just do like it's my favorite one.
dana

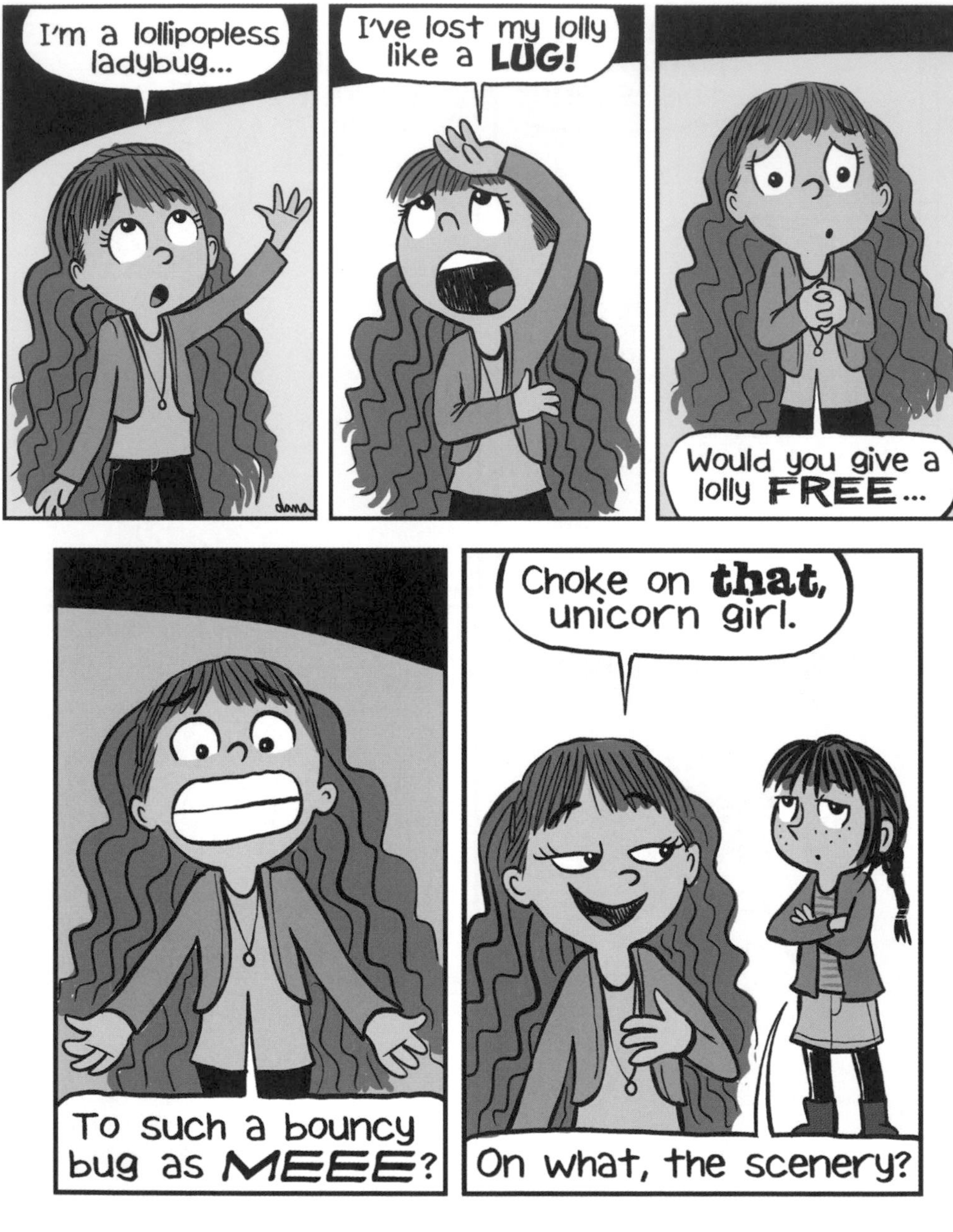
I'm a lollipopless ladybug...
I've lost my lolly like a LUG!
Would you give a lolly FREE...
To such a bouncy bug as MEEE?
Choke on that, unicorn girl.
On what, the scenery?

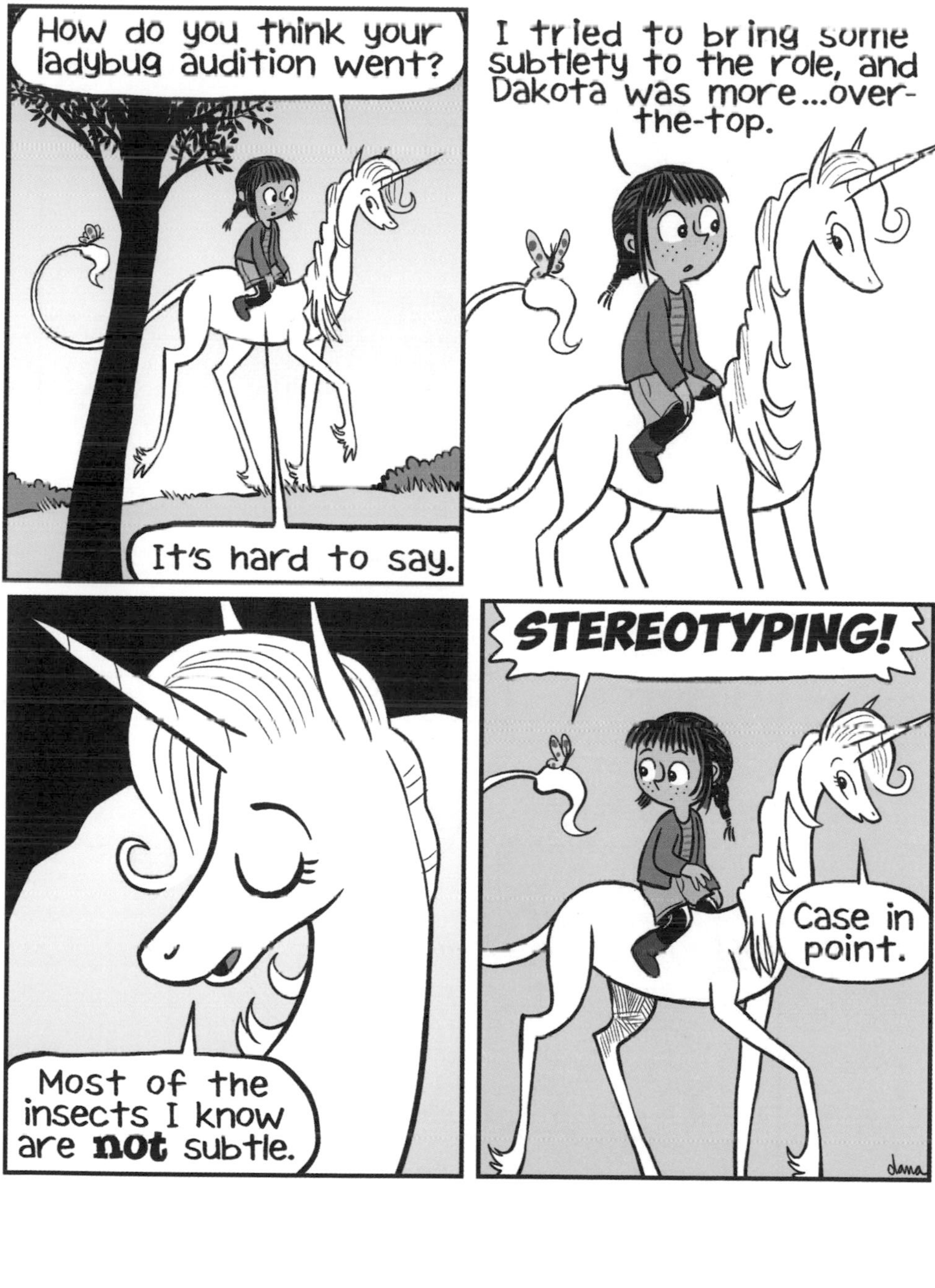
How do you think your ladybug audition went?
It's hard to say.
I tried to bring some subtlety to the role, and Dakota was more...over-the-top.
Most of the insects I know are **not** subtle.
STEREOTYPING!
Case in point.
dana

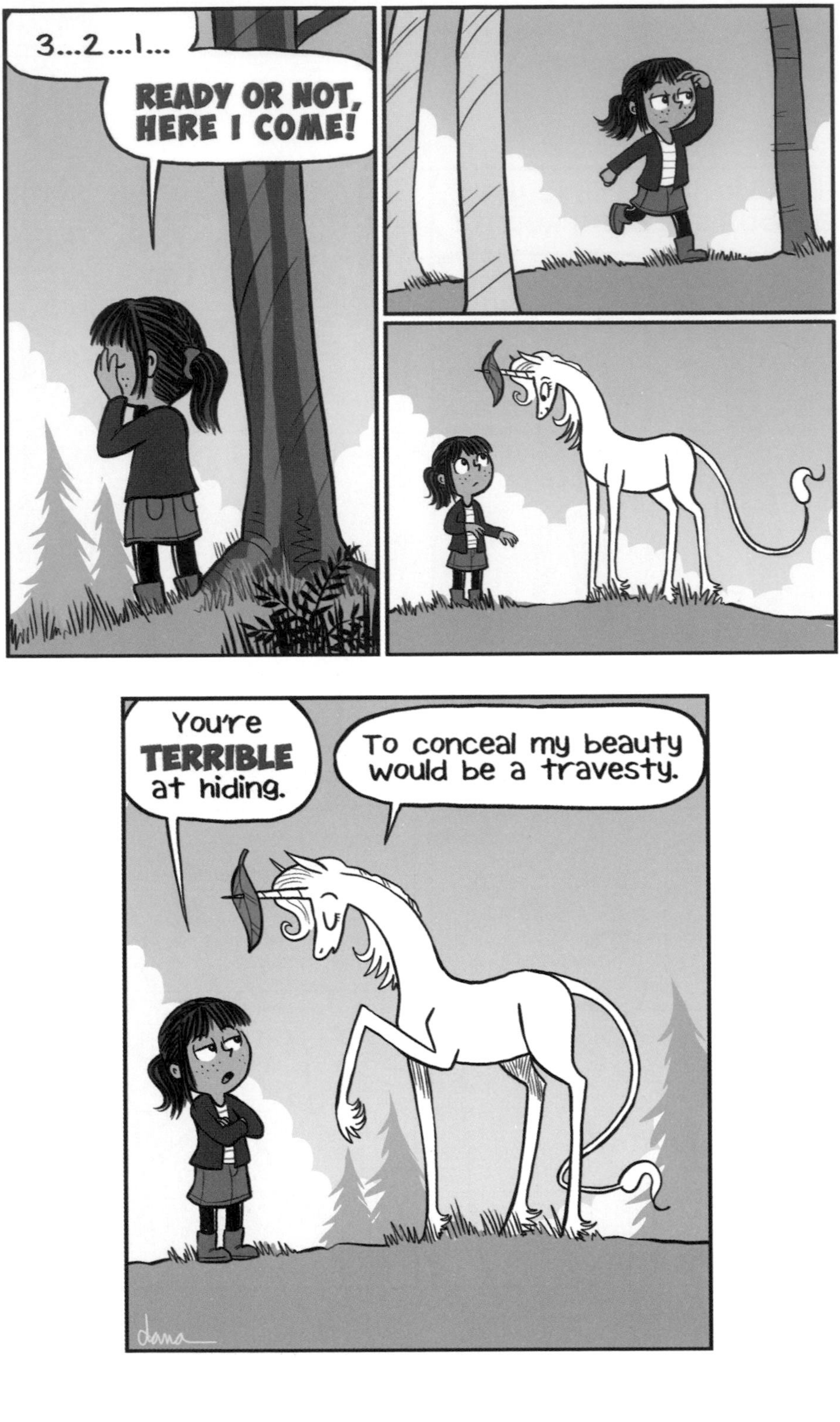
3...2...1...
READY OR NOT, HERE I COME!
You're TERRIBLE at hiding.
To conceal my beauty would be a travesty.
dana

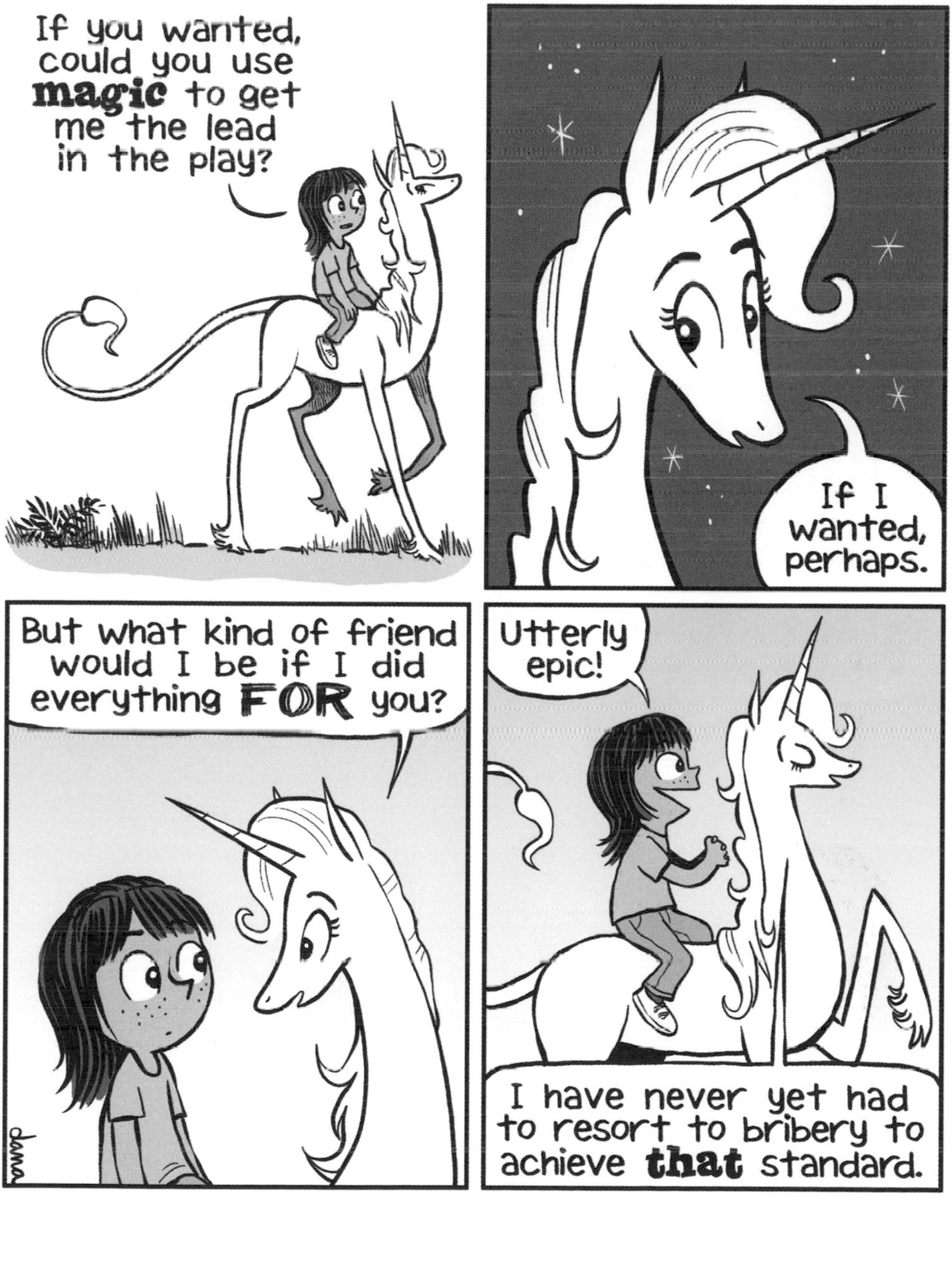
If you wanted, could you use **magic** to get me the lead in the play?
If I wanted, perhaps.
But what kind of friend would I be if I did everything **FOR** you?
Utterly epic!
I have never yet had to resort to bribery to achieve **that** standard.
dana

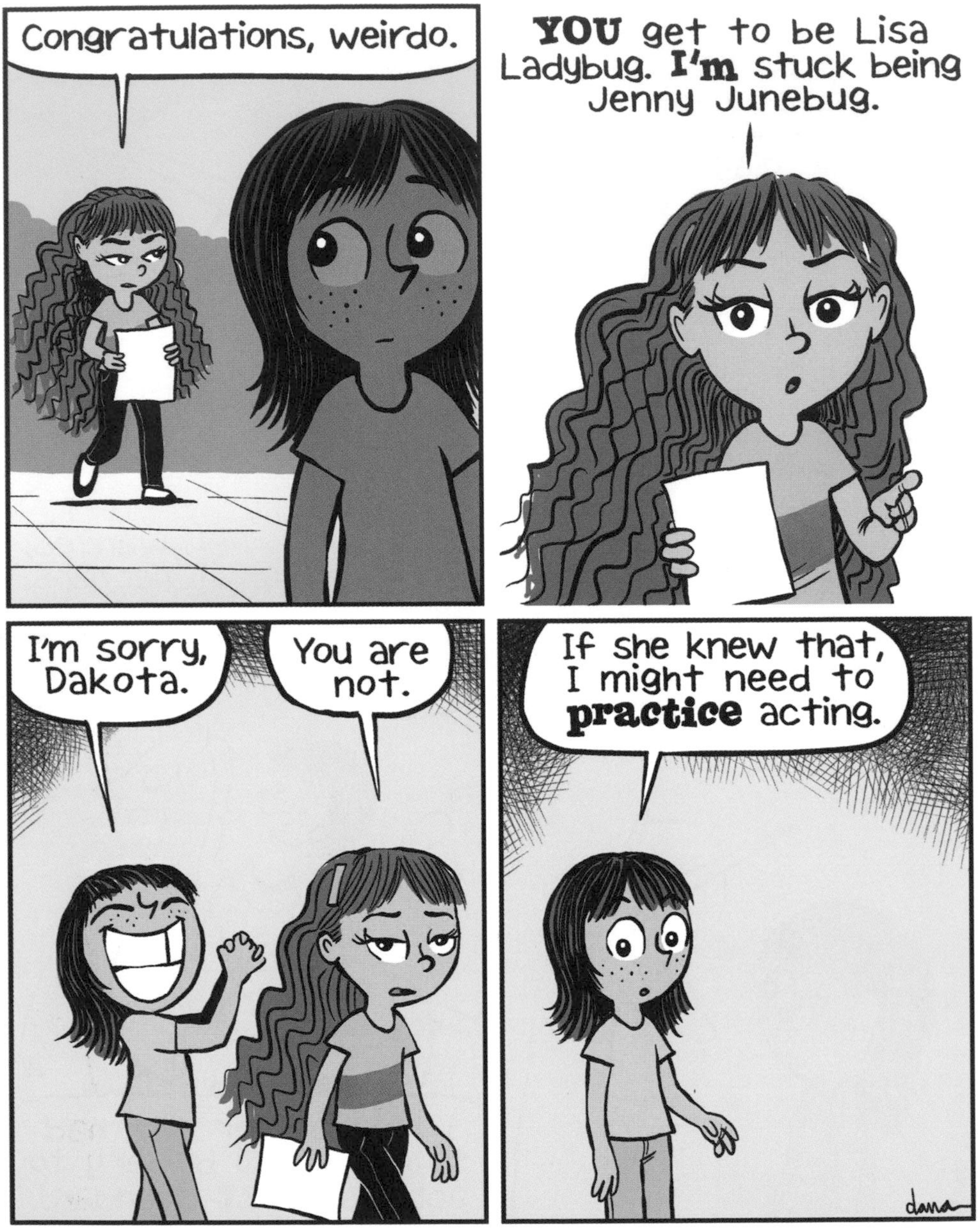
Congratulations, weirdo.
YOU get to be Lisa Ladybug. **I'm** stuck being Jenny Junebug.
I'm sorry, Dakota.
You are not.
If she knew that, I might need to **practice** acting.
dana

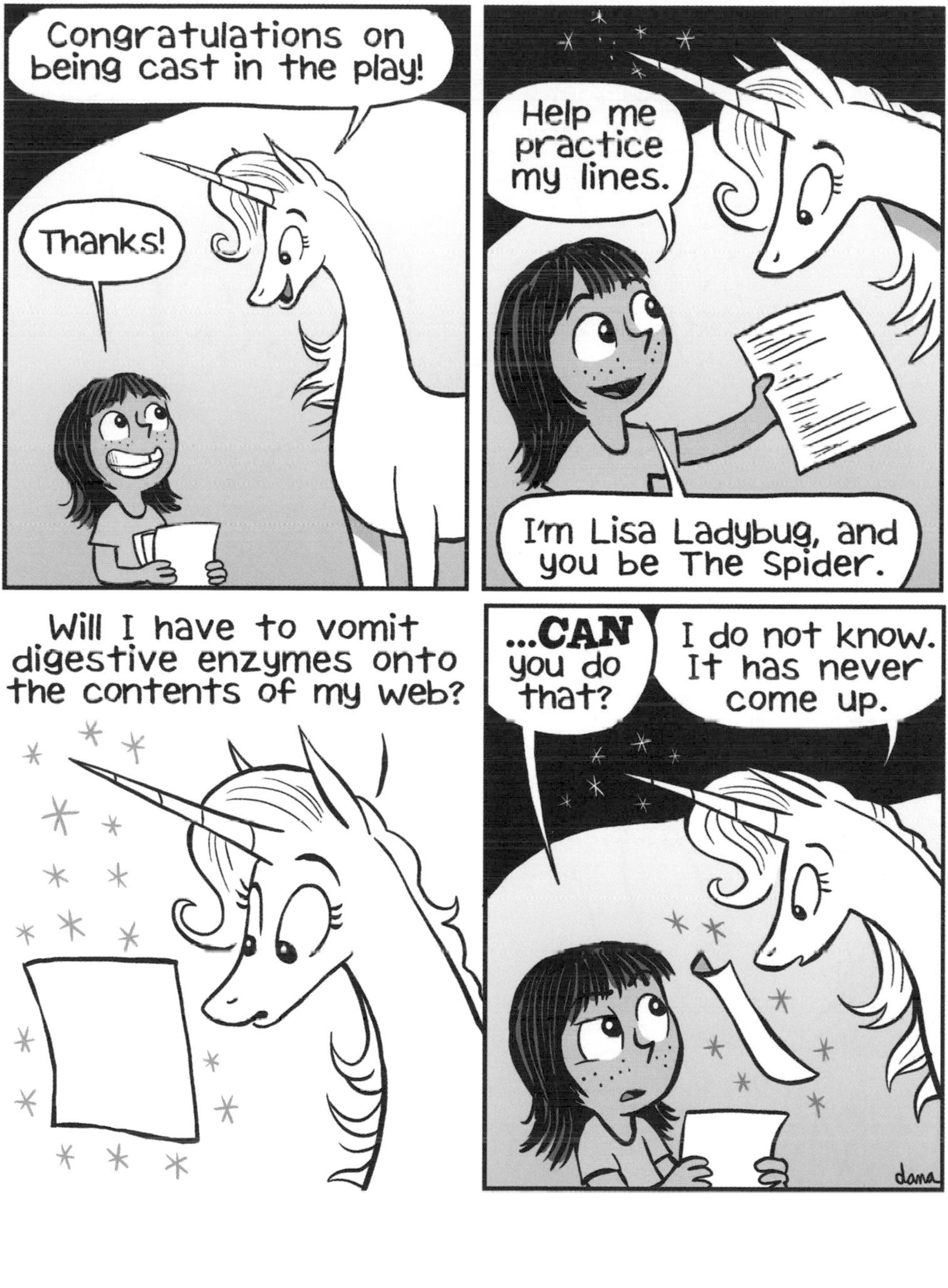
Congratulations on being cast in the play!
Thanks!
Help me practice my lines.
I'm Lisa Ladybug, and you be The Spider.
Will I have to vomit digestive enzymes onto the contents of my web?
...CAN you do that?
I do not know. It has never come up.
dana

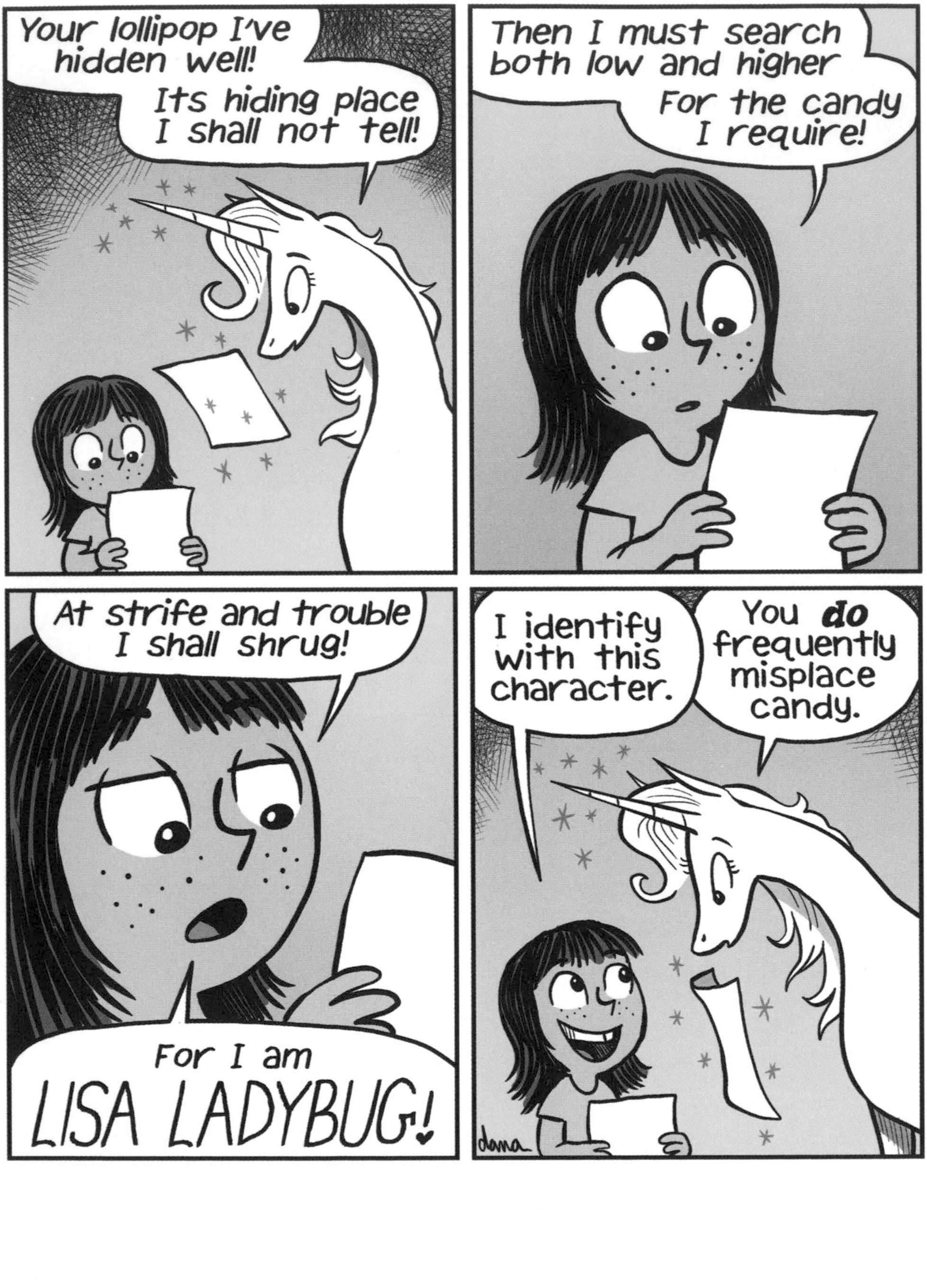
Your lollipop I've hidden well!
Its hiding place I shall not tell!
Then I must search both low and higher
For the candy I require!
At strife and trouble I shall shrug!
For I am LISA LADYBUG!
I identify with this character.
You **do** frequently misplace candy.
dana

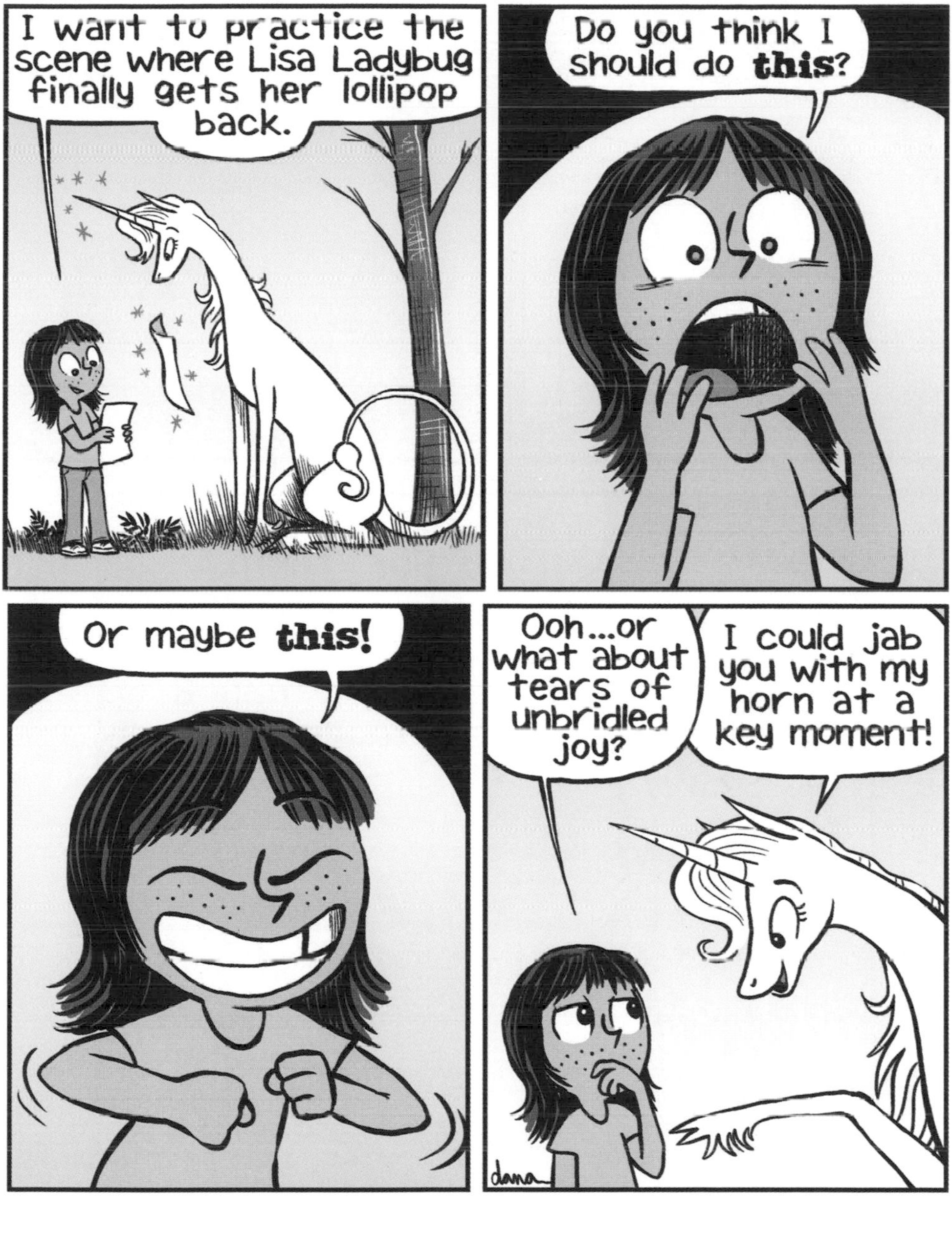
I want to practice the scene where Lisa Ladybug finally gets her lollipop back.
Do you think I should do **this**?
Or maybe **this**!
Ooh...or what about tears of unbridled joy?
I could jab you with my horn at a key moment!
dana

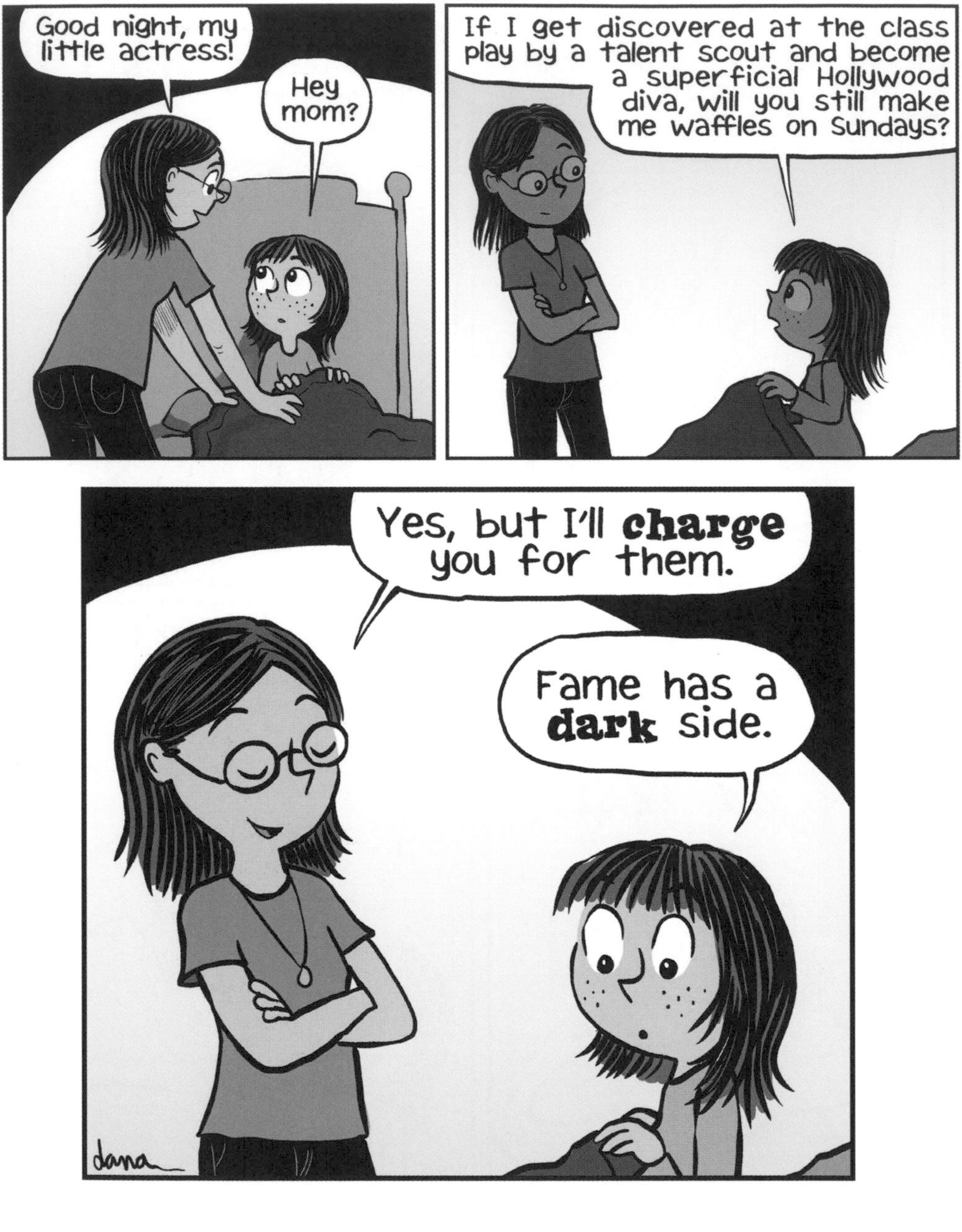
Good night, my little actress!
Hey mom?
If I get discovered at the class play by a talent scout and become a superficial Hollywood diva, will you still make me waffles on Sundays?
Yes, but I'll **charge** you for them.
Fame has a **dark** side.
dana

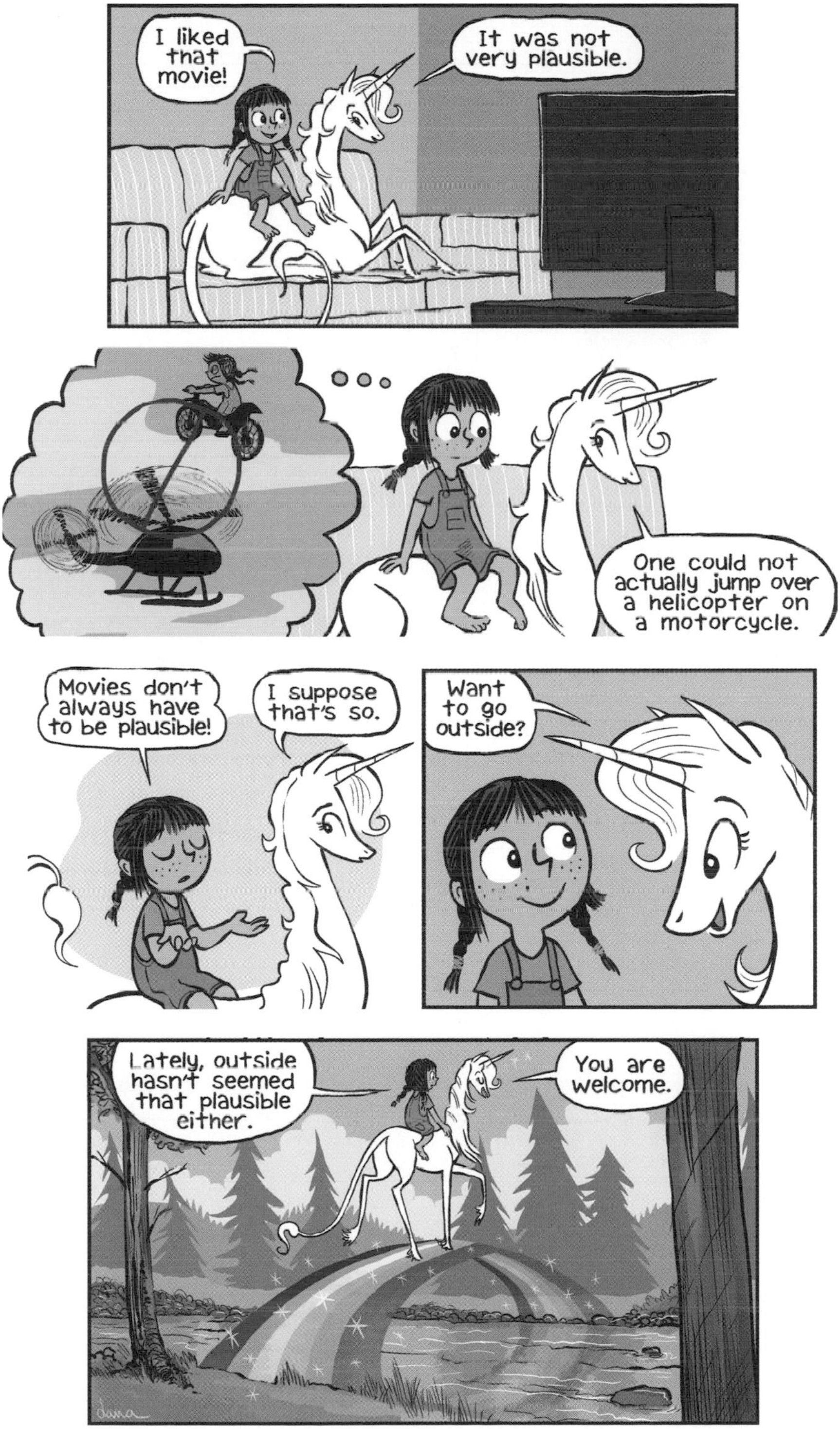
I liked that movie!
It was not very plausible.
One could not actually jump over a helicopter on a motorcycle.
Movies don't always have to be plausible!
I suppose that's so.
Want to go outside?
Lately, outside hasn't seemed that plausible either.
You are welcome.
dana

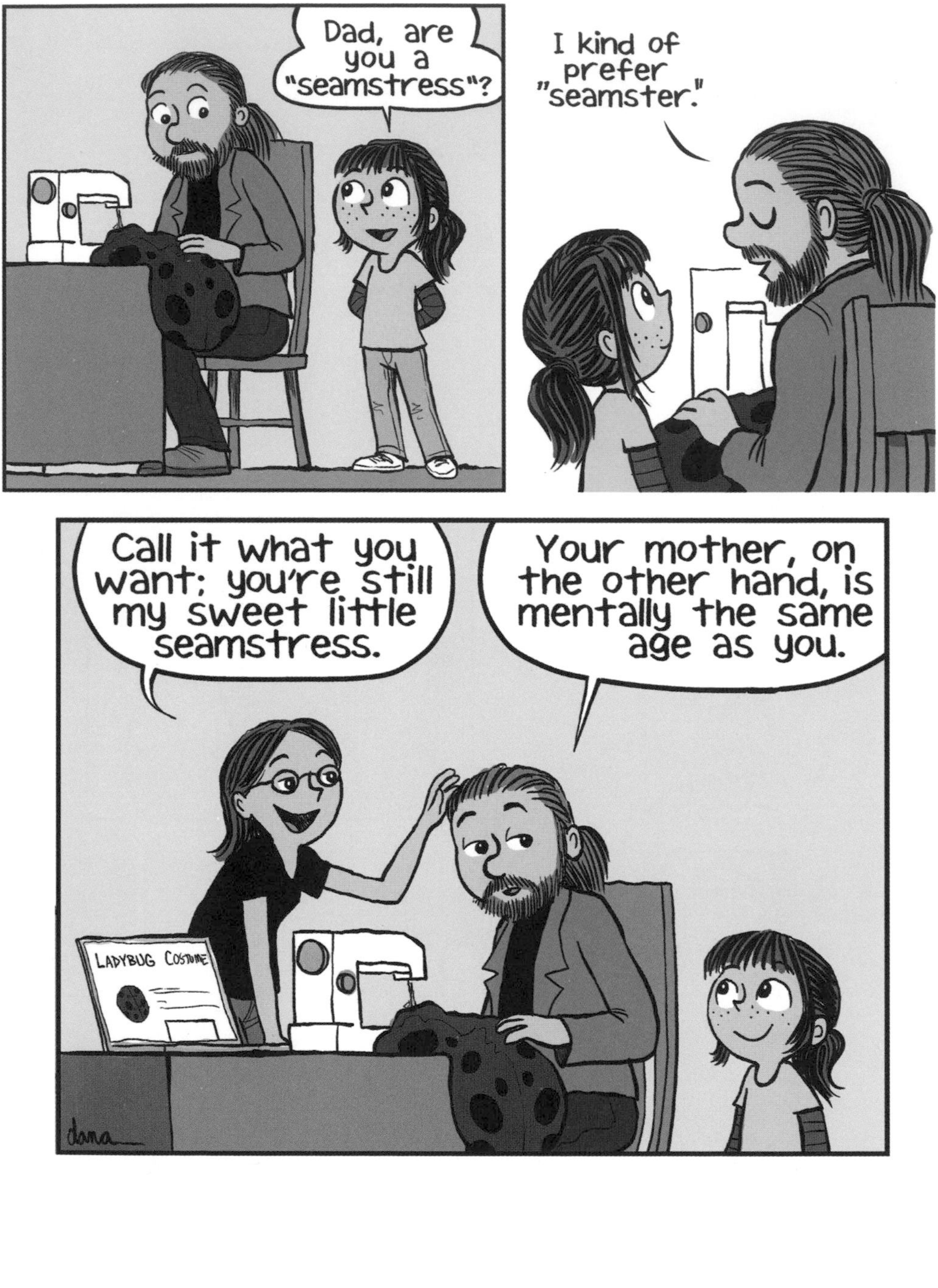
Dad, are you a "seamstress"?
I kind of prefer "seamster."
Call it what you want; you're still my sweet little seamstress.
Your mother, on the other hand, is mentally the same age as you.
LADYBUG COSTUME
dana

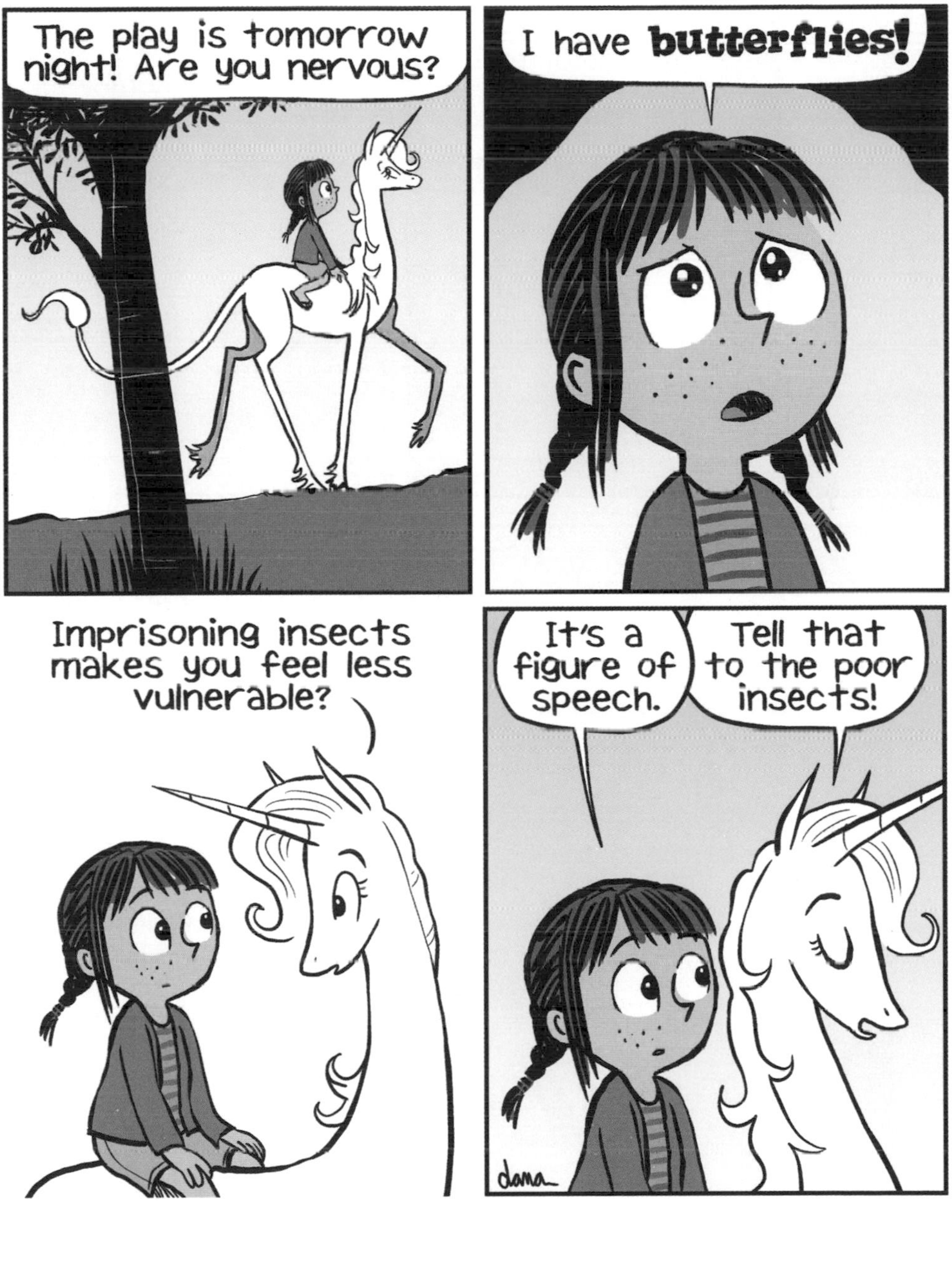

The play is tomorrow night! Are you nervous?
I have **butterflies!**
Imprisoning insects makes you feel less vulnerable?
It's a figure of speech.
Tell that to the poor insects!
dana

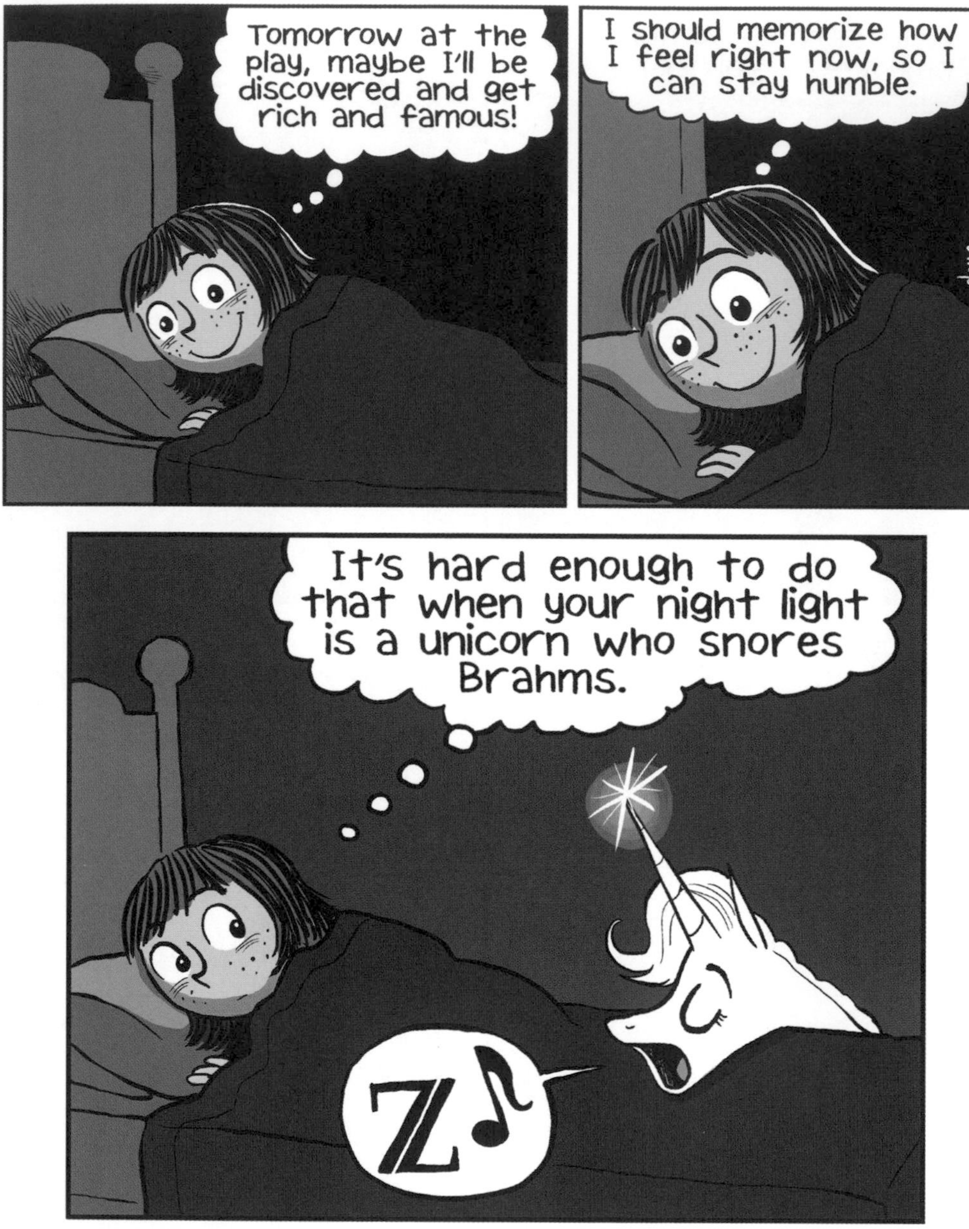
Tomorrow at the play, maybe I'll be discovered and get rich and famous!
I should memorize how I feel right now, so I can stay humble.
dana
It's hard enough to do that when your night light is a unicorn who snores Brahms.
Z

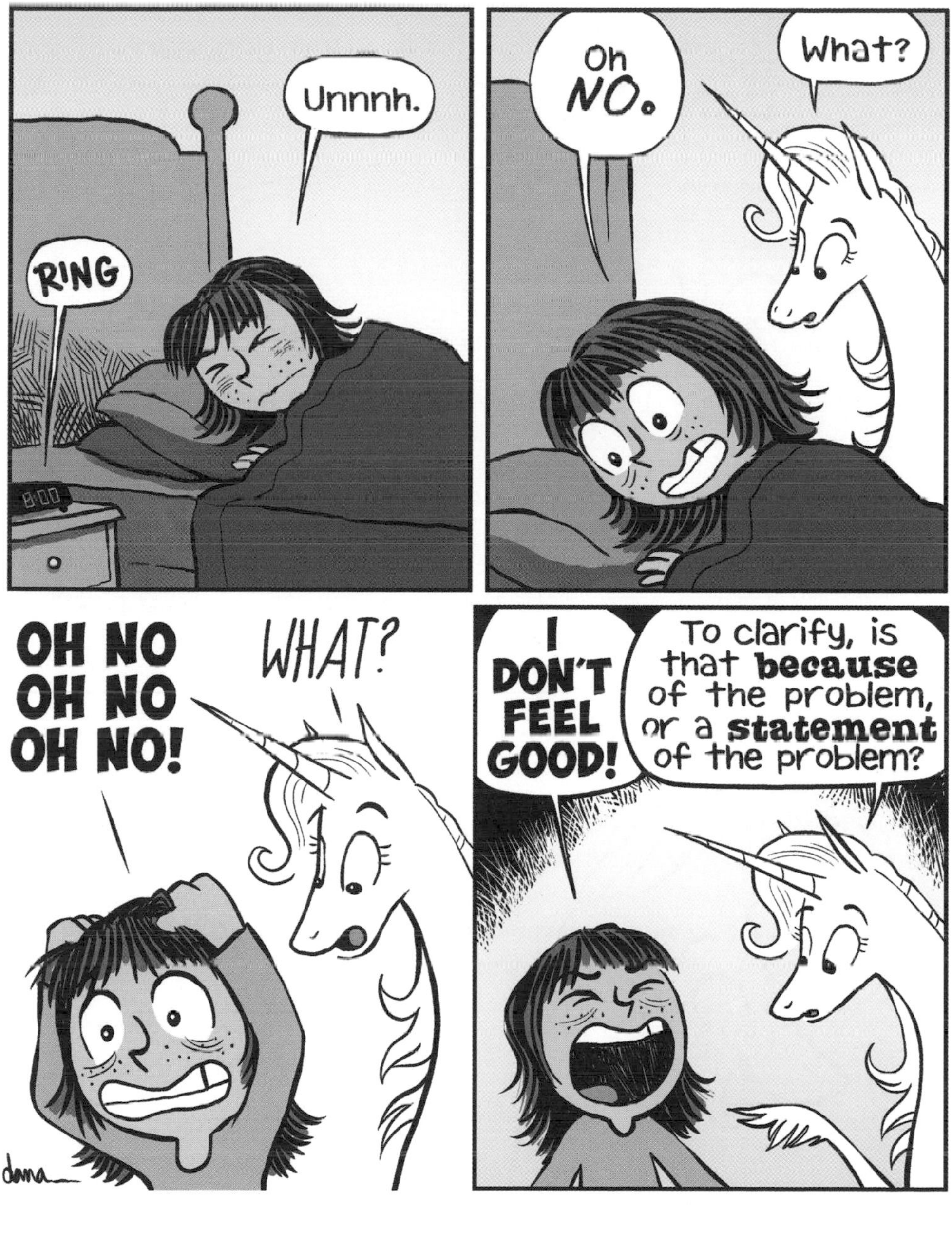
Unnnh.
RING
Oh NO.
What?
OH NO OH NO OH NO!
WHAT?
I DON'T FEEL GOOD!
To clarify, is that **because** of the problem, or a **statement** of the problem?
dana

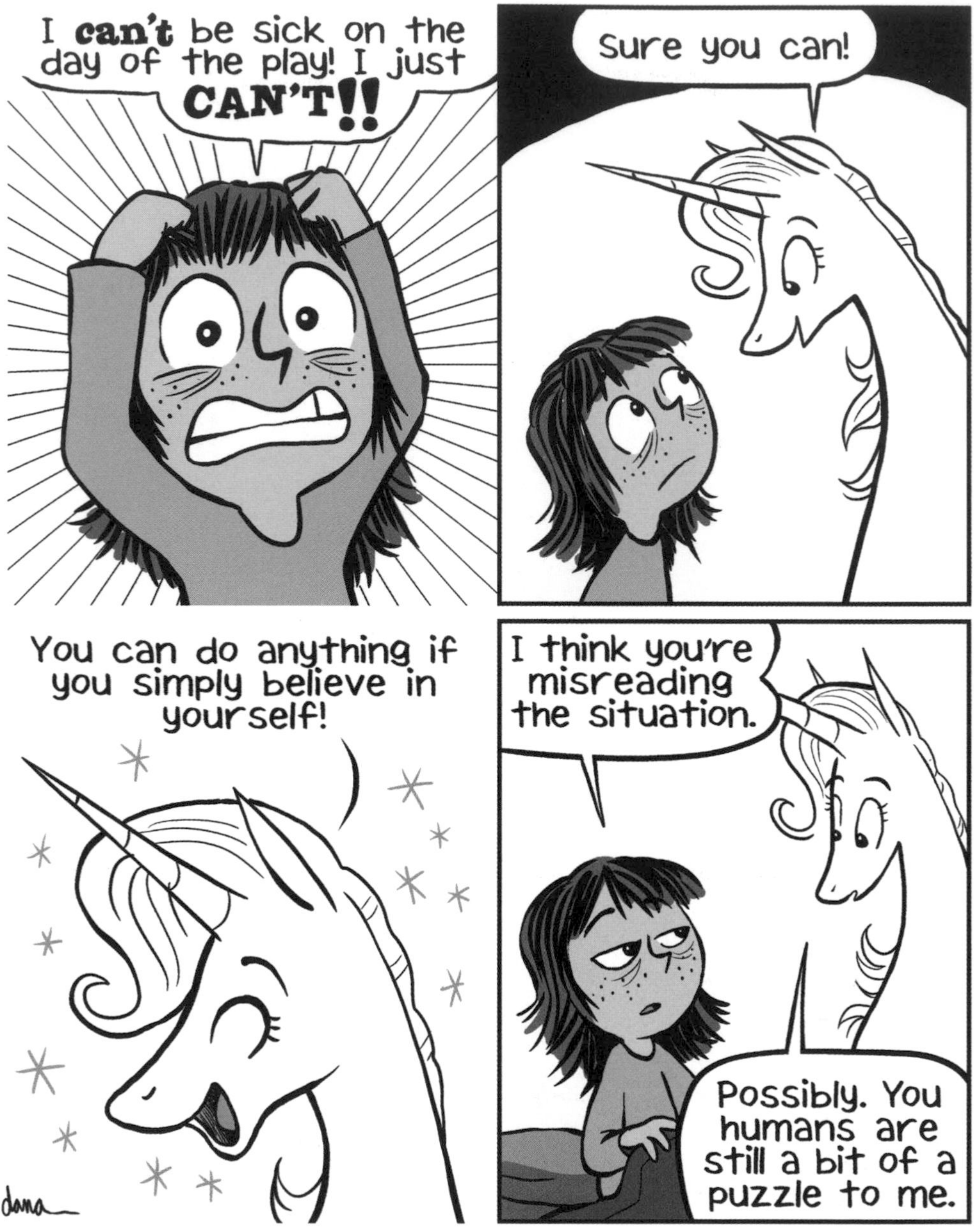
I **can't** be sick on the day of the play! I just **CAN'T!!**
Sure you can!
You can do anything if you simply believe in yourself!
I think you're misreading the situation.
Possibly. You humans are still a bit of a puzzle to me.
dana

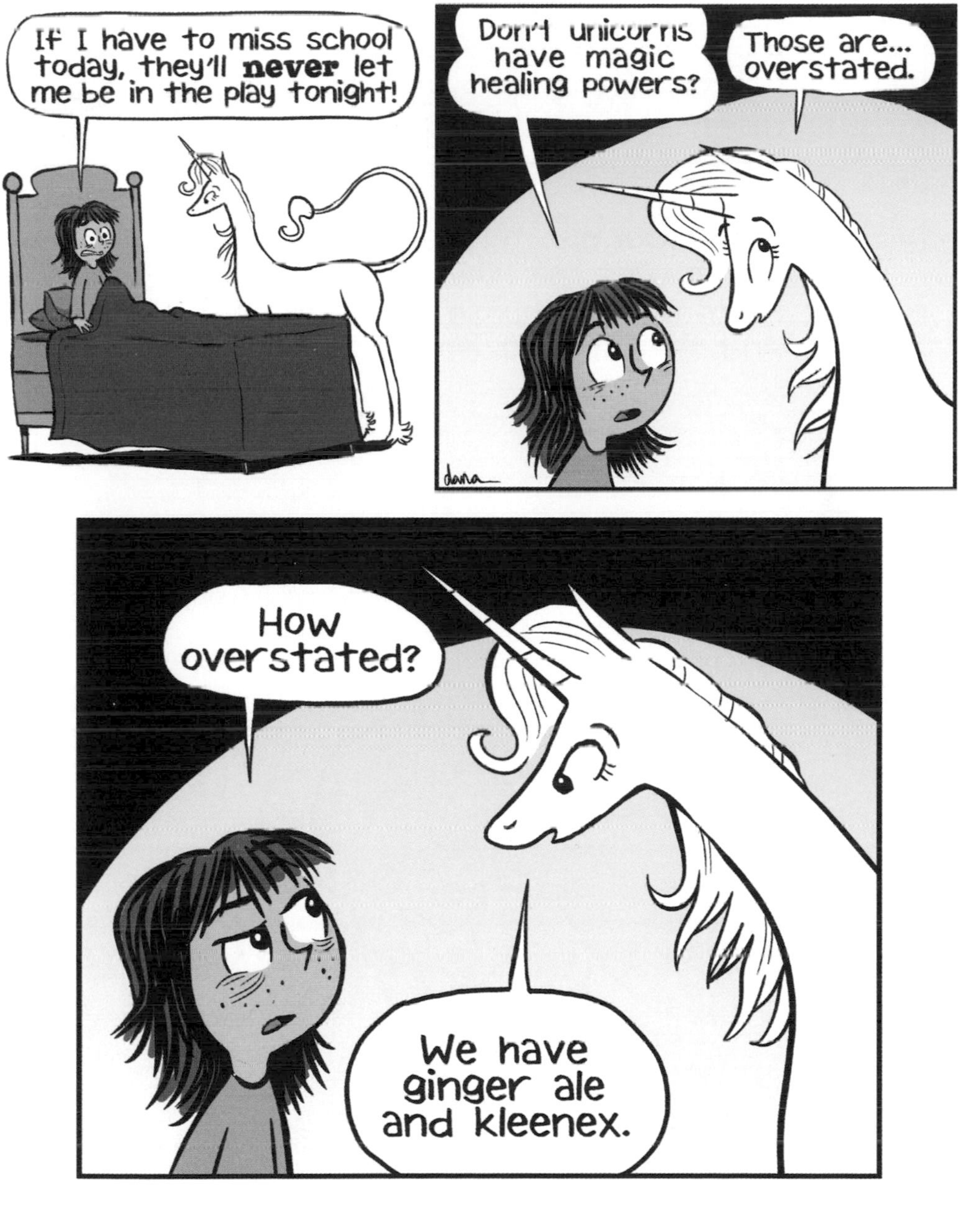
If I have to miss school today, they'll **never** let me be in the play tonight!
Don't unicorns have magic healing powers?
Those are... overstated.
dana
How overstated?
We have ginger ale and kleenex.

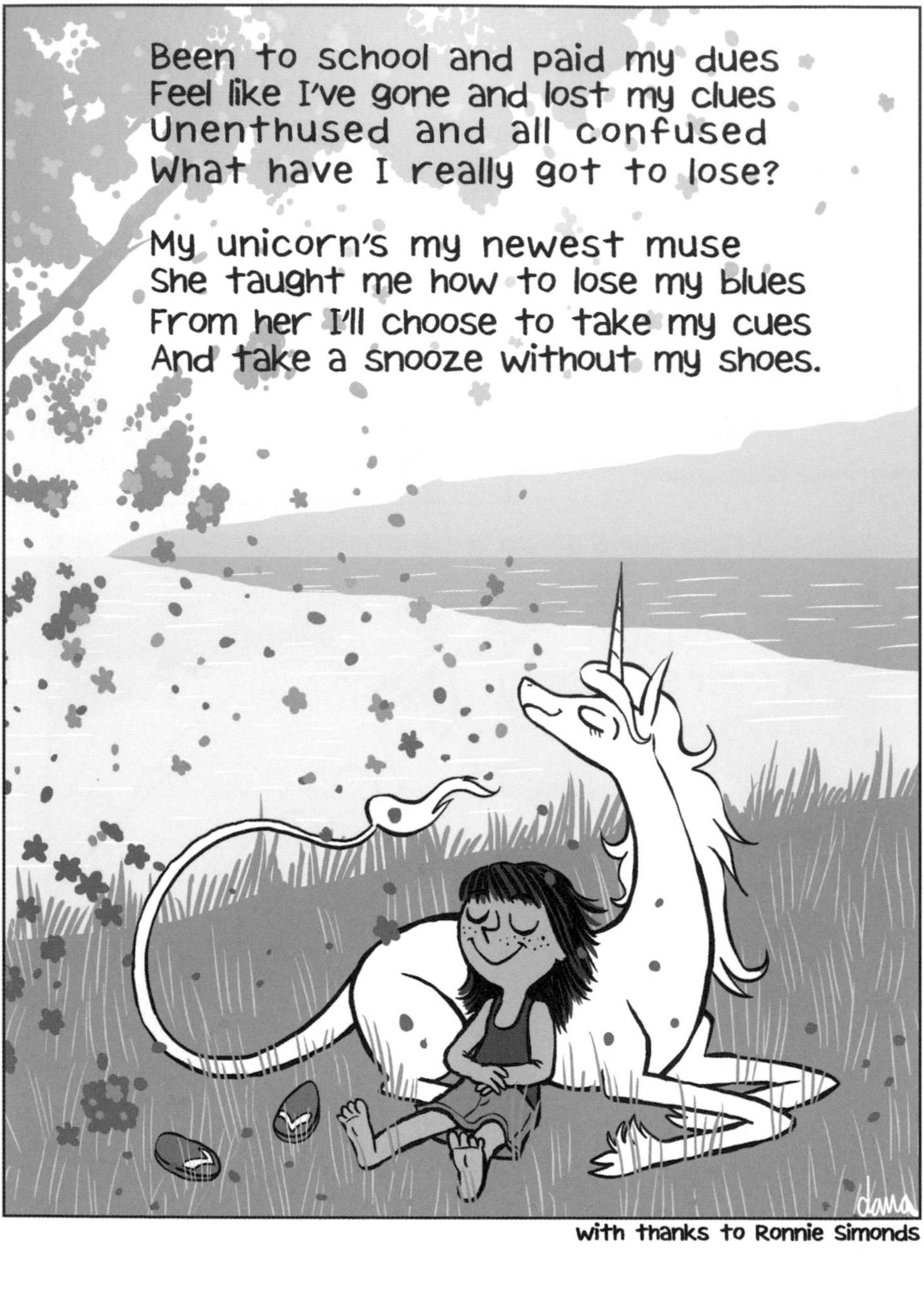
Been to school and paid my dues
Feel like I've gone and lost my clues
Unenthused and all confused
What have I really got to lose?

My unicorn's my newest muse
She taught me how to lose my blues
From her I'll choose to take my cues
And take a snooze without my shoes.
dana
with thanks to Ronnie Simonds

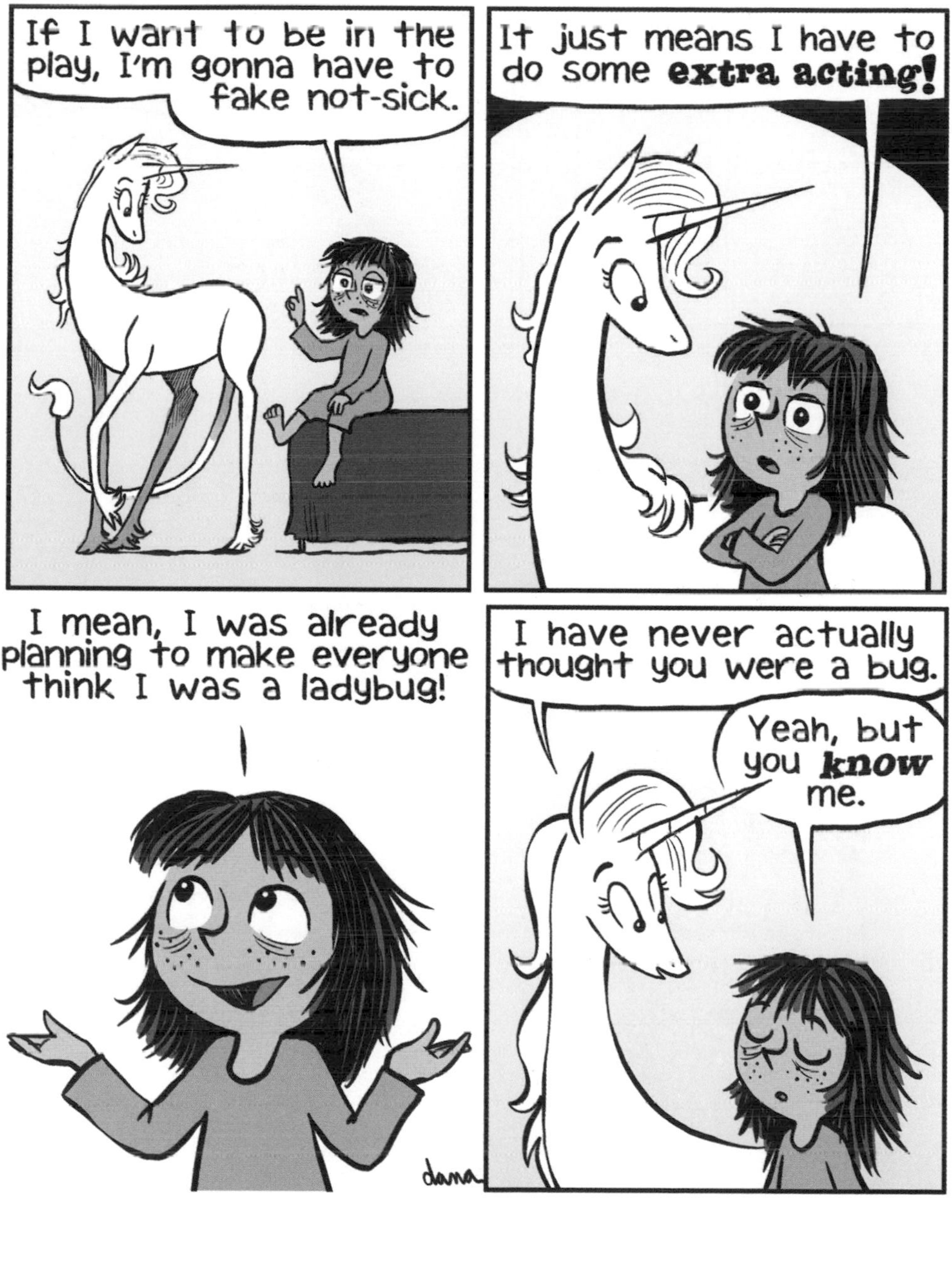
If I want to be in the play, I'm gonna have to fake not-sick.
It just means I have to do some **extra acting!**
I mean, I was already planning to make everyone think I was a ladybug!
I have never actually thought you were a bug.
Yeah, but you ***know*** me.
dana

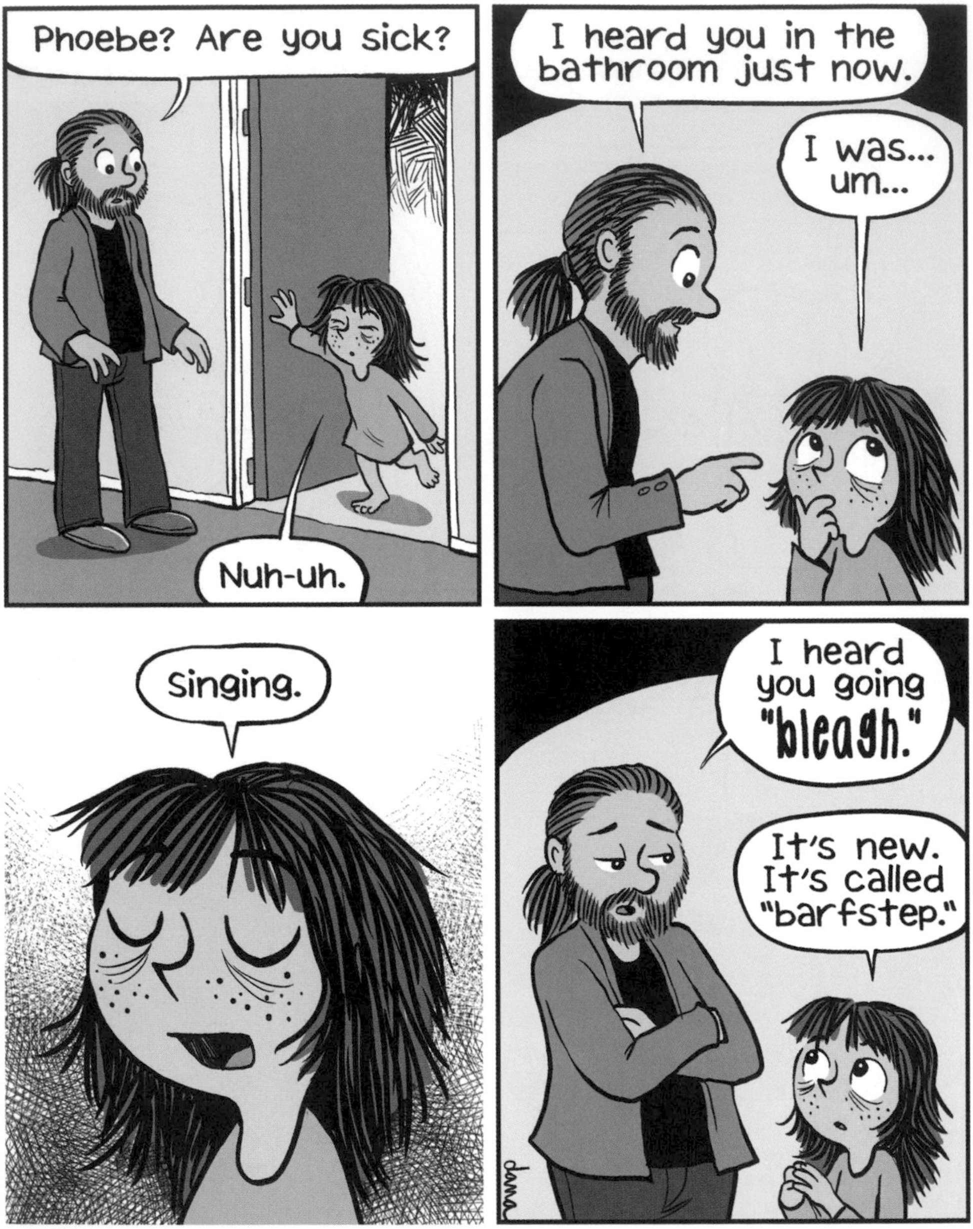
Phoebe? Are you sick?
Nuh-uh.
I heard you in the bathroom just now.
I was... um...
Singing.
I heard you going "bleagh."
It's new. It's called "barfstep."
dana

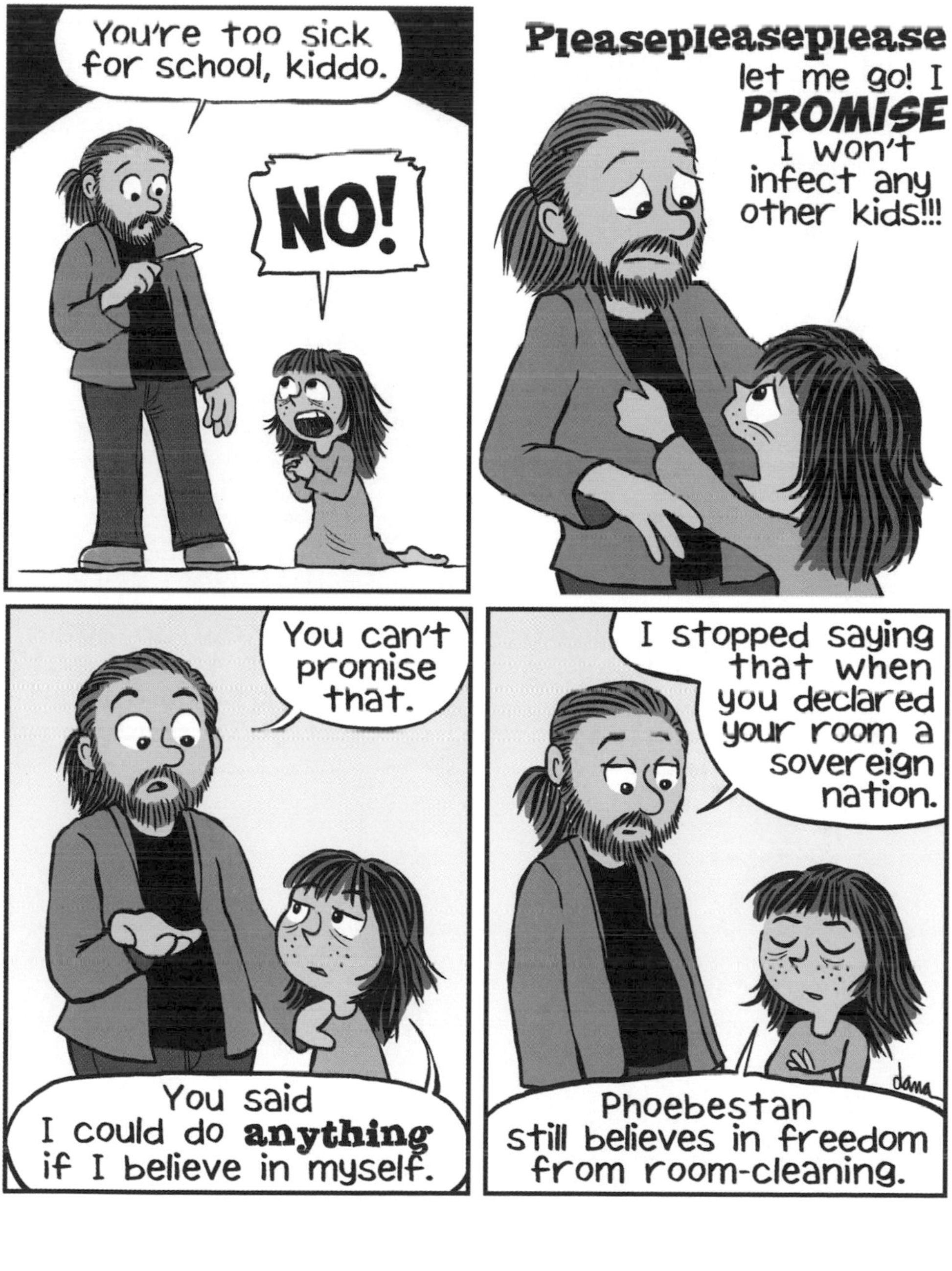

You're too sick for school, kiddo.
NO!
Pleasepleaseplease let me go! I PROMISE I won't infect any other kids!!!
You can't promise that.
You said I could do anything if I believe in myself.
I stopped saying that when you declared your room a sovereign nation.
Phoebestan still believes in freedom from room-cleaning.
dana

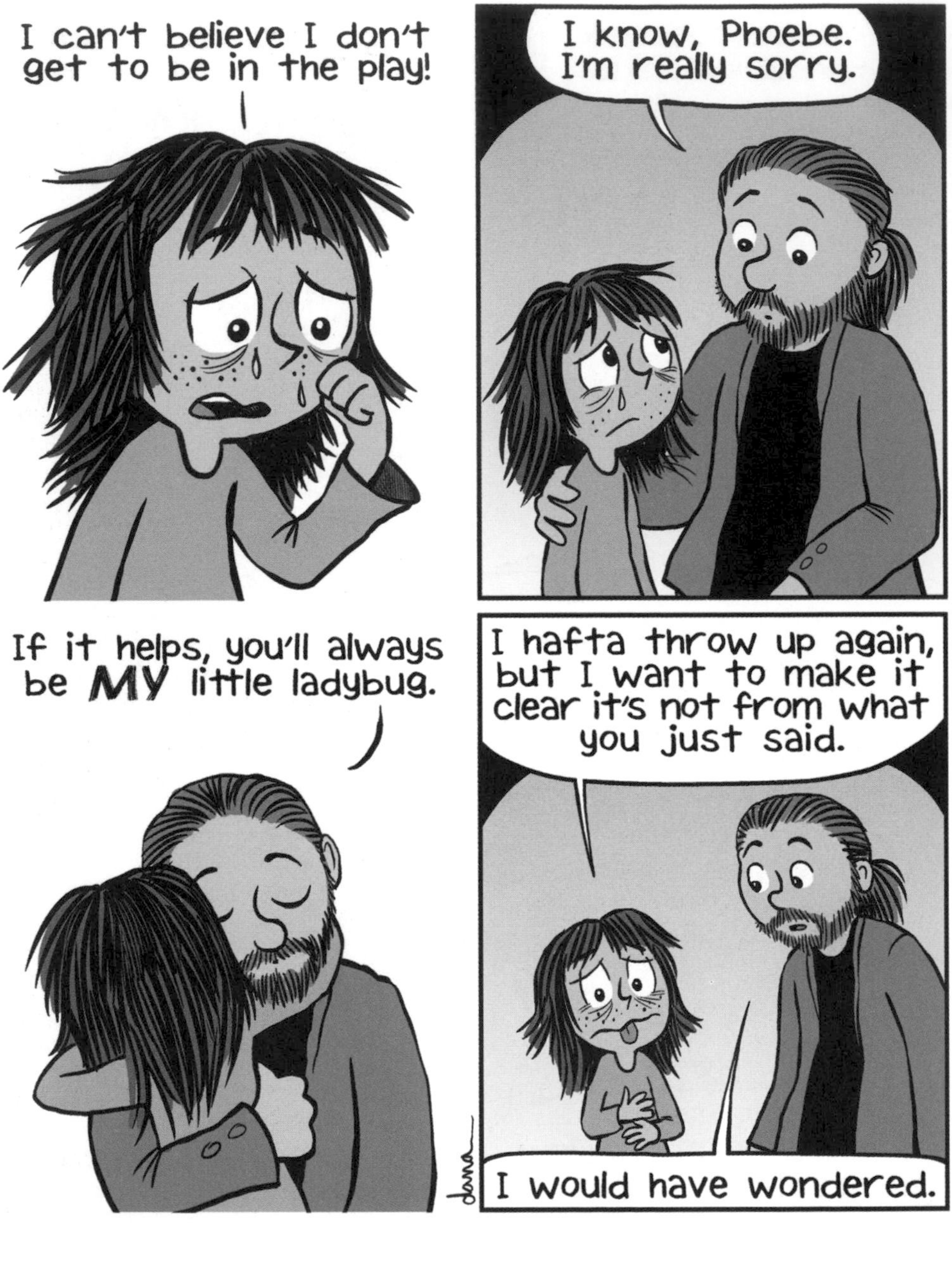
I can't believe I don't get to be in the play!
I know, Phoebe. I'm really sorry.
If it helps, you'll always be MY little ladybug.
I hafta throw up again, but I want to make it clear it's not from what you just said.
I would have wondered.
dana

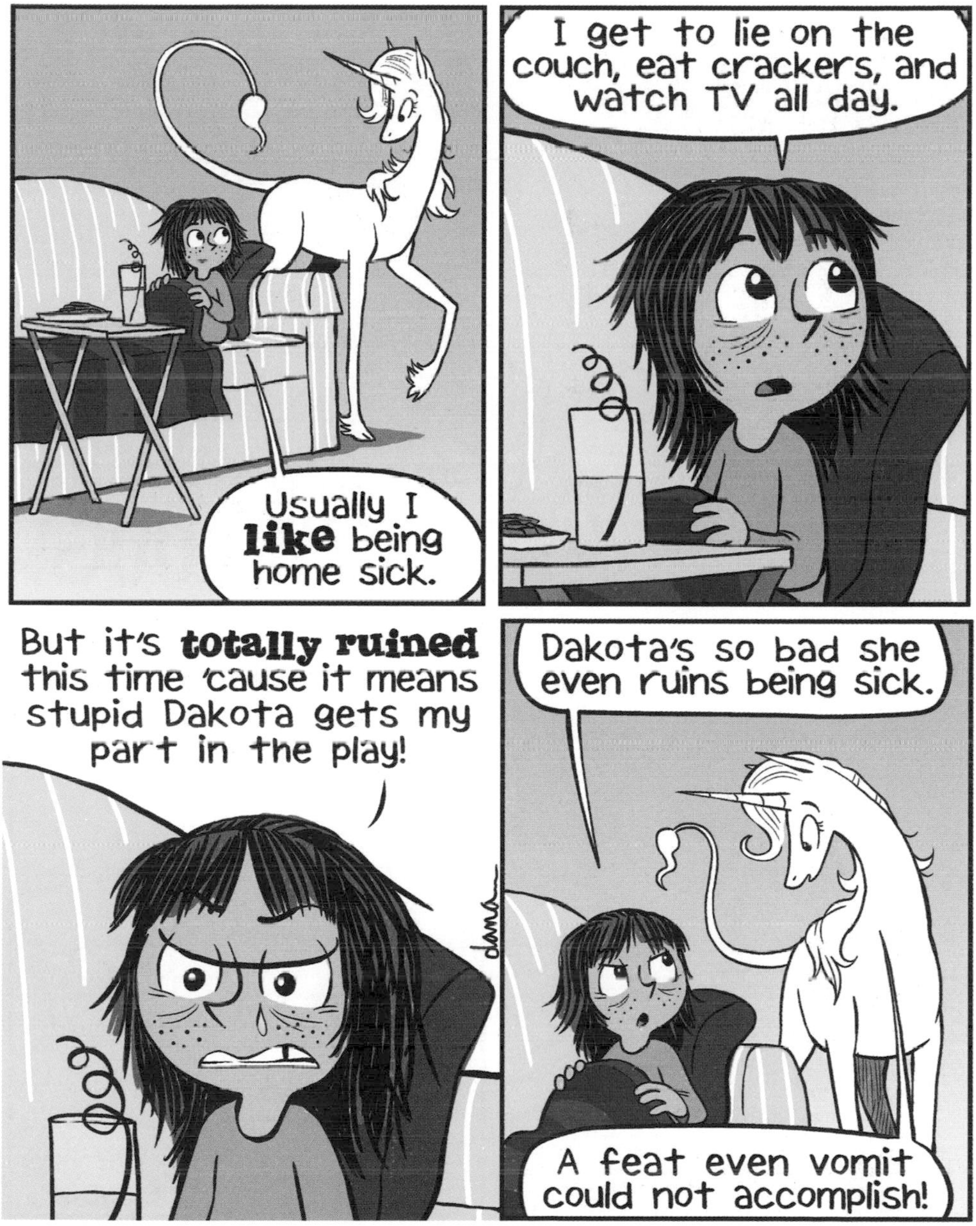

Usually I **like** being home sick.
I get to lie on the couch, eat crackers, and watch TV all day.
But it's **totally ruined** this time 'cause it means stupid Dakota gets my part in the play!
Dakota's so bad she even ruins being sick.
A feat even vomit could not accomplish!

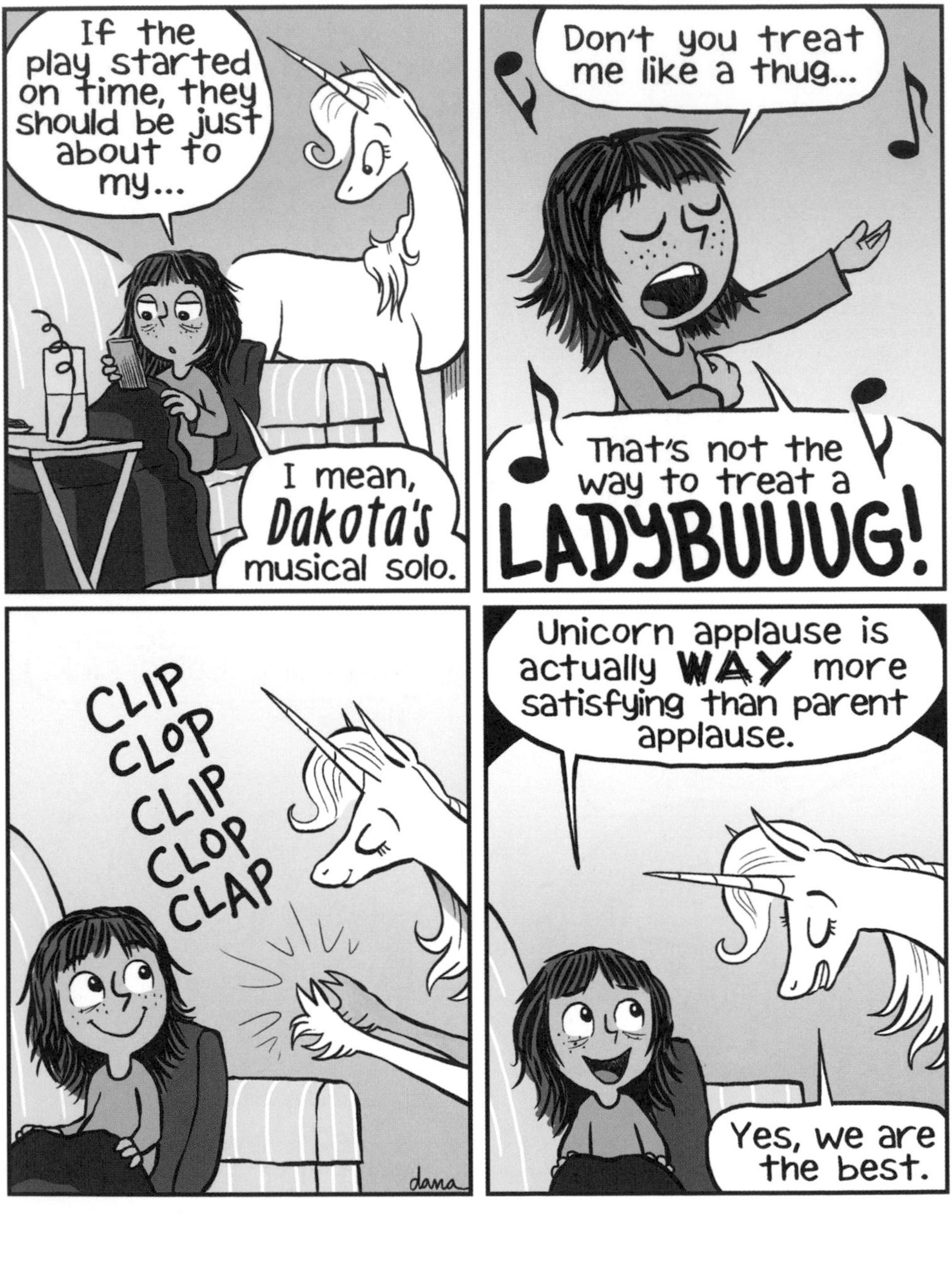

If the play started on time, they should be just about to my...
I mean, Dakota's musical solo.
Don't you treat me like a thug...
That's not the way to treat a LADYBUUUG!
CLIP
CLOP
CLIP
CLOP
CLAP
dana
Unicorn applause is actually WAY more satisfying than parent applause.
Yes, we are the best.

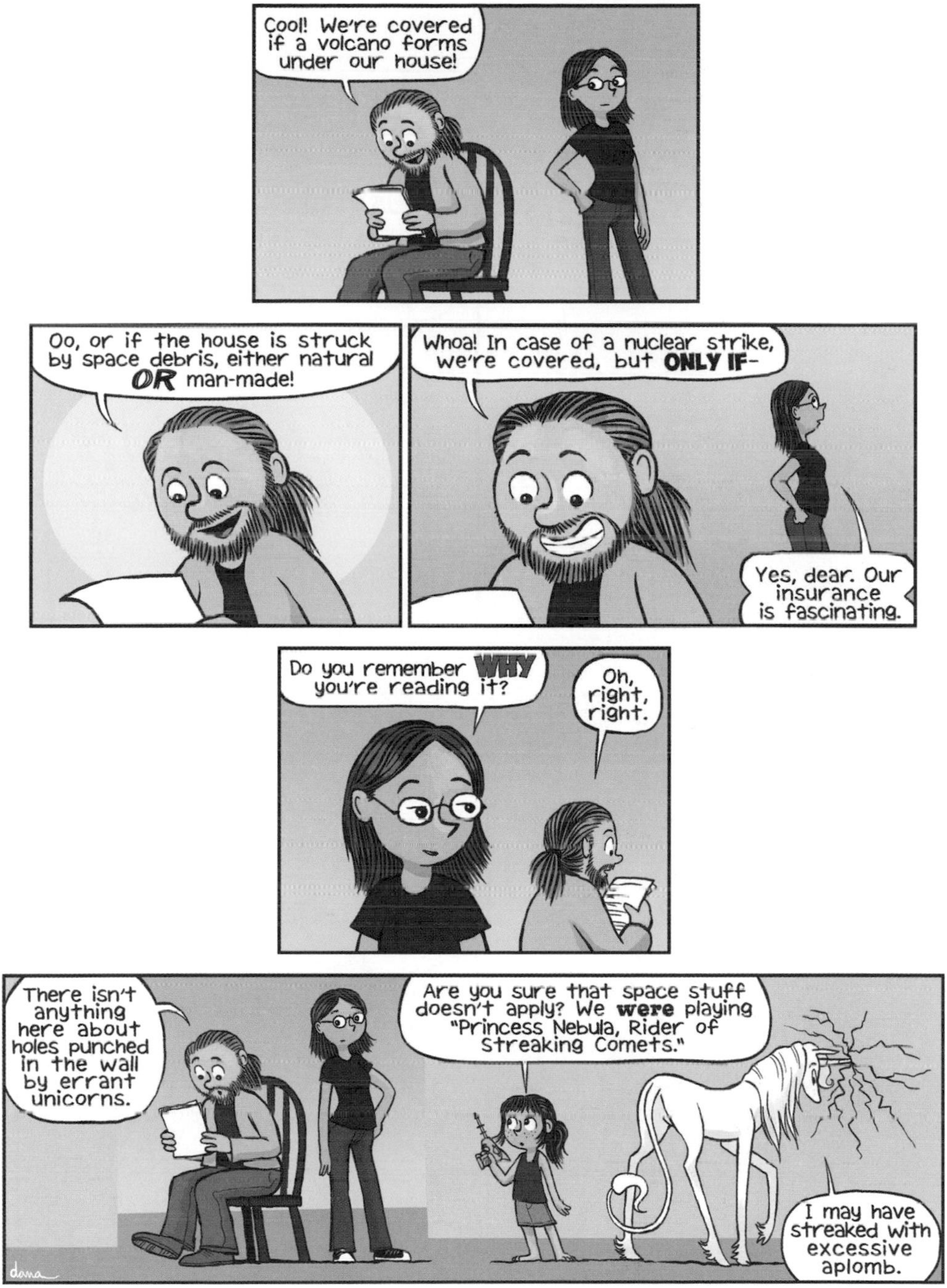
Cool! We're covered if a volcano forms under our house!
Oo, or if the house is struck by space debris, either natural OR man-made!
Whoa! In case of a nuclear strike, we're covered, but ONLY IF-
Yes, dear. Our insurance is fascinating.
Do you remember WHY you're reading it?
Oh, right, right.
There isn't anything here about holes punched in the wall by errant unicorns.
Are you sure that space stuff doesn't apply? We were playing "Princess Nebula, Rider of Streaking Comets."
I may have streaked with excessive aplomb.
dana

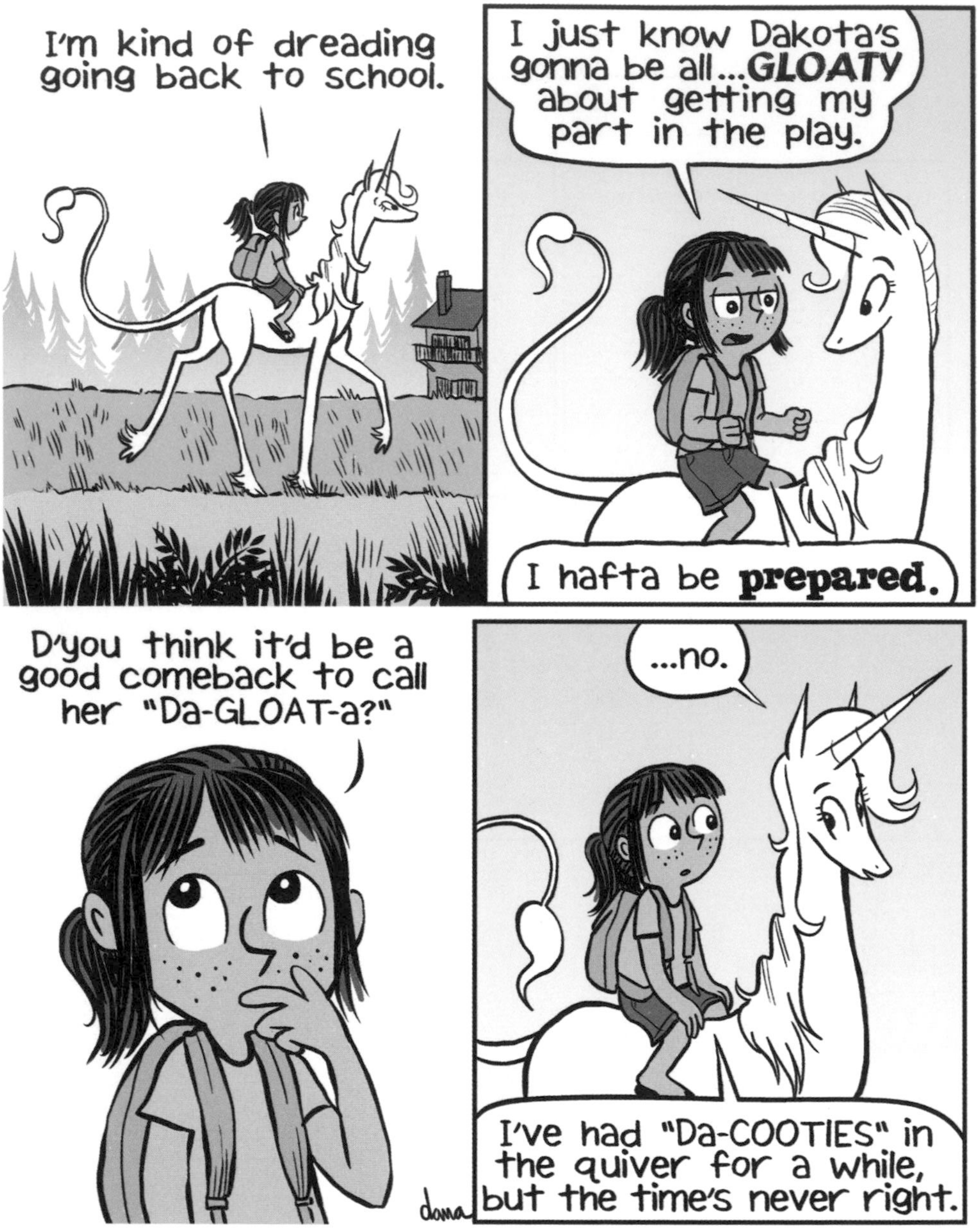
I'm kind of dreading going back to school.
I just know Dakota's gonna be all...**GLOATY** about getting my part in the play.
I hafta be **prepared**.
D'you think it'd be a good comeback to call her "Da-GLOAT-a?"
...no.
I've had "Da-COOTIES" in the quiver for a while, but the time's never right.
dana

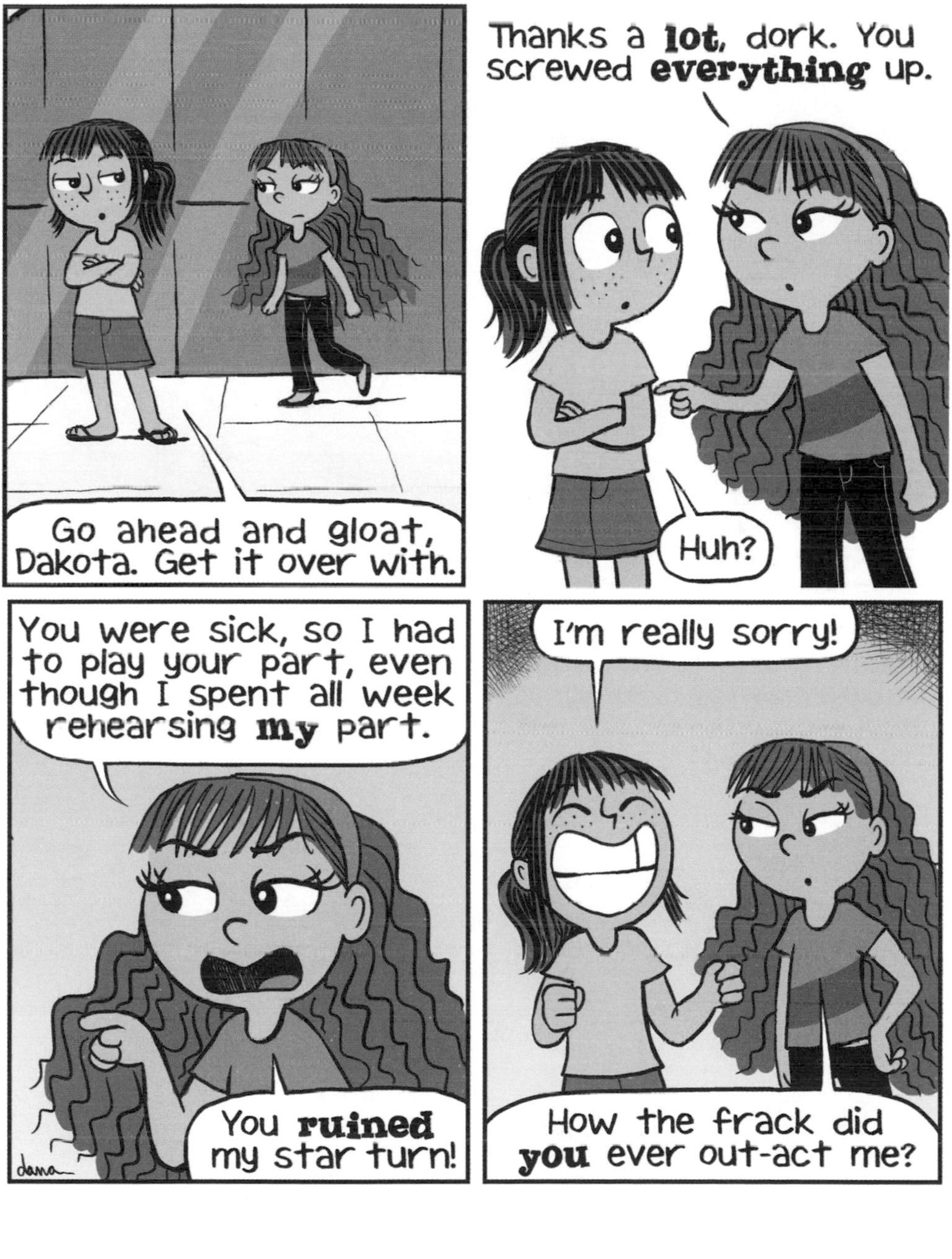
Go ahead and gloat, Dakota. Get it over with.
Thanks a lot, dork. You screwed everything up.
Huh?
You were sick, so I had to play your part, even though I spent all week rehearsing my part.
You ruined my star turn!
dana
I'm really sorry!
How the frack did you ever out-act me?

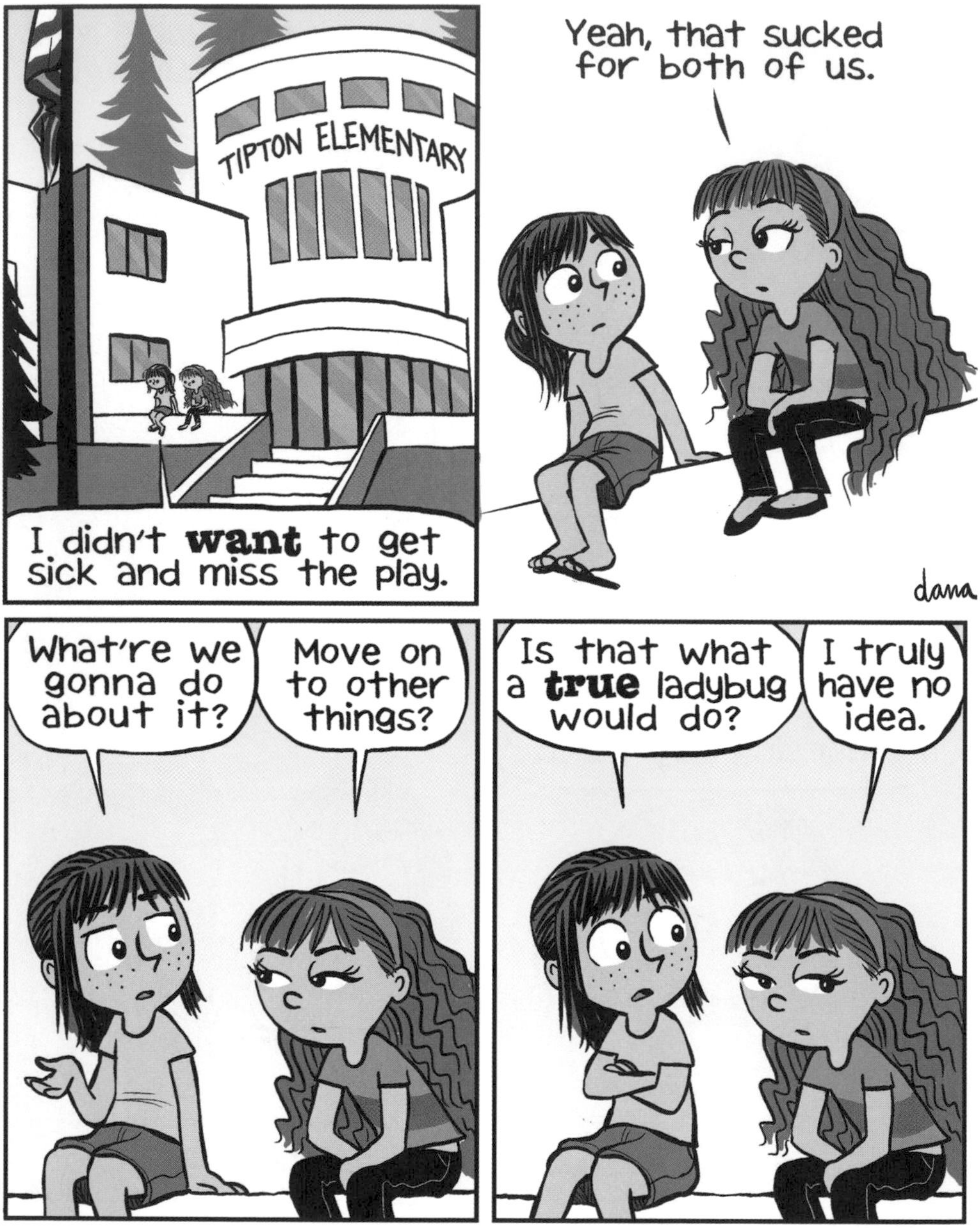
TIPTON ELEMENTARY
I didn't **want** to get sick and miss the play.
Yeah, that sucked for both of us.
dana
What're we gonna do about it?
Move on to other things?
Is that what a **true** ladybug would do?
I truly have no idea.

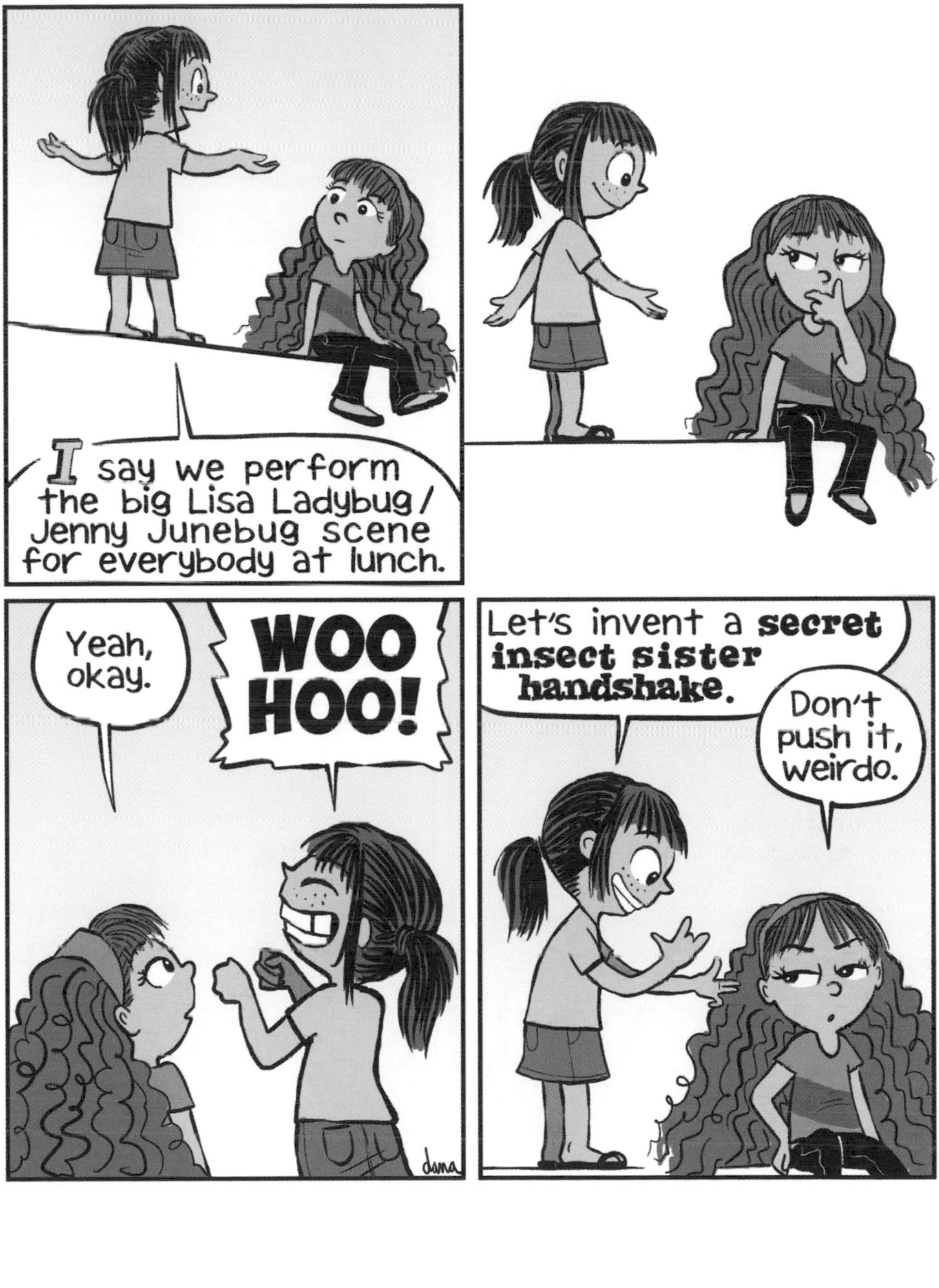
I say we perform the big Lisa Ladybug/ Jenny Junebug scene for everybody at lunch.
Yeah, okay.
WOO HOO!
Let's invent a **secret insect sister handshake**.
Don't push it, weirdo.
dana

My costume's at home.
Mine too, but never fear!
O MAGIC STEED, SWIFT OF HOOF, COME TO MY AID!
We need you to go get-
It can wait until I am done posing.
dana

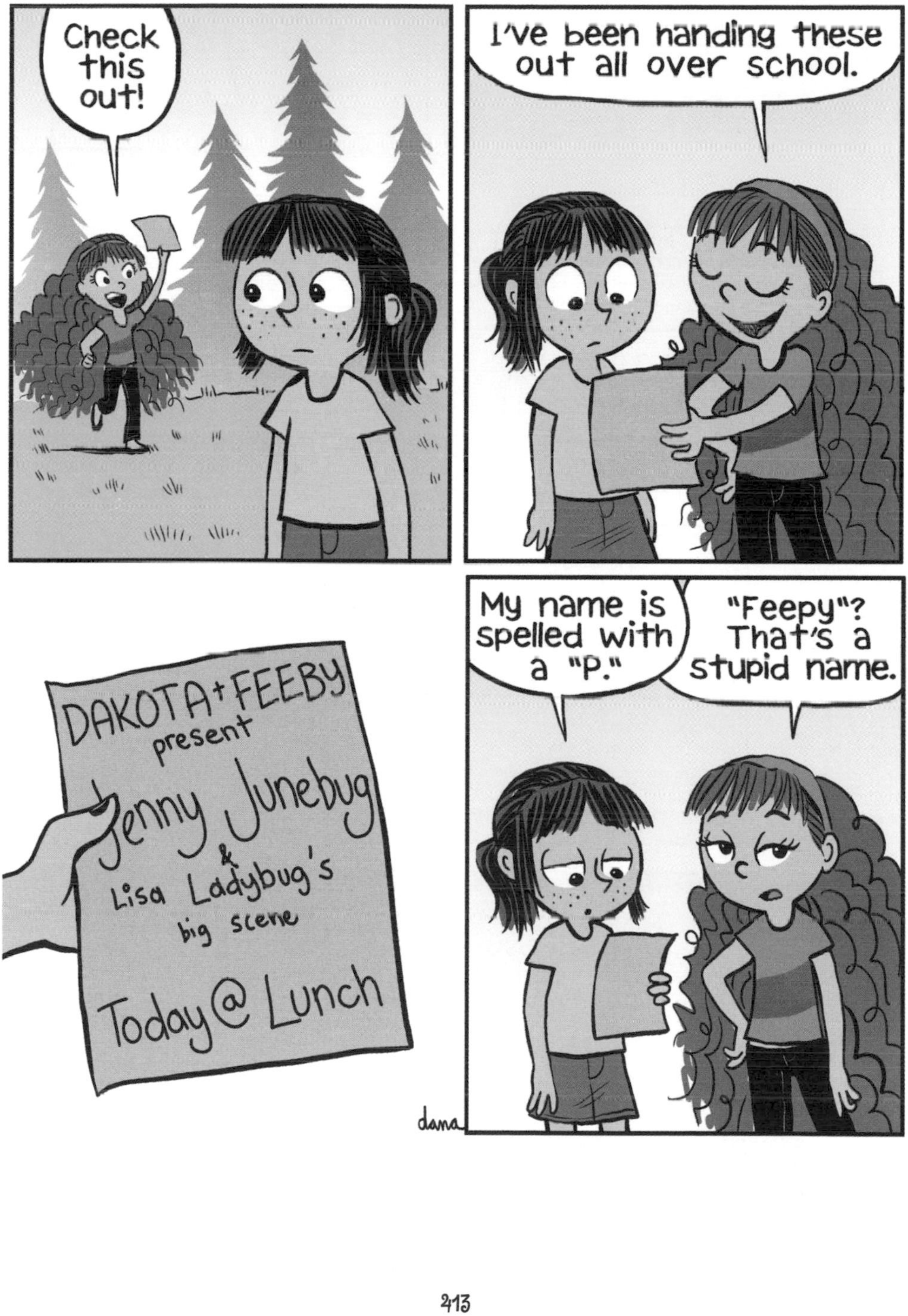
Check this out!
I've been handing these out all over school.
DAKOTA + FEEBY present Jenny Junebug & Lisa Ladybug's big scene Today @ Lunch
My name is spelled with a "P."
"Feepy"? That's a stupid name.
dana

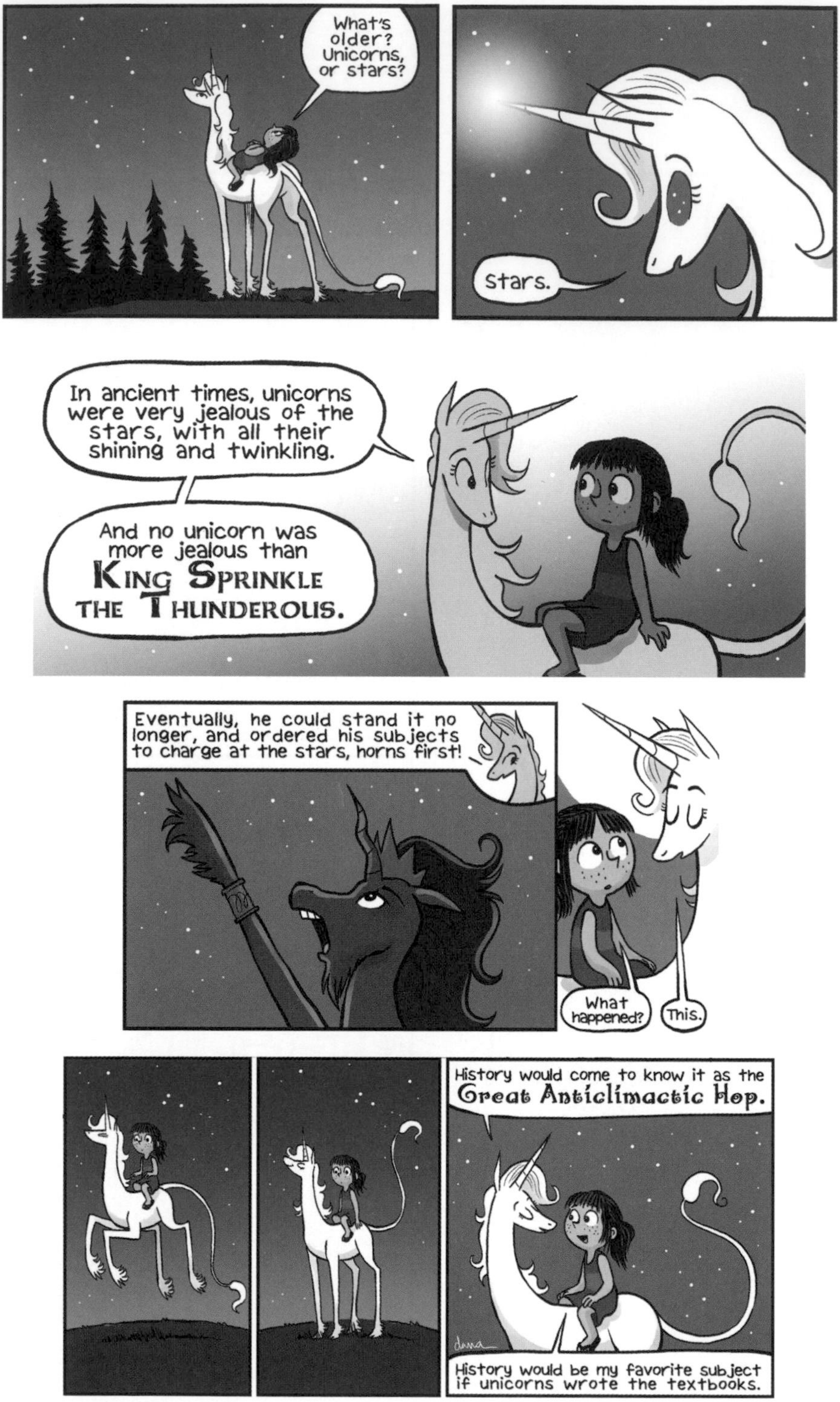
What's older? Unicorns, or stars?
Stars.
In ancient times, unicorns were very jealous of the stars, with all their shining and twinkling.
And no unicorn was more jealous than KING SPRINKLE THE THUNDEROUS.
Eventually, he could stand it no longer, and ordered his subjects to charge at the stars, horns first!
What happened?
This.
History would come to know it as the Great Anticlimactic Hop.
History would be my favorite subject if unicorns wrote the textbooks.

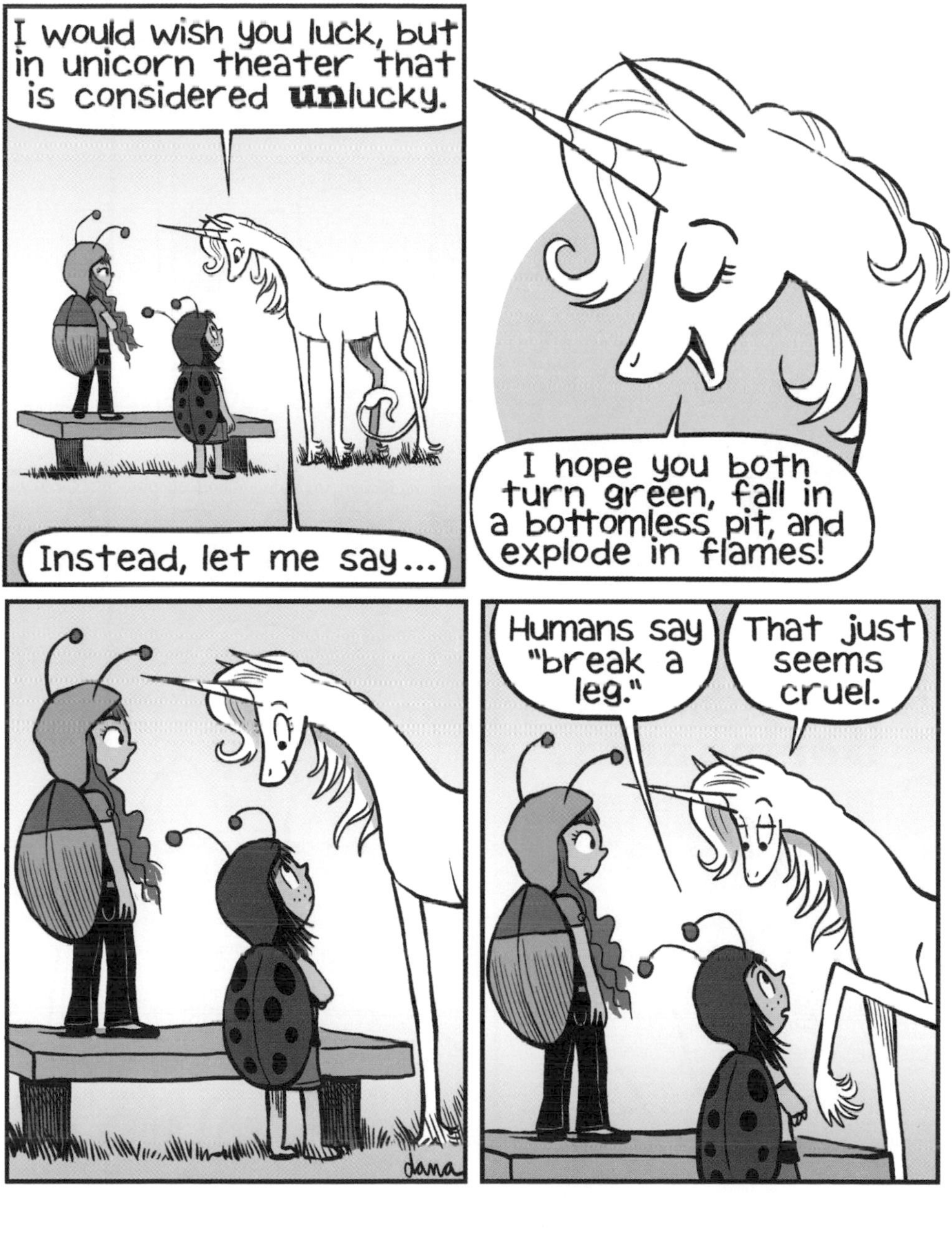

I would wish you luck, but in unicorn theater that is considered **un**lucky.
Instead, let me say...
I hope you both turn green, fall in a bottomless pit, and explode in flames!
Humans say "break a leg."
That just seems cruel.
dana

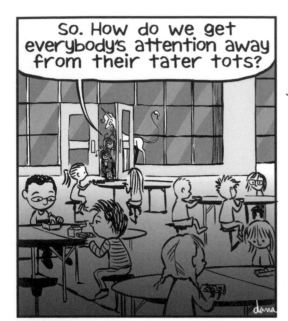

So. How do we get everybody's attention away from their tater tots?

Leave that to me!

I will draw everyone's attention to you with a **Reverse Shield of Boringness.**

Unicorns are more powerful than tater tots!

I would have hoped that was a given.

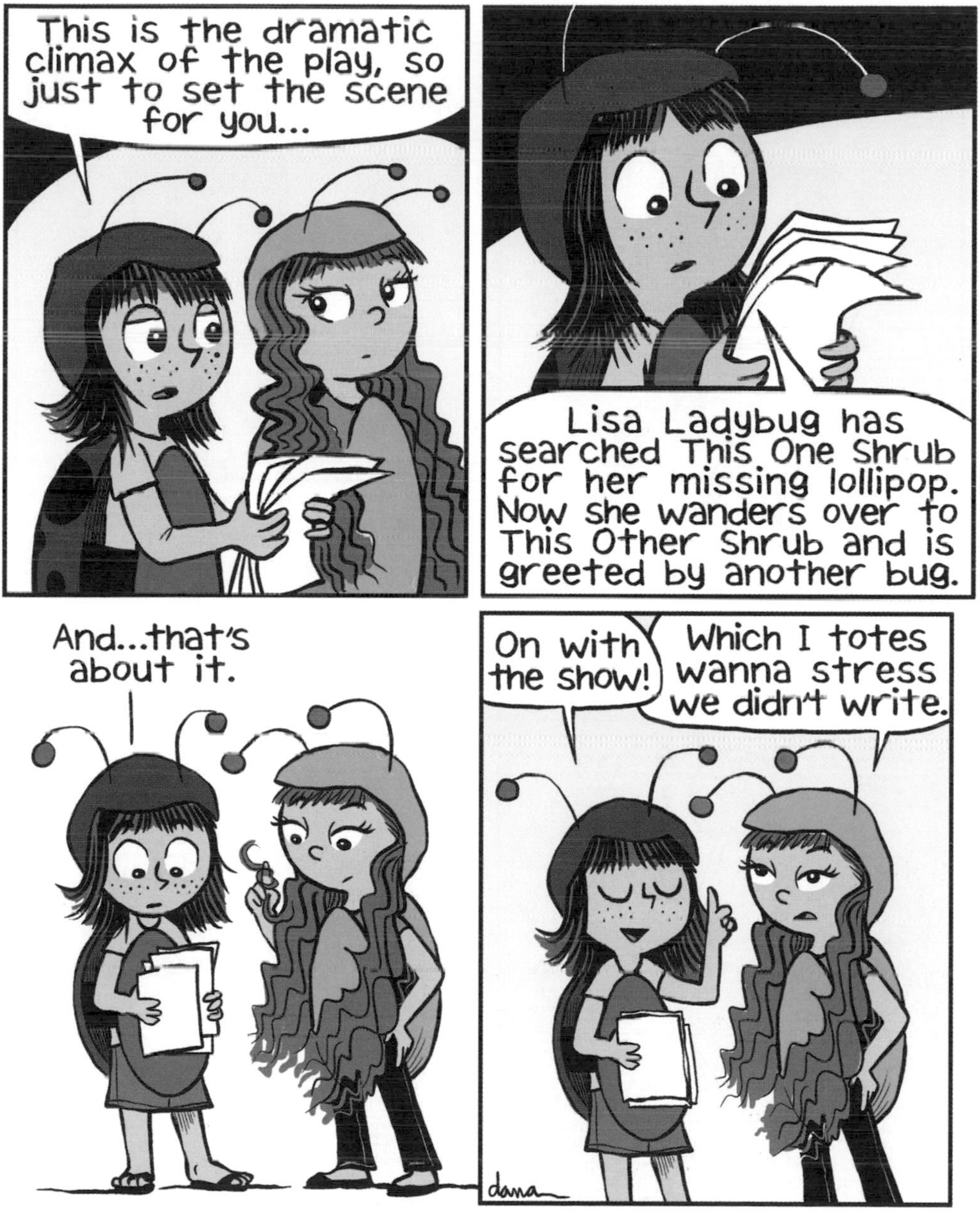
This is the dramatic climax of the play, so just to set the scene for you...
Lisa Ladybug has searched This One Shrub for her missing lollipop. Now she wanders over to This Other Shrub and is greeted by another bug.
And...that's about it.
On with the show!
Which I totes wanna stress we didn't write.
dana

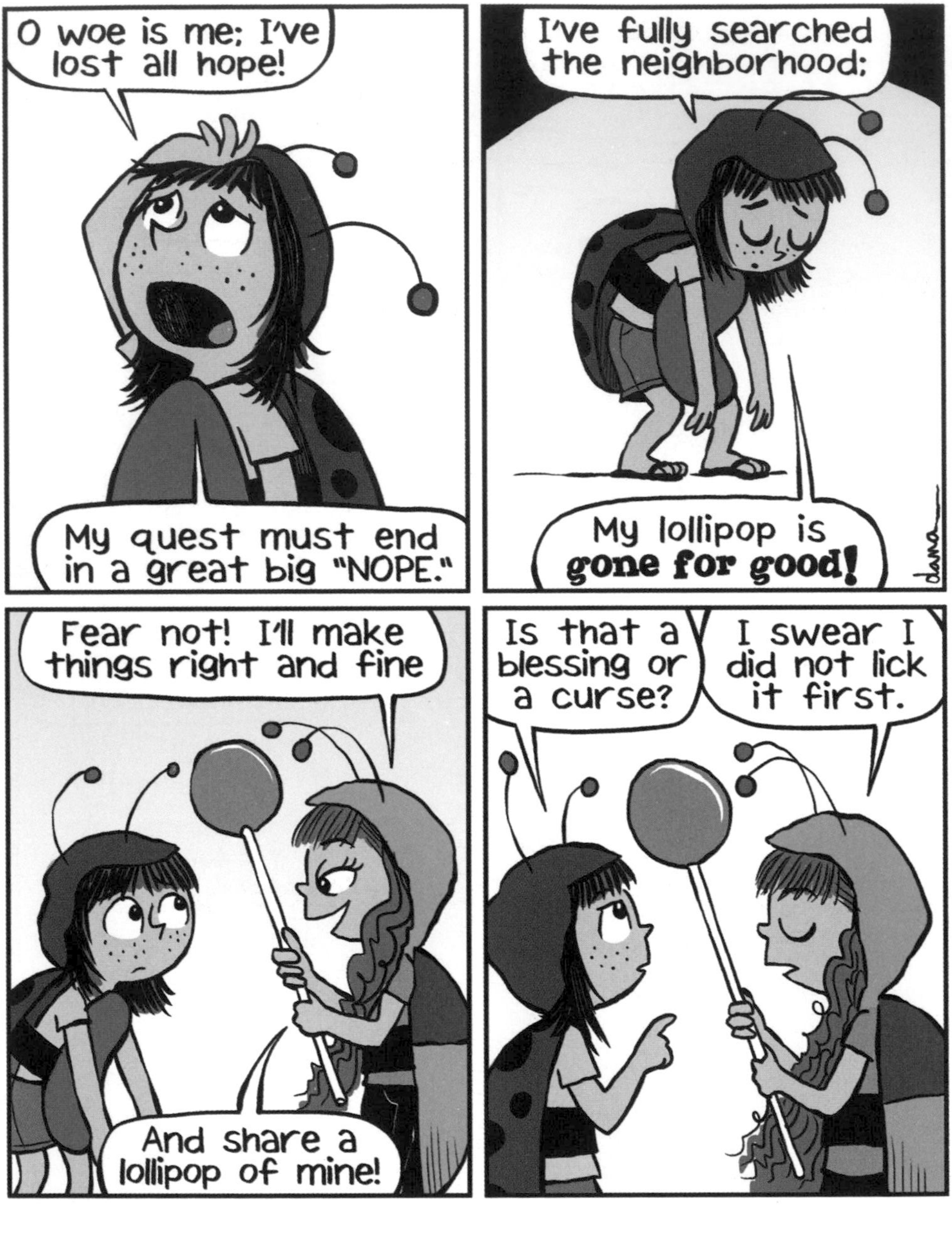
O woe is me; I've lost all hope!
My quest must end in a great big "NOPE."
I've fully searched the neighborhood;
My lollipop is **gone for good!**
dana
Fear not! I'll make things right and fine
And share a lollipop of mine!
Is that a blessing or a curse?
I swear I did not lick it first.

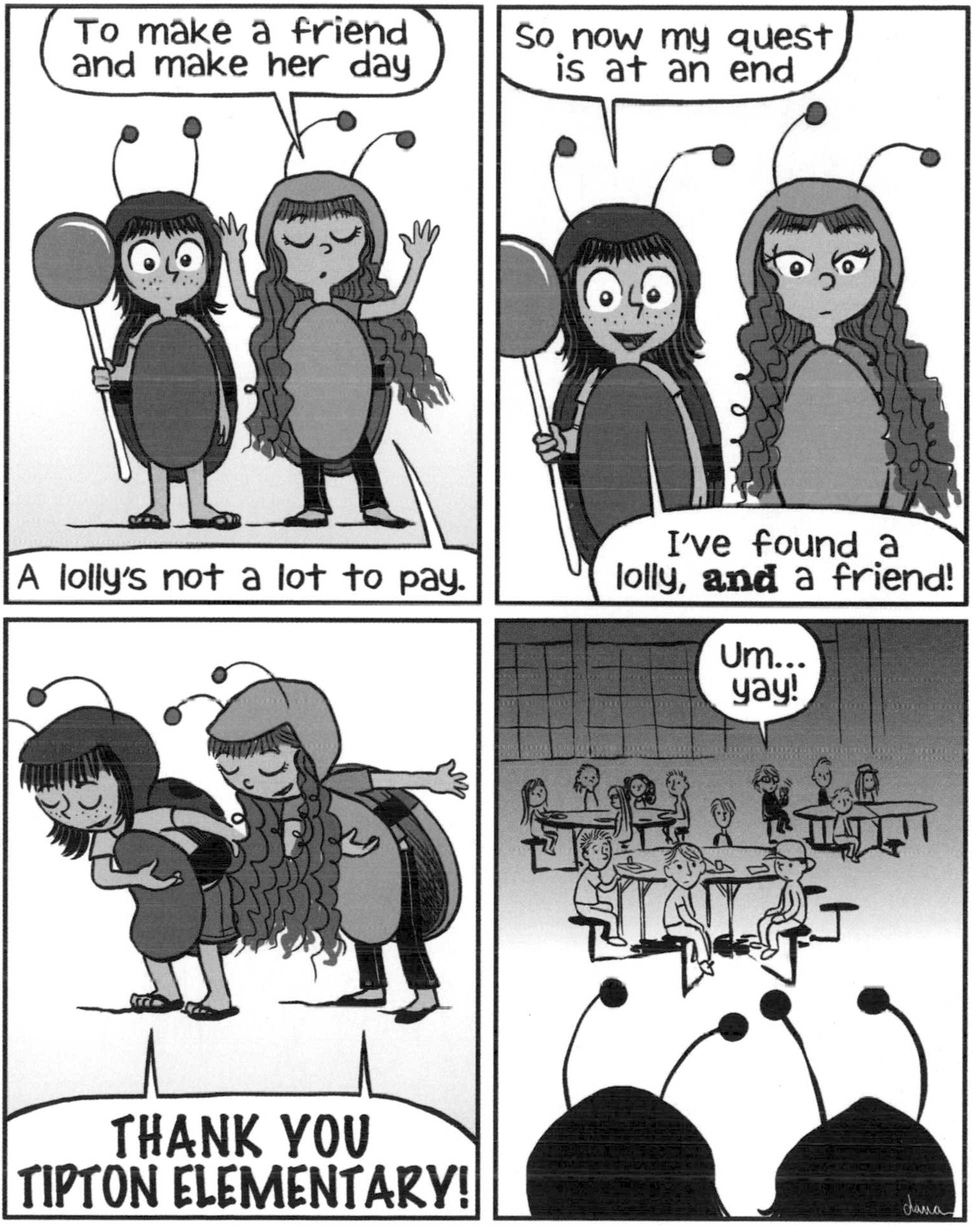
To make a friend and make her day
A lolly's not a lot to pay.
So now my quest is at an end
I've found a lolly, **and** a friend!
THANK YOU TIPTON ELEMENTARY!
Um... yay!

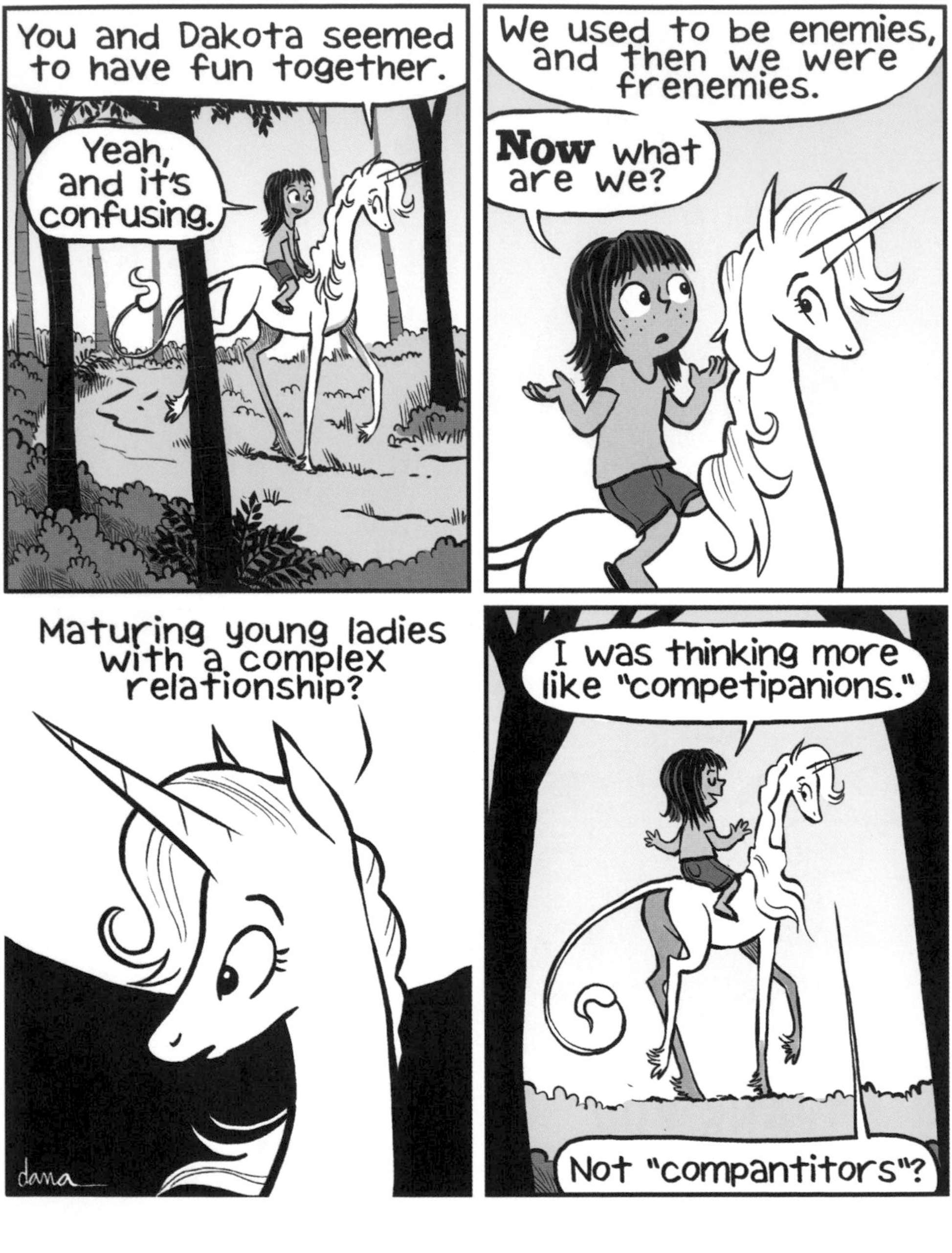

You and Dakota seemed to have fun together.
Yeah, and it's confusing.
We used to be enemies, and then we were frenemies.
Now what are we?
Maturing young ladies with a complex relationship?
I was thinking more like "competipanions."
Not "compantitors"?
dana

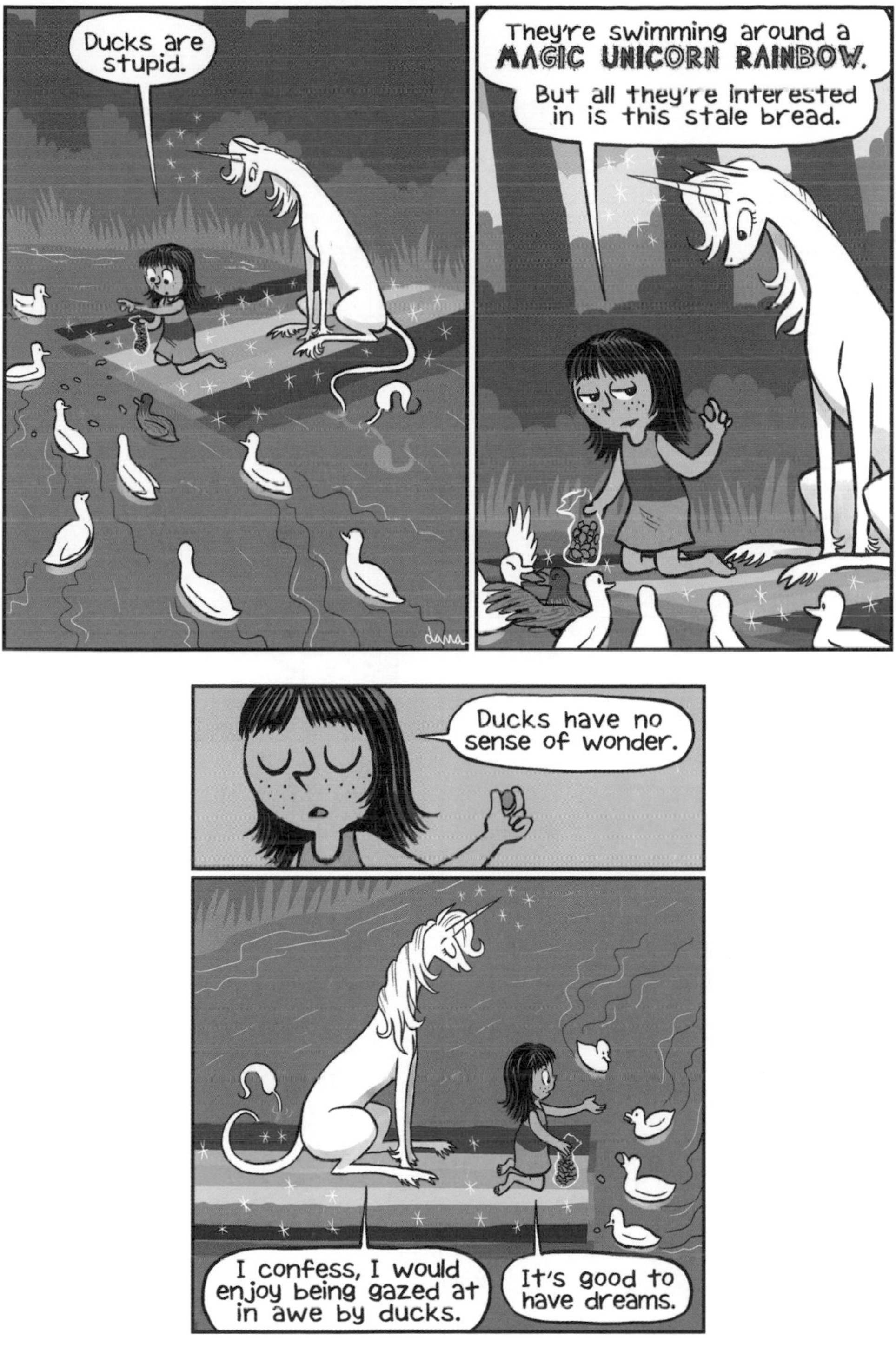
Ducks are stupid.
They're swimming around a MAGIC UNICORN RAINBOW.
But all they're interested in is this stale bread.
dana
Ducks have no sense of wonder.
I confess, I would enjoy being gazed at in awe by ducks.
It's good to have dreams.

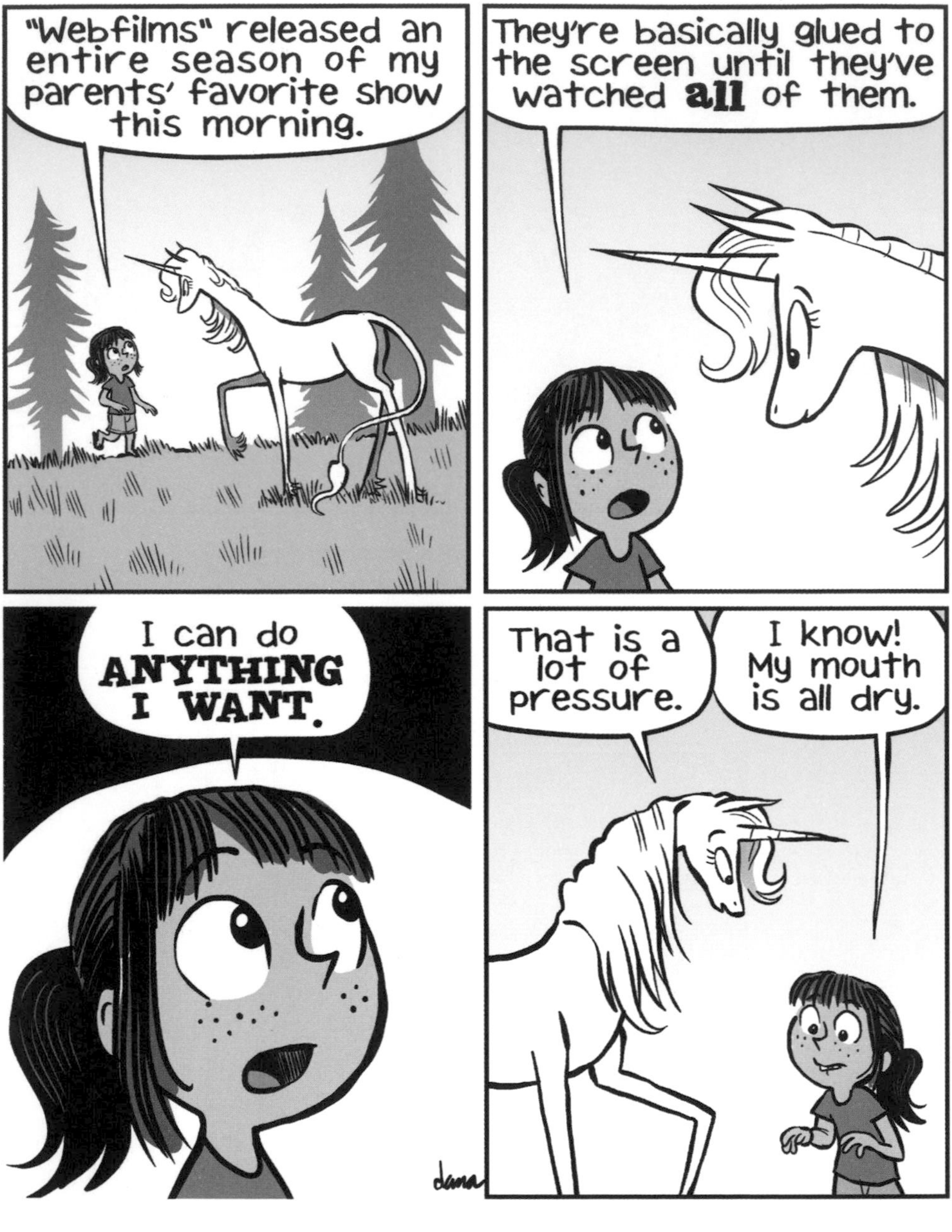
"Webfilms" released an entire season of my parents' favorite show this morning.
They're basically glued to the screen until they've watched **all** of them.
I can do **ANYTHING I WANT**.
That is a lot of pressure.
I know! My mouth is all dry.
dana

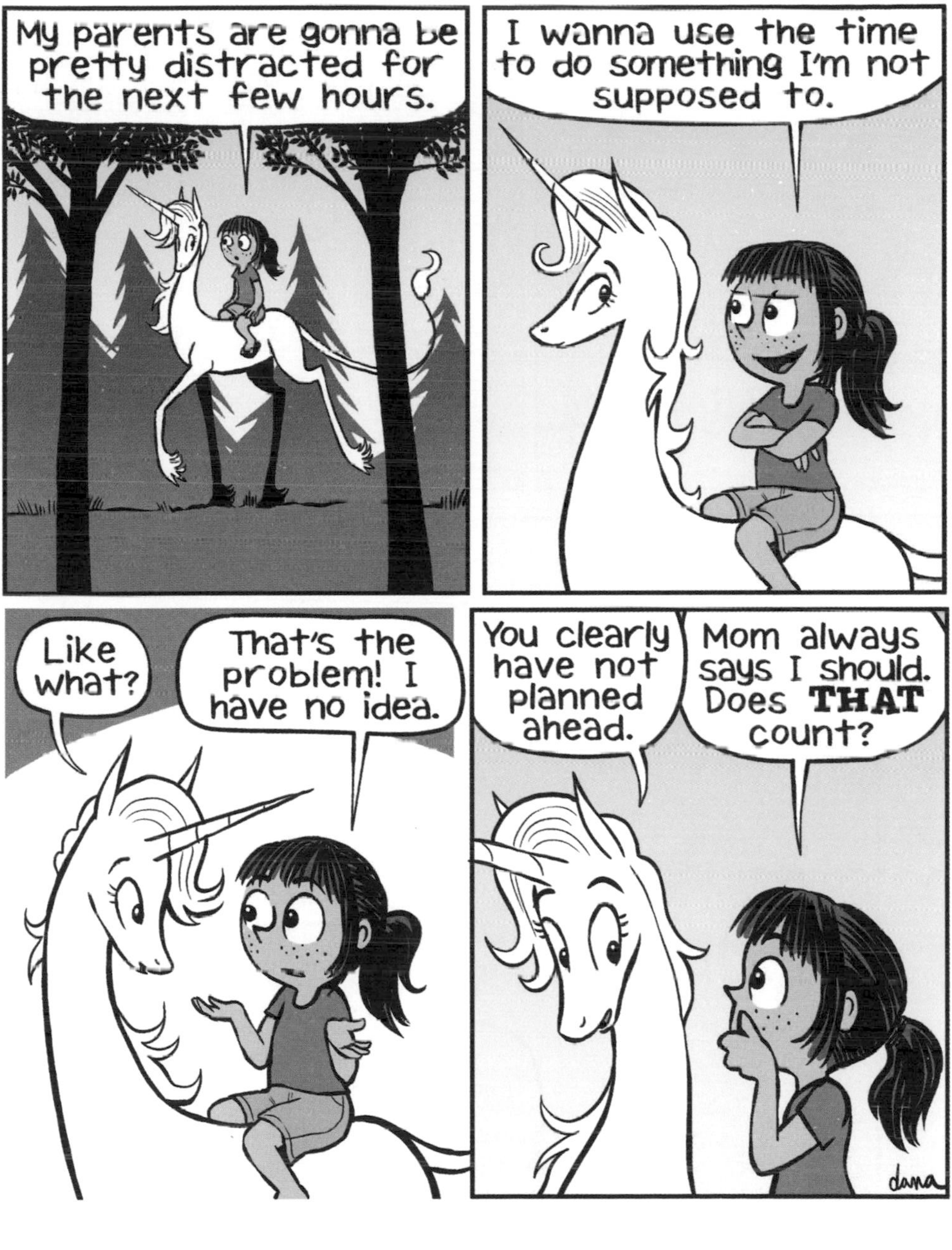
My parents are gonna be pretty distracted for the next few hours.
I wanna use the time to do something I'm not supposed to.
Like what?
That's the problem! I have no idea.
You clearly have not planned ahead.
Mom always says I should. Does **THAT** count?
dana

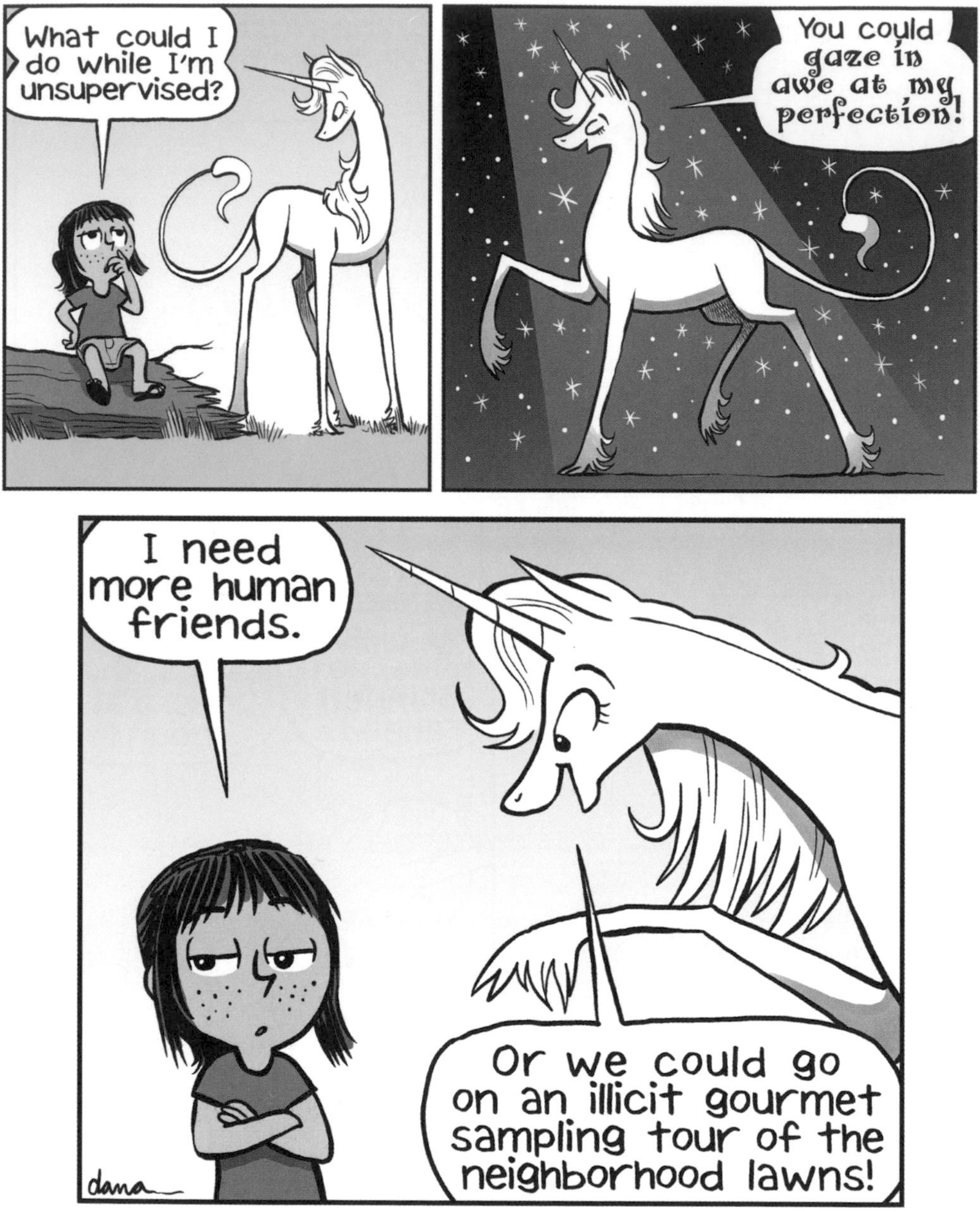
What could I do while I'm unsupervised?
You could gaze in awe at my perfection!
I need more human friends.
Or we could go on an illicit gourmet sampling tour of the neighborhood lawns!
dana

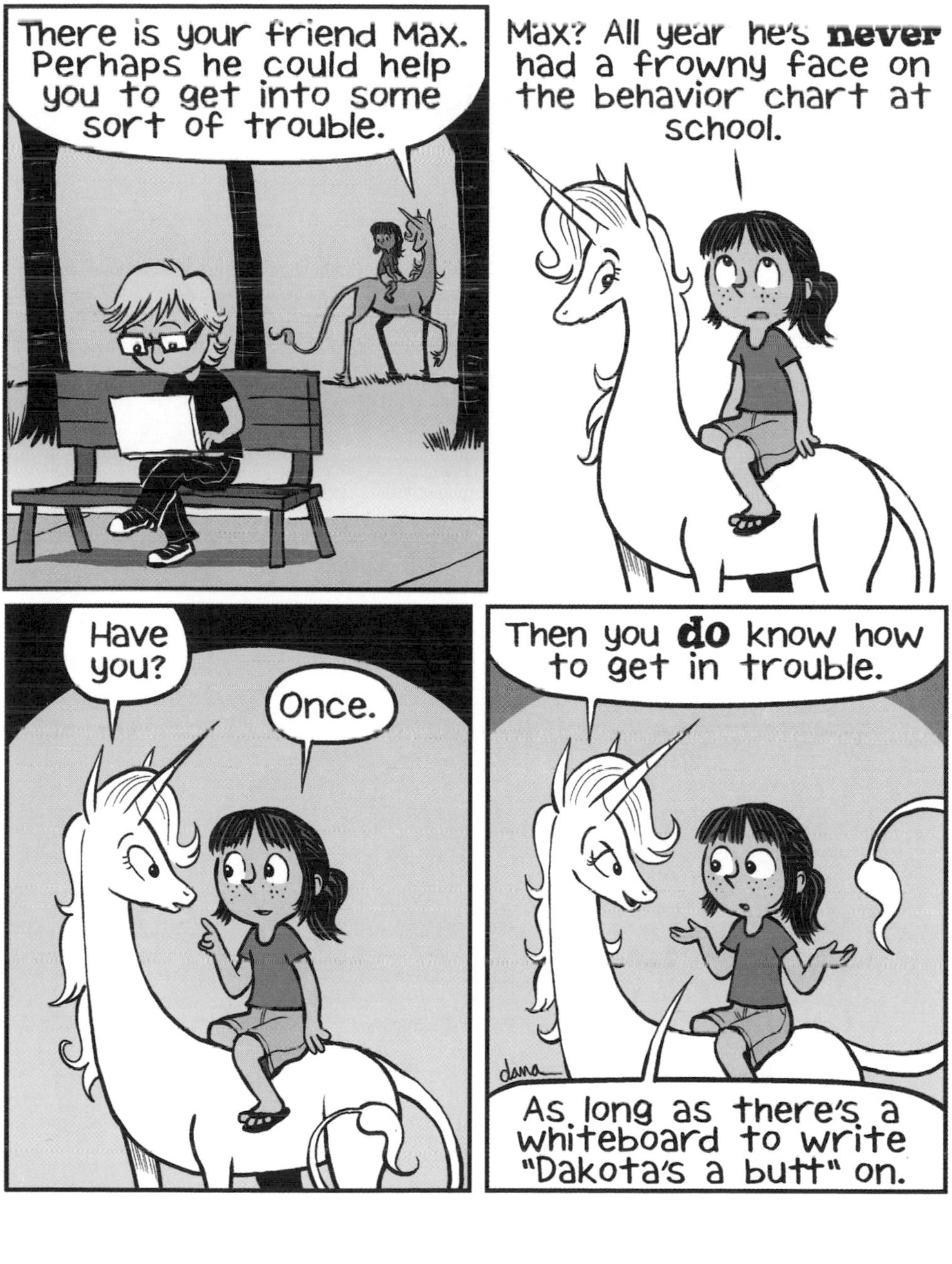
There is your friend Max. Perhaps he could help you to get into some sort of trouble.
Max? All year he's **never** had a frowny face on the behavior chart at school.
Have you?
Once.
Then you **do** know how to get in trouble.
dana
As long as there's a whiteboard to write "Dakota's a butt" on.

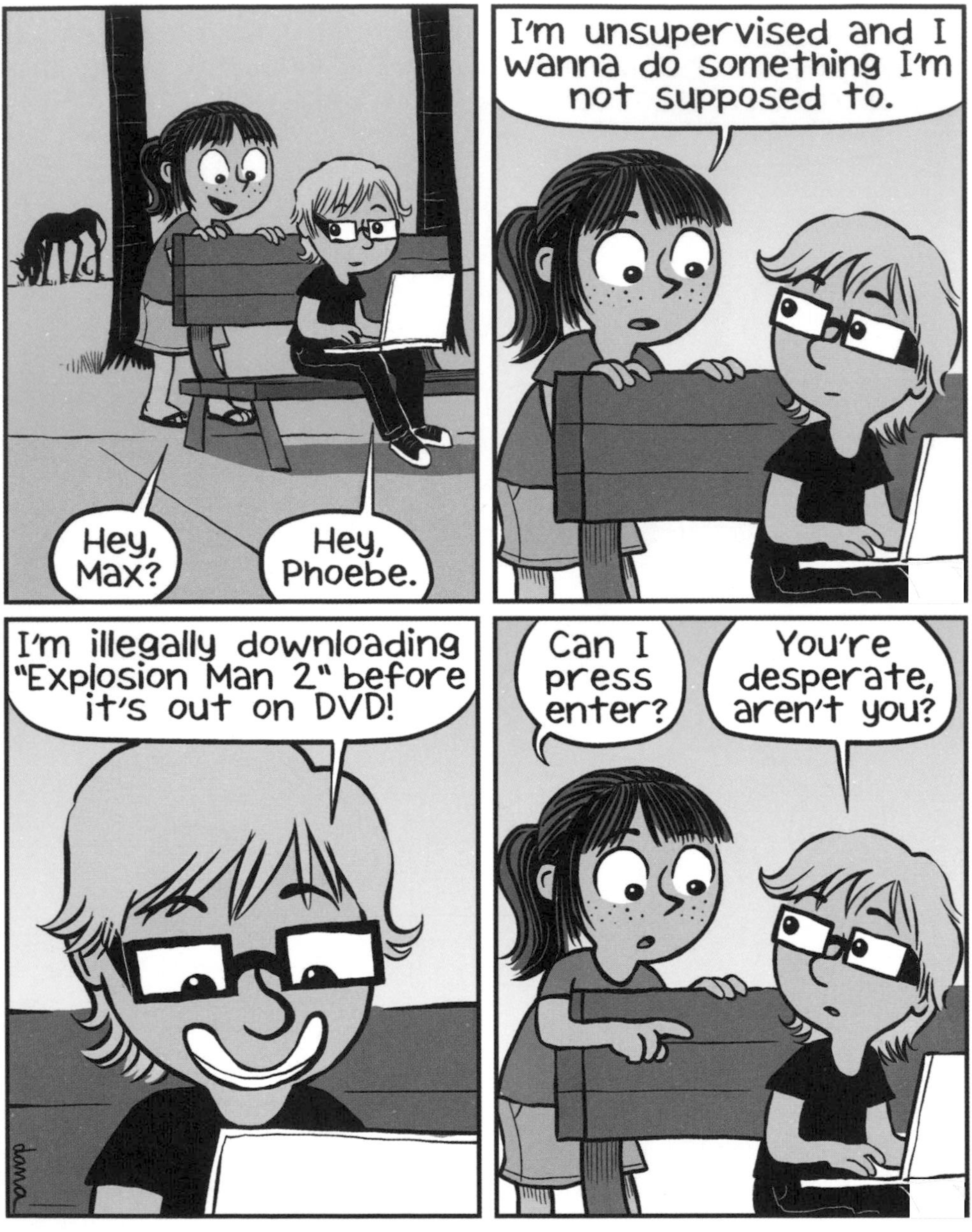
Hey, Max?
Hey, Phoebe.
I'm unsupervised and I wanna do something I'm not supposed to.
I'm illegally downloading "Explosion Man 2" before it's out on DVD!
Can I press enter?
You're desperate, aren't you?

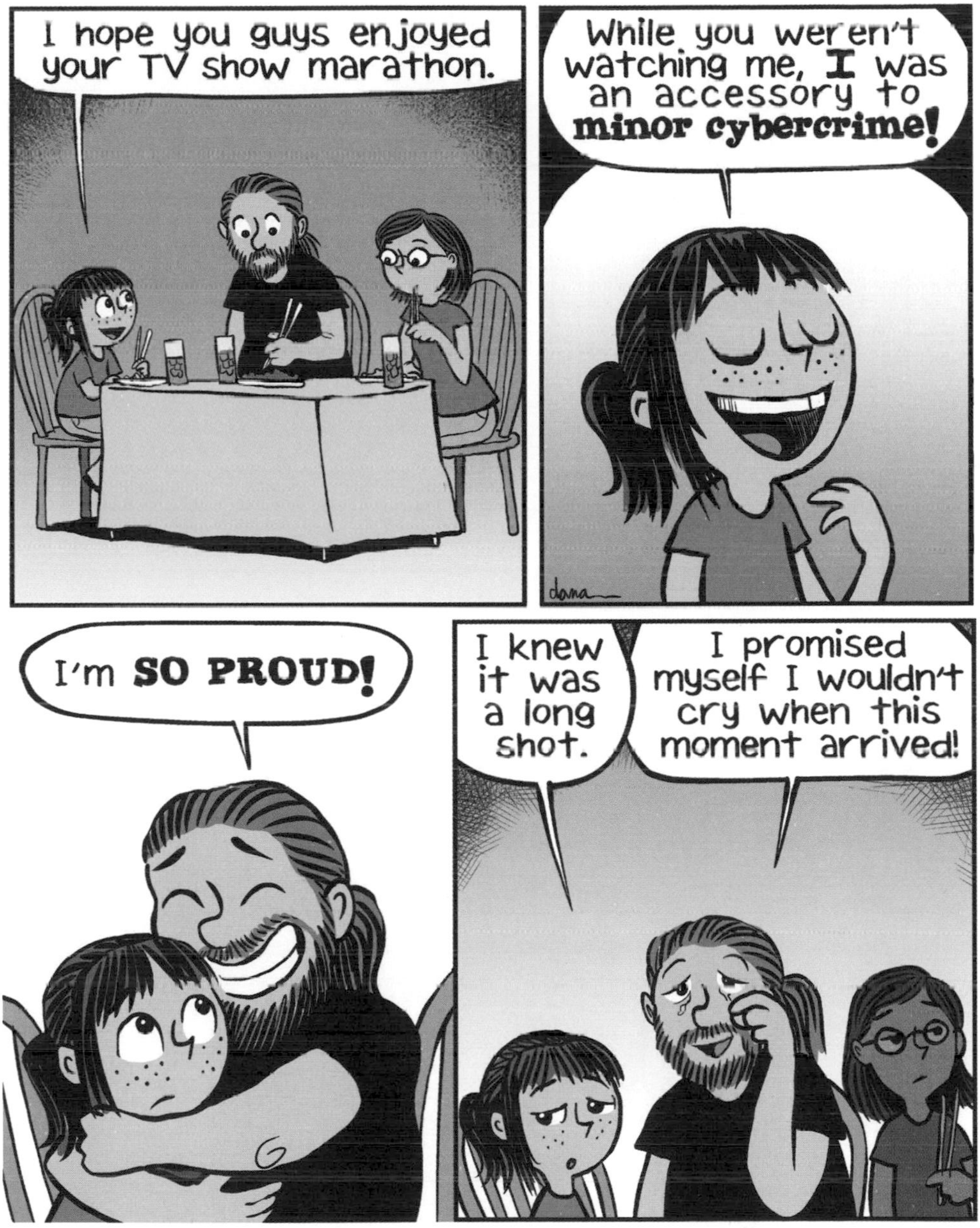
I hope you guys enjoyed your TV show marathon.
While you weren't watching me, **I** was an accessory to **minor cybercrime!**
I'm **SO PROUD!**
I knew it was a long shot.
I promised myself I wouldn't cry when this moment arrived!

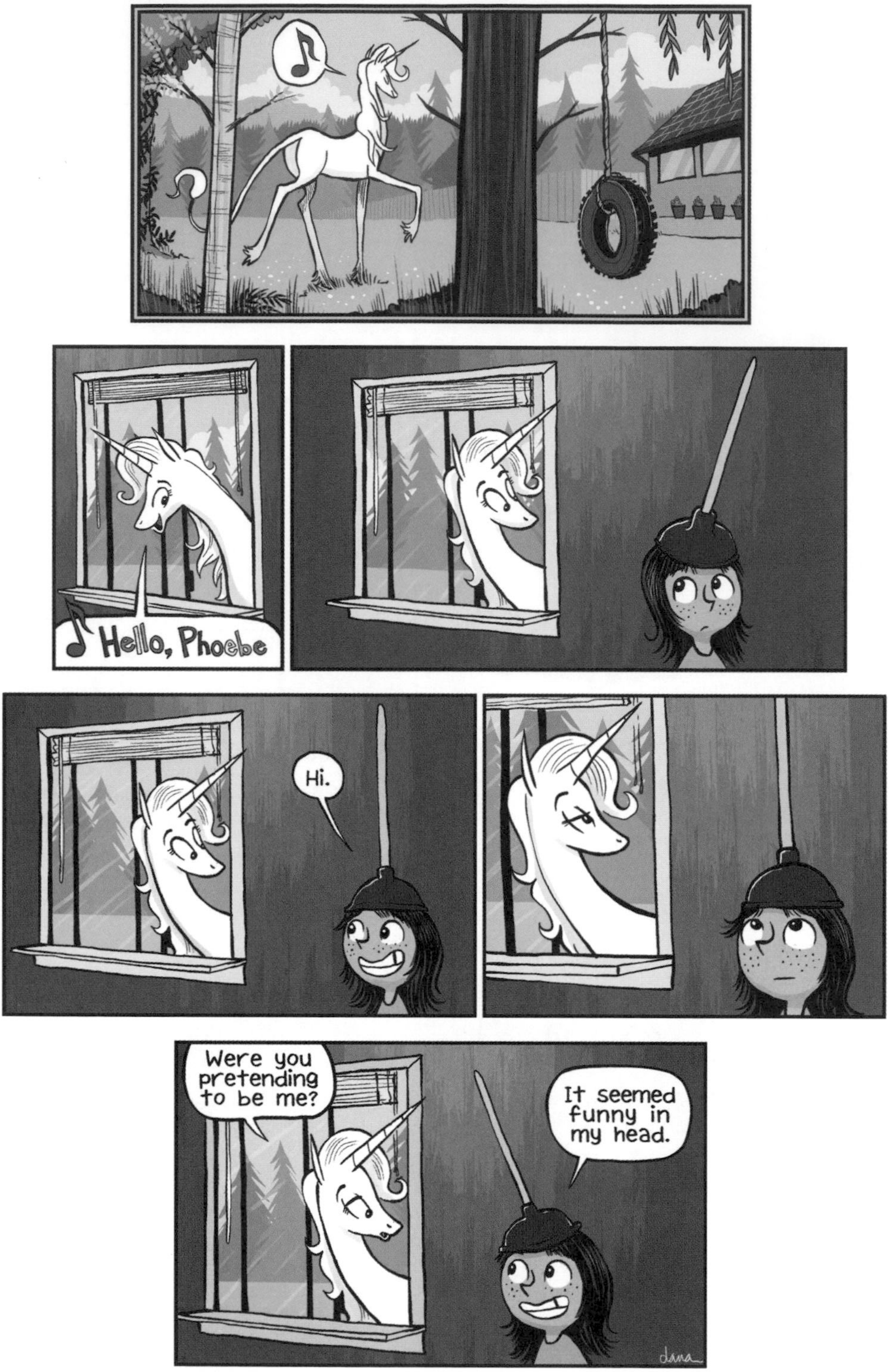
Hello, Phoebe
Hi.
Were you pretending to be me?
It seemed funny in my head.
dana

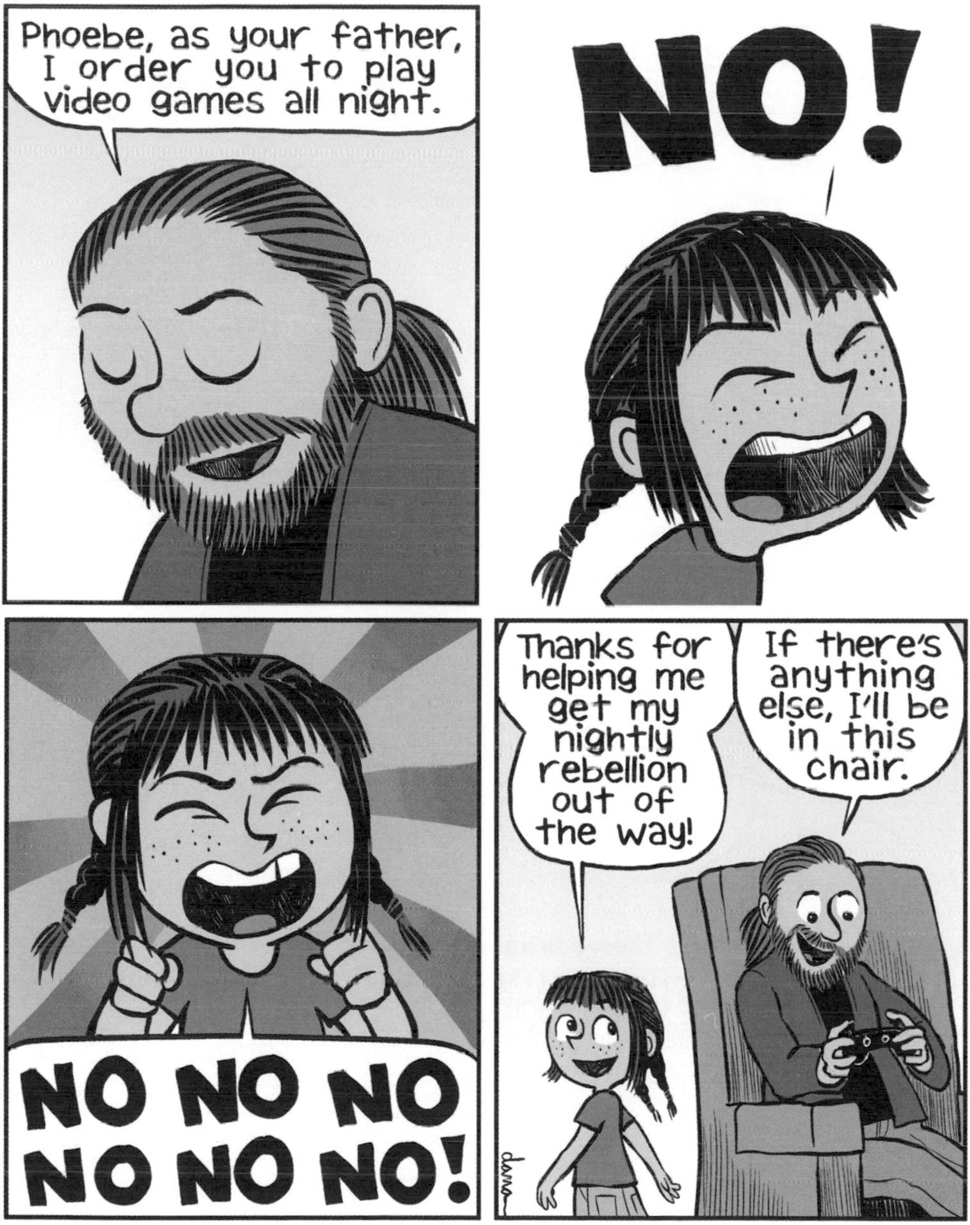

Phoebe, as your father, I order you to play video games all night.
NO!
NO NO NO NO NO NO!
Thanks for helping me get my nightly rebellion out of the way!
If there's anything else, I'll be in this chair.

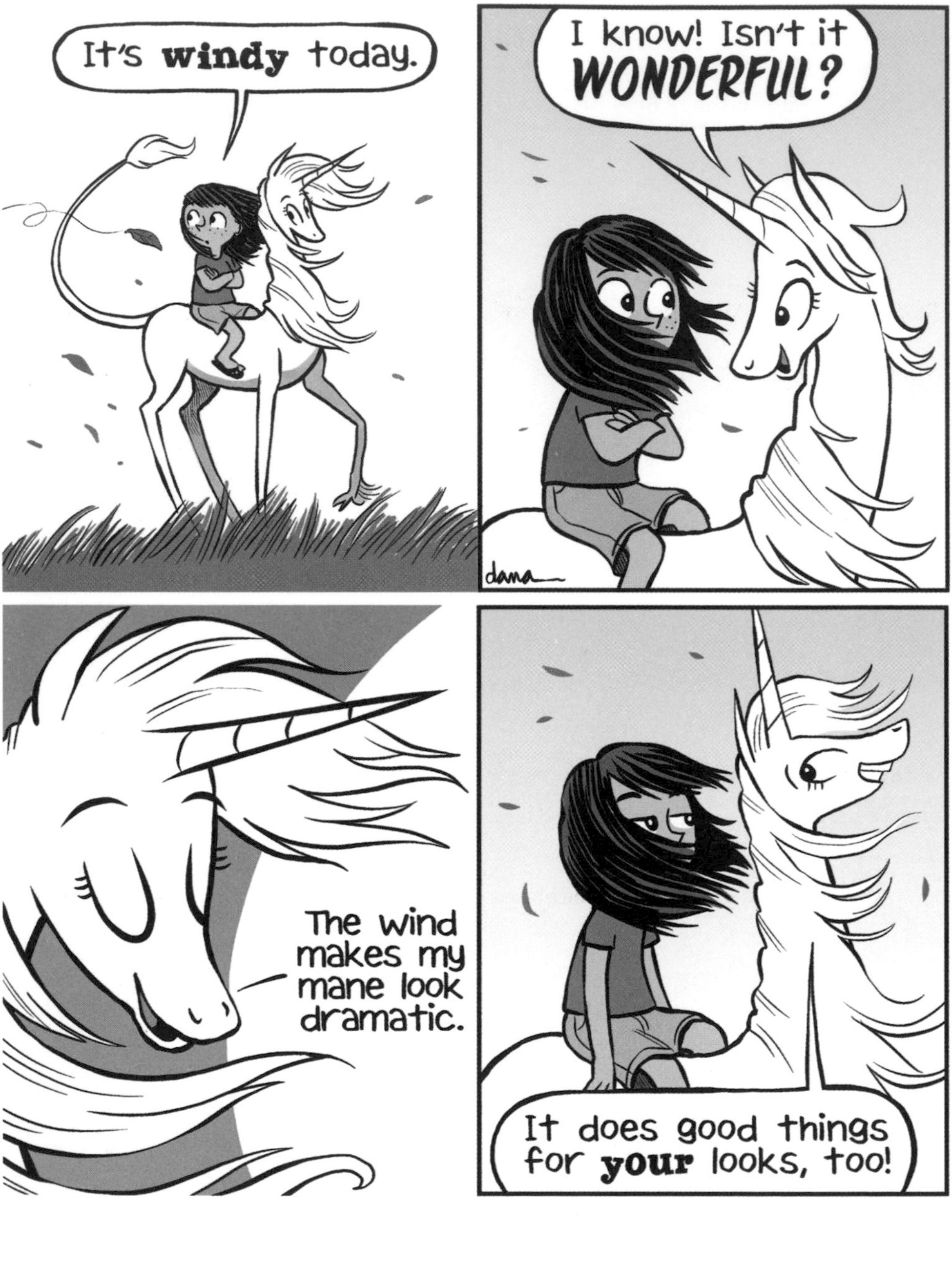
It's **windy** today.
I know! Isn't it **WONDERFUL?**
dana
The wind makes my mane look dramatic.
It does good things for **your** looks, too!

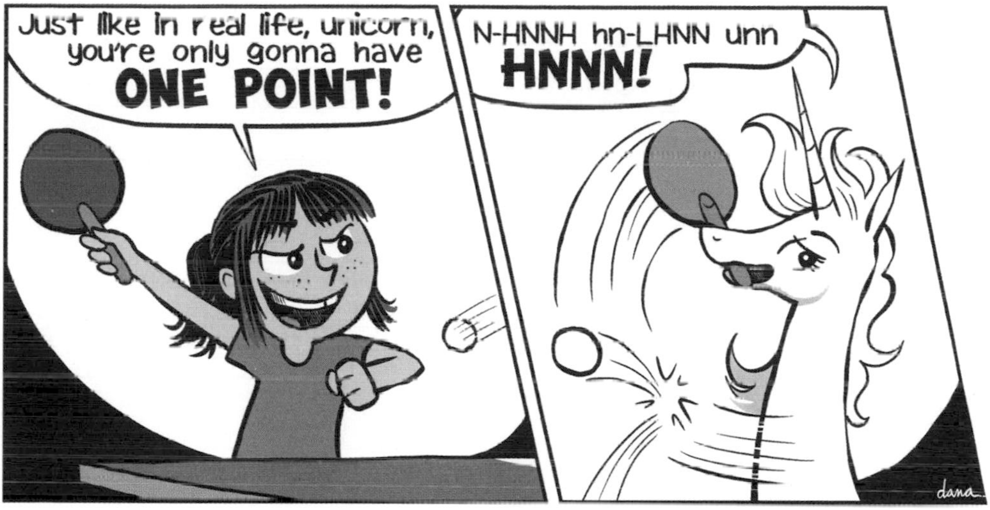
Just like in real life, unicorn, you're only gonna have ONE POINT!
N-HNNH hn-LHNN unn HNNN!
dana

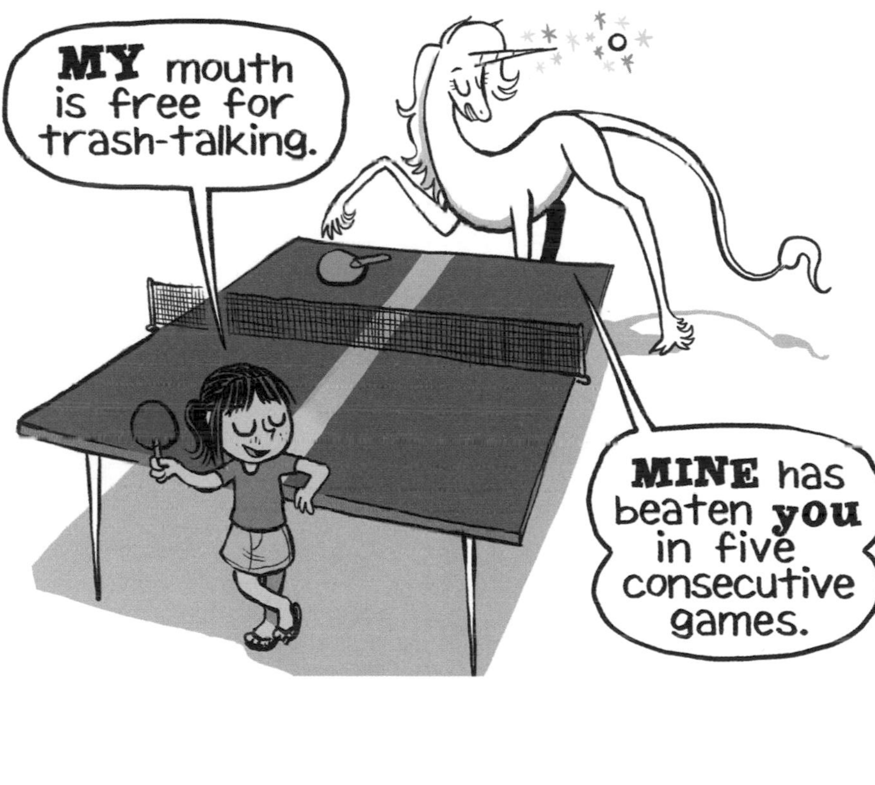
MY mouth is free for trash-talking.
MINE has beaten you in five consecutive games.

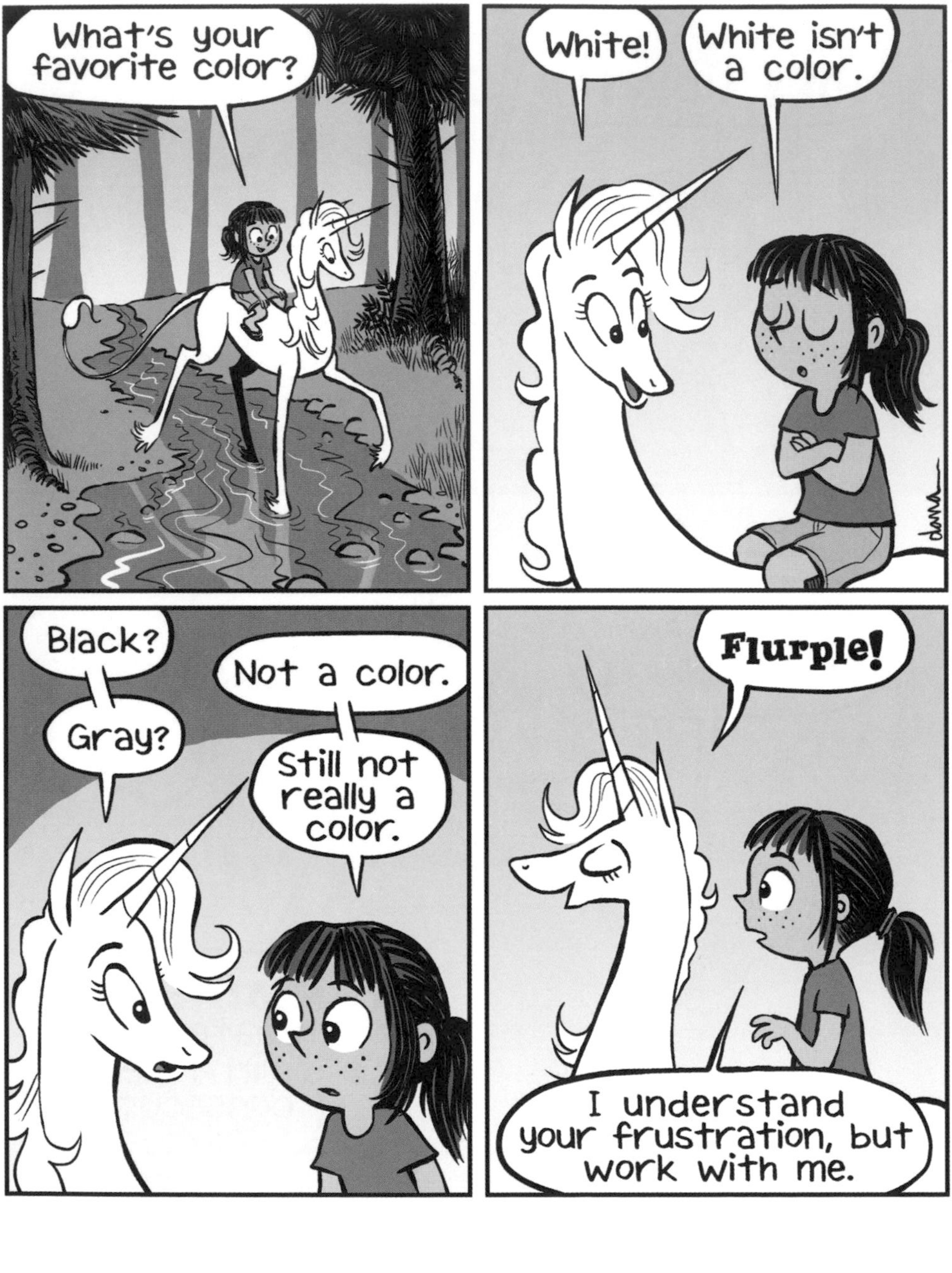
What's your favorite color?
White!
White isn't a color.
Black?
Gray?
Not a color.
Still not really a color.
Flurple!
I understand your frustration, but work with me.
dana

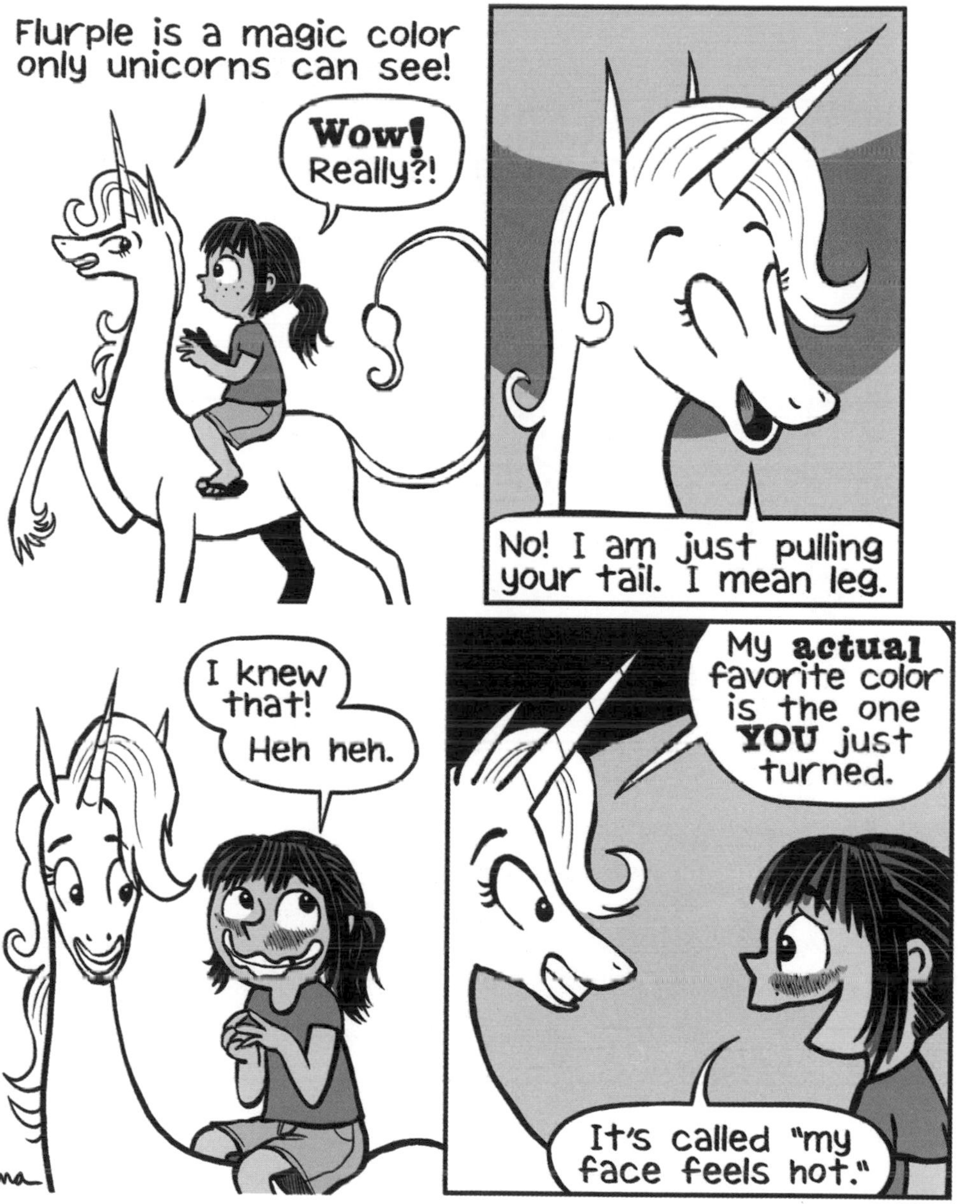
Flurple is a magic color only unicorns can see!
Wow! Really?!
No! I am just pulling your tail. I mean leg.
I knew that! Heh heh.
My actual favorite color is the one YOU just turned.
It's called "my face feels hot."
dana

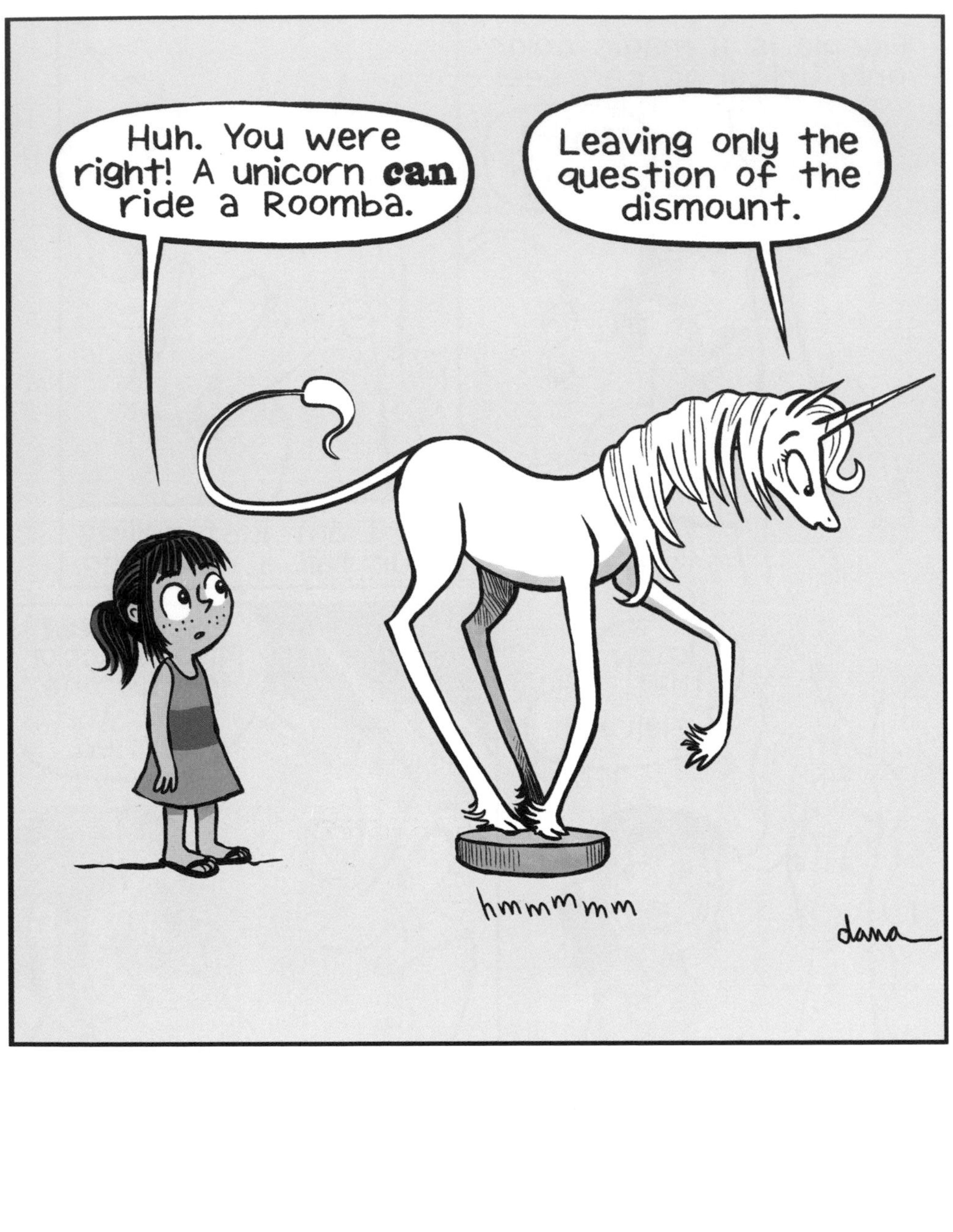
Huh. You were right! A unicorn **can** ride a Roomba.
Leaving only the question of the dismount.
hmmmmmm
dana

Pineapple ring!
Doughnut!
Bagel!
Cookie I drilled a hole in!
A+
A
5
I wish this worked with trail mix.
When we get back from our ride, you are going to wash my horn.
dana

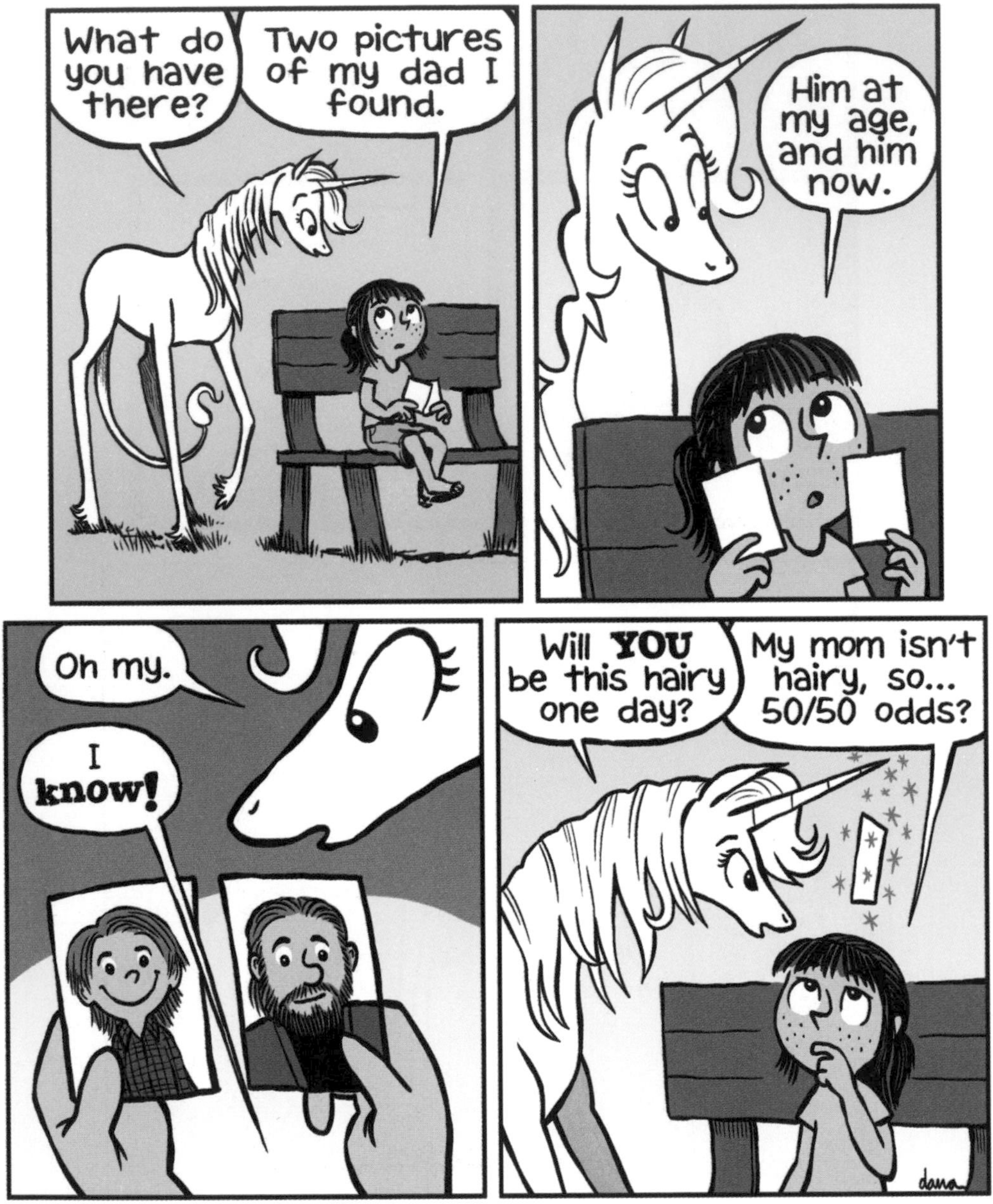
What do you have there?
Two pictures of my dad I found.
Him at my age, and him now.
Oh my.
I **know!**
Will **YOU** be this hairy one day?
My mom isn't hairy, so... 50/50 odds?
dana

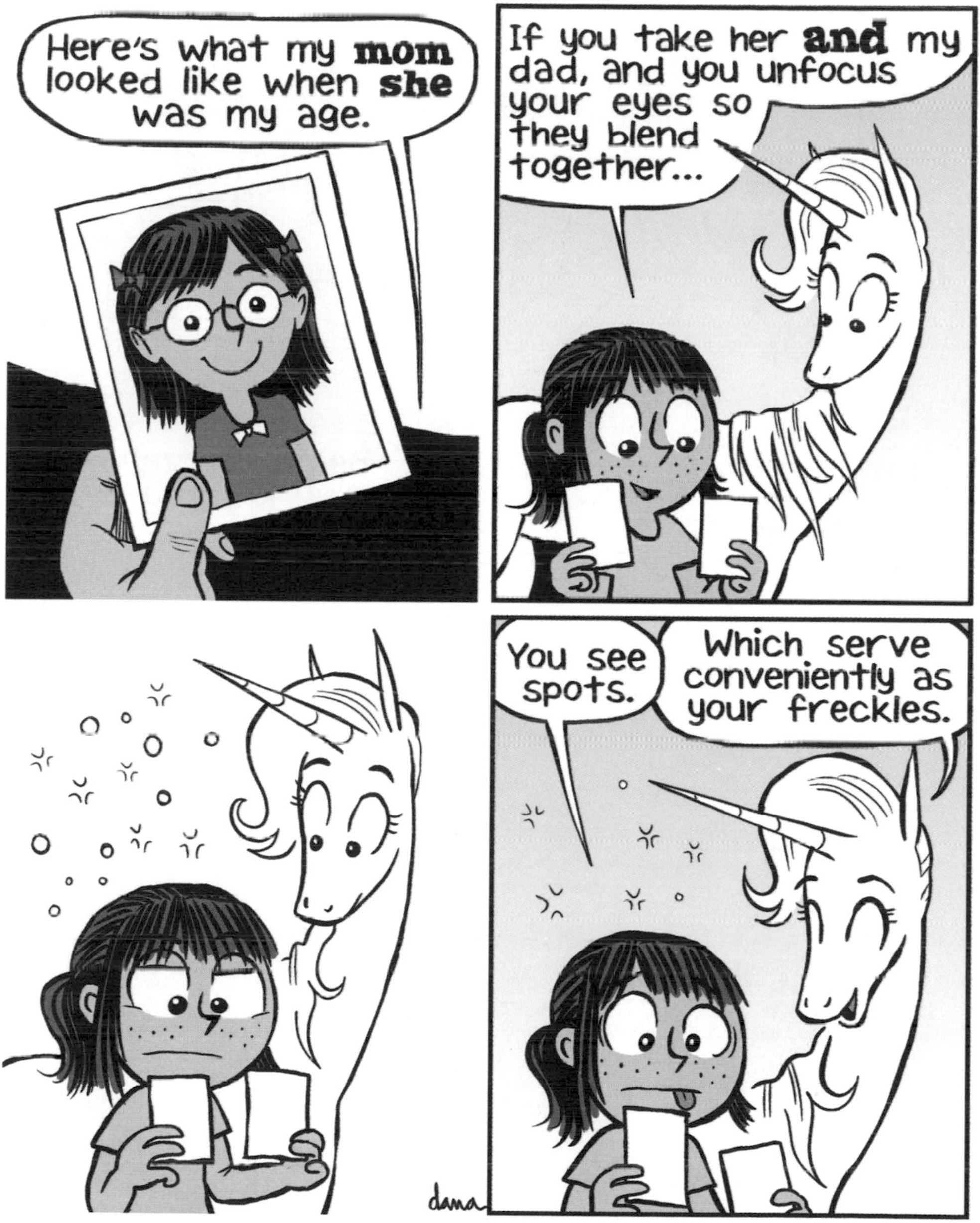
Here's what my mom looked like when she was my age.
If you take her and my dad, and you unfocus your eyes so they blend together...
You see spots.
Which serve conveniently as your freckles.
dana

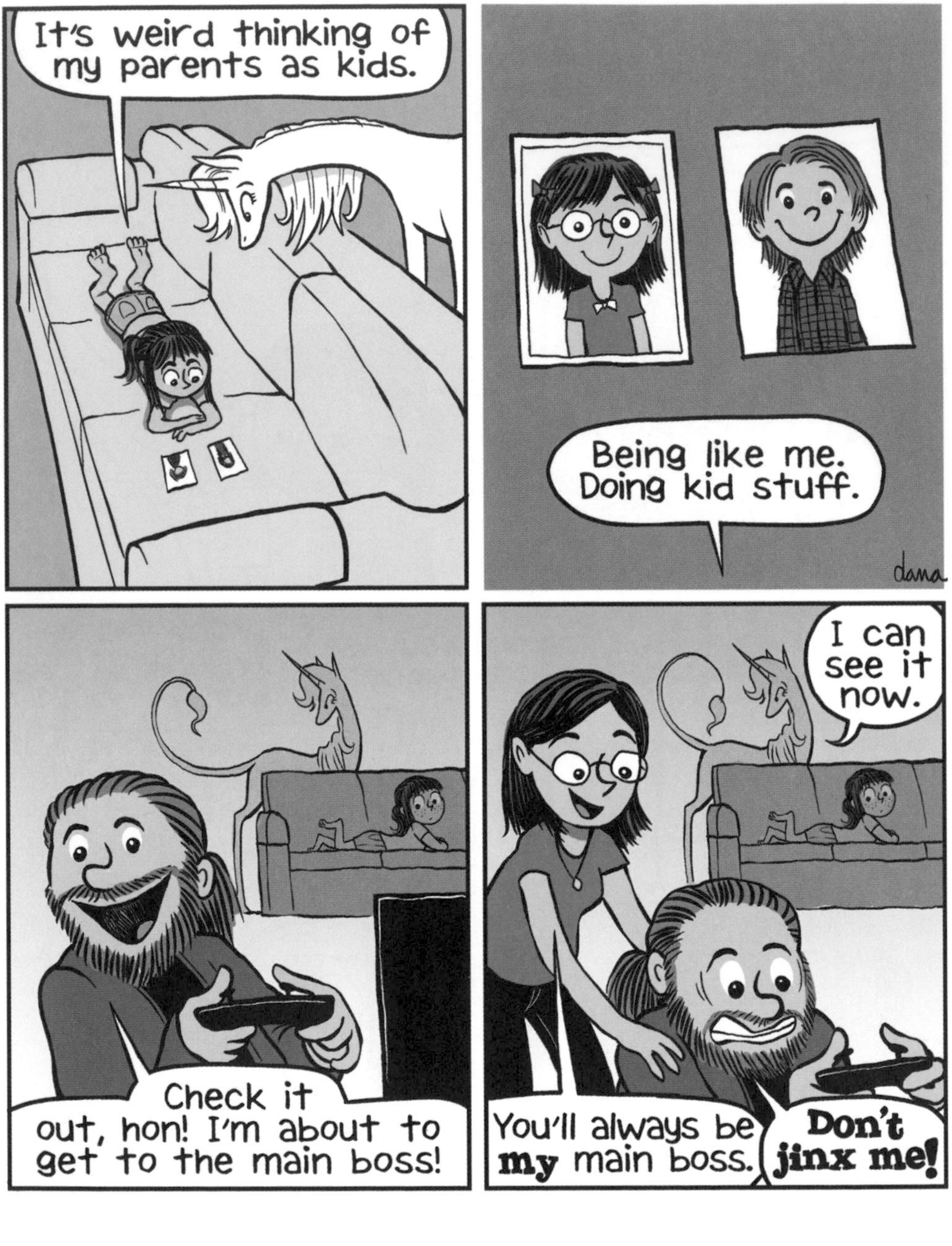
It's weird thinking of my parents as kids.
Being like me. Doing kid stuff.
dana
Check it out, hon! I'm about to get to the main boss!
I can see it now.
You'll always be **my** main boss.
Don't jinx me!

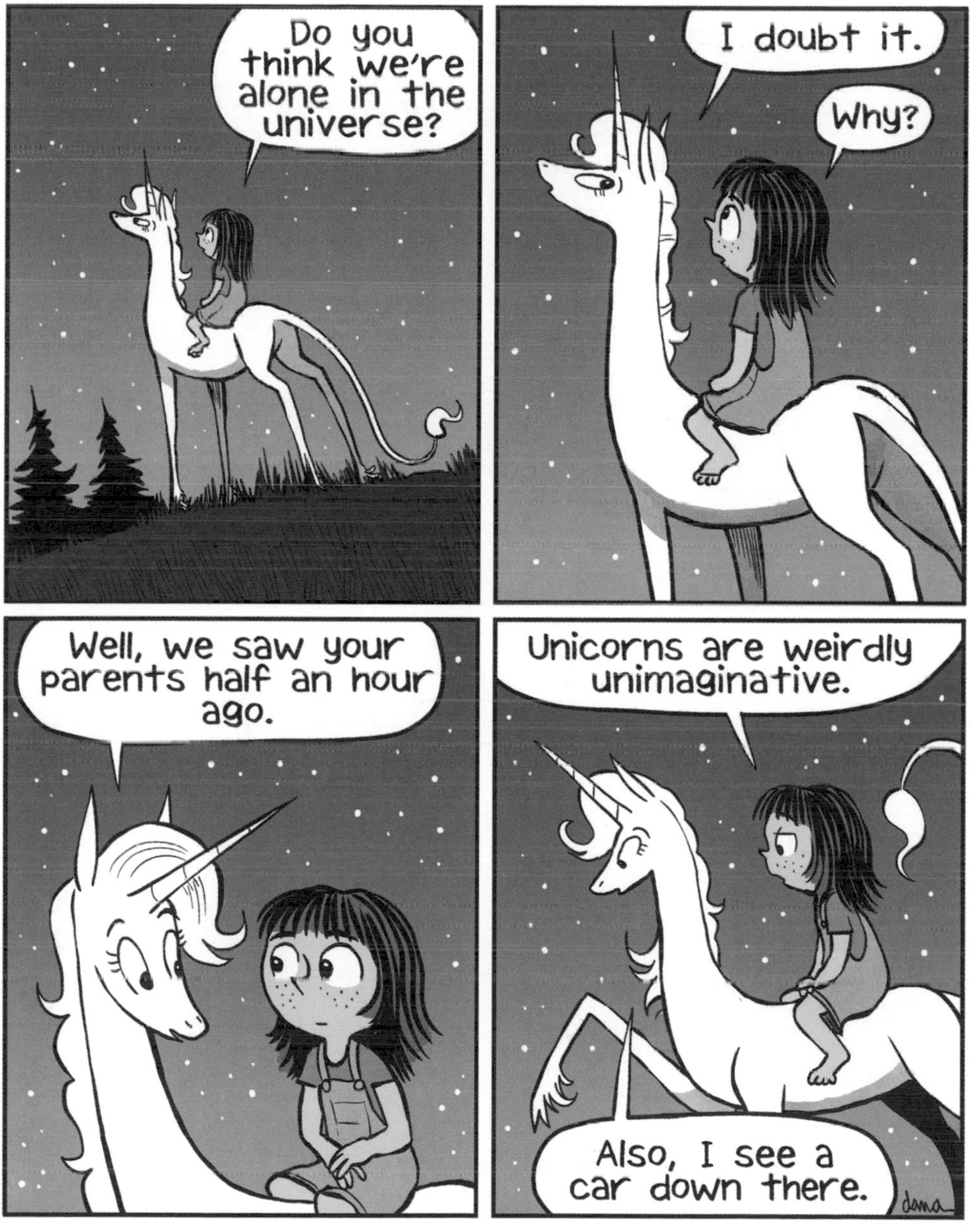
Do you think we're alone in the universe?
I doubt it.
Why?
Well, we saw your parents half an hour ago.
Unicorns are weirdly unimaginative.
Also, I see a car down there.
dana

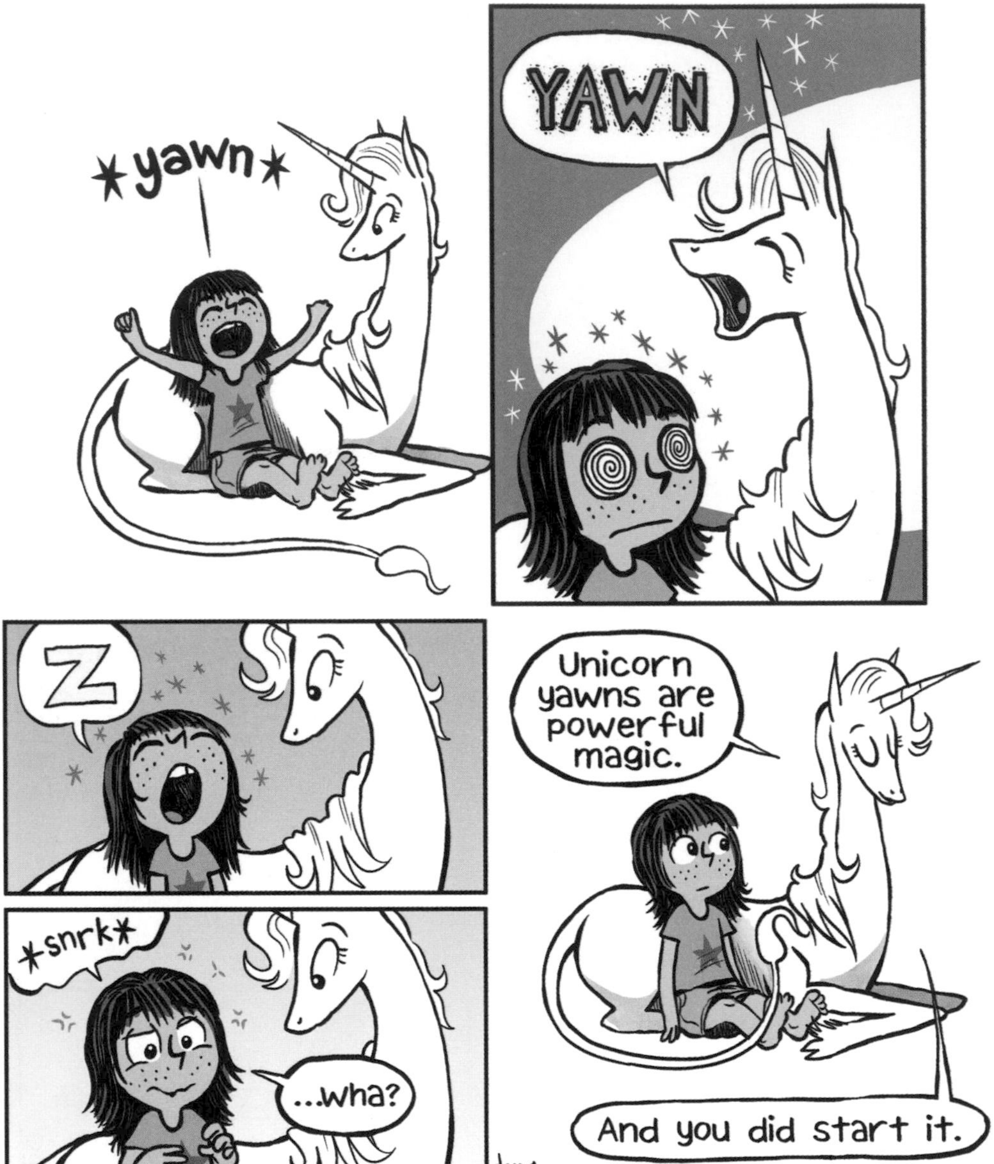
yawn
YAWN
Z
snrk
...wha?
Unicorn yawns are powerful magic.
And you did start it.
dana

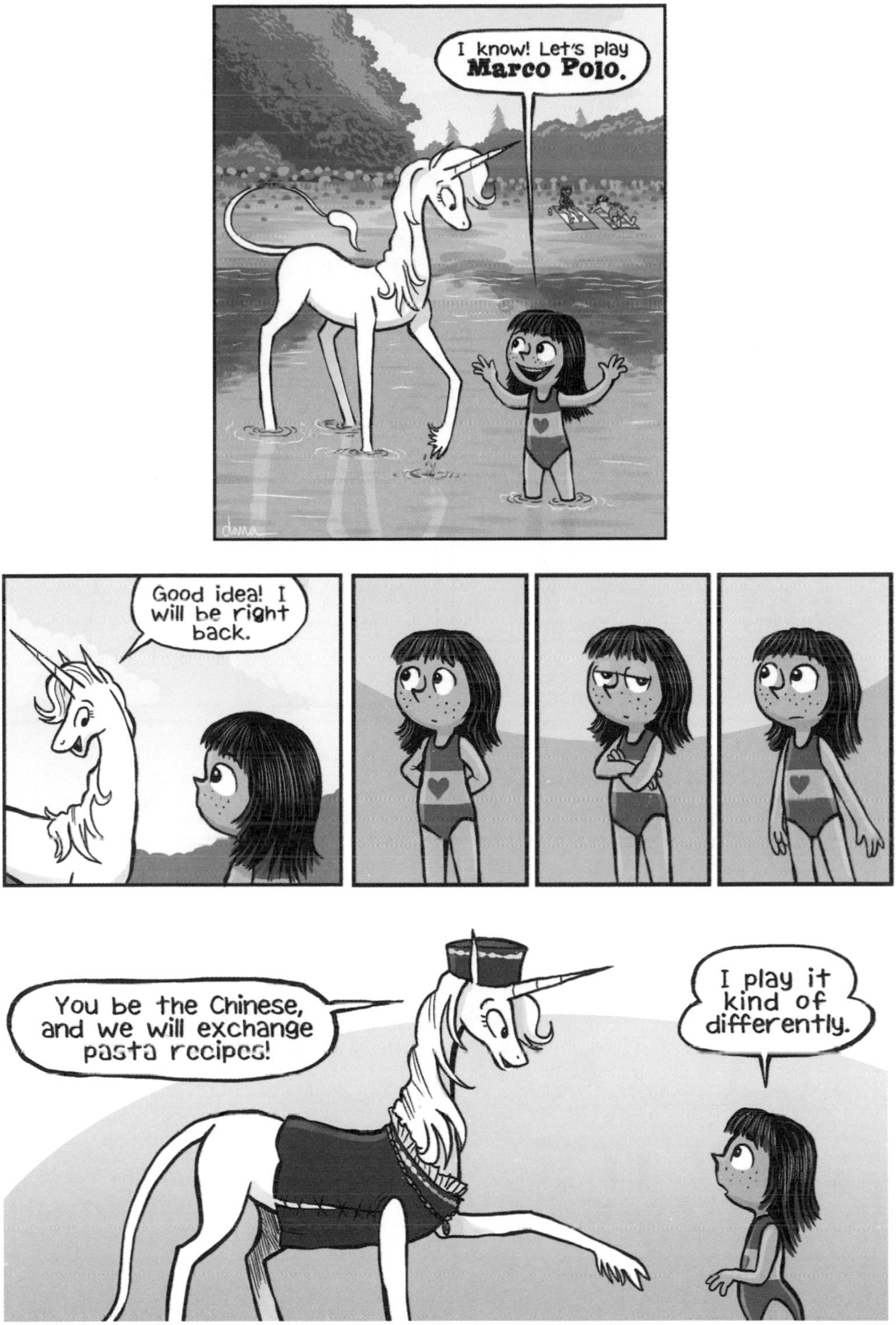
I know! Let's play Marco Polo.
dana
Good idea! I will be right back.
You be the Chinese, and we will exchange pasta recipes!
I play it kind of differently.

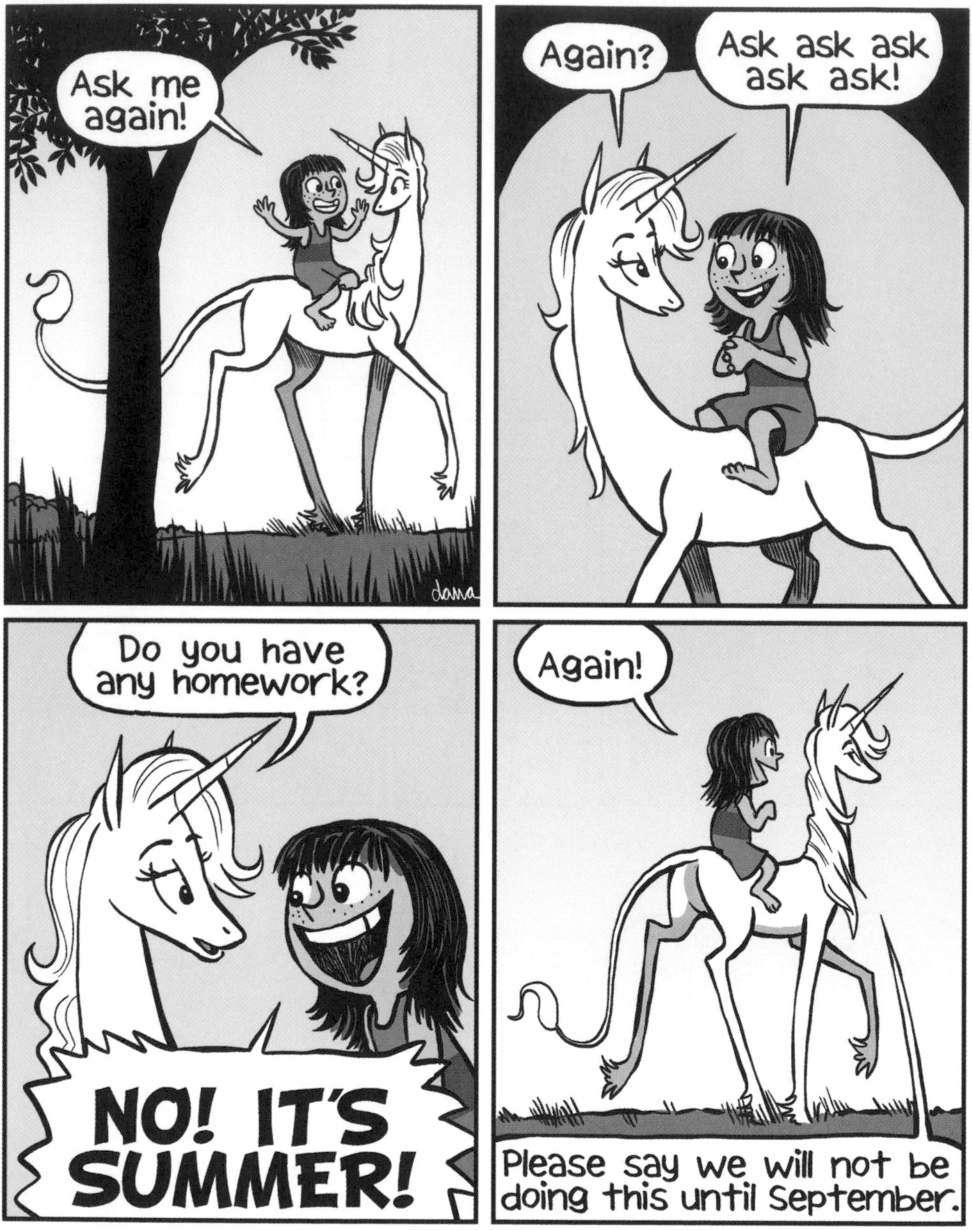
Ask me again!
Again?
Ask ask ask ask ask!
Do you have any homework?
NO! IT'S SUMMER!
Again!
Please say we will not be doing this until September.
dana

How to Draw Expressions

There are a lot of ways to draw expressions! There's really no single right way to draw any of them. But here's some of how I do it.

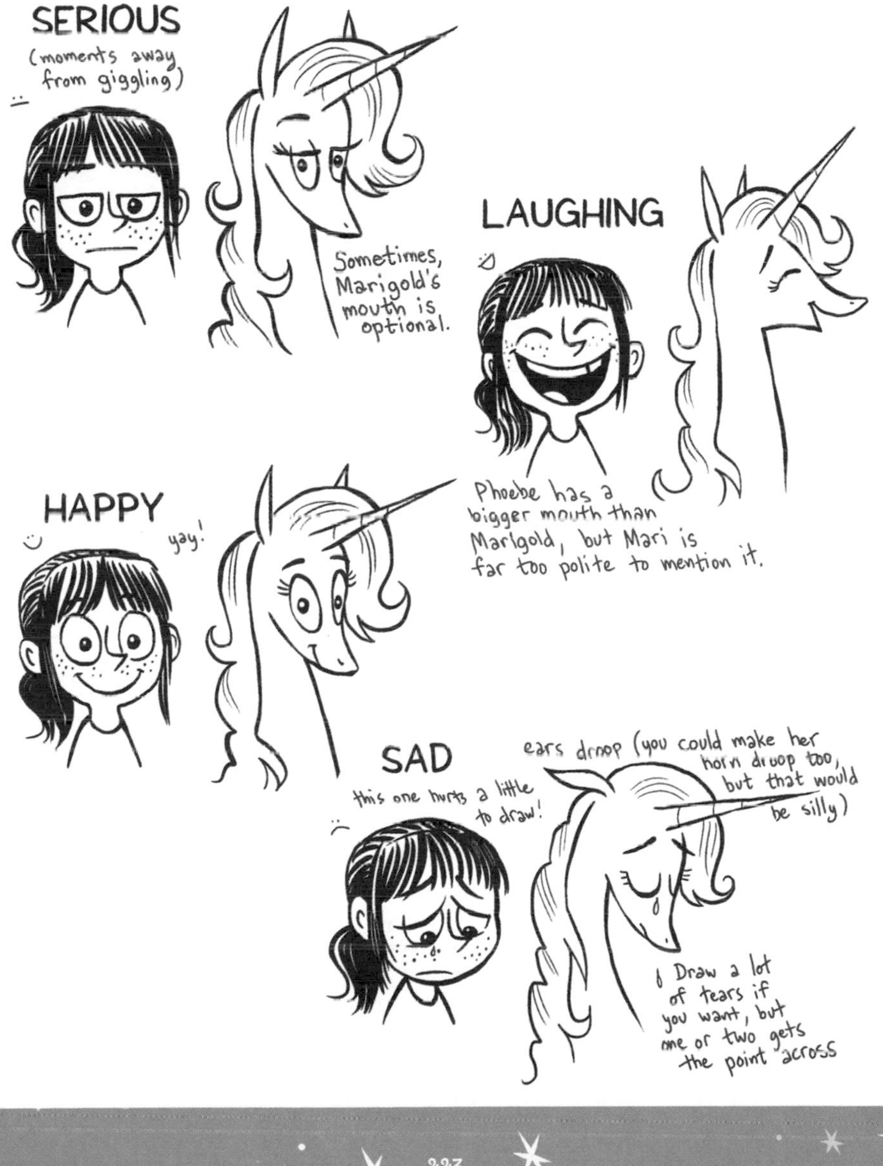
SERIOUS
(moments away from giggling)
Sometimes, Marigold's mouth is optional.
LAUGHING
HAPPY
yay!
Phoebe has a bigger mouth than Marigold, but Mari is far too polite to mention it.
SAD
this one hurts a little to draw!
ears droop (you could make her horn droop too, but that would be silly)
Draw a lot of tears if you want, but one or two gets the point across

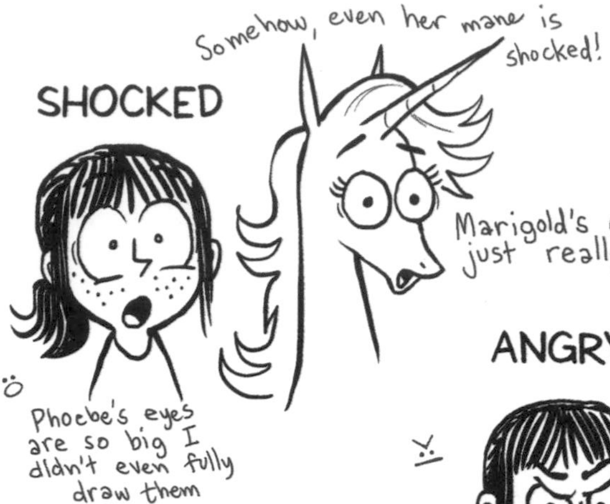
SHOCKED
Somehow, even her mane is shocked!
Marigold's eyes are just really round
ö
Phoebe's eyes are so big I didn't even fully draw them

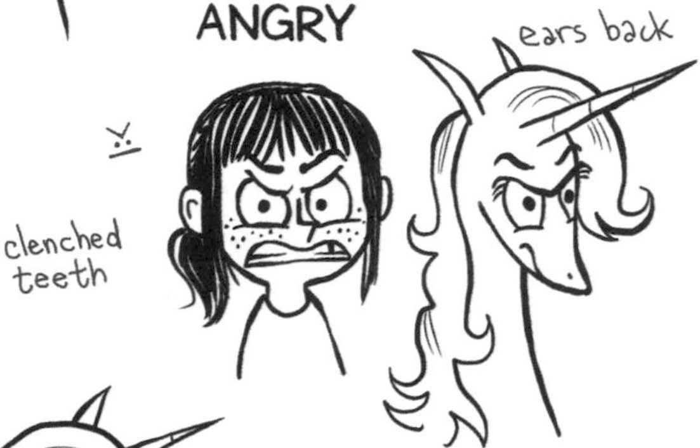
ANGRY
ears back
clenched teeth

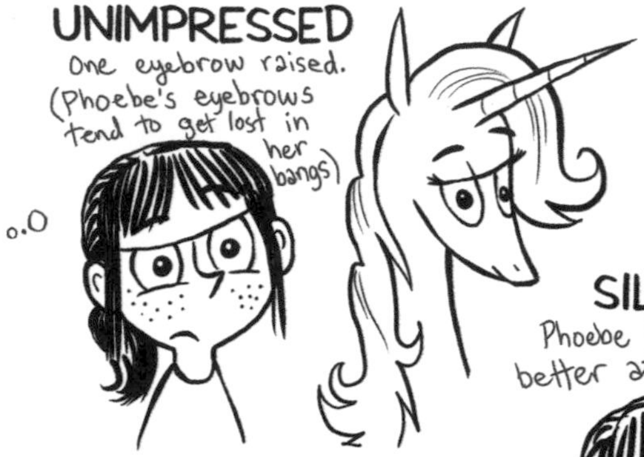
UNIMPRESSED
One eyebrow raised.
(Phoebe's eyebrows tend to get lost in her bangs)
o.O

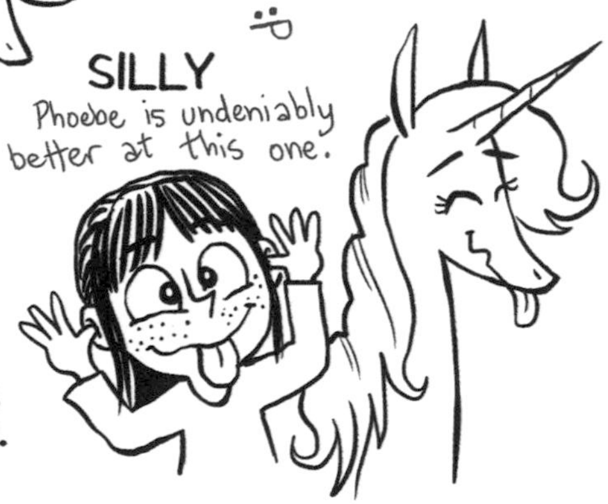
SILLY
Phoebe is undeniably better at this one.

Of course, you can (and should!) also just look at the expressions of people you know, too. Or just find a mirror!

(Fun fact: When I'm drawing facial expressions, I often make those expressions in real life, too, without really meaning to. Sometimes my husband looks at me and just starts giggling.)

Make Sparkly, Colorful Unicorn Poop Cookies!

Marigold is far too refined to ever use the word poop, but Phoebe knows delicious cookies when she tastes them! With an adult's help, make this sweet treat to enjoy with your friends.

INGREDIENTS: Store-bought refrigerated sugar cookie dough, four-pack of food colors, shiny sprinkles, edible glitter

INSTRUCTIONS:

1. Split the dough into four equal pieces and place each one in a separate bowl.
2. Add one food color to each bowl and stir to mix completely with the dough.
3. Refrigerate the bowls for 30 minutes.
4. Take a small piece of dough from each bowl. Roll each one on a counter or cutting board to make a rope-like shape. Then coil the four different colored pieces into a cookie shape until you've used all the dough.
5. Follow the directions on the cookie dough package to bake and cool.
6. Decorate with your favorite colors of sparkly sprinkles and edible glitter.

Makes about 24 cookies.

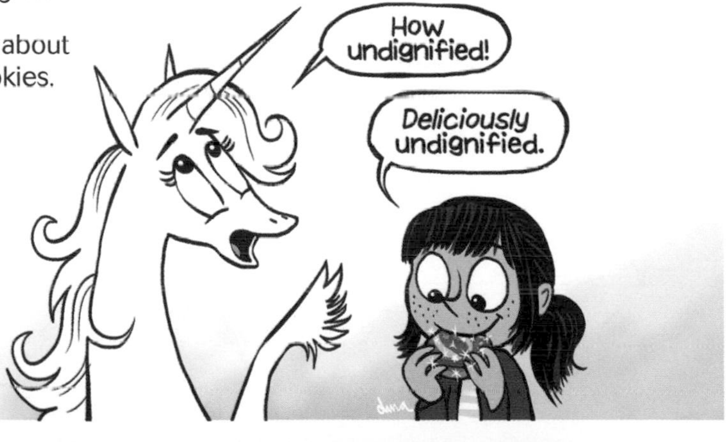
How undignified!
Deliciously undignified.

Make an Origami Figure of Marigold's Far-Removed Relative, the Happy Horse

First, make the Helmet Base.

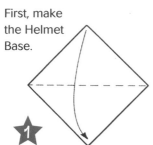

1 Take a square piece of paper and fold it in half as shown.

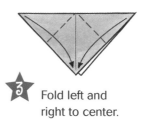

2 Then fold it in half again.

3 Fold left and right to center.

Helmet Base

Then make the Happy Horse.

2 Start with the Helmet Base.

5 Fold sides and bottom to indicated point.

6

7

Happy Horse

Thanks to Jeff Cole, author of *Easy Origami Fold-a-Day Calendar 2015* (Accord Publishing, a division of Andrews McMeel Publishing) for the origami instructions.

Phoebe and Her Unicorn is distributed internationally by Andrews McMeel Syndication.

Andrews McMeel Publishing
a division of Andrews McMeel Universal
1130 Walnut Street, Kansas City, Missouri 64106

www.andrewsmcmeel.com

20 21 22 23 24 SDB 10 9 8 7 6 5 4 3 2 1

ISBN: 978-1-5248-6177-3

Made by:
King Yip (Dongguan) Printing & Packaging Factory Ltd.
Address and location of manufacturer:
Daning Administrative District, Humen Town
Dongguan Guangdong, China 523930
1st Printing—4/6/20

Look for these books!

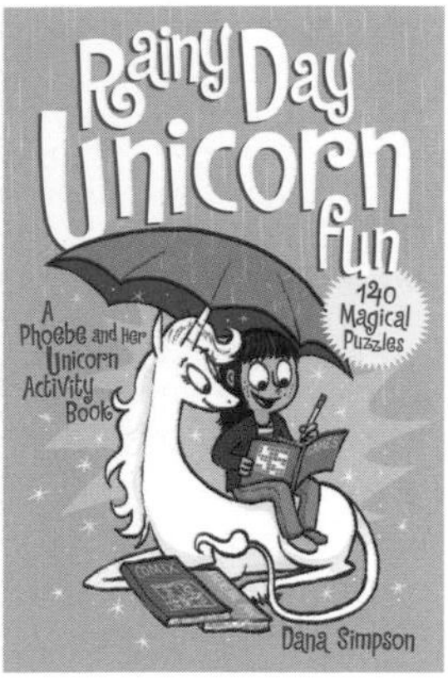
Rainy Day
Unicorn
fun
140 Magical Puzzles
A Phoebe and Her Unicorn Activity Book
Dana Simpson

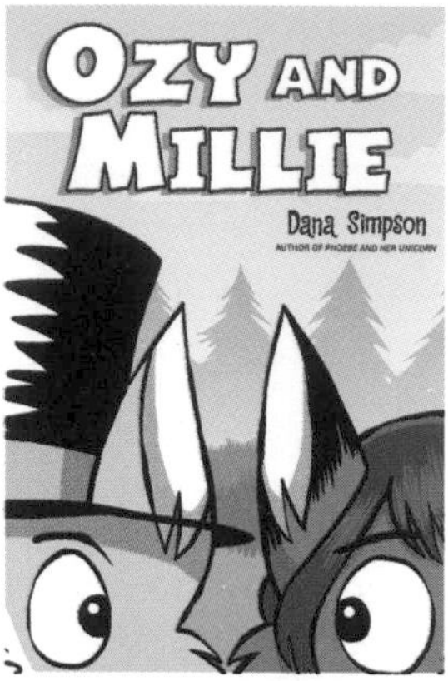
OZY AND
MILLIE
Dana Simpson
AUTHOR OF PHOEBE AND HER UNICORN

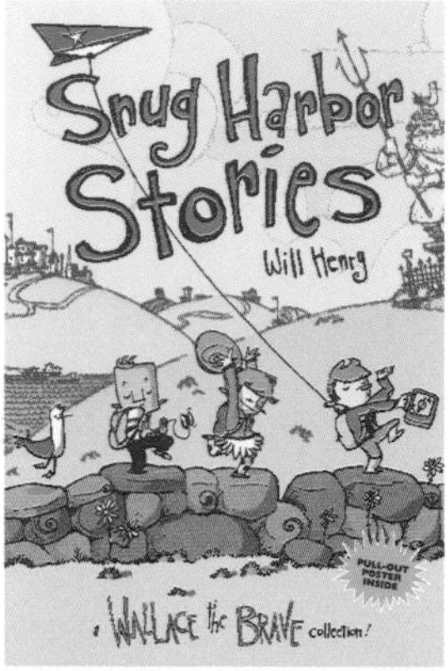
Snug Harbor
Stories
Will Henry
PULL-OUT POSTER INSIDE
a WALLACE the BRAVE collection!

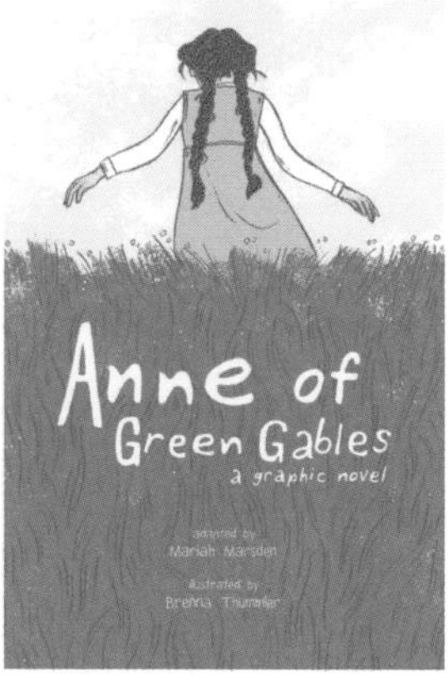
Anne of
Green Gables
a graphic novel

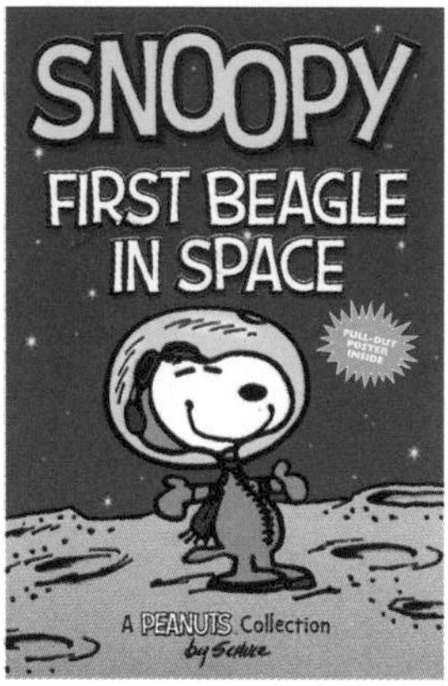
SNOOPY
FIRST BEAGLE
IN SPACE
PULL-OUT POSTER INSIDE
A PEANUTS Collection
by Schulz

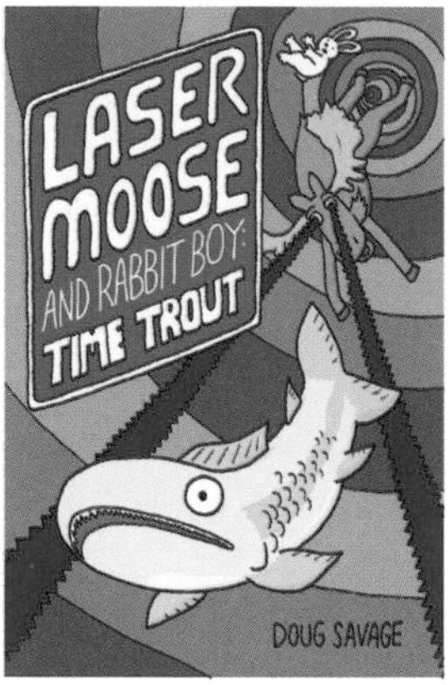
LASER
MOOSE
AND RABBIT BOY:
TIME TROUT
DOUG SAVAGE

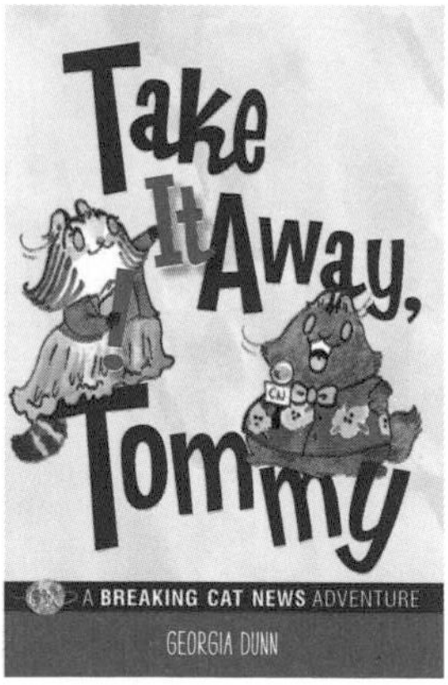
Take
It Away,
Tommy
A BREAKING CAT NEWS ADVENTURE
GEORGIA DUNN

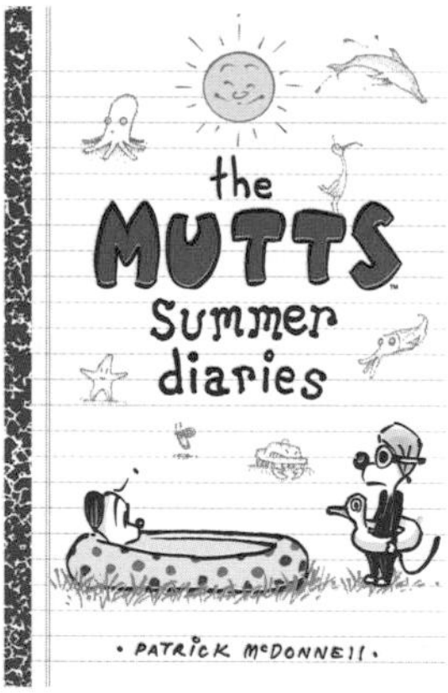
the
MUTTS
Summer
diaries
• PATRICK McDONNELL •

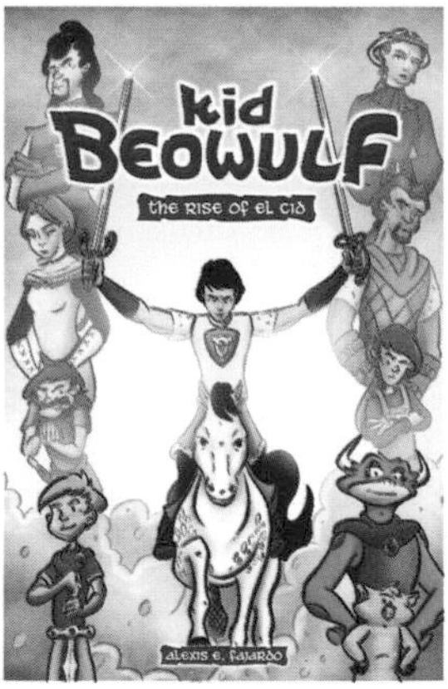
kid
BEOWULF
the rise of el cid
alexis e. fajardo